IAN FLEMING'S
JAMES
BOND
BACK IN ACTION
THREE COMPLETE NOVELS
BY JOHN GARDNER

ABOUT THE AUTHOR

JOHN GARDNER was born in England in 1926. He served in the Royal Navy Air Fleet from 1944 to 1946, and in the Royal Marine Commandos in 1946. He then attended St. John's College, Cambridge, where he earned a B.A. in 1950 and an M.A. in 1951.

From 1952 to 1958 Gardner served as a curate in Evesham, England, and then left the church to become theater critic and arts editor for the *Herald* in Stratford-Upon-Avon from 1959 to 1965. After his employment at the *Herald,* Gardner began his full-time writing career, and his work made him the logical heir to the literary tradition of the legendary James Bond. His continuation of Ian Fleming's vision has drawn praise from all quarters. John Gardner currently lives in Ireland.

IAN FLEMING'S JAMES BOND

BACK IN ACTION

THREE COMPLETE NOVELS
BY JOHN GARDNER

ROLE OF HONOR

NOBODY LIVES FOREVER

NO DEALS, MR. BOND

AVENEL BOOKS · NEW YORK

This omnibus was originally published in separate volumes under the titles: *Role of Honor,* copyright © 1984 by Glidrose Publications, Ltd. *Nobody Lives Forever,* copyright © 1986 by Glidrose Publications, Ltd. *No Deals, Mr. Bond,* copyright © 1987 by Glidrose Publications, Ltd. All rights reserved.

The author gratefully acknowledges permission from Walden Music, Inc., and Sour Grapes Music to reprint lyrics from "Sam Stone" by John Prine, copyright © 1971 by Walden Music, Inc. & Sour Grapes Music, in *Nobody Lives Forever.*

This 1988 edition is published by Avenel Books, distributed by Crown Publishers, Inc., 225 Park Avenue South, New York, New York 10003, by arrangement with the Putnam Publishing Group.

Printed and Bound in the United States of America

LIBRARY OF CONGRESS CATALOGING-IN-PUBLICATION DATA

Gardner, John E.
 Ian Fleming's James Bond back in action.

 Originally published in separate volumes.
 Contents: Role of honor—Nobody lives forever—No deals, Mr. Bond.
 1. Bond, James (Fictitious character)—Fiction. 2. Spy stories, American. I. Fleming, Ian, 1908–1964. II. Title.
PS3557.A712A6 1988   813'.54   88–19240
ISBN 0-517-67250-2

h g f e d c b a

CONTENTS

ROLE OF HONOR

for
BERYL & GIL

CONTENTS

ROBBERY WITH VIOLETS

THE ROBBERY OF security vans can take place at any time of the day, though, as a rule the Metropolitan Police do not encounter hijackers attempting a quick getaway during the rush hour. Nor do they expect trouble with a cargo that is sewn up tight. Only a privileged few knew exactly when the Kruxator Collection would arrive in the country. That it was due to come to Britain was common knowledge, and one had only to read a newspaper to discover that March 15 was the day on which the fabled group of paintings and jewelry was to go on display—for two weeks— at the Victoria and Albert Museum.

The Kruxator Collection is so called after its founder, the late Niko Kruxator, whose fabulous wealth arose from sources unknown, for he had arrived penniless in the United States—or so he had always said—about the time of the Wall Street Crash in October 1929. By the time he died, in 1977, most people thought of him as the Greek shipping magnate, but he still held his interest in Kruxator Restaurants, and the great international chain of Kruxlux Hotels. He was also sole owner of the Kruxator Collection, which he left to his country of adoption—all three hundred paintings and seven hundred fantastic objets d'art, including three incredible icons dating back to the fifteenth century, smuggled out of Russia at the time of the Revolution, and no fewer than sixteen pieces once owned by the Borgias: a collection certainly beyond price, though insured for billions of dollars.

The two-week London showing of the Kruxator Collection would be the last in its tour of European capitals before the whole consignment was returned to its permanent home in New York, Niko having left an endowment for the building in which these priceless objects could be displayed. Niko Kruxator wanted to be remembered, and he had taken steps to make certain that his name would be permanently linked with those of Van Gogh, Brueghel, El Greco, Matisse, and Picasso. Not that he was knowledgeable about art, but he could sense a fair bargain that would appreciate in value.

A private security firm looked after the precious oils, artifacts and gems on a permanent basis, though host countries were expected to provide extra protection. Nobody was in any doubt that the two armored vans, into which the exhibits fitted, were at constant risk. When the collection was on display, the most elaborate electronics protected each item.

The cargo arrived at Heathrow on an unannounced 747 at six minutes past one in the afternoon. The Boeing was directed to an unloading bay far away from the passenger terminals—near the old Hunting Clan hangars, which still display the name of that company, in large white letters.

The pair of armored vans was waiting, having taken the sea route during the previous night after depositing the collection at the Charles de Gaulle airport in Paris. Two unmarked police cars, each containing four armed plainclothes officers, were now in attendance.

The loaders were trusted employees of the Kruxator Collection itself, who knew their task so well that the entire cargo was off the aircraft and packed into the vans within hours. The unassuming convoy, led by one of the police cars, the other taking up the rear, set off to make a circuit of the perimeter before joining the normal flow of traffic through the underpass and out onto the M4 motorway. It was just after five-fifteen and the light was beginning to go, the traffic starting to build up both in and out of the capital. Even so, within half an hour the procession arrived at the end of the motorway where the road narrows to two lanes, taking vehicles onto what is dubiously known as the Hammersmith Flyover and then into the Cromwell Road.

Later reports from the police cars—which were in touch by radio with the armored vans—showed a certain amount of confusion during the early part of the journey. An eye-catching black girl, driving a violet-colored sports car, managed to come between the leading car and the first van, just as the convoy climbed the ramp onto the Flyover; while, at the rear, an equally striking white girl, in a violet dress, driving a black sports car, cut between the second van and the police car in the rear.

At first nothing alarming was reported through the radio links, though the separation of police vehicles and armored vans was soon made even greater by the behavior of the two girls who had tucked a Lancia and a Ferrari neatly into the convoy. The trailing police car made two efforts to overtake and get back into position, but the two sports cars either swung out to prevent traffic from getting in or pulled over to allow other private cars, lorries and taxis to overtake. By the time they reached the Cromwell Road not only had the gap between the police and the armored vans widened, but also the two vans had themselves been separated.

The route had been chosen to ensure maximum security. The convoy was to swing left off the Cromwell Road and proceed into Kensington High Street, then turn right before Knightsbridge into the one-way system at Exhibition Road so as to gain access to the rear of the Victoria and Albert Museum, well away from the exposed garden forecourt at the front of the building.

One police car had reached the Royal Garden Hotel, on the High Street side of Kensington Gardens, and the other was only just entering the far end of the High Street, when radio communications abruptly ceased.

The lead car broke all security regulations, activating its klaxon and U-turning across a blocked mass of traffic to make its way back along Kensington High Street. The rear car, also in some panic, began to move forward aggressively. A chaos of honking, hooting vehicles was suddenly smothered in a thick pall of choking, violet-colored smoke. Later, the drivers—and shotgun riders—of the two vans gave identical accounts of what occurred.

"The colored smoke was just there. No warning, no bombs, nothing, just dense colored smoke out of nowhere. Then everything in the cab went alive, as though we'd developed some terrible electrical fault. Naturally, when that happens, you turn off the engine, but the shocks kept coming, and we realized there was danger of being electrocuted. Getting out was a gut reaction . . ."

No one recalled anything after taking off the electronic locks, and all four men were later discovered, still in safety helmets and flak jackets, neatly laid out on the pavement. They were treated—

like many others—for respiratory problems, for the smoke had had an unpleasant effect on the lungs.

The two vans simply disappeared, as though someone had opened up the road, dropped them into the hole and then closed it perfectly over them.

The police inspector in charge of the investigation told viewers of *News at Ten* that evening that the robbery had been planned to the second. It must have been rehearsed again and again. So precise was the timing that one might well suppose it to have been a computerized theft. The only clues were the two sports cars and the descriptions of their drivers. The Central Registry, however, soon revealed that the sports car number plates—noted accurately by police officers—had never been issued to any vehicle.

The Kruxator robbery was daring, exact, brilliant and very costly. The lack of progress made by the police investigating it remained in the news for the best part of a month. Even sly comments concerning a breach of security, and the sudden resignation of a senior member of the Secret Intelligence Service—by name Commander James Bond—were lost to the Kruxator headlines, pushed back to a corner of page two and soon altogether out of the public eye.

2

A FRIVOLOUS AND EXTRAVAGANT MANNER

IN THE BEGINNING, Standing Orders were quite clear. Paragraph 12(c) instructed that

> *Any officer, classified as being on active duty, who is subject to any alteration in private financial status will*

inform Head of A Section, giving full details, and
providing any documentation that is thought either
necessary or desirable by Head of A.

A Section is, of course, Accounts, but confidential information—
such as James Bond's Australian legacy—automatically went personally to M, Records and the Chief of Staff as well.

In the ordinary commercial world, Bond would naturally have
received numerous warm expressions of congratulations on such
an unexpected windfall. Not so in the Service. Those who work
for Records are tight-lipped by tradition as well as by training.
Neither M, Bond's Chief of Service, nor Bill Tanner, M's Chief
of Staff, would think of bringing the matter up, for both were of
the old school, which, rightly, considered details of private money
to be of a personal nature. The fact that they both knew would
never stop them pretending they did not. It was, then, almost a
shock when M himself mentioned it.

The months before Bond received the news of his legacy had
been dull with routine. He always found the office paperwork of
his job debilitating and boring, but that summer—now eighteen
months ago—was particularly irksome, especially as he had taken
all his leave early, a mistake that condemned him to day after
day of files, memos, directives and other people's reports. As so
often happened in Bond's world there was absolutely nothing—
not even a simple confidential courier job—to alleviate the drudg-
ery of those hot months.

Then came the legacy. It arrived, literally out of the blue, in a
thick manila envelope with a Sydney postmark, and fell with a
heavy plop through his letter box early in the following November.
The letter was from a firm of solicitors who for many years had
acted for the younger brother of Bond's father, an uncle whom
Bond had never seen. Uncle Bruce, it appeared, had died a wealthy
man, leaving every penny of his estate to his nephew James, who
hitherto had enjoyed a little private money. Now his fortunes were
drastically changed.

The whole settlement came to around a quarter of a million
sterling. There was one condition to the will. Old Uncle Bruce
had a sense of humor and decreed that his nephew should spend

at least one hundred thousand pounds within the first four months in "a frivolous and extravagant manner."

Bond did not have to think twice about how he might best comply with such an eccentric proviso. Bentley motor cars had always been a passion, and he had sorely resented getting rid of the old models that he had owned, driven, enjoyed and loved. During the last year he had genuinely lusted after the brand-new Bentley Mulsanne Turbo. When the will was finally through probate, he took himself straight down to Jack Barclay's showrooms, in Berkeley Square, and ordered the hand-built car—in his old favorite British Racing Green, with a magnolia interior.

One month later, he visited the Rolls-Royce Car Division at Crewe, spending a pleasant day with the chief executive and explaining that he wanted no special technology built into the car apart from a small concealed weapon compartment and a long-range telephone, which would be provided by the security experts at CCS. The Mulsanne Turbo was delivered in the late spring, and Bond—having put down the full price with the order—was happy to get rid of the remaining statutory thirty thousand pounds plus by spending it on friends, mainly female, and himself, in a spree of high living such as he had not enjoyed for many years.

But 007 was not so easily brought out of the doldrums. He longed for some kind of action—a craving that he slaked with too many late nights, the excitement of the gaming tables, and a lukewarm affair with a girl he had known for years—a small romance that guttered out like a candle flame after a few months. So even this period of lotus eating failed to remove that unsettled, edgy sense that his life had lost both purpose and direction.

There was one week, in the late spring, when he found some pleasure with the Q Branch Armorer, Major Boothroyd, and his delectable assistant, Q'ute, testing a hand gun the Service was toying with using on a regular basis: the ASP 9mm, an American-made combat modification of the 9mm Smith & Wesson. Bond found it one of the most satisfying hand guns he had ever used.

Then, in the middle of August, when London was crowded with tourists and a torpor hung over the Regent's Park Headquarters, there came a summons from M's secretary, the faithful Miss Moneypenny, and Bond found himself in his chief's office, with Bill Tanner in attendance. It was here, on the ninth floor, over-

looking the dry, hot and dusty park, that M surprised him by
bringing up the matter of the Australian legacy.

Moneypenny was far from her usual flirtatious self while Bond
waited in the outer office, giving him the distinct impression that,
whatever the cause of M's summons, the news could not be good.
The feeling was heightened once he was allowed into the main
office.

Both the Chief of Staff and M looked wary. M's eyes did not
even meet Bond's, and Tanner hardly turned to acknowledge his
presence.

"We have a pair of Russian ambulance chasers in town," M
stated, baldly and without emphasis, once Bond was seated in
front of his desk.

"Sir." There was no other possible response to this opening
gambit.

"New boys to us," M continued. "No diplomatic cover, French
papers, but definitely high-quality ambulance chasers." The Head
of Service was talking about Russian operatives whose specific task
was to recruit potential informants, agents, traitors.

"You want me to put them on the first aircraft back to Moscow,
sir?" Bond's heart rose a little, for even that simple chore would
be better than sitting around the office shuffling papers.

M ignored the offer. Instead he looked at the ceiling. "Come
into money, 007. That's what I hear."

Bond found himself almost shocked by M's remark. "A small
legacy . . ."

M raised his eyebrows, quizzically muttering the word "Small?"

"The ambulance chasers are high-powered professionals." Bill
Tanner spoke from the window. "They've both had some success
in other parts of the world—Washington, for instance—though
there's never been hard evidence. Washington and Bonn. These
fellows got in very quietly on both those occasions, and nobody
knew about them until it was too late. They did a lot of damage
in Washington. Even more in Bonn."

"The orders to expel arrived after the birds had flown," M
interjected.

"So, now you know they're here—in the UK—and you want
some solid evidence?" An unpleasant thought had crept into Bond's
mind.

Bill Tanner came over, dragging a chair so that he could sit close to Bond. "Fact is, we've got wind at an early stage. We presume they imagine we don't know of their presence. Our brothers at 'Five' have been cooperative for once . . ."

"They're here, and active, then." Bond tried to remain calm, for it was not like M or Tanner to beat about the bush. "You want hard evidence?" he asked again.

Tanner took a deep breath, like a man about to unburden his soul. "M wants to mount a dangle," he said quietly.

"Tethered goat. Bait," M growled.

"Me?" Bond slipped a hand into his breast pocket, withdrawing his gunmetal cigarette case, and lit up one of his H. Simmons specials, bought in bulk from the old shop, which still exists in Burlington Arcade.

"Me?" Bond repeated. "The tethered goat?"

"Something like that."

"With respect, sir, that's like talking of a woman being slightly pregnant." He gave a bleak smile. "Either I'm to be the bait, or I'm not."

"Yes." M cleared his throat, plainly embarrassed by what he was about to suggest. "Well . . . it really came to us because of your . . . your little windfall." He stressed the word "little."

"I don't see what that's got to do with it . . ."

"Let me put a couple of questions to you." M fiddled with his pipe. "How many people really know you've, er, come into money?"

"Obviously those with need to know in the Service, sir. Apart from that only my solicitor, my late uncle's solicitor and myself . . ."

"Not reported in any newspapers? Not bandied about? *Not public knowledge?*"

"Certainly not public knowledge, sir."

M and Tanner exchanged quick, knowing glances. "You have been living at a somewhat extravagant pace, 007," M scowled.

Bond remained silent, waiting. As he had thought, it was not good.

"You see, James," Tanner took up the conversation, "there has been some talk. Gossip. People notice things and the word, around Whitehall, is that Commander Bond is living a shade dangerously—

gambling, the new Bentley, er . . . ladies, money changing hands . . ."

"So?" He was not going to make it any easier for them.

"So, even our gallant allies in Grosvenor Square have been over asking questions. They do it when a senior officer suddenly changes his habits."

"The Americans think I'm a security risk?" Bond bridled. "Damned cheek."

"Enough of that, 007," M retorted. "They have every right to ask. You *have* been acting the playboy recently."

"And if they get touchy," Tanner interjected, "then there's no knowing what thoughts are running through the minds of those who watch from Kensington Gardens."

"Rubbish," Bond almost spat. "Those who are not our friends know me too well. They'll ferret out the legacy in no time—if they're interested . . ."

"Oh, they're interested all right," Tanner continued. "You haven't noticed anything?"

Bond's brow creased as he shook his head.

"No? Well, why should you? They've been very discreet. Not a twenty-four-hour surveillance or anything like that, but our people on the street have reported that you're under observation. Odd days, occasional nights, questions in unlikely places."

Bond swore silently. He felt foolish. *Even at home, behave as though you're in the field,* they taught. Elementary, and he had not even noticed.

"Where's this leading, then?" he asked, dreading the answer.

"To the dangle." Tanner gave a half smile. "To a small charade, with you as the central character, James."

Bond nodded. "As I said. I'm going to be the bait."

"It seems reasonable enough." M turned his attention to his pipe. "The situation is ideal . . ."

This time Bond did explode, voicing his feelings with some venom. It was the most stupid ploy he had ever heard of. No recruiting officer from any foreign agency would seriously consider him. And, if they did, their masters would put the blight on it in ten seconds flat.

"You're not really serious about this, are you?"

Absolutely, 007. I agree, on the face of it they'll steer clear of you; but we have to look at the facts—they *are* more than interested already . . ."

"Never in a thousand years . . ." Bond started again.

"We've already written the scenario, 007, and we're going along with it. Do I have to remind you that you're under discipline?"

There were no options, and Bond, feeling the whole business was sheer madness, could only sit and listen to the litany of the scheme as, between them, M and Tanner outlined the bare bones, like a pair of theatrical directors explaining motivation to a reluctant actor.

"At an appropriate moment we haul you in," M said.

"Enquiry in camera," counterpointed Bill Tanner.

"Making certain the Press are tipped off."

"Questions in the House."

"Hints of scandal. Corruption in the Service."

"And you resign."

"Giving the impression that, in reality, we've cast you into outer darkness. And if that doesn't lure the ambulance chasers, then there's something else in the wind. Wait, and do as I say, 007."

And so it had happened—though not because of the ambulance chasers, as they had told him. Rumors ran along the corridors of power; there was gossip in the clubs, tattle in the men's rooms of government departments, hints to the Press, hints *by* the Press, even questions in the House of Commons, and finally the resignation of Commander James Bond.

3

OUTER DARKNESS

IN THE MONTH before the Kruxator robbery, Bond himself had been following a hedonistic routine. He spent days lazing in bed until noon and ventured forth in the evenings, to restaurants, clubs and gaming houses, usually with a pretty girl in tow. The Press, which had hounded him at the moment of his resignation, hardly approached him again. He had no contact at all with his former employers. In fact they went out of their way to avoid him. One evening, he found himself at the Inn on the Park, seated only two tables from Ann Reilly—the attractive and talented assistant to the Armorer in Q Branch. Bond caught her eye and smiled, but she merely looked through him, coldly, as though he did not exist.

Then, toward the end of April, around noon one mild, bright Thursday, the telephone rang in Bond's flat. Bond, who had been shaving, grabbed at the handset, as though he would like to strangle the trilling tone.

"Yes?" he growled in response.

"Oh!" The voice was female, and surprised. "Is that 58 Dean Street? The Record Shop?"

"It's not 58 anything." Bond did not even smile.

"But I'm sure I dialed 734-8777 . . ."

"Well, you didn't get it." He slammed the receiver down.

Later in the afternoon, however, he telephoned his date—a favorite blonde hostess with British Airways—to cancel their evening. Instead of dinner for two at the Connaught, Bond went, alone, to Veeraswamy's, that most excellent Indian restaurant in Swallow Street, where he ate a chicken vindaloo with all the trimmings, lingered over his coffee, then paid the bill and left on the dot of nine-fifteen. The magnificent uniformed and bearded doorman threw him a quivering salute, then loudly hailed a cab. Bond gave the driver his home address, but when the taxi reached the top of St. James's, he told the driver to pull over, paid him, and set off on foot, to follow what appeared to be an aimless route, turning into the side streets, crossing roads suddenly, doubling back on himself a number of times, loitering at corners, making certain he was not being followed. Eventually, clinging to this patient and devious routine, he ended up in a doorway near St. Martin's Lane.

For two minutes, Bond stood looking up at a lighted window across the road. At precisely ten o'clock the oblong of light turned black, then lit again, went black, lit and stayed on.

Quickly Bond crossed the road, disappearing through another

doorway, up a narrow flight of stairs, across a landing and up four more steps to a door that bore the legend RICH PHOTOGRAPHY LTD. MODELS AVAILABLE.

When he pressed the small button to the right of the lintel, the chimes, associated with a well-known brand of cosmetics, ding-donged from far away inside. There were faint footsteps and the click of bolts being drawn.

The door opened to reveal Bill Tanner, who nodded and moved his head in a gesture indicating that Bond should enter. He followed Tanner along a small passage, the paintwork peeling, and a cloying smell of cheap scent hanging in the air, then through the door at the far end. The room was very small and cluttered. A bed with an eye-battering coverlet stood in one corner. A seedy Teddy-Bear lounged on a bright orange, heart-shaped imitation silk nightdress case. A small wardrobe faced the bed, its door half open, displaying a pathetic row of women's clothes, while a tiny dressing table was crammed with bottles and jars of cosmetics. Above a popping gas fire, a print of *The Green Lady* looked down from a plastic frame upon a pair of easy chairs that would not have been out of place in a child's Wendy House.

"Come in, 007. Glad to see you can do simple mathematics." The figure in one of the chairs turned, and Bond found himself looking into M's familiar cold gray eyes.

Tanner closed the door, and now crossed to a table on which were set several bottles and glasses.

"Good to see you, sir," Bond said with a smile, holding out a hand. "Seven and three equals ten. Even I can manage that."

"Nobody in tow?" Bill Tanner asked, sidling toward the window that Bond had viewed from the far side of the street.

"Not unless they've got a team of a hundred or so footpads and about twenty cars on me. Traffic's thick as treacle tonight. Always bad on Thursdays—late night shopping, and all the commuters staying up to meet their wives and girlfriends."

The telephone gave a good old-fashioned ring, and Tanner got to it in two strides.

"Yes," he said, then, again, "Yes. Good. Right." Replacing the receiver he looked up with a smile. "He's clear, sir. All the way."

"I told you—" Bond began, but Tanner cut him short with an invitation to take a gin and tonic with them. Bond scowled, shaking his head. "I've had enough alcohol to float several small ships in the past few weeks . . ."

"So we all noticed," M grunted.

"Your instructions, sir. I could remind you that I said at the outset nothing would come of it. Nobody in our business would even begin to believe I'd left the Service, just like that. The silence has been deafening."

M grunted again, "Sit down, 007. Sit down and listen. The silence has not been so deafening. On the contrary, the isle is full of noises, only you have been on a different frequency. I fear we've led you on a merry dance, but it was necessary for you to remain ignorant of the true object of this operation—that is, until we had established to the various intelligence communities that you were persona non grata as far as we're concerned. Forget what we told you during our last meeting. Now, we have the real target. Look on this picture, and on this, and this."

Like an experienced poker player, M laid out three photographs, one man and two women.

"The man," he said at last, "is presumed dead. His name was Dr. Jay Autem Holy." The finger touched one photograph, then moved on to the next. "This lady is his widow, and this—" the finger prodded toward the third photograph—"this is the same lady. Looks so different that, should her husband come back from the dead, which is in the cards, he would never recognize her."

M picked up the final photograph. "She will give you the details. In fact she'll give you a little training as well."

The woman in question was plump, with mousy brown hair, thick-lensed spectacles, thin lips and a sharp nose too big for the bone structure of her rather chubby face. At least that was how she looked in the photograph taken some years ago when she was married to Jay Autem Holy. M also maintained that Bond would not recognize her now. That did not surprise him when he studied the second photograph.

"You're sending me on another course?" Bond mused rather absently without looking up.

"Something like that. She's waiting for you now."

"Yes?"

"In Monaco. Monte Carlo. Hotel de Paris. Now listen carefully, 007. There's a good deal for you to absorb, and I want you on the road early next week. First, her name is Persephone Proud. Second, you must, naturally, still consider yourself as one cast into outer darkness. But this is what we—together with our American cousins—planned from the start."

M talked earnestly for about fifteen minutes, allowing no interruptions, before Bond was escorted through another elaborate security routine to get him safely clear of the building and on the rest of his way home in a taxi without being followed. Not for the first time, Bond had been given another life, a double identity. But unlike all the many parts he had played for the honor of his country, this was to appear—to all but M and Tanner—as a role of dishonor.

4

PROUD PERCY

Bond PARTICULARLY ENJOYED the drive through France, down to the Midi, for it was the first time he had been able to let the huge Mulsanne Turbo off the leash. The car seemed to revel in the business of doing its job with perfection. It pushed its long, elegant snout forward and then, like a thoroughbred in peak condition, gathered itself together, effortlessly thrusting well in excess of the hundred-mph mark, eating up road without fuss or noise.

He had left London early on the Monday morning, and Ms. Proud was to be in the Casino each evening—from the Tuesday— between ten and eleven.

At a little after 6:00 P.M. on Tuesday the Mulsanne slid into Monaco's Place Casino and up to the entrance of the Hotel de Paris. It was a splendid, clear spring evening, with hardly a breath of wind to stir the palm trees in the gardens that front the Grand Casino. As he switched off the ignition, Bond checked that the small hidden weapon compartment below the polished wooden facia, to the right of the wheel, was locked; and that the safety key was turned on the powerful Super 1000 telephone housed between the front seats. Stepping out he glanced around the Place, nostrils filling with a mixture of bougainvillea, heavy French tobacco, and the soft sea air.

Monte Carlo—like the neighboring cities and towns along the Côte d'Azur—had a smell that was its own, and Bond reckoned someone could make a fortune if they could only bottle it, to provide nostalgic memories for those who had known the Principality in its heyday. For the one-time gambling legend of Europe was no longer the great romantic fairytale place remembered by people who had won, and lost, fortunes, and hearts, there in the old days. The packaged holiday, weekend tours and charter flights had put an end to that. Monaco only managed to keep up its veneer of sophistication through its royal family and the high prices that speculators, hoteliers, restaurateurs and shopkeepers could charge, and even these had not created an adequate buffer against some of the more garish attributes of the 1980s.

On his last visit, Bond had been stunned to find one-armed bandits installed even in the exclusive Salles Privées of the Casino. Now, he would not be surprised if there were Space Invader games there as well.

His room faced the sea and, before taking a shower and preparing for the evening, he stood on the balcony, looking out at the twinkling lights, sipping a martini and straining his ears, as though he might be capable of reaching out to recapture the sounds and laughter of former, brighter days.

After a modest dinner—a chilled consommé, grilled sole, and a mousse au chocolate—he went down to check the car, then walked over to the Casino, paying the entrance fee—which would admit him to the fabled Salles Privées—and purchasing fifty thousand francs worth of plaques, around four thousand pounds sterling.

There was play at only one of the tables, and, as he crossed the floor, he saw Ms. Proud for the first time. M had underestimated the case when he said her husband would not even recognize her. Bond, who had hardly credited the second picture—"the 'after' photograph," as M said—found it difficult to believe that the woman, undeniably the one from *that* photograph, could ever have been either plump or mousy.

She stood, bare-shouldered, her back against the bar, a tall, almost willowy figure, head tilted, small breasts thrusting into relief against the filmy material of her blue dress. Long ash-blonde hair just touched the tanned skin at the nape of her neck, and her light gray eyes were intent on the play at the table. The eyes were twinkling with amusement. A half smile hovered around her "new" mouth, full lips having replaced the original, while the once angular nose was now almost a snub.

Fascinating, Bond thought. Fascinating to see what strict diet, a nose job, contact lenses, and a dedicated course of beauty treatment and hairdressing could accomplish.

He did not pause on his way to the table, where he took a seat, acknowledging the croupier, and studied the game for three turns before dropping twenty-five thousand francs on *Impair*.

The croupier called the ritual *"Faits vos jeux,"* and all eyes watched, as the little ball bounced into the spinning wheel. *"Rien ne va plus."*

Bond glanced at the other three players—a smooth, American-looking man, late forties, blue-jowled and with the steely look of a professional gambler; a woman, in her early seventies, he judged, dressed in last season's fashions; and a heavyset Chinese whose face would never give away his age. Everyone followed the wheel now, as the ball bounced twice and settled into a slot.

"Dix-sept, rouge, impair et manque." the croupier intoned in that particular plainchant of the tables. Seventeen, red, odd and low.

The rake swung efficiently over the green baize, taking in the house winnings and pushing out plaques to the winners, including James Bond, whose *Impair* bet had netted him even money. At the call, he again placed twenty-five thousand on *Impair*. Once more he won: Eleven came up. *Impair* for a third time, and the ball rolled into fifteen. In three turns of the wheel, Bond had made seventy-five thousand francs. The other players were betting complex patterns—*A Cheval, Carré* and *Colonne,* which made for higher odds. James Bond was playing the easy way, high stakes for even returns. He pushed the whole of his seventy-five thousand onto *Pair* and fourteen—red—came up. Stake plus one hundred fifty thousand francs. Time to call it a night. He flipped a five thousand-franc plaque across the table, muttering *"Pour les employés,"* and pushed back the chair. There was a little squeal as the chair touched the girl's legs, and Bond felt liquid run down his left cheek where her drink had spilled—a natural enough incident, for the Englishman had not sensed her standing behind him. It was a move carefully prearranged far away in London, in the safe flat near St. Martin's Lane.

"I'm terribly sorry . . . *Pardon, Madam, je . . ."*

"It's okay, I speak English." The voice was pitched low, the accent clear and without any nasality. "It was my fault, I shouldn't have been standing so close. The game was very . . ."

"Well, at least let me get you a fresh drink." He completed drying off his face, took her elbow and steered her toward the small bar. One of the dinner-jacketed security men smiled as he watched them go. Hadn't he seen women pick up men like this many times? No harm in it, as long as the women were straight, and this one was an American visitor. Silently he wished them luck.

"Mr. Bond," she said, raising her champagne cocktail to his.

"James. My friends call me James."

"And mine call me Percy. Persephone's too much of a mouthful."

Bond's eyes smiled over the rim of his glass. "Percy Proud?" An eyebrow cocked. "I'll drink to that."

Percy was a relaxed young woman, an easy communicator, and blessed with a sense of both humor and the ridiculous.

"Okay, James"—they were at last seated in her room at the Hotel de Paris, both armed with champagne cocktails—"down to cases. How much have you been told?"

"Very little." *She'll give you the fine print,* M had said. *Trust her; let her teach you. She knows more about all this than anyone.*

"You've seen this picture?" She extracted a small photograph from her handbag. "I just have to show it to you and then destroy. I don't want to be caught with it on me, thank you very much."

The photograph was a smaller print of the one they had shown him in the St. Martin's Lane safe flat.

"Jay Autem Holy," Bond said.

The man looked to be very tall, thinning hair failing to disguise a domed head, while the nose was large and beaky.

"*Doctor* Jay Autem Holy," she corrected.

"Deceased; and you are the widow—though I would scarcely have recognized you from the photos."

She gave a quick, melodic giggle. "There've been some changes made."

"I'll say. The other identity wouldn't have been attractive in black. The new one would look good in any color."

"Flattery could get you everywhere, James Bond. But I don't really think Mrs. Jay Autem Holy ever needed the widow's weeds. You see, he never died."

"Tell me."

She began with the story already told by M. Over a decade before, while Dr. Jay Autem Holy had been working solely for the Pentagon, a U.S. Marine Corps Grumman Mohawk aircraft had crashed into the Grand Canyon. It carried but two passengers: Holy and a General Joseph (Rolling Joe) Zwingli.

"You already know that Jay Autem was way ahead of his time," she said. "A computer whizz kid long before anyone had heard of computer whizz kids. He worked on very advanced programing for the Pentagon. The airplane went down in an almost inaccessible place—wreckage dumped deep into a crevasse. No bodies were ever recovered, and Jay Autem had a nice bundle of significant computer tapes with him when he went. Naturally, they were not recovered either. He was then working on a portable battle-training program for senior officers and had almost perfected a computerized system for anticipating enemy movements in the field. At that time his work was, literally, invaluable."

"And the general?"

" 'Rolling Joe'? A nut. A much-decorated, and brave, nut. Believed the United States had gone to the dogs—the Commie Dogs. Said openly that there should be a change in the political system; that the Army should take control; the politicians had sold out; morals had gone to pieces; people had to be *made* to care."

Bond nodded, "And I gather Dr. Holy had a nickname—as 'Rolling Joe' was General Zwingli's nickname."

She laughed again. "They called Zwingli 'Rolling Joe' because, in World War II he had this habit of air-testing his B-17 Flying Fortress by rolling it at a thousand feet."

"And Dr. Holy?" he prompted.

"His colleagues, and some of his friends, called him 'The Holy Terror.' He could be a tough boss." Percy paused before adding, "And a tough husband."

"Late husband." Bond gave her a close, unblinking look and watched her drain the last of her champagne cocktail and place the glass carefully on a side table as she slowly shook her head.

"Oh, no," she said softly. "Jay Autem Holy did not die in that plane wreck. Certain people have been sure of that for some years. Now there's proof."

"Proof? Where?" He led her toward the moment for which M had prepared him.

"Right on your own doorstep, James. Deep in the English rural heart. Oxfordshire. And there's more to it than that. You remember the Kruxator robbery in London? And the £20 million gold bullion job?"

Bond nodded.

"Also the £2 billion air hijack? The British Airways 747 taking foreign currencies from the official printers in England to their respective countries?"

"Of course."

"You remember what those crimes had in common, James?"

He waved his gunmetal cigarette case at Percy, who declined with an almost imperceptible gesture of the hand. Bond was surprised to find the case being returned to his pocket unopened. His forehead creased.

"All large sums," he said. "Well planned . . . wait a minute, didn't Scotland Yard say they were almost computerized crimes?"

"That's it. You have the answer."

"Percy?" There was an edge of puzzlement in Bond's voice. "What are you suggesting?"

"That Dr. Jay Autem Holy is alive, and well, living in a small village called Nun's Cross, just north of Banbury, in your lovely Oxfordshire. Remember Banbury, James? The place where you can ride a cock horse to?" She made a tight movement of her lips. "Well, that's where he is. Planning criminal operations—and probably terrorist ones as well—by computer simulations."

"Evidence?"

"Well." Again a pause. "To say that no bodies were recovered in the plane wreck is not quite true. They got out the pilot's remains. There were no other bodies. Intelligence, security and police agencies have been searching for Jay Autem Holy ever since."

"And suddenly they found him in Oxfordshire?"

"Almost by chance, yes. One of your Special Branch men was in that area, on a completely different case. First he spotted a pair of well-known London crooks."

"And they led him to . . .?"

Percy got up and slowly began to pace the room.

"They led him to a small computer games company called Gunfire Simulations, in the village of Nun's Cross, and there he sees a face from the files. So he goes back and checks. The face is that of Dr. Jay Autem Holy. Only now he calls himself Professor Jason St. John-Finnes—pronounced Sinjon-Finesse: finesse, as in the game of bridge. The name of the house is Endor."

"As in Witch of?"

"Right."

Percy paused in her pacing and leaned over the back of Bond's armchair, her dress brushing his ear. He could not at that moment bring himself to turn his head and look up into the face above his shoulder.

"They even have chummy little weekend wargames house parties there, at which a lot of strange people turn up," Percy continued.

She rose and sidled over to a couch on to which she dropped, drawing her long slender legs up under her.

"Trouble was that none of this happened to be news to the American Service. You see, they've been keeping an eye on that situation for some time. Even infiltrated it, without telling anyone."

Bond smiled. "That would please my people no end. There are rules about operating on other countries' soil and—"

"As I understand it," Percy interrupted in a drawling voice, "there were what is known as frank and open discussions."

"I'll bet!" Bond thought for a moment. "Are you telling me that Jay Autem Holy—strongly prized by the Pentagon, and missing, believed dead—just managed to settle in this village, Nun's

Cross, without benefit of disguise, or cover? Except for some new identity papers?"

Percy stretched out her legs and laid back almost full length on the couch, trailing her arm languidly and brushing the floor with her hand.

"Not an easy man to disguise," she said. "But, yes, that's exactly what he's done. Mind you he rarely goes out, he's hardly ever seen in the village. His so-called wife deals personally with business, and those he genuinely employs just think he's eccentric—which he is. A great deal of ingenuity and a lot of money went into fixing up Jay Autem's hideaway."

Slowly, many of the things M had said, back in London, started to make sense.

"And I'm the one who's supposed to join that happy band of brothers?" Bond asked.

"You've got it, in one."

"And just how am I supposed to do that? Walk in and say, Hi there, my name's James Bond, the famous renegade intelligence officer? I'm looking for a job."

It was Bond's turn to get up and pace the room.

"Something like that," Percy drawled softly.

"Good God!" Bond's face tightened in anger. "Of all the hare-brained . . . Why would he want to employ me, anyway?"

"He wouldn't." She gave a flick of a smile and sat up, suddenly very alert and in earnest. "He's got enough staff to run the Gunfire Simulations business—all legal and aboveboard. And *are* they screened? It makes the British positive vetting look like a kid's crossword puzzle. Believe me, I know. He has to be certain, because that side of things is absolutely straight." She took a little breath, turning her head slightly, like a singer swinging away from the microphone. "No, James, he wouldn't think of employing you but there are people he works with who just *might* find you a great temptation. That's what your people are banking on."

"Mad. Absolute madness! How . . . ?"

"James," she soothed, standing up and taking both his hands in hers. "You have friends at the court of King St. John-Finnes— well, an acquaintance anyhow. Freddie Fortune. The naughty Lady Freddie."

"Oh, Lord!" Bond dropped Percy's hands and swung aside. Once, some years ago, Bond had made the error of cultivating the young woman Percy had just mentioned. In a way he had even courted her, until he discovered that Lady Freddie Fortune—darling of the gossip columnists—suffered from a somewhat slap-dash political education, which had placed her slightly to the left of Fidel Castro.

"You also have to study, James. That's why you're here, with me. To get an entree into Endor you must know something about the job they do at Gunfire Simulations. How much do you really know about computers?"

Bond gave a sheepish smile. "If you put it like that, the technicalities only."

Had he been pressed, computers were the last thing he really wanted to discuss just then with the strangely alluring and un-settling Persephone Proud.

5

TEACHER'S PET

WITH A LUCIDITY born of his years in the Service, Bond outlined to Percy the way in which a microcomputer works, as they both sauntered about the room in almost a ritual dance, carefully avoiding one another. A complex electronic tool, designed to do particular tasks when a series of commands are read into its two memories, he annunciated in a toneless voice like a schoolboy reciting Latin declensions to an indulgent master. A machine that would keep records and work out financial tasks one minute, process data the next, receive and transmit information over thousands of miles in a matter of seconds; that would design your new house, or allow you to play complicated games, make music or display moving graphics. A miracle with an ever-growing memory, but only as good as the program it was given.

"I know the theory—just," Bond said with a smile. "But I haven't a clue how it's all done by the programer."

"That, as I understand it from your wonderful old boss, is the main reason we're here," Percy retorted. Bond was mildly surprised to hear M spoken of as his wonderful old boss. "My job is to teach you programing languages, with special reference to the kind of thing my dark angel of an ex-husband used to do, and probably is doing right now. Oh, yes, he is ex. Dead, missing, whatever, I made sure it was legal."

"And how difficult is that going to be?" Bond asked with feigned innocence.

"Depends on your aptitude. It's like swimming, or riding a bicycle. Once you've got the knack it becomes second nature. Mind you, we're up against a particular kind of genius when it comes to Jay Autem Holy. I'm going to have to tell you a lot about *him*. Seriously, though, it's simply like learning a new language, or how to read music."

Percy walked over to the closet, from which she hauled a pair of large, customized cases, heavily embellished with coded security locks. They contained a very large microcomputer, clearly of exceptionally advanced design, several types of disk drive, and three metal boxes, which, when opened, revealed disks of differing sizes. She asked Bond to move the television set and then began to plug in the micro. The keyboard was twice the size of that on an electronic typewriter. She talked as she set up the equipment. This micro, she told him, was her idea of what Jay Autem would be using now. Bond had already noticed that she referred to Dr. Holy simply as Jay Autem or The Holy Terror.

"When he went missing, his own micro disappeared with him— or, I should say, at the same time. I guess he had it stashed away somewhere safe. In those days we were just beginning to see the full development of the microcompressor—you know, the chip that put a whole roomful of computer circuits on to a 5mm-square piece of silicon. He built his own machine, and we were still mainly using tapes for that. Since then there've been so many developments, and things have become much smaller. I've tried to keep pace with the technology, changing his original design, doing my best to keep one jump ahead, as he would have done. I rebuilt his Terror Six—that's what he called his machine—and altered it as I went on."

Bond stood peering over her shoulder as she made final adjustments.

"This," she waved a hand at the console, "is my equivalent of what would now be the Terror Twelve. Since Jay Autem disappeared, the chips have gotten smaller, but the big leap forward has been the incredible advance in the amount of memory a little thing like this can contain. That, and the way more realistic pictures—real video—can be used in the kind of programs he's interested in."

"And what kind of programs are those, Percy?"

"Well—" she selected a disk from one of the boxes, switched on a drive, inserted the disk and powered up the machine "—I can show you the kind of thing that *used* to fascinate him, when he was doing work for the Pentagon. Then we can take it a stage further."

The television screen had come alive, the disk drive whirring and rasping, a series of rapid beeps emanating from the loudspeaker. The drive continued to grunt and honk when the staccato beeps finally stopped and the screen cleared, showing a detailed map of the border between East and West Germany—the district around Kassel, NATO country.

Unaccountably Bond suddenly felt hot and flushed. He almost reached out a hand to Percy's shoulder, but instead loosened his tie as she withdrew a heavy, functional black joystick from one of her cases and plugged it into the console, pressing the keyboard *S*. Immediately a bright rectangle appeared on the map, which, Bond saw, was as clear as a printed piece of cartography.

"Okay, this may look like some weird game to you, but I promise you, it's a very advanced training aid."

Percy activated the joystick, and the rectangle slid across the screen, moving the map as it reached the outer perimeter, so that it scrolled up and down. The entire area covered was about eighty square miles of border, with a long oblong blue window below the map.

"I type in coordinates, and we go immediately to that section of the map." Percy suited action to words, and the map jumped on the screen, the rectangle staying in place. "Now we can look at what is going on in a smaller area." She positioned the rectangle over a village, about a mile from the border, and pressed the trigger on the joystick. Bond had become aware of the perfume Percy was wearing but couldn't decide what it was. He jerked his mind back to the matter in hand.

It was as if a zoom lens had been applied to the screen, for now he could see detail—roads, trees, houses, rocks and fields. Among this detail Bond could pick out at least six tanks and four troop carriers, while a pair of helicopters sat hidden behind buildings, and three Harrier aircraft could be defined on pads shielded by trees.

"We have to assume that some form of non-nuclear hostility exists."

Percy was typing commands into the micro, asking for information, first on NATO forces. The tanks, troop carriers, helicopters and Harriers blinked in turn, while their designated call-signs and strength ribboned out on the lower part of the screen. Percy noted the call-signs on a pad at her elbow and then typed a command for information concerning Warsaw Pact forces in this small sector, only a few miles square.

They appeared to be facing at least two companies of infantry, with armored support.

"It'll only give you available information, the kind of thing intelligence and reconnaissance would actually have." Percy watched as the screen flashed up known positions, the window running out data concerning the enemy.

Bond could not take his eyes from the soft curl of her hair on an almost exposed shoulder as she began to input orders. Two of the Harriers moved off, as though flying in to attack the enemy armor. At the same time, she activated the NATO tanks and troop carriers.

Individual responses—from the tank and infantry commanders—came up on the screen, while the tiny vehicles moved to her bidding, the tanks suddenly coming under attack, indicated by shell bursts on the screen and audible crumps and whines. Bond stooped slightly for a closer look at the screen and found himself glancing sideways at Percy's face, profiled and absorbed alongside his. He looked quickly back at the screen.

The action, controlled throughout by Percy, lasted for almost twenty minutes, during which time she was able to gain a small superiority over the enemy forces with the loss of three tanks, one helicopter, a Harrier and just under one hundred men.

Bond stood back a pace behind Percy. He had found the whole operation fascinating. He asked if this kind of thing was used by the military.

"This is only a simple computer TEWT," Percy said. A TEWT, she explained, was a Tactical Exercise Without Troops, a technique used in training officers and NCOs. "In the old days, as you know, they did TEWTs with boards, tables, sand trays and models. Now all you need is a micro. This is very simple, but you should see the advanced simulations they use at staff colleges."

"And Dr. Holy was programing this kind of thing for the Pentagon?" For the first time Bond noticed a little mole on Percy's neck that almost made him jump with delight.

"This, and more. When he disappeared, Jay Autem was into some exceptionally advanced stuff. Not only training but also specialist programs, where the computer is given all possible options and works out the one most likely to be taken by an opposing power under a particular set of circumstances."

"And now? If he really is still alive . . . ?"

"Oh, he's alive, James." She flushed suddenly. "I've seen him. Don't doubt it. He's the one I've already told you about—Jason St. John-Finnes, of Nun's Cross, Oxfordshire. I should know. After all, I was his watchdog for three and a half lousy years . . ."

"Watchdog?" Her eyes really were the most incredible color, a subtle shade of turquoise that changed according to the light.

Percy looked away, biting her lip in mock shame. "Oh, didn't they tell you? I married the bastard under orders. I'm a Company lady—from Langley. Marriage to Dr. Holy was an assignment. How else would I know the inside of this operation?"

"He wasn't trusted, then?" Bond tried not to show surprise, even though the idea of a CIA employee being instructed to marry in order to keep surveillance on her husband appalled him.

"At that time, with his contacts—he had many friends among the scientific community in Russia and the Eastern bloc—they couldn't afford to trust him. And they were right."

"You think he's working for the KGB now?"

"No." She went to the small freezer to get another bottle of champagne. "No, Jay Autem worked for Jay Autem and nobody else. At least I discovered that about him." Passing another glass to Bond, she added, "There are almost certainly Soviet connections in what he's doing now, but it'll be on a freelance basis. Jay Autem knows his business, but he's really only dedicated to money. Politics is another matter."

"So what sort of thing do you reckon he's doing?" Bond caught another strong whiff of that strange perfume.

"As they say, James, that's for him to know, and you to find out. And it's my job to teach you how. Tomorrow morning we start, in earnest. Eight-thirty suit you?"

"Hardly worth my going back to my own room." Bond casually glanced at his watch.

"I know, but you're going all the same. I'm to teach you all I can about how to prepare the kind of programs Jay Autem writes, *and* give you a course on how to break into his programs, should you be lucky enough to get your hands on one."

Percy took hold of his wrist and reached up to kiss him gently on the cheek. Bond moved closer, but Percy stepped away, wagging a finger.

"That's a no-no, James. But I'm a good teacher, and, if you prove to be a diligent pupil, I have ways of rewarding you that you never dreamed of when you were at school. Eight-thirty, sharp. Okay?"

"You guarantee results, Proud Percy?"

"I guarantee to teach you, Bond James," she said with a wicked grin. "And about computer programing as well."

Promptly at eight-thirty the next morning, Bond knocked at her door, one arm hidden behind his back. When she opened up, he thrust out his hand to give her a large rosy apple.

"For the teacher," he smiled.

It was the only joke of the day, for Percy Proud proved to be a hard and dedicated taskmaster.

6

HOLY CODE

IT TOOK A little less than a month, and even that was a tribute to Persephone Proud's teaching skill, as well as her pupil's capabilities. For the job—as they both knew—entailed the equivalent of learning a new language, and several complicated dialects in addition. Indeed, James Bond could not remember a time when he had been forced to call so heavily on his mental reserves, to focus his concentration, like a burning glass, on the intellectual matter at hand.

They quickly established a routine, which seldom varied. For the first few days they worked from eight-thirty each morning, but, as the late nights began to take their toll, this was modified to ten o'clock.

They would work until around one, then take lunch in a nearby bar, walking there and back, then resume work until five.

Each evening, at seven, they would go down to Le Bar—the Hotel de Paris' famous meeting place, where, it is said, the wrists and necks of the ladies put the Cartier showcases to shame.

If they intended to stay in Monaco for the evening, the couple would dine in the hotel, but further afield they could be seen at L'Oasis in La Napoule when the Cannes Casino took their fancy, sampling the latest tempting dish invented by the gourmet master chef, Louis Outhier. Sometimes they took a more austere meal at the Negresco in Nice, or even at La Réserve in Beaulieu, or—on occasions—the modest Le Galion, at the Menton port of Garavan. Wherever they ate, the meal was always a prelude to a night at the tables. *Don't go invisible,* M had instructed. *You are bait, and it would be a mistake to forget it. If they're trawling there, let them catch you.* So, the Bentley Mulsanne Turbo slid its silent way along the coast roads each evening, and the tanned, assured Englishman and his willowy elegant American companion became familiar figures on the gambling landscape of the Côte d'Azur.

Bond played only the wheel, and then conservatively—though he tended to double up on bets, plunging heavily on some evenings, coming away thousands to the good on others. Mainly he worked to a system using big money on the *Pair, Impair, Manque* and *Passe,* which paid evens, only occasionally changing to a *Carré*—covering four numbers at odds of just over eight to one.

Within the first week, he was the equivalent of a few thousand pounds, sterling, to the good, and knew the various casinos were watching with interest. No casino—even with the reputation of those along that once glittering coast—is happy about a regular who plays systematically, and wins.

Most nights, Percy and Bond were back at the hotel between three and three-thirty in the morning. Occasionally it was earlier—even one o'clock—giving them a chance to do another hour's work before getting a good sleep before starting all over again.

From time to time, during those weeks, they would not return until dawn—driving the coast roads with windows open to scent the morning air, feasting their eyes on the greenery of palm and plane trees, cacti and the climbing flowers around the summer homes of the wealthy, with their swimming pools fed by spouting marble dolphins. On those occasions, they would get back to the hotel in time to smell the first coffee of the day—one of the most satisfying aromas in the world, Bond thought.

The hotel staff considered it all very romantic—the attractive American lady and the wealthy Englishman (so lucky at the tables, and in love). Nobody would have dreamed of disturbing the lovebirds.

The truth concerning their enclosed life in Percy's room was, in fact, far removed from the fantasies of chambermaids and porters—at least for the first couple of weeks.

Percy began by teaching Bond how to flowchart a program—to draw out, in a kind of graph, exactly what he wanted the program to do. This he mastered in a matter of forty-eight hours, after which the serious business of learning the Basic computer language began. There were extra lessons on the use of graphics and sound. Toward the end of the second week, Bond started to learn various dialects of Basic, gradually grasping the essentials of further, more complex, languages like Machine Code, Cobal, or the high-level Pascal, and Forth.

Even in their spare time, they spoke of little else but the job in hand, though usually with special reference to Jay Autem Holy, and it did not take long for Bond to glean that Holy used his own hybrid program language, which Percy referred to as Holy Code.

"It's one of Jay Autem's main strengths as far as protecting his programs is concerned," Percy told him over dinner. "He's still using the same system, and the games being produced by his little company—Gunfire Simulations—are quite inaccessible to other programers. He always said that, if security was necessary—and by God he believed in it—the simplest protection is the best. He has an almost perfect little routine at the start of all his games programs, one that's quite unreadable by anyone who wants to copy, or get into the disk. It's probably the same piece of code he used to put on to his Pentagon work. Anyone trying to copy, or list, turns the disk into gibberish."

Bond insisted on talking about Dr. Holy whenever he was given the opportunity, for Percy was as close as he could ever get to knowing the man, before meeting him.

"He looks like a great angry hawk: Well, you've seen the photographs." They were dining in the hotel. "Outward appearances are not to be trusted, though. If I hadn't been on a specific job, I could easily have fallen for him. In fact, in some ways I did. There were often times when I hoped he'd prove to be straight." She looked pensive, and, for a moment, it was as though she saw neither Bond nor their plush surroundings. "He has amazing powers of concentration. That knack of being able to close the world out and allow his own work to become the only reality. You know how dangerous that can be."

Bond reflected that it could produce the kind of madness that turned men into devils, and Percy agreed. "Oh, yes, kind, loving and generous one minute: a clawing, ranting, terrifying ogre the next."

It was after this particular dinner, toward the end of the second week, that two things happened, one of which was to change the even tenor of Bond's emotions for some time to come.

"So, are we playing the Salles Privées tonight, or shall we jaunt?" Percy asked.

Bond decided on a trip along the coast, to the small casino in Menton, and they left soon after.

The gaming itself did not make it a night to remember, though Bond came away with a few thousand extra francs in his wallet.

As they pulled away from the casino, taking the road through Carnoles and so back to Monaco, he caught the lights of a car drawing away from directly behind him. He hadn't noticed anybody getting into it. Immediately he told Percy to tighten her seatbelt.

"Trouble?" She betrayed no sign of nervousness.

"I'm going to find out." He gunned the big car forward, letting it glide steadily into the nineties, holding well into the side of the narrow road.

The lights of the car behind remained visible, and when he was forced to slow—for that particular road twists and turns before hitting the long stretch of two-lane highway—it came closer, a white Citroen, its distinctive snout clearly visible behind its lowered headlight. It stuck like a limpet, a discreet distance behind. Bond wondered if it might only be some Frenchman, or an Italian wanting to race or showing off to a girlfriend. Yet the prickling sensation around the back of his neck told him this was a more sinister challenge.

They came off the two-lane stretch of highway like a rocket, and Bond stabbed at the big footbrake in order to drop speed quickly. The road into Monaco was not only narrow but also closed in on both sides, by rockface or houses, leaving little room for maneuver.

The Bentley's speed dropped and he took the next bend at around sixty. Percy gave a little audible intake of breath and, as he heard her, so Bond saw the obstruction: another car, pulled over to the right but still in the Bentley's road space, its hazard lights winking like a dragon's eyes. To its left, hardly moving and blocking most of the remaining space, was an old and decrepit lorry, wheezing and chugging as though about to suffer a complete collapse. He yelled for Percy to hang on, jabbed hard at the brake and slewed the Bentley, first left, then right, in an attempt to slalom his way between the vehicles. Halfway through the righthand skid, it was plain they would not make it. The Bentley's engine howled as he pushed the stalk from automatic drive to low-range, taking the engine down to first.

They were both jarred against the restraining straps of their seatbelts as the heavy machinery halted in midlunge, the speed dropping from fifty-five almost to zero in the blink of an eye. They were angled across the road with the car jamming their right side and the elderly lorry now backing slightly on the left. Pincers. Before they could take any further action, two men jumped down from the lorry and another pair materialized from the shadows surrounding the parked car, while the white Citroen boxed them in neatly from behind.

"Doors!" Bond shouted, slamming his hand against his door lock control, knowing his warning was more of a precaution than anything else, for the central locking system should be in operation. At least three of the team now approaching the Bentley appeared to be armed with axes.

Reaching for the hidden pistol compartment catch, Bond realized even as he did it, was only a reflex action. If he operated the electric window to use the weapon, they had a route in. They could get in anyway, for even a car built like this would eventually collapse under well-wielded axes.

The Bentley Mulsanne Turbo is a little over six-and-a-half feet wide. This one was not quite at right angles across the road. The Citroen behind, Bond judged, was within a foot of his rear bumper, but the Bentley's weight would compensate for that. Ahead, the car with its hazard lights blinking was a couple of inches from his door, the lorry some three inches from the bonnet. Directly in front, eight feet or so away, the roadside reached up into a sloping rock face. The Bentley's engine had not stalled, and still gave out its low grumble.

Holding his foot hard on the brake pedal, Bond adjusted the wheel, and, as one of the assailants came abreast of his window, placing himself between the Mulsanne and the parked car, raising both hands to bring down the axe, Bond slid the gear stalk into reverse, lifting his foot smartly off the brake.

The Bentley slid backwards, fast. Then a judder as they hit the Citroen, and a yelp of pain, loud and clear, from the man about to try to force entry with his axe. Thrown to one side, he had been crushed between the Bentley and the parked car.

With a quick movement, Bond now slid the automatic gear into drive. He had at most an extra six inches to play with and his foot bore gently down on the accelerator.

The car eased forward. Once again the screaming attacker on their right was crushed as the Bentley straightened, then gathered speed and headed for the gap.

The steering on the Mulsanne Turbo is so light and accurate that Bond did not have to wrench at the wheel; he simply used a very light touch of his fingers. The car gathered speed as it closed into the narrow gap between lorry and car. More control to the left. Straight. Hard left. A fraction to the right. Now! His foot went down, and they hurtled forward, clearing the front of the car with less than an inch to spare between the lorry on the left and the rock face to the right.

Then, quite suddenly, they were through, and back on the main, empty road, shooting downhill into Monaco itself.

"Hoods?" He could feel Percy quivering beside him.

"You mean *our* kind?" Bond replied. "Lion tamers?"

She nodded, her mouth forming a small "Yes."

"Don't think so. Looked like a team out to take our money and anything else they could grab. There's always been plenty of that along this coast. In the north of England they have a saying— where there's muck there's money. You can change that to where there's money there's lice."

Deep down, though, Bond knew he was lying. It was just possible that the cars, lorry and team were a group of gangsters, but the setup had been deadly in its professionalism and sophistication. He would report it as soon as he could get a safe line to London. Aloud he told Percy that he would do just that.

"So shall I."

They said nothing more until they got to her room. After that, neither of them would ever be able to say what started it.

"They were pros," she said.

"Yes."

"Don't like it, James. I'm pretty experienced, but I can still get frightened."

She moved toward him, and in a second his arms were around her, and their lips met as though each was trying to breathe fresh energy into the other. Her mouth slid away from his, and her cheek lay alongside his neck as she clung, whispering his name.

So they became lovers, their needs and feelings adding urgency to every moment of their days and nights. And so came a fresh anxiety. The final goal loomed before them: preparing Bond to meet Percy's former husband.

At the start of the third week, Percy suddenly called a halt. "I'm going to show you the kind of thing that Jay Autem could well be writing now," she announced, switching off the Terror Twelve and removing the set of normal disk drives that Bond had just been using.

In their place she fitted a large, hard-disk laser drive, and powering up the system, booted a program into the computer.

What appeared on the screen now were not the standard computer graphics Bond had become used to, even in their highest form, but genuine pictures—real, natural in color and texture, like a controllable movie.

"Video," Percy explained. "A camera interfaced with a hard laser computer disk. Now watch!"

She manipulated the joystick controller, and it was as though they were driving along a city street in heavy traffic.

Certainly the human forms she produced during the demonstration were more like advanced cartoon characters than the genuine background against which she made them move, run and fight. But the difference—using these symbolic figures against genuine places—added an almost frightening reality.

"I call it Bank Robbery," Percy said, and there was no doubt about the intention. By the clever juxtaposition of real film and graphics, you could "play" at robbing a real bank, dealing with every possible emergency that might arise. Bond was more than impressed.

"When I've taught you how to process and copy Jay Autem's work, you'll have the Terror Twelve and three types of drive to take with you, James. Don't say I haven't provided you with all the essential creature comforts. Now, let's really get to it."

Until later that evening, Bond applied himself to the work, but his mind hovered between the tasks at hand and the appalling tool that Jay Autem Holy—or indeed anyone with the necessary knowledge—had at his disposal for evil. Certainly Bond had been aware of the vast changes the micro had made in business, police and security work, but never before had he considered how far the applications of these machines had leaped forward. It should have been obvious, of course. If there were programs to assist the military in learning strategy and tactics, there had to be the possibility of those through which people could learn the best way to rob, cheat and even kill. The idea, combined with Percy's incredible demonstration of "living graphics"—in the shape of video pictures being combined with a game-type program—had brought new dimensions to his own thinking.

"And you really believe training programs, like the one you showed me earlier, are being used by criminals?" he asked much later, when they were in bed.

"I'd be very surprised if they were not." Percy's face was grave. "Just as I'd be amazed if Jay Autem was not training criminals, or even terrorists, in his nice Oxfordshire house." She gave a humorless little laugh. "I doubt if it's called Endor by accident. The Holy Terror has a dark sense of humor."

Bond knew that she was almost certainly right. Every two days, he received a report from England, via Bill Tanner: a digest of the information coming from the surveillance team that had been set up, with exceptionally discreet care, in the village of Nun's Cross. The reports showed that not only criminals but also known link-men with terrorist organizations from the Middle East, Italy, Germany and even closer to home were in constant contact with Professor St. John-Finnes and his small team of assistants at Endor. The sooner he got back to England and insinuated himself into that hornet's nest, the better it would be. London wanted him back, and even though they assured him the incident on the road between Menton and Monaco could only be the work of local gangsters, Bond detected a fresh anxiety.

He even asked Percy what she thought had actually happened on the night Dr. Holy went missing, and she gave a snort. "Well, he certainly didn't go by himself. That should be obvious to a cretin. Dear old Rolling Joe Zwingli must have gone with him, and that guy was as mad as a hatter—they had a file long as your arm on him at Langley. Oh, he was brave, in that foolhardy, unimaginative way some soldiers are, but, as I told you at the start, he was also crazy. Became very bitter after Viet Nam. He turned exceptionally, violently anti-American, so he was just the kind of malleable character Jay Autem could have used to set up a disappearing act."

"Dealt with the pilot first, then jumped, I suppose?" Bond was almost speaking to himself.

Percy nodded, then shrugged. "And did away with Rolling Joe when it suited him."

Bond finished Percy's course two days early having mastered the art of copying all types of programs, even those protected by every method Percy knew to be used by Dr. Holy. They saved the last two days for themselves.

"You're an enchantress," Bond told her. "I know of nobody else who could have taught me so much in such a short time."

"You've given me a few wrinkles as well, and I don't mean on my face," Percy said, putting her head back onto the pillow. "Come on, James, darling, one more time—as the jazzmen say—then we'll have a sumptuous dinner, and you can really show me how to play those tables in the Salles Privées." It was mid-afternoon, and by nine that evening they were both seated at the first table in the Casino's most sacred of rooms.

Bond's run of luck was still high, though he was now gambling with care, harboring his winnings, which had quadrupled since his arrival. During the three hours they played that night he was, at one point, down to forty thousand francs. But the wheel started to run in his favor, and eventually, by midnight, his winnings had increased to three hundred thousand francs.

He waited for two turns to pass, deciding to make the next bet the last of the night, when he heard a sharp intake of breath from Percy.

Glancing toward her, he saw the color leave her face, the eyes shocked and staring at the entrance. It was not so much a look of fear as one of surprise.

"What is it?"

She answered in a whisper. "Let's get out. Quickly. Over there. Just come in."

"Who?" His eyes fell on a tall, grizzled man, straight-backed, and with eyes that swept the room as though surveying a battlefield. He did not really need to hear her reply.

"The old devil. And we thought Jay Autem had done him in.

That's Rolling Joe in the flesh. Joe Zwingli's here, and with a couple of infantry divisions by the look of it!"

Zwingli was now moving into the room, flanked by four other men, neat and smart as officers on parade, and looking as dangerous as an armored brigade about to attack a Boy Scout troop.

7

ROLLING HOME

GENERAL JOE ZWINGLI had been no chicken at the time of his disappearance. He must now be in his middle, or, more probably, late seventies. Yet, from where Bond sat, Rolling Joe looked like a man of sixty, in good physical shape. The other four men were younger, heavier, and not the kind of people you would be likely to meet at Sunday School parties.

For a moment, Bond sat calmly awaiting the worst, convinced that Zwingli and his men were looking for him and Percy. There had to be a connection; one didn't need a crystal ball to work that out. Zwingli had gone missing with Jay Autem Holy, so had been a necessary part of the disappearance plot. If there was collusion at the time of the airplane wreck, there would still be collusion now—for Dr. Holy and General Zwingli were tied together for life, by a much stronger bond than the marriage vows. Conspirators can rarely divorce.

Bond smiled genially. "Don't stare, Percy, it's rude. It also may call the good general's attention to us—if it's us he's looking for." His lips hardly moved as he watched Zwingli and his entourage out of the corner of one eye.

To his relief, the general's craggy face broke into a broad smile. He was not looking in their direction but advancing toward a dark-skinned, muscular man, possibly in his middle thirties, who had been sitting at the bar.

The pair shook hands, warmly, and there were greetings and introductions all round.

"I think, to be on the safe side, it would be prudent for us to take our leave now," Bond muttered. "Be casual and natural."

He went through the business of tipping the croupier, gathering the plaques together as they rose and made their way to the *caisse,* where Bond opted for cash rather than a check. Once outside, he took Percy's arm, leading her firmly back to the hotel.

"It could simply be coincidence, but I'm taking no chances. I don't for a moment think he could recognize you. How well did you know him, Percy?"

"Two or three dinner parties. Washington social functions. I knew him, but he always gave the impression of being completely uninterested. Not just in me, but in all women. It was him all right, James. I've no doubt about that."

During M's briefing Bond had studied a number of photographs, including the two well-documented occasions when General Zwingli had appeared on the cover of *Time* magazine. "For someone who's been dead that long, he looked in exceptionally good shape. No, the only way he could recognize you is if he was forewarned; if he knew you'd changed your . . . well . . . your image."

Percy giggled. "This *is* my real image, James. Mrs. Jay Autem Holy was the disguise. I ate my head off, let my hair go, wore plain, thick, clear-glass spectacles to make it look like I had the worst eyesight since Mr. Magoo . . ."

"And the nose?"

"Okay, so I had a nose job after Jay Autem went missing— nobody's perfect. But you're right, I'd have had to be fingered directly to Rolling Joe for him to know it was me."

"There's always the possibility that someone's fingered *me.*" Bond brushed back the lock of hair that fell, like a comma, over his right eye. They reached the hotel entrance. "You recognize the fellow he met? The swarthy one the general seemed to be expecting?"

"The face was familiar. I've seen him—or a picture of him— before. Maybe he's on file. You?"

"The same. I should know him." Bond continued to talk, telling her they would have to leave, ". . . and fast. It's only a precaution, but we really shouldn't hang around. The best way would be for us both to get away in the Bentley. We can be in Paris by lunchtime tomorrow."

"Wait till we're upstairs," she said, then when they reached her room: "My brief was to leave here on my own. I have a car, and orders that we go separately. Under no circumstances are we to travel together. Those are my instructions, and there's no way I'm going to disobey them."

"So?"

"So I agree with you, James. I think it's merely a coincidence. It's also a useful piece of information—knowing that Zwingli lives. And I think we should leave: the sooner, the better."

They went their different ways, to pack. Bond lugged the cases containing the Terror Twelve into his own room, together with the various disk drives and several utility programs, on disks, to help him copy, or recover, Holy's listings—should he get hold of any. Meanwhile he worried at the identity of the man Zwingli had met in the Salles Privées. Automatically he had broken down the description of him so that his mind registered the main features: average height, muscular, dark-skinned, almost certainly of Middle Eastern origin. Regular, rather straight, nose; neat heavy black hair cut short; eyes to match, set wide on the squarish face; lips normal, no thickness; a small mustache; moved confidently; could have a military background. Worry at it, Bond told himself, and the name will come.

Percy settled her bill separately, and they met, as planned, in the garage, after her luggage had been loaded into the boot of her sporty little blue Dodge 600ES.

They would both be traveling on roughly the same road, for Percy had to return to the CIA Paris Station, while Bond faced the long drive back to Calais, and the ferry to Dover.

"You think we'll ever meet again?" Bond felt uncharacteristically inadequate.

She put her hands on his shoulders, looking into the startlingly blue eyes. "We have to, don't we, James?"

He nodded, knowing they shared each other's private thoughts. "You know how to get in touch with me?"

It was her turn to give a small nod. "Or you can call me—when all this is over." She rattled off a Washington number. "If I'm not there, they'll pass on a message, okay?"

"Okay." He stepped forward, and Percy put her arms around his neck, kissing him, long and lovingly on the mouth.

As she started up the Dodge, Percy leaned out of the window: "Take care, James. I'll miss you." Then she was gone, in a smooth acceleration, along the lane of cars and out—up the ramp—into the streets of Monaco, and the night roads of France.

Half an hour later, as planned, Bond took the Mulsanne Turbo from the same garage, and, within minutes, he was out of the Principality, heading back along the Moyenne Corniche toward the beginning of the main A8 Autoroute.

It was on the first leg—at about four in the morning—when Bond suddenly remembered the true identity of the man Zwingli had met. Yes, there *was* a file. The thick dossier had been across Bond's desk on several occasions, and there was a general watching brief on Tamil Rahani. Part American, part Lebanese, and carrying at least two passports, Rahani was usually in New York, where he was chairman, and principal shareholder, of Rahani Electronics. He had first come to the attention of the Service some five years before, handed on to them by their American counterparts. At this time, Rahani made several attempts to secure defense contracts from both the American and British governments, mainly in connection with aircraft communications electronics.

They had turned Rahani down flat, mainly because of his many contacts with undeniably unfriendly agencies, and uncertain governments. Wealthy; smooth; sharp; intelligent, and slippery as an eel. The flag on the file—Bond remembered—was ciphered *Possible clandestine. Probable subversive.*

Once the truth had settled in his mind, Bond pushed the Mulsanne to its limit. All he wanted to do was get back to England, report to M, and try to move in on Jay Autem Holy—a task that was more inviting than ever, now that he knew something of the doctor's work, plus the fact that Zwingli was alive, well, and—unless he was mistaken—working hand in glove with a highly suspect character.

During the final stage of the long drive—on the Autoroute to Calais—Bond found himself singing aloud. Perhaps, after the enforced idleness, lack of excitement, and intrigues of M's plan to use him as bait, he was starting to feel the fire of action in his belly once more.

"Rolling home," he sang, remembering far-off days when he would literally roll home, with brother officers.

> "Rolling home,
> By the light of the silvery moon;
> I have twopence to lend,
> And twopence to spend,
> And twopence to send home to . . ."

His voice trailed off. He could not bring himself to sing the last line, about sending money home to his wife. For the ghost of his own dead wife, Tracy, still haunted him, even though he consciously missed Percy Proud's clear mind and agile, beautiful body. Weakness, he chided himself. He was trained as a loner, one who acted without others, one who relied on himself. Yet he did miss her . . .

Pull yourself together, he told himself. Yet, undeniably, there were moments when he thought he could still smell her scent, and touch her skin.

Among the bills and circulars of mail awaiting Bond at his London flat was one letter—from a firm of business consultants— that demanded special attention. Embedded within this seemingly innocuous letter were a series of telephone numbers—one for each day of the week—that he could ring and so set up a meeting at the safe house near St. Martin's Lane.

This time it was a truly glorious late spring evening. Summer was around the corner, and you could feel it, even in the heart of the capital.

"Well, 007, the woman's taught you all the tricks of the trade, eh?"

"Some of them, sir. But I really wanted to talk to you about a new development." Without wasting words, or time, he gave them a summary of the final hours in Monaco, and the sighting of Zwingli with Tamil Rahani.

Bond had hardly got Rahani's name out before M ordered the Chief of Staff to check.

"There's a spot and report order on that joker." M looked at Bond, the old gray eyes hard and showing no compassion.

Tanner returned within ten minutes. "Last report from Milan. Seen by our resident there, who had a weather eye on him. Rahani appeared to be on his usual round of business meetings." The Chief of Staff gave a somewhat downcast shrug. "Unhappily, sir, nobody spotted him leaving. Though his airline ticket showed a return booking to New York yesterday, he was not on the flight."

"And I suppose nobody's seen hide nor hair of him since?" M nodded like a Buddha. "Except 007, in Monaco."

"Well, he was in the casino," Bond added. "As I've said, with General Zwingli and four thugs."

M looked at him, in silence, for a full minute. "Incredible," he said, "incredible that Zwingli's still alive, let alone mixed up with Rahani. Where does *he* fit into all this? You'll just have to be alert to Rahani's possible involvement, 007. He's always been a bit of an unknown quantity, so we'll inform those who need to know. You see, we're ready to put you in. Now, here's what I want you to do. First, your old acquaintance Freddie Fortune has . . ."

James Bond groaned loudly.

For the next week, he was to be seen around his old London haunts. He confided in one or two people that his feelings of disillusion had grown considerably. He had been in Monte Carlo where things had run true to the old adage—lucky at cards, unlucky in love—except it had been roulette, not cards.

Carefully, he laid a trail among people most likely to talk, or those whose connections were right for some "salting." Then, on the Thursday evening, in the bar of one of Mayfair's plush caravanserai, he bumped, as if by accident, into Lady Freddie Fortune, the extravagant, extreme, pamphlet-wagging socialite, whom he always called his "Champagne Communist." She was a vivacious, petite, compact and pretty redhead, completely untrustworthy, and always in the gossip columns, either campaigning for some outrageous cause or involved in sexual scandal. "Red Freddie," as some called her, was discreet only when it suited her. That night, Bond dropped a hint that he was now looking for work in the computer field. He also poured out all his troubles—an affair in Monte Carlo that had ended disastrously, leaving him bitter and wretched.

Lady Freddie was, it seemed, titillated to see this man, once a pillar of good form, become so emotional, so she whipped Bond off to her bed, allowing him to cry on her shoulder, which led, inevitably, to other acts of sympathy. The next morning, Bond feigned a hangover and a morose, even waspish, manner. But none of this put Freddie Fortune off in the slightest. As he was leaving, she told him that she had some particular friends who might well be of use to him. If, that is, he really meant to find a job in computers.

"Here." She tucked a small business card into his breast pocket. "It's a nice little hotel. If you can make it on Saturday, I'll be there. Only, for heaven's sake, don't let on I've told you. I leave it to you, James, but, if you do decide to come, be surprised to see me. Okay?"

On the following Saturday morning, therefore—with a weekend case and all the computer equipment in the boot of the Bentley— James Bond drove out of London, onto the Oxford road. Within the hour he had turned off and was threading through country lanes, heading for the village of Nun's Cross, near Banbury.

8

THE BULL

Banbury cross is not an antiquity, but was erected in the late 1850s, to commemorate the marriage of the Princess Royal to the Crown Prince of Prussia. There was a much earlier cross— there were three, to be exact—but the present Victorian Gothic monstrosity was placed where it is today because a local historian believed this to be the site of the ancient High Cross.

Three miles to the north of Banbury, nestling beside a wooded hill, lies the village of Nun's Cross, and there is no cross on view there at all.

James Bond guided the Mulsanne Turbo through the narrow

main street of Nun's Cross, and into the yard of the coaching inn, which rejoices in the name of The Bull at the Cross.

The inn, he considered, hefting the overnight case from the boot, was probably the only going concern in Nun's Cross—a beautiful Georgian building, lovingly kept, and neatly modernized. The Bull, he'd noted in a guidebook, even offered "gourmet weekends for the discriminating."

From the porter who took his case, Bond learned that, as far as the hotel was concerned, it was going to be a very quiet weekend.

"A strange paucity of bookings, sir," the porter told him. "Possibly the recession. Jammed full last weekend, and booked to the rafters next. But now it's very sparse—thank you, sir," as the tip changed hands. "We've had a lot of the recession around here, sir."

Bond unpacked, changed into gray slacks, an open-necked shirt topped by a navy pullover, and his most comfortable moccasins. He was not armed. The ASP 9mm lay comfortably clipped into its hidden compartment in the Bentley. Yet he remained alert as he went down, through the old coach yard and into the village street. His eyes were searching for either a dark blue Jaguar XJ6 or a gray Mercedes-Benz saloon. The license numbers had been committed to memory, for both cars had appeared in his mirror, exchanging places with monotonous frequency, ever since he had taken to the road that morning.

He was under no illusion. For the first time since he had assumed the mantle of a disaffected former member of the Secret Service, someone other than his own people was following him—almost blatantly, for it was as though they wished to be seen as well as to see.

It was too early for a lunchtime drink. Bond decided to have a look around this village, which, if everything added up, harbored a sophisticated villain who was possibly also a traitor.

The Bull at the Cross lay almost on the crossroads that marked the center of the old village—a hodge-podge of mainly Georgian buildings, with a sprinkle of slightly older terraces, houses that were now the village shops, leaning in on one another as though mutually dependent. Small rows of what must, at one time, have been laborers' cottages now housed those who commuted into Banbury, or even Oxford, to labor in different fields.

Almost opposite the coach yard entrance stood the church, while, to the south, the main street meandered out into open country, scattered with copses and studded with larger houses. Gateways and rhododendron-flanked drives gave glimpses of large, sedate Victorian mansions, or glowing Hornton stone Georgian buildings. The third driveway past the church was walled, with heavy, high and modern gates set into the original eighteenth-century stone. A small brass plate was sunk into the wall to the right of the gates: Gunfire Simulations Ltd. In newer stone, carved and neatly blended with the original, was the one word "Endor."

The drive, which turned abruptly into a turmoil of low trees and bushes, appeared to be neatly kept, and a slash of gray slate roof was only just visible some two hundred yards in the distance.

Bond calculated that the grounds were about a square mile in extent, for the high wall continued to his left, the boundary being a narrow dirt track neatly signposted "The Shrubs."

After half a mile or so, he turned back, retracing his steps along the village street and carrying on to the northern extremity, where the cluster of old houses bordered on a scrubby, wooded hill. Here the sharp speculators had been at work and a modern housing estate—as many small brick boxes as possible in the space—had encroached almost on the woodland itself.

It was after twelve when Bond ambled slowly back to the inn. The dark blue Jaguar stood not far from the Bentley. Only the staff appeared to be about. He even found the private bar empty, but for the barman and one other guest.

"James, darling, what a surprise to find _you_ here, out in the sticks!" Freddie Fortune, neat in an emerald shirt and tight jeans, sat in a window seat.

"The surprise is mutual, Freddie. Drinking?"

"Vodka and tonic, darling."

He got the drinks from the barman, carrying them over to Freddie, saying loudly, "What brings you here, then?"

"Oh, I adore this place. Come down to commune with nature—and friends—about once a month. Not your sort of place though, James." Then, quietly, "So glad you could make it."

Bond said he was glad also, although he felt unutterably foolish, chattering after the manner of Freddie's usual London friends.

Freddie took a quick sip of her vodka and tonic. "So you wanted to get out of the hurlyburly, yah?"

"Yah," Bond almost mimicked her affected accent.

"Or did you come because *I* asked you?"

He gave a noncommittal "Mmmm."

"Or, perhaps, the possibility of work?"

"Little of all three, Freddie."

"Three's a crowd." She snuggled up beside him. Freddie's small, excellently proportioned figure was just right for snuggling, thought Bond. Then—almost immediately—his face clouded—as Persephone entered his mind, so clearly that she might really have been there in person. For a second, Bond had a strange, eldritch feeling that Percy was genuinely close by.

They lunched together from a menu that would not have put the Connaught to shame, then walked for some five miles across the fields and through the woodland, getting back around three-thirty—"Just in time for a nice quiet siesta." Freddie gave him the come-to-bed look, and Bond, invigorated by the walk, did not stand a chance. When he entered her room, she was lying on the bed, wearing precious little.

Smiling sweetly, she said, "Come and bore the pants off me, darling."

"Dinner together?" Bond asked later, as they sat over tea in the Residents' Lounge. The hotel had filled up, and three Spanish waiters scurried about with silver teapots, small plates of sandwiches and fancy cakes.

"Oh, Lord, darling," Freddie put on her "devastated" face. "I have a dinner date." Then she smiled—sweet innocence. "So have you, if we play our cards right. You see—I told you so—I've got some old friends who live here." She suddenly became confidential. "Now, listen, James, they could be a godsend. You were serious about going into computers? Programing and all that sort of thing? Micros?"

"Absolutely."

"Super. Old Jason'll be thrilled."

"Jason?"

"My friend—well, friends really. Jason and Dazzle St. John-Finnes."

"Dazzle?"

Freddie gave an impatient back-flip of her hand. "Oh, I think her real name's Davide or something peculiar. Everyone calls her Dazzle. Super people. Into computers in a really big way. They're incredibly clever and invent frightfully complicated war games."

M had already briefed him about the other members of Jay Autem Holy's entourage—the "wife," Dazzle; a young expert called Peter Amadeus ("Austrian, I think," Freddie now added); and the even younger Cambridge graduate, Ms. Cindy Chalmer.

"She's an absolute hoot." Freddie became expansive. "The local peasants call her Sinful Cindy, and she's jolly popular, particularly with the men. Black, you know."

No, Bond said he did not know, but he would like to find out. How did Sinful Cindy get on with Peter Amadeus?

"Oh, darling, no woman has anything to fear—or hope for—from the Amadeus boy, if you see what I mean. Look, I'll give Jason a bell." Freddie, like many of her kind, was apt to lapse into the London vernacular, particularly when out of Town. "Just to make certain they don't mind me having you in tow."

She disappeared for five minutes or so.

"We've got a result, James," she gushed on her return. "They'd absolutely adore to have you as a dinner guest."

Gently he questioned her, in an attempt to discover how long "Old Jason and Dazzle" had been such close friends. She hedged a little, but it finally transpired that she had known them for exactly two months.

They went in the Bentley—"I adore the smell of leather in a Rolls, or Bentley. So positively sexual," Freddie said, curled up in the front passenger seat. Playing out the charade, he was careful to ask for directions, and as they neared the turning she told him—"The gates'll probably be closed, but turn in and wait. Jason's a maniac about security. He has lots of incredible electronic devices."

"I'll bet," Bond said under his breath, but obeyed instructions, turning left and pushing the Mulsanne's snout to within an inch of the great high metal barriers. He would have put money on their being made of steel, worked to give the impression of wrought-iron ornamental bars. The gate-hangings themselves were shielded, behind massive stone pillars. There had to be some kind of closed-circuit television system, for the car sat waiting for only a matter of seconds before the locks clicked audibly, and the gates swung back.

As Bond had already divined, Endor was a large house. It had around twenty rooms. Classical Georgian in style, with a pillared porch and symmetrically placed sash windows like eyes peering out of the high golden stone, as though Endor itself watched the newcomers sliding gracefully up the drive. The crunch of gravel under the Bentley's wheels brought back many memories to him—the older cars he had once owned, and oddly, the books of Dornford Yates he'd read at school, with their adventurers riding forth to do battle in Bentleys or Rolls-Royce cars, usually to protect gorgeous ladies with very small feet.

Jason St. John-Finnes—Bond had learned to think of him by that name—stood by the open door, light shafting onto the turning circle. He had made no attempt at disguise. The decade in which he had been "dead" appeared to have taken no toll, for he looked exactly like the many photographs in his file at the Regent's Park Headquarters. Tall and slim, he was obviously in good physical condition, for he moved with grace and purpose. The famous green eyes were just as startling as Percy had maintained. By turns warm or cold, they were almost hypnotic, lively and penetrating, as though they could look deeply into a person's heart. The nose was indeed large and hooked—a great bill—so that the combination of bright searching eyes and the big sharp nose *did* give the impression of a bird of prey. Bond shuddered slightly. There was something exceptionally sinister about the scientist, but this unsettling facet all but vanished the moment he started to speak.

"Freddie!" He approached her with a kiss. "How splendid to see you, and I'm so glad to meet your friend." He stretched out a hand. "Bond, isn't it?"

The voice was low, pleasant, and full of laughter, the accent mid-Atlantic, almost Bostonian, the handshake firm, strong, warm and very friendly. It was as though a wave of good will and welcome passed through the flesh as their palms touched.

"Ah, here's Dazzle. Darling, this is Mr. Bond."

"James," he said, already in danger of being hypnotically charmed by the man. "James Bond."

For a few seconds his heart raced as he gazed at the tall, ash-blonde, slight-figured woman who had come out of the house.

Then he realized that it was a trick of the light, for at a distance, especially as now at dusk, Dazzle could easily be taken for Percy Proud: the same hair, figure and bone structure, even the same movements.

Dazzle was as warm and welcoming as her husband. The pair of them had a curious effect, as though together they were able to enfold you, pulling you into some circle of enchantment. As they left the car and walked into the spacious hallway, Bond had the ridiculous desire to throw all caution to the wind and immediately face Jason, asking him what had really happened on that day so long ago when he had taken off on the ill-fated flight, what had been the purpose of disappearing, and what he was up to now.

During the whole of that evening, in fact, he had to keep a strong hold on himself not to come out into the open. Between them Jason and the vivacious Dazzle proved to be a daunting couple. Within minutes of being in their company one felt oneself an old friend. Jason, the story went, was Canadian by birth, while Dazzle came from New York, though you would have been hard put to place her accent, which had more of Knightsbridge in it and very little of Fifth Avenue.

The one matter never really discussed in detail during M's briefings had been finance, but now, seeing the house with its brilliant decor ("That's Dazzle," Jason laughed, "she has what the designers call flair") and obviously careful taste, one became aware of wealth. The large drawing room into which they were first taken was a clever blend of original Georgian and comfortable modern—the antique pieces counterpointing the quiet, striped wallpaper (a cream overlaid with lime) and not clashing with the more modern pictures, or the large buttoned-leather wing chairs and Chesterfields. Where, Bond wondered, did all this come from? Where were the (rich) bodies buried?

A Filipino houseboy appeared to serve the drinks, and the talk was almost exclusively about what a wonderful refurbishing job they had done on the house (that from Freddie) and amusing tidbits of local scandal.

"It's what I adore about life in a village," Jason gave a low chuckle. "My work doesn't allow for me to be what you might call socially active, but we still get all the gossip—because everybody does."

"Except the gossip about ourselves, darling," Dazzle said with a grin. Bond realized that her nose was similar to Percy's *before* it had been "bobbed." There was an oddity. Was Jay Autem conscious of it? Bond wondered. Had he always known what the real Percy looked like?

"Oh, I get the gossip about us." Jason's voice was deep with humor. "Cindy and I are having a passionate love affair, while you're in bed most of the time with Peter Amadeus."

"Much good would it do me." Dazzle put a hand over her mouth, mockingly. "Where are they, anyway, dear? Peter and Cindy, I mean," she asked.

"Oh, they'll be up in a minute. They decided to play one more round of The Revolution. We've still got a good deal of preliminary work to do." He turned to Bond. "We're in the computer games business."

"So Freddie mentioned." At last he managed to break the spell, allowing a hint of superior disapproval into his tone.

Jason caught it at once. "Oh, but you're a computer programer as well, aren't you? Freddie told me."

"A little. Not games though. Not really." The stress on the word *games* was exact, designed to give the impression that the use of computers to play mere games was anathema to him.

"Aha," Jason wagged a finger, "but there are games and games, Mr. Bond. I'm talking about complex, highly original and undoubtedly intellectual pastimes, not the whizz-bang-bang-shoot-'em-up arcade rubbish. Who do you work for?"

Bond admitted he worked for nobody at the moment. "My training in programing was done when I worked for the Foreign Office," he said, trying to sound diffident.

"You're *that* Mr. Bond!" Dazzle sounded genuinely excited.

He nodded. "Yes, the notorious Mr. Bond. Also the innocent Mr. Bond."

"Of course." For the first time—like reality showing through a mask—there was a slightly dubious note to Jason's reply. "I read about your case."

"Were you really a spy?" Dazzle tended to become almost breathlessly excited by anything that interested her.

"I . . ." Bond began, then put on a show of floundering, so that Jason came to his rescue.

"I don't think that's the kind of question you're meant to ask, my dear." At that moment, Peter Amadeus and Cindy Chalmer came into the room.

"Ah, the amazing Doctor Amadeus," Jason rose.

"And Sinful Cindy," laughed Dazzle.

"I'd be flattered if they called *me* Sinful Freddie," said Lady Freddie as she greeted the pair.

"Sinful indeed!" Cindy was not black, as Freddie had told Bond, but more of a creamy coffee shade. "The product of a West Indian father and a Jewish mother," she was later to confide in Bond, adding that there were a thousand racist jokes that could be made at her expense.

Dressed in a simple gray skirt and white silk shirt, Cindy had the figure and legs of a dancer, breasts like Ogen melons—the simile was ancient, but exact—and a face that reminded Bond of a very young Ella Fitzgerald. Peter, on the other hand, was around thirty—a few years older than Cindy—short, precise, prematurely balding and with a pedantic streak crossed with occasional glimpses of verbal viciousness that would have been the only hint of his sexual predilection, had he not, as it turned out, been so blatantly honest about it.

After the introductions (Bond wondered if he imagined it, but Cindy Chalmer appeared to give him a long, almost conspiratorial, look), Dazzle suggested they go in to dinner. "Tomas'll be furious if his cooking is spoiled." Tomas was the near-invisible Filipino, and had learned to cook at the feet of Europe's greatest chefs—courtesy of Jason St. John-Finnes.

The meal was almost a banquet—a Lombardy soup, made from pouring boiling consommé over raw eggs sprinkled with Parmesan and laid on bread, partially fried in butter; smoked salmon mousse; venison baked in a sauce of juniper berries, wine, chopped ham and lemons; and a dessert of pears in chocolate sauce, "Specially for Lady Freddie."

To begin with, the conversation mainly concerned the work that Cindy and Peter had just been doing.

"How did it go, then?" Jason asked as they sat down at a long refectory table set on bare polished boards in the dining room.

"We've found another couple of random problems you can set into the early section. Raise the general and search strengths of the British patrols, and you get some very interesting results." Peter gave a lopsided smile.

"And, to equalize, there's a new random for the later stages," Cindy added. "We've put in a random card that gives the colonial militia more uncaptured cannon. If you draw that option the British don't know the strength until they begin assaulting the hill."

Freddie and Dazzle were chattering away about clothes, but Jason caught Bond's interested eye. He turned to Peter and Cindy.

"Mr. Bond does not approve of using such high-tech magic for mere games," he said, smiling, and the comment was made with no malice.

"Ah, come on, Mr. Bond!"

"It's intellectual stimulation."

These remarks made by Cindy and Peter, in that order. Peter continued, "Is chess a frivolous use of wood, or ivory?"

"I said nothing of the kind." Bond laughed, knowing that the interrogation and testing time was getting close. "I was simply trained as a programer of Cobal and databases for government purposes . . ."

"Not military purposes, Mr. Bond?"

"Oh, the military use them, of course. I was a naval man, myself, but some time ago." He paused. "I was, in fact, intrigued. These games of yours—are they really games?"

"They are games in one sense," Peter answered. "I suppose they're also tutorials. We know that a lot of serving military people order our products."

"They teach, yes." Jason leaned over toward Bond. "You cannot sit down and play one of our games unless you have some knowledge of strategy, tactics and military history. They can be taxing—and they do require intelligence. It's a booming market, James." He paused, as though a thought had struck him. "What's the most significant leap forward in the computer arts—in your opinion, of course?"

Bond did not hesitate. "Oh, without doubt the advances being made, almost by the month, in the field of vastly increased storage of data, using smaller and smaller space."

Jason nodded. "Yes. Increased memory, in decreased space. Millions of accessible facts, stored for all time in something no larger than a postage stamp. And, as you say, it's increasing by the month, even by the day. In a year or so, the little home micro will be able to store almost as much information as the large mainframe computers used by banks and government departments. There is also the breakthrough that marries the laser video disk recording with computer commands—movements, actions, scale, response." They were already experimenting with such things, here. "At Endor we have a very sophisticated setup. You may like to look around after dinner."

"Put him on The Revolution and see if a novice player comes up with anything new," suggested Cindy.

"Why not?" The bright green eyes glittered, as though some challenge was in the offing.

"You've made a computer game out of what? The Russian Revolution?"

Jason laughed, "Not quite, James. You see, our games are vast—in a way too large for the home computer. They're all very detailed and require a great amount of memory to use. We pride ourselves on the playability, that area which makes the battles and campaigns 'fun' to fight, as well as being taxing, intellectually and mentally. We don't even like calling them games. Simulations is a better word. No, as yet we haven't got a simulation of any revolution. We are, though, preparing an interesting one of The American Revolution—you know, the final stages prior to the so-called War of Independence: Concord; Lexington; Bunker Hill. September 1774 to June 1775.

"At the moment, we have only six simulations on the market: Crécy, Blenheim, The Battle of the Pyramids—Napoleon's 1798 Egyptian expedition—Austerlitz, Cambrai, which is good, because the outcome could have been very different, and Stalingrad. We're very well advanced with one on the Blitzkrieg of 1940. And we're in the early stages of The American Revolution."

Bond remarked that Cindy and Peter talked as though they were actually playing the game—"I mean simulation," he hastily added.

"Freddie and I are going to look at dresses," Dazzle suddenly interrupted, rather sharply. "It's shop all the time. Very boring. See you later, James Bond."

Jason did not even apologize, merely smiling like a benign eagle. Freddie gave Bond a broad wink as the two ladies left the room, and, as he turned back to the table, he caught Cindy looking at him again, in the same almost conspiratorial way—tinged, this time, with jealousy. Or did he imagine it?

"Yes, to answer your query, James," Jason had hardly paused, "they *are* playing a kind of simulation. Naturally, you're conversant with flowcharting a computer program?"

Bond nodded, recalling the hours spent in Monaco. Once more, with the memory, came that odd sense of Percy's presence. He dragged himself back, for Jason had continued to speak.

"Before we prepare a detailed flowchart, we have to find out what we wish to chart. So we begin to discover the simulation by playing it on a large table. This acts as our graphics guide, and we have counters for units, troops, ships, cannon, plus cards for the random possibilities: weather cards, epidemics, unexpected gains or losses, hazards of war."

"From this," Peter took over, "we learn the scope of the program task. So, when we've played the campaign—"

"About a million times," Cindy added. "It seems like a million, anyway."

Peter nodded. "We're ready to begin flowcharting the various sections. You have to be dedicated in this job."

"Come," Jason's voice became commanding, "we will show James Bond the laboratory, and the board we're working on now. Who knows, he may become interested and return to battle it out with me. If you do," he looked straight at Bond, "make sure you have plenty of time. Campaigns cannot be fought in five minutes." Behind these seemingly pleasant words there was a hint of obsession, a glitter in the eyes that seemed to say that, somehow, the way of Jay Autem Holy led beyond reason.

As they left the room, Bond was conscious of Cindy brushing against him. He felt her hand touch lightly on his right hip, just where the ASP 9mm was holstered. Had that been accidental, or was she carrying out a subtle search? Whatever the answer, Cindy Chalmer, at least, knew that he was armed.

They went through the main hall, and Jason produced a bunch

of keys attached to a thin gold chain. He unlocked a door that had once, he said, been the way down to the cellars. "We've made a few changes, naturally."

Naturally, Bond acknowledged, but was quite unprepared for the nature of the alterations. Below the house there were at least three large, well-equipped computer rooms, with several well-known makes of superior micros sitting in front of their Visual Display Units. But, in the last room—Jason's own office—Bond's heart leaped as he spotted a machine that was almost exactly, on the surface at least, like the Terror Twelve now safe in the Bentley's boot outside.

The walls of each room were filled with metal storage cabinets, and from his office Jason led the way into a long chamber, lit from above by at least thirty spotlights. Below them was a large table, while the walls were covered with charts and maps.

The table was overlaid with a thick plastic grid, below which rested a detailed map of the Eastern seaboard of America—centered on Boston—as it was in the 1770s. The main communicating roads and natural features were clearly marked in color, and the map took up almost the entire table.

In the center of the grid stood a rectangular framework made of black plastic, the size and shape of a large television screen, while two small easels had been placed at the far end, and a series of trays—on opposite sides of the table—contained packs of white three-by-five cards.

There were chairs placed so that players could sit in front of the trays, with desk tops to each player's right, replete with paper, maps and printed forms.

They began to explain the nature of the game, and how it was used to build up all the details of the simulation before anything was committed to a computer program.

The rectangular framework moved freely—though in a strict pattern—both vertically and horizontally across the map.

"That is the area a player will eventually see on his screen, when we have built the game." Jason's manner had become somehow less warm, as though the professional in him had suddenly ousted the friendly side of his nature. Now he explained how they could slot closeups of the terrain into the rectangle. "When we've got the game on computer, you'll be able to scroll around this whole map, but only see one section at a time," he said. "However, there's a zoom facility. You press the Z key, and the screen will give you a blowup of the section you've moved to."

Cindy explained that the two easels contained a calendar and the weather cards—each month's cards shuffled separately before play began. "Weather restricts or enhances movement." She demonstrated how the British patrols could move five spaces—arranged in hexagon shape—on good days, but in heavy rain only three, and in snow, two.

Looking at the map, Bond tried to remember the history of that period, learned too long ago in dusty schoolrooms. He thought of the frustration among officers of the colonial militia, of the British inability to protect the cities and towns; the unrest; then rebellion and open hostility.

Then there was a general—was it General Gage?—caught between his situation on the ground and the necessity to await orders from England. Of the patrols searching for the rebels' arms caches, the great warning ride of Paul Revere—which allowed the militia's weapons and ammunition to be moved out of Concord—and the skirmishes around that town and Lexington. All had finally led to a British withdrawal into Boston, dominated by the militia cannon on Bunker Hill. It was Bunker Hill that was remembered as a kind of Dunkirk by the Americans, for the British garrison had won the battle and taken the hill, but with such terrible losses that they had to retreat, by sea, to Halifax.

Bond thought of these things as Jason, warming to his theme, went on about the way the simulation was played. The players took turns in issuing orders, moving forces—some of the moves could be secret, and had to be noted on paper—then challenging and, possibly, skirmishing.

"The thing I find interesting is that you can alter history. I am, personally, very attached to the idea of changing history." Again, the hint of obsession hovering just below the surface. The eyes glazed slightly, and the voice altered—a faraway, menacing sound. "Perhaps I *shall* alter history. A dream? Maybe, but dreams can turn into reality, if one man of brilliance is put to proper use. You think my spark of genius is put to proper use? No?" He expected no answer, and his next words really concerned something far and away beyond the game, or simulation. "Perhaps, James, we could look at this in more detail—even play a few sequences—say, tomorrow?"

Bond said he would like that, sensing more than an ordinary challenge. St. John-Finnes continued to talk of revolution, change and the complexity of wargames like this. Cindy made an excuse to leave, nodding at Bond and remarking that she hoped they would meet again.

"Oh, I'm certain you will," Jason appeared to be very sure of himself. "I'm inviting him to have another look, say, six tomorrow evening?"

Bond accepted, noticing that Jason did not even smile.

As they left, he walked on ahead, but Peter lingered to the rear, with Bond, taking the opportunity to whisper, "If you do play with him, he likes to win. Bad loser, and plays by the historical book. The poor dear always thinks his opponent will do exactly what was done in reality. Be warned. The man's a paradox." He gave Bond a wink that made it all too clear that Peter Amadeus was not particularly fond of his boss.

Upstairs, Dazzle awaited them. Cindy had gone to bed, and she had, herself, driven Freddie back to the Bull. "She seemed very tired. Said you had dragged her all around the countryside this afternoon, Mr. Bond. You really shouldn't subject her to so much physical exercise. She's very much a town mouse, you know."

Bond had his own thoughts about this. He also could do with a good night's sleep, but accepted the offer of a nightcap from his host. Peter and Dazzle made themselves scarce, leaving the two men alone.

After a short silence, Jason raised his drink.

"Tomorrow," he said, the green eyes like glass. "Maybe we won't play games, James. But I would welcome the chance of taking you on. Who knows? Computers, yes . . ." He was away again, in some world of his own with a different time, place and set of values. "Computers are either the greatest tool mankind has invented, the most magnificent magic, capable of destruction or the construction of a new age." He laughed, one sharp rising note. "Or they're the best toy God has provided." In a couple of seconds the more familiar Jason seemed to return, as though the tall commanding figure was inhabited by two spirits, one benign and one evil. "Can I share my thoughts about you, James?"

Throughout the evening, Bond had been conscious that the man who called himself Jason St. John-Finnes had been asking questions designed to entrap, and to lead the questioner into his subject's very soul.

"I think," Jason was not waiting for Bond's reply, or consent. "I think that you are a small fraud, Mr. Bond. That you know very little about the art of computer programing. Some, but not as much as you pretend. Am I right?"

"No." Bond was firm. "No, you're not right. I've had the standard courses that they give people like myself. I reckon that I'm adequate. Not in your class, though. But who is?"

"Plenty of people." Jason's voice was quiet. "Young Cindy, and Peter, to name two. It's a young people's profession, and future, James Bond. Yes, I have a lot of knowledge, and some flair for strategy. But young people who are brought up with the machines acquire flair very quickly. You know the age of the biggest, richest software tycoon in the United States?"

"Twenty-eight."

"Right. Twenty-eight years of age, and some of the really advanced programers are younger. I know it all, but it's up to people like Cindy, or Peter, to translate the agility of my ideas into reality. Brilliance, genius, requires nurturing. Programers like my two may not really know that they feed my great conceptions. As for you, a man with minimal training—you cannot be of real use to me. You don't stand a chance in this field."

Bond shrugged. "Not against you," he said, not understanding if this was some devious wordplay, some psychological ploy.

At the door, Jason told him he looked forward to the next meeting. "If you feel you can take me on—at a game I mean— I'll be happy to oblige. But, maybe, we'll find something more interesting than games, eh? Six tomorrow."

Bond was not to know how the game of life itself would have changed by the time he saw Jay Autem Holy again. Nor what was really at stake in the games this tall, unhinged man liked to play. He did know that Holy was a man possessed, a dangerous, possibly psychotic case. Beneath the bonhomie and charm, he thought, lay the mind of one who would play God with the world, and he found this deeply disturbing.

The renovations at the Bull were very much in keeping with

the inn's original style, so no modern knob-locks or cards had been fitted to the bedroom doors. Just good old-fashioned mortise locks. Bond retrieved his large key from a dozing night porter and went up to his room. But, on putting the key in his lock, he found the door already open. Freddie, he thought, with some irritation, for he wanted very much to have time in which to think.

He remained cautious, slipping the automatic pistol from its holster, holding it just behind his right thigh, turning the handle and gently kicking the door open.

"Hallo, Mr. Bond." Cindy Chalmer smiled up at him from one of the chairs, her long legs sprawled out in front of her, like an invitation.

Quietly, Bond closed the door.

"I bring greetings from Percy," Cindy's smile broadened into a bewitching grin.

Bond remembered the looks she had given him during the evening. "Who's Percy?" he asked evenly, holding her eyes with his, trying to detect either truth or deception.

9

ENDOR GAMES

"COME ON, MR. BOND. Percy Proud. Persephone. We're in cahoots."

"Sorry, Cindy. Nice of you to drop by, but I've never heard of Percy, Persephone, or Proud." He quietly slipped the automatic pistol back into its holster. Cindy would have to do better than this, if he was going to accept her. Face value and a mention of Percy was not enough.

We've even infiltrated Endor, he heard Percy whisper into the echo chamber of his mind.

"You're very good." Cindy spoke like a cheeky schoolgirl. "Percy said you were. She also told me that I had to mention you liked treats, and an apple for the teacher always brought great rewards."

Bond remained cautious. Certainly only Percy and he knew about his byplay with the apple—in Monte Carlo—and their jokes concerning rewards for pupils. But . . . ? "You're in cahoots—as you put it—with someone called Percy?" he went on, staring her out.

Cindy bobbed her head, teeth like an advertisement against the cream coffee of her face. "Cahoots; intrigue; in league with. We both belong to the same outfit, Mr. Bond."

It made some sense. If the American Service already had someone in the house, close to Jay Autem Holy, they would not broadcast the fact. Persephone, as a true professional, would not tell Bond either. The circle of knowledge would be confirmed until the last minute. So, was this the last minute?

"Tell me more."

"She said—Percy said—you'd know what to do with these." The girl produced two hard disks from her shoulder bag. They were encased in plastic, making thin square boxes a little over five inches to a side and less than a quarter of an inch deep. On one side of the square there was a hinged flap, like those on much fatter video cassettes. The square wafers were both colored in brilliant blue and had small labels stuck on one corner.

He made no move to even touch them. "And what, Miss Chalmer, are those?"

"A couple of our target's less conventional programs. And I can't hang on to them for long. At about four in the morning I turn into a pumpkin."

"I'll get a couple of white mice to drive you home, then."

"Seriously. I can manage to get past the security without being detected, until about four. They change shifts then."

"We're talking of getting back into Endor, I take it?"

"Of course we're talking about Endor. The place is electronically buttoned like Fort Knox—you remember Fort Knox?" A small, almost mocking smile. "Well, Endor has code and lock combinations that change with each security shift. I have to go back during the current phase. Otherwise I'll be right up the proverbial tributary without oars, as they say."

Bond asked if she did this often.

"In the mating season, yes. That's why I've cultivated a certain reputation in the village. So's I have a kind of alibi if I ever get caught. But, if they cop me with these stuffed down my shirt . . . Well." She ran a finger over her throat. "So, Mr. Bond, I'd appreciate it if you'd copy these little beauties."

"How unconventional are they?" He reached out to take the disks, feeling as though something irrevocable could happen once he laid hands on them. To actually handle the things implied that he *could* do as Cindy asked. If, though, this was an attempt to frame him, there would be no going back.

"You'll see. But please do what has to be done as quickly as you can. I have no way of copying them at the house . . ."

"You can borrow them, but not make copies? I find that difficult to believe, Miss Chalmer. Your boss told me, not long ago, that you're a wizard with these things."

She made an irritated, spluttering noise that inexplicably reminded him of M, when the Head of Service became annoyed. "Technically, of course I can copy. But in fact, it would be exceptionally dangerous to try it in the house. I'm never left alone with the essential hardware for very long at one time. Either the great man's around, or the Queen of the Night is fussing about . . ."

"The who?"

"Queen of . . . Oh, Peter. That's my pet name for him. I think he may well be quite trustworthy—he certainly loathes the boss—but it's not worth the risk. Percy wouldn't hear of it."

Bond smiled inwardly.

She raised her eyes, indicating a ready response for any question.

"How well do you know this Percy?"

"You're dreadfully coy, James." They now slipped easily into first-name terms.

"No, I'm dreadfully careful."

"I know her quite well. Have done for the past, what? Eight years?"

"Has she been hospitalized since you've known her? Medical operations of any kind?"

"A nose job. Spectacular. That's all."

"And you?"

"I've never had a nose job."

"Background, Cindy. What? Who? And why?"

"All of it? Okay. I spent eight months in a hospital for infectious diseases after I left high school. There are medical records, doctors and nurses who remember me. I know because Old Bald Eagle's ferrets checked them out. Only I wasn't there. I was at the Farm, being trained. Then, surprise, I won a scholarship to Cambridge University, England. From then on, as pure as the proverbial driven. A good, hardworking girl. I'm untouchable, fully sanitized, as we say. The Company kept me on ice. I worked for IBM and with Apple before I applied for the job with Jay Autem Holy, and his boys checked, double-checked and then didn't trust me for eighteen months."

Bond gave a brisk nod. There were no real options left. Trust, between him and the girl, had to be entered into quickly, though not lightly. "Okay, just tell me about these two programs."

"Why don't you take a look for yourself? Percy gave me to understand you had the means."

"Tell me, Cindy. Concisely as you can, then we'll get on with it."

She talked rapidly, reducing the information, telescoping her sentences to the minimum. They had games weekends at Endor— he knew about that—and some very strange people turned up along with the usual dedicated wargames freaks. "There are two particular characters—Balmer and Hopcraft."

"Tigerbalm and Happy, yes." M had briefed him on this pair, nicknames included.

"Tigerbalm's about as balmy as a force ten blizzard. Kill you quick as look at you; and Happy's probably only that way when he's raping or pillaging. Happy would've made a good Viking raider."

The Gunfire Weekends, as they were called in the computer magazines, all appeared to be run with a military flavor—"Strict discipline. Order Groups at 0900 hours. Lights out at 2230, and all that." It was what happened after lights out that became interesting.

"The oddballs are detailed to rooms near one another, and always near Tigerbalm and Happy. The weekends cover three nights. The oddballs all leave looking as though they've been awake for a week. In fact they get very little sleep, because, around midnight—*on each night*—they're down in Old Bald Eagle's private den, behind the filing cabinets in the War Room, where we looked at The Revolution plotter.

"And there they stay, all night, working on their own little games, two of which I'd like to get back into their files before the dawn's early light."

Bond told her to wait in his room while he went quietly down to the car, selected the equipment he required, and brought it back to the room.

"For God's sake." Cindy looked at the Terror Twelve with undisguised pleasure. "She certainly got it right. I only hope the circuit diagrams I provided are accurate."

He'd buy that: Cindy monitoring the technology advance at Endor to provide Percy with all the ammunition required to build a computer identical to the one Holy had devised over the years. It also provided another motivation for Bond's infiltration. Maybe he was there only to get the latest programs out. After that, others could step in and clean out the stables, armed with evidence provided by himself, Percy and Cindy. Who knew?

With the console, and hard laser drives plugged in, Bond took the first disk and booted up. The moment the first menu of options came onto the screen he knew what it was about: in a series of flashing colored letters on the television screen, the menu read:

Phase One—Airport to Ken High Street
  A. First Girl Driver.
  B. Second Girl Driver.
  C. Advance Car.
  D. Trail Taxi.

He accessed the First Girl Driver and the screen showed him to be in heavy traffic, inbound from Heathrow Airport. Ahead lay the small convoy of police and security vans. The program was obvious, and Bond flipped through the phases—Turn Off; Kensington High Street: Phase One; Kensington High Street: Phase Two; Abort; Kensington High Street: Phase Violet Smoke, and on to Getaway, passing things like Security Teams (Electrics) and Security Teams (Way Out). He did not need to run the whole simulation to know that the disk currently resting in his top drive was a training program for the Kruxator Collection robbery—that superbly planned heist which had taken place on the day of his own setup Press conference.

Taking a virgin disk, Bond began to go through the careful procedure of breaking down Jay Autem Holy's protection program in order to make a clean second copy of the original.

The process was slow, for Holy had used not only the regular, easy system of "scribbling" on some sectors of the disk, but also the small "routine" Percy had shown to Bond. In effect this was a program in itself, designed to "crash" the disk, making it completely useless if anyone even attempted to copy it. Following Percy's tuition, he was now able to, first, detect the program, and then remove it, line by line, before matching up his virgin disk so that it would be in a format to exactly copy the original. The work took over an hour, but at the end there was a true clone of Holy's training program for the Kruxator robbery. A further twenty minutes was spent in returning the protect program to the original disk.

The second of Cindy's disks was, as they found very quickly, a similar training program—this time, they presumed, for the hijacking of an aircraft. As there had been a monumental hijacking of an especially chartered freight plane, carrying newly printed money from the Royal Mint printers to several countries, the chances were that this was the blueprint for that particular piece of villainy.

Once more, the cloning process began, but this time with more urgency, for Cindy had become anxious about her return.

"There is one other thing." She looked tired and concerned.

Without taking his eyes off the screen, Bond grunted a "Yes?"

"Something very big's going on. Not a robbery, I'm pretty sure of that, but a criminal—probably violent—operation. There've been callers in the night, and I've heard several references to a special program."

"What kind of special program?"

"I've heard the name only—they call it The Balloon Game, and there seem to be specialists involved."

Bond was concentrating, writing back the protect program onto the hijack simulation original. "They're all specialists, Cindy. Even Tigerbalm's a specialist."

"No, I've seen some of these guys. Oh, certainly some of them are hoods and heavies; but others are like pilots and parsons."

"Parsons?"

"Well, not exactly. Doctors and dentists, if you like. Upright. Professional."

"The Balloon Game?"

"I heard Tigerbalm use the expression, and one of the others—talking to the Holy Terror. Will you report it, please, I think it's something nasty."

Bond said he would be getting the copies of these two programs to London with speed. He'd mention The Balloon Game at the same time. "You think they're using it now? Training on it?"

"Positive."

"If we could get a copy . . ."

"Not a chance. Not yet, anyway."

He fell silent, finishing off the job in hand. Presently he rattled off a description of Rolling Joe Zwingli. "Ever see anyone like him around Endor?" He asked.

"General Zwingli? I recognize the description, and the answer's no. I had some garbled message from Percy that he's alive." She paused, adding that this seemed incredible.

"Stranger than fiction." Bond completed his tasks and started to close things down, returning the original disks to Cindy, asking, finally, about the routine at the house—did Jason and Dazzle ever go out? Or away? How many security people did they have around?

She usually referred to Jay Autem as the target, or Old Bald Eagle. Yes, he went away for a couple of days or so about once a month—always left, and returned, at night. Never left the house during the day; never showed his face in the village. "Very cagy, our target. Dazzle's out and about a great deal—the village, Oxford, London and trips abroad. I suspect she's really the liaison officer."

"Where abroad?"

"Middle East. Europe. All over. Percy's got the list. I try to keep track—mainly from hotel book matches, or flight labels. But she's cagy as well. Gets rid of a lot of stuff before she comes home."

As for the household, there was one Filipino boy and four security men. "He has six genuine sales reps who wouldn't suspect anything. But they're on the outside. The four security blokes double as reps and staff. It's very good cover. Would've had me fooled if I hadn't known better. They're all quiet, efficient guys—two cars between them; out and about a great deal; managing the telephones, taking orders, distributing the genuine Gunfire Simulations packages. But two of them never leave the house. They work on a strict rota, and the electronics are highly sophisticated. Breakable, but clever. I mean you have to know the system to fiddle it. What's more, as I've already told you, they alter the codings for every shift. You can only get in and out if you know the numbers for a particular six-hour period; and, even then, the machines have to know your voice-print.

"Visual?" Bond asked.

"Quite a lot—the main gates, large areas of the walls, front and rear of the house. You can only dodge the closed-circuit visual stuff at the back, and then only if you know the pattern: they change that with the lock codings, so you really do need to know each six-hour period to get in, or out, without being detected. An intruder wouldn't last three minutes."

"Ever had any?"

"Intruders? Only a tramp, and one false alarm—at least they presume it was a false alarm."

"Weapons?"

"I was around when the false alarm was triggered. Yes, one of the guys on duty had a hand gun. So I've seen one. There're probably more. James, can I get going? I can't afford to get caught with these disks on me. There are blank fakes in the cabinets, and they rarely get taken out. But if I . . ."

"On your way, Cindy, and good luck. I'll see you tonight. The little tournament I'm fighting against our target. By the way, your friend Peter tipped me off about Jason's style of play . . ."

"He doesn't like to lose," she grinned. "Almost pathological, like a child. It's a matter of honor with him."

Bond did not smile. "And me," he said softly. "It's a matter of honor with me."

It was past three-thirty in the morning. Bond packed up the equipment and took it down to the car, locking it away in the boot but leaving the cloned programs in a FloppiPak disk mailer, wryly contemptuous of the revolting nomenclature of trade items such as this.

Addressing the label to himself, at one of the "convenience" box numbers, he weighed the small, flat package in his hand, making an intelligent guess before taking a folder of postage stamps from his briefcase. He wanted to deliver the package in person, but was not going to leave anything to chance.

Sitting at the small dressing table, Bond next wrote a short note, on hotel paper, to Freddie.

> Gone to Oxford for the morning. Didn't want to wake you, but will be back for lunch. How about a return match this afternoon?
>
> —J.

Stripping off, he ran a cold shower and stepped under it, holding his face against the stinging needle spray, and gasping at the initial shock. After a minute or so, he added some warm water, soaped himself, then rubbed down, toweling his body with brisk, tingling ruthlessness before shaving and climbing into his underwear, a pair of black Ted Lapidus cords, and a black cotton rollneck. Then he strapped the ASP automatic in its holster so that it lay hard against his right hip, before putting on a light suede jacket and pushing his feet into the old favorite moccasins.

It was just getting light, the darkness changing to gray, and then that pearl, cold-washed sky which heralded unsettled weather.

With the detested FloppiPak in his briefcase, Bond went downstairs, left his key and the note for Freddie at a deserted Reception, and went out to the car.

The Bentley's engine growled into life at the first turn of the key, and he allowed it to settle to its normal, gentle purr, fastening the seatbelt and watching the red warning lights flick off one by one.

Releasing the foot brake, he slid the selector into drive and let the car roll forward. If he took the Oxford road, turned onto the Ring Road, and then headed for the M40, he could be in London within ninety minutes.

It began to rain as he reached the big roundabout on the periphery of the Ring Road, taking the dual freeway, heading toward London. He was a mile or so along this stretch when the gray Mercedes of the day before appeared in his mirror.

Bond cursed silently, tightened his seatbelt and eased his foot down on the accelerator. The car slid forward, gathering power, the speedometer rising to 100, then 120.

There was little traffic as yet, and he slid neatly in and out among the stray cars and lorries, mainly keeping to the fast lane.

The Mercedes held back, but, even at speed, Bond could not throw him. Ahead the signs came up for an exit, and, flicking the indicator at the last moment, he left the dual carriageway still well in excess of the 100 mph mark, the Bentley responding to his fingertips, holding the road tightly in the turn.

The Mercedes seemed to have disappeared. He hoped that the driver had not been able to reduce speed in time to get off the main two-lane highway. Ahead, the road narrowed, fir trees shadowing either side, and a lumbering heavy transporter grumbling along at fifty behind a petrol tanker.

The Bentley's speed dropped off, and, as he rounded the next bend, Bond caught a flash of headlights, blinking on and off from a layby. The next time he looked there was another Mercedes—white—hooking itself onto his tail.

Radio contact, he thought, and probably five or six cars covering him. Taking the next left, he picked up the telephone and, without allowing his eyes to leave the road, punched out the numbers that would access the duty officer, on a scrambled radio line, at the Regent's Park Headquarters.

The road narrowed and the second Mercedes was still there as he negotiated the next turn and the DO answered.

"Gamesman flash for Dungeonmaster," Bond spoke rapidly. "Am being followed, south of Oxford. Important package for Dungeonmaster. Will attempt mail. Addressed myself. The Programer is definitely involved all illegal actions as thought. Investigate Balloon Game. Speak to the Goddess." He was Gamesman; M the Dungeonmaster; Jay Autem Holy the Programer; while, naturally, Persephone Proud had been cryptoed Goddess.

"Understood," the duty officer said, and the line was closed. As he took the next bend, Bond realized he had outdistanced the Mercedes, and there was a village coming up. He pumped the big central footbrake, slowing dramatically, looking ahead and to the left.

The car was almost out of the village before he spotted it—the welcome brilliant red of a post box. The Bentley slid to a halt beside the box, and Bond had the straps off before the car stopped rolling.

It took less than twenty seconds to slip the package into the open maw of the box and return to the driving seat. This time he did not rebuckle the belt until later, rolling the Bentley out and gathering speed as the Mercedes came into view again.

He passed an electric milk float, doing the early rounds, and held the left-hand bend, which took him into open country, then through trees again. As he reached the trees, Bond caught a glimpse of a picnic area sign, then saw the other two cars emerge from the trees, their bonnets coming together to form a V, blocking his path.

"Playing for keeps," he muttered, ramming the footbrake and hauling on the wheel with his left arm.

As the Bentley began to slew, broadside on, he was conscious of the white Mercedes, now close behind him.

The speedometer was touching sixty as the Bentley left the road, plunging among the trees, over bracken, zigzagging wildly and trying to negotiate a path that would bring him back to the road.

The first bullet made a grating, gouging sound on the roof, and Bond could only think of the damage it would do to the coachwork. The second hit his rear offside tire, sending over five thousand pounds weight of custom-built motor car side on into a tangle of bushes.

Slammed against the seatbelt, Bond reached simultaneously for the 9mm automatic pistol and the electric window button.

10

EREWHON

THE ASP 9MM is a small, very lethal weapon. Essentially a scaled-down version of the Smith & Wesson Model 39, the ASP has been in use with United States Intelligence agencies for more than a decade. With a recoil no greater than that of a Walther .22, it has the look of a target automatic rather than the deadly customized hand gun it really is, for Armaments Systems and Procedures—the organization that carried out the conversion—produced the weapon to exacting specifications: concealability; a minimum eight-round capacity; reliability; an ammunition indicator, by way of Lexon see-through butt grips; and an acceptance of all known 9mm ammunition.

The rounds in Bond's magazine were particularly unpleasant: Glaser Safety Slugs. A Glaser is a prefragmented bullet that contains several hundred Number 12 shot, suspended in liquid Teflon. The velocity of these slugs, from the ASP, is over seventeen hundred feet per second; they will penetrate body armor before blowing, and a hit from a Glaser—on any vital area of the body—is usually fatal.

He fired two rounds from the lowered window almost before the car had come to a halt—both eyes open and looking down the revolutionary Guttersnipe sight, back-mounted, with three triangular yellow walls that give instant target acquisition.

Through the bushes, trees and bracken, men were visible around the cars—waving, gunning motors to get the vehicles off the road, while others clambered toward the Bentley. Bond's rapid shots were aimed at the clear outline of a tall man, wearing a dirty-white raincoat, but he did not stop to find out what happened to the target. Jerking open the door, he rolled from the car, low into the undergrowth.

Branches seemed to clutch and scratch at him, but Bond continued to roll, determined to get as far away as possible from the Mulsanne Turbo.

He moved to the right, putting about twenty yards distance between himself and the car in less than sixty seconds. He twisted, flat on his belly, gun up and ready, eyes constantly moving—left, right, center—covering a wide sweeping sightline.

The cars had been backed off the road, and he guessed they now simply contained drivers. Only two figures were visible, but, almost by intuition, he reckoned there had to be at least four others fanning out, moving low and trying to encircle him.

Bond lay quite still, allowing his breathing to settle and his body to adjust in the undergrowth as he assessed the situation.

If they were methodical—and he had no reason to doubt it—

these men would eventually find him: It was even possible they might call up reserves. Certainly there had to be more men available. How else could they have been certain of picking him up on the road, unless the Bentley had a location homer stuck onto it?

They would, Bond reasoned, find him later, rather than sooner. There should be time for him to coordinate a plan and make good his escape. Who were they? he found himself asking—some of Jay Autem Holy's hoods? There had to be a connection, but Holy—or St. John-Finnes—would have had ample opportunity to get him dead to rights that evening, at Endor. Unless . . . ? Unless . . . ? There were two possibilities—either Cindy had set him up, or Cindy, herself, had been caught. If the latter, a watch on him had been activated with great speed. Another "unless"— unless he had been under close surveillance from the word go, and Bond did not think that was on. He was operational and rarely left things to chance. The surveillance team would have to be very good indeed, and, apart from the obvious Mercedes—and Freddie's Jaguar—yesterday—he was ninety-eight percent certain that there had been no large team locked on to him.

It was now raining quite hard. One could hear the steady pattering from the branches, and the hiss coming from tires on the road. There was some shelter in this stretch of woodland, but, if the rain kept up, the day would become soggy.

To attempt a move now would be suicidal. He was at least one hundred and fifty yards from the road, and even if he reached the cars without being intercepted—which was unlikely—he would still be outnumbered three to one. Wait, he told himself. Patience. He must try to follow their search, and make sure nobody bounced him from behind.

He continued to watch the arc to his front, gently turning his head to look to the rear when he reached far left and far right, straining his ears to catch any sound or word.

There was silence now that the cars were off the road, as though, by a prearranged signal, the pursuers had reverted to hand signals. The two men originally visible to his front had disappeared, while the sounds of movement would now be successfully blotted out by the audible rain.

The minutes ticked by, and, from his own reckoning, Bond had been lying in cover for the best part of fifteen minutes before he got a positive fix on any of them. The sharp crack of a branch and a flicker of movement on the far left caught ear and eye at the same moment. With tediously careful slowness he swiveled his neck. There, not more than twenty paces away, a man crouched against a tree, looking to the right of where Bond lay.

From his attitude, the compact alert manner, the way he kept low, using the bottom of the tree trunk for cover, and the small revolver, steady in the right hand held against left shoulder, the man signaled professionalism—a man well trained, a soldier of one kind or another. He was also searching in the calm, cautious manner of a hunter—eyes not just moving around, but methodically examining every square foot of ground within a specified arc.

That meant there was probably another like him to his left, or right, or both. What was more, it could only be a matter of time before his eyes came to rest on the ground where Bond lay.

The searcher appeared to be olive-skinned. His complexion seemed to match the denim trousers, shirt and military jacket he wore. Moving each limb about half an inch at a time, Bond began to turn. If need be he wanted to at least get a shot in before anyone else closed on him.

Another stir—this time on the right—caused Bond to change pace, his reflexes and intuition warning of danger, the ASP coming up in the direction of this new threat.

The triple, three-dimensional yellow walls that angle to form the Guttersnipe sight fell automatically into their correct triangular patterns, right on target—another figure, running, low between the trees, and much too close for any real comfort.

In the wink of an eye, Bond's brain instructed his muscles, fingers, eyes and reflexes to deal with both men, roll to the left and then check for a third, and maybe fourth, target. He was conscious of the first man bringing his revolver up in a two-handed grip, then—

The unmistakable click of a revolver hammer being drawn back, very close behind him, and the sharp burning cold of a muzzle placed gently on the side of his neck.

"Drop it, Mr. Bond. Please don't try to be silly. Just drop the gun."

Bravery was one thing; sheer recklessness another. Bond had no desire to get himself killed at this point in his career. He tossed the ASP onto the ground in front of him.

"Good." The voice was unfamiliar, soft, slightly lilting. "Now, hands on the head, please."

The two who had caused Bond to move too late were now standing, coming forward, the one to his left with arms outstretched, holding a snub-nosed revolver in the two-handed grip, the arms steady as iron bars, his eyes never leaving their captive. Bond was in no doubt that two bullets would reach him fast if he made any wrong move.

The other came in quickly, scooping up the fallen ASP like a predatory bird swooping onto its prey.

"Right, now get to your feet very slowly," the voice continued, the gun muzzle detaching itself from just behind Bond's ear. There was the sound of feet shuffling as the unseen man stepped back. "That maneuver is rather good, isn't it? We knew the rough area where you had gone to ground, so it was merely a matter of showing you someone with stealth, and another with speed. The lads went through that little farce three times before they found the right place. It's the kind of fieldcraft we teach. Please turn around."

"Who teaches?" He turned, and found himself facing a tall, well-built man in his mid-thirties—tight curly hair, dark above jet eyes, a square face, large nose and full lips. For all that, women would find him attractive, Bond thought. The complexion was overlaid with a hard, sunbaked tan, with which he could well have been born. It was the eyes that really gave him away, for they had that particular look, as if, for years, they had searched horizons for the telltale sign of dust; or the sky for a speck that could easily turn itself into a shrieking dive of death; or outcroppings of rock, for movement—even doorways and windows, the muzzle flashes. Those eyes had probably been doing that kind of thing since childhood. Nationality? Who could tell? One of the Middle Eastern countries obviously, but whether he came from Jerusalem, Beirut or Cairo was impossible to tell.

"Who teaches?" he asked again, and the young man lifted an eyebrow. "You may get to find out, Mr. Bond, Who knows?" The smile was not unfriendly. "Now," he said, "we have to move you, and I cannot be certain you'll sit still." He gave a short laugh, "I rather think my superiors want you alive and in one piece, so could you take off your jacket and roll up your sleeve?"

One of the other men had come into view—the one Bond had first spotted, and whom he now thought of as the Shootist, for he was obviously a very careful fighter with a hand gun. Two more figures rose from the bushes, as the senior man holstered his own weapon, reaching into a hip pocket to bring out a hard oblong box.

One of the newcomers helped to remove Bond's jacket while the other's hands rested firmly on his shoulders. Unresisting, Bond allowed them to roll up his sleeve while the leader, with great professionalism, filled a hypodermic syringe, lifting it so that the needle pointed upward. A tiny squirt of colorless liquid arced into the air.

Bond felt a damp swab on the upper part of his arm.

"It's okay," the leader smiled again. "We do want you in one piece, I assure you." The smile broadened. "As the actress said to the bishop, just a little . . . er . . . a little jab."

One of the men laughed aloud, and Bond heard another say something in a language he did not recognize. He did not even feel the needle slide home, only saw the mist creeping up around the trees to envelop him. Cloud—damp, gray and clammy. Then darkness.

At first he thought he was in a helicopter, lying flat on his back while the machine bucked under him. He could hear the chug of the engine turning the rotor blades. Then, far away, the rip of automatic fire.

For a time, Bond drifted away again, then the helicopter sensation returned, and he realized that his consciousness had been cut into by a series of loud explosions near at hand.

Opening his eyes, he saw the fan, turning slowly on its electric motor above his head. The fan, white walls, a simple metal bedframe on which he lay, fully dressed.

He propped himself on one elbow to take stock. No ill effects. Physically he felt fine: no nausea, no headache, eyes focused properly. He held out his right hand, fingers splayed—not a tremor.

The fan kept turning, and he looked around the room. Nothing.

Just the bed. No furniture. Nothing on the walls. One door, a window covered with bars and steel mesh on the outside, and another kind of mesh inside. Sunlight forced its way through the aperture, and as he swung his feet onto the floor there was another explosion—a dull, double crump, at a distance, so that the room did not even shudder at the force.

He stood up and still felt normal. Halfway to the door, there was the brip of machine-gun fire—again at a distance. The door was, of course, locked, and he could make out little through the window. The mesh on the inside was a thick papery adhesive substance that had been applied to the panes of glass, making it impossible to get any clear view. It would also prevent fragmentation from blast. Bond was convinced of two things. He was certainly not in England. The warmth inside the little white room, even with the fan phutting round and round, was not induced by the kind of heat you ever got in England, even during the most brilliant of summers. Also, the sounds of small arms fire, punctuated by the occasional explosion, made it appear likely that he was in some war zone.

He tried the door again, then had a look at the lock. No way. It was solid, well-made, and more than efficient.

Methodically he went through his pockets. Nothing. They had cleaned him out. Even his watch was missing, and the metal bedframe appeared to be a one-piece affair. Given time, and some kind of lever, he might well force a piece of thick wire from the springs. But it would be an arduous business, and—whoever they were—it was not in the cards that he would be left alone for long at a stretch.

When in doubt, do nothing.

He went back to the bed and stretched out, going back, in his mind, over the events still fresh on the track of his memory.

The attempt to get away with the computer programs. Posting them. The trailing cars. The wood and his capture. The needle. He was the only one to have fired a shot. Almost certainly he had hit—probably killed—one of them. Yet apart from their natural caution, they had been careful to make sure that he was unharmed.

Conclusions? None. A connection between his visit to Jay Autem Holy and the current situation was probable, though not absolutely certain. Take nothing for granted. Wait for revelations. Expect the worst.

Bond lay there, mentally prepared, for the best part of twenty minutes. At last there were footsteps, muffled, as though boots crunched over earth, but the tread still retained a military flavor. Bolts were drawn back.

As the door opened, he caught a glimpse of sand, low white buildings, and two armed men, dressed in olive-drab uniforms. A third person stepped into the room. He was the one who had administered the knockout injection in the Oxfordshire wood. Now he wore a uniform—simple olive-drab battledress; no insignia or badges of rank; desert boots; a revolver, of high caliber, holstered on the right of his webbing belt; a long sheathed knife on the left. His head was covered by a light brown, almost makeshift, *kaffiyeh* held with an Apache-type red band.

One of the men outside reached in and closed the door.

"Have a good sleep, Mr. Bond?" The man's smile was almost infectious. As he looked up, Bond remembered his feelings about the eyes.

"I'd rather have been awake." Give nothing until you were given; share nothing; accept nothing.

"You're all right, though? No ill effects?"

Bond shook his head.

"Right." Crisp, businesslike. "My name's Simon." An extended hand, which Bond did not take.

A slight pause, then: "We hold no grudge concerning our man. You killed him, by the way. But he was being paid to risk his life." Simon shrugged. "We underestimated you, I fear. My fault. Nobody thought you'd be carrying. After all, you're not in the trade any more. I reasoned that, if you were armed, it would be for old time's sake, and nothing as lethal as that thing. It's unfamiliar to us, incidentally. What is it exactly?"

"My name is James Bond, formerly Commander, Royal Navy. Number CH 4539876. Formerly Foreign Service. Now retired."

Simon's face creased into a puzzled look for a couple of seconds, then cleared. "Oh yes. I see. Name, rank and number." He gave a one-note laugh. "Sorry to disappoint you, Commander Bond, but you're not a prisoner of war. When you outran us in that beautiful motor car there was no way to let you know we came as emissaries. Friendship. A possible job."

"You could have shouted. In the wood, you could have shouted, if that was the truth."

"And would you have believed us?"

Silence.

"Quite. No, I think not, Commander Bond. So we took action to bring you in alive and well, using only minimal force."

Bond thought for a moment. "I demand to know where I am, and who you people are."

"In good time. All in—"

"Where am I?" he snapped.

"In Erewhon." Simon gave a low chuckle. "Like so many organizations that don't wish to come under public scrutiny, we go in for atrocious code names, cryptonyms. For safety, security and our peace of mind—just in case you turn down the job; or even prove to be not quite the man we require—this place is called Erewhon." His smile switched on and off, wry and humorless as he added, "Now sir, the officer commanding would like a word."

Bond slowly got off the bed, reaching out a restraining arm, clasping his hand around Simon's left wrist, and aware of the man's other hand drifting very quickly to the revolver butt. "Commander, I wouldn't advise . . ."

"Okay," Bond said, releasing Simon's wrist. "I just don't recall having applied for a job. Not with anybody."

"Oh, really? No, I suppose you haven't." There was mocking disingenuousness in Simon's voice. "But you're out of work, Commander Bond. That's true, surely?"

"Yes."

"And, by nature, you're not an idle man. We wanted to—how would you say it? We wanted to put something your way." The on-off smile again. "That's why the officer commanding Erewhon wishes to talk to you."

Bond appeared to think for a moment, then he nodded. "I'll see your OC, then."

"Good." Simon rapped on the door, and one of the men outside opened up.

As they stepped outside, the two guards took station on either side. Bond sniffed the air. It was warm, but clear. Rare. They were fairly high above sea level, that was plain. They were also in a small depression, the flat bed of a hollow surrounded by hills. On one side the hills were low—a curving double mound, like a woman's breasts, but pitted with rock among the dry, sandy earth. The rest of the circle was more forbidding, crests and peaks running up several hundred feet, with ragged outcrops of unforgiving rock. The sun was high, almost directly above them, and along the flat sand bottom of the hollow were ranged a series of low white buildings laid out in one long rank, with divisions, and another terrace with three out-strokes, like a large letter E. Away, hard under the high ground there were other, similarly built structures: planned, but not regimented. Simon led them across the five or six hundred yards toward one of these latter blocks.

As they went, Bond kept his eyes alert. Smoke drifted up from some of the smaller buildings. To his left there was a firing range, with a group of uniformed people preparing to use it. Back, toward the hills, a clutter of gutted brick houses—looking almost European—suddenly erupted to the sound of heavy explosions and small arms fire. Figures dashed between these houses as though fighting a street battle, flashes among the smoke as grenades exploded.

As he turned at the noise, Bond also caught sight of some kind of bunker dug into the rock toward the top of one of the hills. A great defensive position, he thought. Easy to defend and almost impossible to attack by air, though helicopter-borne landings would, presumably, be possible.

"You like our Erewhon?" Simon asked cheerfully.

"Depends what you do here. Do you run package tours?"

Simon's forehead lifted, "Almost." He sounded quite amused.

They reached the building—about the size of a modest bungalow. There was a notice, neatly executed, to the right of the door. *Officer Commanding,* it said in a dozen languages, including Hebrew and Arabic.

The front door opened into a small, empty anteroom. Simon crossed to another door at the far end and knocked.

A voice ordered them to "Come," and Simon gestured, smartly barking out, "Commander James Bond, sir."

Given everything that he'd seen outside, and with the myriad questions unanswered, Bond would not have been shaken to find Rolling Joe Zwingli on the other side of the door. But the identity of the man seated behind the folding table that dominated the office made him catch his breath with surprise.

There was certainly some connection between this man and Zwingli, for the last time Bond had seen him was in the Salles Privées at Monte Carlo.

"Come in, Commander Bond. Come in. Welcome to Erewhon," said Tamil Rahani, their suspect tycoon. "Do sit down. Get the commander a chair, Simon."

11

TERROR FOR HIRE

THE ROOM, LARGE and utilitarian, contained the folding table, four chairs, and filing cabinet that could have been found in the quartermaster's stores of most armies the world over. The furnishings also appeared to reflect the character of Tamil Rahani, the officer commanding.

From a distance, when Bond had viewed him briefly in Monte Carlo, Rahani had looked like any other successful businessman—sleek, well-dressed, needle-sharp and confident. At close quarters, the confidence certainly remained, but instead of sleekness a kind of dynamism stood out—harnessed and controlled. One usually got the same sense of self-discipline from very good military leaders, a kind of quiet calm, through which one detected, rather than viewed, an immense, unflinching resolve, coupled with authority and the subject's own firm belief in his ability. All these things were present, emanating from Tamil Rahani like static electricity.

As Simon brought the chair—and took one for himself—Bond glanced quickly around the office. The walls were lined with maps, charts, large posters displaying the silhouettes of aircraft, ships, tanks and other armored vehicles. There were also year- and month-planners, their red, green and blue markers giving the only splash of color to an otherwise functional ambience.

"Don't I know you, sir?" Bond was careful to observe military courtesy, for Rahani's final detectable attribute was danger.

Rahani laughed, throwing back his head a fraction. "You may have seen pictures in newspapers, Commander. Possibly we shall speak of it later. At the moment I'd rather talk about *you*." His smile puffed out his cheeks, slightly out of character, more like some pompous little chairbound British major. "You come to us highly recommended."

"Really?" It was meant to sound as though Bond could not care a damn whether he came recommended or not.

"Yes," Rahani tapped his teeth with a pencil. The teeth were perfect—white, regular and well-tended, the mustache above them trimmed as if to a regulation length. "Let me be completely frank with you, Commander. Nobody knows whether you can be trusted or not. Everybody—and by that I mean most of the major intelligence communities of the world—knows that you have been a loyal and active officer of the British Secret Intelligence Service for a long time. You ceased to be either a member or active some time ago. It is said that you resigned in a fit of bitterness." He made a small questioning noise, like a hum in the back of his throat. "It is also said that *nobody* ever goes private from the SIS, the CIA, Mossad or the KGB—is that the correct term? Going private?"

"So the espionage writers tell us." Bond maintained his couldn't-care-less attitude.

"Well," Rahani continued, "quite a number of people wanted to find out the truth. A number of agencies would have liked to approach you. One very nearly did. But they got cold feet. It was argued that, having been loyal for so long, you would most probably rediscover your loyalty if put to the test—no matter how disaffected you felt."

There was a pause, during which Bond remained poker-faced until the officer commanding spoke again.

"You're either an exceptional actor, Commander, working under professional instructions, or you are genuine. What appears to be true is that you're a man of uncommon ability in your field; alas, you're out of work. If there is truth in the rumors surrounding your resignation, then it seems a pity to allow you to remain unemployed. The purpose of bringing you here is to test the story, and, possibly, offer you a job. You would like to work? In intelligence, of course?"

"Depends," his voice flat as a board.

"On what?" Sharp, the man of authority showing through.

"On the job." Bond's face relaxed a fraction. "Look, sir. I don't wish to appear rude, but I *was* brought here—wherever it may be—against my will. Also, my previous career is nobody's business but mine—and, I suppose, the people for whom I used to work. To be honest, I'm so fed up with the trade that I'm not at all certain if I really want to get mixed up in it again."

"Not even as an adviser? Not even with a very high salary? With little to do, and less danger in doing it?"

"I just don't know."

"Then would you consider a proposition?"

"I'm always open to propositions."

Rahani took a long breath through his nose. "An income in excess of a quarter of a million pounds, sterling, a year. The occasional trip, at short notice, to advise in one country or another. One week out of every two months spent giving a short series of lectures here."

"Where's here?"

For the first time, Rahani's brow puckered with displeasure. "In good time, Commander. As I've said, in good time."

"Advise on what? Lecture on what?"

"Lecture on the structure and methods of the British Secret Intelligence Service, and the Security Service. Advise on the intelligence and security aspects of certain operations."

"Operations carried out by whom?"

Rahani spread his hands in a gesture of openness. "That would depend. It would also alter from operation to operation. You see, the organization I command bears no allegiance to any one country, group of people or ideal. We are—a much-used word, but the only one—we are apolitical."

Bond waited, as though asking for more details before he committed himself.

"I am a soldier," Rahani finally gave in. "I have been a mercenary in my time. I am also a highly successful businessman. We have certain things in common, I think. One of them being a liking for money. Some time ago, and in cooperation with one or two other like-minded people, I saw a possibility of combining the two things—mercenary activities and very profitable business returns. Being apolitical myself, owing nothing to political ideologies or beliefs, it was easy. Countries, and groups of so-called revolutionaries, are always in need of specialists. Either a particular man, or a group of men—even a planning group, and the soldiery to carry out the plan."

"Rent-A-Terrorist," Bond said, with a touch of distaste. "Who does not dare hires someone else to dare for him. It's a truly mercenary activity, in all senses of the word."

"Well put. Yes, but you'd be surprised, Commander Bond. The so-called terrorist organizations are not our only customers. Bona fide governments have been known to ask for an operation, with percentage payment on results. Anyway, as a former intelligence officer you cannot allow yourself the luxury of politics, or ideals."

"I can allow myself the luxury of opposing certain ideals. Even of intensely disliking them."

"And, it seems, you have an intense dislike for the British and American way of intelligence—yes?"

"Let's just say I'm disillusioned; that I'm embittered that an official organization can call me to question after many years of loyal service."

"Don't you ever feel that revenge could be sweet?"

"I'd be a liar if I said it hadn't crossed my mind, but it's never been an obsession. I don't harbor grudges."

Rahani made the querying, humming noise again. "We shall need your cooperation; and your decision. You understand what I mean?"

Bond nodded, saying he was no fool. Having disclosed the existence, and purpose, of his organization, Tamil Rahani was committed to making a decision about Bond. If he could offer a job—and if Bond accepted—there was no problem. If, however, he decided Bond was a risk, or his motives were in doubt, there could only be one answer. During this last summary, Bond never once used Rahani's real name. It would not do, at this stage, to disclose the knowledge.

Rahani heard him out. Then—

"You won't mind if I ask a few pertinent questions?"

"What do you call pertinent?"

"I'd like to know the things you would not discuss with the Press. The *true* reason for your resignation, Commander Bond. An interdepartment disagreement, I believe you said. Accusations, which were withdrawn, but taken most seriously by yourself."

"If I don't choose to tell you?"

Rahani's smile was there. "Then we have to conclude that you are not trustworthy, my friend. A conclusion that may have unpleasant consequences."

Bond went through the process of looking as though he was giving the situation some thought. With M and Bill Tanner he had put together a story that would hold water up to a point. To prove, or disprove, this version would mean getting hard information from the Judicial Branch—a number of experienced barristers retained by the Service, also from three definite individuals working in the Registry and someone who had easy access to the documents held by S Department.

After a couple of minutes Bond gave a short nod. "Right. If you want the truth . . ."

"Good. Tell us then, Commander Bond." The voice and manner were equally bland.

He told the story, just as they had concocted it in M's office. Over a period of some six months it had been discovered that several highly sensitive files had been taken from the Service Headquarters and kept out overnight. It was an old story, and one that was technically possible, even with the stringent security, spot checks, and signing in and out of files.

However, the system was double-checked by using an electronic bar code, appended to each file, and read in every time the file was taken out or returned. The files went in—and out—via a machine that read the code and stored the information in the Registry databank, which was examined at the end of each month. It was impossible to alter the bar codes on the files, or to duplicate them. But because the information, stored away on the big computer tapes, was only read out at the end of each month, one person could return a dummy file each night—if he so wished—putting back the original the following night. By alternating dummy and original it was possible to examine at leisure around twenty files over a month before anyone discovered the tampering. This, Bond maintained, had occurred—though Registry had spent so much time cross-checking, and looking at the data, because they imagined it to be a program error in the computer, that a further week had passed before a report went up to Head of Service.

In all, only eight files had been at risk. But, on the relevant dates, James Bond had been one of those with access to the files. Five people were under suspicion, and they had hauled Bond in before anybody else.

"Someone of my rank, experience and service would normally be given the courtesy of a private interview with the Head of Service," he said, his tone verging on rising anger. "But no. It didn't seem to matter that the other four were junior, relatively inexperienced, and without field records. It was as if I was singled out because of my position; because I had been in the field; because of my experience."

"You were actually accused?" It was Simon who asked.

Bond simulated the anger now boiling up and breaking the surface. "Oh, yes. Yes, I was accused. Before they even talked to anyone else they carted in a couple of very good interrogators, and a QC. 'You removed these files from the headquarters building, Commander Bond. Why? Did you copy them? Who asked you to take them?'—It went on for two days."

"And did you take them from the building, Commander?"

"No, I did not," Bond shouted. "And it took them another two days to haul in the other four, and then a day for Head of Registry to come back off leave and recall that special permission had been given to one officer to take the wretched files over for study by a Civil Service mandarin—adviser to the Ministry. They had left spaces in the records, just to keep the data neat. Head of Registry was supposed to put a special code into the databank. But he was off on leave, and forgot about it. Nobody had a go at him, or offered his head on a salver."

"So no files went missing at all. You got an apology, of course?"

"Not immediately," Bond glowered, like a schoolboy. "And nobody seemed the least bit concerned about my feelings. Head of Service didn't appear to even understand why I got annoyed."

"So you resigned? Just like that?"

"More or less."

"It's a very good story," Tamil Rahani looked pleased. "But it is one that will be difficult to prove, if I know anything about government departments."

"Exceptionally difficult," Bond agreed.

"Tell me, what did the questionable files contain?"

"Ah," Bond tried to look as charming as possible. "Now you're really asking me to betray."

"Yes." Matter-of-fact.

"Mainly updated material concerning the disposition of Eastern bloc tactical nuclear weapons. One concerned agents on the ground and their proximity to the Eastern bases."

Rahani's eyebrows twitched. "Sensitive. I see. Well, Commander, you've started, so you might as well finish. I shall make a few tiny inquiries. In the meantime, perhaps Simon will show you around Erewhon, and we'll continue to have our talks."

"You mean interrogations?"

Rahani shrugged. "If you like. Your future, salary and work, depend on what you tell us now. Quite painless, I assure you."

As they reached the door, Bond turned back. "May I ask *you* a question, sir?"

"Of course."

"You bear a striking resemblance to a Mr. Tamil Rahani— chairman of Rahani Electronics. I believe you've been in Monte Carlo recently?"

Rahani's laugh had all the genuine warmth of an angry cobra. "You should know, Commander. You were raising a fair amount of hell at the gaming tables on the Cote d'Azur at the time, I think."

"Touché, sir." He followed Simon out into the sunshine.

They went first to a mess hall where around eighty people were enjoying a lunch of chicken, seasoned and cooked with peppers, onions, almonds and garlic.

Everyone wore the same olive-drab uniform, and some carried sidearms. There were men and women, mainly young and from many different countries. They sat in pairs, or teams of four. That was how the training went, Simon explained. They worked with a partner, or in teams. Sometimes two teams would be put together, if the work demanded it. Also, some of the pairs were training to be lone specialists.

"In what?"

"Oh, we cover the usual spectrum. Big bang merchants; take-away artists; removal men; monopoly teams. You name it, we do it—electricians, mechanics, drivers, all the necessary humdrum jobs also."

Bond translated the jargon as meaning explosives experts; kidnappers, or thieves; assassins; and hijack or hostage teams. He identified a number of different tongues being spoken—there were Germans, French, Italians, Arabs, Israelis, Irish, and even English. He almost immediately identified a pair of German terrorists whose names and details were on file with his Service, M15 and Scotland Yard.

"If you want anonymity, I shouldn't use those two in Europe," he told Simon, quietly. "They've both got star billing with our people."

"That's good. Thank you. We prefer unknowns, and I had a feeling about that couple. Everyone has had some field work behind them when they come here—how else would they lose their ideals?—but we do not like 'faces.' " He gave a pleasant grin. "But we have need of them. Some have to be lost, you know. It comes in handy during training."

Throughout the afternoon, they walked around the training area, which was incredibly well-equipped, and Bond experienced the odd sensation of having seen all this before—taking part in it, but as though through a different end of a telescope.

It took an hour or so to work out exactly what was wrong. These men and women were being trained in techniques he had seen used by the SAS, Germany's GSG9, the French GIGN, and several other elite police, military and paramilitary units that deal with antiterrorist activities. There was one difference, however. The trainees at Erewhon were receiving expert tuition on how to counter antiterrorist action.

Apart from classes in weaponry of all kinds, explosives and the like, there was very special training on hijacking and takeover, leaving little to chance. They even had two real flight simulators within the compound, while one building was devoted solely to the techniques of bargaining with authorities while holding either hostages or kidnap victims.

One of the most spectacular training aids lay around the gutted buildings Bond had earlier noticed. Here a team of four would be taught how to counter attempted rescues by men using all the known techniques of well-trained counterterrorist forces. It was disturbing to note that most eventualities appeared to be covered.

That night he slept again in the same unfurnished, secure building in which he had woken; and, on the following day, the hours of interrogation began.

It was done on a classic one-to-one basis—Tamil Rahani and James Bond—with Rahani ingeniously asking seemingly ordinary questions that, when expanded and probed, turned out to be attempts to pry loose highly sensitive information concerning Bond's Service.

They began with reasonably harmless stuff—organization and channels of command; but soon, the detail was being called for, and Bond had to use all his native ingenuity to give the appearance of telling everything, while keeping back truly vital information.

But Rahani was like a terrier. Just when Bond thought he had managed to retain some real piece of information, the officer commanding Erewhon would change tack, going in a circle to return to the nub of the question. Soon, it became all too obvious that, once they had milked him dry, Bond would be quietly thrown to the wolves.

It happened on the sixth day. Rahani had been hammering away at the same questions—which concerned minutiae of protection for heads of state, the Prime Minister, the Queen and other members of the Royal Family. This, naturally, was no part of Bond's own work, nor the work of his Service, but Rahani, quite rightly, assumed that he would have a great deal of knowledge about the subject.

He even wanted names, possible weaknesses in those assigned to such duties, and the kind of schedules they worked.

At about five o'clock in the afternoon, a message was brought in. Rahani read it, then slowly folded the paper neatly, and looked at Bond.

"Well, Commander, it seems your days here are numbered. There is a job for you back in England. Something very important is at last coming to fruition, and you are to be part of it. You are on salary as of now." He picked up one of his two telephones, asking for Simon to come over as quickly as possible. They all used simple first names at Erewhon, with the exception of the officer commanding.

"Commander Bond is with us," he told Simon. "There's work for him, and he leaves for England tomorrow. You will escort him." An odd look passed between the two men before Rahani continued. "But, Simon, we have yet to see the gallant commander in action. Would it be a good idea to put him through the Charnel House?"

"He'd like that, I'm sure, sir." The Charnel House was a gallows-humor nickname for the gutted buildings they used for training in defense against a counterterrorist force.

Simon said he would set things up, and they all left for the short walk over to the area where Simon left to make the arrangements. "I've got just the team for you, James." He gave a knowing look, which Bond felt had some hidden meaning that he should be able to decipher. Ten minutes later, Simon returned, taking Bond inside the house.

Though the place was gutted and bore the marks of many simulated battles, it had been remarkably well built. A large entrance hall stood inside the solid main door. Two short passages led off to left and right, ending in doors that opened onto large rooms. The rooms were uncarpeted but contained one or two pieces of furniture. A solid staircase climbed from the hall to a wide landing. The wall was blank except for one door, through which one reached a long passage running the length of the house's rear. Doors on the front-facing wall led into two rooms built directly above the ones on the ground floor.

Simon led him upstairs. "They have a team of four. Blank ammunition, of course, but real 'flashbangs,' "—flash-bangs were stun grenades, not the nicest thing to be near on detonation. "The brief is that they know you are somewhere upstairs," he pulled out the ASP 9mm. "Nice weapon, James. Very nice. Who would think it has the power of a .44 Magnum?"

"You've been playing with my toys."

"Thoroughly. There, one magazine of blanks, and one spare.

Use initiative, James. Good luck." Simon looked at his watch. "You have three minutes."

Bond quickly reconnoitered the building and placed himself in the upper corridor, knowing it had no windows. He remained close to the door that opened onto the landing, but well shielded by the corridor wall. He was crouched against the wall when the stun grenades exploded in the hallway below—two ear-splitting crumps, followed by several withering bursts of automatic fire. Bullets hacked and chipped into the plaster and brickwork on the other side of the wall, while another burst almost took the door beside him off its hinges.

They were not using blanks. This was for real, and he knew with sudden shock that it was as he had earlier deduced. He was being thrown to the wolves.

12

RETURN TO SENDER

Two more explosions came from below, followed by another heavy burst of fire. The second team of two men was clearing the ground floor. Bond could hear the feet of the first team on the stairs. In a few seconds there would be the dance of death from the landing—a couple of stun grenades, or smoke canisters, through the door to his right, then lead would hose down the passage, taking him on that short trip into eternity.

Simon's voice kept running in his head like a looped tape— "Use your initiative . . . Use your initiative . . ." Was that a hint? A clue?

Move. Bond was off down the corridor, making for the room to his left. He had some vague idea that he could leap from the window—anything to remove his vulnerable body from the immediate vicinity of the vicious, inevitable hailstorm of bullets.

He took rapid strides, hand closing on the doorknob. He turned it, trying to make as little noise as possible, closed the door behind him and slid a small bolt above the lock, in which there was no key. He started to cross the floor, heading for the windows, clutching the useless ASP as though his life depended on it. Halfway, as he sidestepped a chair, he saw them—two ASP magazines, cutaway matt black oblongs, lying on a rickety table between the high windows. Grabbing at the first, he saw immediately that they were his own reserves, both full, loaded with Glasers.

There is a fast routine for reloading the ASP—a fluid movement that quickly jettisons an empty magazine, replacing it with a full one. Bond went through the reload in a matter of five seconds, including the action of dropping his eyes to check that a live round had entered the chamber.

He performed the whole maneuver on the move, turning his body so that he was hard against the wall to the left of the door. The team would leap in after the grenades had accomplished their disorientating effect—one left and one right. They would be firing as they came, but Bond gambled on their first bursts going wide across the room. As he reloaded, he was conscious of them running down the corridor, then the bangs and rattle of their textbook assault through the door.

Flattening himself against the wall, he held the powerful little weapon at arm's length—the two-handed grip.

Bullets splintered the woodwork to his right. A boot smashed in the handle and lock, while a pair of stun grenades hit the bare boards with a heavy clunk, one of them rolling for a split second before detonation.

He closed his eyes, head turning slightly to avoid the most distressing effect of the little metal eggs—the flash that temporarily blinds—though nothing could stop the great crump that seemed to explode from within his own cranium, putting his head in a vise and ringing in his ears like a magnified bell. His head was crammed with noise and a great buzzing. It blotted all external sounds, even the noise of his own pistol as he fired, and the death-rattle of the submachine guns from the two-man team as they stepped through the lingering smoke.

At the first movement through the door, Bond sighted—the three little yellow triangles on the Guttersnipe all falling equally onto the dark moving shape. He squeezed the trigger twice, re-sighted and squeezed again. In all the four bullets were off in less than three seconds—though the whole scene appeared to be frozen in time, slowed like a cinematic trick so that everything happened with a ponderous, even clumsy, brutality.

The man nearest Bond leaped to his left, the wicked little automatic weapon tucked between upper arm and rib cage, the muzzle already spitting fire as he identified and turned toward his target. Bond's first bullet caught him in the neck, hurling the man sideways, pushing him, his head lolling as though it had been ripped from its body. The second slug entered his head, which literally exploded into a cloud of fine pink and gray.

The third and fourth bullets both caught the second man in the chest, a couple of inches below the windpipe. He was swinging outward and to his right, realizing, too late, where the target was situated, the gun in his hand spraying bullets toward the window. The ASP's impact lifted the man from his feet, knocking him back so that he was momentarily poised in midair, angled at forty-five degrees from the floor, the machine pistol still firing and ripping into the ceiling as a mushroom of blood sprouted from his torn body.

Because of his temporary deafness, Bond felt as though he stood outside time and action, but experience pushed him on. Two down, he thought, two to go, for the second team would—almost certainly—be covering the entrance hall, might even be coming to their comrades' assistance.

Bond stepped over the headless corpse of the first intruder, his foot almost slipping in a lake of blood. It always stunned him how there was so much blood from one man. This was something they did not show in movies, or even newsreel film—the gallon, and then some, of blood that fountained from a human body that has been violently cut to pieces by a pair of well-placed shots.

In the doorway, he paused for a second, ears straining to no effect.

Glancing down, he saw that the number two of the team still had a pair of grenades tucked firmly into his belt, hooked on by the safety levers. He slid one out, removed the pin, holding the oval egg in his left hand, and advanced back down the corridor toward the landing door, calculating the amount of force he would need to hurl the object down the stairs. It had to be done right, for he would not get a second chance.

He paused, just short of the landing door, and something made him turn—that sixth sense which, over the years, had been fine-tuned to emergencies. He spun around, just in time to see the figure emerging gingerly, negotiating his way through the gore and shattered bodies on the far side of the door.

Later, Bond reasoned they had planned some kind of pincer maneuver, one man scaling the wall to attack through the window while his comrades stormed through the interior. He aimed two shots at the man in the doorway, while his left hand lobbed the stun grenade out of the landing door in the direction of the staircase.

He saw the man in the doorway spin as though caught by a violent whirlwind and, at the same instant, felt the flash from the landing.

Five seconds to release the magazine, in which there were now only two rounds left, and replace it with the fully charged one. Then two paces through the door, firing as he went—two slugs going nowhere while he located his target.

The last man was struggling at the bottom of the stairs, for the grenade had caught him napping. From the scorch marks and his agonized flapping at the smoldering cloth around his loins it was obvious that the grenade, which rarely kills, had hit him squarely in the groin.

Still deaf, Bond saw the man's mouth opening and closing, his face distorted. From the top of the stairs, he shot him once—neatly blowing off the top of his head so that he fell onto his back, then bounced a foot or so on impact.

Quietly, Bond retraced his footsteps, once more stepping over the bodies and crossing to the window. Below, and about twenty yards away, Tamil Rahani stood, watching, with Simon and half a dozen members of Erewhon's permanent staff. They were quite still, heads held as though listening. There was no sign of an unholstered weapon, and Bond could not see any other guns trained on the house—from rooftops or other vantage points.

He moved back from the window, not wanting to show himself yet uncertain of the best, and safest, way to get out of the place.

He had gone only two steps, when the decision was partially made for him.

"Are you still with us, Commander Bond?" Rahani's voice drifted up from the warm air outside, followed by Simon's calling, "James? Did you figure it out?"

He returned to the window, standing to one side, showing as little of his head as possible. They were all in the same place as before. Still no visible armament.

Withdrawing, Bond shouted, "You tried to kill me, you bastards. Let's make it fair. I'll take on one of you at a time." He dropped to the ground and snake-crawled along the wall below the window to the next aperture.

They were all looking at the first window as he fired, putting the bullet about ten yards in front of them, kicking up a great cloud of dust.

"Right, Bond." It was Tamil Rahani calling. "Nobody wanted to do you any harm. A test, that's all. A test of your efficiency. Just come out now. The test is complete."

"One of you—unarmed. Just one—Simon, if you like. In now. At the front. Otherwise I start taking you out, very quickly." A quick peek. Their reaction was very fast, for Simon was already unbuckling his belt, letting it fall to the ground as he walked forward.

Seconds later, Bond was at the top of the stairs, and Simon stood in the entrance hall, hands on his head, staring with some admiration.

"What's going on exactly?" Bond asked, and Simon looked up.

"Nothing. You did as we expected. Everyone told us how good you were, so we sent in four quite expendable men—two of them were the ones you pointed out to me the other day—the German fellows who you said were known faces. We have others like them. This is a standard exercise."

"Standard? Telling the victim everyone's only using blank ammunition . . . ?"

"Well, you soon discovered you had live rounds, like the others. They also thought they had blanks."

"But I only had live ammunition if I could find it—which I did, partly by luck."

"Rubbish. You had the real thing from the word go, and there were spare magazines all over the place, James. Can I come up?"

Keeping his hands on his head, Simon slowly mounted the stairs, while Bond began to wonder. Fool, he said to himself. You merely took the man's word for it. He said you had blanks, but . . .

Five minutes later, Simon had proved his point—first by retrieving Bond's original magazine, which proved to be fully, and correctly, loaded with Glasers; second, by showing him other full magazines—on the corridor floor and in the second room upstairs, as well as on the landing.

Even with this evidence, it had still been a foolhardy and exceptionally dangerous business. Four men armed with, as it turned out, MP 5K submachine guns, against one.

"I could have been wiped out within seconds."

"But you weren't, were you, James? Our information was that you would get out alive, if set this kind of challenge. It merely shows that our informants were correct."

They walked down the stairs and out into the air, which felt very good. Bond had a feeling that he was, indeed, lucky to be alive. He also wondered if his luck was merely a stay of execution.

"And if I had died in there?"

Rahani did not smile at the question. "Then, Commander Bond, we would've only had one body to bury instead of four. You lived; you showed us your reputation is well deserved. Here only survival matters."

"And it was, as Simon said, a challenge? A test?"

"More of a test."

They had dined alone, the three of them. Now they sat in Tamil Rahani's office.

"Please." The officer commanding Erewhon made an open gesture with his hands. "Please believe me, I would not have put you through this ordeal, had it been up to me."

"It's your organization. You were offering me a job."

Rahani did not look him in the eyes. "Well," he said, his voice low. "I have to be perfectly truthful with you. Yes, the idea of founding an organization that rented out mercenary terrorists *was* my original idea. Unhappily, as so often happens in matters like this, I needed specialist assistance. In turn this meant taking in partners. The end product gives me a large return, but . . . well, I take my orders from others."

"And in this case your orders were . . . ?"

"To make a decision regarding the possibility of using you. To see if you were trustworthy, or merely some kind of undercover plant. To obtain certain information from you, the strength of which we could easily test, and then—when we were satisfied on those points—to put you up against a real challenge: to see if you could survive a genuine situation of danger."

"And I've passed on all points?"

"Correct. We are satisfied. Now, you can be returned to our planners. It was true when I said there was a job waiting for you. There has been from the word go. That is why you were manipulated—and why you were brought here, where we have facilities. You see, once here, if you had turned out to be—how do you people say it?—A double? Is that correct?"

Bond nodded.

"If you had been exposed as a double, we had the facilities here for losing you. Permanently."

"So what's this job you have for me?"

"It is a large and complex operation, with many tiny details. But one thing I *can* tell you." He looked up at Bond, his eyes blank as though each was made of glass. "What is being planned at the moment will be the so-called terrorist coup of the decade, even the century. If things proceed normally, they will spark off the ultimate revolution. A unique and complete change in the course of world events, the beginning of a new age. And those of us taking part in it will inherit a large and privileged position within the Phoenix that will undoubtedly spring from what is to be done."

"I saw the film."

Simon rose, going over to the filing cabinet on which rested a few bottles. He poured himself a liberal glass of wine, then disappeared from Bond's view.

"Scoff, Mr. Bond. But I think even you will find this to be an operation without parallel in history."

"And it won't work without me?" Bond raised a cynical eyebrow.

"I did not say that. But it may not work without somebody *like* you, Commander Bond."

"Okay." He leaned back in his chair. "So tell me all about it."

"I'm afraid *I* can't do that." The cold eyes bored into him, so that, for a second or two, Bond thought the man was trying out some elementary hypnosis.

"So?"

"So, you have to be returned. You have to go back."

"Back? Back to where?"

Too late Bond felt Simon's presence behind him.

"Back from whence you came, James."

Bond was conscious of the small, sharp pinch through his shirt, on his arm just below the right shoulder.

Tamil Rahani continued to speak.

"We're not talking about the stories dreamed up by pulp novelists. No blackmail through concealed nuclear devices hidden in the heart of great Western cities; no plots to kidnap the President, or hold the world to ransom by setting all the major currencies at naught. We're not talking about extortion; nor . . . are . . . we . . ." His voice slowly receded, fogged over, and then—like life itself—went out.

13

THE NUMBERS RACKET

THE SKY WAS gray, almost leaden. He could see it through the window—the sky and part of an old apple tree. That was all.

Bond had woken from what seemed to be natural sleep. He was still fully dressed, and the ASP, complete with holster and one extra clip of ammunition, lay on the bedside table. The room appeared to be very English—white gloss paint on the woodwork and Laura Ashley wallpaper, with contrasting fabrics for curtains. Only most of the window was bricked up; and the door would not budge when he tried to open it.

There was a depressing sense of déjà vu. He had been along this road before, only last time it was Erewhon. Rahani had said they had accepted him, but he wondered how and why. Certainly the long interrogation sessions had been searching, and M had instructed him to give away anything they could check on, even if it was highly sensitive. Fences, his Chief maintained, could be mended later. But what would be the state of play by the time they came to mend fences? At Erewhon preparations were steaming forward for something earth-shattering. What was it that Rahani had said?—"A unique and complete change in the course of world events." The dream of revolutionaries—to change the march of history; to crush the status quo; to alter in order to build a new society. Well, Bond thought, it had been done before, but only within countries. Russia was the prime example, though Hitler's rise in Germany had been a revolution as well. The problem with revolutions, so history taught, was that the ideal usually fell short because of human frailty.

Also, Rahani had specifically told him that he—Bond—or somebody like him, was essential to whatever was about to take place. They needed a man, or woman, with the skills or contacts or knowledge of an experienced Secret Intelligence field officer. What part of those skills, or what particular piece of knowledge was required?

He was still pondering on these things when somebody knocked at the door, and a key turned in the lock.

Cindy Chalmer looked bright and crisp. She wore a laboratory coat over jeans and shirt, and was carrying a large tray. "Breakfast, Mr. Bond," she beamed at him. In the background, he glimpsed a tall, muscular man—a hood if ever he had seen one.

Bond nodded toward him. "Someone to watch over me?"

"And me, I guess." She set the tray down on the end of the bed. "Can't be too careful with hot shots like you around. Nobody knew what you'd like, so Dazzle did the full English breakfast— bacon, eggs, sausages, toast, coffee." She lifted the silver cover from the steaming plate, holding it with the inside toward Bond. There was a folded paper neatly taped to the inside of the cover.

"That'll do fine." He gave her an understanding nod. "Do I call room service when I've finished?"

"Don't call us, we'll call you," she said brightly. "We will, Mr.

Bond. I gather the Professor wants to talk with you later. Good to see you feeling better. They said you had a nasty bump when you went off the road. The Professor was genuinely worried, that's why he persuaded the hospital to let him bring you here."

"Very good of him."

She seemed to linger by the door. "Well, it's nice to know we'll all be working together."

"Good to have a job in these difficult times," Bond countered, not knowing how much Cindy knew. Had they told her he'd been in a motor accident? That he was being given a job at Endor? Well, presumably the latter was more or less true. He waited until the key clunked home in the lock. There was nothing else to hear, no retreating footsteps, for the passage outside—like this room—was overlaid with thick carpet.

The paper came away easily from the inside of the lid. Cindy had filled it with small, neat writing and, in spite of the steam, the ink had not run. The note started abruptly, without any salutation.

> I don't know what's happened. They say you've had a car smash, but I don't know whether to believe them. The facts are simple. They brought your Bentley back here, and there's been a lot of talk about you joining the team as a programer. I wondered if they knew you had computer equipment with you, and felt you would not want them to find it. Very difficult, but I got hold of the Bentley's keys and cleaned out the boot. All your private stuff is now hidden in the garage, and not likely to be found, unless we're unlucky. A good thing I did it straight away, because security's been tightened for the weekend. A lot of people are coming down, and—from what I've heard—the game I spoke of (remember the balloons?) is going to be in use. It is possible that I may be able to get hold of it. Do you wish to copy? Or is that superfluous now that you are "One of Us?" C.

So, the place was going to be crowded, The Balloon Game was to the fore, and Bond, so he'd been told, was essential. Therefore, if The Balloon Game was a training simulation for the operation, then Bond and the game were closely interconnected. QED.

He tore the message into tiny pieces and ate them with the bacon and some toast. He could not stomach the eggs or sausage, but the coffee was good, and he drank four cups, strong and black.

There was a small bathroom attached to his bedroom and set neatly on the glass shelf, above the handbasin, were his toilet articles—everything from razor to his favorite cologne. Already he had seen his weekend case beside the small wardrobe, and on examination discovered his clothes had all been washed and neatly pressed.

Don't believe it all, he told himself. On the face of it, he was trusted—weapon, shaving kit, everything intact. But they kept the door locked, and there was no immediate way out of the window.

He showered, shaved and changed, retaining the casual clothes that allowed him to move easily and fast. Even the ASP was strapped to his right hip by the time a second knock and the turning of the key announced the arrival of two muscular men whose faces were definitely familiar from the files—"Tigerbalm" Balmer and "Happy" Hopcraft.

"Mornin', Mr. Bond." Tigerbalm smiled, his eyes not meeting Bond's but sliding around the room, as though measuring it.

"Hallo, James, nice ter meecher." Happy stuck out a hand, but Bond pretended not to notice.

"Balmer and Hopcraft," Tigerbalm said. "At your service. The Professor wants a word." Behind the expensive mohair suits and the cheerful bonhomie lay a sinister spark of menace. One knew, just by looking at them, that this pair would have your head, stuffed and mounted, if it suited them, or if they were so ordered by someone paying them for the favor.

"Well, if the Professor calls, we must answer." Bond looked at the key, clutched in Tigerbalm's hand. "That really necessary?"

"Orders." From Happy.

"Let's go and see the Professor, then."

They did not exactly crowd him as the three of them went down the corridor, then the stairs, and on to the working area that had once been the cellars, but their presence had a certain intimidating effect. Bond felt that one false move—any inclination to go in another direction—would bring about a fast, restraining action.

There was no sign of either Cindy or Peter, but St. John-Finnes sat at his desk, the large computer console in front of him, and the VDU giving out a glow of color.

"James, it's nice to have you back." He signaled with his head, indicating that Tigerbalm and Happy should leave, then gestured to an easy chair.

"Well," when they were settled, "I'm sorry you were put to some inconvenience."

"I could've been killed, quite easily." Bond spoke in a level, calm manner.

"Yes. Yes, I'm sorry about that; but it was actually *you* who did the killing, I gather."

"Only because I had to. Habits take a long time to die. I think my reactions are reasonably fast."

The high, birdlike head moved up and down in comprehension. "Yes, the reports all say you're rather good. You must understand that we had to be sure of you. I mean, one error and a great deal of money, and planning, would have been in jeopardy."

Bond said nothing, so St. John-Finnes continued: "Anyway, you passed with flying colors. I'm glad, because we need you. You're now aware of the connection between things here at Endor and the training camp, Erewhon?"

"I gather that you and your partner, Mr. Tamil Rahani, run a rather strange enterprise—hiring out mercenaries to terrorist and revolutionary groups."

"Oh, a little more than that." It was the benign large bird, smiling and nodding. "We can offer complete packages. A group can come to us with an idea, and we do everything else—from raising the money to performing the operation. For instance, the job for which you have been recruited has been on the drawing board for some time now, and we stand to gain a great deal from it."

Bond said he realized that he had been vetted, tested; also he knew there was some particular job for him, within the organization, and connected to an operation. "But I've no idea of the . . ."

"Details? No, of course you have no idea. Just as in your old profession people worked on a need-to-know basis, so we must be exceptionally careful—particularly with this current work. No one person is in possession of the full picture, with the exception of Colonel Rahani and myself, of course." He made a slight movement of the fingers and head, which was meant to convey modesty. It was a curiously Oriental gesture, as though he wished Bond to realize that he was really unworthy to be granted the honor of knowing such plans. Bond also noted that it was now *Colonel* Rahani, and he wondered where that title came from.

". . . particularly careful concerning you, I fear," St. John-Finnes had spoken again. "Our principals were very much against giving you a situation of trust, but I think—since Erewhon—we have made them think twice."

"This job? The one you've recruited me for . . . ?" Bond started.

"Has been in the making for a considerable time. Much money was needed, and our principals in the matter were, shall we say, short of funds. This suited us. We're packagers, Bond. So we packaged some money-making projects to finance the main thrust."

"Hence the Kruxator Collection, and other pieces of high-tech thieving."

Jay Autem Holy remained blizzard cold. Only in his eyes could Bond detect a tiny wariness. "You come to interesting deductions, my dear Bond. For one who knows nothing . . ."

"Stab in the dark." Bond's face betrayed nothing. "After all, there have been several imaginative robberies lately—all with the same handwriting. A case of putting two and two together, and, maybe, coming in with the correct answer."

Holy made a noncommittal grunt. "Good. I am satisfied that you're clean, Bond. But my orders are to segregate you. There is knowledge, and skill, which you possess. We require you to put that knowledge into action now."

"Well?"

"Well, as a former field officer of the Secret Intelligence Service, you must have a working knowledge of the diplomatic, and military, communications network."

"Yes."

"Tell me, then, do you know what an EPOC Frequency is?"

"Yes." Bland as before, though Bond was now beginning to worry. The last time he had heard of EPOC Frequencies was when he had been called upon to guard against possible aggressive monitoring of signals during a visit to Europe by the President of the United States. EPOC stood for Emergency Presidential

Orders Communications. So an EPOC Frequency was the cleared radio band frequency upon which flash—or emergency—messages were sent out by the United States President during an official tour outside the United States.

"And what kind of signal is sent over an EPOC Frequency?"

Bond paused, as though giving the matter some thought. "Only vital military instructions. Sometimes a response to a military query that demands action from the President only. Sometimes action inaugurated by him."

"And how are these orders transmitted?"

"Usual high-speed traffic, but on a line kept permanently clear, via one of the communications satellites."

"No, I mean the nature of the transmissions. The form they take."

"Oh. A simple group of digits. Data, I suppose. The orders that can be given through the EPOC Frequency are very limited. It's rarely used, you know."

"Quite." Holy gave what could only be described as a knowing smile. "Rarely used, and very limited—but limited in a most far-reaching way, yes?"

Bond agreed. "The President would use the EPOC Frequency only on strong recommendation from his military advisers. The subjects are usually concerned with rapid deployment of conventional troops and weapons . . ."

"The raising, or lowering, of any readiness state as far as nuclear strike capacity is concerned?"

"That's a priority, yes."

"And tell me, would the instructions be obeyed? Immediately, I mean? Suppose the President was, for the sake of argument, in Venice and wished to bring NATO forces to a top level of readiness and prepare his nuclear strike forces for imminent action. Would it simply be done? Without consultation?"

"Quite possibly. The code for that kind of action is, in effect, a computer program. Once it's fed into the system it works. In the scenario you're suggesting, the British Prime Minister and the Commander-in-Chief NATO would consult back. But the readiness state would persist."

"And if the British Prime Minister, and the C-in-C NATO

forces, were known to be with the President at the moment of transmission?"

Suddenly they were on very dangerous ground. Bond felt his stomach turn over. Then he remembered Rahani's words: *No blackmail . . . no plots to kidnap the President, or hold the world to ransom . . .*

"In those circumstances," he said calmly, thinking meanwhile that something far more devious, more ingenious, than a hare-brained revolutionary plot was involved, "the instructions would go to all local commanders automatically. They would be fed into the mainframe computers, the program would begin to run, globally, straight away. No question. But surely you know all of this yourselves."

"Indeed I do." There was a weird, unsettling tranquility in the way Jay Autem answered. "Yourselves" became "I," Bond noticed, and the tone was of an almost glacial imperturbability. "Yes, *I* know the minutiae of it. Just as I know who has access to the daily ciphers for use through the EPOC Frequency; and who also has access to that Frequency."

"Tell me?" Bond gave the impression of not knowing such details.

"Come, Mr. Bond. You know as well as I do."

"I'd rather hear it from you, sir."

"There are only eleven ciphers that are capable of being sent via EPOC. These are seldom altered, for, as you say, they are programs designed to automatically be set in motion while the President is out of the country. The eleventh is, incidentally, a countermand program to stop an order, returning things to the status quo. But that one can be used in only a limited time scale. The Frequency itself is altered at midnight every two days. Correct?"

"I believe so."

"The ciphers are carried by that omnipresent, and somewhat frightening official known as the Bag Man. Correct?"

"The system has been found reliable," Bond observed. "There was a Bag Man present in JFK's entourage in Dallas. It's never been changed. He's always around—in the United States as well as when the Chief Executive travels abroad. The penalty for having your President as C-in-C Armed Forces."

"The Bag Man can only part with the ciphers and EPOC Frequency to the President, or the Vice-President, should anything happen. If the President should meet with a fatal accident overseas, the ciphers are immediately null and void, unless the Vice-President is with him."

"Yes."

"So, if someone—anyone—was in possession of the EPOC Frequency, and the eleven ciphers, it would be possible to relay a particular command that would automatically begin to run?"

For the first time since they had started talking, Bond smiled, slowly shaking his head. "No. There is a failsafe. The EPOC Frequency is a beamed satellite signal. It goes directly through one of the Defense Communications Satellite Systems, and they are very tricky little beggars. When the signal is initiated, the program will only run if the satellite confirms that it has come directly from the area in which it knows—because it has been told—the President is located. You'd have to be *very* close to the President of the United States before you could beat the system and plunge the world into chaos."

"Exactly." To Bond's surprise, Jay Autem Holy looked quite happy. "Would you be surprised to learn that we already have the eleven ciphers, the programs?"

"Nothing surprises me anymore. If you're playing games with an Emergency Presidential Order you still have to get hold of the Frequency for the particular forty-eight hours in which you plan to operate. Then you have to get close to the President, and have means of using the Frequency. I'd say the last two were the hardest—getting near to the President with the equipment needed to transmit, and obtaining the necessary frequency."

"So who else knows the EPOC Frequency—always?" Jay Autem raised his eagle brows, questioning. "I'll tell you, Mr. Bond. The duty Intelligence officer at the NATO C-in-C's headquarters; the duty Communications officer at the CIA HQ, Langley; the duty Communications officer, NSA; the senior communications officer in the United States Armed Forces; and, Mr. Bond, the senior monitoring officer at GCHQ, Cheltenham; plus the Duty Security Officer at the British Foreign Office—who is always a member of the Secret Intelligence Service. It's quite a list, when you consider that the President himself has no knowledge of the EPOC Frequency until he has occasion to use it."

"They're so very rarely used. Yes, as I remember it, you've got the list right—but for one other person."

"Who?"

"The officer who controls the ciphers and frequency at the outset. Usually a communications security officer with the NSA—the National Security Agency."

"Who usually, Mr. Bond, has forgotten the details within five minutes. What we shall need from you is the precise EPOC Frequency on a particular day—which means we need it twenty-four hours in advance. All other details are taken care of."

"And how do you expect me to give you the EPOC Frequency?"

Jay Autem Holy gave a throaty laugh. "You have done service as Duty Security Officer at the Foreign Office. You know the system, and the routine. We know you can be ruthless, and that you are a professional. Someone of your background, with your expertise and knowledge, should have no difficulty in obtaining what we require. Using your knowledge, and what contacts are left to you, there should be no problem. Just put your mind to it. Then report your scheme to me. This is why you were the obvious candidate, Bond. Providing you're as straight as we believe. There is an old proverb—When you want something from the lions, send a lion, not a man."

"I've never heard that before."

"No? You are the lion going to the lions. You are trusted, but if you should fail us . . . Well, we are not forgiving people, I'm afraid. Incidentally, I'm not surprised you didn't recognize the proverb. I just invented it!" And the man who was Jay Autem Holy threw back his head in a guffaw of laughter.

James Bond did not think it was that funny.

"You'll get the Frequency for us, won't you, Bond?" The query came out through a series of deep breaths, as Holy gained control of himself. "Think of it as your revenge. I promise you it will be used for good, and not to create havoc and disaster."

There was no other option, for the moment. "Yes, yes, of course I'll do it. It's only a few numbers you want, after all."

"That's right. You're in the numbers racket now. A few simple digits, James Bond." He paused, the amazing green eyes boring into Bond's skull. "Did you know the Soviets use almost an identical method when the General Secretary and Chairman of the Central Committee is abroad? They call it the Panic Frequency—but in Russian of course."

"You need access to this Panic Frequency as well?" Casual, but with antennae twitching.

"Oh, we *have* access. You're not the only person in the numbers racket, Bond. Our principals in this operation have little money to spare, but they certainly have contacts. Light on cash but heavy on information."

"Ah, your principals, yes." Bond turned down the corners of his mouth. "Even though my part in all this is vital—essential—I am not allowed to know . . . ?"

"The name of our principals? I should have thought a man like you would have already guessed. A once powerful and very rich organization, which has fallen on bad times—mainly because they have lost their last two leaders under tragic circumstances. Our principals, Mr. Bond, are a group who call themselves SPECTRE. The Special Executive for Counterintelligence, Terrorism, Revenge and Extortion. I rather like the Revenge element, don't you?"

14

BUNKER HILL

TIGERBALM AND HAPPY, the strong-arm men in residence, cheerfully took Bond back to his room and left him. Yet there was something different on the return trip. He knew it, but for the moment, preoccupied, could not work out what it was.

Stretching out on the bed, Bond stared at the ceiling and concentrated on the current problem. It all seemed so unreal, particularly in this pleasant room, with its white gloss paint, straight out of a television ad, and the chintzlike pattern of the wallpaper. Yet here he was, with the full knowledge that somewhere below him a scientist who had already run simulations for criminal activities, was now training people for some other, more dangerous mission, this time in the service of Bond's old, long-standing enemy, SPECTRE.

It didn't surprise him in the least to have learned that SPECTRE—as principals in the matter—had not approved of Bond's recruitment. After all, their death feud had gone on for more years than either party cared to remember.

But that was neither here nor there at this moment. Jay Autem Holy had disclosed the reason for Bond's being on the payroll: They needed him. Now, it was up to him to be convincing, to Holy, Rahani and SPECTRE, in the role they had designed for him.

M had been clear on this point. "If they take you in—if any organization takes you in—then you will have to split yourself in two," M had ordered. First, Bond should not believe any recruitment was either serious or long-term; second, he *had* to believe it was serious. "If they want you for a specialist job, then you must, at all costs, treat it as a reality. Work it out, as they would expect you to: like a professional."

So now, lying on the bed, with part of his mind reviewing the situation with grave suspicion, James Bond began to tackle the problem of how to get hold of the EPOC Frequency.

First, there was a small ray of hope. To secure the set of numbers they required, he would have to get in touch with the outside. More, it would mean communication with his old professional world. It was also ninety-nine percent certain that this contact would, at some point, have to be physical—which meant escape. In this context, M's paradox became crystal clear. He really *had* to set up a method of laying hands on the EPOC Frequency. At the same time, a way had to be devised for him to do it with full knowledge of his own Service.

It took half an hour for Bond to develop two possible methods, though both presupposed a situation in which he alone would be let loose to gain access to the Frequency. The first plan also needed Cindy Chalmer's assistance, and a method of reaching his Bentley. If this was not possible, then the second plan would have to suffice, though it contained a number of imponderables, some of which could come unbuttoned with worrisome ease.

He was still mentally wrestling with this reserve plan when he suddenly realized what was different. Once Tigerbalm and Happy left, there had been no click of key in lock.

Sliding quietly off the bed he went over to the door. It opened without resistance. An error? Or a message from the master of Endor, telling him he was free to go wherever he liked? If the latter, then Bond would have put money on it being a very limited rein. Then why not put it to the test?

The corridor took him out to a landing, the landing to the main staircase, which brought him into the hall, familiar from his previous visit. There, all possibility of real freedom ended. Seated near the door, dressed in jeans and a rollneck, was a young man he recognized from Erewhon. Another graduate from that particular alma mater lounged near the door to the cellar, or laboratory, stairs.

Giving each guard a friendly nod of recognition—returned with only a hint of uncertainty in the far reaches of their eyes—he strolled through to the main drawing room, in which he had last sat with Freddie, Peter, Cindy and the two St. John-Finneses that first night before dinner.

The room was empty. He looked around, in the hope of spotting some newspapers. None—not even copies of the television guides. There was a television, however, and he took four strides to get to it. The set was dead. Plugged in, switched on at the mains, but dead as a stone. The same applied to the tuner radio facility on the stereo system.

Nothing, it seemed, was coming into Endor through normal means. Bond assumed that any other television or radio would also be inoperable, which signaled a need for him, and possibly the others, to be separated from world events. Cut off. In isolation.

He stayed downstairs for five minutes or so before retracing his steps to his room.

An hour or so later Tigerbalm came, alone, to tell him they were going to have a meal shortly. "The chief says you can join us." He showed no particular feelings for Bond, either friendly or hostile, only the terse, necessary cordiality of a messenger. Somewhere along the morning road Tigerbalm's bouncy bonhomie had dissipated.

The dining room was bare of its good furniture and trappings. In place of the refectory table, a series of functional, military trestle tables had been set up, while the food was collected from another cloth-covered table—soup, bread, cheese, several salad dishes. All very simple with only mineral water to drink.

The room, however, was crowded, and Bond recognized most of the faces from Erewhon. Only Tigerbalm and Happy appeared out of their depth, bulky and furtive among the serious, sunburned, soldierly young men.

"James, good to see you." Simon stood at his elbow.

"I wondered where you'd got to," Bond replied. He studied the face carefully. The openness, so visible at Erewhon, had now turned to camouflage—a change that confirmed the situation every bit as much as the alterations in the decor. Whatever plot, plan or caper had been set in motion by SPECTRE, it was already running. D minus two, three, four or five, Bond reckoned. Then he drastically reduced the odds in his head as he spotted Tamil Rahani, seated on one side of St. John-Finnes, and—guess who?— good old Rolling Joe Zwingli on the other. The three men sat apart from everyone else—alone at a smaller table, and were being served with food by a pair of younger "soldiers." Like the others, the leaders were dressed in uniform khaki slacks and drab green pullovers, their heads bent together as though sitting for a portrait to be titled *The Conspirators.*

For a second Bond's mind drifted off to the surveillance team in the village. Had they noted the comings and goings? Were they aware of the dangerous powers gathered together in this place?

"I said, did you rest well?" Simon was speaking to him.

"Rest? Oh, rest, yes." Bond managed a smile. "I had no option, Simon. You saw to that."

"Security," Simon grinned, answering Bond's last remark. "You know all about security, James. You go to sleep in a hot dusty climate, and wake up in a quiet English village. Come, have some food." Simon began piling salads and cheese onto a plate until Bond had to stop him with a gesture of his hand.

They sat together at the end of one of the longer tables, Simon seeing to it that Bond had his back to the three "brains." Bond watched as his partner took a mouthful of bread and cheese, chewing on it, sucking the juices back into his throat. Every inch a trained soldier, he thought.

"Hallo, Old Bald Eagle's coming your way, James. Looks like he's got orders for you."

Then "Old Bald Eagle"—St. John-Finnes—was leaning over them. "James," his voice took on a quiet, confiding tone, as though trying to calm a tantrum-beleaguered child. "Can you spare an hour or two?"

Bond checked himself from making a fatuous remark, nodded and rose, winking at Simon as he followed his employer. He could feel the eyes of both Rahani and Zwingli on his back as they left.

A young man guarded the stairs down to the laboratory and offices. He did not even signify that he had seen them, almost ostentatiously looking the other way.

"I thought I'd give you a chance to lose the American Revolution to me," Jay Autem said as they began the descent. "It's an easy enough simulation at this level, so we can, perhaps, talk about your plans as we fight. Yes?"

"Whatever you say." Noncommittal, but running the high-speed tape of his plan for getting the EPOC Frequency through his mind.

In the main laboratory area, some drastic rearrangements had also taken place. The largest space was now filled up with collapsible wooden chairs, arranged in rows to give the place the look of some small school assembly hall, or a World War II briefing hut. One modern touch, however: Instead of the expected white screen at the far end, facing the chairs, there was a large television projection screen with Jay Autem Holy's version of the Terror Twelve before it.

Bond could not help seeing the two modern typing chairs nearby, or the big chunky joystick controllers.

A training session had obviously been going on for most of the morning. The Balloon Game? Almost certainly.

Then they were through the office and into the large room with its spotlights and map board of the Eastern coastline of late-eighteenth-century America. There was Boston with Bunker Hill and Breed's Hill to the north, Dorchester Heights jutting out to enclose the harbor, and the townships of Lexington and Concord inland. For no apparent reason, Bond recalled hearing Americans pronounce Concord with a shortened second syllable so that it sounded like Conquered. Jay Autem was smiling down at the

board, with its movable open rectangle and all the games paraphernalia set at the two adjacent tables.

Bond saw the smile, and the look, and in that one second
abruptly realized that, for all the man's brilliance in his chosen
field, the chink in his armor was glaringly obvious.

His interest in strategy and tactics had evolved into an obsession—an obsession with winning; just as his simulations of war,
on computer, were his brain-children only because through them
he could beat his own system and win. Like an overindulged
child, Dr. Jay Autem Holy was only interested in winning. To
lose was the ultimate failure. Had he lost some internal Pentagon
battle when he dropped out of life all those years ago? Bond
speculated, steeling himself meanwhile, then concentrating on the
rapid instructions issued by his Games Master.

Certainly the rules were simple enough. Each player took a
turn, which was divided into four phases—Orders; Movement;
Challenge; and Resolution. Some of these moves could be made
in secret—and, therefore, not seen by the opponent—by marking
the location of troops, or matériel, on a small duplicate map of
the playing area, a pile of which rested in front of each player.
"When we transfer the whole thing onto computer there's an even
more ingenious method of making the 'unobserved moves,' " Jason
told him, with all the pride of a small boy showing off a collection
of toy soldiers.

The playing area itself, on the grid of the large map, was marked
out in hundreds of black hexagons. Each side had counters that
represented number, strength and type of unit—black for one
piece of cannon, with horses and crew; green for five men; blue,
ten; red, twenty, and so on. There were also counters overprinted
with a horse, denoting mounted troops, while special counters
were set out to represent arms caches and leading members of
the revolutionary cause.

In good weather men on foot could move five hexes, seven on
horseback, and cannon only two. These moves were restricted by
bad weather, and by woodland or hills.

Once Orders had been noted, the player moved and then chal-
lenged—either by coming within two hexes of an enemy counter,
or by declaring that he had sight over five hexes, thereby revealing
any "hidden" moves. After the Challenge came the Resolution,

in which various strengths, fatigue, weather and so on, were taken into consideration, and the outcome of the Challenge—which could be a skirmish or a full-scale bloody battle—would be noted, one or the other player losing troops, matériel or the action itself.

As each turn, at the beginning, covered a timescale of one day— and the whole episode lasted from September 1774 to June 1775, Bond realized they could be at it for many hours.

"Once we get it onto the computer, the whole business becomes faster, of course," Holy remarked as they both began their Orders phase—with Bond playing the British. He recalled Peter Amadeus' remarks: that his opponent almost expected the British to make the same moves—and mistakes—they had in history.

As Bond recalled it, the garrison commander had been hamstrung by the length of time orders took to reach him from England. Had he acted decisively in the first weeks and months, this opening period could have had a very different outcome. History would have been changed and—while independence would almost certainly have followed at some point—lives, as well as face, might have been saved.

He opened by showing patrols going out of Boston to search the surrounding countryside, but also made secret forays in order to gain control of the high ground—Bunker and Breed's hills, together with Dorchester Heights, at an early stage.

He was surprised to find how, once playing, the game moved much faster than expected.

"The fascination for me," Holy observed as Bond took out two arms caches and around twenty revolutionaries on the Lexington road, "is the juxtaposition of reality and fiction. But, in your former job, this must have been a constant problem."

Bond secretly took three more cannon toward Breed's Hill, a section of thirty men in a final move to the top of Dorchester Heights, while showing more patrols on the ground along the Boston-Concord line. "Yes," he answered, reminding himself to be truthful, "yes, I have lived a fictitious life within a reality—it is the daily bread of field agents."

"I trust you are living in reality now, friend Bond. I say that because what is being planned in this house can also change the course of history." Holy revealed two strong bodies of the colonial militia along the road, attacking the British patrols so fiercely that

Bond lost almost twenty men and was forced to withdraw and regroup. Secretly, though, he still poured men, and weapons, onto the dominating ground. The Battle of Bunker Hill—if it ever came—would be completely reversed, with the British forces in a strong and dominant position defending instead of attacking under the withering fire of the entrenched militia.

"One hopes that any change can only be for the good, and that lives are not put at risk."

"Lives are always at risk." The master of Endor found himself losing four caches of weapons and ammunition in a farmhouse on the far side of Lexington, realizing as he did so that Bond had also begun to move his forces on Concord. He shrugged. "But, as for your own life, I know there is no point in threatening you with sudden death. Any threat to your person is of little importance."

"I wouldn't say that," Bond found himself smiling. "We all like life. The thought of being separated from it is as good a lever as any."

The date pages on the calendar easel showed them almost at the end of December, and the weather was against both sides. All either of them could do now was consolidate—openly, or using the clandestine option. Bond decided to divide his forces, encircling the road between Lexington and Concord, while his remaining troops continued to fortify the hills and heights. Holy appeared to be playing a more devious game—sniping at British patrols and, Bond suspected, moving forces toward the high ground already occupied by the British. They played, turn after turn as the weather grew worse and movement was further restricted. Yet throughout this phase, the master of Endor carried on a conversation that appeared to have little to do with the simulated battle.

"Your part in our mission," he took out five of Bond's men, "is of exceptional importance, and you will undoubtedly have to use much fiction, and illusion, to accomplish it."

"Yes. I've been giving it a lot of thought."

"Have you given thought to the way in which governments mislead their gullible peoples?"

"In what way?" he now had sizable forces on all three sections of ground overlooking Boston.

"The obvious, of course, is the so-called balance of power. The

United States does not draw attention to the fact that it is out-numbered in space by Russian satellites—not to mention things like the fractional orbital bombing system, in which the Soviets hold a monopoly of seventeen to zero."

"The figures are there for anybody." Bond would soon have to make a serious challenge from the high ground, as colonial forces struggled upward in increasing numbers, restricted by both the climb and the snow.

"Oh, yes, but neither side makes a big thing about figures." Jason scanned the board, brow creased. "Except when Russia takes umbrage at the deployment of Cruise and Pershings in Europe—even when she can more than adequately match them. But James, I may call you James? What is the real conspiracy here? The British tie up many policemen against antinuclear protesters. Yet nobody says to these well-meaning people, 'If it happens, brothers and sisters—which it will not—it's not going to happen with a big nuclear bang. The Cruise and Pershing are for rattling only. What could occur will be ten thousand times worse.' "

"Nobody tells the protesters in the United States, either." Bond watched as his opponent edged even larger numbers of men toward the waiting British guns and fought a small skirmish along the constant battlefront of the country between Boston and Concord.

"And yet, if it came, James, what *would* happen?"

"Your guess is as good as mine. Certainly not the big bang and mushroom cloud. More like the bright lights, and a very nasty chemical cloud."

"Quite—I challenge from this hex," his arm moved out, to an area between Concord and Lexington, where British troops were now much thinner on the ground. "No, it will be neutrons and chemicals. A lot of death, but little destruction—then a Mexican stand-off in space, with the Soviets holding the big stick up there."

"Unless the United States and the NATO forces have done something to equalize things. That's what's going on, isn't it?" Why this? Bond asked himself. Why this chatter about the balance of power, and the place nuclear weapons played in that balance? Why talk of this to me?

Then he recalled the sound advice always given in classes on interrogation—don't listen to the words, let your ears hear the music. The orchestration makes the banal words seem more intelligent; the clever, soaring strings took your mind from the cheap potency of simple, emotional ideas.

It was late January, and, at a challenge, Bond had to reveal there were British forces ringing the far side of Concord. Holy started to cut them apart with his colonial militia, sniping across the winter landscape. Readily, Bond saw how addictive this kind of exercise could become. Using imagination, one could almost feel the cold and fatigue that played havoc with men's strength and fighting ability. One even heard the crack of musket fire, and saw the blood staining the dirty snow in some farmer's field.

Holy was not really talking about the lopsided balance of power. He was talking about the need to end the whole system that controlled that balance.

"Would the world not really be a better, and safer, place if the real strength was removed? If the stings were drawn from the superpowers' tails?" he asked, making another foray into the bleak Massachusetts winter scene.

"If it was possible, yes," Bond agreed. "It would be better, but I doubt safer. Slingshot or nuclear weapon, the world's always been dangerous." One more turn and he would have to declare his presence in the hills.

Jay Autem Holy leaned back, temporarily stopping play. "We're involved in halting the race to the holocaust—nuclear, neutron or chemical. To you is entrusted the task of getting that EPOC Frequency. Now, do you yet have a way?" As though he did not expect an answer, he played through his turn, concentrating on bringing men well into the British zone of fire.

"I have the makings of a plan. It will require certain information in advance . . ."

"What kind of information?"

"When you need the Frequency, I shall have to know, a little ahead of time, exactly who the Duty Security Officer is, for the night in question, at the Foreign Office . . ."

"That presents no problem. One man does the job for a whole week, yes?"

"As a rule."

"And he is a senior officer?"

Bond spread the fingers of his right hand, making a rocking movement. "Let's say middle management."

"But you are likely to know him?"

"That's why I really have to get a name. If you can't provide it, then I shall have to telephone."

"We can provide."

"Then, if I know him, I shall still have to make a call. If he is unknown to me—unlikely but possible—I'll have to think again."

"If you know him . . .?"

"I have a way of getting in. I should only need an hour, at the most, in his company." Bond prayed it would work. "I challenge you here," his finger hovered around the upper reaches of Breed's Hill.

"But . . ." his opponent began, then realized the trap that Bond had sprung.

A few minutes later, as he faced slaughter on the slopes of Bunker Hill, having lost the majority of his men and arms on Dorchester Heights and Breed's Hill, Jay Autem angrily told Bond that he would have plenty of warning. "You'll *know* who the officer is. That I promise you!" He watched as Bond revealed two more cannon to counterattacking militia on the far side of the hill. "This is the wrong way round," he said, barely controlling his rage. "And Bunker Hill can't happen until June—it's hardly February!"

"And this is the fiction," Bond answered calmly, feeling a measure of satisfaction in spite of himself. "The reality's history—even though a great deal of history happens to be fiction also."

Then, suddenly, the storm broke. Jay Autem Holy's chest seemed to swell, and his cheeks went crimson. "You . . . You . . . You . . ." The voice rising to a scream. "You've beaten me! ME!" One huge hand swept the papers from his playing area, then descended in a fist. "How dare you? How dare you even . . ." It was an awesome rage as the man spluttered. He stamped his feet; he literally kicked the table. Awesome, and yet funny, as a child's tantrums are amusing yet distressing.

Then, as suddenly as the rage had begun, it stopped. There was no dusk, no twilight, for sanity appeared to return, and Holy stood, looking for a brief moment like a chastened child.

"The militia could rally yet," the voice small, throaty. "But we've played too long," with a wave of the hand, "I have other things to do. Better things."

He stood, as though winning or losing a game were now of little consequence to him. When he spoke, the tone was completely normal, as if nothing unusual had taken place. "The object of spending this time with you, though, was to hear how your thoughts were shaping up—regarding your part in the operation." Quiet and conversational, making it all the more bizarre. "Tell me, if you happen to know the man on duty, how do you propose to get the Frequency from him?"

Bond, who was amazed to see by his watch that it was already eight in the evening, began to recite the method he had mentally prepared. Silence stretched out—the hush in the aftermath of a battle fought with counters instead of men, and on a board and map instead of ground. No reaction. As the seconds ticked by, he thought perhaps there had been a miscalculation. He sifted through his mind. Was there any really weak point? Anything that Jay Autem Holy could grab at to prove the whole idea a mere insubstantial fiction—which it surely was?

Then the silence ended, and a laugh began to rise from the tall man's throat, the head nodding in great beaky movements, as if preparing to tear his prey apart, savaging it with that sharp bill.

"Oh, yes, James Bond. I told them you were the only possible choice. If you can pull that off we'll *all* be happy, not that . . ."

He broke off suddenly, appearing to pull himself together, eyes darting around, as though he had been on the brink of an indiscretion.

The laughter subsided, and Bond was aware of movement. People were entering the main laboratory area.

"We have been down here for too long," Jay Autem snapped. "I took the trouble to ask Cindy to make up a tray for you. In your room. I shall eat later."

Superman, thought Bond. He's telling me that he's a survivor. Go without food and drink for long periods. "In the desert," he said softly, "when you were with General Zwingli—after you jumped from that airplane—did you have to go long without food and drink?"

The green eyes went bitterly cold, all sign of normal human life ebbing from them.

"Clever, Mr. Bond. How long have you known?"

Realizing that he had overplayed his hand, and not really certain why he had done so, Bond said he had suspected it from their first meeting. "It just happened that I'd read the old file. They resurrect it from time to time, you know. I thought I knew your face the moment we met—when I came here with Freddie. During the evening, I became more convinced, but still not one hundred percent sure. After all, if you *are* Jay Autem Holy, you've been dead a long time."

"And what if you had still been on active service, Mr. Bond? Would you have gone running to your superiors? And why, incidentally, is the file resurrected regularly?"

"You know what the Colonial militia is like," Bond tried to inject humor into his voice. "*Your* Colonial militia. They jump at ghosts. Spooks."

Jay Autem made a growling noise. "Tamil was right. It's a pity we didn't pull you in sooner. His people tried, against my advice. You see, I did not wish to deal with yet another hostage; another woman—you had some woman with you, yes? Anyway, the job was bungled; you were quick, and used cunning. So." The tense atmosphere changed yet again. There were no advance warnings with Holy. "Well, I have work to do. You stand by, James, and thank heaven we have you now."

They were gathering in the main laboratory, all young and bronzed—except Tigerbalm and Happy. Bond saw that Zwingli was still in deep conversation with Tamil Rahani, as though they had not stopped since lunch.

"Just see Mr. Bond up the stairs," Holy spoke to Tigerbalm, giving Bond a small pat on the shoulder, as if reassuring himself that all was well.

Tigerbalm went as far as the landing and watched as Bond walked to his room. He recalled being told that, appearances to the contrary, Jay Autem was a genius of sorts—was it Percy who had told him? The man obviously lived in that odd world of unreality. If he said he was dead, then that was exactly what the world should believe. Holy had been genuinely shaken by the idea that others might not be convinced. Then there was the question of Percy—"You had some woman with you, yes?" Well, who was it who had said that not even Holy would recognize his own wife?

He opened the door, and there—for the second time—was Cindy Chalmer, a finger of one hand to her lips, a hard computer disk clutched in the other.

Bond closed the door. "More greetings from Percy?" he asked softly.

15

THE BALLOON GAME

"**N**O. THIS ONE'S on me." She saw the look in Bond's eye, and followed his gaze, for he had suddenly become hesitant, wary, moving quietly around the room.

Softly she spoke again, "It's okay, James. They have visual surveillance, and a superabundance of military detection gear, but this lot don't seem to have caught up with the all-powerful bug."

"You certain?" he mouthed.

"Swept the place myself. In my first week; and I've kept abreast of all the security developments since. If they've put any sound in, I'll turn back into a virgin."

Bond nodded. There was nothing to be amused about now. Even though he appeared satisfied, throughout the time they were together in the room all conversation was conducted in a low murmur. Foolish, he thought, for that would be as audible to sophisticated equipment as yelling should Cindy be proved wrong.

"The Balloon Game." She held out the hard disk to him, a small flat square encased in plastic.

So she had got it, stored away on the wafer-thin magnetic disk, the program that would provide the answer to what SPECTRE had proposed to Rahani and Holy. Yet he did not move to take it from her.

"Well, don't just stand there. At least say thank you."

He remained silent, wishing to draw her out. The trick was as old as the trade itself, practiced constantly by case officers and agent handlers the world over. Remain silent and let them come to you, tell you all there is to tell.

"They've got four backup copies," she said at last, "and I just hope to heaven the Old Bald Eagle doesn't need to run the fourth, 'cause this is it."

"I thought they'd buried it, locked it behind steel and sprinkled man-eating spiders in the vault." He still did not smile.

"The original, and its backups, have been kept in the chief's safe—the one in his office that does have everything except the man-eating spiders." Once more she held it out. "But today it's all systems go, and they're using it all the time. As often happens, Peter and I have been banished from the lab. But the guards have got used to us going up and down. You beat him at his own game, I gather?"

"Yes." As though there had been no pleasure in it.

"Heard some of it. Now perhaps you'll believe he's insane—had one of his tantrums. Heard that as well."

"How did you get down?"

"Looked as though I belonged. Clipboard under one arm. They've seen me before. I just walked past the young thugs on the door. You were with Bald Eagle. Like a lot of people who become paranoid about security, he has a blind spot. The safe was left open. I did a swift switch, and tucked this up my shirt."

It was all he was going to get. "You haven't seen it run, then?"

She shook her head. Her negative gestures, he noticed, were always performed with the head tilted slightly to the right—a distinctive mannerism—a flourish, like the way some people curl the last letter of their signature, underlining the name to give it more importance. It was a habit they should have caught during training where the mohair-suited psychiatrists note, and expunge, mannerisms. He waited again.

"There's been no way, James. Only the inner circle've seen it, played with it—if that's the right word."

At last Bond took the disk. "Trained on it," he corrected. "And there's little chance of us having a look-see. My gear's where exactly?"

"In the garage. Under a pile of rubbish—tires, old tins, tools. In one corner. I had to improvise, and it was better to hide it there than let them find it in the car. It's not safe by any means, so we just have to hope nobody goes rooting around."

He seemed to give the situation a lot of thought. Then said, "Well, I for one don't fancy trying to unlock this," he touched the disk. "What's on it is big, and, I suspect, exceptionally dangerous. I just hope you're right—that the disk isn't missed, and that nobody goes rooting through the garage."

"So what good's it going to do? You want me to try and get it out?"

He walked over to the window, where the chintz Laura Ashley curtains had been drawn. The promised supper tray was on a table nearby, and he noticed it had been set for two—prawns in little glasses, cold chicken and tongue, salads; a bottle of wine; bread rolls. Did anybody get hot food at Endor when the heat was on? he wondered. Then he started thinking about the disk, still clutched in his hand. Better if he kept it close. Yet there were few really possible hiding places. In the end, he banked on there being no search, walked over to the wardrobe and stuck it among his clothes.

"There are friends," he confided at last. "Quite near. I would have thought that by now . . . No, you don't move from the house. Nobody tries to get out except me." Bond turned, and dropped quietly into a chair, signaling she should also sit. He nodded toward the wardrobe. "No risks, not with that. It's like a time bomb."

Cindy perched on the end of the bed, her skirt riding up to show a slice of smooth thigh. "We just sit, and wait until the cavalry arrive?"

"Something like that." He was thinking, trying to reckon what time they might have; whether the surveillance team, with their cameras, log books, directional microphones and all their other Boy's Book of Spies gear had advised M that something major was imminent. Would M sweat it out? Possibly. The cautious, diplomatic intriguer had waited before—until the very last moment.

"I want an educated guess from you, Cindy. You've been here before—I mean when they've prepared for some caper . . . ?"

Okay, she had been at Endor when the hard men came and spent hours down in the converted cellars, training.

"This is the biggest gathering yet?"

Since she had been here it was. Yes.

"In your estimation, Cindy, what's the timing? How long've we got before things start to roll?" In his mind the question was really, how long have *I* got before they ask me to filch the EPOC Frequency?

"It can only be a guess, but I'd say forty-eight hours, max."

"And your little playmate, Peter . . . ?"

She sprang to Peter's defense, like a sister. "Peter is okay. He's a brilliant worker, dedicated . . ."

"Would you trust him? Really trust, when the chips are down, as they say?"

She gnawed her upper lip. Only in a real emergency. Nothing against him; he couldn't stand the boss. "He's been looking for a different job. Says this place is too claustrophobic for him."

"I expect it's going to be even more claustrophobic. That you, Peter and myself are destined for oblivion. Anybody who isn't completely in their confidence." Once more he stayed silent, for nearly a full minute, his mind slicing through every morsel of information. Jay Autem had indicated that SPECTRE's current ploy was destined to change history. If it wasn't just some outrageous piece of stupidity, then it was quite possible the evil organization had latched on to something earth-shattering. Afterward, they would not want anybody around who could name names, or draw faces. Certainly not in the immediate wake of whatever they planned.

"My car," he began.

"The Bentley? Yes?"

"You took my gear from the boot. How?"

It was just before the present crowd arrived. Cindy had been through the kitchens and spotted large amounts of food being loaded into the two big deep freezes. She had also heard Old Bald Eagle on the telephone. "I knew they were bringing you back. What did happen, by the way? They said you were in hospital . . ."

Bond brusquely told her to get on with it.

She knew the car had been driven back and put into the garage, and she wondered about the micro and drives he had used in the hotel. The Bentley's keys were left in a security cabinet ("Where they keep all the car keys. I've been in and out of that one since I first arrived.") and she chose her moment.

"It was a risk, but I only had the keys out for five minutes. Everyone was busy, so I took the keys, unloaded the boot and stashed the stuff in the garage. It's not a hundred percent safe, but it seemed to be the only way. Bad enough doing that, and far too risky to attempt getting it any further away."

"And the car itself? Have they done anything with it? Gone over it?"

She gave her angled negative head shake. "No time. Not enough troops either."

"The keys?"

"Jason'll have them."

"And it's still there? In the garage?"

"Far as I know. Why?"

"Can we . . . ?"

"Forget it, James. There's no way we can drive out of here in one piece."

"I hope to be going officially. But, if they haven't messed about with it, I wouldn't mind spending fifteen minutes in that car now. Possible?"

"The keys? . . . How? . . . Lord, I don't . . ."

"Don't worry about keys. Just tell me, Cindy, can we get into the garage?"

"Well, I can." She explained that her room had a window looking out on the garage roof. "You just drop down, and there's a skylight. Opens upward. No problem."

"And security?"

"Damn. Yes, they've got a couple of young guys out front." She explained the layout. The garage itself held four cars, and was, in effect, an extension to the north end of the house. Her room was on the corner, just above the flat roof—one window looking down on the garage, two more to the front.

"And these guards? They're out front? Specifically watching the garage?"

"Just general duties. Keeping an eye on the north end. If we could . . . wait a minute. If my curtains aren't drawn they can see straight up into my room. I caught one lot at it last night. They just move a shade farther down the drive and they have a good view. How would it be if I gave them a peep show?"

Bond smiled for the first time. "Well, I'd appreciate it."

Cindy leaned back on the bed. "You, James, you male chauvinist pig, have the opportunity to appreciate it any time you want: and that's an offer."

"Which I'd love to take up, Cindy. But we have work. Let's see how good they've been with my luggage." He went over to the weekend case and dumped it on the bed beside the girl, then knelt to examine the locks. After a few seconds he nodded and took out the black gunmetal pen, unscrewing the wrong end to reveal a tiny set of miniature screwdriver heads. In turn, these were threaded at their blunt ends, the threads matching a small hole in the pen's cap. "No traveler should be without one," Bond smiled, selecting one of the drivers, and screwing it into place.

He then carefully started to remove the tiny screws around the right lock of his case. They turned easily, the lock coming off in one piece to reveal a small oblong cavity containing one spare set of keys for the Mulsanne Turbo, which he slipped into his pocket, before replacing the lock, and putting away the miniature tool kit.

The plans—for Cindy's diversion, and Bond's crawl from her window—were quickly arranged. "Diversion's no problem," she said, lowering her lids, "I've got exceptional quality tart's stuff on under the skirt." A small pout. "Thought I might even turn you on." She outlined her room, suggesting that she should enter in the dark, open the side window—with its drop onto the garage roof—and pull those curtains before switching the light on. "I'll be able to see exactly where the guards have placed themselves, and you'll have to crawl to the side window on your belly."

"How long can you . . . Well, tantalize them?"

If she performed the full act, Cindy said, putting on a throaty voice, she could keep them more or less happy for an hour. "To be on the safe side, I guess about ten minutes, give or take five."

He gave her a look reserved usually for the more cheeky jumpers and pearls set at the Regent's Park Office, checked the ASP, and said the sooner they got on with it, the better. Bond's common sense told him that, if they had not yet tampered with the car, it would certainly be given a going over before they let him out— *if* they let him out—to perform his allotted task.

Nobody appeared to be stirring in the house. The men still lounged in the hall—they saw them tiptoeing across the landing, but the rest was quiet, and the corridor leading to Cindy's room, at the far end of the house, was in darkness. Her smooth palm touched his, their fingers interlocking for a moment as she guided him toward her door.

She was young, supple, very attractive, and obviously available— to him at least. For a second he wondered, not for the first time, how genuine she was. But that option of trust had long since passed. There was nobody else.

Cindy opened her door, whispering, "Okay, down boy." He dropped onto his stomach, beginning to wiggle across the floor. Cindy was humming to herself, and interspersing the low tuneful bluesy sound with soft comments, "Nobody at the side . . . I'm closing the curtains . . . Okay, going to the front windows . . . Yes, they're down there . . . Right, James, get cracking, I'm putting the lights on . . ." And on they flooded, with Bond halfway across the floor, moving fast toward the window, in front of which the curtains billowed and sighed like a sail.

As he reached it, he saw her out of the corner of his eye, standing near the far front window, hands to her shirt, swaying slightly as she sang softly:

> He shakes my ashes, freezes my griddle,
> Churns my butter, stokes my pillow
> My man is such a handyman.

> He threads my needle, gleans my wheat,
> Heats my heater, chops my meat,
> My man is such a handyman.

The last words were barely distinguishable to Bond, who was out of the window, dropping silently onto the garage roof, by then.

Flat against the roof, his body pressing down as if to merge with the lead surface, Bond let his eyes adjust to the darkness. Then he froze, hearing first the noise of feet on gravel—to his left, at the front of the house—then the voices, alerted.

They spoke in heavily accented English, and there were, as Cindy had said, two of them.

One made a hushing sound. Then—

"What?"

"The roof. Didn't you hear it?"

"A noise? What?"

"Sounded like someone on the garage roof . . ."

Bond tried to will his body into the flat surface, pressing down, his head turned away, heart thudding in his ears.

"On the roof? No."

"Move back. Take a look. You know what he said—no second chances."

The feet on the gravel again.

"I can't see any . . ."

"You think we should go and . . . ?"

Bond's hand inched toward the ASP.

"There's nobody there. No . . . Hey, look at that!" The scuffle of feet moving back off the gravel.

Bond turned his head, and saw the clear silhouettes of the two guards below, in front of the house. They were close to one another, looking up like a pair of astronomers studying a new planet, eyes fixed on the windows out of his line of vision.

Carefully he started to move over the roof toward its center, where he knew the skylight lay. Then, suddenly, flat again as the guards also moved—his own breathing sounding violently loud, as though it would draw everyone to him. But the two men were now backing away from the house, heads tilted, trying to get a better view—a clearer angle—on what was happening just inside Cindy's lighted, open window.

Again he edged forward, going as fast as safety would allow, conscious of each minute slipping away.

The skylight moved at his first touch. Very gently he slid it back, staring down into the darkness below.

They had made it easier for him by parking the gray Mercedes directly underneath. One swing and he was down, feet on the car's roof, head less than a foot below the edge of the skylight.

Bond slipped the ASP from its holster. Once more he waited, stock still, letting eyes adjust and ears strain. No sound, except the beating of his own heart, no sign of any movement, but certainly the long outline of the Mulsanne Turbo parked to his right.

He dropped to the floor, one hand still grasping the ASP, the other now clutching the keys.

The lock of the Bentley thumped open, and there was that solid, satisfying sound as the catch gave way to his thumb and the heavy door swung back.

He slid into the driving seat and checked the connections around the Super 1000 long-range telephone, which Communications Control Systems had provided for the electronics wizards of Rolls-Royce to wire in. Then he picked up the handset, letting out a breath of relief as the small pin of red light came on to signify the telephone was active. His one fear had been that Jay Autem's or Tamil Rahani's men had cut the connections. Now, all he could do was pray nobody was monitoring the closed waveband.

Quickly he punched out the number, and, before the distant end had time to say "Transworld Exports," he rasped out, "Predator! Confuse!" hitting the small blue scramble button as he said it, then counting to twenty, waiting for the distant to come up again.

"Confused!" the voice of the duty officer at the Regent's Park Headquarters said clearly.

"I say this once only. Predator, emergency," and Bond launched into a fast two-minute message that he hoped would cover all the angles if Jay Autem Holy really intended to send him out from Endor to steal the United States EPOC Frequency within the next few days.

Putting the telephone back into its cradle, between the seats, he retrieved the ASP, which had rested only a cobra-strike from his hand, above the polished wooden dashboard, and returned it to the holster.

Now he had to make it back to Cindy's room as fast as possible. The thought of the girl slowly stripping, singing to herself, was highly erotic, but his mind flitted to other thoughts—about Percy Proud, to his passing surprise. A trick of the subconscious, he decided, closing the Bentley's door as quietly as its weight allowed, and operating the locking system.

He had just turned, to head back to the Mercedes, when a sharp double metallic click brought him to a halt.

There was an old game—from back in World War II—which they still played in training courses. You sat in darkness while tapes of noises were run. The object was to identify each noise. Often it was the distinctive cocking action of an automatic pistol (in training they ran this with sounds of door handles, toys, even metal snap fastenings). The sharp double click that he heard now came from the far side of the Mercedes, and Bond would know it anywhere. It was the automatic pistol.

The ASP was in his hand again, but as the gun came up, so the spotlight flashed on, and a familiar voice spoke softly:

"Put that nasty thing away, dear. It's not really worth it, and neither of us wants to get hurt, do we?"

16

EPOC

Bond could see him quite clearly, outlined against the lighter coloring of the wall. In a fraction of a second, his brain and body calculated the situation and made a decision.

Normally, with all his training and the long built-in reflexes, Bond would have taken him out with one shot—probably straight from the hip. But several factors intervened.

The voice was not aggressive, denoting room for barter; the words had been plain, simple and to the point—"neither of us wants to get hurt, do we?"—and, most important, there was no noise-reduction system fitted to the ASP. A shot, from either side, would bring unwanted company into the garage. Bond's reactions concluded that Peter was as anxious as himself to keep the wolves at bay.

"Okay, Peter. What's the score?" Almost a whisper, as Peter Amadeus came closer. Bond sensed, more than saw, that the small pistol, just visible, held away from the body, was moving around like a tree in a gale. The precise little man was very nervous.

"The score, Mr. Bond, is that I want out—and as far away from here as possible. I gathered from your one-way talkabout that you're thinking of going as well."

"I'm going when I'm told—by your boss and the others. Do they know you're out, by the way?"

"If the gods happen to be on my side, they won't notice. If the hue and cry is raised, I just pray they won't come looking here."

"Peter, you won't get out at all unless I go back the way I came pretty damned quickly. Wouldn't it be better for you to stay put?"

The pistol sagged in Amadeus' hand, and this time his voice edged one notch toward hysteria. "I can't, Mr. Bond! I can't do it. The place, those people—particularly Bald Eagle . . . I just can't stay in the house any longer!"

"Right," Bond soothed, hoping the young man's voice would not rise too high. "If we can think of a way, would you give evidence if necessary? Make a clear statement?"

"I've got the best evidence in the world," he seemed calmer, on safer ground. "I've seen it run—The Balloon Game; I know what it's about, and that's enough to terrify any red-blooded man, let alone me."

"What? Tell me."

"You haven't got time, and it's my only ace. You get me out, and I'll give any help you may need. Deal?"

"I can't promise." Bond was acutely aware that time was slipping by. Cindy would not be able to distract the two guards much longer. He told Peter to put the gun away, going very close to him now. "If they're letting me out, to do a bit of their dirty work, it's pretty certain they'll go through the Bentley with the finest of toothcombs. You've also got to realize that your absence puts a lot of people at risk."

"I know, but . . ."

"Okay, it's done now. Listen, and listen carefully . . ." As quickly as he could, Bond instructed Amadeus on the best way of hiding under the other cars in the garage. Then he pressed the keys into the young man's hand. "You only use these *after* they've played around with the Bentley. It's a risk. Anything could happen, and I haven't any assurance they'll even let me go in my own car. One other thing. If you're found here, you get no help—I deny you completely. Right?"

Amadeus, Bond said, should hide in the boot after the car had been examined. Then there was a final instruction should all else fail, or if he, himself, was prevented from going.

Time had just about run out. He patted the little programer's shoulder, wishing him luck, then climbed back onto the Mercedes, hauled himself up through the skylight, and back to the flat roof.

Lying in the chill night air, pressed hard against the lead, he realized that Cindy had exhausted her repertoire. The guards were very close, just below the garage roof. He could hear them muttering—making comments about what they had seen.

He lay, tense and listening, for around five minutes until they moved away, following their routine pattern of covering the front of the house from all angles.

It took a good ten minutes for Bond to snake his way back to the window. After each move he stopped, lying still, ears cocked against the guards, who passed under the garage twice during his uncomfortable crawl. At last he negotiated the sill, climbing back into Cindy's room.

"You took your time."

She was stretched out on the bed, her dark body glistening, the gorgeous long legs moving as she rubbed thigh against thigh. Cindy was quite naked, and Bond, with the tension released, went to her.

"Thank you. I've done all I can."

He was going to say something about Amadeus, but changed his mind—sufficient to the day. Abruptly Cindy lifted her arms to his shoulders, and Bond, with no power to resist, let himself be dragged down. Only once, as he entered her, did Percy's face and body flash through his head—a picture so vivid that he thought he could smell her particular scent—before these too vanished in the swirling whirlpool.

It was almost dawn when he crept back to his own room, and the house was still silent, as though sleeping in preparation for action. He ate some of the food, threw more down the lavatory, and flushed three times to clear it away. Then at last he lay down on his own bed, still fully dressed, and dropped into a refreshing sleep.

* * *

At the first noise he was awake, the right hand reaching for the ASP.

It was Cindy. She carried a breakfast tray, and was followed by Tigerbalm, who smiled his inane grin, saying that Professor St. John-Finnes wished to see him at noon. "That's sharp midday," he added. "I'll come up and fetch yer."

"Please do." Bond moved on the bed, but Cindy was already halfway out the door.

"Cindy," he called.

She did not even look back. "Have a nice day," flung over her shoulder, not unpleasant, but peremptory.

Bond shrugged, worried a little, and then began to help himself to black coffee and toast. It was ten-thirty by his watch. By eleven-forty-five he was showered, shaved and changed, thinking as he went through his routine that even M could not leave it much longer before moving against Endor.

At three minutes to twelve, Tigerbalm reappeared, and they went downstairs to the rear of the house, where Jay Autem Holy awaited him in a small room he had never seen before.

There was a table, two chairs and a telephone. No pictures, windows or distractions of any kind. The room was lit by two long neon strips, and Bond saw immediately that the chairs and table were bolted to the floor. It was familiar ground: an interrogation room.

"Come in, friend Bond," the head came up in a swooping movement, the green eyes piercing, hostile as laser gun sights. He told Tigerbalm to leave, motioning for Bond to sit down. Then Holy wasted no time.

"The plan you outlined to me—the way of getting your eyes on the current EPOC Frequency . . ."

"Yes."

"It is imperative that we have the Frequency that comes into operation at midnight tonight—covering the next two days."

"I can but . . ."

"You will do more than any buts, James. Our principals—SPECTRE—are still, the way it turns out, most unhappy about using you. They have sent you a message, which I am to deliver, alone."

Bond waited. A pause of around three beats.

"Those who speak for SPECTRE say that you already know they are not squeamish. They also say that it is useless for us to threaten you personally with death, or anything else—if you do not carry out orders to the letter." He gave the ghost of a smile. "I happen to believe that you're with us, all the way. If you're doubling, then I'd have to admit you've fooled me. However, just so that we all know where we stand, I am to tell you the worst that can happen."

Again Bond did not reply, or allow any change in his expression.

"The operation to which we are all now committed has peaceful aims—I must stress this. True, it will alter history; certainly it will bring about some chaos; there will undoubtedly be resistance from reactionaries. But the change will come, and with it Peace. With a capital P."

"So?"

"So, the EPOC Frequency is a prerequisite to this peaceful solution embedded within SPECTRE's operation. If all goes well, and the very simplicity of the idea appeals to me, there will be little or no bloodshed. If anyone is hurt, it will be the fault of those trying to make a stand against the inevitable.

"What I am instructed to tell you is that, should you fail us, or try any tricks to foil what cannot be foiled, the operation will still go ahead, but the accent on peaceful solutions will be changed. Without the EPOC Frequency there is one way only—the way of horror, terror and the ultimate holocaust."

"I . . ." Bond began, stopped short by Holy's glare.

"They wish me to make it clear to you that, should you be tempted to cut and run, not provide the Frequency, or—worse— try to alter it, then the blood, death, ravage of millions will be on your head, and yours alone. They are not joking, James. We have worked for them now. We have come to know them. To tell you the truth, they terrify me."

"Do they terrify Rolling Joe as well?"

"He's a tough old bird." Holy relaxed a little. "A tough, but disillusioned, old bird. But, yes, they also frighten him." He spread his hands on the table, near the telephone, palms down. "Joe Zwingli lost all faith in his country, roughly at the same time that I came to the conclusion that the United States had become a degenerate, self-serving nation, led by corrupt men. I deduced that

America—like Britain—could never be altered from the inside. It had to be done from without. Together we cooked up the idea of disappearing, of working for a truly democratic society, and world peace, from the obscurity of . . . what shall I call it? . . . the obscurity of the grave?"

"How about the obscurity of a whited sepulcher?"

The green eyes hardened, diamonds reflecting light. "Not worthy, James. Not if you're with us."

"I was thinking it was what the world might say." Too late, Bond checked his impulse to be less than friendly with the scientist.

"The world will be a very different place within the next forty-eight hours. Few will be concerned with what I did. Many will look with hope to what I have made possible."

"So I go tonight? If you've decided my ploy's the best?"

"You go tonight, and you set things in motion before you go. The Duty Security Officer's name is Denton—Anthony Denton."

"Good."

"You know him?"

In fact, Bond knew Tony Denton well. They had done some courses together in the past and, a few years ago, had been on a bring-'em-back-alive trip—a defector who had walked into the Embassy in Helsinki. Yes, he knew good old Tony Denton, though it would make no difference at all if his instructions had been taken to heart at the Regent's Park Headquarters.

"He goes on duty at six in the evening, I understand," Holy prompted.

Bond said that certainly used to be the old routine; and Holy suggested he should make the telephone call at about six-thirty. "In the meantime, I suspect you'd better get some rest. If you do the job properly, as you *must,* we can all look to a brighter future—to those broad, sunlit uplands of which a great statesman once spoke."

"I go in my own car." He was not asking but telling Holy.

"If you insist. I shall have to instruct that the telephone be disconnected—but you'll not object to that."

"Just leave me an engine and complete set of wheels."

Holy allowed himself the glint of a smile. Then the face hardened again. "James . . ." Bond knew suddenly that he was going to say something unpleasant.

"James, I'm giving you the benefit of the doubt. I understand the nubile Miss Chalmer was in your room last night, furthermore that you were in hers until the early hours. I must ask you, did Cindy Chalmer give you anything? Or try to pass something to you?"

"I trust not," he began, then realized this was not the time for facetious remarks. "No. Nothing. Should she have?"

Holy stared at the table. "She says not. Idiot girl. Sometime yesterday she removed what she imagined to be a rather important computer program from the laboratory. She's shown signs of willfulness before now, so I personally set a small trap for her. The program she stole was rubbish, quite worthless. She says that you knew nothing of her action, and I'm inclined to believe her. But the fact remains that she hid the disk among your clothes— where, James, it has been found. Cindy made quite a speech about it. She seems to have concluded that we're—as she puts it—up to no good. So she took the disk, as some kind of evidence, and hid the thing in your room until she could think of some way to use it against me." He became hesitant. "We've kept it in the family, James—by which I mean that we've not let it go beyond Dazzle and myself. My partners—Rahani and Zwingli—could become alarmed, might pass it on to the representatives of SPECTRE. I don't think we'd want that, would we? A domestic problem. None of their business."

So, thought Bond, as serious a matter as stealing even a dummy backup program of The Balloon Game—on which, he presumed, the whole operation for SPECTRE was based—could be overlooked and kept "in the family." It was an interesting turn of events. One thing it suggested was that Jay Autem Holy lived in fear of SPECTRE; and that was a piece of deduction that might well be put to valuable use later.

"Cindy?" Bond mused. "What . . . ?"

"Will happen to her? She is regarded as one of my family. She will be disciplined—like a child—and kept very close, under guard, lock and key. Dazzle is seeing to it."

"I haven't seen your wife recently."

"Dazzle? No, she prefers to remain in the background. But she has certain tasks to perform, tasks necessary to success. What I really wish to ask of you, James, is that we keep this business about Miss Chalmer to ourselves. Keep it as a personal matter. I mean, we don't mention it to anybody. Personal, between us, eh?"

"Personal," Bond echoed, keeping his thoughts to himself. What else was there to say?

Tigerbalm came for him shortly after six o'clock. They had not locked him in, though food was served on a tray, brought up by a young Arab.

They went to the same room as before—with its bolted-down table and chairs. The only difference this time was that a tape recorder, with a separate set of earphones, had been hooked up to the telephone.

"It's time, then." Holy was not alone. Tamil Rahani stood beside him, while the large, craggy face of Rolling Joe Zwingli, peered out from behind them.

"I can't promise this part will work," Bond said, his voice flat and calm. So calm that it appeared to activate something within General Zwingli, who pushed his way through his partners, sticking out a leathery hand.

"We haven't met, Commander Bond." The voice had a slightly Texan tang to it. "My name's Joe Zwingli, and I just want to wish you luck. Get in there and *make* it happen for us, Commander. It's in a great cause—to put your country and mine back on their feet."

Bond did not want to disillusion the man. Heaven knew, the day SPECTRE did anything that was not for their own good would be, he reckoned, the first day of never. He played it, however, to the hilt.

"I'll do what I can, sir," he said, then he sat down, waited for Holy to ready the tape monitor, don the headphones and indicate they were set.

He picked up the handset and punched out the digits, which, or so he had led them to believe, would access the special small complex where the SIS Duty Security Officer to the Foreign Office spent his twelve-hour watches, together with specialist teleprinter, cipher, radio and computer operators. In fact, the number he punched was a screened telephone number known only to the field officers of his Service. It was also manned day and night, and hid many identities—depending upon what operations were being run.

That night it was a Chinese laundry based in Soho; a radio cab firm; a French restaurant; and—if the matter arose—the Foreign Office Duty Security Officer's direct line. For that purpose it had been alerted for special action ever since Bond's flash radiophone call from the garaged Bentley, the previous evening. If the call came, it would be passed to one person only.

It rang four times, before anyone picked it up. "Hallo?" The voice was flat.

"Tony Denton, please—the DO, please."

"Who wants him?"

"Predator." He saw Holy give a wry smile, for, when outlining his plan, Bond had refused to give the last cryptonym he had used as a member of the Service. Apparently Jay Autem Holy thought this one very apt.

"Hang on, please." They were switching the call through to the instrument near wherever Bill Tanner was currently situated, and it was his old friend Tanner's voice that next sounded in Bond's ear.

"Denton. I thought you were out, Predator? This is an irregular call, which I really must terminate."

"Tony! Wait!" Bond hunched over the table. "This is priority. Yes, I'm out—as far as anyone can be out—but I have something vital to the Service. But *really* vital."

"Go on." Unconvinced.

"Not on the phone. Not safe. You're the only person I could think of. I must see you. I *have* to see you. Imperative, Tony. Consul." He used the standard cipher word for extreme emergency.

At the far end there was a fractional pause. "When?"

"Tonight. Certainly before midnight. I can get to you, I think. Please, Tony, give me the all-clear."

Again the deep, breathless pause. "If this isn't straight I'll see you in West End Central, and in Court by morning, charged under the Official Secrets Act. As quickly as you can. I'll clear you. Right?"

"Be with you before midnight." Bond sounded relieved, but the line had gone dead long before he took the handset from his ear.

"First hurdle." Holy jabbed down on the recorder's stop button.

"Now, you have to be convincing when you get there."

"So far, it's playing to packed houses." Tamil Rahani sounded pleased. "And the dispatch rider brings the Frequency up from Cheltenham at around eleven-forty-five, yes?"

"If the President of the United States is away from his own country, yes." Bond held the man's eyes, trying to discern his state of mind.

Rahani laughed. "Oh, he's out of the country. No doubt about that, Commander Bond. No doubt at all."

"If you leave here at nine-forty-five you should make it with time to spare," Holy said, removing his headset. "We'll be with you all the way, James. All the way."

17

DOWN ESCALATOR

THE METAL FORESTS of antennae that rise above the massive pile of government buildings, running from Downing Street along Whitehall and Parliament Street, conjure thoughts of communications flitting in through the night, of telephones ringing in darkened houses, wakening ministers, calling them to deal with important crises, of the fabled "telegrams" crossing the airwaves from distant embassies.

In fact, only clear, precise and open messages run into those government offices. Sensitive signals, and urgent information messages, are usually routed from the GCHQ complex outside Cheltenham, or one of its many satellites. From Cheltenham they pass through the mystery building known as Century House, or to the Regent's Park Office. Ciphers, for the Foreign Office only, then go, not to Whitehall and Parliament Street, but to an unimposing, narrow, four-story house off Northumberland Avenue.

They are sent by a variety of methods, ranging from the humble dispatch rider to teleprinter by land-line; or even through a closed telephone circuit, often linked to a computer modem. Certainly there are plenty of dedicated computers in the house near Northumberland Avenue; dedicated, that is, to the art of quick deciphering.

If the romantically minded also imagined that someone with the title of Duty Security Officer, Foreign Office, prowls the great corridors of power with flashlight and uniformed accomplices, they would be wrong. The DSOFO does not prowl. He sits, in the house off Northumberland Avenue, and his security job is to ensure that all ciphers, for Foreign Office only, remain secure and get to the right person. He also deals with a mass of restricted information concerning communications from abroad, both from British sources and those of foreign powers. Leaders of friendly foreign powers, in particular, look for assistance from the Foreign Office. They usually find it with the DSOFO.

It was to the little-noticed turning off Northumberland Avenue that James Bond was now heading in the Mulsanne Turbo.

They had taken him out to the garage shortly after nine-thirty, made sure he had money, credit cards, his ASP and petrol in the tank. Holy, Rahani and Zwingli had, in turn, shaken his hand and promptly at nine-forty-five, the Bentley eased onto the gravel turning circle, flashed lights once and swept on its stately way up the drive, onto the road toward Banbury.

From Banbury, Bond followed the route they had ordered him to take—straight to the M4 motorway, and so into London.

He did not spot any shadows. No doubt they were there, but the possibility caused him little concern. The street in which he would finally stop would have been well cleared of all but authorized vehicles, and, unless SPECTRE had someone with supernatural powers, there was little chance of his being observed once he'd entered the parking area.

Risking the wrath of police patrols, Bond made the journey at speed. From numerous telltale signs and bumps he was certain Peter Amadeus had managed to let himself into the car's boot. He could survive for long enough, but the little programer would, by now, be suffering great discomfort. He stopped once, at the service station near Heathrow Airport, to fill the tank. There he was able to let a little air into the boot and satisfy himself that

Amadeus was, indeed, alive, well, and living in the Mulsanne. Whispering, he explained the impossibility of releasing his traveling companion—reassuring him that it would not be long now.

Less than forty minutes later, Amadeus was freed, speechless and stiff from the cramped, uncomfortable ride, but duly grateful.

"Well, this is where you show your gratitude," Bond said. He took the programer's arm firmly and led him toward the lighted doorway of the terraced house.

Swing doors opened onto a marble-tiled hallway with a lift that took them to the second floor and a minuscule landing watched over by a government guard, who half rose from his desk to ask what they required.

"Predator," Bond snapped at him. "Tell them, Predator and friend."

Less than a minute later, they were led quickly through a passage and into a larger room. The red velvet curtains were drawn, a portrait of the Queen hung over the Adam fireplace—there was another, of Winston Churchill, on one wall—while a long board-room table gleaming like a wooden flight deck occupied a large portion of the available space.

Six faces turned as one. M, with Bill Tanner on his right, and another officer Bond recognized to the left: Major Boothroyd, the Armorer—Head of Q Section—sat to Tanner's right with Lady Freddie Fortune next to him.

Bond did not have time to be surprised at Freddie's presence, for the sixth member of the reception committee left her chair almost at a run.

"James, darling. Oh, it's so good to see you!" And Percy Proud, oblivious to the officialdom around her, held him close, as though she would never let go again.

"Commander Bond! Miss Proud!" M was genuinely embarrassed. "I, er, think we have important work to do."

Bond detached himself from Percy, acknowledged the others, and introduced Peter. "I think Dr. Amadeus will be able to contribute." He glanced often and suspiciously at Freddie Fortune, so often that M finally said, "Lady Freddie's been on the team for some years. Done good work. Sound woman, 007, very deep cover indeed. You are to forget you've ever seen her here."

Bond caught Freddie's steady gaze, returned it with a sardonic smile and cocked eyebrow. Then M drew the conference to order.

"I trust you've gone into Endor, sir . . ." Bond started.

"Yes, 007. Yes, we went in about an hour after you drove out, but the birds had flown. I don't think many could have been left there by the time you departed. They have vanished into thin air. Bag and baggage. We thought you could tell us . . ."

"I'm instructed to return there. By the same route as I came." He recalled the deserted feel of the place that morning, and the fact that he had only seen Cindy and the Arab, then Tigerbalm, Holy, Rahani and Zwingli later on. "The cars were still there, though." It sounded a lame comment, even as he said it. "Three of them. Still in the garage."

"Two when our people arrived," the officer said, the one Bond recognized but could not name.

"How about mine? How about Cindy?" Percy touched his sleeve, and Bond could not meet her eyes.

"I'm not certain. She was a great deal of help, last night. Even tried to steal a copy of their main program—the simulation of whatever they're doing." He turned to M. "It's on SPECTRE's instructions, this business, sir. Did you know?"

"Is it indeed?" M could give the iceberg treatment when he had a mind. "That villainous scum is on the warpath again, eh?"

"You still haven't told me about Cindy?" Percy had her hand tightly on his arm now.

"I just don't know, Percy. I've no idea." He told her about the previous night, leaving out all that happened after he got back to her room but repeating Holy's comments of the morning.

"So we have no ideas about this simulation?" M sucked at his pipe.

"If I could have a word." They all turned toward the forgotten man, Peter Amadeus. "I've seen the simulation running. It was a couple of weeks ago. I couldn't sleep. I went down to the laboratory in the middle of the night, and Jason was in what we call the War Room—Mr. Bond knows: It's at the far end. Jason was engrossed. Just didn't hear me," he passed a hand across his forehead. "That was before all those great oafs—the gun-happy boys—turned up. Before I got the vapors about being there."

M looked uncomfortable, sucking noisily at his pipe.

"Well, thinks I, have a look, Pete. See what the crooks are after next. They refer to it as The Balloon—"

"The Balloon Game, yes," Bond interrupted.

"I've seen it and you haven't. I have the floor, Mr. Bond, please." Peter Amadeus looked around him—a minuscule prima donna. "As I was saying, they all called it The Balloon Game, but it's to do with something they've named Operation Down Escalator."

M's brow creased as he repeated the words under his breath.

"The simulation," Amadeus raised his voice, "appears to be set in a commercial airport. Not large. I didn't recognize it, but that's nothing to go by. The scenario begins in an office complex just to the left of the main terminal building. There's a lot of stuff with cars and positioning men. As far as I could see, the idea was to lift one man."

"Lift?" From M.

"Kidnap, sir," Bond clarified.

Amadeus scowled at them, as though to say he didn't like being interrupted. "They lift this chap, and there's a lot of changing around in cars—you know, he's taken to one point, then switched to another car. Then the location alters. A smaller field—an airfield. Tiny, with a mini control tower and one main building, a hangar, and—guess what? An airship."

"Airship?" From Bond.

"Hence Balloon Game. They get onto this field using the man they've lifted. It does appear to be terribly clever—there are three cars, twelve men, and the hostage, if that's what he is. Result? They take over the whole shooting match. There is a final scenario, and that's to do with flying the airship to a certain point. It got very technical and—"

"Chief of Staff," M almost butted in. "Go and check it out. We know the thing's there, because it's on the itinerary. Saw it myself. They cleared it with the President's people, the Prime Minister, and the Russians. Doing a sort of fly-past tomorrow morning."

Bill Tanner was out of the room before he finished.

Bond looked at his chief, the questions clear on his face. "Sir, I haven't seen, or heard, any news since . . . They even immobilized the car radio . . . Could you?"

"Yes," M leaned back. "At least we've now got a small conception of what it's about. We know where, and how. What? Well, that's a very different matter."

"Sir," Bond prompted.

"It's been kept under wraps for some time—a good few months in fact," M began. "These things always take the devil of a time to organize, and the participants wanted it to remain very low profile. Tonight, members of a summit conference are to arrive in Geneva. In fact the first main session *is* this very night. They've taken over the whole of Le Richemond Hotel for three days . . ."

"Who, sir?"

"Russia, the United States of America, Great Britain, France and West Germany. The President of the United States; the French President; the Chairman of the USSR; the German Chancellor; our Prime Minister—with all advisers, secretaries, military, the entire circus. Aim? To come to a collective agreement regarding arms control, and to seek a more positive and prosperous future. The usual pie-in-the-sky impossibilities."

"The airship?" The more Bond heard, the less he liked it.

"Goodyear. They have their ship, *Europa,* in Switzerland at the moment. When they heard about the summit, Goodyear asked permission to fly what they called "a goodwill mission," taking them straight over Le Richemond. They've got the blimp tethered just up the lake, on a small strip—a tiny satellite field you can only approach from the lake itself. Mountain rescue boys and some private flyers use it."

"But when did Goodyear arrange this?" Bond had not heard a whisper about any summit conference.

M grunted. "You know what it's like, 007. They arrange their flights a year in advance. The *Europa* would have been there in any case. Would've been flying. However, they had to get permission once the conference was announced."

Percy, it seemed, had caught on. "Dr. Amadeus, when did you first hear about The Balloon Game?"

About four months ago, he told her. Four or five.

"And the Summit . . . ?"

"Has been penciled in for a year," M nodded. "Information available through diplomatic channels. The Press have been good boys for a change. Not a whisper, even though they must have known."

Bill Tanner returned with the news that he had been in contact with Geneva. "I talked to the Goodyear security man out at the strip. No problems, and we've alerted the Swiss police. They're going to close the field to everyone but accredited Goodyear staff. That means around thirty—thirty-five—people, handlers, publicity and PR, mechanics, two pilots. Nobody's going to get in unless the Goodyear representatives okay bona fides. Sewn up, sir."

"Right. Well, Bond, all we have to do now is sew up the remainder of this unpleasant lot. Any ideas?"

Bond had one idea, and one only. "You give me the EPOC Frequency, sir—the real one, just in case they already have it. Because I wouldn't put anything past SPECTRE and this crowd who're doing their dirty work for them."

"Oh, yes, the EPOC Frequency. That was mentioned in your message. Made us think. Tell me about that, 007."

He went through the essentials of the story, from start to finish, leaving out nothing. "They claimed to have the Russian equivalent, sir. And the Emergency ciphers for both Russia and the United States of America. I tend to believe them."

M nodded. "Yes, SPECTRE's never been backward in acquiring information. Good job we've got the Goodyear field under wraps, Chief of Staff. Chivvy the Swiss, would you; and keep in contact with the Goodyear people." He began to expand on his own theory.

If they did have the Emergency ciphers of the United States, and Russia, together with the frequencies, there was no theoretical reason why—if SPECTRE's agents could get very near to the leaders of the two superpowers—they should not activate any one of the Emergency ciphers.

"That means," Bond caught up with him, "they could hijack the airship, load enough shortwave hardware, plus a computer on board. Do the Goodyear goodwill flight, taking them right over the very spot where heads of state are gathered together . . ."

"That's it, Bond! Directly overhead would be enough for the United States' communications satellite to justify the cipher, and, I presume, the Russian one also."

It meant there were several possibilities. Full nuclear strikes by one or the other country, or a simultaneous strike by both, knocking out the superpowers in one preposterous cloud of death, with nothing but desolation on the two great continents for years to come. It was unthinkable. M said so, loudly. Bond, in turn, pointed out that Jay Autem Holy had talked only of peace. "There would be danger, but only in the event of my not returning with the EPOC Frequency."

"There's one alternative." M looked around the room, receiving no help from the faces gathered about the table. "Ploughshare," he said, as though this was the answer to everyone's dreams. "Ploughshare, and the Russian equivalent—whatever that is."

Percy asked what Ploughshare was, and M, with a rare smile, explained. A way, he said, of consigning all nuclear weapons— the bulk of them anyway—to the scrap heap. "The last great failsafe. The final hope." Quietly he told them of the one cipher that could be sent over the EPOC Frequency that would set in motion the destruction of all arming codes, and the disarming of all nuclear weapons—"strategic and tactical. It's been reckoned that the process will take around twenty-four hours, in the United States. I should imagine a little longer in the Soviet Union. Just as there's always been a Doomsday Machine, we've had a Swords-to-Ploughshares Machine for the last three decades.

"It's there in the event of some catastrophe—like a sixty-seventy percent paralysis of the armed forces; some disastrous nerve gas; or a genuine stalemate, a Mexican stand-off, where the only way out is for everyone to drop their guns, if you follow me. Of course it's always been hoped that, if the Ploughshare option was taken, it would be by mutual understanding. But it's there. And it's just as potentially dangerous as blowing two great nations to pieces, because what would be the easiest way of destabilizing the two superpowers? Remove their nuclear balance at a stroke. Do that, and the stage is set for real revolution, economic disaster, and survival of the fittest."

Yes, M continued, Bond was right. Let him be supplied with the EPOC Frequency, plus a homing device, one or two of the Armorer's more fancy pieces of equipment, and a good surveillance team in addition. "You can then go back from whence you came, 007. Somewhere along the way, they'll pick you up, and we'll track you—safe enough if the team stays well back."

They took him off into a side room, where Major Boothroyd wired three homing devices into his clothes, and one for luck into the heel of his right shoe. The Armorer then handed over a couple of other small weapons—"Just in case"—and they gave him five minutes with Percy.

She clung to him; kissed him; told him to take care. There would be time enough, once this was over. He said there was no doubt about it, and the haymaking season would last all summer. Percy smiled the knowing smile women the world over smile when they've got what they really want.

Back in the conference room, they gave him the EPOC Frequency that had come into effect at midnight. It was now one in the morning, and Bill Tanner gave the final hasty briefing.

"We've already got your homers on two scanners," he said. "Don't worry, James, they've a range of almost ten miles. The car behind will stay only a mile or so away. The one riding point is already on his way. We know the route, so as soon as you go astray, we'll be in action. One SAS team standing by. They'll be anywhere in a matter of minutes, in a straight line, as the chopper flies. Good luck."

Even the center of London was starting to slow down, and Bond had the Bentley on the Hammersmith Flyover, heading out toward the M4, in less than twelve minutes. He began to burn up the road, thinking—as they all thought—that Holy and Rahani wouldn't try anything until he was well along the motorway.

It happened just after the Heathrow Airport turnoff.

First, a pair of cars, traveling at great speed, forced the Bentley to give up the fast lane. Bond cursed them for a couple of fools and pulled into the middle lane.

Before he realized what was happening the two cars reduced speed, riding beside him, keeping him in the center, while two heavy goods lorries came up in the slow lane.

Bond increased speed, trying to slip away in the center, but both cars and lorries were well souped up, and—too late—he saw the way ahead was blocked by a big, slow-moving, slab-sided refrigerated truck.

He braked to hold back from the truck and, unbelieving at first, saw the rear doors open, and a ramp slide out, its rear end riding on buffered wheels, fishtailing to the road surface, the whole thing being driven with exceptional precision.

The cars to the right, the lorries on the left, crowded him like sheep dogs working together until he had no option left. With a slight jerk, the Bentley's front wheels touched the ramp. With the wheel bucking in his hands, Bond glided into the great white moving garage.

The doors clanged shut behind him. Lights came on, and his side door was opened. Simon stood beside the car, an Uzi tucked under one arm. "Well done, James. We couldn't give you any warning. Now, there's not much time. Out of those clothes—off with everything. We've brought the rest of your gear. Everything off, shoes as well, just in case they smelled a rat and bugged you."

Hands grasped at his clothing, tearing it from him, handing over other things—socks, underwear, gray slacks, white shirt, tie, blazer, and soft leather moccasins.

When he turned around, Simon was behind him, now dressed in a chauffeur's uniform, and the van seemed to have slowed down, taking one of the exits. The ASP was handed back to him—a sign of good faith? He wondered if it was loaded. Certainly the whole team had worked with such speed and proficiency that Bond hardly had time to take in what was going on.

As the truck shuddered to a halt, Simon opened the Bentley's rear door, half pushing Bond into the back, and in a second the truck's doors were again open, and they were reversing out. Simon, the chauffeur, driving; the Arab boy, who had served breakfast that morning—no, yesterday morning—next to him, and—

"Well done, James. You got the Frequency, I presume?" Jay Autem Holy said from beside him.

"Yes," his voice sounded numb.

"I knew it. Good. Give it to me now."

Bond parroted the figures, and the decimal point. "Where're we going?"

Holy repeated the Frequency, asking for confirmation, and by now they were moving smoothly back on to the motorway.

"Where are we going, James? Don't worry, we're going to live through an important moment in history. First, Heathrow Airport. All the formalities have been taken care of. We are just a little late and we're cleared to drive straight up to the private jet. We're going to Switzerland. Be there in a couple of hours. Then another short journey. Then yet another kind of flight. You see—I shall explain it in detail later—yesterday morning, long before you woke for breakfast, while it was still dark, the team from Erewhon carried out a smooth, and very successful, raid. They stole a small landing strip, and an airship. In the morning, James, we're all going for an airship ride. To change history."

A mile or so back down the road, the trail car observer had noted that their target seemed to pull off the motorway for a few minutes. "We're closing on him. Can't make it out. You want me to call in?"

"Give it a minute," the driver shifted in his seat.

"Ah. No," the observer stared at the moving blip that was James Bond's homer. "No, it's okay. Looks as though they were right. He's on his way to Oxford. Lay you odds on them picking him up between Oxford and Banbury."

But the Bentley had, in fact, just passed them, going in the opposite direction, hurling itself back toward Heathrow and a waiting executive jet.

18

THE MAGIC CARPET

THE EXECUTIVE JET had Goodyear symbols all over it: a smart livery, with the words *Good Year* flanking the winged sandal. It also had a British registration.

The realization that he was outnumbered and outgunned held Bond back from making a run for it. Whoever had really laid out the ground plan of the operation—Holy, Rahani, or the inner council of SPECTRE itself—had done so with exceptional attention to detail.

For all he knew, the whole gang on board could prove genuine affiliation to Goodyear. In any case he did not even know if the ASP was loaded, and—so far—there was at least a small residue of trust between him and the main protagonists. Exploit the trust to the full, he told himself, so he just went along for the ride.

After takeoff, an attractive girl served coffee. Bond then excused himself and went to the pocketsized lavatory at the rear of the aircraft.

Simon sat near the door and eyed him with amused wariness. But there was no attempt at restraint.

Instead Bond took out the ASP and slipped the magazine from the butt. It was, as he had thought, empty. Whatever else happened, ammunition, or another weapon, was a top priority.

Back in his seat, Bond tried to work out a logical sequence of events. M and his staff, in London, were obviously unaware of the situation near Geneva. The takeover of the Goodyear base, together with the airship *Europa,* had already happened hours before Bill Tanner had checked. True, the Swiss police were now alerted, but they would only make SPECTRE's task more secure by keeping out unwanted meddlers.

The Goodyear man to whom Tanner had spoken would have been one of Holy's or Rahani's men. The only possibility of action being taken by his Service would come from the surveillance cars losing him, but heaven knew how long it would take for them to discover he was gone.

Not for the first time in his career, Bond was truly alone. On the face of it, there was very little he could do to stop the airship's scheduled flight over Geneva and the use of the Russian and United States EPOC ciphers. Even the high security classification of these ciphers would work against them. If M was correct, and the plan turned out to be the operation of the American Ploughshare cipher together with its Russian equivalent, there would be no worldwide alerts. And if the Russian and American leaders remained incommunicado, locked within their summit talks, the damage would already have been done by the time they learned of it.

Sitting next to Jay Autem Holy, Bond reflected on the ingenuity of the plan. The two superpowers almost denuded of their one great strength—their one true weapon in the power balance. It was, of course, what many people had dreamed of, protested for and argued over for years. M had stressed this at the meeting in the house off Northumberland Avenue. He had also underlined that an agreed reduction of stockpiled nuclear arms and a steady phasing out of these instruments of potential doom was one thing, but for the two superpowers to be suddenly stripped, overnight, would cause a collapse of the system that had allowed a certain calm and sanity, however precarious, to prevail over the globe since World War II.

M had gone on to say that any historian, or economist, could map out the events that would follow the undercutting of stability. First would come a financial panic and market crash of enormous proportions, for who would have confidence in the great nations once their most terrible power was gone? The United States and Russia would be at the mercy of any other nation—however small—that possessed its own nuclear capability: China, France, possibly Iraq, Iran, Libya, Argentina, Israel. As his mind reviewed the pictures that M had drawn, vividly describing what would happen in this new world, Bond became more determined. He had to stop Down Escalator from proceeding, no matter what the cost to himself; for if it succeeded, history would indeed be changed.

"Anarchy will rule," M had declaimed in a rare burst of almost Churchillian oratory. "The world, as we know it, will divide into uncertain alliances and the man in the street—no matter what his birthright, nationality or politics—will be forced to accept a way of life that will drop him, like a handful of sand, into a dark and bitter well of misery. Freedom, even the compromise freedom we now enjoy, will be erased from the dictionary of life."

"Seatbelt, James." Bond opened his eyes. He hadn't been asleep, only lost in thought, but Jay Autem Holy was shaking his shoulder. "We're coming in to land."

Bond glanced at his watch. It was not yet six in the morning, and out of the cabin window, as the aircraft banked on its final approach, the sky was beginning to brighten in a dark gray colorwash sprinkled with lights.

"Where are we landing?" In Geneva, he guessed? He knew the airport well. Maybe—just maybe—he could get away there and raise the alarm.

"Bern, Switzerland. You remember, don't you? We're flying into Switzerland?"

Bern. That meant an overland trip of some duration. It also meant he would have to bide his time.

"Nice place, Bern," he casually observed, and Holy nodded.

"We go on by car. An hour—hour and a half. There'll be plenty of time. What has to be done doesn't start until eleven."

They came in, engines throttled back, then a final short burst of power to lift them over the threshold, and hardly a bump as the wheels touched. They parked well away from the main terminal, and two Audi Quatros and a police car pulled up alongside.

From his window, Bond watched the transaction take place: the small pile of passports handed over, inspected and returned, with a brisk salute—a combination of Swiss efficiency and SPECTRE's cunning. There would be no customs inspection, he guessed. The Goodyear jet must have been running in and out of Switzerland for a month or more now. They would have the formalities cut down to the fine art of mutual trust.

By the time they left the aircraft, in single file, Bond hemmed in neatly by the Arab boy and Simon, the police car was already slowly disappearing toward the terminal building in the half light of dawn.

The Audis had Goodyear VIP stickers on the windshields and rear windows. Bond recognized both drivers, in their gray uniforms, as men he had spotted in Erewhon.

Within minutes, he was sitting next to Holy in the rear of the second car, and they swept away from the airport. Behind them, another plane started its engines. Most of the houses on Bern's outskirts still slept, while others appeared to be just waking—lights coming on, green shutters open. Always, in Switzerland, Bond thought, you knew you were in a small, rich country, for—however big—the houses, offices, churches and railways looked as though they had been assembled in some sterile room, from a plastic kit complete with small details of greenery and flowers.

They took the most direct route—straight to Lausanne, then along the lake road, following the line of the toylike railway.

Holy was quiet for most of the journey, but Simon, sitting in the front passenger seat, occasionally turned back to ask fatuous, insignificant questions—"You know this part of the world, James?" "Fairytale country, isn't it?"

Bond remembered, for no apparent reason, that he'd been sixteen the first time he had visited Lake Geneva. He had spent a week with friends in Montreux, had a small affair with a waitress from a lakeside café, and developed a taste for Campari–soda.

Between Lausanne and Morges they stopped at a lighted lakeside restaurant where Simon and the Arab boy went, in turns, to bring coffee and rolls out to the cars. The sheer normality of their actions grated on Bond's nerves, like a probe on a raw tooth. Half of his mind and body urged him to take drastic action, now; the other, more professional, half told him to wait, and to seize the moment only when it came.

"Where're we actually heading?" he asked Holy, soon after the breakfast break.

"A few kilometers this side of Geneva." The Holy Terror remained relaxed, in perfect control of himself. "We turn off the lake road. There's a small valley and an airstrip. The team from Erewhon will be waiting for us. You ever flown in an airship, James?"

"No."

"Then it will be a new experience for us both. I'm told it's totally fantastic." He peered from the windows. "And it looks as though we'll have a clear day for it. The view should be wonderful."

They went through Nyon, where the houses clustered together as though to keep themselves from falling into the lake. Then, soon after, Geneva came into view at the western end, a misty blur of buildings, while a toy steamer, ploughing a lone furrow of spray, chugged across the water.

They also met their first police checkpoint. The cars slowed almost to a standstill before the sharp-eyed uniformed men waved them on.

There was a second police roadblock just before they turned inland. A car, two motorcycle cops. These too started to flag them down, until they spotted the Goodyear stickers. Then they waved them through, and as Bond looked back, he saw one of the men talking into a radio. The police, he realized, were assisting, however innocently, in the events planned to take place over the lake in a few hours.

The great cleft in the mountains seemed to widen as the road climbed. The sun was up now, and up the slopes one could see tiny farmhouses, plateaus with animals grazing. Then, suddenly, the valley floor and the tiny landing strip appeared a little below them—the grass a painted green, the control tower, hangar and one building as neat, and unreal, as a movie set.

Out on the grass, two mountain rescue aircraft were parked like stranded birds, and at the far end of the field the sausage shape of the Goodyear airship *Europa* swung lazily, tethered to her low portable masthead.

Then the road dipped, the airfield disappeared, and they were twisting through the S-bends that would carry them to the final destination.

Before the two cars reached the airstrip, two more police checkpoints were negotiated. The Swiss police had certainly snapped into action. London, Bond decided, would feel very satisfied.

There were no less than three more police cars at the airstrip entrance, which was little more than a metal gateway set into an eight-foot chain-link fence, circling the entire strip. In the distance, a police car patrolled the perimeter, as slowly and thoroughly as only the Swiss perform their official duties.

The Audis drew up to the gate, and Bond saw two faces—again recognized from Erewhon. This time, though, the men were dressed in smart suits and smiled broadly as the two-vehicle convoy came to a halt. They exchanged a few words with the senior policeman on the gate, then climbed into the Audis, one to each car.

The man who entered Bond's car was a German, fair-haired, suspicious-looking, and with features cut from a solid block of rough stone. He appeared to be in his mid-twenties, and the smart suit bulged around the breast pocket. Bond did not like the look of him. He liked him even less when the talking started.

The two cars headed not for the little office building but for the hangar, where the two slab-winged Pilatus aircraft sat. Meanwhile, Holy confined himself to only the most pertinent questions, and was given precise, military answers, in an American-tinged accent.

Rudi—that was the German's name—had all the answers and then some. Posing as the Goodyear head of PR he had taken the call from Bill Tanner, which he now described in detail, saying the man was certainly English, and also undoubtedly represented one of the major British security agencies. The police—he said—began to arrive within half an hour of his call.

Jay Autem then asked about the timing. It didn't take him long to deduce that the first call had come even while Bond was in the Foreign Office house off Northumberland Avenue.

"James," he said, turning to Bond, the great bird eyes narrowing. "How much did you tell your friend . . . uh, what was his name?"

"What friend?" Bond answered.

"Denton. Last night. Anthony Denton."

"Me?" Bond looked surprised and startled, as though he hadn't been paying attention to the conversation. "What *could* I have told him?"

Holy stared at him. "Don't be naive, James. Tamil's people took over this airstrip yesterday morning. Nobody suspected, there was no trouble. Not until last night, that is, when you were getting the EPOC Frequency for us. Why, I ask myself, should the Swiss police begin to take an interest in us at that time of night?"

Bond shrugged, indifferent. He had no idea, he said. In any case, whatever had happened had nothing to do with him.

The cars came to a halt. Holy shifted again in his seat.

"I do hope you've given us the correct frequency, James. If you haven't . . . Well, I've already warned you of the consequences. Consequences for the entire world, my friend . . ."

"You've got it," Bond snapped back. "That's the current EPOC Frequency. Have no doubt about that, Dr. Holy."

Holy winced at the sound of his true name. Then he leaned forward to open the door.

Bond saw a moment of opportunity. As the others got out, he was left briefly with the Arab boy, who watched him with alert bright eyes, a small Walther automatic clutched in his right hand. The safety, Bond noticed, was off, but he could, he calculated, take the Arab out.

As abruptly, the moment faded. Even as Simon, Holy and the German, Rudi, were joined by Rahani and Joe Zwingli in a little procession walking to the hangar, Bond now saw Rahani's men everywhere he looked. Spread out, half concealed by what cover they could find in the shadows of the hangar and the aircraft, with a full armament of automatic weapons.

A small door, inserted in the great sliding panels of the hangar, was opened, and the party stepped inside. About two minutes later, Simon came out, striding quickly to the car.

"Colonel Rahani wants you inside," he said. His manner had become one of indifference—that of a man who wants no involvement with anyone outside his own tight comradeship. Bond recognized the psychology. They had come, it seemed, to some cutoff point.

It could be, Bond thought, as they walked the few paces toward the hangar, that the end was now. They'd decided he'd talked, and they had no further use for him. Curtain time.

The little group stood just inside the small door, and it was Tamil Rahani who greeted him.

"Ah, Commander Bond. We thought you should see this." His hand came up to gesture toward the center of the hangar. "A part of your education in our methods."

About forty men sat, close together on the floor, held into a tight knot by three machine guns, tripod-mounted, each with a crew of four.

"These are the good men from Goodyear," he split the Goodyear, as though making a joke. "They will remain here until our mission is completed. You should know about this. They will be quickly dispatched—all of them—if one person makes an attempt to break out. Or if anything else goes wrong.

"It is uncomfortable for them, I know," Rahani continued. "But if all goes well, they will be released unharmed. You will notice, of course, there is one lady. I believe you know her, Commander."

From the middle of the group, Cindy Chalmer gave Bond a wan smile, and Tamil Rahani lowered his voice: "Between ourselves, Commander Bond, I think the delightful Miss Chalmer has little chance of surviving. But we want no bloodshed as yet. Not even your blood. You see, it was the original intention that you should be put with this group of prisoners, once you'd fulfilled your mission. The representative from SPECTRE—who did not trust you from the start—is not at all happy with you now. However," his lips widened, not into a smile, but rather a straight thin slash across his face. "However, I think you can be of use in the airship. You can fly, yes? You have a pilot's license?"

Bond nodded, adding that he had no experience of airships.

"You'll only be the copilot. The one who sees to it that the pilot does as he's told. There'll be a certain poetic irony in it, if by any chance you *have* doubled on us, Commander Bond. Come!"

Back to the cars, and a swift drive over the few hundred yards to the office building.

Inside, around forty of Rahani's trained men from Erewhon were sitting around, smoking and drinking coffee. "Our handling team, Commander Bond. They have learned by simulation. At Erewhon. It was something we did not show you, but they are very necessary when we weigh out the airship before takeoff; and, to a greater extent, when we get back from our short excursion."

Only one man looked out of place, and he sat at a table just inside the door. He wore a navy-blue pilot's uniform, and his peaked cap lay on the table in front of him. One of Rahani's hoods sat opposite, well clear of the table, with an Uzi machine pistol ready to blow the man's stomach out should he make a fuss.

"You are our pilot, I presume?" Rahani smiled politely at the man, who looked at him coldly and said yes, he was a pilot, but that he wouldn't fly under duress.

"I think you will." Confident, and quite unmoved. "What do we call you?"

"You call me Captain," the pilot replied.

"No. We're all friends here. Informal." Then, with a commanding snap: "Your first name."

The pilot did not seem one to be intimidated, but he hesitated, then cocked his head on one side. "Okay, you can call me Nick."

"Right, Nick," Tamil Rahani carefully explained what was going to happen. Nick was to fly the airship, just as he would have under normal circumstances. Up to Geneva, along the lakefront. After that he would change course, cutting straight over Le Richemond Hotel. "You will stay over the hotel for approximately four minutes," Rahani expressed himself as an officer used to being obeyed. "Four minutes at the outside. No more. Nothing will happen. Nobody'll be hurt, as long as you do what you're told. After that, you bring the ship back here and land. You will leave unharmed."

"Damned if I'll do it."

"I think you will, Nick. For one thing, we have forty of your fellow employees in the hangar. Should anything go wrong, they will die, instantly. For another, if you don't fly it, someone else will. This gentleman here, for instance," he touched Bond's shoulder. "He's a pilot—without airship experience, true—and will do it if we give him enough encouragement. Our encouragement to you is that we kill you, now, if you don't agree."

"He means it, Nick," Bond interrupted.

"Thank you, Commander," said Rahani.

The pilot thought for a moment, then seemed to lose his resolve under Rahani's implacable stare.

"Okay. Okay, I'll fly the blimp."

"Good. Now I'll tell you what we have in store for Commander Bond. Like God, he is your copilot. You will tell him, now, about the differences in flying an aircraft and handling an airship. In turn we are going to give him one round of ammunition for his automatic pistol. One round only. He can only kill, or wound, one person with that, and there'll be five of us on board. Five, not counting Commander Bond and yourself. Bond, here, will do exactly as I tell him. If you try to be clever, I will tell him to kill you—which will leave him with no ammunition. If he does not kill you, Simon—or one of us—will do it for him, and force him to take over. If he still resists, then we'll kill him also, and another of us will fly the ship. Do you understand me?"

"Yes, I understand you."

"Well, Commander Bond will look after you, and we'll all have a pleasant trip—how long? Half an hour?"

"About that. Maybe three-quarters."

"Commander Bond, talk to your pilot. Learn from him. We have things to get on board the gondola."

Bond lowered his head, letting his lips come near to the pilot's ear as he sat down. "I'm working under duress too. Just do what I tell you. We have to stop them." Then, in a normal voice: "Okay, Nick, you'd better tell me about this ship."

The pilot looked up, puzzled for a moment, but Bond nodded encouragement, and he began to talk.

Around them, Rahani's men were carrying equipment out of the office. Among the hardware, Bond saw one shortwave transmitter—a powerful one, from the look of it—and a micro as well.

Bond listened attentively to the pilot's instructions. Flying the airship, he said, was more or less the same as handling an aircraft. "Yoke, rudder pedals, same flight instruments, throttles for the two little engines. Only difference is in trimming the blimp." He explained how the two ballonets—fore and aft within the helium-filled envelope—could be inflated with air, or have the air valved off. "It's more or less the same principle as a balloon, except, with the air-filled ballonets, you don't have to bleed off expensive gas. You just take on or dump air. The ballonets take care of the gas pressure, give you extra lift, or allow you to trim down, or up. The only tricky part is knowing when to dump the pressure as you come in to land, to give the ground crew a shot at the guy ropes. The rest is a piece of cake."

It was all technically straightforward. Nick had hardly finished when Simon came over, glancing at his watch. The office was almost deserted.

"You're both needed at the ship." Simon held up one round of 9mm ammunition, and Bond saw that it was one of his original Glaser slugs. "You get this when we're aboard," he said, his eyes showing no compassion. "Now let's get moving."

At the airship, Rahani's men had readied themselves to take up the strain on the forward guy ropes. The others were already aboard the curved gondola which hung from the great gleaming sausage of the ship.

Nick climbed up first, through the large door that took up a third of the gondola's right-hand side. Bond followed, Simon taking up the rear and pulling the door closed behind him.

Tamil Rahani sat next to Holy at the back of the gondola. In front of them, they had arranged the transmitter, linked to the computer. The Arab boy sat directly in front of Holy, General Zwingli across the narrow aisle from him. Bond went to the front, taking his place on Nick's right. Simon now hovered between them.

As soon as he was in his seat, Nick became the complete professional, showing Bond the instrumentation, and pointing out the valves for the ballonets.

"Whenever you're ready," Rahani called out. Nick proceeded through his preflight checks, then slid his window open to shout down to the man in command of the ground crew. "Okay," he called. "Tell your crew to stand by. I'm starting up, and I'll give you a thumbs-up when they have to take strain." To Bond, he said he would be starting the port engine first. Immediately afterward, the starboard would fire. "We fill the ballonets and while they're filling, I'll release us from the mooring mast. The boys outside, if they've been trained correctly, will take the strain, dump the hard bags of ballast hanging from the gondola." He turned, grinning. "After that, I trim the ship, lift the nose and we'll see if they have the sense to let go of the ropes."

Reaching forward, Nick started both engines, one after another, very fast, and set the air valves to fill.

As Bond was watching, Simon leaned forward, felt inside his jacket and removed the ASP. There was a double click, as the one round went into the breech, then the weapon was handed back. "You kill him, if the colonel gives the order. Otherwise I shoot you first, straight through the head."

Bond did not even acknowledge. By now he was following everything that Nick was doing, opening the throttles, pulling the lever that moored them to the mast, monitoring the pressure.

The airship's nose tilted upward, and Nick waved to the ground crew as he gave the engines full throttle. The nose slid higher and there was a slight sense of buoyancy, then, very slowly, they moved forward and upward: rock-steady, no tremor or vibration as they climbed away from the field. It was like riding on a magic carpet.

19

PLOUGHSHARE

IN HIS TIME James Bond had either flown, or flown in, most types of aircraft—from the old Tiger Moth biplane to Phantom jets—yet never had he experienced anything like the *Europa*.

The morning was clear and sunny, and could have been specially cleaned and prepared, as one so often suspects the Swiss of doing.

With its two little engines humming like a swarm of hornets—the single-blade, wooden pusher airscrews blurring into twin disks—the fat silver ship emerged from the wide cleft in the mountains, over the road and railway lines, and climbed above the lake. At a thousand feet, gazing out at the spectacular view, Bond even forgot—for a few seconds—his most dangerous mission.

It was the stability of the ship that amazed him most—that, and the lack of any buffeting of the kind one would get at a thousand feet in a conventional aircraft, over this type of terrain. No wonder those who traveled on the great airships of the twenties and thirties had fallen in love with them.

The blimp dipped its nose, almost stood on it. It turned a full circle—fifteen hundred feet now—so they caught a glimpse of the entire lake: the mountain peaks rising, touched with snow against the light blue sky; Montreux in the distance, with the Château Chillon a miniature poking into the water; the French side of the lake and the town of Thonon, peaceful and inviting.

Then Nick eased the ship around, so the view was of Geneva, and they approached at a stately fifty miles an hour.

Bond slewed his mind back to the present. He turned to look at the rear of the gondola. Rahani and Jay Autem Holy, oblivious to the view, were hunched over the transmitter. They had removed some of the seat backs, leaving Bond a good view of the radio, and he saw that it was linked up to the micro with its built-in drive.

Holy appeared to be muttering to himself as he tuned to the frequency. Rahani watched him closely—like a warder, Bond thought, while Zwingli half-turned in his seat to give advice. Both Simon and the Arab boy stood guard. The boy never took his eyes off the pilot and Bond, while Simon leaned against the door, almost as though he was covering his masters as well.

Below them, the lakeside of Geneva slid into view. The airship slowed, stood on its nose and turned gently.

"No playing around, Nick," Rahani called, warning. "Just do what you normally do. Then take her straight over Le Richemond."

"I'm doing what I normally do," the pilot said laconically. "I'm doing it by the book."

"And what," Bond called back, "are we really doing anyway? What is this caper that's supposed to change history?"

Holy lifted his eyes toward the flight deck.

"We are about to put the stability of the world's two most powerful nations to the test. Would you believe that the ciphers that can be sent through the emergency networks of both the American President and the Russian Chairman include programs to deactivate their main nuclear capabilities?"

"I'd believe anything." Bond didn't need to hear any more. M was right. The intention was to send the United States Ploughshare program, and its Russian counterpart, into their respective satellites, and from there into irreversible action.

"Well, that's precisely what we're going to do, James," Holy went on, the messianic tone entering his voice. "An end to the nuclear menace. Peace in our time. Peace on our planet."

Peace at the point of a gun, Bond thought but did not say. He glanced again at the armed Arab. It was at this moment that he decided upon his best, indeed his only, option.

His whole adult life had been dedicated to his country; now he knew his own life would be forfeit. There was one Glaser slug in the ASP. With luck, in the confined gondola it would blow any one of the men in half—but only one: So what was the use of a human target? Kill one, then be killed. But if he chose the right time, and the Arab boy could be distracted, the one Glaser slug, placed accurately, would decimate the radio, and possibly the micro as well.

He would die, very quickly, after taking out the hardware, but, for Bond, this was nothing compared to the satisfaction of smashing SPECTRE's plans one last time. Maybe they would try again, but there were always others behind him, others like himself, and the Service had been alerted.

The clean, ordered, picturesque Micropolis of Europe now lay to their right, as Nick gently turned the ship. Mont Blanc towered away above them. They began to descend to a thousand feet for his pass along the lakeside.

"How long?" It was the first time General Zwingli had spoken.

Nick glanced back. "To Le Richemond? Four minutes or so."

"You locked into that Frequency?" The old general now addressed Holy.

"We're on the Frequency, Joe. I've put the disk in. All we have to do is press the Enter key, and we'll know if Bond has been true to his word."

"You're activating the States first, then?"

"Yes, Joe." Rahani replied this time. "Yes, the United States of America get their instructions in a couple of minutes." He craned forward to look from the window. "Yes, there it is, coming up now."

Bond slid the safety off the ASP.

"Ready, Jay. Any minute." Rahani did not shout, yet the words carried clearly over the length of the gondola.

The luxurious hotel—a jewel among Geneva's resting places—was coming up below them. Nick held the blimp on a true course that would take them straight over the palatial building and its perfect gardens.

"I said ready, Jay."

"Any second. Okay," Holy answered.

At that precise moment, Bond, gripping the ASP, turned toward the Arab boy, shouting, "Your window! Look to your window!"

The Arab turned his head slightly, and Bond's hand came up, his brain telling him he had one chance, and one chance only.

He squeezed the trigger, and over the whirling engine noise, the solid clunk of the pistol's firing mechanism echoed through his ears.

For a second he could not believe it. A misfire? A dud round? Then came the laugh from Simon, echoed with a grunt from the Arab boy.

"Don't think of throwing it, James. I'll cut you down with one hand. You didn't honestly think we'd let you on board with a loaded gun, did you?"

"Damn you, Bond." Rahani was half out of his seat. "No gunplay—not in here. Have you given us the Frequency, or is that as false as your own treachery?"

The bleep and whir, from the back of the gondola, indicated that Holy had activated the cipher program. Now, he gave a whoop of joy: "It's okay, Tamil! Whatever else Bond's tried, he *has* given us the Frequency. It's been justified. The satellite's accepted it!"

Bond dropped the pistol, now a useless piece of metal. He had blown it. They had done it. At this moment, the massive machines in the Pentagon—or wherever they were located—would be sorting the numbers at that unbelievable rate of speed with which computers perform huge mathematical tasks. The instructions would be pouring out to similar machines, the length and breadth of the country—even to Europe and the NATO forces.

Now it was done. He felt only a terrible anger, and a sickness deep in his stomach.

What happened in the next few seconds took time to sink in. Holy was still whooping as he half rose, stretching out a hand, fingers snapping, toward Rahani. "Tamil, come on, the Russian program. You have it. I've locked onto their Frequency . . ." His voice rose with urgency. "Tamil!" Now shouting, "Tamil! The Russian program. Quickly."

Rahani gave a great bellowing laugh. "Come on, yourself, Jay. You didn't think we were really going to allow Russia to suffer the indignity of being stripped of her assets as well?"

Jay Autem Holy's mouth opened and closed, fishlike. "Wha . . . ? Wha . . . ? What d'you mean, Tamil? What . . . ?"

"Watch them!" Rahani snapped, and both Simon and the Arab boy appeared to stiffen to his command. "You can begin the return journey, Nick." Rahani spoke so quietly that Bond was amazed he could be heard above the steady motor buzz. "Look at the reality, Jay. Face the reality. Long ago, I took over as the chief executive of SPECTRE. Now we have done what we set out to do. I even gambled on your pawn, Bond, actually getting the EPOC Frequency to lead us on. Down Escalator was always simply intended to deal with the imperialistic power of the United States, which we should now be able to hand on a plate to our friends in the Soviet Union. You were only brought in to provide the training programs. We have no use for emotionally motivated fools like Zwingli and yourself. Do you understand me now?"

Jay Autem Holy let out a long and desperate keen, echoed only by General Zwingli's roar of anger.

"You bastard!" Zwingli started to move. "I wanted my country strong again, by putting both Russia and the United States on the same footing. You've sold out—You . . . !" Whereupon he launched himself at Rahani.

The Arab boy shot him. Once. Fast and accurate. One bullet split the old general's skull. He toppled over without a sound, and as the blast of the boy's weapon echoed in the confined space, a long bell-like boom, Jay Autem Holy leaped toward Rahani, arms outstretched to claw at his throat, the scream of his voice turning to a banshee wail of hate.

Rahani, with no room to back off, shot him in midspring, two rounds from a small hand gun Bond had not even noticed. But Holy's powerful leap, goaded by fury, carried his body on, so that he crashed, lifeless, on top of SPECTRE's leader, the man who had inherited the throne of the Blofeld family.

"Get us down!" Bond shouted at the pilot, Nick. "Just get us down!" In the confusion, he propelled himself toward the nearest target—Simon, who, his back to the flight deck, had taken a pace toward the tangle of bodies piled on the seats. Bond landed hard on Simon's back, one arm locking around his neck, the other delivering a mighty chopping blow that connected a fraction below the right ear.

Three things happened simultaneously. Off balance, Simon's weight shifted to the left just before Bond's blow landed. His hand, scrabbling for some kind of hold, hit the gondola door's locking device and the door swung open, bringing an urgent draft of air into the gondola. Second, as Simon went limp from the blow, the Arab boy fired at Bond, a fraction of a second late, for the bullet hit Simon's chest, making it a moot point as to how he died—whether from Bond's death chop or the Arab's bullet.

Whichever way he died, Simon's long military training produced a final reflex action. At the moment of his death, a great power seemed to force itself through his muscles. He broke free from Bond's grasp, turned and with a deathly grip on the Uzi machine pistol, fired half a burst of fire, rap, rap, rap, that cut the Arab almost in two.

Simon did not let go of the gun, not even then. He collapsed backward. No sound came from his throat. Simon simply fell through the gondola door, through a thousand feet of air until he reached his grave in the lake water below.

Bond made to grab at the Arab's Walther, now lying on the floor. He felt the sting of a bullet cutting a shallow furrow along the flesh above his right hip, and another sing past his ear.

His hand reached the Walther, feet slipping on the floor. But, as he turned, instinctively, toward where Tamil Rahani should be, finger taking up the pressure on the trigger, he realized the instigator of their whole drama was already gone.

"Parachute," Nick said calmly. "Little bastard had a parachute. Taken the dive."

Bond took a pace toward the gondola door, hanging on to the grab rail, and leaned out.

There, below, against the blue-gray water of the lake, was the white shape of Rahani's parachute, a light breeze carrying him away from Geneva toward the French side of the lake.

"Bound to pick him up," Bond said aloud.

"Could you close the door, please?" Nick's voice, calm as only an experienced pilot can sound under stress. "I've got to find somewhere to drop this blimp in." He switched on the flight radio, flicking the dial with finger and thumb, adjusting the headset he had not worn throughout the flight of disaster.

A few seconds later, he turned his head slightly as Bond slumped into the seat beside him. "We can go back to the strip. Apparently the Swiss military cleared it soon after we left. Looks as if we've had guardian angels watching over us."

They sat together around the balcony of M's room in the lakeside hotel. Bill Tanner, M himself, Cindy Chalmer, Percy and Bond, whose side still stung from the long bullet burn.

"You mean," Bond said, with cold anger, "that you already knew they had taken over the airstrip? You *knew* when you sent me off from London."

M nodded. He had recounted how—because of the tight security surrounding the summit conference—many interested parties had been given cipher words by which they could prove their authenticity by radio or telephone. On the night Bond had visited the Communications house off Northumberland Avenue, Bill Tanner's call to the Goodyear people had not elicited the correct sequence of identification.

"Therefore we knew something had gone wrong." M did not appear to be in the least bit concerned. "We alerted everyone with need to know; arranged with both the United States and the Soviet Union that any messages on their current emergency satellite frequencies should be accepted, but then stopped."

"I was to be thrown to the wolves, then," Bond retorted. "It wasn't necessary to the operation that I should be left in outer darkness, as you once so neatly put it. But you let me go, knowing full well . . .''

"Come, come," M put in tartly. Suddenly he leaned forward and placed a hand gently on Bond's arm. "It was for your own good as much as ours, James. After all, you might have found a way of bringing in Holy—or Rahani, come to that. But that wasn't uppermost in our minds. We had to find a way of restoring your good name. Look on it as a sort of rehabilitation."

"Rehabilitation?"

"You see," M went on quietly, "there had to be some role you could play for the sake of your public image. The Press aren't going to fail to notice hijinks on an airship overhead while the summit talks were going on. Geneva's been stiff with journalists these past few days. We told the Swiss authorities they could let a certain amount of reporting go through. Saves us a tricky hushing-up job in a way. I think you'll be pleased with what the papers say tomorrow."

Bond was silent. He gazed at M, who gave his arm a couple of reassuring pats.

"I suppose you'll want to take some sick leave because of that scratch," M said distantly.

Bond and Percy exchanged looks. "If it wouldn't inconvenience the Service, sir."

"A month, then? Let all this fuss die down. We can't have the whole department going public for the sake of your honor, 007."

Cindy spoke for the first time. "What about Dazzle? Mrs. St. John-Finnes?"

Tanner told them there had been no trace of the lady who called herself Dazzle, just as Rahani had disappeared into thin air. "A launch picked up his chute. He had drifted well inshore, on the French side."

"Damn. I wanted a little time alone with that bastard." The delightful Cindy Chalmer could be lethal when roused.

Percy gave her a wicked smile. "You, Cindy, are going straight back to Langley. The order came through this morning."

Cindy pouted, and Bond tried hard not to catch her eye. "And what about Dr. Amadeus?" he asked.

"Oh, we're taking care of him," Bill Tanner answered. "We've always room for good computer men in the Service. Anyway, Dr. Amadeus turned out to be a brave young man."

"There is something else," M grunted. "The Chief of Staff did not know this, but in checking back through the files when you alerted us to Rahani, 007, we found some interesting information. You recall we've been keeping surveillance on him for some time?"

Bond nodded as M slid a matte black-and-white print from the folder on his lap.

"Interesting?"

The photograph showed Tamil Rahani locked in an embrace with Dazzle St. John-Finnes. "Looks as though they had plans for the future."

Bond asked about Erewhon and was told that the Israelis had pinpointed the site.

"Nobody there. Deserted. But they're keeping an eye on it. I doubt if Rahani will visit it again. But he'll probably show up somewhere."

"Yes." Bond's voice was flat. "Yes, I don't think we've heard the last of him, sir. After all, he boasted that he was Blofeld's successor."

"Come to think of it," M mused. "I wonder if you should forgo that leave, 007. It may be vital to follow up . . ."

"He's got to rest, sir." Percy was almost ordering M. "For a short time at least." The Head of Service looked at the willowy ash-blonde, astonishment on his face.

"Yes. Yes. Well, if you put it like that . . . I suppose . . . yes."

20

END OF THE AFFAIR

THEY FIRST FLEW to Rome, for a week at the Villa Medici. Percy had never been to Rome, and James showed her almost everything one can see in seven short days.

From Rome they moved to Athens, and from Athens the couple traveled light on an island-hopping tour. First, the Aegean, then, doubling back, to the Ionian Sea, where they managed to find some secluded beaches, and tavernas, off the package deal routes.

It was a time of distant voices from the past. They told each other long tales of their youth, made their separate confessions, and became totally immersed in each other's bodies. For Percy and Bond, the world became young again, and time stood still, as only time can within the dark, secret mysteries of the Greek islands.

They ate lobster fresh from the sea, and Greek salads, and drank their fill of retsina. Sometimes the evenings ended with them dancing with the waiters, under the vines of a roadside taverna, doing all the arm-stretching, calf-slapping, and graceful swaying that goes with it. They discovered, as many have before, that the taverna owners of the islands know, and recognize, the signs of love and take lovers into their hearts.

All along—out of habit perhaps, for Percy was a lady of the same trade, but also out of some sixth sense—they kept a wary eye on strangers. They did not, though, spot a familiar face. Vehicles, even motorcycles, did not show twice. They were free, or so it seemed.

But SPECTRE's teams were numerous, and clever. Neither James Bond, nor Percy Proud, could know or see the shadows closing in around them.

The teams were usually five-handed, and they changed daily, never using the same car twice, always having a man or woman ready to follow on to the next island. A girl here, a happy Greek boy there; first a student, then a middle-aged English couple; old VWs, brand-new Hondas, middlebrow Peugeots. The leader's orders were clear, and, when the right moment came, he also arrived.

Bond and Percy spoke much of the future, but by the last week, while heading for Corfu—for they had decided they would fly to London direct from that island of cricket and ginger beer—they could still not come to any sure conclusion. They found a small bungalow of a hotel, away from the razzmatazz of the beehive modern glass and concrete palaces. It was close to a secluded beach, which could only be reached by clambering over rocks, and to a taverna. Their room looked out on a slope of dusty olive trees, and oddly Victorian-looking scrub.

In the late afternoon of each day, they would return to their room, and, as dusk closed in and the cicadas began their endless song, the couple would make love—long and tender, with a rewarding fulfillment of a kind that neither remembered experiencing before.

On their last night, with the small packing yet to be done and a special dinner ordered at the taverna, they followed their usual pattern, walking hand in hand up the slope, entering their room from the scrubby olive grove, leaving the windows open and the blinds drawn.

They soon became lost in each other, murmuring the sweet words of intimacy, enjoying their private island of physical pleasure.

They were hardly aware of the darkness, or the song of the night closing from the cicadas. Neither of them heard Tamil Rahani's car pull up quietly on the road below the hotel, for the heir to SPECTRE had chosen to be in at their death. Nor were they aware of his emissary, who moved up from the road sure-footed in rope-soled sandals, treading softly through the olives until he reached the window.

Tamil Rahani, the true and rightful successor to the Blofelds, had decreed they should both die. His one regret was that it would be quick.

The short, sallow-faced man, who was the best of SPECTRE's silent killers, peered through the lattice of the blinds, smiled, and carefully withdrew a six-inch ivory blowpipe. With even greater care he loaded the tiny, sharp wax dart—filled with deadly pure nicotine—and began to slide the end of the pipe through the lattice.

Percy lay, eyes closed, nearest the window. Her reaction was conceived in long training—for she was like an animal in her instinct for danger.

With a sudden move, she slid from under a startled Bond, one hand going for the floor and the small revolver that always lay at her side of the bed.

She fired twice, rolling naked on the floor as she did so—a

textbook kill, for the man clearly outlined through the blinds was lifted back, as though in slow motion, his dying breath expelling the wax dart into the air.

Bond was beside her in a second, the ASP in his hand, and, as they emerged into the night air, both heard the sound of Rahani's car on the road below the hotel. They needed no superiors to tell them who it was.

Later, when the body had been removed, calls made to London and Washington, the police and other authorities satisfied, Bond and Percy drove into Corfu itself, to spend the night in one of the larger hotels.

"Well, at least that settles it. We should both know, now," Percy began.

"Know?" They had managed to get a meal of sorts in their room, though Bond found it hard to relax.

"The future, James. We should both know about the future after this episode."

"You mean that until Blofeld's successor is dead, neither of us will have peace?"

"That's part of it. Not all though." She paused to sip her wine. "I killed, James, automatically and . . ."

"And most efficiently, darling."

"Yes, that's what I mean. We're not like other people, are we? We're trained, and readied, and we obey orders—fly into danger at a moment's notice."

Bond thought for a moment. "You're right, of course, darling. What you mean is that people like us can't just stop, or live normal lives."

"That's it, my dear James. It's been the best time. The very best. But . . ."

"But now it's over?"

She nodded, and he leaned across the table to kiss her. "Who knows?" Bond asked of nobody in particular.

The next morning they rebooked tickets, and Bond saw her off, watching her aircraft climb over the little hillock at the end of the runway, then turning to set course for the west.

In an hour, he would be on his way, back to London and one

of his other lives, to play some other role for his country.

Bond went into the airport bar to wait for his flight to be called, passing the time with a large brandy, and musing on time past, and future. Percy had been right. It had been the best of times with her, but now his work called, and James Bond knew it would forever entice him back to new dangers—and new sweetness.

NOBODY LIVES FOREVER

for
PETER & PEG
with affection

CONTENTS

1

NO WAY TO START
A VACATION

JAMES BOND SIGNALED late, braked more violently than a Bentley driving instructor would have liked, and slewed the big car off the E5 motorway and onto the last exit road just north of Brussels.

It was merely a precaution. If he was going to reach Strasbourg before midnight it would have made more sense to carry on, follow the ring road around Brussels, then keep going south on the Belgian N4. Yet even on holiday, Bond knew that it was only prudent to remain alert. The small detour across country would quickly establish whether anyone was on his tail, and he would pick up the E40 in about an hour or so.

Lately there had been a directive to all officers of the Service advising "constant vigilance, even when off duty, and particularly when on leave and out of the country."

He had taken the morning ferry to Ostend, and there had been over an hour's delay. About halfway into the crossing the ship had stopped, a boat was lowered, and they began to move—in a wide searching circle. After some forty minutes the boat returned and a helicopter appeared overhead as they set sail again. A little later the news spread throughout the ship. Two men overboard, and lost, it seemed. "Couple of young passengers skylarking," said the barman. "Skylarked once too often. Probably cut to shreds by the screws."

Eventually they arrived and, once through customs, Bond pulled into a side street, operated the secret compartment in the dashboard of the Bentley Mulsanne Turbo, checked that his 9mm ASP automatic was intact, with the spare ammunition clips, and took out the small concealable operations baton, which lay heavy in its soft leather holster.

Unobserved, he closed the compartment, loosened his belt and threaded the holster into place so that the weapon hung at his right hip. The baton was an effective piece of hardware: a black rod, no more than six inches long. When used by a trained man it could be lethal.

Shifting in the driving seat now, Bond felt the hard metal dig comfortably into his hip. He slowed the car to a crawl of 40 kph, scanning the mirrors, taking corners and bends and automatically slowing again once on the far side. Within half an hour he was certain that he was not being followed.

Even with the memo in mind, he reflected that he was being more careful than usual. A sixth sense of danger? Or, possibly, M's remark a couple of days ago?

"You couldn't have chosen a more awkward time to be away, 007," his Chief had grumbled, typically begrudging when it came to matters of leave.

"It's only my entitlement, sir. You agreed I could take my month now. Don't forget, I had to postpone it earlier in the year."

M grunted.

"Moneypenny's going to be away as well. Off gallivanting all over Europe. You're not . . . ?"

"Accompanying Miss Moneypenny? No, sir."

"Off to Jamaica or one of your usual Caribbean haunts, I suppose?" M frowned.

"No, sir. Rome first. Then a few days on the Riviera dei Fiori before driving across to Austria—to pick up May. I just hope my housekeeper'll be fit enough to be brought back to London by then."

"Yes . . . Yes." M was not, however, appeased. "Well, leave your full itinerary with the Chief of Staff. Never know when we're going to need you."

"Already done, sir."

"Well, take care, 007. Take particular care. The Continent's a hotbed of villainy these days, and you can never be too careful." There was a sharp, steely look in his eyes—as though he knew something that was being hidden from Bond.

As Bond left M's office, the old man had the grace to say he hoped there would be good news about May.

At the moment, May, Bond's devoted old Scottish housekeeper, appeared to be the only worry on an otherwise cloudless horizon.

During the winter she had suffered two severe attacks of bronchitis and seemed to be physically deteriorating. She had been with Bond more years than either cared to remember. In fact, apart from the Service, she was the one constant in his not uneventful life.

After the second bronchial attack, he had insisted on a thorough checkup by a Service-retained doctor with a Harley Street practice, and though May had resisted—insisting she was "tough as an auld game bird, and no yet fit for the pot"—Bond had taken her personally to the doctor's consulting rooms.

There had followed an agonizing week, with May being passed from specialist to specialist, complaining all the way. But the tests had proved undeniably positive. The left lung was badly damaged, and there was a distinct possibility that the disease that now showed itself might spread. Unless the lung was removed immediately—followed by a good three months of enforced rest and care for the patient—May was unlikely to see her next birthday.

The operation was carried out by the most skillful surgeon Bond's money could provide, and once she was well enough, May had been packed off to one of the best convalescence clinics in the world, the Klinik Mozart, in the mountains south of Salzburg, where, they informed Bond when he regularly telephoned, she was making amazing progress.

He had even spoken to her personally the evening before, and he now smiled to himself at the tone of her voice, and the somewhat depreciating way she had spoken of the Klinik. She was, no doubt, reorganizing its staff and calling down the wrath of her Glen Orchy ancestors on everyone from maids to chefs.

"They dinna know how to cook yon decent wee bite here, Mr. James, that's the truth of it; and the maids canna make a bed for twopence. I'd no employ any the one of them—and you paying all this money for me to be here. Yon's a downright waste, Mr. James. A *criminal* waste." May had never been able to get her tongue round the word "criminal."

He checked the fuel, deciding it would be best to get the tank filled before the long drive that lay ahead on the E40. Having established there was nobody on his tail, he now concentrated on looking for a garage. It was after seven in the evening, and there was little traffic about. He drove through two small villages, and saw the signs indicating proximity to the motorway; then, on a straight, empty stretch of road, he spotted the garish signs of a small filling station.

It appeared to be deserted, though the door to the tiny office had been left open and the two pumps were unattended. A notice in red warned that the pumps were *not* self-service, so he pulled the Mulsanne up to the "super" pump, switched off the engine and climbed out, stretching his muscles, almost immediately alert to the noises coming from behind the little glass and brick building. Growling, angry voices, and a thump, as though someone had collided with a car.

Bond operated the central locking device on the car and strode quickly to the corner of the building. Within seconds he was moving with real speed.

Behind the office lay a garage area, in front of which stood a white Alfa Romeo Sprint. Two young men were beside the bonnet, across which they held down a third person, a girl. The driver's door was open and a handbag lay on the ground, its zipper ripped open and contents scattered.

"Come on," one of the young men spoke in rough French. "Where is it? You must have some! Give." Like his companion, the thug was dressed in faded jeans and sneakers. Both men were short and broadshouldered, with tanned muscular arms.

The girl protested, and the man who had spoken raised his hand to hit her across the face.

"Stop that!" Bond's voice cracked like a whip as he moved forward.

Both men looked up, startled. Then one of them smiled. "Two for the price of one," he said softly, grabbing the girl by the shoulder and throwing her away from the car, his partner standing over her as she sprawled on the ground.

The man who faced Bond now held a large wrench and obviously thought Bond was easy meat. His hair was tight and curly, and the surly young face already showed the scars of a street fighter. He came forward fast, in a half crouch, holding the wrench low. He moved like a large monkey, Bond thought, reaching for the baton on his right hip as the mugger sprang.

The baton, made by the same firm which developed the 9mm

ASP pistol, looks harmless enough—six inches of nonslip rubber-coated metal. But, as he drew it from its holster, Bond flicked down hard with his right wrist. From the rubber-covered handle sprang a further, telescoped ten inches of toughened steel, which locked into place.

The sudden appearance of the weapon took the young thug off guard. His right arm was raised, clutching the wrench, and for a second he hesitated. Bond stepped quickly to his left and swung the baton. There was an unpleasant cracking noise, followed by a yelp, as the baton connected with the attacker's forearm. He dropped the wrench and doubled up, holding his broken arm, cursing in violent French.

Again Bond moved, delivering a lighter tap, this time to the back of the neck. The mugger went onto his knees and then pitched forward, out for the count as, with a roar, Bond hurled himself at the second thug.

But the man had no stomach for a fight, turning and starting to run. Not fast enough, though, for the tip of the baton came down hard on his left shoulder, certainly breaking bones.

He gave a louder cry than his partner, then raised his hands and began to plead. But Bond was in no mood to be kind to a couple of young *voyous* who had preyed on a virtually helpless woman. He lunged forward, burying the baton's tip in the man's groin, eliciting a further screech of pain that was cut off by a smart blow to the left of the neck, neatly judged to bring unconsciousness and do little further damage.

Bond kicked the wrench out of the way and turned to give the girl assistance, but she was already gathering her things together by the car.

"You all right?" He walked toward her—taking in the long tangle of red hair, the tall, lithe body, oval face, large brown eyes and Italianate look.

"Yes. Thank you, yes."

She had no trace of accent, and, as he came closer, he noted the Gucci loafers, the very long legs encased in tight Calvin Klein jeans, and the silk Hermes shirt.

"Lucky you came along when you did," she said. "You think we should call the police?"

She gave her head a little shake, stuck out her bottom lip, and blew the hair out of her eyes.

"I just wanted petrol." Bond looked at the Alfa Romeo. "What actually happened?"

"I suppose you might say that I caught them with their fingers in the till, and they didn't take kindly to that. The attendant's out cold in the office, by the way."

The thugs, posing as attendants, had apologized when she drove in, saying the pumps out front were not working: Could she take the car to the pump around the back? "I fell for it, and they dragged me out of the car."

Bond asked how she knew about the attendant.

"One of them asked the other if he'd be okay. He said the man would be out for an hour or so." Her voice betrayed no sign of tension, and as she smoothed the tangle of hair, her hands were steady. "If you want to be on your way, I can telephone the police. There's really no need for you to hang about, you know."

"Nor you," he smiled. "Those two'll also be asleep for some time. The name's Bond, by the way. James Bond."

"Sukie," she held out a hand, the palm dry and the grip firm. "Sukie Tempesta."

In the end, they both waited for the police, though it cost Bond over an hour and a half's delay. The pump attendant had been badly beaten and urgently required medical attention. Sukie did what she could for him, while Bond telephoned the police. Then, as they waited, he talked to the girl, dropping innocent questions designed to find out more about her, for the whole affair had begun to intrigue him, and he had the impression she was holding out on him. But, however cleverly he phrased the queries, Sukie managed to sidestep, giving him answers that told him nothing.

There was little to be gleaned from observation either. She was very self-possessed, with a businesslike manner, and could have been anything, from a lawyer to a high-class tart. She looked well-off, judging by her clothes and the jewelry she wore. Certainly an attractive young woman, all in all, with a low-pitched voice, precise economic movements, and a reserved manner that was possibly a touch diffident.

One thing Bond did discover, quickly, was that she spoke both English and French fluently, which pointed to both intelligence and a good education. As for the rest, he could not even discover her nationality, though the plates on the Sprint were—like her name—Italian.

Before the police arrived with a flurry of sirens, Bond went back to his car and stowed away the baton—an illegal weapon in any country. He submitted to an interrogation, at the end of which he was asked to sign a statement. Only then was he allowed to fill up the car and leave, with the proviso that he gave his likely addresses for the next few weeks, and his address and number in London.

Sukie Tempesta was still being questioned when he drove away, feeling strangely uneasy. He recalled the look in M's eyes, and began to wonder about the business on the ferry.

The incident at the petrol station led to yet another, which happened just after midnight, on the E25 between Metz and Strasbourg.

Bond had again filled the tank, and drunk some passable coffee at the frontier post, when crossing into France. Now the road was almost deserted, so he spotted the tail lights of the car ahead a good two miles before overtaking it.

Out of habit, his eyes flicked to the number plate. It was a big white BMW and the number registered in his mind, as did the international *D* that proclaimed its German origin.

After crossing the frontier, he had set the cruise control at 110 kph and sailed past the BMW, which appeared to be pottering along in the eighties.

A minute or so later, Bond became alert. The BMW had picked up speed, moving into the center lane, yet remaining close to him, the distance varying between a quarter of a mile and a few hundred yards.

He touched the brakes, taking out the cruise control, and accelerated. One hundred and thirty. One hundred and fifty. The BMW was still there.

Then, with about ten miles to run before reaching the outskirts of Strasbourg, he became aware of another set of headlights, directly behind him in the fast lane and coming up at speed.

He switched into the middle lane, eyes flicking between the road ahead and the mirror. The BMW had fallen back a little, and in seconds the oncoming lights grew, and the Bentley was rocked slightly as a little black car went past like a jet. It must have been touching 180 kph and, in his headlights, Bond could only get a glimpse of the plates splattered with mud. His main impression was that they were Swiss; he was almost certain that he had caught sight of the Ticino Canton shield to the right of the rear plate. There was not enough time for him to identify the make of the vehicle—just low, black and very fast.

The BMW remained in place for a few moments only, appearing to slow and lose ground. Then Bond saw the flash in his mirror: a brutal crimson ball erupting in the middle lane behind him. He felt the Bentley shudder as the shock waves hit and watched in the mirror as a series of violent flaming shapes appeared to dance across the motorway.

Bond increased pressure on the accelerator. Nothing would make him stop and become involved at this time of night, particularly on a lonely stretch of road. Within a few minutes he realized that he felt oddly shaken at the unexplained violence that appeared to have surrounded him during the day.

At one-eleven in the morning, the Bentley nudged its way into Strasbourg's Place Saint-Pierre-le-Jeune to stop outside the Hotel Sofitel. The night staff was deferential—"Oui, Monsieur Bond . . . Non, Monsieur Bond." But certainly they had his reservation. The car was unloaded, his baggage whipped away, and he personally took the Bentley to the hotel's private parking.

The suite proved to be almost too large for the overnight stay, and there was a large basket of fruit, compliments of the manager. Bond did not know whether to be impressed or to be on his guard. He had not stayed at the Sofitel for at least three years.

Opening the minibar, he mixed himself a martini—pleased the bar stocked Gordons and a decent vodka, though he had to make do with a simple Lillet vermouth instead of his preferred Kina. Taking the drink over to the bed, Bond selected one of his two briefcases, the one that contained the sophisticated scrambling equipment, which he attached to the phone before dialing Transworld Exports—the Service headquarters' cover—in London.

The duty officer listened patiently while Bond recounted the two incidents in some detail. The line was quickly closed, and Bond, tired after the long drive, took a quick shower, rang down for a call at eight in the morning and, naked, stretched out under the down cover.

Only then did Bond start to face up to the fact that he was more than a little edgy. He kept thinking of that strange look in M's eyes. Then he thought about the Ostend ferry and the two men overboard; the girl—Sukie—in distress at the filling station; and the deadly explosion on the road. It was too much to be mere coincidence, and a shadow of menace started to creep into his head.

2

THE POISON DWARF

BOND SWEATED THROUGH his morning exercise routine—the normal twenty slow pushups with their exquisite lingering strain; then the leg lifts, performed on the stomach; and lastly the twenty fast toe-touches.

Before going to the shower, he called room service and gave exact instructions for breakfast—two thick slices of whole-wheat bread, with their best butter and, if possible, Tiptree "Little Scarlet" jam and Cooper's Marmalade. Alas, monsieur, there was no Cooper, but they had Tiptree. It was unlikely they could supply De Bry coffee, so, after a question and answer routine, he settled for their special blend. While waiting for the tray to arrive, he took a very hot shower, followed by one with the water freezing cold.

He did not like change, being a man of habit, but had recently altered his soap, shampoo and cologne to Dunhill Blend 30— deciding they held a more masculine tang—and now, after a vigorous toweling, he rubbed cologne into his body before slipping into his silk traveling "Happi-coat" to await breakfast, which came complete with all the local morning papers.

The BMW, or what small amount of debris was left, seemed

to be spread across all the front pages, while the headlines proclaimed its destruction to be everything from an atrocious act of urban terrorism to the latest assassination in a criminal gang war that appeared to have been sweeping France over the last few weeks.

There was little detail, except for the police claim that there was only one victim—the driver—and that the car was registered in the name of Conrad Tempel, a German businessman from Freiburg. Herr Tempel was missing from his home, so they presumed he was mixed up in shreds among the pieces of blasted motor car.

While reading the story, Bond drank his two large cups of black coffee, without sugar, reflecting that he would skirt Freiburg later that day, after driving into Germany. He planned to cross the Swiss frontier later, at Basel, and, once in Switzerland, would make his way down to Lake Maggiore in the Ticino Canton, and spend a night in one of the small tourist villages on the Swiss side of the Lake. Tomorrow he could plan for a final long run into Italy—a lengthy sweat over the autostradas to Rome and a few days with the Service's Resident and his wife—Steve and Tabitha Quinn.

Today's drive would not be so taxing. He did not need to leave until noon, so had a little time to look around and relax, but first there was the most important ritual of the morning—the telephone call to the Klinik Mozart, near Salzburg, to inquire after May.

He dialed the French "out" code, 19, followed by the 61 that would take him into the Austrian system, then the number. Once the Klinik answered he asked to be put through to the Herr Direktor—Herr Doktor Kirchtum—who came on the line almost immediately.

"Good morning, Mr. Bond. You are in Belgium now, yes?"

Bond said no, he was in France, tomorrow Switzerland and Italy on the following day.

"You are burning a lot of the rubber, as they say." Kirchtum was a large man, and his voice was full of boom and resonance. At the Klinik he could be heard in a room long before he arrived. The nurses called him *das Nebelhorn*—"the Foghorn."

Bond asked after May.

"She still does well. Orders us around, which is a good sign of recovery." Kirchtum gave a guffaw of laughter. "I think the chef is about to cash in his index, as I believe you English say."

"Hand in his cards." Bond smiled to himself. The Herr Doktor, he was sure, made very studied errors in colloquial English. He asked if there was any chance of speaking with the patient, and was told that she was undergoing some treatment at the moment and would not be able to talk on the telephone until later in the day. Bond said he would try to phone during his drive through Switzerland, thanked the Herr Doktor and was about to hang up when Kirchtum stopped him.

"There is someone here who would like a word with you, Mr. Bond. Hold on, I'll put her through."

To his surprise, the next voice was that of M's personal assistant, Miss Moneypenny. "James," she said with that hint of affection always present when she spoke to Bond, "how lovely to talk to you."

"Well, Moneypenny. What on earth're you doing at the Mozart?"

"I'm on holiday, like you, and spending a few days in Salzburg. I just thought I'd come up and see May. She's doing very well, James." Moneypenny's voice sounded light and excited.

"Nice of you to think of her. Be careful what you get up to in Salzburg, though, Moneypenny—all those musical people looking at Mozart's house and going to concerts . . ."

"Nowadays they all want to go off to see the locations used in *The Sound of Music*," she laughed.

"Well, take care all the same, Penny. I'm told those tourists are after only one thing from a girl like you."

"Would you were a tourist, then, James," she sighed. Moneypenny still held a special place in her heart for Bond.

After a little more conversation Bond again thanked her for the thoughtful action of visiting May.

His luggage was ready for collection, the windows were open and the sun streamed in. He would take a look around the hotel, check on the car, have some more coffee and get onto the road. As he went down to the foyer he realized how much he needed a holiday. It had been a hard year, and for the first time Bond wondered if he had made the right decision. Perhaps the short trip to his beloved Royale-les-Eaux would have been a better bet, in more ways than one.

He went down to the foyer, pleased to see that the hotel had kept up its excellent standards. It was good to know there were still hotels that provided real service, in a world so often given to the shoddy and easy way out.

He had started for the main doors in order to make his way to the parking area and check the car, when a familiar face slid into the periphery of his vision. He hesitated, turned and gazed absently into the hotel shop window, the better to examine the reflection of a man sitting near the main reception desk.

The man gave no sign of having seen him, as he sat casually glancing through yesterday's *Herald Tribune.* He was short—not even five feet, Bond guessed. Neatly and expensively dressed, he had the look of many small men: one of complete confidence. Bond always mistrusted people of short stature, knowing they had a tendency to overcompensate with pushy ruthlessness, as though it was necessary to prove themselves.

He turned away, having made his identification. The face was known well enough to him—unpleasant features, thin, ferretlike, with the same bright darting eyes as the animal. What, he wondered to himself, was Paul Cordova—or "the Rat" as he was known in underworld circles—doing in Strasbourg? Bond knew him only because, some years ago, there had been a suggestion that the KGB—posing as a United States government agency—had used him to do a particularly nasty piece of work in New York.

Paul "the Rat" Cordova was what the American Mob called an "enforcer" for one of the New York families—a polite way of saying he was a killer, with his photograph and record on the files of the world's major police, security and secret intelligence departments. It was part of Bond's job to know faces like this, even though Cordova moved in criminal rather than intelligence circles. Moreover, Bond did not think of him as "the Rat." To him, the man was "the Poison Dwarf." Another "coincidence"? he wondered.

Going down to the parking area, he checked the Bentley with great care, telling the man on duty that he would be picking it up within half an hour. He refused to let any of the hotel staff move the car, and there had been a certain amount of surliness on his arrival because he would not leave the keys with the concierge. On his way out, Bond could not fail to notice the low, black, wicked-looking Series 3 Porsche 911 Turbo. The rear plates were mud-splattered, though the Swiss Ticino Canton shield showed clearly.

Whoever had shot past him on the motorway, just before the BMW's explosive disintegration, was now at the hotel. Bond's antennae told him that it was time to get out of Strasbourg as quickly as possible. The small cloud of menace had grown a shade larger.

Cordova was not in the foyer when he returned, so, on reaching his room, Bond put through another call to Transworld Exports in London—again using the scrambler. Even on leave it was his duty to report any sightings—particularly of anyone like the Poison Dwarf so far away from his own turf.

Within twenty minutes, Bond was again at the wheel of the Bentley, heading for the German border.

He crossed without incident, skirted Freiburg and by early afternoon again changed countries, going into Switzerland at Basel. A few hours later he was aboard the car train rattling through the St. Gotthard Pass, and by early evening the Bentley had purred through the streets of Locarno and onto the lakeside road, through Ascona, that paradise for artists, both professional and amateur, to the small and pleasing village of Brissago.

In spite of the beauties of the day, the sunlight, clean little Swiss towns and villages, the towering, awesome mountains and breathtaking views, a sense of impending doom remained with Bond as he drove south. At first he put it down to the odd events of the previous day, and the vaguely disconcerting experience of seeing a known New York Mafia hood in Strasbourg. Yet, as the day had progressed, and he neared Lake Maggiore, he wondered if this mood could be due to a slightly dented pride. The girl he had saved, Sukie Tempesta, had appeared so self-assured, calm and unimpressed by Bond's charm that he felt distinctly annoyed. She could, he thought, at least have shown some sort of gratitude. In the event, she had hardly smiled at him.

As the red-brown roofs of the Maggiore lakeside villages came in sight, Bond began to laugh. Suddenly his gloom, and its possible reasons, came into perspective and he saw the pettiness of his attitude. He slid a tape into the stereo system, and, a moment later, the combination of the view and the great Art Tatum rattling out "The Shout" banished the darkness, putting him into a new, happier mood.

Though his favorite part of the country lay around Geneva, Bond also loved this little slice of Switzerland that rubbed shoulders with Italy. As a young man he had lazed around the shores of Lake Maggiore, eaten some of the best meals of his life in Locarno, and once, on a hot moonlit night, with the waters off Brissago alive with lamplit fishing boats, made unforgettable love to an Italian countess in the very ordinary little hotel by the pier.

It was to this hotel—the Mirto Du Lac—that he now headed: a simple, clean and friendly family place, below the church with its arcade of cypresses, and hard by the pier where the lake steamers put in every hour or so.

The padrone greeted him like an old friend, and Bond was soon ensconced in his room, where the little balcony looked out over the lake.

He made himself comfortable, and before unpacking his few needs for the night, dialed the Klinik Mozart. The Herr Direktor was not available so they put him through to one of the junior doctors, who said he was sorry but Mr. Bond could not speak with May. She was resting. There had been a visitor and she was a little tired. For some reason the doctor's words did not ring true. There was a slight hesitation that worried Bond. He asked if May was all right, and the doctor assured him that she was perfectly well, just a little tired.

"This visitor," he went on, "I believe a Miss Moneypenny . . ."

"This is correct." The doctor was the one who sounded most correct.

"I don't suppose you happen to know where she's staying in Salzburg?"

He was sorry but he did not. "I understand she is coming back to see the patient tomorrow," he added.

Bond thanked him and said he would call again. By the time he had showered and changed, it was starting to get dark. Across the lake the sunlight slowly withdrew from Mount Tamaro, and lights went on along the lakeside. Insects began to flock around the glass globes, and one or two couples took seats at the tables outside.

At the moment Bond left his room to go down to the bar that stood in the corner of the restaurant, a black Porsche 911 crept quietly into the forecourt, parking with its nose thrust toward the lake. Its occupant climbed out, carefully locked the car and walked, with neat little steps, back the way he had driven, up toward the church.

It was a good ten minutes later that those sitting outside the Mirto, or, like Bond, in the bar, heard the series of piercing screams.

The steady murmur of talk and laughter petered out as people realized the screams were not some silly girl playing catch and kiss games with her boyfriend. These were shrieks of terror. Several people started toward the door, already some of the men outside were on their feet, others looking around to see where the noise was coming from.

Bond was among those who dashed and pushed to get outside. The first thing he saw, through the confusion of people, was the Porsche, then the woman, face white, her mouth an open gash that seemed to have taken the place of features, hair flying as she ran down the steps from the churchyard, screaming, hands wild, going to her face, then wringing the air, then clutching her head. Between the screaming she kept shouting, *"Assassinio! Assassinio!"* Murder! Murder! As she yelled the word, one hand would point back, up to the churchyard with its cypresses and rough stones.

Six men beat Bond up the steps, and there were already several others clustered around a small bundle lying across the cobbled path, their voices raised for a moment, then stilled as they came to the object.

Bond moved quietly to the perimeter of this knot of men. Paul "the Rat" Cordova—his Poison Dwarf—lay on his back, knees drawn up, one arm flung outward, his head at an angle, for it seemed to have been almost severed by the single deep slash across the throat.

Bond moved away, pushing through the gathering crowd and heading back down to the lakeside and the hotel. He had never been a man who believed in coincidences. The drowned passengers; the affair at the filling station; the explosion on the motorway;

the fact of Cordova's presence—first near him in France, now here on the Swiss-Italian border—were linked. He was the common denominator, and already he knew that his holiday was shattered. He would telephone London, report and await orders.

But, on reaching the hotel, another surprise awaited him. There, standing by the reception desk, looking just as trim as ever, but now wearing a short blue-tinged leather number, probably a Merenlender, stood yesterday's damsel in distress, Sukie Tempesta.

3

SUKIE

"JAMES BOND!" THE delight appeared to be genuine enough, but, with beautiful women, Bond considered you could never be sure.

"In the flesh." He moved closer, and for the first time really saw her eyes—large, brown with violet flecks, oval, like her face, and set off by exceptionally long, curled and certainly natural lashes. They were eyes, he thought, that could be the undoing of a man, or, conversely, the making of him. His own eyes flicked down to the full firm curve of her breasts under the well-fitting leather.

She stuck out her lower lip, to blow hair from her forehead, as she had done the day before. "I didn't expect to see you again." Her wide mouth tilted in a warm smile. "I'm so glad. I didn't get a chance to thank you, properly. For yesterday, I mean." She bobbed a mock courtsy. "Mr. James Bond, I might well owe you my life. Thank you *very* much. I mean it—*very* much."

He had moved to one side of the reception desk in order to watch her and keep an eye on the main doors. Instinctively, he felt danger close at hand. Danger in being close to Sukie Tempesta, perhaps.

Outside, police moved among the crowd, and the sound of sirens floated down from the main street and church above them. Bond knew he needed his back against a wall at all times now.

She asked him what was going on, and he told her. She shrugged, "It's more commonplace where I spend most of my time. In Rome, murder is a fact of life nowadays, but, somehow, you don't expect it here, in Switzerland."

"It's commonplace anywhere." He tried his most charming smile. "But what are *you* doing here, Miss Tempesta—or is it Mrs., or even Signora?"

She wrinkled her nose, prettily, and raised her eyebrows. "Principessa, actually—if we have to be formal."

Bond lifted an eyebrow. "Principessa Tempesta." He dropped his head in a formal bow.

"Sukie." The wide smile again, and the large eyes, innocent, yet with a minute tinge of mockery. "You call me Sukie, Mr. Bond. Please."

"James."

"James." And at that moment the padrone came bustling up to complete the paperwork of booking her in. As soon as he saw the title on the registration form everything changed to a hand-wringing, bowing comedy at which Bond could only smile wryly.

"You haven't yet told me what you're doing here," he continued, over the padrone's effusive deference.

"Could I do that over dinner? At least I owe you that." Her hand touched his forearm and he felt the natural exchange of static. Bells of warning rang in his head. No chances, he thought, you must take chances with nobody, particularly with those to whom you are naturally attracted. "Dinner would be fine," he replied, then, once more, asked what she was doing here on Lake Maggiore.

"My little motor car has broken down. There's something very wrong, according to the garage here—which probably means all they'll do is change the plugs. But they say it's going to take days."

"And you're heading for . . . ?"

"Rome, naturally." She blew at her hair again.

"What a happy coincidence," Bond gave another bow, "if I can be of service."

She hesitated a fraction, "Oh, I'm sure you can. Shall we say dinner, down here, in half an hour?"

"I'll be waiting, Principessa."

He thought he saw her nose wrinkle and her tongue poke out, like a naughty schoolgirl's, as she turned to follow the padrone to her room.

In the privacy of his own quarters, Bond telephoned London yet again, giving them the news concerning Cordova. He had the scrambler on, and, as an afterthought, asked them to run a check with the Interpol computer, as well as their own, on the Principessa Sukie Tempesta.

Hoods like Cordova were not nickel and dime men, but contract killers who came at Cartier prices. Principessa Tempesta looked as though she came at a usurious rate of interest. He finally asked the duty officer if they had yet gotten information on the BMW's owner, Herr Tempel of Freiburg. Nothing yet, he was told, but some material had gone to M that afternoon. "You'll hear soon enough if it's important. Have a nice holiday."

Very droll, thought Bond, packing away the scrambling device— a CC500, which could be used on any telephone in the world and allowed only the legitimate receiving party to hear the caller *en clair*. Eavesdroppers of any kind—from the exchange to the professional wiretapper—heard only sounds that were completely indecipherable, even if they tapped in with a compatible system, for each CC500 had to be individually programed. It was standard Service practice nowadays for all officers—on duty or leave—out of the country to carry a CC500, and the access codes were altered daily.

There were ten minutes to spare before he had to meet Sukie— if she was on time—so he washed quickly, rubbing cologne hard into face and hair, then put on a blue cotton jacket over his shirt and went rapidly downstairs and out to the car. There was still a great deal of police activity in the churchyard above, and he could see that a scene-of-crime team had set up lights where Cordova's body had been discovered.

Inside the car he waited for the courtesy lights to click off before activating the switch on the main lighting panel, allowing the concealed compartment to drop down below the facia.

Slipping off his jacket, he buckled the compact holster in place, checking the 9mm ASP before getting the jacket on again and securing the baton's holster to his belt. He had no idea what was going on around him, but it had already cost at least two lives—probably more. Care would ensure that he did not end up as the next cadaver, for he was now more than certain that the proximity of these deaths was no accident. Coolly, Bond had already accepted that some unseen menace was stalking him—and him alone.

To his immense surprise, Sukie was already at the bar when he got back into the hotel. "Like a dutiful woman I didn't order anything while I waited." She blew at her hair again—it was like a nervous tic.

"I prefer dutiful women." Bond slid onto the bar stool next to her, turning it slightly so that he had a clear view of anyone coming through the big glass doors at the front. "What'll you drink?"

"Oh, no, tonight's on me. In honor of your saving *my* honor, James." Again the hand lightly brushed his arm, and he felt the same electricity.

Bond capitulated, "Well, we're in Ticino where they think grappa is good liquor, so I'd best stick to the comic drinks—a Campari soda, if I may."

She ordered the same, then the padrone bustled over with the menu. It was very *famiglia,* very *semplice,* he explained. It would make a change, Bond said, and Sukie asked him to order for them both. He said he would be difficult and change the menu around a little, starting with the *Melone al kirsch,* asking them to serve his plain, without the kirsch—Bond disliked any food soused in alcohol, and deplored the current fashion in many English restaurants for cooking practically everything in wine, or worse, vermouth. He was pleased to note that Sukie agreed, pulling a face to indicate the fact.

"For the entrée there's really only one dish, pasta excepted, in these parts, you'll agree . . . ?"

"The *coscia d' agnello?*" She smiled as he nodded. In the north these spiced lamb chops were known as Lamm-Gigot. Here, among the Ticinese, they were less delicate to the palate but made delicious by the use of much garlic. Like Bond, Sukie refused any vegetables but accepted the plain green salad that he also ordered, together with a bottle of Frecciarossa Bianco, apparently the best white wine they could supply. Bond had taken one look at the champagnes and pronounced them undrinkable, but "probably reasonable for making a dressing," at which Sukie laughed. Her laugh was, Bond thought, the least attractive thing about her, a shade harsh, difficult to detect as genuine.

When they were seated, Bond wasted no time in making an offer to help her on her journey. "I'm leaving for Rome in the morning. If you want a lift, I'd be very pleased. That is if the Principe won't be offended at a commoner bringing you home."

She gave a little pout, "He's in no position to be offended. Principe Pasquale Tempesta died last year."

"I'm sorry, I . . ."

She gave a dismissive wave of the right hand, "Oh, don't be sorry. He was eighty-three. We were married for two years; it was convenient, that's all." She did not smile or try to make light of it.

"A marriage of convenience?"

"No, it was just convenient. I like good things. He had money; he was old; he needed someone to keep him warm at night—he could do precious little else. In the Bible didn't King David take a young girl—Abishag—to keep him warm?"

"I believe so. My upbringing was a touch Calvinistic, yet I seem to recall the Lower Fourth sniggering over that story."

"Well, that's what I was, Pasquale Tempesta's Abishag, and he enjoyed it. Now, I enjoy what he left me."

"For an Italian you speak excellent English."

"I should." The smile again, and then the laugh, a shade more mellow this time. "I *am* English."

"You speak excellent Italian, then."

"And French, and German." She reached forward, putting out a hand to cover his as it lay on the table beside his glass. "Don't worry, James, I'm not a witch. But I can spot nosy questions, like all those you put to me yesterday, however subtly. Comes from the nuns, then living with Pasquale's people."

"Nuns?"

"I'm a good convent-educated girl, James. You know about girls who've been educated in convents?"

"A fair amount."

She gave another little pout. "I was pretty well brainwashed.

Daddy was a broker, all very ordinary: home counties; mock-Tudor house; two cars; one scandal. Daddy got caught out with some funny checks and drew five years in an open prison. Collapse of stout family. I'd just finished at the convent, and was all set to go to Oxford. That was out, so I answered an ad in *The Times*—nanny, with a mound of privileges, to an Italian family of good birth: Pasquale's son, as it happened. It's an old title, like all the surviving Italian nobility, but with one difference—they still have property and money."

To cut the amusing story short, for she took a long time in its telling, the Tempesta family had taken their new English nanny into the family as one of their own. The old man, the Principe, had become a second father to her. She became very fond of him, so, when he proposed a marriage—which he described as *comodo* as opposed to *comodita*—Sukie, whose maiden name was Susan Destry, saw a certain wisdom in taking up the offer.

Yet even in that she showed shrewdness, careful to be certain that the marriage would in no way deprive Pasquale's two sons of their rightful inheritance. "It did, to some extent, but they're both wealthy, and successful in their own right, and they put forward no objections. You know old Italian families, James. Papa's happiness; Papa's rights; respect for Papa . . ."

Bond asked in what way the two sons had become successful, and she hesitated a fraction too long before airily saying, "Oh, business. They own companies and that kind of thing, and, yes, James, I'll take you up on your offer of a ride to Rome. Thank you."

They were halfway through the lamb when the padrone came hurrying forward, excused himself to Sukie, and bent to whisper that there was an urgent telephone call for Bond, pointing toward the bar, which had its phone off the hook.

"Bond," he said quietly into the receiver.

"James, you somewhere private?" He recognized the voice immediately—Bill Tanner, M's Chief of Staff.

"No. I'm having dinner."

"This is urgent. Very urgent. Could you . . . ?"

"Of course." He closed the line and went back to the table to make his apologies to Sukie. "It won't take long." He told her about May being ill in the Klinik. "They want me to ring them back."

In his room he set up the CC500 and called London. Bill Tanner came on the line straight away. "Don't say anything, James, just listen. The instructions are from M, do you accept that?"

"Of course." He had no alternative, if Bill Tanner said he was speaking for the Chief of the Secret Service. Bond's discipline was obedience, like a monk to his abbot.

"You're to stay where you are and take great care." There was anxiety in Tanner's voice.

"I'm due in Rome tomorrow, I . . . ."

"Listen to me, James. Rome's coming to you. You, I repeat *you*, are in gravest hazard. Genuine danger. We can't get anyone to you quickly, to watch your back, so you'll have to do it for yourself. You stay put and stay tight. Understand?"

"I understand." When Bill Tanner spoke of Rome coming to him, he meant Steve Quinn, the Service resident in Rome. The same Steve Quinn with whom he had planned to spend a couple of days. He asked why Rome was coming to him.

"To put you fully in the picture. Brief you. Try to get you out." He heard Tanner take a quick breath at the other end of the line. "I can't stress the danger strongly enough, old friend. The Chief suspected problems before you left, but we only got the hard intelligence in the last hour." M had flown to Geneva. Rome—Steve Quinn—was on his way there to be briefed, then he would come straight to Bond. "Be with you before lunch. In the meantime, trust nobody. For God's sake just stay close."

"I'm with the Tempesta girl now. Promised her a ride to Rome. What's the form on her?" Bond crisp and terse.

"We haven't got it all, but the people to whom she's related seem clean enough. Certainly not connected with the Honored Society. Treat her with care, though. Don't let her get behind you."

"I was thinking of the opposite, as a matter of fact," Bond's mouth moved into a hard smile.

Tanner ordered him to keep her at the hotel. "Stall her about Rome, but don't alert her. You really don't know who are your friends and who your enemies. Rome'll give you the full strength tomorrow. Lock your door; keep your back to the wall."

"We won't be able to leave until late morning, I'm afraid," he told Sukie, once back at the table. "That was a business chum who's been to see my old housekeeper. He's passing through here tomorrow morning, and I really can't miss the chance of seeing him."

She said it did not matter. "I was hoping for a lie-in tomorrow anyway." Could he detect an invitation in her voice?

They talked on, had coffee and a *fine* in the dining room, neat with its red and white checkered tablecloths, gleaming cutlery, and the two serious waitresses, who went about their business as though serving writs instead of food. The girls, he thought, probably came from the north. There, the stolidness of the waitress often belied a fire of good clean lust lurking beneath the sensible shoes and uniforms. At least Bond had often discovered so in his youth.

Sukie suggested they should go outside, to sit at one of the tables fronting the Mirto, but Bond made an excuse not to. "Mosquitoes and midges tend to congregate around the lights," he said. "You'll end up with that lovely skin blotched. Safer indoors."

She asked what kind of business he was in, and he answered in his usual vague way, which she appeared nonetheless to accept. They talked of towns and cities they both enjoyed, and of food and drink.

"Perhaps I can take you to dinner in Rome," Bond suggested. "Without seeming ungrateful, I think we can get something a shade more interesting at Papa Giovanni's or Augustea."

"I'd love it. It's a change to talk to someone who knows Europe well. Pasquale's family are very Roman, I fear. They don't really see much further than the Appian Way."

In all, it was a pleasant evening, though Bond had to put up a show of being relaxed after hearing the news from London. Now he had to get through the night.

They went up together, with Bond offering to escort Sukie to her room. They reached the door, and he had no doubt as to what would happen. She came into his arms easily enough, but, when he kissed her, she did not respond, her lips closed and tight, her body rigid.

So, he thought, one of those. But he tried again, if only because he wanted to keep her in sight. This time she pulled away, gently putting her fingers to his mouth, "I'm sorry, James. But no." There was the ghost of a smile as she said, "I'm a good convent girl, remember. But that's not the only reason. If you're serious, be patient. Now, goodnight, and thank you for the lovely evening."

"I should thank *you,* Principessa," he said with a shade of formality, watched as she closed her door, then went slowly to his own room, swallowed a couple of Benzedrine tablets and prepared to sit up all night, ready for anything.

4

THE HEAD HUNT

STEVE QUINN WAS a big man, tall, broad, bearded and with an expansive personality—"a big, bearded bastard," Steve's wife, the petite, blonde Tabitha, was often heard to remark. Not the usual kind of person who made it to a responsible position in the Service. The Service preferred what it liked to call "invisible men"—ordinary, gray people who could vanish into a crowd like illusionists.

Now, Bond—wearing only the silk Happi-coat—watched from the shadows of his half-closed shutters as the big, bearded bastard alighted from a hired car and walked toward the hotel entrance.

A few seconds later, the telephone rang and Bond said they should allow Mr. Quarterman up to his room. Quarterman was the name under which Quinn traveled.

The man from Rome was inside, with the door closed and locked, almost before the knock had died in the air.

Quinn did not speak immediately, going straight to the window, glancing down onto the stretch of forecourt and the lake steamer that had just docked to disgorge its local and tourist passengers. The sight of the sheer magnificent beauty usually took people's breath away when they disembarked, but this morning the loud yah-yah-yahing of an affected Englishwoman's voice could be heard even in Bond's room—"I wonder what there is to see here, darling?"

Bond scowled, and Quinn gave a little twisted smile almost hidden by his beard. He looked at the detritus of breakfast still on its tray and mouthed a few words, asking if the place was clean.

"Spent the night going over it. Nothing in the telephone, or anywhere else."

Quinn nodded. "Okay."

Bond asked why they could not have flown Geneva up to him—they usually spoke of Service residents by the name of their area of influence.

"Because Geneva's got problems of his own," Steve Quinn's finger stabbed out toward Bond, "but not a patch on *your* personal problems, James."

"Talk then. The Chief met you for a briefing?"

"Right. I've done what I can, within limits. Geneva doesn't like it, but two of my people should be here by now to watch your back. M wants you in London—in one piece if possible."

"So, there *is* someone on my tail." He sounded unconcerned, but pictures of the shattered car on the motorway and the American hood's body lying in the churchyard reeled through his mind.

Quinn lowered his considerable bulk into a chair. When he spoke it was low, almost a whisper. "No," he said, "you haven't got someone on your tail. It seems to us that you've got just about every willing terrorist organization, criminal gang and un-friendly foreign intelligence service right up your ass. There is, to use a gangland expression, a contract out for you. A unique contract. Somebody has made every alien organization—to coin a phrase—an offer they can't refuse."

Bond gave a hard half smile. "Okay, break it to me gently. What am I worth?"

"Oh, they don't want all of you. Just your head."

Quinn began. It appeared that M had received some indication about two weeks before Bond went on leave. "The firm that controls South London tried to spring Bernie Brazier from the Island." In plain language, this meant that the most powerful underworld organization in South London had tried to get one

Bernie Brazier out of the high-security prison at Parkhurst, on the Isle of Wight. Brazier was doing life for the cold-blooded killing of a quite notorious London underworld figure, noted for his professional skills. Scotland Yard knew he had carried out at least twelve murders for money, but could not prove it. In short, Bernie Brazier was Britain's top "mechanic," which is a very polite name for hired killer.

"The escape was bungled. A real dog's breakfast. Then, after it was all over, friend Brazier wanted to do a deal," Quinn continued, "and, as you know, the Met don't take kindly to deals. So he asked to see somebody from the sisters"—he spoke of their sister Service, M15. This had been refused, but the details were passed to M, who sent the Grand Inquisitor to Parkhurst Prison, where Brazier claimed that he was being sprung for a particular job, that it was important to the country's security and that he had details. But, in return for the goods, he required a new identity, in the sun, with money to singe if not actually to burn.

Bond remained oddly detached, for the scenario, as Quinn explained it, had a dreamlike, nightmarish quality. He knew the devil incarnate in M would promise the world for hard intelligence, and then give the source of supply a very small plot of earth. So it had been. Another pair of interrogators had gone to Parkhurst and had a long talk with Brazier. Then M had taken the trip, himself, to make the promises.

"And Bernie told all?" he finally asked.

"Some of it. The rest was to come once he was nicely tucked away in some tropical paradise with enough birds and booze to give him a coronary within a year." Quinn's face went very hard. "The day after M's visit they found Bernie in his cell—hanged with piano wire."

From outside came the sound of children at play near the jetty, the toot of one of the lake boats and, far away, the drone of a light airplane. Bond asked what they had gotten from the late Bernie Brazier.

"That you were the target for this unique contract. A kind of competition."

"Competition?"

"There are rules, it appears, and the winner is the group that physically brings your head to the organizers—on a silver charger, no less. Any bona fide criminal, terrorist or intelligence agency can enter. They have to be accepted by the organizers. The starting date was four days ago, and there's a time limit. Three months. Winner gets ten million Swiss."

Bond gave a low whistle.

"Quite." Quinn did not smile.

"Who in heaven's name . . . ?" Bond started.

"M discovered the answer to that less than twenty-four hours ago, with the help of the Metropolitan Police. About a week back, they pulled in half of the South London mob, and let M's heavy squad have a go. It paid off—or M's paying off, I don't quite know which. I do know that four major London gangland chiefs are pleading for round-the-clock protection, and I guess they need it. The fifth one"—he mentioned the name—"laughed at M and walked out of the slammer. I gather they found him last night. He was not in a good state."

When Quinn went into the details of this particular man's demise, even Bond felt queasy. "Jesus . . ."

"Saves," Quinn showed not a shred of humor. "One can but hope He's saved that poor bastard. Forensic say he took an unconscionable time a'dying."

"And who's organized this grisly competition?"

"It's even got a name, by the way," Steve Quinn interrupted in a somewhat offhand manner. "It's called the Head Hunt. No consolation prizes, just the big one. M reckons that around thirty professional killers went through the starting gate . . ."

"Who's behind it?"

Quinn nodded, making placating movements with his hands. "In general, your old friends the Special Executive for Counterintelligence, Terrorism, Revenge and Extortion—SPECTRE. In particular, the inheritor of the Blofeld dynasty, their leader, with whom you've had one nasty brush, M tells me . . ."

"Tamil Rahani. The so-called Colonel Tamil Rahani."

"Who will be the late Tamil Rahani in a matter of three to four months. Hence the time limit."

Bond was silent for a minute. He was fully aware of how dangerous Tamil Rahani could be. They had never really discovered how he had managed to take over as chief executive of SPECTRE, that organization which seemed to have always kept its leadership embedded in a sort of right of succession within the Blofeld family. But certainly the inventive, ruthless, brilliant strategist of terror, Tamil Rahani, *had* become SPECTRE's leader. He could see the man now—dark-skinned, muscular, radiating self-discipline and a controlled dynamism. Short, full of fire and guile. A smooth, ruthless and internationally powerful leader.

He recalled the last time he had seen him, drifting by parachute over Geneva—Tamil Rahani's great forte as a terrorist commander was that he led from the front. He had tried to have Bond killed a month or so after that last meeting. Since then there had been few sightings, but 007 could well believe in this bizarre competition SPECTRE titled the Head Hunt—especially if it was the brainchild of the truly sinister Tamil Rahani.

"You're implying the man's on his way out? Dying?"

"There was a sudden and dangerous escape by parachute . . ." Quinn did not look him in the eyes.

"Yes."

"Information is that he jarred his spine on landing. In turn this caused problems. The man has a cancer affecting the spinal cord. Apparently M knows of six specialists who've seen him. There is no hope. Within four months, Tamil Rahani's going to be the late Tamil Rahani."

Bond nodded. "Who's involved? Apart from SPECTRE, who am I up against?"

Quinn slid a hand down his dark beard. "M's working on it. A lot of your old enemies, of course, whatever they call the former Department V of the KGB these days—what used to be SMERSH . . ."

"Department Eight of Directorate S: KGB," Bond snapped.

Quinn went on as though he had not heard, ". . . Also practically every known terrorist organization, from the old Red Brigade to the Puerto Rican FALN—the Armed Forces for National Liberation. With ten million Swiss francs as the star prize you've attracted a lot of attention."

"You mentioned the underworld."

"Of course—British, French, German, at least three Mafia families and, I fear, the Union Corse. Since the demise of your ally, Marc-Ange Draco, they've been less than helpful . . ."

"All right!" Bond stopped him, sharply.

Steve Quinn lifted his large body from the chair. There was no effort, as is so often the case with heavy men, just a fast movement, a second between being seated and facing Bond, one large hand reaching out and holding 007's shoulder. "Yes. Yes, I know. This is going to be a bitch." He hesitated, as though something even more unpleasant had to be said. "There's one other thing you've got to know about Head Hunt . . ."

Bond shook off the hand. Quinn had been tactless in reminding him of the special relationship he had once nurtured between the Service and the Union Corse—that Cosa Nostra-like underworld link which could be even more deadly than the Mafia. Bond's contacts with the Union Corse had led to his marriage, followed quickly by the death of his bride, Marc-Ange Draco's daughter. "What other thing? You've made it plain I cannot trust anybody— can I even trust you?" With a sense of disgust, Bond realized he meant the last remark. Nobody. He could not even trust Steve Quinn—the Service's man in Rome.

"It's to do with SPECTRE's rules for Head Hunt." Quinn's face would have done credit to Mount Rushmore. "The organizations, or criminal fraternities, who've applied to enter the competition are restricted to putting one man in the field—one only. The latest information is that four of these contestants have already died violently within the past twenty-four hours—one of them only a few hundred meters from where we're sitting."

"Tempel, Cordova, and a couple of thugs on the Ostend Ferry."

"Right. The ferry passengers were two opposing London gang representatives—South London and the West End. Tempel had known links with the Red Army faction—he was an underworld-trained hood, with money and influence, a barroom politician who thought there were rich pickings in the politics of terrorism. The American, Paul Cordova, you know about."

All four of them, Bond thought, had already been near to him, and very close indeed when they were murdered. What were the odds on that being a coincidence? Aloud, he asked Quinn what M's orders were.

"You're to get back to London at the speed of light. We honestly haven't the manpower available to look after you loose on the Continent. My own two boys'll see you to the nearest airport and then take care of the car . . ."

"No." Bond whirled on him. "No, I'll get the car back, nobody else is going to take care of it for me—right?"

Quinn shrugged. "Your funeral. You're terribly vulnerable in that vehicle."

But Bond did not appear to notice. He was already moving about the room, neatly finishing his packing, yet all the time his senses were centered on Quinn. Trust nobody: Right, he would not even trust this man. "Your boys?" he asked. "Give me a rundown."

Quinn nodded in the direction of the window. "They're out there. Look for yourself," he said, going toward the shuttered balcony, peering through the louvered slats.

Bond placed himself just behind the big man. "There," Quinn said. "One standing by the rocks, in the blue shirt. The other's in the silver Renault, parked at the end of the row of cars." It was a Renault 25 V6i. Not Bond's favorite kind of car. If he played his cards properly he could outrun that pair with ease. "I wanted information on one other person." He stepped back into the center of the room. "An English girl who's inherited an Italian title . . ."

"Tempesta?" There was a sneer on Quinn's lips.

Bond nodded.

"M doesn't think she's part of the game, though she could be bait. He says you should take care—what he actually said was, 'exercise caution.' She's around, I gather."

"Very much so. I've promised to give her a lift to Rome."

"Dump her!" An order.

"We'll see. Okay, Quinn, if that's all you have for me, I'll sort out my route home. It could be scenic."

Quinn nodded and stuck out his hand, which Bond ignored. "Good luck. You're going to need it."

"I don't altogether believe in luck. Really I believe in only one thing—myself."

Quinn frowned, nodded and left Bond to make his final preparations. Speed was essential, but his main thought at this moment was what he should do about Sukie Tempesta. She was there, an unknown quantity, yet he felt she could be used somehow. A hostage, perhaps? The Principessa Tempesta would make an adequate hostage, a shield even, if he felt that ruthless.

As though by some act of clairvoyance, the telephone rang and
Sukie's voice came, mellow, on the line, "I was wondering what
time you wanted to leave, James?"

"Whenever it suits you. I'm almost ready."

She laughed, and the harshness seemed to have gone—there
was some humor in her voice as she said she only had to finish
packing. "Fifteen minutes at the most. You want to eat here,
before we leave?"

Bond said he'd prefer to stop for a snack en route if she did
not mind, then added, "Look, Sukie, I've got a very small problem.
A minor thing, but it might effect our journey—the odd detour.
May I come and talk to you before we go?"

"To my room?"

"It would be better."

"It could also cause a small scandal for a well-brought-up
convent girl."

"I can promise you there'll be no scandal. Shall we say ten
minutes' time?"

"If you insist." She was not being unpleasant, just a shade more
formal than before.

"It's quite important, and you truly need not concern yourself
with any scandal. I'll be with you in ten minutes."

Hardly had he put down the telephone and snapped the locks
on his case when the instrument rang again.

"Mr. Bond?" He recognized the booming voice of Herr Doktor
Kirchtum, director of the Klinik Mozart, but the voice appeared
to have lost its ebullience.

"Herr Direktor?" Bond heard the note of anxiety in his own
tone.

"I'm sorry, Mr. Bond. It is not good news . . ."

"May!"

"Your patient, Mr. Bond. She is vanished. The police are here
with me now. I'm sorry not to have made contact sooner. But
she is vanished—with the friend who visited yesterday, the
Moneypenny lady. There has been a telephone call and the
police wish to speak with you. She has been, how do you say it?
Napped . . ."

"Kidnapped? May, kidnapped, and Moneypenny?" A thousand
thoughts went through his head, but only one of them made sense.

Someone had done his homework very well. Kidnapping May could just possibly be a byproduct of the kidnapping of Moneypenny, whose situation always made her a likely target. What was more likely, though, was that one of the Head Hunt entrants wanted Bond under close control, and how better than to lead him in a search for May and Moneypenny?

5

NANNIE

A<small>LL THINGS BEING</small> considered—Bond thought—Sukie Tempesta showed that she was an uncommonly cool lady.

He had showered and shaved before Quinn's arrival, so now he worked out a plan to deal with Sukie as he dressed—casual slacks, with his favorite soft leather moccasins and a sea island cotton shirt, over which he threw a battledress-style gray Oscar Jacobson Alcantara jacket. The jacket was mainly to hide the 9mm ASP. He then placed his case, and the two briefcases, near the door, checked the ASP and went quickly downstairs where he settled both his own and Sukie's accounts with a credit card, returning with equal speed to the second floor, going straight to her room.

Of course she had Gucci luggage—one medium-size case, a dressing case and the briefcase. They stood in a neat line near the door, which she opened to his knock. She was back in the Calvin Klein jeans, this time with a black silk shirt that looked very Christian Dior.

He gently pushed her back into the room, though she did open her mouth to protest, saying she was ready to leave, but his face was set in a serious mask that made her ask, "James, what is it? Something's really wrong, isn't it?"

"I'm sorry, Sukie. Yes. Very serious for me, and it could be dangerous for you also."

"I don't understand . . ."

"I have to do certain things you might not like. You see, I've been threatened . . ."

"Threatened? How threatened?" She continued to back away.

"I can't go into details now, but it's clear to me—and others—that there's a possibility you could be involved."

"Me? Involved with what, James? Threatening you?"

"It *is* a serious business, Sukie. Don't be fooled, my life's at risk, and we met in rather dubious circumstances . . ."

"Oh, dubious my eye. What was dubious about it? Except for those unpleasant young muggers?"

"It appeared that I came along at a fortunate moment. It seems I saved you from something unpleasant. Then your car breaks down—conveniently near where I'm staying. Being, I trust, a gentleman, I offer you a lift to Rome. Some people might see this as a scenario for a setup, with me as the target."

"But I don't—"

"I'm sorry, I—"

"You can't take me to Rome?" Her voice was level. "I understand, James. Don't worry about it, I'll find some way, but it does present me with a little problem of my own . . ."

"Oh, you're coming with me—maybe even to Rome eventually. I have no alternative. I *have* to take you—even if it's as a hostage. I must have a little insurance with me. You'll be my policy."

He paused, letting it sink in, then, to his surprise, she smiled. "Well, I've never been a hostage before. It'll be a new experience." She looked down and saw the gun in his hand. "Oh, James! Melodrama? You don't need that. I'm on a kind of holiday anyway. I really don't mind being your hostage, if it's necessary." She paused, her face registering a fascinated pleasure. "It could even be exciting, and I'm all for excitement."

"The kind of people I'm up against are about as exciting as tarantulas, and lethal as sidewinders. I hope what's going to happen now isn't going to be too nasty for you, Sukie. I have no other option, and I *have* to be very careful. I promise you this is no game. You're to do everything I say, and do it very slowly. No disrespect is intended, but just turn around—right around, like a model—with your hands on your head."

Initially, he was looking for two things, the makeshift weapon or the one more cunningly concealed. She wore a small cameo brooch, holding together the neck of her shirt. He made her unpin the brooch and throw it gently onto the bed, where her shoulder bag lay. The brooch was followed by her shoes.

He kept the cameo—it looked safe, but technicians could do nasty things with brooch pins. All his examining moves were accomplished deftly with one hand, while the ASP stayed well back in the other.

The shoes were clean—he knew every possible permutation with shoes—as was her belt. He apologized for the indignity, but her clothes and person were the first priorities. If she carried nothing suspicious he could deal with the luggage later, making sure it was kept out of harm's way until they stopped somewhere, so he emptied the shoulder bag onto the bed. The usual junk spilled out onto the white quilt—checkbook, credit cards, cash, Kleenex, comb, a small bottle of pills, about twenty-five crumpled Amex and Visa receipts, a small scent spray—Cacharel Anais Anais— lipstick and a gold compact, plus a dozen or so other miscellaneous, useless items, thrust into the bag out of habit or sentiment.

He kept the comb, some book matches, a small sewing kit from the Plaza Athénée, the scent spray, lipstick and compact. Comb, book matches and sewing kit were immediately adaptable weapons for close-quarter work. The spray, lipstick and compact needed closer inspection. In his time he had known scent sprays to contain liquids more deadly than even the most repellent scent; lipsticks to house razor-sharp curved blades, propellants of one kind or another, even hypodermic syringes; and powder compacts to conceal miniature radios, or worse.

She was more embarrassed than angry about having to strip. Her body was the color of rich creamed coffee, smooth and regular, with the kind of tan you can get only through patience, the right lotions, a correct regimen of sun and nudity. It was the sort of body that men dreamed of finding alive and wriggling in their beds: a designer body.

He would have given much to examine the body in detail, but now was not the time, so Bond went through the jeans and shirt, making doubly sure there was nothing inserted in linings or stitching. When he was satisfied, he apologized again, told her to get dressed and then call down to the concierge. She was to use exact words—that the luggage was ready in her room and in Mr. Bond's. It was to be taken straight to Mr. Bond's car.

Sukie did as she was told, and as she put down the receiver, gave a little shake of the head, "I'll do exactly as I'm told, James. You're obviously desperate, and you're also undoubtedly a professional of some kind. I'm not a fool. I like you. I'll do anything, within reason, but I also have a problem." Her voice shook slightly, as though the whole experience had unnerved her.

Bond nodded, indicating that she should tell him her problem.

"I've an old school friend in Cannobio, just along the lakeshore . . ."

"Yes, I know Cannobio, one-horse Italian holiday resort. Picturesque in a guide-booky kind of way. Not far."

"I took the liberty of telling her we'd pick her up on our way through. I was supposed to do it last night—meet her, that is. She's waiting at that rather lovely church on the lakeside—the Madonna della Pieta. Going to be there from noon onward."

"Can we put her off? Telephone her?"

She shook her head. "After I arrived, with the car problems, I telephoned the hotel where she was supposed to be staying. That was last night. She hadn't arrived. I called her again after dinner, and she was waiting there. They were booked up. She was going in search of somewhere else. You'd said we might be late setting off so I just told her to be at the Madonna della Pieta from twelve noon. I didn't think of getting her to call back . . ."

She was interrupted by the padrone himself, arriving to collect the luggage.

Bond thanked him, said they would be down in a few minutes and turned his mind to the problem. There was a lot of road to cover whatever he did, and his aim was to get safely to Salzburg and the Klinik Mozart, where there would be a certain amount of police protection in the current search for May and Moneypenny. He had no desire to go into Italy at all, and, from what he could recall of the center of Cannobio, it was the perfect place for a setup. The lakeside road, with the square in front of the Madonna della Pieta, was always busy: plenty of people, and a lot of traffic—both tourist and local, for Cannobio was a thriving industrial center as well as a lakeside paradise for holiday makers.

The area in front of the church was ideal territory for one man—or a team on a motorcycle—to make a kill. Was Sukie, knowingly or not, putting him on the spot?

"What's her name? This old school friend?" he asked.

"Norrich." She spelled it out for him. "Nannette Norrich. Everyone calls her 'Nannie,' as in babies, not goats. Norrich Petrochemicals, that's Daddy."

Bond nodded as though he had already guessed. "We'll have to leave her. She'll just have to stew. Sorry."

He took her by the elbow, firmly to let her know that he was in charge.

In the back of his head, Bond already knew that the trip to Cannobio would hold him up for an hour—thirty minutes there, and another half hour back—before he could head off toward the frontier, and Austria.

It would mean two hostages, not one. He could position them in the car to make a hit more difficult, and there was also comfort in the fact that it was *his* head that would gain the prize. Whoever struck would do it on a lonely stretch of road, or, possibly, during a night stop. It was easy enough to sever a human head. You did not even have to be very strong. A flexi-saw—like a bladed metal garrote—would do it in no time. The only thing you did need was a certain amount of privacy. Nobody would have a go in front of the Madonna della Pieta, Cannobio, on the Italian side of Lake Maggiore.

Outside, the padrone stood, at the rear of the British Racing Green Mulsanne Turbo, waiting patiently with the luggage.

Out of the corner of his eye, Bond saw Steve Quinn's man, the tall one standing above the rocks, begin to saunter casually back along the cars toward the Renault. The man did not even look in his direction, but kept his head down, as though searching for dropped coins. He was tall, with the face of a Greek statue that had been exposed to a great deal of time and weather.

Bond contrived to keep Sukie between himself and the car, reaching forward from behind her to unlock the trunk.

When the luggage was stowed, they all shook hands with a certain gravity, and he escorted Sukie to the front passenger side.

"I want you to fasten the seatbelt, then keep your hands in sight on the facia," he smiled. She smiled back, and along the line of cars the Renault grumbled into life.

Bond settled into the driving seat with engine running. "Sukie, please don't do anything stupid. I promise that I can act much faster than you. Don't make me do anything I might regret."

She smiled very prettily. "I'm the hostage. I know my place. Don't worry."

They backed out, headed up the ramp and, seven minutes later, crossed the Italian frontier with the minimum of fuss.

"If you haven't noticed, there's a car behind us," her voice quavered slightly.

"That's right." Bond gave a grim little smile. "They're babysitting us, but I don't want that kind of protection. We'll throw them off eventually."

He had told her that Nannie would have to be handled with care—not given any details, except the option that she could go on to Rome under her own steam. Plans had changed and they had to get to Salzburg in a hurry. "Leave it to her. Let her make up her own mind. Be apologetic, but try to put her off," he cautioned. "Follow me?"

She nodded.

There was a lot of action around the Madonna della Pieta when they arrived—tourists and traffic, as he had expected—but there, standing by a small suitcase, looking supremely elegant, was a very tall girl with hair the color of a moonless night pulled back into a severe bun. She wore a patterned cotton dress, which the breeze caught for a second, blowing it against her body to reveal the outline of long, slim thighs, rounded belly and well-proportioned hips. In spite of the hair, and an attempt to make her appear a Plain Jane, the body—what one could see of it—revealed possible depths that any red-blooded male would be eager to plumb.

"My, how super! A Bentley. I adore Bentleys." She grinned when Sukie called her over to the passenger side of the car.

"Nannie, meet James. We have a problem." She explained the situation, just as Bond had instructed her. All the time, he watched Nannie's face—calm, rather thin features, granny glasses, behind which a pair of dark gray eyes peered out brightly, full of intelligence. The long dark hair looked as though it had been cut by someone who should have known better, and her eyebrows were unfashionably plucked, giving the attractive features a look of almost permanent sweet expectation.

"Well, I'm easy." Nannie had a low-pitched drawl, not unpleasant, certainly not affected, but giving the impression that she did not believe a word of Sukie's tale. "It *is* a holiday after all— Rome or Salzburg—it mattereth not. Anyway, I adore Mozart."

"Are you coming with us, Nannie?" Bond felt vulnerable, out in the open, and could not allow the girls to start chattering— that could go on for hours. His voice pushed urgency into the situation.

"Of course. Wouldn't miss it for the world." Nannie had the door open, but Bond stopped her. "Luggage in the boot," he said a little sharply, then very quietly to Sukie, "hands in sight, like before. This is too important for games."

She gave a nod of understanding, placing her hands above the facia, as Bond got out and watched Nannie Norrich put her case into the trunk. "Shoulder bag as well, please." He smiled his most charming smile.

"I shall need it. On the road, I'll need it. Why . . . ?"

"Please, Nannie, be a good girl. The problems Sukie told you about are mine, and they're dangerous. I can't have *any* luggage in the car. When the time comes, I'll check your bag and let you have it back, okay?"

She gave a funny little worried turn of the head and a puzzled look, but did as she was told. The Renault, Bond noticed, was parked ahead of them, the engine idling. Good, they thought he planned to route through Italy.

"Nannie, we've only just met and I don't want you to get any ideas, but I have to be slightly indelicate," he said quietly. The trunk was still open, he could see Sukie plainly through the rear window and there were a lot of people around, but what he had to do was necessary. "Don't struggle or yell at me. I have to touch you, but be assured I'm not taking liberties. Lives are in danger."

With fast expert movements he ran his hands over her body, using fingertips and trying not to make it embarrassing for the girl. "I don't know you," he said as he went through the quick frisk, "but my life's at risk, so if you get into the car you're also in danger. As a stranger you could also be dangerous to me. Understand?"

To his surprise, she smiled at him. "Actually, I found that rather pleasant. I *don't* understand, but I still liked it. We should do it again sometime. In private."

They settled back in the car and he asked Nannie to fasten her seatbelt in the rear, telling them there was fast driving ahead.

He started the engine again and waited, both for the road traffic to clear and to be certain there was space free of pedestrians, and vehicles, behind him. When things seemed right, he slid the Bentley into reverse, spun the wheel, banged at accelerator and brake, slewing the car backward into a skid, bringing the rear around in a half circle, then roaring off, cutting between a peeping VW and a truckload of vegetables—much to the wrath of the drivers.

Through the mirror he could see the Renault in trouble and taken by surprise. He increased speed as soon as they were through the restricted zone, and began to take the bends and winds of the lakeside road at expert, if dangerous, speed.

At the frontier he told the guards that he thought they were being followed by brigands, making much of his spare passport— the diplomatic one always carried against emergencies.

The carabinieri were suitably impressed, called him *Eccellenza,* bowed to the ladies and promised to question the occupants of the Renault with vigor.

"Do you always drive like that?" Nannie hummed from the rear. "I suppose you do. You strike me as a fast-cars, horses and women kind of fellow. Action man."

Bond did not comment. Violent man, he thought, concentrating on the driving, allowing the girls to slip into talk of schooldays, parties and men.

There were some problems—particularly when the girls wished to use restrooms—but they managed it twice during the afternoon, by stopping at service areas with Bond positioning the car so that he had full view of any pay telephones, and of the restroom doors. He let them go one at a time, making pleasantly veiled threats as to what would happen to the one left in the car, should either of them do anything foolish. His own bladder had to be kept under control, but just before they started on the long, awesome mountain route that would take them into Austria, they rested together at a roadside café and had food. It was here that

Bond took the chance of leaving the girls alone.

When he returned they both looked as though butter would not melt, though they seemed surprised when he popped a couple of Benzedrine tablets with his coffee.

"We were wondering . . ." Nannie began.

"Yes?"

"We were wondering what the sleeping arrangements are going to be when we stop for the night. I mean, you obviously—for some unspecified reason—can't let us out of your sight . . ."

"You sleep in the car. I drive. There'll be no stopping at motorway hotels. This is a one-hop run . . ."

"Very Chinese," Sukie muttered.

". . . and the sooner we get to Salzburg the sooner I can release you. The local police will take charge of things after that."

"What are these *things,* James?" Again from Sukie. "Look, you've explained a little bit. We both think you're a nice guy with some pretty heavy problems. We accept that we're hostages, but we'd like to help . . ."

"I can't trust you—I can't trust anyone," Bond said soberly. "Thanks for the offer, Sukie, but truly you'd be out of your depth. I just want you here in the car until Salzburg."

Nannie spoke up, level-voiced, the tone almost one of admonition: "James, we hardly know each other, but you have to understand that, for us, this is a kind of adventure—something we only read about in books. It's obvious that you're on the side of the angels, unless our intuition's gone right up the spout. This could be routine for you, but it's so abnormal for us that it's exciting."

"We'd better get back to the car," Bond said flatly. "I've already explained to Sukie that it's really about as exciting as being attacked by a swarm of killer bees." Inside, he knew the girls were either going through a form of transference, like hostages starting to identify with their captors, or trying to establish a rapport in order to lull him into complacency. To increase chances of survival he had to remain detached; and that was not an easy option with a pair of young women as attractive and desirable as Sukie and Nannie.

Nannie gave a sigh of exasperation, and Sukie started to say something, but Bond stopped them with a movement of his hand.

"Into the car," he ordered.

They made exceptional time on the long run up through the twisting Malojapass, through St. Moritz, finally crossing into Austria at Vinadi, so that just before seven-thirty in the evening they were cruising at speed along the A12 Autobahn, having skirted Innsbruck, now heading northeast. Within the hour they would turn further east onto the A8, which would lead them to Salzburg. The day had been blazing hot, even high among the mountains, and the girls, when not indulging themselves in the trivial pursuits of their world—which ranged from haute couture to the latest scandals of their particular sets—proved not to be insensible to the rugged and incredible grandeur of the terrain through which they passed.

Bond drove with care and relentless concentration, cursing the situation in which he found himself. So beautiful was the day, so impressive the scenery, that, had things been different, the ever-changing landscape, combined with the two girls, would have made this a memorable holiday indeed.

His eyes searched the road ahead, scanning the traffic, their signals, then swiftly crossing the instruments to check speed, fuel consumption and temperature.

"Remember the silver Renault, James?" Nannie, in an almost teasing voice from the rear. "Well, I think it's behind us, moving up fast."

"Guardian angels," Bond breathed. "The devil take guardian angels."

"The plates are the same," from Sukie. "I remember them from Brissago. But I think the occupants've changed."

Bond glanced into the mirror. Sure enough, a silver Renault 25 was coming up fast, about half a mile behind them. From the mirror he could not make out the passengers. "Might have changed crews," he said. He was calm about it; after all they were only Steve Quinn's people—angered probably by being given the slip, but on guard just the same. "Let them have their day," he said, then touched the brakes and pulled into the far lane, watching from his offside wing mirror.

He was conscious of a tension between the two girls, like game that sensed the hunter. Fear suddenly seemed to flood the interior of the car, almost tangible, a scent of danger.

The road ahead was empty, ribbon straight, with grassland curving upward toward outcrops of rock and the inevitable pine and fir, abundant and thick. Bond's eyes flicked to the wing mirror again, and he glimpsed the hard, screwed-up concentration on the face of the Renault's driver.

The red dropping ball of the sun was behind them, so the silver car was using the old fighter pilot tactic—coming out of the sun. As the Bentley swung for a second, the crimson fire filled the wing mirror. The next moment, Bond was depressing the accelerator, feeling the proximity of death.

The Bentley responded as only that machine can, a surge of power, effortlessly pushing them forward. But he was a fraction late. The Renault was already almost abreast of them and going flat out.

He heard one of the girls shout, and felt a blast of air as a rear window was operated. One hand came off the wheel as he drew the ASP, dropping it into his lap, the hand moving to the row of switches that operated the electric windows. Somehow he realized that Sukie had shouted for them to get down, while Nannie Norrich had lowered her window with the individual switch.

"Onto the floor!" He heard his own voice as a second blast of air began to circulate within the car, his own offside window sliding down to the pressure of his thumb on the switch.

He heard Nannie shout from the rear, yelling, "They're going to shoot," and the distinctive barrel of a pump-action sawn-off Winchester showed, for a split second, from the rear window of the Renault.

Then came the two blasts, one sharp and from behind his right shoulder, filling the car with a film of gray mist bearing the unmistakable smell of cordite. The other was louder, but farther away, almost drowned by the engine noise, the rush of wind into the car and the ringing in his own ears.

The Mulsanne Turbo bucked to the right, as though some giant metal boot-tip had struck the rear with force; the push was accompanied by a rending, clattering noise, like stones hitting them. Then another bang from behind him.

He saw the silver car to their left, almost abreast of them, a haze of smoke being whipped from the rear where someone crouched at the window. The Winchester's barrel was trained on them.

"Down, Sukie!" he shouted, his voice rising to a scream as his own hand came up to fire through the open window—two rounds, precise and aimed toward the driver.

There was a lurching sensation, then a grinding as the sides of the two cars grated together, then drifted apart, followed by another crack from the rear of the Bentley.

They must have been touching 100 kph, and Bond knew he had almost lost control of the big car as it veered and snaked across the road. He pumped the brakes, watched the road now, touched the brakes twice more and felt the speed bleed off as the front wheels mounted the grass verge.

There was a sliding sensation, then a rocking bump as they stopped. "Out!" Bond yelled, "Out! On the far side! Use the car for cover!"

When he reached the relative safety of the car's side, he saw Sukie had followed him and was lying as though trying to push herself into the earth. Nannie, on the other hand, was crouched behind the trunk, her cotton skirt hitched up to show a stocking top and part of a white garter belt. The skirt had hooked itself onto a neat, soft leather holster, on the inside of her thigh, and she held a small .22 pistol very professionally, in a two-handed grip, pointing across the trunk.

"The law would be very angry," Nannie shouted, "they're coming back. Wrong side of the motorway."

"What the hell . . . ?" Bond began.

"Get your gun and shoot at them," Nannie laughed. "Come on, Master James, Nannie knows best."

6

THE NUB

Over the long snout of the Bentley, Bond saw the truth. He had no time to go into the whys and wherefores of Nannie's professional actions, her gun or how he had missed finding it.

The silver Renault was streaking toward them, up the slow lane, moving in the wrong direction, regardless of two other careening cars and a lorry, all three of which weaved and screeched over the wide autobahn to avoid collision.

"The tires," Nannie said coolly. "Go for the tires."

"*You* go for the tires," Bond snapped, angry at being given instructions by the girl. He had his own method of stopping the car, which was now almost on top of them.

In the fraction of time before he fired, a host of things crossed his mind. The Renault had originally contained a two-man team. When the hit had come, there were three of them: one in the back with the Winchester, the driver and a back-up who seemed to be using a high-powered revolver. Somehow the shotgun-wielding killer had disappeared, but the one in the passenger seat now had the Winchester. The driver's side window was open, and in a fanatical act of lunacy, the passenger seemed to be leaning across the driver, to fire the Winchester as they came rapidly closer to the Mulsanne Turbo, which was slewed, like a beached whale, just off the hard shoulder of the road.

Bond looked straight over the Guttersnipe sight on the ASP— three long bright grooves that gave a marksman the perfect aiming coordinates by showing a triangle of yellow when it was on target.

He was on target now: aiming not at the tires but at the petrol tank, for the ASP was loaded with those most horrific projectiles, Glaser Slugs—prefragmented bullets, each containing hundreds of number 12 shot suspended in liquid Teflon. The effect of an impact from just one of these appalling little bullets was devastating, for the projectile would penetrate skin, bone, tissue or metal, before almost literally exploding the mass of tiny steel balls. They would cut a man in half at a few paces, take out a leg or arm and certainly ignite petrol in a vehicle's tank.

Bond began to take up the first pressure on the trigger, and, as the rear of the Renault came fully into the triangle of his sights, he squeezed hard. As he got the two shots away he was conscious of the double crack from his left—Nannie giving the tires hell.

Several things happened quickly. The nearside front tire crossed the great divide in a terrible burning and shredding of rubber— Bond remembered thinking that she had been very lucky to get a couple of puny .22 shots close to the inner section of the tire.

The car began to slew inward, toppling slightly, looking as though it would cartwheel straight into the Bentley, but the driver struggled with wheel and brakes, and the silver car just about stayed in line, hopelessly doomed, but running fast and straight toward the hard shoulder.

This all happened in a millisecond, for, as the tire disintegrated, so the two Glaser Slugs from the ASP scorched through the bodywork and into the petrol tank.

Almost in slow motion, the Renault seemed to continue on its squealing, tippling way. The effect of the Glasers appeared to take minutes, but it happened just as the car had passed the rear of the Bentley—a long, thin sheet of flame, like natural gas being burned off, hissing from the rear of the car. There was even time to notice that the flame was tinged with blue before the whole rear end of the Renault became a rumbling, irregular, boiling, growing crimson ball.

The car now began its cartwheel, and was, in fact, a burning, twisted wreck—a hundred yards or so to the rear of the Bentley— by the time the noise reached them: a great hiss and whump, followed by a screaming of rubber and metal as the vehicle went through its spectacular death throes.

Nobody moved for a second. Then Bond reacted. Two or three cars were approaching the scene, and he was in no mood to be involved with the police at this stage.

"What kind of shape are we in?" he called.

"Dented, a lot of holes in the bodywork, but the wheels seem okay." Nannie was at the other side of the car. She unhitched her skirt from the garter belt, showing a fragment of white lace as she did so. "There's a very nasty scrape down this side. Stem to stern."

Bond looked towards Sukie, asking if she was okay. "Shaken, but undamaged, I think."

"In!" Bond commanded crisply. "Into the car. Both of you," as he dived toward the driving seat, conscious of at least one car, containing people in checked shirts, floppy hats and the usual impediments of tourists, drawing up cautiously to the rear of the burning wreckage.

He twisted the key, almost viciously, in the ignition. The huge engine throbbed into life immediately, and, without ceremony, he knocked off the main brake with his left hand, slid into drive and smoothly gunned the Mulsanne Turbo back onto the motorway.

The traffic remained sparse, giving Bond the opportunity to run through checks on the car's engine and handling. There was no loss of fuel, oil or hydraulic pressure; he went steadily up the steps, through the gears and back again. Brakes appeared unaffected. The cruise control went in and came out normally, while whatever damage had been done to the body did not appear to have affected either suspension or handling.

After five minutes he was satisfied the car was relatively undamaged. There was, he did not doubt, a good deal of penetration from the couple of Winchester blasts.

The car, with its damage, would now be a sitting target for the Austrian police who, like the forces of most Western countries, were not enamored of shoot-outs between cars on their relatively safe autobahns—particularly when one of the vehicles, and its occupants, ends up incinerated.

There was need to reach a telephone quite quickly, alert London and get them to call the Austrian dogs off. Bond was also concerned about the possible fate of Steve Quinn's team.

Something else nagged at his mind. Nannie Norrich swam, an image, into his head—the lush thigh, and the .22 pistol being expertly handled.

"I think you'd better let me have the armory, Nannie," he said quietly, hardly turning his head.

"Oh, no, James. No, James. No," she sang, quite prettily.

"I don't like women roving around with guns, especially in the current situation, and within this car. How in heaven's name did I miss it anyway?"

"Because, while you're obviously a pro, you're also a bit of a gent, James. You failed to grope the inside of my thighs when you frisked me in Cannobio."

He recalled her flirtatious manner, and the cheeky smile. "So, I suppose I now pay for the error. Are you going to tell me it's pointing at the back of my head?"

"Actually it's pointing toward my own left knee, back where it belongs. Not the most comfortable place to have a weapon." She paused. "Well, not *that* kind of weapon anyway."

A sign came up indicating a picnic area, ahead and to their

right. Bond slowed, pulling off the road, down a track through dense fir trees and into a clearing. Rustic tables and benches stood in the center of the clearing. There was not a picnicker in sight.

To one side—praise heaven—a neat, clean and unvandalized telephone booth awaited them.

Bond brought the car to a halt in the shade of the trees, turning it so that they could make a quick exit if necessary. He cut the engine, clicked off his seatbelt and turned to face Nannie Norrich, holding out his right hand, palm upward. "The gun, Nannie. I have to make a couple of important calls, and I'm in enough danger already. Just give me the gun."

Nannie smiled at him, a gentle, fond smile. "You'd have to take it from me, James, and that might not be as easy as you imagine. Look, I used that weapon to help *you*. Sukie's given me my orders. I *am* to cooperate—to assist—and I can assure you that, had she instructed otherwise, you would have known it within a very short time of my joining you in the car."

"*Sukie's* ordered you?" Bond felt lost.

"She's my boss. For the time being anyway. I take orders from her, and . . ."

Sukie Tempesta put a hand on Bond's arm. "I think I should explain, James. Nannie *is* an old school friend. She is also president of NUB."

"And what the devil's the NUB?" Bond was cross now.

"Norrich Universal Bodyguards."

"What?"

"Minders," said Nannie, still very cheerful.

"Minders?" For a second he was incredulous.

"Minders, as in people who look after other people for money. Minders. Protectors. Heavies." Nannie began again. "James, NUB is an all-women outfit. Staffed by a special kind of woman. My girls are exceptionally trained—weaponry, karate, all the martial arts, driving, flying, you name it, we do it. Truly, we're good, and with an exceptional clientele."

"And the Principessa Sukie Tempesta is among that clientele?"

"Naturally. I try to do that particular job myself whenever possible."

"Your people didn't do it very well the other evening in Belgium," Bond said sharply. "At the filling station. I ought to charge commission."

Nannie sighed, "It *was* unfortunate . . ."

"It was also my fault," added Sukie. "Nannie wanted to pick me up in Brussels, when her deputy had to leave. I said I'd make it without any problems. I was wrong."

"Of course you were wrong. Look, James, you've got problems. So has Sukie, mainly because she's a multimillionaire who insists on living in Rome for most of the year—and that's damned dangerous. Kidnappings of the wealthy are daily happenings, so she's a sitting duck. Now, you go and make your telephone calls. Just trust me. Trust us. Trust NUB."

Eventually Bond shrugged, took the keys out of the ignition, and climbed from the car, locking the two girls in behind him.

After retrieving the CC500 from the trunk, he went over to the telephone booth, made the slightly more complex attachments needed for pay phones and dialed the operator, placing a call to the Resident's number in Vienna.

The conversation was short and to the point, ending with the Resident agreeing to fix the Austrian police, and even arranging for a patrol to come out to where he was parked—if possible with the senior officer in charge of the May/Moneypenny kidnapping. "Sit tight," he counseled. "They should be with you in an hour or so."

Bond hung up, redialed the operator and within seconds was speaking to the duty officer at the Regent's Park HQ in London.

"Rome's two men are dead," the officer told him, without emotion. "Found shot through the back of the head in a ditch. Stay on the line, M wants a word."

A moment later his Chief's voice sounded, gruff, in his ear. "Bad business, James." M only called him James in moments of great stress.

"*Very* bad, sir. Moneypenny as well as my housekeeper."

"Yes, and whoever has them is trying to strike a hard bargain."

"Sir?"

"Nobody's told you?"

"I haven't seen anyone to speak to, sir."

There was a long pause. Then, "The women will be returned,

unharmed, within forty-eight hours in exchange for you."

"Ah," said Bond, "I thought it might be something like that. The Austrian police know of this?"

"I gather they have some details."

"Then I'll hear it all when they arrive. I understand they're on their way. Please tell Rome I'm sorry about his two boys."

"Take care, 007. We don't give in to terrorist demands in the Service. You know that policy, and you must abide by it. No heroics. No throwing your life away. You are not, repeat *not* to comply."

"There might be no other way, sir."

"There's always another way. Find it; and find it soon." He closed the line.

Bond unhooked the CC500. Already he knew that his life was possibly forfeit for those of May and Moneypenny. If there *was* no other way, then he would have to die. He also knew that he would go on to the bitter end, taking risks, but in the last resort . . . well, they would have to see. Slowly he walked back to the car.

It took exactly one hour and thirty-six minutes for the two police cars to arrive: just time enough for Bond to hear how Nannie, always good at sports, in spite of what she called "my odd eyeballs," had put her natural talents to good use by founding the thriving Norrich Universal Bodyguards—"The nub of the matter," as she said.

In five years she had established branches in London, Paris, Rome, Los Angeles and New York, yet never once had she advertized the service. "If I did, there would be people who'd imagine we were call girls. It's been a word-of-mouth thing from the start. What's more, it's fun."

Bond wondered why he, or his Service, had never heard of them. NUB appeared to be an excellently kept secret, operating within the enclosed confines of the ultra-rich. "We don't usually get spotted," she told him. "Men out with a girl minder look as though they're merely on a date, and when I go to some function with somebody like Sukie we always make certain we both have safe men with us." She laughed. "I've seen poor Sukie through two dramatic love affairs in the last year alone."

Sukie opened her mouth in apparent retort to Nannie's remark, but at that moment, the police arrived—two cars, unheralded by klaxons, sweeping into the glade in a cloud of dust.

There were four uniformed officers in the second car and three in the first, plus another in civilian clothes. The plainclothed man unfolded himself from the rear of the first car and stretched, as though sitting in the vehicle had done terrible things to his long bones.

He was immensely tall but immaculately dressed. The latter was necessary, for his whole frame was built out of proportion and only an expert tailor could possibly make him even half presentable. His arms were long, ending with very small hands that seemed to hang almost down to his knees, like an ape's, while his face, crowned with a gleaming full head of hair, was too large for the oddly thin shoulders.

He had the apple cheeks of a fat farmer and large horn-rimmed spectacles that gave him an owlish look, while a pair of great jug-handle ears made the head almost aerodynamic. The man could be taken for a freak, a walking joke.

"Oh, my God," Nannie's whisper filled the interior of the car with a shiver of fear. "Put your hands in sight. Let them see your hands." It was something Bond had already done instinctively.

"*Der Haken!*" Nannie whispered again.

"The hook?" Bond hardly moved his lips as he queried her German.

"Real name's Inspector Heinrich Osten. Well over retirement age and stuck as an inspector, but he's the most ruthless, corrupt bastard in Austria." She still whispered, as though the man, who had now started to shamble toward the Bentley, could hear every word. "They say nobody's ever dared ask for his retirement because he literally knows where all the bodies're buried."

"He knows you?" Bond asked.

"Never met him. But he's on our files. The story is that as a very, *very,* young man he was an ardent National Socialist. They call him Der Haken because he favored a butcher's hook as a torture implement. If we're dealing with this joker, James, don't trust him, don't believe him and, for God's sake, don't be taken in by him."

Inspector Osten had reached the Bentley, and now stood, backed by two uniformed men, on Bond's side of the car. He stooped, as though folding his body straight from the waist—Bond had the mental picture of an oil pump—and waggled his small fingers outside the driver's window. The fingers rippled, as though he was trying to attract the attention of a baby.

Bond activated the window.

"Herr Bond?" The voice was high-pitched, low in volume.

"Yes. Bond. James Bond."

"Good. We are to give you protection to Salzburg. Please to get out of your car for a moment."

Bond opened the door, climbed out and looked up at the beaming, polished-apple cheeks, and grasped the obscenely small hand, outstretched in greeting. It was like touching the dry skin of a snake.

"I am in charge of the case, Herr Bond. The case of the missing ladies—a good mystery title, *ja?*"

There was silence. Bond was not prepared to laugh at May's or Moneypenny's predicament.

"So," the inspector became serious again. "I am pleased to meet you. My name is Osten. Heinrich Osten." His mouth opened in a grimace that revealed blackened teeth. "Some people like to call me by another name. Der Haken. I do not know why, but it sticks. Probably it is because I hook out criminals." He laughed again. "I think, perhaps, I might even have hooked you, Herr Bond. The two of us have much to talk about. A great deal. I think I shall ride in your motor so we can talk. The ladies can go in the other cars."

"No!" Nannie objected violently.

"Oh, but yes." Osten reached for the rear door and tugged it open.

Already a uniformed man was half helping and half dragging Sukie from the passenger side.

The girls went, kicking and screaming, to the other cars. Bond hoped Nannie had the sense not to reveal, or use, the .22.

Osten gave his apple smile again. "We shall talk better without the tattle of women, I think. In any case, Herr Bond, you do not wish them to hear me charge you with being an accessory to kidnapping and, possibly, murder, do you?"

THE HOOK

BOND DROVE WITH exaggerated care. For one thing, the man who now sat next to him gave off incredibly sinister vibrations of danger. It was like being close to an unstable bomb. The grotesque Inspector Osten had about him an aura of sweating gelignite, mixed with an odd sensation of latent insanity. Bond had felt the presence of evil many times in his life, but now it was as strong as he could ever recall.

Osten smelled of something else, and it took time to identify the old-fashioned bay rum that he obviously used in large quantities on his thatch of hair.

They were several kilometers along the road before the silence was broken. "Murder and kidnapping," Osten said quietly, almost to himself.

"Blood sports," Bond answered placidly, and the policeman gave a low rumbling chuckle.

"Blood sports is good, Mr. Bond. Very good."

"And you're going to charge me with them?"

Once more the laugh. "I can have you for murder. You and the two young women. How do you say in England? On toast, I can have you."

"I think you should check with your superiors before you try anything like that. In particular your own Security and Intelligence Department."

Osten gave a short, rough, contemptuous laugh. "Those skulking, prying idiots have little jurisdiction over me, Mr. Bond . . ."

"You're a law unto yourself, Inspector?"

There was a slow sigh, which seemed to go on for a long time. Then, "In this instance I *am* the law, and that's what matters. You have been concerned for two English ladies who have disappeared from a clinic . . ."

"One is a Scottish lady, Inspector."

"Whatever." He raised a tiny hand, like that of a doll, grafted onto the long stump of arm, an action at once dismissive and full of derision. "You are the only outside key; the linking factor in this small mystery; the man who knew both victims. It is natural, then, that I must question you—interrogate you—thoroughly regarding these disappearances . . ."

"I've yet to learn the details myself. One of the ladies is my housekeeper."

"The younger one?" The question was asked in a particularly unpleasant manner, and Bond replied with some vehemence.

"No, Inspector, the elderly Scottish lady. She's been with me for many years. The younger lady is a colleague, and I think you should forget about interrogations until you hear from people of slightly higher status than yourself."

"There are other questions—bringing a firearm into the country, a public shoot-out that caused not only the deaths of three men, but also great danger to innocent people using the autobahn."

"With respect, the three men were trying to kill *me,* and the two ladies who were in my car."

Osten nodded, but it was a gesture that contained reservations. "We shall see. In Salzburg we shall see." Casually, the man they called the Hook leaned over, his long arm stabbing forward, like a reptile, the tiny hand moving like a rock crab. The inspector was more than just very experienced, Bond thought, he also had a highly developed intuition, for, within seconds, the little hands had removed both the ASP and the baton from their respective holsters.

"I am always uncomfortable with a man armed like this." The apple cheeks puffed, like a balloon blowing up, into a red, shiny smile.

"If you take my wallet, you'll find that I have an international licence to carry the gun." Bond sat, grim, behind the wheel.

"We shall see." Osten gave another sigh, repeating, "In Salzburg we shall see."

It was late when they reached the city, and Osten began to give him terse instructions—a left here, then a right and another right. Bond caught a glimpse of the River Salzach, the bridges and, behind him, the old town, with the Hohensalzburg castle—once the stronghold of the prince-archbishops—standing, floodlit on its great lump of dolomite rock, above the town and river.

They were heading for the new town, which was no surprise, and Bond quite expected to be guided towards police headquarters. Instead, he found himself driving through a maze of streets, past a pair of very modern apartment blocks and down into an underground car park.

The other two cars, which they appeared to have lost on the outskirts of the city, waited, parked neatly with a space between them for the Bentley. The police were still sitting in their vehicles, and the girls had been separated, one to each car.

An uneasy sensation, like a facial tic, flashed through Bond's nervous system. He had been assured by the Resident that the police were there to get him safely into Salzburg. Now, he was faced not only with a very unpleasant and probably corrupt policeman, but also with what was obviously some plan to bring him, and the girls, into a possibly unofficial building—for he had no doubt that the car park belonged to the second of the modern blocks of luxury apartments.

"Lower my window," Osten spoke quietly. One of the policemen had come over to the passenger side of the Bentley, and another stood forward of the vehicle. The second man had a machine pistol tucked into his hip, the evil eye of the muzzle pointing directly at Bond.

Now, through the open window, Der Haken muttered a few rapid, commanding sentences in German to the officer beside the car. His voice was pitched so low, and his German, tinged with that odd high-piping Viennese accent, was so rapid that Bond caught only a few words—"The women first," then a mutter, "separate rooms . . . under guard at all times . . . until we have everything sorted out . . ." He ended with a question, which Bond did not catch at all. The answer, however, was clear.

"You are to telephone him as soon as possible."

Heinrich Osten nodded, the oversized head like that of a souvenir doll designed to sit in the rear of a car window. He told the uniformed man to carry on. The one with the machine pistol did not move.

"We sit, quietly, for a few minutes." The head turned, red cheeks puffed in a smile.

"I think, as you have only hinted at possible charges against

me, I should be allowed to speak to my embassy in Vienna."
Bond clipped out the words, as though they were parade ground
orders.

"All in good time. There are formalities." Osten was terrifyingly
calm, sitting with hands folded, as one who has complete command
of the situation.

"Formalities? What *formalities?*" Bond shouted. "People have
rights. In particular, I am on an official assignment. I demand
to—"

Osten gave the hint of a nod toward the machine-pistol-toting
policeman. "You can demand nothing, Mr. Bond. Surely you
understand that. You are a stranger in a strange land. By the very
fact that I am the law—and you have an Uzi trained on you—
your rights are forfeit. No demands can be met."

He saw the two girls being hustled from the other cars. They
were kept well apart and both looked considerably frightened.
Sukie did not even turn her head in the direction of the Bentley,
but Nannie glanced toward him. In a fragment of time the message
was clear in her eyes. She was still armed and biding her time.
A remarkably tough lady, he thought: tough, and attractive in a
scrubbed kind of way, for—on purpose, he presumed—she made
no concession to glamor, with the granny glasses and no-nonsense
hair.

The women disappeared from Bond's line of vision, and a
moment later Osten prodded him in the ribs, with his own ASP.
"Leave the keys in the car, Mr. Bond. It has to be moved from
here before the morning. Just get out, showing your hands the
whole time. My officer with the Uzi is a little nervous."

Bond did as he was bidden. It felt quite cool in the almost bare
underground park—eerie and smelling, like all car parks, of gas-
oline, rubber and oil.

The man with the machine pistol motioned to him to walk
between the other cars, through a small exit passage and toward
what appeared to be a brick wall. Osten made a slight movement,
and Bond caught sight of a flat remote controller in his left hand.
Without even a click, a door-sized section of the brickwork moved
silently inward, and then slid to one side, revealing steel elevator
doors. Somewhere, far away in the car park, an engine fired,
throbbed and settled as a vehicle made its exit.

The elevator arrived with a brief sigh, and Bond was signaled to enter. The three men stood, silent, as the lift cage made its noiseless upward journey. The doors slid open and, again, Bond was ushered forward, this time into a passageway, lined with modern prints, a thick pile carpet underfoot. A second later they were in a large apartment of obvious luxury and impeccable taste.

The carpets were Turkish, and of value; the furnishings modern, but obviously custom-built—wood, steel, glass and expensive fabrics—while the walls sported paintings and drawings by Piper, Sutherland, Bonnard, Gross and Hockney. The entrance passage led to a large, open room, with great glass windows, firmly shut, but disclosing a wide balcony. To the left an archway revealed the dining area and kitchen, while two other, lower arches faced them showing only long passages studded with gleaming white doors. A police officer stood in each of the passages, as though on guard.

Through the huge glass windows, you could just glimpse the floodlit Hohensalzburg, and Osten must have seen Bond's head turn to look, for he quickly commanded that the curtains be closed. Light blue velvet slid electronically on soundless rails.

"Nice little place you have, for a police inspector," Bond said.

"Ah, my friend. Would it were mine. I have only borrowed it for this one evening."

Bond nodded, trying to indicate this was obvious, if only because of the style and elegance. He turned to face the inspector, and began speaking rapidly. "Now, sir. I appreciate what you've told me, but you must know that the embassy, and officers of the department I represent, have already given instructions, and received assurances from your own people. You say I have no right to demand anything, but you make a grave error there. In fact I have the right to demand everything."

Der Haken looked at him glassy-eyed, then gave a distinct chuckle. "If you were alive, Mr. Bond. Yes, if you were still alive you would have the right; while I would have the duty to cooperate if I were also alive. Unhappily we are both dead men."

Bond scowled, puzzled, though the first glimmer of truth was starting to force itself into his head.

"The problem is actually yours," the policeman continued, "for you *really* are a dead man."

Osten, smiling, glanced around him. "I shall be living in this kind of world very shortly. A good place for a ghost, yes?"

"Enchanting; and what kind of place will I be haunting?"

Any trace of humanity disappeared from the policeman's face. The muscles turned to hard rock, and the glassy eyes broke and splintered. Even the apple cheeks seemed to lose color and become sallow. "The grave, Mr. Bond. You will be haunting the cold, cold grave. You will be nowhere. Nothing. It will be as though you had never existed." His small hand flicked up so that he could glance at his wristwatch, and he turned to the man with the Uzi, sharply ordering him to turn on the television. "The late news will be starting any moment." Still no humor. "My death should already have been reported. Yours will be announced as probable—though it will be more than probable before dawn. Please sit down and watch. I think you'll agree that my improvisation has been brilliant, for I had only a very short time to set things up."

Bond slumped into a chair, half his mind on the chances of dealing with the policeman and his accomplices, the other half working out what had been planned and why.

There were commercials on the big color screen. Attractive Austrian girls stood against mountain scenery and told the world of the essential value of a sun barrier cream; a young man arrived, hatless, from the air, climbed from his light aircraft cockpit and said the view was *wunderschön* but even more *wunderschön* when you used a certain kind of camera to capture it; while a badly dubbed American advertisement extolled the value of a preparation for hemorrhoids.

The news graphics filled the screen, and a serious brunette appeared. The lead story was about a shooting and tragedy on the A8 autobahn. One car, carrying seemingly innocent tourists, had been fired at and crashed in flames—the pictures showed the recognizable wreckage of the silver Renault, surrounded by police and ambulances. The young woman, now looking very grave, appeared again to say that the horror had been compounded by the deaths of five police officers in a freak accident as they sped from Salzburg to the scene of the shooting. One of the police cars had gone out of control, and was hit, broadside on, by the other. Both cars had skidded into woodland and caught fire.

There was another series of pictures showing the remains of the two cars. Then Inspector Heinrich Osten's official photograph came up in black and white, and the newsperson informed Austria that the country had lost one of its most efficient and long-serving officers in this disaster. The inspector had been traveling in the second car, and his body, like those of his companions, was incinerated beyond identification.

Next, Bond saw his own photograph, and the number plate of the Bentley Mulsanne Turbo. He was a British diplomat, traveling on private business, probably with two young women—unidentified—and was wanted for questioning regarding the original shoot-out. A statement from the embassy said he had telephoned appealing for help, but they feared he might have been affected by stress and run amok. "He has been under great strain during the last few days," a bland embassy spokesman told a television reporter. So the Service and Foreign Office had decided to deny him. Well, that was standard. The car, diplomat and young women had disappeared, and there were fears for their lives. Police would resume the search at daybreak, but the car could easily have gone off one of the mountain roads. The worst was expected.

Der Haken began to laugh. "You see how simple it all is, Mr. Bond? When they find your car, smashed to pieces at the bottom of a ravine—probably sometime tomorrow—the search will be over. There will be three mutilated bodies inside."

The full impact of the inspector's plan had struck home. "And mine will be minus its head, I presume?" Bond asked calmly.

"Naturally." He scowled. "It would appear that you know what's going on."

"I know that, somehow, you've managed to murder five of your colleagues . . ."

The tiny hand came up. "No! No! Not my colleagues, Mr. Bond. Tramps, vagrants. Scum. Yes, we put an end to some scum—"

"With two extra police cars?"

"With the two original police cars. The ones down in the garage are the fakes. We have kept a pair of white VWs, complete with detachable police decals and plates, for a long while, on the off chance that the time would come when I might need them. The moment arrived suddenly."

"Yesterday?"

"When I discovered the true reason for the kidnapping of your friends—and the reward. Yesterday. I have means. Ways and means to contact people. Once the ransom demand was clear I made inquiries, and came up with . . ."

"The Head Hunt."

"Precisely. You're very well informed. Those who are offering the very large prize for what appears to be the second-most-important piece of your anatomy gave me the impression that you were in the dark—that is correct? In the dark?"

Bond nodded. "For a late starter, Inspector, you seem to be well organized," he said.

"Ach! Organized!" The polished cheeks blossomed with unpleasant pride. "When you have spent most of your life being ready to move at short notice, you make certain you are ready to go, and have ways, means, papers, friends, transport."

Obviously the man was very sure of himself, as well he might be with Bond caught in a building high above Salzburg, which had been his territory for a long time. He was also expansive. "I always knew the moment for wealth and personal escape would come through something like a blackmail or kidnapping case. The petty criminals could never supply me with the kind of money I really need to be independent. If I was able to do a private deal, in, as I have said, a blackmail or kidnapping case, then my last years were secure. Though never, even in my craziest dreams, did I expect the luck and riches that have come with you, Herr Bond." He beamed, like a malicious and evil child. "In my time here I have made sure that my personal team had the correct incentives. Now they have a great and always good reason for helping me and moving with me. They're not really uniformed men, of course. They are my squad of detectives. But they would die for me . . ."

"Or for the money," Bond said coldly. "They might even dispose of *you* for the money."

Der Haken growled a laugh. "You have to be up early in the morning to catch an old bird like me, Herr Bond. They could try to kill me, I suppose, but I doubt it. What I do not doubt is that they will help me to dispose of you." He rose. "You will excuse me, I have an important telephone call to make."

Bond lifted a hand. "Inspector! One favor! The girls are here?"

"Naturally."

"They have nothing to do with me. A chance meeting. They're uninvolved, so I ask you to let them go."

Der Haken did not even look at him, muttering, "Impossible," as he strode off down one of the passageways.

The man with the Uzi smiled at Bond over the barrel, then spoke in bad English, "He is very clever, Der Haken, yes? Always he promised us that, one day, there would be a way to make us all rich. Now he says we shall all be sitting in sunshine and luxury soon. There will be women." His smile turned into a leer, and Bond thought how easy it was to manipulate men with the glint of fairy gold. Like as not, Osten would see his four accomplices at the bottom of some ravine before he made off with the reward— if he ever got the reward. In German, he asked the Uzi-holder how they had concocted a plan so quickly.

It appeared that they had been working on the kidnapping at the Klinik Mozart. There were various telephone calls. Suddenly the inspector disappeared for about an hour. On his return he was jubilant. He had brought them all to this apartment and explained the situation. All they had to do was catch a man called Bond. Once they had him, the kidnapping would be over—only there was a bonus. The people who owned this very apartment would see the women returned to the Klinik *and* provide a huge amount of money for Herr Bond's head.

"The inspector kept calling in to headquarters," the man told him. "He was trying to find out where you were. When he discovered, we left in the cars. We were already on the way when the radio call told us you were waiting off the A8. There had been shooting and a car was destroyed. He thinks on his feet, the inspector. We picked up five vagrants, from the worst area of the town, and drove them to the place where we keep the other cars. The rest was easy. We had uniforms with the cars; the vagrants were drunk, and easy to make completely unconscious. The accident was simple to stage. Then we came on to pick you up." He was not certain of the next moves in the game but knew his chief would get the money; and, at that moment, Der Haken returned.

"It is all arranged," he smiled. "I fear I shall have to lock you in one of the rooms, like the girls, Herr Bond. But only for an hour or two. I have a visitor. When my visitor has gone we will all go for a short drive into the mountains. The Head Hunt is almost over."

Bond nodded, thinking to himself that the Head Hunt was *not* almost over. There were always ways. He now had to find a way—and quickly—to get himself and the girls out of Der Haken's clutches. The grotesque Inspector Osten was gesturing with the ASP, indicating that Bond should head down the righthand passageway.

Bond took a step toward the arch, then stopped. "Two questions—last requests, if you like . . ."

"The women have to go," Osten said quietly. "I cannot keep witnesses."

"And I would do the same in your shoes. I understand. No, my questions are merely to ease my own mind. First, who were the men in the Renault—they were obviously taking part in this bizarre hunt for my head? I'd like to know."

"Union Corse, so I understand." Der Haken was in a hurry, agitated, as though his visitor would arrive at any moment.

"And what exactly happened to my housekeeper and Miss Moneypenny?"

"Happened? They were kidnapped."

"Yes, but the events. How did it take place?"

The policeman gave an irritated snarl, "I haven't got time to go into details now. They were kidnapped. You do not need to know anything else." He gave Bond a light push, heading him in the direction of the passage.

They came to a door—third on the right. Osten unlocked it, and almost threw Bond inside. He heard the key turn and the lock thud home.

It was a guest bedroom: bright, with a single modern four-poster, more expensive prints, an armchair, dressing table and built-in wardrobe. The single window was draped with heavy and expensive cream curtains.

He moved quickly, first checking the window. He appeared to be at the side of the building, and thought the long balcony off the main room probably ran around the angle of the wall, for the casement window looked out on to a narrow section of balcony—almost certainly an offshoot of the large main terrace.

The window glass was thick and unbreakable. The locks were high-security, and while not completely beyond him, would take time to remove. Already he realized an assault on the door was out of the question. The lock had been Chubb—a deadlock—not easy to manipulate without a great deal of noise, and the only tools hidden on him were small. At a pinch he might just do the window, but what then? He was at least six stories above ground, unarmed, and without any aids to assist a climb down a well-lit apartment block.

He checked the wardrobe, which, like every drawer in the place, was empty. As he did so, a series of sharp rings came from far away in the main area of the flat. The visitor had arrived—Tamil Rahani's emissary, he supposed, certainly someone of authority within SPECTRE. Time was running out, so it would have to be the window.

Oddly, for a policeman, Osten had left him with his belt. Thank heaven, for there, sewn carefully, and almost undetectably, between the thick leather strips was a long, thin multipurpose tool, built like a very slim Swiss Army knife. Fashioned in toughened steel, it contained a whole set of miniature tools ranging from screwdrivers and picklocks to a tiny battery and connectors that could, in emergency, be used in conjunction with three small explosive charges, the size and thickness of a fingernail, hidden in the casing.

The Toolkit had been designed by the Armorer's—Major Boothroyd's—brilliant assistant in Q Branch, Anne Reilly, known to all within the Regent's Park Headquarters as Q'ute. Now Bond silently blessed her ingenuity as he set to work on the security locks, which were screwed tightly into the metal frame of the casement.

There were two, plus the actual lock on the window handle, and the first took a good ten minutes to remove. At this rate he had at least another twenty minutes' work—possibly more—and he guessed that kind of time was not at his disposal.

He worked on, blistering and grazing his fingers, knowing the alternative—trying to blow out the Chubb deadlock on the door—was of no value, for they would cut him down almost before he could reach the passage.

From time to time he stopped, standing to listen for any noise that might indicate action from within the apartment. Not a sound reached him, and he finally disposed of the second lock. All that remained was the main window catch, and he had just started to work on it when a blaze of light came on outside. Somebody in the main room had switched on the terrace balcony lights, one of which, he now saw, was bracketed to the wall just outside this particular window.

He still could hear nothing—the place probably had some sound-proofing in the walls, while the windows were so toughened and thick that little exterior noise would seep through. After a few seconds, his eyes adjusted to the new light, and he was able to continue his attack on the main lock. Five minutes passed and he only managed to get one screw away. He stopped, leaned against the wall and decided to have a go at the lock mechanism itself, which held down the catch and handle that would at least lead him to the freedom of the balcony.

He tried three different picklocks before hitting on the right one. There was a sharp click as the bar was withdrawn, and a glance at his Rolex told him the whole business had, incredibly, taken over forty-five minutes. There could be very little time left, and he had no firm plan in mind once he reached the terrace.

Quietly, Bond lifted the handle and pulled the window in toward him. There was no squeak, as the hinges were obviously well-oiled, and he was able to draw the small, doorlike window noise-lessly into the room. A chill blast of air hit him, and Bond took several deep breaths to clear his head as he stood, ears straining for any sound that might come from the well-lit terrace out of sight, around the corner to his right.

Silence.

The whole thing was odd. Time must now really be trickling out for Der Haken, the crooked police officer who had somehow managed to become a late entrant for this macabre chase, the object of which was, literally, Bond's own head.

It had long been obvious that one of the competitors was looking out for himself, watching, lurking and waiting for the moment to strike—carefully taking out the opposition as he went along. But Der Haken had arrived, unexpectedly, on the scene and, almost certainly, with an offer SPECTRE's leader, Rahani, could not refuse. Among the professional terrorist, criminal and espionage organizations, Osten was the wild card, the joker—the outsider who had suddenly solved SPECTRE's problems.

Carefully, making no noise, Bond eased his way through the window and pressed against the wall. Still no sound. Carefully, he peered around the angle to view the wide terrace, high above Salzburg—a terrace complete with lamps, flowers and white-painted garden furniture. Even Bond took in a quick, startled breath as he looked at the scene.

The lamps were lit, the panorama of the new and old towns twinkled as a beautiful backdrop. The furniture was neatly positioned—as were the bodies.

Der Haken's four accomplices had been laid out in a row between the white wrought-iron chairs, each man with the top of his head blown away—the blood stippling the furnishings and walls, seeping out over the flagstones set into the thick concrete balcony.

The long series of windows leading into the main room had been opened, and above them huge pots of geraniums hung, scarlet, on hooks embedded in the wall. One of the pots had been removed. In its place hung a rope, which ended in a reinforced small loop. To the loop, a long, sharp butcher's hook was attached, and from the great spike of the hook, Der Haken himself had been hung.

Bond wondered when he had last witnessed a sight as revolting as this. The policeman's hands and feet were tied together, while the point of the hook had been inserted into his throat. It was long enough to have penetrated through the roof of the mouth, to exit straight through the left eye. Someone had taken great trouble to see that the big, gangling and ungainly man had suffered slowly and unmercifully. If the old Nazi stories were true, then whoever had done this knew Inspector Heinrich Osten's death to be poetic justice.

The body, still dripping blood, swung slightly in the breeze, the neck almost visibly stretching as it moved, and what was left of the face contorted in horrible agony.

Bond swallowed and stepped toward the window. As he did so, there came a strange, dramatic background sound, mingling with the creak of rope on hook. From across the street, a group of rehearsing musicians began to play. Mozart, naturally—Bond thought it was the somber opening of Piano Concerto no. 20, but his knowledge of Mozart was limited. At the same moment, from further down the street, came the sound of an experienced jazz trumpeter—a busker probably, playing as though shaking his musical fist at the godlike composition of the great Mozart.

It was an odd counterpoint—the precise notes of a Mozart concerto mingling with the old 1930s "Big House Blues." Bond wondered if this was mere coincidence.

8

UNDER DISCIPLINE

Bond NEEDED TIME to think, but standing on the terrace, in the midst of the carnage, was not the best way to concentrate. It was now three o'clock in the morning and, apart from the music floating from below, the city of Salzburg was silent—a glitter of lights, with the outline of mountains showing pitch black against the dark navy sky.

He walked back into the main room. The lights were still on and there was no sign of any struggle. Whoever had blown away Der Haken and his crew must have operated very quickly. There had to have been more than one of them to deal with five men at speed; also, whoever had done it needed to be known and trusted, at least by Osten. The weapons, it went without saying, must have been silenced.

As his thoughts centered on weapons he realized there were signs of the violent deaths—traces of blood on the wall between the two archways, and more patches on the deep-pile cream carpet. Also, there, in plain sight on one of the tables, was his ASP and the baton. Bond checked the weapon, which was still loaded and unfired, before returning it to the holster. He paused, weighing the baton for a moment before slipping it into the cylindrical holder still attached to his belt.

Then he went over and closed the windows—Der Haken's body bumping heavily against the glass—and found the button that operated the curtains, blotting out the gruesome sight on the terrace.

He had moved from the balcony with some speed, being very conscious that whoever had put the police officers into permanent sleep could still be in the apartment. Drawing the ASP, Bond now began a systematic search. The apartment appeared to be empty, but for three of the rooms, the doors of which were firmly locked. One was the guest room he had recently vacated; the other two, he reasoned, probably contained Sukie and Nannie. There was no response from either of them when he knocked, and certainly no sign of keys.

His first duty was, naturally, to release the girls—if, indeed, they were there—but he also needed some direction. As he had thought earlier, somebody—one of the Head Hunt competitors—was playing a careful and devious game. Any other competitor who came near to the prize was being eliminated: first the German on the Belgian motorway; then the Poison Dwarf; then the three men killed in the Renault, whom Der Haken had identified as Union Corse. All were criminals, and now the amateur—the rogue policeman—had been taken out, together with his assistants.

Two things worried Bond. Why, when their quarry—himself—was on toast, here in this flat, had they not used the opportunity and killed him on the spot? Second, who were the most likely people to be running this kind of interference? The obvious choice was SPECTRE itself, of course, for it would be their style to mount a competitive kind of operation, with a fabulous price on the victim's head, and then monitor results in order to step in at the last moment. That was the way to save money: to have your cake and eat it.

But, if SPECTRE was responsible for knocking out the opposition, they would certainly have disposed of him by now, so who was left? Possibly one of the unsympathetic espionage organizations that were natural entrants—the first choice among these would, naturally, be the current successors to Bond's old enemy SMERSH.

Since he had first encountered this black and devious arm of the KGB, SMERSH—an acronym for *Smiert Shpionam,* Death to Spies—had undergone a whole series of changes within the constantly altering structure of the KGB. For many years it was known as Department Thirteen, until it became the completely independent Department V. In fact, Bond's Service had allowed all but its inner circle to go on referring to Department V for a long time after it had also disappeared from the secret Russian scene.

What had occurred was very much the business of the Secret Intelligence Service, which had been running an agent of its own—Oleg Lyalin—deep within Department V. When Lyalin defected, in the early seventies, it took little time for the KGB to discover he had been a long-term mole, and when that happened, Department V suffered a purge that virtually put it out of business.

Even Bond had not been informed, until relatively recently, that his old enemies were now completely reformed under the title Department Eight of Directorate S. So, he now thought, the most possible dark horses in the race for his head would be Department Eight of Directorate S, KGB.

In the meantime, though, there were very pressing problems. Check out the rooms that he thought contained the girls, and do something about getting out of the apartment block. The Bentley Mulsanne Turbo, beautiful and efficient car though it is, cannot be called the most discreet of vehicles. Bond reckoned that, with the alert still on, he could get about half a kilometer before being picked up.

Searching Der Haken's swinging body was not pleasant but it did yield the Bentley keys, if not those to the guest bedrooms or to the elevator. The telephone was still working, so at least there was communication with the outside world, though he had no way of making a clandestine call.

Carefully he dialed the direct number for the Service Resident in Vienna. It rang nine times before a fuddled voice responded.

"It's Predator," Bond spoke quickly, using his field cryptonym. "I have to speak clearly, even if the Pope himself has a wire on your phone."

"Right." The resident was wide awake as soon as he recognized that it was Bond. "Where the hell are you? There's a great deal of trouble. A senior Austrian police officer—"

"And four of his friends got killed," Bond completed.

"They're out in droves looking for you . . . How did you know about the cop?"

"Because he didn't get killed."

"What?"

"Well, he did, but not in the accident. The bastard was doubling. Set it up himself," Bond went on to explain the situation in the simplest possible terms, telling the truth about everything that had occurred.

"Where are you?" The Resident's even voice carried undertones of concern.

"Somewhere in the new town, in a very plush apartment block, together with five corpses and, I hope, the two ladies who were with me. I haven't a clue about the address, but there's a telephone number you can work from." He read out the number on the handset.

"Enough to be going on with. I'll call you back as soon as I get something sorted, though I suspect they're going to ask you a lot of questions."

"The hell with the questions, just let me get out to the Klinik and on with the job. Quickly as you can." Bond took the initiative in closing the line. He then went to the first of the two locked rooms and banged on the door, hard. This time, he thought he could hear muffled exasperated grunts coming from inside.

The lock was Chubb—a deadlock again, like the one on the room he had been put into. It would have to be brute force, he thought, and to hell with the noise.

On his way to search for a suitable instrument in the kitchen, he went through the same procedure with the other locked room. The results were similar, and in the kitchen he found a heavy meat cleaver. The cleaver was sharp and, though he could never claim it went through the door like a warm knife through butter, it did the job on the first lock in around four minutes.

Sukie Tempesta lay on the bed, bound, gagged and stripped to her underwear. "They took my clothes!" she shouted angrily when he got the ropes untied and the gag off.

"So I see," Bond smiled, and she reached for a blanket as he went quickly to the other room. The lock took less time—two minutes flat.

Nannie was in the same situation, and she yelled, "They stole my clothes, and my garter belt with the holster on it."

At that moment the telephone started to ring.

"A very senior officer's on the way with a team," the Resident said. "For heaven's sake be discreet, and tell only what truth is necessary. Then get to Vienna with all speed. That's an order from on high."

"Tell them to bring women's clothes," Bond snapped, giving a rough estimate of the sizes, but by the time he was off the telephone he could hear squeals of delight from the girls. They had found the clothes bundled in cupboards in one of the bathrooms.

Sukie came through, fully dressed; but, almost blatantly, Nannie appeared doing up her stockings to her retrieved garter belt, which still had holster and pistol in place.

"Let's get some air in here." Sukie went toward the windows and Bond had to put his body in front of her, saying that he would not advise opening even the curtains, let alone the windows. Quietly, he told both girls why, cautioned them to stay in the main room and then made his own way behind the drapes to let air into the room.

By the time he was back in the room the main doorbell was ringing violently.

Half the Salzburg police force appeared to have arrived, but they were headed by a smart, authoritative, gray-haired man whom they treated with great respect. He introduced himself as Kommissar Becker and allowed the investigative team to get on with their job on the terrace while he talked to Bond. The girls were taken away by plainclothes men—presumably to be interrogated separately in other rooms.

Becker came quickly to the point, and knew the score—"I have been instructed by our Foreign Ministry, and Security Department," he began. "I also understand that the Head of the Service to which you belong has been in touch. All I want from you is a detailed statement. You will then be free to go, but, Mr. Bond, I think it would be advisable for you to be out of Austria within twenty-four hours."

"Is that an order? Official?"

Becker shook his head. He had a long patrician nose and eyes in which a kindly streak moved when he allowed it. "No, not official. It is merely my personal opinion. Something I would advise. Now, Mr. Bond, let us take it from the top, as they say in musical circles."

Bond had a foolish image of Mozart, in front of a small orchestra, saying, "From the top—a-one-two-three-four."

He recounted the whole story—leaving out all he knew about Tamil Rahani and SPECTRE's Head Hunt, so passing off the autobahn shoot-out as one of those occupational hazards that can unexpectedly befall any person in the kind of clandestine work in which he was involved.

"There is no need to be coy about your status." Becker gave him an avuncular smile. "In police work, here in Austria, we come into contact with all kinds of strange people, from many walks of American, British, French, German and Russian life—if you follow me. We are almost a clearinghouse for spies, only I know you don't like to use that word."

"It is a touch old-hat," Bond found himself smiling back. "In many ways we are outdated, old-fashioned people whom many would like to see consigned to the scrap heap. Electronics, satellites, computers and analysts have taken over much of our day-to-day operations."

"The same with us," the policeman shrugged. "However, nothing can replace the policeman on the beat, and I'd wager there is still a need for the man on the ground in your business. It applies to war also. However many tactical or strategic missiles appear over the horizon, the military needs live bodies in the field of action. Here we are geographically placed at a dangerous crossroads. We have a saying especially for the NATO powers—if the Russians come they will be with us, in Austria, for breakfast; but they will have their afternoon tea in London."

With a detective's knack of moving from a digressional tributary back to the mainstream of interrogation, Becker asked about the motives of Heinrich Osten—Der Haken—and Bond gave him a word-by-word account of what had passed between them, again leaving out the core of the business concerning the Head Hunt. "He has apparently been looking for a chance to line his pockets, and get away, for many years."

Becker gave a wry smile. "It doesn't surprise me. Der Haken, as most people called him, had an odd hold over the authorities. There are still many folk, some in high office, who recall the old days, the Nazis. They remember Osten all too well, I fear. Whoever brought him to this unpleasant end has done us a favor." Again, he switched his tack. "Tell me, why do you think the ransom has been set so high on these two ladies?"

James Bond tried his innocent expression. "I don't really know the terms of the ransom. In fact, I have yet to be told the full story of the kidnapping."

The distinguished police officer repeated his wry smile, this time wagging a finger as though Bond was a naughty schoolboy. "Oh, I believe you know the terms well enough. After all, you were in Osten's company for some time following the exaggerated reports of his death. I took over the case last night. The ransom is *you* Herr Bond, and you know it. There's also the little matter of ten million Swiss Francs lying, literally, on your head."

Bond made a capitulatory gesture. "Okay, so the hostages are being held against me, and your colleague found out about the contract, which is worth a lot of money . . ."

"Even if you *had* been responsible for his death," Becker cut in, "I don't think many police officers, either here or in Vienna, would go out of their way to charge you—Der Haken being what he was." He lifted an inquisitorial eyebrow.

"You didn't kill him, did you?"

"You've had the truth from me. No, I didn't, but I think I know who did."

Becker gave a sage nod. "Without even knowing the details of the kidnapping?"

"Yes. Miss May—my housekeeper—and Miss Moneypenny are bait. It's me they want. The two ladies are but a lure: tethered goats. These people know I will not hesitate to try to rescue the ladies and, I suspect, they're also certain I'd give myself up to save them."

"I thought English gentlemen only saved damsels in distress— fair maidens, young and innocent, held against their will by dragons. You are prepared to give your life for an elderly spinster and a colleague of uncertain age . . . ?"

"Also a spinster," Bond smiled. "The answer to your question is yes. Yes, I would do that—though I intend to do it without losing my head."

"From my information about you, Herr Bond, you have many times almost lost your head over . . ."

"What we used to call a bit of fluff?" Bond smiled again.

"That is an expression I do not know—bit of fluff."

"Bit of fluff; piece of skirt—young woman," he supplied.

"Yes. Yes, I see, and you are correct. Our records show you as a veritable Saint George slaying dragons to save young, attractive women. This is an unusual situation for you. I—"

Bond cut in, sharply. "Sir, can you tell me what actually happened? How the kidnapping took place?"

Kommissar Becker paused as a plainclothes officer came into the room and there was a quick exchange, the officer telling his superior that the women had been interrogated. Becker dismissed him, saying they should all wait for a short time. Out on the balcony the scene-of-the-crime team was finishing up its preliminary investigation.

"Inspector Osten's case notes are, naturally, a shade hazy," the Kommissar finally said. "But we do have some bare details—his interviews with the Director of the Klinik, Herr Doktor Kirchtum, and others."

"Well?"

"Well, it appears that your colleague, Miss Moneypenny, visited the patient twice. After the second occasion she telephoned the Herr Direktor asking permission to take Miss May out—to a concert. It was all very innocent, and untaxing. The doctor gave his consent. Miss Moneypenny arrived, as arranged, in a car with a chauffeur and another man."

"There is a description?"

"The car was a BMW . . ."

"The man?"

"A silver BMW. A Series 7. The chauffeur was in uniform, and the man went into the Klinik with Miss Moneypenny. The staff who saw them said he was young, in his mid-thirties—light hair, neat, well-dressed, tall and muscular."

"And Moneypenny's behavior?"

"A little edgy, but nothing to speak of. Just a shade nervous. Miss May was in good spirits. One nurse noticed that Miss Moneypenny treated her with great care. The nurse said it was as though your Miss Moneypenny had nursing experience; she also said she had the impression that the tall, fair young man knew something about medicine. He stayed very close to Miss May the whole time." He sucked in breath through his teeth.

"They got into the BMW and drove off. Four hours later, Herr Doktor Kirchtum received a telephone call saying they had been abducted. You know the rest."

"I do?" Bond queried.

"You were told. You started out toward Salzburg—then the shoot-out and your experience with the late unmourned Heinrich Osten."

"The car? The BMW?"

"Has not been sighted, which means that it was out of Austria very quickly, with plates changed—maybe a respray—or it's tucked away somewhere until all goes quiet."

"And there's nothing else?"

It was as though the Kommissar remained uncertain whether to pass on any further information. He did not look at Bond, but away, toward the scene-of-the-crime people taking their photographs and measurements on the terrace. Then, "Yes. Yes, there is one other thing. It was not in Osten's investigation notes, but they had it on the general file at headquarters." He hesitated again, and Bond had to prompt him.

"What was on file?"

"At 15:10, on the afternoon of the kidnapping—that is, around three hours before it took place—Austrian Airlines received an emergency booking from the Klinik Mozart. The caller said they had two very sick ladies who had to be transported to Frankfurt. There is a flight at 19:05—OS 421—arrives Frankfurt (Main) at 20:15. On that particular evening there were few passengers. The booking was made and accepted."

"And the ladies made the flight?"

"They were accommodated in first class. On stretchers. Both ladies were unconscious, and their faces covered with bandages . . ."

Classic KGB ploy, Bond thought. They had been doing it for years. He particularly recalled the famous Turkish incident, and there had been two at Heathrow, London.

"They were accompanied," Kommissar Becker continued, "by two nurses and a doctor. The doctor was a young, tall, good-looking man with fair hair."

Bond nodded, "And further inquiries showed that no such reservation had been made from the Klinik Mozart."

"Exactly," the Kommissar raised his eyebrows. "One of our men followed up the booking—sort of freelance, certainly Inspector Osten did not instruct him to do it."

"And?"

"And they were met by a genuine ambulance team at Frankfurt. They transferred onto another flight—the Air France 749, arriving Paris 21:30. It left Frankfurt on schedule, at 20:25. The ambulance people just had time to complete the transfer. We know nothing about what happened at the Paris end, but the kidnap call was placed to Doctor Kirchtum at 21:45. So, they admitted the abduction as soon as the victims were safely away."

"Paris?" Bond queried, absently. "Why Paris?" and, as though in answer to his thoughts, the telephone began to ring. Becker himself picked it up and said nothing, just waiting for an identification on the line. His eyes flicked toward Bond, alarm stirring deeply within them. "For you," he mouthed quietly, hand over the mouthpiece.

He took the handset and identified himself. There was a moment's pause, after which Bond heard the voice of the Herr Doktor Kirchtum. His voice still had its resonance, but the Herr Doktor was obviously a very frightened man, for there was a definite tremor in his tone, and a number of pauses, as though he was being prompted. "Herr Bond," he began, "Herr Bond, I have a gun . . . They have a gun . . . It is in my left ear, and they say they will pull the trigger if I don't give you the correct message."

"Go on," Bond said calmly.

"They know you are with the police. They know you have been ordered to go to Vienna. That is what I must first tell you."

So, Bond thought, they had a wire on this telephone and had listened to his call to the Resident in Vienna.

Kirchtum continued, very shaky indeed. "You are not to tell the police of your movements."

"No. Okay. What am I to do?"

"They say they have booked a room for you at the Goldener Hirsch . . ."

"That's impossible. You have to book months ahead . . ."

The quaver in Kirchtum's voice became more pronounced. "I assure you, Herr Bond, for these people, nothing is impossible.

They understand you have two ladies with you. They say they have a room reserved for them also. It is not the fault of the ladies that they have been . . . have been . . . I'm sorry, I cannot read the writing . . . Ah, have been implicated. For the time being these ladies will stay at the Goldener Hirsch, you understand?"

"I understand."

"You will stay there and await instructions. You will tell the police to keep away from you. You will on no account contact your people in London, not even through your man in Vienna. I am to ask if this is understood."

"It is understood."

"They say, good, because if it is not understood, the ladies— Miss May and her friend—will depart, and not peacefully."

"IT IS UNDERSTOOD!" Bond shouted at the mouthpiece.

There was a moment's silence. "The gentlemen here wish to play a tape for you. Are you ready?"

"Go ahead."

There was a click at the other end of the line, then May's voice, unsteady, but still the same old May, "Mr. James, some foreign friends of yorn seem to hae the idea that I can be afeard easy. Dinna worry aboot me, Mr. Jam—" There was a sudden slap as a hand went over her mouth, then Moneypenny's voice, thick with fear, sounded as though she was standing behind him. "James!" she cried, "Oh, God, James . . . James . . ." and then an unearthly scream cut into his ear, loud, terrified, gibbering, and obviously coming not from Moneypenny, but from May.

It was the kind of prolonged, agonized shriek of horror that one associated with nightmares, ghosts and more especially, medieval devils. Coming from May, it made Bond's blood run cold. It was enough to put him under new orders—the orders and discipline of those who had May and Moneypenny in their power, for it would take something particularly terrifying to make the tough May scream like this. Bond was, at that moment, ready to obey them to the death.

He looked up. Becker was staring at him. Deep in the policeman's eyes there lurked a shocked expression. "For pity's sake, Kommissar, you didn't hear any of that conversation."

"What conversation?" Becker's expression did not alter.

9

VAMPIRE

Salzburg was crowded—a large number of United States citizens were out to see Europe before they died, and an equally large number of Europeans were out to see Europe before it completely changed into Main Street Common Market, with the same plastic frozen food everywhere and identical dull souvenirs from Taiwan on sale in all the major historic cities. Many thought they were already too late, but Salzburg, with the ghost of Mozart, and its own particular charm, did better than most.

The hotel Goldener Hirsch—the "Golden Hind," if one fancied loose translations—held up exceptionally well, especially as its charm, comfort and hospitality reached a long arm back through eight hundred years.

They had to use one of the Festival Hall car parks and send over for the luggage—with the exception of Bond's two special briefcases—as the Goldener Hirsch stood right in the old town, where no car had ever gone before—between the Festival Hall and the crowded, colorful Getreidegasse, with its exquisite carved window frames, and the gilded wrought iron hanging shop signs, which gave it a clean air of distinction.

Sukie and Nannie were slightly bemused at the abrupt end to the night's dramas, both talking at once, trying to discover the whys and wherefores of the past twenty-four hours.

Bond calmly told them that the problem was his; that he would try to make it up to them somehow at a later date, and that they would almost certainly only have to bear with him for another twenty-four hours or so. "There are bookings for us at the Goldener Hirsch."

"Whaaat?" From Sukie.

"How in the name of Blessed Saint Michael did anyone get reservations?" From Nannie.

"Influence," Bond countered soberly. Then, after a short pause, "Why Saint Michael?"

"Michael the Archangel. Patron saint of bodyguards and minders."

Bond thought grimly that he needed all the help the angels could provide. Heaven alone knew what instructions would come to him within the next twenty-four hours at the Goldener Hirsch—or whether the instructions would be in the form of a bullet or knife.

Before they left the Bentley, Nannie cleared her throat and began a lecture. "James," she began primly, "you just said something that Sukie finds offensive, and that doesn't make me happy either."

"Oh?"

"You said we'd only have to bear with you for another twenty-four hours or so."

"Well, it's true."

"No! No, it isn't true."

"I was accidentally forced to involve you both in a potentially very dangerous situation. I had no option but to drag you into it. You've both been courageous, and a great help, but it couldn't have been fun. What I'm telling you now is that you'll both be out of it within twenty-four hours or so."

"We don't want to be out of it," Nannie said calmly.

"Yes, it's been hairy," Sukie began, "but we feel that we're your friends. You're in trouble, and—"

"Sukie's instructed me to remain with you. To mind you, James, and, while I'm at it, she's coming along for the ride."

"That just might not be possible." Bond looked at each girl in turn, his clear blue eyes hard and commanding.

"Well, it'll just have to become possible," Sukie was equally determined.

"Look, Sukie, it's quite probable that I shall be given instructions from a very persuasive authority. They may well demand that you be left behind, released, ordered to go your own sweet way."

"Well," Nannie was just as firm, "it's just too bad if our own sweet way happens to be the same as your own sweet way, James. That's all there is to it."

Bond shrugged. It was possible that he would be ordered to

take the women with him anyway. If not, there should be opportunity to leave quietly when the time came. The third possibility was that it would all end here, at The Goldener Hirsch, in which case the question would not arise.

"I might need some stamps," Bond said, quietly, to Sukie as they approached the hotel. "Quite a lot. Enough for a small package to the UK. Could you get them? Send a few innocuous postcards via the porter, and gather some postage stamps for me, would you."

"Penny stamp and a Chinese burn," muttered Nannie.

"I beg your pardon?" He looked at her curiously.

"It's the bully in her," Sukie said with a grin. "Schooldays. Penny stamp—on the foot—and a Chinese burn—twisting the wrist. Or didn't you do things like that at school, James?"

"Where did you two go to school, anyway?" he asked, giving them a suspicious look.

Sukie hung her head, "Sorry, James, *not* a convent. That's a fiction I find useful."

"A coeducational, so-called 'progressive' school in Surrey, actually." Nannie's face was set in innocence as she mentioned the name of a very expensive school, which, a few years ago, had been notorious. "Back in the bad old days when it got into the tabloids, and the local law turned it over for drugs every other week."

"Happiest days of your life." Sukie's grin had not left her face. "Oh, it's very respectable now, but when we were there—Oh my, oh my. There was one boy who had a secret still in the woods . . ."

"And we had an arsonist."

"They've cleaned it up now," Sukie sounded a shade sad. "*We're* not invited to open day because we were there during the dark age. Might corrupt the present flock, I suppose."

"Will you get me stamps?" Bond hissed.

"Of course, James." Sukie playfully trod on his foot. They reached the hotel entrance.

The Goldener Hirsch is perhaps the best hotel in Salzburg—enchanting, elegant and picturesque, though entering it is rather like walking onto the stage set of a superior production of *The White Horse Inn,* for the staff dressed in the local loden and the atmosphere was heavy with Austrian history. This in no way spoiled the charm, and the trio were met, by all, with a courtesy that successfully avoided the pseudo-fawning found in so many good European hotels.

Bond reflected that his room could easily have been especially prepared for shooting *The Sound of Music II,* but soon forgot that aspect as he set to work preparing for the possible dangers ahead.

He heard Kirchtum's warning again, clear in his head: "You will . . . *await instructions.* . . . You will on no account contact your people in London, not even through your man in Vienna." So, for the time being at least, it would be unwise to telephone London. Yet he *must* keep people informed.

From his second briefcase Bond extracted two minute tape recorders, checked battery strength, set them to voice activation, made certain the tapes were fully rewound and attached one— via a sucker microphone no larger than a grain of wheat—to the telephone; the other he placed in full view on top of the minibar, which looked more like an eighteenth-century commode than a minibar.

Fatigue had caught up with all of them, and he had arranged to meet the girls for dinner that evening in the famous snug bar around six. Until then, they had agreed to rest. He rang down for a pot of black coffee and a plate of scrambled eggs, and as he waited, Bond examined the rest of his room—and the small, windowless bathroom, with a neat shower, protected not by a curtain but by sliding, very solidly built glass doors. He approved, deciding to take a shower later. In the meantime, he unpacked, and was hanging suits in the wardrobe when the waiter arrived, in his fancy costume, with excellent coffee and exceptionally well-prepared eggs.

The ASP was near at hand and, having put the *Do Not Disturb* sign, in four languages, on the door, Bond settled into one of the comfortable armchairs and began to doze.

The exhaustion had really caught up with him, for he eventually fell into a deep sleep, during which he dreamed, oddly, that he was a waiter in some continental café, the clientele of which included Sukie and Nannie. He seemed to spend the day dashing between the kitchen and the tables, waiting on M, Tamil Rahani, the now-deceased Poison Dwarf and the two girls.

Just before waking he had served Sukie and Nannie with tea and a huge cream cake, which turned to a lump of sawdust as soon as they tried to cut it. This appeared not to worry either of them, and they paid the bill, each one leaving a piece of jewelry as a tip. He reached to pick up a gold bracelet—left by Sukie—and it slipped, falling with a heavy crash onto a plate.

Bond woke with a start, convinced the noise was real. But now there only appeared to be the normal street noises drifting in through his window. He stretched, uncomfortable and stiff after sleeping in a chair, then glanced at the stainless steel Rolex on his wrist, amazed to see that he had slept for hours and that it was almost four-thirty in the afternoon.

He went, bleary-eyed, to the bathroom, feeling vaguely doped with sleep, turned on the lights and opened the tall doors to the shower. A strong hot shower, followed by one of icy temperature, would freshen him up. Then a shave and change of clothes. He just had good time to be ready for the girls at six o'clock.

It crossed his mind that whoever had made the present arrangements, and instructed him to await orders, was taking his time. He began to run the shower, closed the door and started to strip. If he had been manipulating this kidnapping and death hunt, Bond would have struck almost as soon as his victim had registered at the hotel, given orders for a move quickly and had his quarry out in the open while he was still groggy from a night without sleep. So far, there had been no contact, no directions. It was, of course, quite possible that his shadowy pursuers were preparing to, literally, take him out of the hotel itself.

Naked, he went back into the main room for the ASP and the baton, which he placed on the floor, under a couple of hand towels, just outside the shower. Then, after testing the water to check it was not too scalding for him to bear, Bond stepped under the spray, closed the sliding door and began to soap himself, rubbing his body vigorously with a rough flannel.

Thoroughly drenched with the hot spray, and rejoicing in a luxurious sense of cleanliness, he altered the settings on the taps, allowing the water to cool quickly, until he stood under a shower of almost ice-cold water. The shock hit him, like a man walking from the warmth of his home into a blizzard. Refreshed, he turned off the water, shaking himself like a dog, feeling a new, revitalized person. He rubbed his face with the flannel and reached out to open the sliding door.

As he did so, Bond became suddenly alert, his extra intuitive senses clicking on like a guidance system. In a fraction of a second he could almost smell danger nearby, and before his hand touched the door handle the lights went out, leaving him disoriented for a second, and in that second his hand missed the handle, though he heard the door slide open a fraction and close again with a thud.

This time, in the darkness, he knew he was not alone. There was something else in the shower with him, brushing his face, and then going wild, thudding against his body and the sides of the shower.

The thing's panic all but transferred itself to Bond, who scrabbled for the door with one hand, whirling the flannel about his face and body to ward off the unseen evil that flapped and bounced around the confined space of the shower, but when his fingers closed over the handle and pulled, the door would not move. The creature was becoming more violent, and, as he tugged hopelessly at the door, so its attacks seemed to become more vicious—he felt something claw at his shoulder, then at his neck, but managed to dislodge it, still hauling on the door, which refused to budge, jammed tight from outside.

The attacks ceased for a moment, as though whatever it was had paused to align itself for a final assault.

He waited, still tugging at the door, the flannel held in front of him, whirling in the darkness. Then Sukie's voice from far away, bright, even flirtatious, "James? James, where the hell are you?"

"Here! Bathroom! Get me out, for heaven's sake!" A second later, the lights went on again. He was aware of Sukie's shadow in the main bathroom, but he could now see his adversary. It was something he had only come across in zoos before this, and even then never one as big. Hunched on top of the spray attachment sat a giant vampire bat, its evil eyes bright above the razor-toothed mouth as it crouched, wings spreading as it prepared to launch another attack.

He lunged at it with the sopping flannel, shouting as he did so, "Get the shower open!"

A second later, the door began to slide. "Get out of the bathroom, Sukie. Get out!" and he pulled back the door as the creature moved.

Bond fell, sideways, into the bathroom, slamming the shower door closed as he did so and rolling across the floor, one hand going for the weapons under the towels.

By itself a vampire bat could not kill instantly, he knew that, and it gave him confidence, but the thought of what it could inject into his bloodstream was enough to make Bond feel true terror in the pit of his stomach; and he had not been quick enough, for the beast had also escaped into the main bathroom.

He shouted again for Sukie to close the door and wait. In a matter of two heartbeats all he knew of the *Desmodus rotundus*— even its Latin name—flashed through his head. There were three varieties; they usually hunted, quietly, at night, creeping up on their prey, clamping onto a hairless part of the body with the incredibly sharp canine teeth, sucking blood and pumping out saliva to stop the blood clotting. It was the saliva that could transmit disease—anything from rabies to forms of deadly virus.

This particular bat—now out of its element of darkness—was obviously a hybrid, which probably meant it carried something particularly horrible in its saliva. The lights of the bathroom had completely disoriented it, though it obviously needed blood badly and would fight to sink its teeth into Bond's flesh. The body, he saw now, was about 27 cm long, while the wingspan spread a good 60 cm—over three times the length of a normal member of its species.

It was certainly not possible to train a creature like this, but if you could develop a hybrid of the *Desmodontidae* family, it would be quite feasible to do it along aggressive, belligerent lines.

As though sensing Bond's quick thoughts, the huge bat raised its front legs, opening the wings to full span and gathering its body up for the fast attack.

Bond's right hand flicked downward, clicking the baton into its open position and smashing the weapon hard in the direction of the oncoming creature. It was luck more than fast judgement, for bats, with their strange radarlike senses, can, more often than not, avoid objects. Probably the unnatural light had something to do with it, but the steel baton caught it directly on the head, throwing it across the room to strike against the shower doors.

Bond could not let it rest there. With a stride he was over the twitching, flapping body, and like a man demented with fear, he hit the vile squirming animal again and again. He knew what he was doing, and was aware that fear played no small part in it, but as he struck the shattered body time after time his thoughts were of the man, or men, who had prepared such a thing as this, warping and redeveloping nature especially to kill him—for he had little doubt that the saliva of this particular vampire bat contained something that would bring a painful death much more quickly than rabies.

When he had finished, he dropped the baton into the shower, turned on the spray and walked toward the door. He had some disinfectant in the small, comprehensive first-aid kit that Q Branch provided.

He had forgotten about his nakedness.

"Well, now I've seen everything. Quits," said Sukie, unsmiling, from the chair in which she waited. There was a small pistol, similar to the one Nannie carried, in her right hand. It pointed steadily midway between Bond's legs.

10

THE MOZART MAN

SUKIE LOOKED HARD at Bond, and then down at the gun. "It's a pretty little thing, isn't it?" She smiled, and he thought he could detect relief in her eyes.

"Just stop pointing it at me, put on the safety catch and then stow it away, Sukie."

She broadened the smile—and he could now see distinct relief flood her face. "Same goes for you, James."

Suddenly, Bond was aware of his nakedness, and grabbed at a hotel toweling robe, thrown over a chair, as Sukie, showing a remarkable slash of thigh, fitted the small pistol into a holster attached to her white garter belt. "Nannie fixed me up with this. Just like hers." She looked up at him, primly pulling down her skirt. "I brought your stamps, James. What was going on in there?" A nod toward the bathroom. "For a horrible moment I thought you were having real trouble."

"I *was* having trouble, Sukie. Very unpleasant trouble in the shape of a large hybrid vampire bat, which is not an animal one usually comes across anywhere in Europe, let alone in Salzburg. This one was definitely prepared by somebody."

"A vamPIRE BAT?" Her voice rose to a screech. "James! Jeerusalem! Something like that could have . . ."

"Probably killed me. If some expert has been clever enough to breed a thing that size, they've almost certainly made sure it's carrying something more quickly lethal than rabies or bubonic plague. How did you get in, by the way?"

"I brought your stamps, as I said." She laid the little colored gummed strips on the table. "I knocked. No reply. Then realized the door was open. It wasn't until I heard the noises coming from the bathroom that I switched the light on. Someone had jammed the shower door with a chair. To be honest with you, I thought it was a practical joke—it's the kind of thing Nannie gets up to—until I heard you shout. I kicked the chair out of the way and ran like a deer."

"And waited in here with a loaded gun."

"Well, Nannie's teaching me to use it. She seems to think it's necessary."

"And I think it's really necessary for the two of you to disappear, but thinking won't make it happen, if women have set their minds on something. Like to do me another favor?"

"Whatever you want, James." Her attitude was suspiciously soft, even yielding. Bond wondered if a girl like Sukie Tempesta could have the guts to handle a box containing a very dangerous hybrid vampire bat and let it loose in his shower. Someone had, and he would put money on the Principessa Tempesta being quite capable of such an act.

"I want you to get me some rubber gloves and a large bottle of antiseptic."

"Done." She stood up. "Any particular brand?"

"Something very strong." The small bottle of stuff in his first-aid kit would not be enough, he had realized, and nobody but an idiot would touch the bat's corpse without taking every possible precaution.

She left without either word or question, and Bond—now dry under the robe—got the small bottle of antiseptic from the first-aid kit and rubbed it hard over every inch of his flesh. By the time he finished, he smelled like a hospital casualty ward, so Bond tried to counteract the strong antiseptic smell with cologne. Only then did he start to dress.

There were considerable worries about disposing of the bat's body. Really it should be incinerated, and the bathroom needed a specialist's attention. Heaven knew what loathsome germs were carried by the creature. Bond knew he could not very well go to the hotel manager and explain the circumstances. Antiseptic, a couple of hotel plastic carriers, a quick visit to the kitchens and their waste-disposal unit, then hope for the best, he thought.

In honor of an evening with the two girls, and in spite of the cloud of danger hanging over all of them, he put on his grey Cardin suit, a light blue shirt by Hilditch & Key of Jermyn Street and a navy white-spotted tie—Cardin again. He was just setting the tie when the telephone rang. As Bond picked it up he glanced at the tape hookup and saw the tiny cassette begin to turn as he answered with a curt "Yes."

It was Herr Doktor Kirchtum again. He sounded, if possible, even more frightened than before. "Mr. Bond?" a heavy, uneven breath. "Is that you, Mr. Bond?"

"Yes, Herr Direktor, are you all right?"

"Physically, yes. They say I am to speak the truth and tell you what a fool I've been."

"Oh?"

"Yes, I tried to refuse to pass any further instructions to you. I told them they should do this job themselves."

"And they did not take too kindly to that." Bond paused, then added, "Particularly as you had already told me I must come,

with the two ladies, to the Goldener Hirsch, here in Salzburg."
This last was for the sake of the tape.

"They took most unkindly," he sounded on the verge of tears,
and the tremor in his voice became more apparent. "I must now
give you instructions quickly, they say, otherwise they will use
the electricity again."

"Go ahead. Fast as you like, Herr Doktor." He knew what
Kirchtum was talking about—the brutal, old, but effective method
of attaching electrodes to the genitals. Outdated methods of per-
suasion were often quicker than the drugs used among more
sophisticated interrogators nowadays.

Kirchtum's voice became rapid and high with fear, so that Bond
could almost see a pair of hoods—from one organization or
another—standing over him, hands poised on the switch. "You
are to go to Paris. Tomorrow. It should only take you one day.
You must drive on the direct route, and there are rooms booked
for you at the George V."

"You mean the ladies have to accompany me?"

"This is essential . . . you understand? Please say you understand, Mr. Bond."

"I—" He was interrupted by a hysterical, terrible scream. The
hood had obviously pulled the switch just for encouragement.

"I understand."

"Good." It was not the Herr Doktor's voice now, but a hollow,
distorted sound, as though the speaker was using some voice
distortion electronics. "Good. Then you will save the two ladies
that we hold from a most unpleasant and slow end to their earthly
travails. Do it, Bond. We shall speak in Paris."

The line closed, and Bond picked up the miniature tape machine,
running the tape back and replaying it through its tiny speaker.
At least he could now get this to either Vienna or London so
that they would know the course of his movements. Also, the
final echoing voice on the line might be some small help to them.
Even if the hoods who were terrorizing Kirchtum had used an
electronic "voice handkerchief," there was still the chance that Q
Branch might take an accurate voice print from it. At least, if
they could make some identification, M would know which particular organization Bond was dealing with.

He went over to the desk, removed the micro-cassette from the tape machine, nipping off the little plastic safety lug in order to prevent the tape from being accidentaly recorded over. He then took out the usual leather folder containing stationery, wrote a few words on a sheet of hotel notepaper and chose the stoutest envelope from the selection in the folder.

He addressed it to M's cover name as chairman of Transworld at one of the safe post office box numbers, folded the cassette into the paper and sealed the envelope.

Consulting the postage guide in the folder, he then selected a rough estimation of the correct stamps—he could only guess the weight of the package.

He had just finished this important chore when a knock at the door heralded Sukie's return. She carried a brown paper sack containing her purchases, and appeared inclined to stay in the room until Bond firmly suggested that she join Nannie and wait in the snug bar for him.

The job of cleaning up the bathroom, wearing the rubber gloves and using almost the entire bottle of antiseptic, took fifteen minutes and left him with a cleansed security baton and the ASP, together with a neat, sinister parcel containing the remains of the disgusting live weapon that had been used against him. Before completing the job he added the gloves to the parcel, and was 99 percent confident that no germs could have entered his system.

While he worked, Bond thought of the possibilities regarding the perpetrator of this last attempt on his life. He was almost logically certain that it was his old enemy, SMERSH—now Directorate S's Department Eight of the KGB—that was holding Kirchtum and using him as their personal messenger. But was it really their style to use such a thing as a hybrid vampire bat against him?

Who, he wondered now, would have the resources to work on the breeding and development of a weapon as horrible as this large vampire bat? It struck him that it must have taken a number of years to bring the creature to its present state, and that indicated a large organization, with funds and the specialist expertise required. The work would have been carried out in, at least, a simulated warm forestlike environment, for if his memory was correct, the original of the species could be found only in the jungles and forests of Mexico, Chile, Argentina and Uruguay.

Money, special facilities, time and zoologists without scruples. SPECTRE was the obvious bet, though any well-funded outfit with an interest in terrorism and killings would be on the list, for the creature would not have been developed simply as a one-off to inject some terrible terminal disease into Bond's bloodstream. The Bulgarians and Czechs favored that kind of thing, and he would not even put it past Cuba to send some agent of their well-trained internal G-2 out into the wider field of international skulduggery. The Honored Society (a polite term for the Mafia) was also a possibility—for they were not beyond selling the goods to terrorist organizations, as long as they were not used within the borders of the United States, Sicily or Italy.

When the chips were down, Bond plumped for SPECTRE itself—but once more during the strange choreography of this dance of death, someone had saved him, at the last moment, from another attempted execution, and this time it was Sukie, a young woman, met, seemingly, by accident. Could she, possibly, be the truly dangerous ace in the hole?

He sought out the kitchens and put on a great deal of charm, giving them a story about food left accidentally and embarrassingly in his car. There was an incinerator, and an odd-job man was summoned to lead him there to dispose of the bundle. The man even offered to do the thing himself, but Bond tipped him heavily, saying he would like to see it burned.

It was now six-twenty, but in spite of being late for his meeting with the girls, he made a last visit to his room to douse himself in cologne lest any traces of the antiseptic remained.

The girls were solicitous and anxious to hear his story, but Bond merely said they would be told all in good time. For the moment they must be content with the more pleasant things of life. They had a drink together in the famous snug bar, and then a splendid dinner—Nannie had been sensible enough to reserve a table—of that famous Viennese boiled beef dish they called Tafelspitz, which is like no other boiled beef on earth and is a gastronomic delight with its piquant vegetable sauce, served with sauteed potatoes that even Bond, not really a potato man, failed to resist.

They had no first course, as it is sacrilege not to eat dessert in an Austrian restaurant. They chose the obvious light, fragile queen of puddings, the Salzburg Souffle, said to have been created nearly three hundred years ago by a chef in the Hohensalzburg. It arrived, to the girls' consternation, topped by what looked like the north face of the Eiger in *Schlag*—as the locals call their rich whipped cream.

Thus replete, Bond led the girls outside into the warm air and among the strolling window-shoppers in the *Getreidegasse*. He wanted to be far away from any possible eavesdropping equipment for what he had to say.

"I'm bloated." Nannie appeared to be hobbling, one hand to her stomach.

"You're going to need the food with what the night has in store for us," Bond spoke quietly. "After today, dinner was not a time for nouvelle cuisine, I promise you."

"Promises, promises," Sukie muttered, breathing heavily. "I feel like a dirigible. So what's in store, James?"

He told them about the orders to drive to Paris. "You've made it plain that you're coming with me, whatever. The people giving me the run-around have also been clear in their demands. You *are* to accompany me, and I have to be sure that you do. The lives of a very dear friend and an equally dear colleague are genuinely at risk. I can say no more."

"Of course we're coming," Sukie bridled.

"Try and stop us," from Nannie, still bent almost double by the intake of food.

"I'm going to do one thing out of line," he explained. "The orders are that we make the drive tomorrow—which I presume means they expect us to do it in daylight. I'm starting just after midnight. That way I can plead that we did start the drive tomorrow, but we might just be a jump ahead of them. It's not much, but I'll do anything to throw them, even slightly, off balance."

The girls agreed to meet him by the car on the dot of midnight, and after a few more words, they started to retrace their steps toward the Goldener Hirsch.

On the return journey, Bond paused, for a brief moment, turned quickly toward a mailbox set into the wall, and slid his package from breast pocket to the box. It was neatly done, taking a minimum of time, and only very close surveillance would have spotted it. He was fairly certain that the action was not noticed even by the girls.

It was just after ten when he got back to his room, and by ten-thirty the briefcases and his bag were packed, and he had changed into casual jeans and jacket—the ASP and baton nestling in their appropriate hiding places. With an hour and a half to go before his meeting with the girls, James Bond sat down and concentrated on how he could possibly gain the initiative in this wild and dangerous death hunt.

So far, the attempts on his life had been cunning, or only in their early stages, when someone else had stepped in to save his hide and, he presumed, set him up for the final act in the drama. Rule one was to trust nobody—especially Sukie, now that she had revealed herself as his savior, however unwitting, in the vampire bat incident. Next came the question of how to take some command. There appeared to be no possibility until he thought of the Klinik Mozart and its Herr Direktor, being held there. The last thing whoever was in control at the Klinik would expect was an assault on this power base.

It was a fifteen-minute drive out of Salzburg to the Klinik Mozart and time ran short. If he could find the right car, perhaps it was just possible.

Moving rapidly, Bond left the room and hurried downstairs to reception to ask what self-drive hire cars were available quickly. For once, Bond seemed to be making his own luck. There was a Saab 900 Turbo—a car to which he was well used—which had only just been returned. A few rapid telephone calls and it was waiting for him, only four minutes' walk from the hotel.

As he waited for the cashier to take details of his credit card, he walked the few paces to the interhouse telephones and rang Nannie's number. She answered straight away. "Say nothing," he spoke quietly. "Wait in your room. I may have to delay departure for an hour. Tell Sukie."

She muttered a surprised affirmative, and by the time he got back to the desk, all formalities had been completed.

Five minutes later, having collected the car from a smiling representative, Bond was driving skillfully out of Salzburg, taking the mountain road south, passing the strange Anif water tower, which rose, like an English manor house, from the middle of a pond in the Salzburg suburbs, then on, up almost as far as the town of Hallein, which originated as an island bastion in the middle of the Salzach and had its own musician to remember— Franz-xavier Gruber, composer of "Stille Nacht, Heilige Nacht," the carol known in all languages to all Christian people.

The Klinik Mozart stood back from the road, about a mile on the Salzburg side of Hallein, surrounded by woodland that screened the converted seventeenth-century house from passing view.

Bond pulled the Saab into a layby, switched off the headlights, cut the engine, put on the reverse lock and climbed out. A few moments later he had ducked under the wooden fencing and was moving carefully through the trees, peering into the darkness for his first glimpse of the Klinik—which he had seen only once before, when visiting to make arrangements for May. Now, he had no idea how those who held the Klinik had arranged for its defense; nor did he know how many people were there, using it as a tactical headquarters from which to maneuver Bond into the final net.

He reached the edge of the trees just as the moon came out. There were no exterior lights burning, so all he could see was the classic oblong block of the big house with light streaming from many of the twenty or thirty windows that fronted the building.

As his eyes adjusted, Bond tried to pick up movement across the hundred yards or so that separated him from the house. There were four cars parked on the wide gravel frontage, but no sign of life, except for the lighted windows. Gently he eased out the ASP, gripping it in his right hand, while his left removed the baton, which he flicked open, ready for instant use. Then he broke cover, moving fast and silently, remaining on the grass and avoiding the long drive that ended in the gravel parking area.

Nothing moved or cried out. He reached the gravel and tried to recall where the Herr Direktor's office lay in relation to the front door. Somewhere to the right, he thought, remembering how he had stood at the tall windows on his last visit, looking out at the lawns and drive. Now he had a fix, and more, for he recalled they were French windows—the French windows immediately to his right, brightly lit and with the curtains closed.

Moving sideways, he eased himself toward the windows, realizing, with heart thudding, that they were open and voices, muffled by the drapes, could be heard from inside. Now he was close enough to actually hear what was being said.

"You cannot keep me here forever—not with only three of you." It was the Herr Direktor whose voice he recognized first. The bluffness completely gone, replaced by a pleading note. "Surely you've done enough."

"We've managed so far." Someone else spoke. "You have been cooperative—to a point—Herr Direktor, but we cannot take chances. Only when the man Bond is secure, and with our people far away, can we leave. The situation is ideal for the short-wave transmitter and electronic surveillance on Bond; your patients have not suffered. Another twenty-four—maybe forty-eight—hours will make little difference to you. Eventually we shall leave you in peace."

" 'Stille Nacht. Heilige Nacht,' " another voice chuckled, gruffly, and Bond's blood ran cold. He moved closer to the windows, the tips of his fingers resting against the inch-wide crack in their opening.

"You wouldn't . . . ?" There was real terror in Kirchtum's voice now—not hysterical fear, but the genuine, eighteen-carat terror that only strikes a man facing inevitable death by extreme torture.

"You've seen our faces, Herr Direktor. You know who we are."

"I would never . . ."

"Don't think about it. You have one more message to pass for us yet, when friend Bond gets to Paris. After that . . . well, we shall see."

Bond physically shivered at the voice, which he had already recognized and never thought, in a thousand years, to hear in this situation. He took a deep breath and slowly pulled, widening the crack between the windows, then inserting his fingers between the curtains to peer into the room.

Kirchtum was strapped into an old-fashioned desk chair—a round-bottomed affair made of wood and leather, with three legs on castors, the kind of chair one saw in newspaper editors' offices in old movies, shown late on television. The bookcase behind him had been swept clean of books, which had been replaced by a powerful radio transmitter. One broad-shouldered man sat in front of the radio; another stood behind Kirchtum's chair, and their leader, legs apart, faced the Herr Direktor. Bond recognized him at once, just as he had known his voice, yet he could not believe it was he.

He breathed in through his nose, lifted the ASP and lunged through the windows. There was no time for sentiment, and what he had heard told him that the three men constituted the entire enemy force at the Klinik Mozart.

The ASP thumped four times, two bullets shattering the chest of the man behind Kirchtum's chair, the other two wrecking the back of the hood who sat before the radio.

The third man whirled around, mouth open, hand moving to his hip.

"Hold it there, Quinn! One move and your legs go—right?"

Steve Quinn, the Service's man in Rome, stood statue-still, his mouth curving into a snarl.

"Herr Bond? How . . . ?" Kirchtum's voice assumed a whisper.

"You're finished, James. No matter what you do to me, you're finished." Steve Quinn had not regained his composure, but he gave a reasonable impression of doing so.

"Not quite," Bond smiled, without triumph. "Not quite yet, though I admit being surprised to find you here, at the Mozart. Who're you really working for, Quinn? SPECTRE?"

Quinn gave him a fast grimace of a smile. "No. Pure KGB. Their mole. First Chief Directorate, naturally, for years, and not even Tabby knows. Now on temporary detachment to Department Eight, which at one time was your sparring partner, SMERSH. Also, unlike yourself, James, I've always been a Mozart man. I prefer to dance to good music."

"Oh, you'll dance." Bond's face showed the hard, cold and cruel streak that was the darkest side of his nature. "But it won't be to soft music."

11

HAWK'S WING AND MACABRE

JAMES BOND WAS not prepared to waste time. He knew, to his cost, the danger of keeping an enemy talking—it was a technique he had used to his own advantage, and Steve Quinn was quite capable of trying to play for time. Crisply, still keeping his distance, Bond ordered the man to stand a good five feet from the wall, spread his legs, stretch out his arms and then lean forward, palms against the wall. Once Quinn was in that position, Bond made him shuffle his feet back even further so that the man could not possibly use any leverage for a quick attack.

Only when he felt it was safe did Bond approach his captive, whom he frisked with great care. There was a small S & W Chief's Special revolver tucked into the waistband of his trousers, hard against the small of his back; a tiny automatic pistol—a Steyr 6.35mm Austrian weapon—taped to the inside of his left calf and a nasty little flick knife secured, with similar tape, to the outside of his right ankle.

"Haven't seen one of these in years." Bond tossed the Steyr onto the desk. "No grenades secreted up your backside, I trust." He did not smile. "You're a damned walking arsenal, man. You should be careful, terrorists might be tempted to break into you."

"In this game, I've always found it useful to be like a Boy Scout and be prepared." As he spoke the last word, Steve Quinn let his body sag. He collapsed onto the floor and, in the fraction of a second, flip-rolled to the right, his arm reaching toward the table where the Steyr automatic lay.

"Don't try it!" Bond snapped, bringing the ASP to bear.

Quinn was not ready either to meet his Maker or die for the cause to which he had allied himself—a traitor to the Service. He stopped, lying on the floor, the hand still raised, looking like a huge child playing the old game of statues.

"Face down! Spreadeagled!" Bond commanded, looking around the room for something to secure his prisoner. Keeping the ASP leveled at Quinn, he sidled behind Kirchtum, using his left hand to unbuckle the two short and two long straps, obviously made for restraining violent patients. As he moved he continued to snap orders at Quinn. "Face right down, eat the carpet, you bastard, and get your legs wider apart, arms in the crucifixion position."

He obeyed, grunting obscenities as he did so, and, as the last buckle gave way, Kirchtum started to rub his wrists, arms, legs and ankles. The wrists were marked where the hard leather thongs had bitten into his flesh.

"Stay seated," Bond whispered. "Don't move. Give the circulation a chance." Taking the straps, he went toward Quinn, keeping his gun hand well back, knowing that a lashing foot could possibly catch his wrist. "The slightest move and I'll blow a hole in you so big that even the maggots'll need maps. Understand?"

Quinn grunted and Bond kicked his legs together, viciously planting the steel-capped toe of his shoe against the man's ankle so that he yelped with pain. While the agony was obviously sweeping through him, Bond swiftly slid one of the straps around the ankles, pulled hard and buckled the leather tightly.

"Now the arms! Fingers laced behind your back!" As though to make him understand, Bond gave the right wrist a jar with his foot. There was another cry of agony, but Quinn did as he was told, and another strap went around the wrists.

"This is old-fashioned, but it'll keep you quiet until we've made arrangements for something more permanent," Bond muttered as he buckled the pair of long straps together, fastening one end around Quinn's already secured ankles, then bringing the elongated strap up around his captive's neck and back to the ankles. He pulled tightly, bringing the prisoner's head up and forcing the legs toward his trunk. Indeed, it was a method old and well-tried. If the captive struggled all he did was strangle himself, for the straps were pulled so tightly that they made Quinn's body into a bow, the feet and neck being the outer edges. Even if he tried to relax his legs, the strap would pull hard on the neck.

Quinn let out a stream of obscene abuse, and Bond—very angry now at the thought of an old friend being revealed as a defector—kicked him hard in the ribs, took out a handkerchief and stuffed it into the trussed man's mouth with a curt, "Shut up!"

Now, for the first time since coming through the windows, he had a real chance to look around the room.

It was all very solid—heavy desk, the bookcases rising to the ceiling, the chairs with curved backs, circa 1850. Kirchtum still sat in the castored working chair, face pale, hands shaking—a big, expansive man turned to terrified blubber.

Bond went over to the bookcase that contained the radio, stepping over the books that lay in disorderly piles where they had fallen when the thugs had swept them from the shelves.

The radio operator remained slumped in his chair, blood still dripping onto the thick carpet, bright against its faded pattern. Bond pushed the body unceremoniously from the chair. He did not recognize the face, twisted in the surprised agony of death. The other hood was sprawled against the wall, as if he were a drunk, collapsed at a party—except that drunks do not usually leave long trails of blood down the wall. This one was recognizable. Bond could not put a name to him, but had seen the photograph in the files—East German heavy, a criminal with terrorist leanings. It was amazing, he thought, how many of Europe's violent villains were turning into mercenaries for the terrorist cells. Rent-a-Thug, he thought, turning to Herr Doktor Kirchtum. "How did they manage it?" he asked—bland, as though all sensitivity had been drained from him by the discovery that Quinn had sold out.

"Manage . . . ?" Kirchtum appeared to be at a loss.

"Look . . ." Bond almost shouted, and then realized that he was facing a man whose English was not always perfect, and who was a gibbering wreck. He walked over and laid an arm on the man's shoulder, speaking quietly and comfortingly. "Look, Herr Doktor, I have to get information from you very quickly. Especially if we are to ever see the two ladies alive again."

"Oh, my God." Kirchtum covered his face with his banana bunch hands. "It is my fault that Miss May and her friend . . .

Never should I have allowed Miss May to go out." He was near to tears.

"No. No, not your fault. How were you to know? Just tell me certain things. Be calm and answer my questions as carefully as you can. First, how did these men manage to get in and hold you here?"

Kirchtum let his fingers slide down his face. The eyes were full of desolation. "Those . . . those two . . ." he gestured at the bodies, "they came as repair men for the *Antenne*—what you call it? The pole? For the television."

"The television aerial."

"Ja, yes, the television ayrial. The duty sister let them in, and onto the roof. She thought it good, okay. Only when she was comink to me did I smell a mouse."

"They asked to see you?" He did not correct the doctor.

"In here. My office, they ask. Only later I find they had been putting up *Antenne* for their radio equipment. They lock the door. Threaten me with guns and torture. Tell me to put the next doctor in charge of the Klinik. To say I would be tied up, in my study on business matters for a day or two. They laughed when I had to say 'tied up.' They had pistols. Guns. What could I do?"

"You do *not* argue with loaded guns," Bond agreed, "as you can see," nodding to the pair of corpses. He turned his eyes to the grunting, straining Steve Quinn. "And when did this piece of scum crawl out of the gutter?"

"Later that night. Through the windows, like yourself."

"What night *was* this?"

"The day after the ladies disappeared. The two in the afternoon, the other at night. By then they had me in this chair. All the time, they had me here, except when I had to perform functions . . ."

Bond looked surprised, and Kirchtum said he meant natural functions. "In the end I refused to give you messages on the telephone. Until then they had only threatened me. But after that . . ."

Already Bond had seen the bowl of water and the electric socket containing a plug from which hung wires and a set of large crocodile clips. He nodded, knowing only too well what the Herr Doktor must have suffered. "And the radio?" he asked.

"Ah, yes. They used it quite often. Twice, three times a day."

"You hear any of it?" Bond looked at the radio. There were two sets of earphones jacked into the receiver.

"Most of it. They wear the earphones sometimes, but there are speakers there, see."

Indeed, there were two small circular speakers set into the center of the system. "Tell me about the messages."

"What to tell? They listen to you like magic. They spoke. Another man spoke from far away . . ."

"Who spoke first? Did the other man call them?"

Kirchtum appeared to be lost in thought for a moment. Then, "Ah, yes. The voice would come with a lot of crackling."

Bond, standing beside the sophisticated, high frequency unit, saw that the dials were glowing. There was a mild, almost distant hum from the speakers, and he noted the dial settings. They were talking to someone quite a long way off—it could be four hundred or four thousand miles, give or take a mile.

"Can you recall if the messages came at any specific times?"

Kirchtum's brow creased, and the large head nodded, "Yes. Ja. Yes, I think so. In the mornings. Early. Six o'clock. Then at noon . . ."

"Six in the evening and again at midnight?"

"Something like that, yes. But not quite."

"Just before the hour, or just after, yes?"

"This is right."

"Anything else?"

The doctor paused, thought again, and then nodded. "Ja. I know they had to send a message when news came that you had left. They have a man watching . . ."

"The hotel?"

"No. I heard the talk. He is watching the road. He is to telephone when you drive away and they were to make a signal with the radio. It is special words . . ."

"Can you remember them?"

"Something about the package being posted to Paris."

That sounded par for the course, Bond thought. Cloak and dagger. The Russians, like the Nazis before them, read too many bad espionage novels. "Were there any other special words?"

"Ja, they used others. The man to the other end calls himself Hawk's Wing—I thought it strange."

"And here?"

"Here they call themselves Macabre."

"So, when the radio comes on, the other end says something like 'Macabre, this is Hawk's Wing . . .' "

"Over."

"Over, yes. And 'Come in Hawk's Wing.' "

"This is just how they say it, yes."

Suddenly, as though he had just thought of it, Bond asked about noise. "Why haven't any of your staff come to this office, or alerted the police? There must have been noise. I have used a gun."

Kirchtum shrugged. "The noise of your pistol might have been heard from the windows, but the windows only. My office is soundproofed. Sometimes there are disturbing noises from the Klinik. This is why the windows were open. They had them open only a few times a day for the circulation of air. It can get most heavy in here with the soundproofing. Even the windows are soundproofed with the double glaze."

Bond nodded and glanced at his watch. It was now almost eleven-forty-five. Hawk's Wing would be making his call at any time, and he had already figured that Department Eight's watchdog would be stationed somewhere near the E-11 Autobahn. In fact they probably had all exit roads watched. Nice and professional. Far better than just one man at the hotel.

But he was now playing for time. Quinn had stopped twisting on the floor, and Bond was already beginning to work out a scheme that would take care of him. Quinn was an old professional, and even though he had defected, his experience and training would make him a hard man to influence. It would take days, even weeks, to crack him under ideal interrogation conditions; violence would be counterproductive. There was, he knew, only one possible way to get at Stephen Quinn.

He went over to the strapped figure, going down on one knee near his head. "Quinn," he said softly, and saw the hate in the man's eyes as they gave him a sidelong, painful and uncomfortable look. "We need your cooperation."

The man grunted through the makeshift gag. It was the kind of grunt which meant that in no way would Quinn cooperate.

"I realize the telephone is insecure, but I'm calling Vienna for a relay to London. I want you to listen very carefully." He went over to the desk, lifted the receiver and dialed 0222–43–16–08—the Tourist Board offices in Vienna, where he knew there would be an answering machine at this time of night.

He held the receiver away from his ear so that Quinn would at least hear a muffled answer.

It came, and Bond simultaneously pressed the receiver very close to his ear and softly closed the line with his finger on the rest.

"Predator," he said, softly. Then, after a pause, "Yes. Priority for London to copy and action taken immediately—and I mean within minutes. Rome's gone off the rails." He paused again, as though listening. "Yes, working for Center. I have him, but we need extreme measures. I want a snatch team in Rome at Flat 28, 48 via Barberini—it's next to the JAL offices. Lift Tabitha Quinn and hold for orders, and tell them to alert Hereford to call one of the 'psychos' in if M doesn't want dirty hands."

Behind him, he heard Quinn grunting, trying to move, getting agitated. A threat against his wife was about the only thing that would keep the man in line.

"That's right. Will do. I'll run it through you, but termination or near termination might be necessary. I'll get back within an hour or so. Good." He put down the instrument, going to kneel beside Quinn again. This time the look in the man's eyes had changed, hatred was edged with anxiety.

"It's okay, Stephen Quinn. Nobody's going to hurt *you*. But I fear it could be different with Tabby. I'm sorry."

There was no way that Quinn could even suspect a bluff or double bluff. He had been in the Service for a long time himself, and was well aware that calling in a "psycho," as the Service called its mercenary killers, was usually no idle threat. He knew it could happen. Worse, he was versed in the many ways his wife could suffer before death. Most of all, he had worked with Bond and was, therefore, sure 007 would show no compunction in carrying out the threat.

Bond went on talking. "I gather there will be a call coming

through. I'm going to strap you into the chair in front of the radio. Make the responses fast. Get off the air quickly. Feign bad transmission if you have to. But, Steve, don't do anything out of line—no missing out words, or putting in 'alert' sentences. I'll be able to tell, as you know. Just as you'd be able to detect a dodgy response. If you *do* make a wrong move everything'll go black, and you'll wake up in Warminster to a long interrogation and a longer time in jail. You'll also be shown photographs of what they did to Tabby before she died. That I promise you. Now," he manhandled the man into the chair recently vacated by the dead radio operator, adjusting the straps from the strangulation position and rebinding him tightly into the chair.

He felt confident, for the fight appeared to have gone out of Steve Quinn. But you could never tell. The defector might well be so indoctrinated that he could bring himself to sacrifice his wife.

At last, he asked if Quinn was willing to play it straight. The big man just nodded his head sullenly, and Bond pulled the gag from his mouth.

"You bastard!" Quinn said, sounding breathless and throaty.

"It can happen to the best of us, Steve. Just do as you're told and there'll be a chance that both of you will live."

Hardly had he completed the words when the radio hummed and crackled into life. Bond's hand went out to the receive-and-send switch, set to *Receive.*

Across the airwaves a disembodied voice recited the litany, "Hawk's Wing to Macabre. Hawk's Wing to Macabre. Come in Macabre."

Bond nodded to Quinn, clicked the switch to *Send,* and for the first time in years, prayed.

12

ENGLAND EXPECTS

"'M ACABRE, HAWK'S WING, I have you. Over." Steve Quinn's voice sounded too steady for Bond's liking, but there was no other option.

The voice at the distant end crackled through the small speakers. "Hawk's Wing, Macabre, routine check. Report situation. Over."

Quinn paused for a second, and Bond allowed the muzzle of the ASP to touch him behind the ear. "Situation normal. We await developments. Over."

"Call back when package is on its way. Over."

"Wilco, Hawk's Wing. Over and out."

There was silence for a moment as the switch was clicked to the *Receive* position again. Then Bond turned to Kirchtum, asking if it all sounded normal.

"It was usual," he nodded.

"Right, Herr Doktor. Now you come into your own. Can you get something that'll put this bastard to sleep for around four or five hours, and make him wake up feeling reasonable—no slurred speech or anything?"

"I have just the think." For the first time, Kirchtum smiled, easing his body painfully from the chair and hobbling off toward the door. Halfway there he realized that he was wearing no shoes or socks, so he limped back, retrieved the articles, put them on and slowly left the room.

"If you have by any chance alerted whoever that was on the line, you must remember that Tabby won't last long once we've found you out. You do everything by the book, Quinn, and I'll do my best for you as well. But the first person to be concerned about is your wife. Right?"

"Right." Quinn glared at him with the kind of hatred shown only by traitors who have been caught and cornered.

"This applies to honesty as well. I want straight answers, and I want them now."

"I might not know the answers."

"True, but if you do know them, you talk . . . otherwise—well, we'll know truth from fiction in the long run."

Quinn did not reply.

"First, what's going to happen in Paris? At the George V?"

"Our people're going to get you. At the hotel, at the George V."

"But you could've got me here. Heaven knows, enough people have already tried."

"Not my people. Not KGB. We banked on you coming down here after May and Moneypenny. Yes, *we* organized the kidnapping. The idea was to start manipulating you from here. Getting you to Salzburg was like putting you into a funnel."

"Then it wasn't your people who had a go in the car?"

"No. One of the competition. They took out the Service people. None of my doing. You seem to have had a guardian angel all the way. The two men I put on to you were from the Rome station. I was to burn them once they saw you safely into Salzburg."

"And send me on to Paris?"

"Yes. Blast you. If it was anyone else but Tabby, I'd . . ."

"But it *is* Tabby we're thinking about." Bond paused. There was a lot still to be done, and he had to know more. "Paris?" he asked again. "Why Paris?"

Quinn locked eyes with him. Deep in the eyes, Bond detected an indecision. The man *did* know something more. "Why Paris? Remember Tabby."

"It was either Berlin, Paris or London. They want your head, Bond. But they want to see it done. We were out to claim the reward, and to be away with the money once you'd been handed over. Just taking your head wasn't enough. My instructions were to get you to Paris. The people there have orders to pick you up, and—" He stopped, as though he'd already said enough.

"And deliver the package?"

Another fifteen seconds' silence. "Yes."

"Deliver it where?"

"To the Man."

"Tamil Rahani? The Head of SPECTRE?"

"Yes."

"Deliver it where?" Bond repeated.

No response.

"Remember Tabby, Quinn. I'll see Tabby suffer great pain before she dies. Then they'll come for you. Where am I to be delivered?"

The silence stretched for what seemed to be minutes. Then, "Florida."

"Where in Florida? Big place, Florida. Where? Disney World?"

Quinn looked away. "The southernmost tip of the United States," he said.

"Ah," Bond nodded. The Florida Keys, he thought. Those linked islands that stretched out one hundred miles into the ocean. Bahai Honda Key, Big Pine Key, Cudjoe Key, Boca Chica Key, the names of the most famous ones flicked through his head. Somewhere in there was Key Largo where, in an old movie, Bogart had bested Edward G. Robinson. But the southernmost tip—well, that was Key West, onetime home of Hemingway, a narcotics route, a tourist paradise, with a sprinkle of islands outside its reef. Ideal, thought Bond. Key West—who would have imagined SPECTRE setting up its headquarters there? "Key West," he said aloud, and Quinn gave a small, ashamed nod. "Paris, London or Berlin. Presumably they could have included Rome and other major cities. Anywhere they could get me onto a direct Miami flight, eh?"

"I suppose so."

"It's not a big place, but where, exactly, in Key West?"

"*That* I don't know. In all truth, I just do not know." He convinced Bond, who shrugged as though to say it did not matter.

The door opened and Herr Doktor Kirchtum came in. He looked better and was smiling. "I have what you need, I think," flourishing a kidney bowl overlaid with a cloth.

"Good," Bond smiled back, "and I think I have what *I* need. Put him out, Herr Doktor."

Quinn did not resist as Kirchtum rolled up his sleeve, swabbed a patch on the upper right arm and slid the hypodermic needle in. It took less than ten seconds for the man's body to relax and the head to loll over.

"He will have a good four to five hours' sleeping. You are leaving?"

"Yes, when I've made sure he can't get away once he wakes up." Bond was already busy with the straps again. "Just a precaution," he told the Herr Doktor. "One of my people should arrive here before he wakes—to make certain he gets the telephone call from his watcher, and then relays it to his source. I have to arrange that. My man will use the words, 'Ill met by moonlight.' You reply, 'Proud Titania.' Got it?"

"This is Shakespeare, the *Summer Midnight Dream,* Ja?"

"*A Midsummer Night's Dream,* Ja, Herr Doktor."

"So, Summer Midnight, Midsummer Night's, what's the difference?"

"It obviously mattered to Mr. Shakespeare. Better get it right," Bond smiled at the bearlike doctor. "Can you deal with all this?"

"Try me, Herr Bond. I deal in aces."

Five minutes later, Bond was heading back to where he had left the Saab. Within twenty he had returned to the hotel.

In his room he called Nannie to apologize for keeping them waiting. "Slight change of plan," he told her. "Just stand by. Tell Sukie. I'll be in touch soon. With luck we'll be leaving within the hour."

"What the hell's going on?" Nannie sounded peeved.

"Just stay put. Don't worry, I won't leave without you."

"I should jolly well think not," she snapped, banging down the receiver.

Bond smiled to himself, opened the briefcase containing the CC500 scrambler unit and attached it to the telephone. Though he was, to all intents and purposes, on his own in this situation, it was time to call for some limited assistance from the Service.

He dialed the London Regent's Park number, knowing the line would be safe now he had taken out the team at the Klinik, and asked for the duty officer, who came on the line almost straight away. After identifying himself, Bond began to issue his instructions. There were matters he wanted relayed quickly to M, and from him to the Vienna Resident. He was precise and firm, saying that there was only one way to deal with the matter—his way. If M would not—or could not—comply, then they had lost the chance, literally, of a lifetime. SPECTRE was a sitting target that only he could smash. But his instructions had to be carried out to the letter. He ended by repeating the hotel number and his room, asking for a call-back as quickly as possible.

It took just over fifteen minutes. M had okayed all the instructions and the operation was already running from Vienna. A private jet would bring in a team of three men and two girls. They would wait at Salzburg airport for Bond, who should get clearance for a private flight to Zurich on his Universal Export passport B. Bookings were made on the Pan American Flight 115 from Zurich to Miami, departing at 10:15 A.M. local time.

Bond thanked him and was about to close the line. "Predator." The duty officer stopped him, using 007's identification code name.

"Yes?"

"Private message from M."

"Go on."

"He says, 'England Expects.' Nelson, I suppose—'England expects that every man will do his duty.'"

"Yes," Bond countered irritably. "Yes, I *do* know the quotation."

"And he says 'good luck,' sir."

Bond thanked him. He knew that he would need every ounce of luck that came his way. He unhooked the CC500 and dialed Nannie's room. "All set. We're almost ready for the off."

"About time," her voice had a small smile in it. "Where're we going?"

"Off to see the Wizard," Bond laughed without humor. "The Wonderful Wizard of Oz."

13

GOOD EVENING, MR. BOLDMAN

"JAMES?" SUKIE SOUNDED almost wheedling, as they left the hotel, lugging their suitcases. "James, you're going the wrong way. You left the Bentley in the car park to the left."

"Yes," Bond spoke quietly. "Don't tell the whole world, Sukie. We're not using the Bentley." On his way back, after parking the Saab, he had made a quick detour and used the old trick of sticking the Bentley's keys up the exhaust pipe. It was not as safe as he would have liked, but it would have to do.

"Not . . . ?" An intake of breath from Nannie.

"We have alternative transport." Bond was crisp, his voice sharp with authority. The whole of his plan to outflank Tamil Rahani and SPECTRE depended on caution and timing. For a few moments, during the drive back from the Klinik, he had even considered ditching Sukie and Nannie—leaving them in the hotel. But, unless there was a way to isolate them, it was a safer course of action to take them along with him. They had already shown their determination to remain with him anyway. Dumping them now was asking for trouble.

He led them toward the Saab, Nannie muttering something about their being unable to be of help if they didn't know what was going on.

"I hope your American visas are up to date," Bond said, once they were packed into the car and he started the engine.

"American?" Sukie's voice rose in a petulant squeak.

"Visas not okay?" He edged out of the parking place and began to negotiate the streets to take them onto the airport road.

"Of course!" Nannie cross.

"I haven't a thing to wear," Sukie said loudly.

"Jeans and a shirt, where we're going," Bond smiled as he turned onto the Innsbruck road, the *Flughafen* sign illuminated for a second in his headlights. "Another thing," he added. "Before we leave this car you'll have to stow your hardware in one of my cases. We're heading for Zurich, then flying direct to the States. I have a shielded compartment in my big case and all weapons'll have to go in there. From Zurich it'll be commercial airlines until we get to our final destination."

Nannie began to protest, and Bond shut her up quickly. "You both decided to stay with me on this. If you want out, then say so now and I'll have you taken back to the hotel. You can have fun going to all those Mozart concerts."

"We're coming, whatever," Nannie said firmly. "Both of us, okay, Sukie?"

"You bet your sweet—"

"As arranged, then." Bond could see the *Flughafen* signs coming up fast now. "There's a private jet on its way for us now. I shall have to spend some time with the people who're arriving on it. *That* you cannot be in on, I'm afraid. Then we take off for Zurich."

In the airport car park, Bond opened the hatchback and unzipped his folding case—which took up to four suits and an incredible amount of shirts and accessories. Q Branch had taken the brown lightweight Samsonite case apart and fitted a sturdy extra zipped compartment into the center. This pocket was shielded against all known airport surveillance and X-ray equipment, and even though it meant weapons had to travel in commercial aircraft freight compartments, Bond had found it invaluable when traveling with airlines that did not give him permission to carry a personal weapon.

"Anything you should not be carrying, ladies, please." He held out a hand while both Sukie and Nannie hoisted their skirts and unclipped identical holsters, complete with automatic pistols, from their garter belts.

In the odd light of the sodium lamps surrounding the car park, Bond could not see if there were any blushes, but he recalled the odd anomaly of Sukie's being modest, while the seemingly strait-laced Nannie had pranced around the apartment where Der Haken had died wearing the most flimsy apparel.

When the case was zipped again and returned to the luggage compartment, he ordered the girls back into the car. "Remember, you're unarmed. If anything happens either stay put or run for it. I shall be with the airport manager. As far as I can tell there's no danger, because the people who're really on my trail now have, I hope, been diverted." He said he would not be long, and then walked toward the small cluster of airport buildings.

The airport manager had been fully alerted and treated the arrival of an executive aircraft as a perfectly normal and routine matter—just as it was supposed to be. "They are about fifty miles out, and just starting their approach," he told Bond. "I gather you need some kind of room for a small conference while the aircraft is being turned around."

Bond nodded, apologizing for the inconvenience of having the airport opened at this time of night.

"Just thank heaven the weather is good," the manager gave an uncertain smile. "It's not possible at night if things close in."

They went out onto the apron, and Bond saw that the airport had been lit for the arrival. A few minutes later he spotted the flashing red and green lights creeping down the invisible path of the approach to the main runway. A few seconds later the little HS 125 Exec jet came hissing in over the threshold to touch down neatly, pulling up with a sharp deceleration. The pilot had obviously used Salzburg before and knew its limits.

Within a short time the aircraft, bearing a British identification number and no other markings, pulled up, guided toward its parking area by an expert "batsman" using a pair of illuminated batons.

The forward door opened and the airsteps unfolded, like old-fashioned sugar tongs. Bond did not recognize the two girls, but was glad to see that at least two of the three men who came down onto the tarmac were people he had worked with before. The most senior was a bronzed, well-honed young man called Crispin Thrush, whose experience was almost as varied as that of Bond.

The two men shook hands, and Crispin introduced him to the other members of the team as the manager led them to a small, deserted conference room, already prepared, with coffee, bottles of mineral water, and note pads set out on a circular table.

"Help yourselves." Bond looked around at the team. "I think I'll go and wash my hands, as they say." He cocked his head at Crispin, who nodded and followed him out of the room, along the passage, and finally out into the airport parking lot.

When they spoke it was with lowered voices.

"They briefed you?" Bond asked.

"Only the basics. Said you'd put the flesh on it."

"Right. You and one of the other boys take a rented Saab—the one with the couple of girls in it, over there—and go straight up to the Klinik Mozart. You've got the route?"

Thrush nodded. "They gave us that. Yes. And I was told something almost unbelievable . . ."

"Steve?"

He nodded again.

"Well, it's true. You'll find him there, sleeping off some dope the Klinik's director, Doctor Kirchtum, gave him. You'll find Kirchtum a godsend. Quinn and a couple of heavies have been holding him there . . ." He went on to explain that part of the situation—that there was some cleaning up to be done, and Quinn to be ready to take a telephone call from the KGB man watching the road for the Bentley. "When he makes his radio report, listen to him and watch him, Crispin. He's a rogue agent, and I've no need to tell you how dangerous that can be. He knows all the tricks, and I've only got his cooperation because of threats against his wife."

"They pulled Tabby in, I understand. She's stashed in one of the Rome safe houses. Gather the poor girl's a bit bemused."

"Probably doesn't believe it. He claims she had no idea that he'd defected. Anyway, if the whole team'll fit into the Saab you'd better drop your two girls and the other lad off at the Goldener Hirsch." He told Crispin where the Bentley could be found, with the keys in the exhaust, and the route he wanted it to take to Paris. "If we all get a move on—ten minutes for a bit of nonsense chat in the conference room—you can get the Bentley team on their way. The car'll be spotted, so make sure you've got time to get settled into the Klinik, with Quinn awake, before the Bentley leaves. Their watcher'll take it for granted that I'm in it, with my companions, heading for Paris. That should throw them for a while."

Once the messages had been passed on, Crispin and his man were to get Steve Quinn out and on to Vienna. "Quickest way possible. The car, I should think."

There were a couple of questions and a final backtrack on the plan, then Crispin reached into his jacket and pulled out a heavy, long envelope. "Tickets." He passed the envelope over. "With the Resident's compliments." Bond slid the papers into his breast pocket, and the pair returned, walking slowly, to the building and conference room.

They stayed there for less than fifteen minutes, drinking coffee and ad libbing a business meeting concerning an export deal in chocolate. Eventually Bond rose. "Right, ladies and gentlemen. See you outside, then."

Already he had arranged to get his party, and their luggage, out of the Saab so that Sukie and Nannie would not even see the team that had flown in. He used some charm to get a man to assist with the luggage, and then gave the girls rapid instructions to follow him into the airport building, where the manager would be waiting.

He joined them a few minutes later, having passed on the Saab keys to Crispin and wished the new team good luck. "M's going to boil you in oil if this goes wrong," Crispin smiled at him.

Bond cocked an eyebrow, sensing the small comma of hair had fallen over his right temple. "If there's anything left of me to boil." As he said it, Bond had a strange premonition of impending disaster coming from some unsuspected source.

"VIP treatment," Sukie sounded delighted when she saw the executive jet, complete with crew and one steward. "Just like the old days with Pasquale."

Nannie simply took it in her stride. Within minutes they were buckled into their seatbelts, whining down the runway and lifting into the black hole of the night.

The steward came around with drinks and sandwiches, then discreetly left them alone.

"So where are we going, James, for the umpteenth time?" Sukie raised her glass.

"And what's more to the point, why?" Nannie sipped her un-iced mineral water.

"The where is Florida. Miami first, and then onward. The why's more difficult."

"Try us," Nannie smiled, peering up over her granny spectacles.

"Oh, we've had a rotten apple in the barrel. Someone I trusted. He set me up, so now I've set him up, arranged a small diversion so that his people imagine we're all on the way to Paris. In reality, as you can see, we're traveling, in some style, to Zurich. From thence we go on, by courtesy of Pan American Airlines, to Miami. First class, naturally, but I suggest that we separate once we reach Zurich. So, tickets, ladies."

He opened the envelope given to him by Crispin and handed

over the long blue and white folders containing the Zurich–Miami segment of the flight. The girls' were made out in their real names— The Principessa Sukie Tempesta and Miss Nannette Norrich. He held back the Providence and Boston Airlines tickets that would get them from Miami to Key West. For some reason he sensed it was better not to let them know the final destination until the last minute. He also glanced at his own ticket to check it was in the name of Mr. J. Boldman—the alias used on what was known as his "B" passport, in which he was described as a company director. All appeared to be in order.

They arranged with the captain, via the steward, to disembark separately at Zurich; to travel independently on the Pan Am flight, and to meet again by the Delta Airlines desk in the main concourse at Miami International. "Get a Skycap to take you there," Bond counseled. "I know the way, but the place is vast and you can get lost at the drop of a boarding pass. Also, beware of legal panhandlers—Hare Krishna, nuns, whatever, they're—"

"Thick on the ground," completed Nannie. "We know, James, we've been to Miami before."

"Sorry. Right. We're set then. If either of you have second thoughts . . ."

"We've been over that as well. We're going to see it through." From Nannie.

"To the bitter end, James." Sukie leaned forward and covered his hand with her own. Bond nodded.

He caught sight of the girls at Zurich, having a snack in one of the splendid cafés that littered that clean and pleasant airport. Bond drank coffee and ate a croissant, then checked in for the Pan Am flight.

On the 747, Sukie and Nannie were seated right up in the front, while Bond occupied a window seat on the starboard side. Neither girl gave him a second look, and he admired the way Sukie had so quickly picked up field technique; Nannie he almost took for granted—already she had shown how good she could be.

The food was reasonable, the flight boring, the movie violent and cut to ribbons by the powers that control in-flight movies. At last, though, they landed at Miami International soon after eight in the evening, local time.

It was hot and crowded, but the girls were already at the Delta counter when he reached them.

"Okay," he greeted them. "Now we go through Gate E, to the PBA departures." He handed them the last tickets.

"Key West?" queried Nannie.

"The 'Last Resort,' they call it," Sukie laughed. "Great, I've been there."

"Well, now's your chance. I want to arrive—"

The ping-pong of an announcement signal on the loudspeaker system interrupted him. He opened his mouth to continue, expecting it to be a routine call for some departure, but the voice mentioned the name Boldman, so he waited, listening for the repeat.

"Would Mr. James Boldman, passenger recently arrived from Zurich, go to the information desk opposite the British Airways counter for an urgent message."

Bond shrugged, "I was going to say that I wanted to arrive incognito. Well, that's my incognito. There has to be some development from my people. Wait for me."

He made his way through the crowds, pressing through lines of people with baggage waiting to check in at various airlines, finally arriving at the information desk.

A blonde with teeth in gloss white and lips in blood red batted eyelids and asked, "Can I help y'awl?"

"Message for James Boldman," he said and saw her glance behind his left shoulder and nod.

The voice was soft in his ear, and unmistakable, "Good evening, Mr. Boldman. How nice to see you."

Steve Quinn pressed close as Bond turned. He could feel the pistol muzzle hard against his ribs, and knew his face to be an etching of surprise.

"Hallo, nice for us to be meeting again, Mr.—what you call yourself now?—Mr. Boldman. Is this right?" Herr Doktor Kirchtum stood on the other side, his big face molded into what appeared to be a big smile of welcome.

"What . . . ?" Bond began.

"Just start walking quietly out of the exit doors over there." Quinn's smile remained, perfect. "Forget your traveling companions, and the PBA flight. We're going to Key West by a different route."

14

FROST-FREE CITY

THE AIRCRAFT WAS very silent in flight—a low rumbling whine from the jets, and that was all. Bond, who had only managed a quick look at the plane before boarding, thought it looked like an Aérospatiale Corvette, with its distinctive long nose-probe.

The interior was sleek and luxurious—customized, as they said in the trade, with six swivel armchairs, a long central table and plush decor in blue and gold.

Below them there was darkness, only the occasional pin of light flashing in the distance, so he presumed they were now high over the Everglades, or turning to make the run to Key West across the sea.

The initial shock of finding himself flanked by Quinn and Kirchtum had passed very quickly. In his job one learned to adapt with speed, think on the run and act accordingly; and in this situation his only option was to go along with Quinn's instructions: In fact it was his only chance of survival.

There had been a moment's hesitation after he felt the gun pressing through cloth into his flesh and saw the faces, then he obeyed, walking calmly between the two men—both big, and crowding him like a pair of cops making a discreet arrest.

Now, he thought, he was really on his own and with nothing up his sleeve. The girls had tickets to Key West, but he had told them to wait for him. They also had the luggage, and his case contained all the weapons—Nannie's two little automatics, the ASP and the steel telescopic baton.

The long black limo with tinted windows stood, parked, directly outside the exit. Kirchtum moved forward a pace to open the rear door, bent his heavy body and entered first.

"In!" Quinn prodded with the gun, almost pushing Bond into the leather-scented interior, quickly following him so that he was closely sandwiched between the two men.

The motor started before the door slammed shut, and the vehicle pulled smoothly away from the curb. Quinn had the gun out now—a small Makarov, Russian made and based on the German Walther PP series design. Bond recognized it immediately, even in the dim glow thrown into the car from the external lights dotted and sprouting from the driveways and airport access roads.

By the same light he could see the driver's head, like a large, elongated coconut, topped with a peaked cap.

Nobody spoke, and no orders were given.

The limo purred onto a slip-road leading, Bond guessed, to the airport perimeter tracks, for Quinn whispered, "Not a word, James. On your life, and May's and Moneypenny's as well." They were approaching a high chain-link fence, into which large gates were set, with a security shack, complete with two uniformed guards.

The car stopped, and there was the whine of the driver's window coming down as one of the guards approached. The driver's hand came up, clutching a fistful of IDs, and the guards said something. The nearside rear window slid down, the guard peering in, looking at the cards in his hand and then glancing in at Quinn, Bond and Kirchtum. "Okay," he said, at last, in a gravel voice. "Through the gate and wait for the guide truck."

They moved forward and stopped, lights dipped. Somewhere ahead of them there was a mighty roar as an aircraft landed, slamming on its reverse thrust so that the noise blanketed everything.

Dimmed light appeared ahead, and a small truck did a neat turn in front of them. It was painted with yellow stripes, a red light revolved on the canopy. The rear was well lit with a large *Follow Me* sign.

They moved off again, obeying the truck, driving very slowly past aircraft of all types—commercial jets, loading and unloading, big piston-engined planes, freighters, small private craft, the insignias ranging from Pan Am, British Airways and Delta to Datsun and Island City Flying Service.

Their aircraft—the one Bond thought was a Corvette—stood well apart from the main gaggle, near a cluster of hangars and buildings on the far side of the field. They pulled up so close that Bond had a moment's concern that they might even touch a wing.

For large men, Quinn and Kirchtum moved with efficient speed, like a well-drilled team, Kirchtum leaving the car almost before it had come to a standstill, and Quinn edging Bond toward the door, so that he was constantly covered from both sides.

Once out in the open, Kirchtum's hand grasped his arm like a steel trap until Quinn was out. The rest was very fast—an armlock and pressure, forcing Bond toward the airdoor and up the steps. He was in the cabin, with Quinn, pistol now in full view, behind him in seconds, and Kirchtum closing the door, the airsteps folding inward and the door locking with a solid clunk.

"That seat," Quinn indicated with the pistol, while Kirchtum moved in with two pairs of handcuffs, which clicked around their victim's wrists and were fitted solidly with small steel D-rings into the padded arms of the seat.

"You've done this before," Bond smiled. There was no edge in showing fear to people like this.

"A precaution." Quinn stood clear, the pistol leveled, as Kirchtum looped shackles around Bond's ankles and secured them to similar steel D-rings on the lower part of the seat. "It would be foolish to be forced to use this once we're airborne." Quinn indicated the pistol as the engines rumbled into life. Seconds later they were moving.

There had been a short wait as they taxied, in line, waiting for other airplanes to be cleared, then the little jet swung onto the runway, burst into full life and rocketed away, climbing fast.

"I apologize for the deception, James." Quinn was now relaxed and leaning back in his seat with a drink. "You see, we thought you might just possibly visit the Mozart, so we stayed prepared for that possibility—even with the torture paraphernalia on show, and the Herr Doktor looking like an unwilling victim. I admit to one serious error: I should have ordered my outside team to move in after you entered. However, these things happen. But the Herr Doktor was excellent in his role of frightened captive, I thought."

"Oscar nominee." Bond's expression did not alter. "I hope nothing nasty's going to happen to my two lady friends."

"I don't think you need bother yourself about them," Quinn smiled happily. "We sent them a message that you would not be leaving tonight. They think you're joining them at the Airport Hilton. I should imagine they're waiting there for you now. If they do get suspicious, I fear they won't be able to do much about

it. You have a date in the morning—I should imagine about
lunchtime—with what the good old French revolutionaries called
Madame La Guillotine. I shall not be there to witness it. As I
told you before, my department merely has orders to hand you
over to the self-styled Colonel Rahani and his organization,
SPECTRE. We take the money and see to the release of May
and Moneypenny—you can trust me regarding that. They will be
returned, 'unopened,' as the jargon has it, though it would be
useful to interrogate Moneypenny."

"And where is all this going to take place?" Bond asked, his
voice showing no concern regarding his appointment with the
guillotine.

"Oh, quite near Key West. A few miles offshore. Outside the
reef. Our timing isn't that brilliant, because we'll have to hole up
with you until dawn. The channel through the reef is not the
easiest to navigate, and we don't want to end up on a sandbar.
But we'll manage. Arrangements have been made. I promised my
superiors that *we* would hand you over and deal with the competition. I like to keep promises."

"Especially to the kind of masters you serve," Bond muttered.
"Failure isn't exactly appreciated in the Russian service. At best
you'd be demoted, or end up running exercises for trainees; at
worst it would be one of those nice hospitals where they inject
you with Aminazin—such a pleasant drug. Turns you into a living
vegetable. I reckon that's exactly how you'll end up." He turned
to Kirchtum, "You as well, Herr Doktor. How did they put the
arm on you?"

The burly doctor gave a huge shrug. "The Klinik Mozart is my
whole life, Herr Bond. My entire life. Some years ago we had—
how do I put it?—a financial embarrassment . . . ?"

"You were broke," Bond said, placidly.

"So. Ja. Yes, broke. No funds. Friends of Mr. Quinn—the
people he works for—made me a very good offer. I could carry
on my work, which has always been in the interests of humanity,
and they would see to the funds."

"I can guess the rest. The price was your cooperation. The odd
visitor, to be kept under sedation for a while and then moved.
Sometimes a body. Occasionally some surgery."

The doctor nodded sadly. "Ja. All those things. I admit that I did not expect to become involved in a situation like the present one. But Mr. Quinn tells me I shall be able to return with no blot on my professional character. Officially I am away for two days. A rest."

Bond laughed. "A rest? You believe that? It can only end with arrest, Herr Doktor. Either arrest, or one of Mr. Quinn's bullets. Probably the latter."

"Stop that," Quinn said sharply. "The doctor is well and truly involved. He has been of great help. He will be rewarded, and he knows it." He smiled at Kirchtum. "Mr. Bond is using an old, old trick, trying to make you doubt our intentions; attempting to drive a wedge between us. You know how clever he can be. You've seen him in action."

Again the doctor nodded. "Ja. The shooting of Vasili and Yuri was unexpectedly unfunny. That I did not like."

"But you were also clever—giving Mr. Quinn some harmless injection . . ."

"Water."

"And, presumably, following me."

"We were on your track very quickly." Quinn glanced toward the window. Outside there was still darkness. "But you changed *my* plans, I fear. My people in Paris were supposed to deal with you. It took some very fast and fancy choreography, James. But we managed."

"You did indeed." Bond swiveled his seat, leaning forward to edge his head close to the window. He thought there were lights in the distance.

"Ah," Quinn sounded pleased, "there we are. Lights—Stock Island and Key West. About ten minutes to go, I imagine."

"And what if I make a fuss when we land?"

"You won't make a fuss."

"You're very confident."

"I have faith. Just as you had faith that I would comply because of Tabitha, I really do believe that you will do as you're told in order to secure the release of May and Moneypenny. It's the one chink in your armor, James. Always has been. Yes, you're a cold fish; ruthless. But you're also an old-fashioned English gentleman at heart. Saint George and all that. You'd give your life to save a damsel in distress, only this time we're not talking of damsels, but of an aging housekeeper, to whom you're devoted, and your Chief's personal assistant—a lady who has loved you hopelessly and from afar for years." He shook his head, smiling. "Not damsels held under spells or captured by dragons. People you *care* for in thrall to one of the dragons you hate most in all the world. You'd give your life for them. It's, unhappily, in your nature. Unhappily, did I say? I really meant happily—for us, happily."

Bond swallowed. Deep down inside he knew that Steve Quinn had played the trump card. He was quite right: 007 would go to his own death to preserve the lives of people like May and Moneypenny.

As the glitter of lights grew closer and brighter, James Bond reflected on the irony. Many times, he had put himself in jeopardy for young and beautiful women. Now, unless some miracle saved him, he was about to die for an elderly woman and a pleasant lady, whom he liked, yet could never fall in love with in a million years.

"There is another reason why you won't make a fuss." Quinn's smile, which one had to search for under the bushy beard—it did not show in his eyes—was still there. "Show him, Herr Doktor."

Kirchtum lifted a small case that lay in the magazine rack between the seats. From the case he drew out what looked like a child's space gun made of clear plastic. "Is an injection pistol." Kirchtum gave a sort of grin. "Before we land I shall fill it. Look, you can see the action." He drew back a small plunger from the rear, lifted the barrel in front of Bond's face and touched the tiny trigger—the whole thing was no more than three inches long, with a couple of inches for the butt. As he touched the trigger, a hypodermic needle appeared, fast as a piece of magician's equipment, from the muzzle. "Injection is given in 2.5 seconds." The Herr Doktor nodded gravely again. "Very quick. Also the needle is very long. Goes easily through cloth."

"You show the least sign of making a fuss, and you'll get the needle, right?"

"Instant death."

"Oh, no. Instant facsimile heart attack. You'll come back to us within half an hour, as good as new. Rahani and SPECTRE want your head. If the worst comes to the worst, then we must kill you and do the unpleasant business with a power tool. But we'd rather deliver the whole body, alive and intact. We owe Rahani several favors, and the poor man hasn't long to live. Your head is his last request, and it'll make his deathbed day to watch that clever, cruel head leave your restless body. So, you won't make a fuss."

"No fuss," Bond agreed, and a moment later the pilot came on the intercom system to ask that seatbelts be fastened and cigarettes extinguished. "We'll be landing in about four minutes," he announced.

Bond watched from the window as they dropped toward the lights. He saw buildings, water, tropical palms, roads, traffic and multicolored signs coming up to meet them.

"Interesting place, Key West," mused Quinn. "Hemingway once called it 'The poor man's St. Tropez'; Tennessee Williams lived here, and many more creative folk. President Truman established a 'Little White House' near what used to be the naval base; John F. Kennedy brought the British PM—Harold Macmillan—to visit; Cuban boat people landed here; but, long before that, it was a pirates' and wreckers' paradise. I'm told it's still a smugglers' heaven, and the United States Coast Guard operates a tight schedule out of here." They swept in over the threshold and touched down with hardly a bump.

"There's history in this airport as well," Quinn continued. "First regular United States mail flight started from here, and Key West is both the beginning and end of Highway Route One." They were rolling to a halt, turning to taxi toward a shacklike hut, with a veranda, which looked as though it had come straight off the back lot of some Hollywood company in the 1940s. Bond saw a low wall with faded lettering—*Welcome to Key West, the Only Frost-Free City in the United States.*

"And they have the most spectacular sunsets," Quinn added. "Really incredible. Pity you won't be around to see one."

The heat hit them like a furnace as they left the aircraft. Even the mild breeze was like a light wind blown from an inferno.

They had organized the departure from the jet as carefully as the boarding, leaving Bond in no doubt that—even though his hands and feet were now free—he would be unconscious very quickly if he did anything to cause suspicion. "Smile and pretend to talk," muttered Quinn, glancing toward the veranda where a

dozen or so people were waiting to welcome passengers off a newly
arrived PBA flight. Bond scanned faces, but saw nobody who
looked remotely like a friend.

They passed through a small gate in the wall abutting the arrivals
and departures shack, Quinn and Kirchtum nudging him forward
toward a sleek dark automobile. They followed the same routine
they had performed at Miami, and in a matter of moments, Bond
was again seated between the two men, though this time the driver
was visible—young, open-necked shirt, blonde long hair. "Y'awl
okay?" he asked.

"Just drive," Quinn ordered. "There's a place arranged, I understand."

"Sure thing. Git y'there in no time." He drew out onto the
road, turning his head slightly, "Y'awl mind if'n I have some
music playin'?"

"Go ahead. As long as it doesn't frighten the horses." Quinn
was very relaxed and confident. If it had not been for Kirchtum,
tense on the other side, Bond would have made a move. But the
Herr Doktor was wound up like a hair trigger. He would have
the hypo into 007 even if he moved quickly.

A burst of sound filled the car, a rough voice singing, tired,
cynical and sad.

> There's a hole in Daddy's arm,
> Where all the money goes . . .

"Not that!" cracked Quinn.

"Ah'm sorry. I kinda like rock and roll. Rhythm and blues.
Man, it's good music."

"I said not *that*."

The car went silent, the driver sullen. Bond watched the lights
and signs—*South Roosevelt Blvd.* A restaurant alive with people
eating—*Martha's.* Lush tropical foliage, the swish of tires, the
ocean on their right; they appeared to be following a long bend
taking them away from the Atlantic, and there were clapboard
houses, white with fretted gingerbread decorations along the porches
and verandas; lights flashed—*Motel; No Vacancy.* Then they turned,
quite suddenly, at a sign—*Searstown*—and Bond saw they were
in a large shopping area.

The car pulled up between a supermarket—the lights blazing and people still buying—and an optician's shop. Between the two there was a narrow alley.

"It's up there. Door on the right. Up above the eye place, where they sell reading glasses. Guess y'awl want me to pick you up."

"Five o'clock." Quinn spoke quietly. "In time to get to Garrison Bight at dawn."

"Y'awl goin' on a fishin' trip, then." The driver turned around and Bond saw his face for the first time. He was not a young man, as Bond had thought—or at least life had been unkind to him in his true youth, for, though he had long blonde hair, half the man's face was missing, sunken in and patched with skin grafts. He must have detected shock in Bond for he looked at him straight with his one good eye and gave an unearthly grimace. "Don't you worry about me none. That's why I work for these gentlemen here. I got this brand new face in Nam, so I thought I could put it to use. Frightens the hell outa some folks."

"Five o'clock," Quinn repeated, opening the door.

The routine did not vary. They had Bond out, along the alley, through a door and up one flight of stairs in no time.

It was a bare room. Two chairs and two beds. Curtains, a noisy air-conditioning unit, and precious little else. Again they used the handcuffs and shackles on Bond, and Kirchtum sat near him—hypo-gun in hand—while Quinn went out for food. They ate melon, some bread and ham, washing it down with mineral water. Then Quinn and Kirchtum took turns guarding Bond, who, giving himself up to the inevitable, went to sleep.

It was still just dark when Quinn shook him awake and stood over him in the little bathroom—bare and functional as the rest of the place. After ten minutes or so, with Bond trying to fight off the grogginess of travel and time, they led him downstairs.

The car was waiting, and they drove out, unnoticed by the very few who were showing signs of life at this time in the morning. The sky looked hard and gray, but Quinn said it was going to be a beautiful day, and that it was a pity Bond would not be around to sample all of it.

North Roosevelt Blvd. Then some kind of marina to their left—yachts and big powered fishing boats. Water to their right as well. Quinn pointed, "That'll be where we'll be heading. Gulf of Mexico.

The island's out on the far side of the reef."

They came up to a restaurant sign—*Harbor Lights*—and hustled Bond out, along the side of the dead, sleeping restaurant and down onto the marina quayside where a tanned, tall and muscular man waited near a forty-foot powered fishing boat, complete with a high laddered and skeletal superstructure above the cabin, its engines idling.

Quinn and the captain exchanged nods, and they bundled Bond aboard, down into the narrow cabin. Once more the handcuffs and shackles went on, the motor noise rose and Bond could feel the swell as the craft started out from the quayside, cruising its way into the marina, under a bridge, and then picking up speed. Kirchtum had put away the hypo and seemed to be calm, while Quinn appeared to have joined the captain at the controls.

Five minutes out they really started to make way, the boat rolling slightly and bounding, slapping hard down into the water. Everyone was concentrating on the navigation, and Bond began to think seriously about his predicament. They had spoken of an island outside the reef, and he wondered how long it would take them. He then concentrated on the handcuffs, realizing before he even began that there was little he could do to get out of them. Houdini, he thought, would have had problems.

Then, unexpectedly, Quinn came down into the cabin. "I'm going to gag you and cover you up." He looked slightly concerned. "There's what looks like another fishing powerboat to starboard, and they appear to be in some kind of trouble. The captain says we should at least offer help. If they have a radio they could report us, and I don't want to raise any alarms. Stay still."

He pushed a handkerchief into Bond's mouth, and then tied another around it, so that for a moment he thought he would suffocate. Then, after checking the shackles, Quinn threw a blanket over him. In the darkness Bond listened.

They were slowing, rolling a little, but definitely slowing. Above, he heard the captain shouting, "Are you in trouble?" Then, a few seconds later, "Right, I'll come aboard, but I have an RV. May have to pick you up on the way back."

There was a sharp bump, as though they had made contact with the other boat, and then all hell broke loose.

Bond lost count after the first dozen shots—cracks: hand guns, he thought. Then the stutter of a machine pistol. A cry, which sounded like Kirchtum, and a number of thumps on the deck above him. Then silence, until he sensed someone nearby. The sound of bare feet descending into the cabin.

The blanket was hauled back roughly and Bond tried to turn his head, eyes widening as he saw the figure above him.

"Well, well, Master James." Nannie Norrich had her small automatic in one hand. "We do have to get you out of some scrapes, don't we?" She turned her head. "Sukie, it's okay. He's down here, trussed up and oven ready by the look of it."

Sukie appeared, also armed. She grinned appealingly. "Bondage, they call it, I believe." She began to laugh as Bond loosed off a stream of obscenities, which were completely inaudible from behind his gag.

They began to work on the handcuffs and shackles. Sukie went aloft again, returning with keys.

"I hope those idiots weren't friends of yours," said Nannie. "I'm afraid we had to deal with them."

The gag came away. "What do you mean, 'deal'?" Bond spluttered. She looked so innocent that his blood ran cold at her answer.

"I'm afraid they're dead, James. All three of them. Stone dead. But you must admit we were clever to find *you*."

15

THE PRICE FOR A LIFE

INDEED, THE CAPTAIN, Steve Quinn and Herr Doktor Kirchtum *were* dead. Stone dead, as Nannie had said, though "stone dead" was not an accurate description. They were bone dead—bone, tissue, cell, muscle, flesh and blood dead.

The captain lay on his back in the little wheelhouse—his shirt bloodied and ripped by at least two bullets that had hit him high, near the throat. Herr Doktor Kirchtum was crumpled in the stern well, his face strangely happy, his body like a beached baby whale. There was not much blood—a trickle coming from the folds of flesh, and Bond guessed he had caught his lethal wounds in the stomach. Nearby lay an Uzi machine pistol.

Steve Quinn was the worst. Obviously he had moved forward, trying to take shelter and shoot from behind the superstructure. The glass around the wheelhouse and upper cabin was starred and shattered, while Quinn lay flat on his back, what was left of his head pointing toward the prow. Two, maybe three bullets, Bond thought: meticulously aimed for the head. Quinn had been thrown back against the guard rail, probably hitting the three neatly rolled life jackets and then bouncing onto the deck.

None of it was pretty, and Bond felt an odd sense of surprise that the two relatively young girls who had brought about this carnage remained buoyant, even elated, as though killing three men were like swatting flies in a kitchen. He also realized that he was suffering from a certain amount of resentment—he had taken the initiative; he had been duped by Quinn and Kirchtum; he had fallen into their quickly devised trap. Yet he had not been able to effect his own escape—the girls had rescued him, and he felt vaguely resentful about it. A peculiar reaction when he should have been very grateful.

A power fishing boat—almost identical to the one in which Bond had been held—lay alongside, rising, falling and gently bumping the boat of death. The sea was smooth, the sky turning from pearl to deep blue as the sun cleared the horizon. It was going to be a beautiful day.

They were well outside the reef, and in the far distance little low mounds of island rose from the sea.

"Well?" Nannie stood near him, looking around while Sukie appeared to be busying herself on their boat.

"Well what?" Bond asked flatly, his voice tinged with diffidence.

"Well, weren't we clever to find you?"

"Very." Sharp, clipped and almost angry. "Was this all necessary?"

"You mean blowing away your captors?" The expression sounded strange coming from the prim-looking Nannie Norrich. "Yes," she flushed with anger now. "Yes, very necessary. Can't you even say thank you, James? We tried to deal with it peacefully, but they opened up with that damned Uzi." She pointed toward their boat and the nasty jagged row of holes in the hull, abaft the high skeleton superstructure above the cabin. "They gave us no option."

Bond nodded, muttering his thanks. Then, "You were, indeed, *very* clever to find me. I'd like to hear more about that."

"And so you shall." Nannie had adopted a waspish attitude. "But first we really have to do something about this mess," waving a hand around her to indicate boat and bodies alike.

"What weapons're you carrying?"

"The two pistols from your case—your stuff's back at the hotel in Key West. I had to force two of the padlocks, I'm afraid—couldn't work out the combinations, and we had become fairly desperate by then."

"Any extra fuel around?"

She pointed, past Kirchtum's body in the stern well. "A couple of cans there. We've got three aboard our boat."

"It's got to look like a catastrophe," Bond frowned. "What's more, they mustn't find the bodies. An explosion would be best—preferably with us well out of the area. It's easy enough, but we really need some kind of fuse, and that's what we haven't got."

"We have a signal pistol—flares."

Bond nodded. "Then that's the only possible way. What's the range—about a hundred yards? You get back with Sukie. Break out the pistol and flares, I'll do what's necessary here."

She nodded, turned away and sprang lightly onto the guard rail, jumping aboard their boat and calling to Sukie.

Bond then set about the somewhat grim task, working with efficient speed, his mind still churning the facts. How *did* the girls manage to find him? How *could* they be in the right place at the right time? He needed the answers to those questions, and until they satisfied him there was no possible way he could trust either of the young women.

He searched the boat carefully, carrying everything that might be of use up onto the deck—rope, wire, boxes of fishing gear that included the ultra-strong lines used for bringing in large fish like sharks and swordfish.

All the weapons went overboard, except for Quinn's automatic—

a prosaic Browning 9mm—and some spare clips.

Next came the grisly job of moving the bodies into the stern well. Kirchtum, being already there, only needed turning over, a task accomplished with Bond's feet; the captain's body stuck in the wheelhouse door, and he had to tug hard to get him free, while Quinn was the most difficult of all, for he had to be dragged along the narrow gap separating cabin from guard rail.

He arranged the bodies in a row, lashing them loosely together with fishing line, positioning them directly over where he knew the fuel tanks to be located. He then went forward again, gathering as much inflammable material as he could—sheets and blankets off the four bunks in the cabin, cushions, pillows and even pieces of rag. These he bundled together, well forward, weighting them with life jackets and other heavier pieces of equipment. He left one piece of coiled rope near the bodies and then transferred himself to the other boat, where Sukie and Nannie were standing close to each other—Sukie forward in the wheel house, Nannie behind her, on the steps leading down to the cabin.

"There it is. One flare pistol." Nannie held the bulbous flare projector by the muzzle.

"Plenty of flares?"

She pointed to a metal box containing a dozen or so stumpy cartridges, each marked with their colors—red, green and illuminating. Bond picked out three of the last. "These should do us." He rapidly told them what was required, and Sukie started the engines as Nannie began to cast off all but one rope amidships.

Bond returned to Quinn's boat to make the final preparations. He dragged the rope from the bodies to the pile of material forward, secured it under the pile and gently played it out back to the stern well, laying it alongside the inlets to the fuel tanks.

He then went forward again carrying one of the two cans of emergency fuel, saturating the material at the front of the boat and running plenty of the liquid over the rope, shuffling backward toward the bodies and fuel caps.

Last he opened the second can, dowsed the bodies in fuel and unscrewed the main fuel cap, inserting the saturated rope, lowering it into the tank. Then he turned and yelled "Stand by!" to the girls, ran from the stern well, mounted the guard rail and was aboard the other boat just as Nannie let go of the one rope that attached the vessels one to the other. Sukie slowly eased the engines open, and they pulled away, gently turning stern-on to the boat from which he had been rescued.

Bond positioned himself aft of the superstructure, slid a flare into the pistol, checked the wind and watched the gap slowly widen between the two craft. At around eighty yards he raised the pistol high and fired an illuminating flare, using a low, flat trajectory. The flare hissed right across the bow of the other boat, but by the time he realized it was a miss, Bond had already reloaded and taken up another position.

This time, the fizzing white flare performed a perfect arc, leaving a thick stream of white smoke behind it, to land in the bow of the other craft. There was a second's pause before the material ignited with a small whumph, and Bond saw the flames being carried straight along the rope fuse toward the fuel tanks, above which the bodies lay.

"Give her full power and weave as much as possible!" Bond shouted to Sukie. The engine note rose, bow lifting, almost before he had completed the order.

Rapidly they bounced away from the blazing fishing boat.

The bodies caught fire, the stern well sending up a crimson flame and then a dense cloud of black smoke. They were a good mile and a half away when the fuel tanks went up—a great roaring explosion with a dark red center, ripping the boat and, he presumed, the bodies apart in a ferocious fireball.

It was the end—just the smoke, the scarlet center of flame, a rising cascade of debris, then nothing. The water appeared to boil around what little remained of the powerful fishing boat, then settled, steamed for a few seconds, and flattened. The shock waves hit the rear of their boat a second or two after the explosion. There was a slight burn on the wind, which they all felt on their cheeks.

At three miles there was nothing to be seen, but Bond remained leaning against the superstructure, gazing in the direction of what had been a small and violent inferno.

"Coffee?" Nannie asked.

"Depends how long we're staying at sea."

"We hired this thing for a day's fishing," she grinned. "I don't think we should make it too obvious."

"No, we'll even have to try to fish. Sukie okay at the wheel?"
Sukie Tempesta turned, nodded and smiled.

"She's an expert." Nannie gestured toward the steps down under the wheelhouse. "There's coffee on."

"And I want to hear how you managed to find me." Bond gave her a steady, suspicious look.

"I told you. I was minding you, James." They were seated in the cramped cabin, he on one bunk facing Nannie, who sat on the other. They both nursed mugs of coffee, and the power boat rolled and thudded against the sea. Sukie had reduced power, and they appeared to be performing a series of gentle, wide circles. "When members of Norrich Universal Bodyguards take it upon themselves to look after you, you get looked after." She had her long legs tucked under her on the bunk, and had unpinned her hair so that it fell, dark and thick, to her shoulders, giving her face an almost elfin look, and somehow making the gray eyes softer and very interesting.

Take care, Bond thought, this lady has to explain herself, and she had better be convincing.

"So I got looked after." He did not smile.

She explained that as soon as he was paged at Miami International, she had told Sukie to stay with the luggage while she followed at a discreet distance. "I had plenty of cover—you know that, the place was crowded—but I saw the routine and I'm experienced enough to know when a client is being pulled."

"But they took me away by car."

"Yes, I had its number, though, and made two quick telephone calls—my little NUB has a small branch here, and they put a trace on the limo. I said I'd call them back if I needed assistance. I then called the flight planning office."

"Resourceful lady."

"James, in this game you have to be. Apart from the scheduled flights to Key West there was one private Exec jet that had a filed flight plan. I took down the details—"

"Which were?"

"Company called Société pour la Promotion de l'Ecologie et de la Civilisation."

SPEC, Bond thought. SPEC. SPECTRE.

"We had about six minutes to catch the PBA flight to Key

West, so I gambled we'd make it just before the private flight."

"You also gambled on my being on board the SPEC jet."

She nodded, "True, but you were. If you hadn't been on it, I would have had egg on my face. However, we were in, and off the aircraft a good five minutes before you came along. I even had time to hire a car, send Sukie to the best hotel in town and follow you to that shopping center in Searstown."

"And then what?"

"I hung around," she paused, not looking at him. "To be honest, I didn't really know what to do, then, like a small miracle, the big bearded guy came out and went straight to the telephone booth. I was only a few paces away, but—in spite of the spectacles—I've got good eyesight. I watched him punch out a number and talk for a while. He went to the supermarket and I took his place in the booth and dialed the number—he called the Harbor Lights Restaurant."

She had got a map and guide with the little rented VW ("They said a small car would be best"), so the Harbor Lights was easy enough to find. "As soon as I got inside I realized it was a fishing and yachting people's paradise—full of bronzed, muscular men who rented boats, and themselves to sail them. I just asked around. One guy—the one who went up in smoke just now—let it slip that he had been hired for an early start. He'd had a bit to drink and even told me what time he was leaving, *with three passengers.*"

"So you hired another powered fishing boat."

"Right. Told the captain I didn't need help—knowing Sukie could really navigate the trickiest of waters blindfolded and with her hands tied. He took me down to this boat, made a pass, got rebuked, showed me the charts, told me about the currents, the channels—which are not easy—talked about the reef, the islands and the 'drop-off' into the Gulf of Mexico, eighteen miles out, and gave me the keys."

"So you went back to Sukie at the hotel . . ."

"Pored over the charts half the night, got down to Garrison Bight early and were outside the reef when your boat came out. We shadowed at a safe distance for a while, and then overtook, just out of sight, watching you on the radar. Positioned ourselves near enough to your course, stopped engines and started firing distress flares. You know the rest."

"You tried to take her by reason, but they opened up with the Uzi."

"To their cost." She cocked her head, and gave a sigh. "Lord, I'm tired."

"You're not alone—and what about Sukie?"

"She seems happy enough. Always is with boats." She put down the empty coffee mug, her hand moving to her shirt, slowly starting to undo the buttons. "I really think I'd like to lie down, James. Would you like to lie down with me?"

"What if we hit a squall? We'll be thrown all over the place." Bond leaned forward to kiss her gently on the mouth.

"I'd rather meet a swell." Her arms came up around his neck, drawing him toward her.

Later, she said that she'd rarely been thanked so well for saving somebody's life.

"You should do it again sometime." Bond kissed her, running one hand over her naked body.

"Why not now?" asked Nannie with an implike grin. "It seems a fair price for a life."

16

GOING DOWN TONIGHT

"As far as I can tell, there are three islands, outside the reef, that are privately owned, with some kind of building on them." Sukie's finger roamed around the chart of waters in the Key West vicinity.

It was early afternoon and they had hoved to, with fishing lines out. So far four large red snapper had come their way, but nothing big—no sharks, no swordfish.

"This one here," Sukie indicated an island just outside the reef, within easy distance of Key West, "is owned by the man who

initially built the hotel we're booked into. There's another to the
north, and this one," her finger circled a largish patch of land,
"just on the shelf, before you reach the drop-off—the edge of the
Continental Shelf, where the depth goes straight from eight hundred
to eighteen hundred. Great fishing water around the drop-off.
There've also been treasure seekers by the dozen in the area."
She prodded the island on the map. "Anyway, it looked very
much as though that was where you were heading."

Bond peered closer to see the name. "Shark Island," he said
aloud. "How cozy."

"Someone appears to think so. I asked around the hotel last
night. A couple of years ago a man who called himself Rainey—
Tarquin Rainey—bought the place. The boy at the hotel is from
an old Key West family, and knows all the gossip. Says this fellow
Rainey isn't seen by people—mystery man; arrives by private jet
and gets ferried out to Shark Island by helicopter or a launch,
which usually stays out there. He's also a bit of a go-getter. People
who build on the islands usually take a lot of time; there's always
difficulty getting the materials taken out, but Rainey had his place
up in the space of one summer. The second summer saw the
island landscaped—he's got tropical trees, gardens, the lot. They're
very impressed, the people in Key West, and it takes a great deal
to impress them—particularly as they claim to be a republic: the
Conch Republic, pronounced 'Konk.'"

"*Nobody's* seen him?" Bond asked, knowing that the alias Tarquin Rainey was just too good to be true. It had to be Tamil
Rahani, which meant Shark Island was SPECTRE property.

"Not officially, no. There are folk who've had a glimpse, of
course—at a distance. Nobody's encouraged to get near him,
though. Apparently some boats have approached Shark Island and
been warned away—politely, but very firmly—by large men in
fast motorboats."

"Mmmmm." Bond thought for a few minutes, then asked Sukie
if she could navigate to within a mile or so at night.

"If the charts are accurate, yes. It'll be slow going, but it's
possible. When did you want to go?"

"I thought perhaps tonight." Bond looked steadily from Sukie
to Nannie. "If that was where I was being taken, then it's really

only courteous for me to call on Mr. Rainey at the earliest possible opportunity."

The girls looked dubious.

"I think we should head back to Garrison Bight now. See if you can keep up the boat hire for a couple of days; then let me get myself one or two bits and pieces I'm going to need, have a look around Key West—see and be seen—and sail about two in the morning. I won't put you in danger, *that* I promise. You simply wait offshore. If I don't return by a certain time, then you get the hell out of it and come back tomorrow night."

"Okay by me." Sukie got to her feet.

Nannie just nodded. She had been quiet all day since they had come back on deck—silent, with many warm glances in Bond's direction.

"Right. Let's get the lines hauled in. We sail at two. In the meantime there's a great deal to be done."

The local police were at Garrison Bight, checking on the boat hired by Steve Quinn. There had been a report from another powerboat that had seen a plume of smoke, and from a Navy helicopter that had spotted wreckage, and sighted *Prospero*—the name of the boat hired by Nannie—some miles from the spot. They had seen the chopper, an hour or so after Quinn's boat had exploded—even waved to it, knowing they were well distanced from Quinn's vessel.

Nannie went ashore and talked to the law, while Sukie stayed in sight on deck and Bond remained in the cabin. It took around half an hour, and Nannie returned, all smiles, saying she had charmed the pants off the cops and hired the boat for a week.

"I hope we're not going to need it that long," Bond grimaced.

"Better safe than sorry, as we Nannies are supposed to say." She poked her tongue out before adding, "Master James."

"I've had enough of that little joke, thank you." He sounded genuinely irritated. "Now, where are we staying? Where's my luggage?"

"Only one place to stay in Key West," Sukie joined in. "The Pier House Hotel. You get a wonderful view of the famous sunset from there."

"I've a lot to do before sunset," Bond said sharply. "The sooner we get to this—what's it called, Pier House?—the better."

As they set off in the hired VW, Bond suddenly felt very naked without his own weapons. He sat next to Nannie, with Sukie squeezed into the back giving an occasional running commentary, having been to the island before.

The place, to Bond, seemed an odd mixture of down-market resort tackiness, sudden snatches of great beauty and large patches of luxury that spelled money. It was hot, palm trees shimmered and moved in the light breeze, and they passed numerous clapboard gingerbread houses, which had a satisfying, pleasing look to them, most of them bright, well-painted and kept in good order, their yards and gardens bright with the color of sub-tropical flowers.

The odd thing was that you could see several of these houses, in perfect condition, but next to rundown places, or even rubbish dumps. The sidewalks were also either in fine order or cracked, broken or nearly nonexistent.

At an intersection, they had to wait for an extraordinary-looking train—a kind of model railroad engine, built onto what appeared to be a diesel-powered jeep, pulled a series of cars, full of people, sitting interested under striped awnings.

"The Conch Train," Sukie informed them. "That's the way tourists get to see Key West."

Bond could hear the driver, all done out in blue overalls and peaked cap, going through a litany of the sights and history as the train wound its way around the island.

They finally turned into a long street that was a mixture of wood and concrete and appeared to house a mile or so of jewelry, tourist junk and art shops, together with great batches of restaurants, which looked very prosperous indeed.

"Duval," announced Sukie, giving them the name of the street and commenting on restaurants and places of interest as they went. "It goes right down to the ocean—to our hotel in fact—and it's great at night. There, see, that's the famous Fast Buck Freddie's Department Store; Antonia's, a great Italian restaurant; and here comes Sloppy Joe's Bar. They say it was Ernest Hemingway's favorite haunt when he lived here."

There was no doubt that Hemingway had lived in Key West. Even if Bond had not known it through reading *To Have and Have Not* he would certainly be apprised of the fact now, for many of the shops had souvenir T-shirts or drawings of Hemingway, while Sloppy Joe's Bar proclaimed the fact loudly, from an inn sign and a tall painted legend on the wall.

The sidewalks were crowded, and the order of dress ranged from straight casual to casual bizarre—the shortest of shorts, the most ragged of cutoffs, T-shirts with weird slogans decorating chests and bosoms: *I owe, I owe, so off to work I go;* and *Sex Tuition Here: First Lesson Free.*

As they reached the bottom of Duval, Bond saw what he was looking for and made a note that it was within very quick walking distance of the hotel, the grounds of which were on their right.

"You're already registered, and your luggage is in your suite," Nannie told him, as she parked the car, and, together, the girls hustled him through the main reception area—all light, friendliness and bamboo—through doors into an enclosed courtyard. In the center a fountain played among flowers and a tall wooden statue of a naked woman. Above, large fans revolved silently, sending a downdraft of cool air.

He followed them down a passage and out into the garden, with its twisting flower-bordered pathways, a pool deck to the left, and beyond that more wood and bamboo; a line of bars and restaurants ran beside a small beach—a pier (after which the hotel was named) held out over the water on big wooden piles.

The whole building appeared to be U-shaped—the gardens, pool and beach located in the center of the U. They entered the main hotel again at the far side of the pool, and went into an elevator and up one floor.

There were two suites, next to each other. "We're sharing," Sukie said, inserting her key into one of the doors. "But you're right next to us, James, in case there's anything we can do for you." For the first time since they had met, Bond thought he could detect an invitation in Sukie's voice. He certainly saw a small angry flash of fire in Nannie's eyes. Could it be that the pair were fighting over him?

"What's the plan?" Nannie asked, a shade sharply.

"Where's the best place to watch this incredible sunset you've been telling me about?"

She allowed him a smile. "The deck outside the Havana Docks Bar—or so they tell me."

"And what's the witching hour?"

"Around six."

"The bar's in the hotel?"

"Right over there," she waved a hand, vaguely, in the direction from which they had come. "Up above the restaurants. Right out toward the sea."

"Meet you both there at six, then." Bond smiled, turned the key in his door and disappeared into what proved to be a pleasant and functional—if not altogether luxurious—suite.

The pair of briefcases and his special Samsonite folding case stood in the middle of the room, and it took Bond less than ten minutes to organize his unpacking. He felt better with the ASP back on his person and the concealable operations baton hidden away under his jacket.

He checked the rooms carefully, made certain the window catches were secure, then quietly opened the door. The corridor was deserted. Silently he closed the door, making his way quickly to the elevator, then back down into the gardens, through an exit to the car park he had noted on the way through, and then out into the hot and humid air.

At the far end of the parking lot stood a low building—the Pier House Market—access to which could be gained from either the hotel or Front Street.

Bond walked straight through, pausing for a moment to look at the fruits and meats on sale, then made his way onto Front Street, turning right and crossing the cracked and lumpy road, walking fast to the corner of Duval. He passed the shop he really wanted to visit, and went on until he found a small male boutique where he bought some faded jeans, a T-shirt without any tasteless slogan and a pair of soft loafers. When in Rome, he thought. Finally he chose an overpriced short linen jacket. For people in Bond's job some kind of jacket or blouse was always necessary, if only to hide the hardware.

He came out of the boutique, turned and made his way back to the place he had spotted from the car. It had an open front decorated with a dummy clad in scuba gear, and the legend above the big walk-in front read *Reef Plunderers' Diving Emporium.*

The bearded, tanned salesman started to try to sell him a three-and-a-half-hour snorkeling trip on board a dive boat called, predictably, *Reef Plunderer II,* but Bond knew exactly what he wanted.

"Captain Jack knows all the best places to dive along the reef," the salesman protested, wasting his breath.

"I want a wet suit, snorkeling mask, knife, flippers, undersea torch, and a shoulder bag for the lot," Bond told him, using the soft yet commanding tone that always demanded attention.

The salesman looked at Bond, took in the physique under the lightweight suit and the hard look in the icy blue eyes. "Yes siree. Sure. Right," he said, leading the way to the rear of the shop. "Gonna cost a ransom, but you sure know what y'awl're after."

"That's right." Bond did not allow his voice to rise above the almost whispering softness.

"Right," the salesman repeated. He was dressed to look like an experienced man of the sea, with a striped T-shirt and jeans. A gold ring hung, piratically rather than fashionably, from one ear. He gave Bond another sidelong look and began to collect equipment from the back of the store. It took ten minutes before Bond was completely satisfied with the purchases—adding a belt with a waterproof zipper bag to his list, and producing a Platinum Amex Card, made out in the name of James Boldman, with which to pay.

"Guess I'll have to just run a check on this, sir, Mr. Boldman."

"You don't *have* to, and you know it." Bond's eyes held less humanity in them than small chips of ice. "But if you're about to make telephone calls, I'm going to stand next to you, right?"

"Right. Right." The pirate salesman repeated, leading the way to a tiny office at the rear of the store. "Yes sir-bub. Yes siree." He picked up the telephone and dialed the Amex clearance number. They okayed the card in five seconds flat. It took ten minutes for the purchases to be stashed into the shoulder bag, and as he left Bond put his mouth very close to the pierced ear with the ring in it. "Tell you what," he began. "I'm a stranger in town, but now you know my name."

"Sure." The pirate gave him a trapped look.

"If anyone else gets to know I've been here, excepting you, Amex and myself, I shall personally return, cut that ring from your ear and then do the same job on your nose, followed by a more vital organ." He dropped his hand, fist clenched, so that it lay level with the pirate's crotch. "You understand me? I mean it," and he certainly sounded and looked as though he did.

The pirate knew the score. He was a good, hard-working man, but recognized the type of character Bond was projecting.

"I already forgot your name, Mr. . . . er . . . Mr. . . ."

"Keep it like that," and Bond was off, out of the shop and into the street, walking briskly, then slowly to the more leisurely pace of those around him.

Back in his suite he lugged the CC500 from its briefcase, hooked it to the telephone and put in a quick call to London, not waiting for a response, merely giving them his exact location and saying he would be in touch as soon as the job was completed.

"It's going down tonight," he finished. "If I'm not in touch within forty-eight hours, look for Shark Island, off Key West. Repeat, it's going down tonight."

It was a very apt phrase, he thought as he changed into his newly acquired jeans, shirt, loafers and jacket. The ASP and baton were in place, so he did not feel naked, but, he thought, surveying himself in the mirror, he would blend in nicely with the tourist scene.

"Going down tonight," he said softly to himself, then left to join the girls on the Havana Docks Bar deck.

17

SHARK ISLAND

THE DECK IN front of the Havana Docks Bar at the Pier House was made of wooden planks, raised on several levels and strategically decorated with metal chairs and tables—the whole thing gave one a feeling of being on board a ship at anchor.

Globe lights on poles stood at intervals along the heavy wooden guard rail, and at sunset in Key West it was *the* place to be.

The deck was crowded and the lights had come on, attracting the night bugs that swarmed around the globes. Inside, someone was playing a piano—"Mood Indigo"—and the rails were lined with camera-hung tourists, eager to capture the sunset for posterity.

As the clear sky turned to a deeper navy blue, an occasional speedboat crossed in front of the hotel, while a light aircraft buzzed a wide circuit, its lights flashing. All was chatter, and to the left, along the wide Mallory Square, which fronted the ocean, jugglers, conjurers, fire eaters and acrobats performed among a crush of people. It was the same on every fine night—a celebration of the day's end and a look toward the pleasures night might bring.

A "Sunset Cruise" boat slid by, so loaded that it looked as if some macabre immigrant ship were leaving Key West, its passengers escaping peril—political or natural.

James Bond, sitting at a table, looking out to sea and the two dark green humps that were Tank and Wisteria islands, close inshore, thought that if he had any sense he would be on a boat or plane moving out. He was in no doubt of the peril close at hand; that Tarquin Rainey was "Colonel" Tamil Rahani, Blofeld's successor; that Shark Island, with its recently built house and landscaping, was his old enemy SPECTRE's new headquarters; and that this could well be his last chance to smash the organization for good and all.

In the warm and pleasant surroundings, Bond's mental antenna reached out and recorded the signals of malevolence nearby. As far as he and SPECTRE were concerned it was a question of smash or be smashed.

"Isn't this absolutely super?" laughed Sukie. "There really is nothing like it in the whole world." It was unclear whether she was talking about the huge shrimp they were eating, with that very special delicious tangy and hot red sauce, the calypso daiquiris they drank or the truly beautiful view.

Bond sipped his daiquiri, took a bite of a shrimp and muttered, "Super," unconvincingly.

"It *is* incredible." Nannie squeezed his hand. "Just look at that sky."

The sun appeared to become larger as it dropped slowly behind Wisteria Island—larger and more crimson, throwing a huge patch of blood-red light across the sky, the great fire of color hitting the water, spreading as though an invisible artist were controlling a giant laser display.

"God's own light show," said Bond, now also mesmerized by the extraordinary beauty of a spectacular sunset on the southernmost tip of the United States.

Above them, a United States Customs helicopter clattered on its way, running from south to north, red and green lights twinkling on and off as it turned, heading toward the naval air station. Bond wondered if SPECTRE had become involved in the huge drug traffic that was reported to pass into America by this route—landing the drugs on isolated sections of the Florida Keys, to be taken inland and distributed. The Navy and Customs kept a very close eye on places like Key West.

A great cheer went up—echoed from the hundreds of people farther up the coastline on Mallory Square—as the sun finally appeared to plunge into the sea, filling the whole sky with deep scarlet for a couple of minutes before the velvet darkness took over.

"So what's the deal, James?" Nannie asked in almost a whisper.

All three of them lowered their heads over the plates of shrimp, conspirators sharing a secret with seafood.

Bond spoke low, saying that those who were after him were, first, almost certainly on Shark Island, and, second, they *knew* he had arrived in Key West. "I want them to think that I'm taking my time," he murmured. "They could well act tonight, here, at the Pier House. That's why we've got to make the first move."

He told them that, until midnight at least, he wanted all three of them to stay visible. "We'll stroll out into town, get a good dinner and come back to the hotel. Then I want us out—separately. We must each go our own way. You're not to use the car, and you'll both have to keep an eye out for anyone on your tails. Nannie, you're trained in this kind of thing, so give Sukie the benefit of your experience. Brief her; tell her the best way to do the trick. I have my own plans. But the most important thing is that we all meet at Garrison Bight, aboard the *Prospero,* around one in the morning, okay?"

The two girls nodded, and Bond noticed a small concerned furrow take shape between Nannie's eyes. "What then?" she asked.

"Has Sukie looked at the charts?"

"Yes, it's not the easiest trip by night." Sukie's eyes showed nothing, neither fear nor elation. "It's a challenge, though. The sandbars are not well marked and we'll have to show a certain amount of light to begin with. Once we're beyond the reef it's not too bad."

"Just get me to within a mile of the island." Bond gave her a hard look, and his voice was edged with authority.

They finished their drinks and the shrimp, rose and began to saunter casually from the deck. At the door to the bar, Bond paused, asking the girls to wait for a moment as he went back to look over the rails, down into the sea. Earlier he had noticed the hotel's little pull-start speedboat making trips just off the beach. It was now neatly tied up between the big wooden piles that held this section of the hotel out over the water. Smiling to himself, he rejoined the girls, and they went through the bar—the pianist was now playing "Bewitched"—and down toward the reception area. They passed along the wooden walkway running alongside the hotel's crowded eating places—the Pier House Restaurant, the Beach Club Bar and Pete's Raw Bar ("Doing a raw-ring trade," Sukie said, and they all groaned).

A small dance floor had been set up across from the bars, on the beach, and a three-man combo had started to pound out rhythms for the cognoscenti; the paths were lit by small lamps, and people were still swimming, diving into the floodlit pool, laughing with pleasure. It was fairyland magic: certainly fairyland when one took a close look at the waiters.

Outside, the streets were as crowded as they had been in mid-afternoon, and few people appeared to have changed from their leisure clothes into anything more formal.

They strolled, arms linked—one girl on each side of Bond—down Duval, looking into windows and peering into the restaurants, which all seemed to be booked solidly for the evening.

Halfway along the street a crowd stood in front of the light gray, Victorian English-looking church staring across the road where, in front of Fast Buck Freddie's Department Store, half a dozen kids were breakdancing to the music of a ghetto-blaster.

Eventually, they retraced their footsteps and found themselves in front of Claire, a restaurant that, while busy, looked exceptionally good. They walked in through a small garden to the maître d', who hovered by a tall desk, in the open air outside the main restaurant.

"Boldman," lied Bond with conviction. "Party of three. Eight o'clock."

The maître d' consulted his book, looked troubled and asked when the booking had been made.

"Yesterday evening," Bond kept up the fantasy, and prayed that the girls would not let him down by giggling.

"There seems to be some error, Mr. Boldman," the bemused man said, a shade too firmly for Bond's liking.

"I reserved the table specially. It's the only night we can make it this week. I spoke to a young man, last night, and he assured me I had the table."

"Just one moment, sir." The maître d' disappeared into the restaurant and they could see he was deep in an agitated conversation with one of the waiters. Finally he came out all smiles. "You're lucky, sir. We've had an unexpected cancellation . . ."

"Not lucky," Bond clenched his jaw. "We had a table *reserved*. We're simply getting our table."

"Certainly, sir," and they were shown into a pleasant room decorated in white, to a corner table where Bond took a seat with his back to the wall and a good view of the entrance.

The tablecloths were made of paper, and there were packets of crayons beside each plate, so that guests could create their own art—perhaps the restaurant's owners were still hoping Picasso would arrive and pay the bill with the tablecloth.

Nannie leaned forward. "I haven't spotted anyone. Are we being watched?"

"Oh, yes." He opened the large menu, with a smile. "Two of them. Possibly three. At least two, working each side of the street. A guy in a yellow shirt and jeans, tall, black and with a lot of rings on his fingers. The other's a little runt, dark trousers, a white shirt, deep tan and a tattoo on his left arm—mermaid being indecent with a swordfish by the look of it. He's across the street now." Bond doodled on the paper tablecloth, drawing a skull and crossed bones. Nannie had sketched something vaguely obscene, in red.

"Got 'em." Nannie also consulted her menu.

"And the possible third?" asked Sukie.

"An old blue Buick. Big fellow at the wheel, alone and cruising. Not easy to tell, but he's been up and down the street a lot—so have others—but he was the only one who didn't seem to take any interest in people on the sidewalks. I'd say he was the backup. They're around, so watch out for them."

A waiter appeared and they all made the same decision about food—conch chowder, the Thai beef salad and, inevitably, Key Lime pie. They drank a California champagne, which slightly offended Bond's palate. They talked constantly, keeping off the immediate business in hand. Eventually, when the waiter went off with the bill and the credit card, Bond told them to be wary. "I want you all there, on board and with nobody on your backs, by one."

They nodded, Bond signed the account and within a couple of minutes they were out on the street again, walking west toward the Front Street intersection. The black man with the yellow shirt kept well back on the other side of the street, and the little tattooed man let them pass him, then overtook them and let them pass again before they got back to the Pier House.

The blue Buick had cruised by twice, and was parked outside the Lobster House, almost opposite the main entrance to the Pier House. "They have us well staked out," Bond murmured as they crossed the street and walked up the drive to the main entrance, where they all made a great show of saying good-night.

Bond was taking no chances. The moment he got to his room he checked the old but well-tried alarm signals he had left behind. The slivers of matchstick were still in place, wedged into the doors of the clothes cupboards, while the threads on the drawers were unbroken.

He looked at the similar traps left on his luggage. Everything was intact. Now was the time to move. It was barely ten-thirty, but he wanted to get out and running as quickly as possible. He doubted that SPECTRE's surveillance team would expect anyone to make a move before the early hours. Nor had he let either of the girls know that he had quietly slipped the spare set of charts from the *Prospero* inside his jacket before leaving the fishing boat that afternoon.

He now spread them out on the round glass table in the center of his living room and began to study the course from Garrison Bight to Shark Island, making notes on headings, the dangerous sections of sandbar, and other hazards, as he ran a thick pencil line along the route. When he was satisfied that he had all the compass bearings correct, and a very good idea of how he could guide a boat to within safe distance of the island, Bond began to dress for action.

He took a light cotton black rollneck from his case, peeled off the T-shirt and wriggled into it. The jeans were replaced by a pair of black slacks, which he always packed—on a duty journey or holiday. Next, he spread out the wide belt that had been so useful when Der Haken had him locked up in Salzburg.

He removed the Q Branch Toolkit and checked the contents, spreading everything out on the table and paying special attention to the small explosive charges and their electronic connectors, adding to them another four small flat packets of plastique explosive, each no larger than a stick of chewing gum. These he took from the false bottom of his second briefcase, together with four short lengths of fuse, some extra-thin electric wire, half a dozen tiny detonators, a miniature pinlight torch, not much larger than the filter of a cigarette—and one other very important item. All these things would fit neatly into the inner pockets of the belt.

Together the explosives would not dispose of an entire building, but they could be useful with things like locks or door hinges. He secured all the equipment and then buckled on the belt, threading it through the loops on his trousers, before opening up the shoulder bag in which he had stowed the wet suit and snorkeling equipment.

Sweating a little, he struggled into the wet suit, and once comfortable clipped the knife into place on the belt he had bought with the suit. The ASP, two spare magazines, the charts and the baton went into the waterproof pouch, already threaded onto the belt, leaving flippers, mask, underwater torch and snorkel in the shoulder bag. Bond then prepared to make his exit from Key West.

He remained inside his wing of the hotel for as long as possible. There was still a great deal of action going on in the bars, restaurant and makeshift dance floor laid out on the beach, and he finally emerged through one of the exits on the ocean side of these festivities.

Squatting with his back against the wall, Bond unzipped the shoulder bag and pulled on the flippers, then slowly edged himself toward the water. The noise, music and laughter behind him were loud as he climbed over the short stretch of rock that marked the righthand boundary of the hotel bathing area. He washed the mask out, slipped it over the upper part of his face, grasped the torch, adjusted the snorkel and slid into the water, going straight down and swimming gently around the metal shark guard that ran in a wide circle to protect swimmers using the hotel beach. It took a good ten minutes for him to find the long, thick wooden piles under the Havana Docks Bar deck, but he surfaced only a few feet from where the motorboat he had seen earlier was tied up.

Any noise he made clambering aboard would not be heard from above, or on the beach, and once inside the neat little craft, he quickly used the torch to check the fuel gauges. The beach staff was efficient and the tank had been filled, presumably ready for the next morning's work.

He cast off and used his hands to maneuver the speedboat from under the pier, then allowed it to drift, occasionally guiding it with the flat of his hand in the water, heading north, into the Gulf of Mexico, silently passing the Standard Oil Company pier, which he had seen from the Havana Docks.

He allowed the boat to drift a good mile out before switching on the riding lights and moving aft to prime and start the motor. It fired at the first pull, and he had to scramble quickly forward to swing himself behind the wheel, one hand on the throttle. As he opened up, glancing down at the small luminous dial of the compass, Bond mentally thanked the Pier House for the care it took in keeping the boat in order.

Minutes later, he was cruising carefully around the coast, fumbling with the pouch to pull out the charts and take his first visual fix.

He could not risk letting the speedboat run at anywhere near its full speed, but within ten minutes he had spotted the exit point from Garrison Bight, and was able to begin negotiating the tricky sandbars, watching his heading and the chart, cruising slowly, occasionally feeling the shallow draft of the boat touch the sand. Twenty minutes later he cleared the reef and set course for Shark Island.

The night was clear, and the moon was up, but Bond still had to watch speed and strain his eyes into the dark stretch of water ahead. Ten minutes; then another ten, before he caught a glimpse of lights. Less than five minutes after the first sighting, he cut the engine, drifting in. The long dark slice of land stood out against the horizon, twinkling with lights from buildings he could see clearly, set among trees. He leaned over, washed out his mask again, took up the torch and, for the second time that night, dropped into the sea.

He remained on the surface for a while, judging that he was around a mile offshore. Then he heard the thrum of engines and saw a small craft rounding the island, to his left, searching the waters with a powerful spotlight—Tamil Rahani's regular patrol, he thought. There would be at least two boats like this keeping up a constant vigil—someone had said people were warned off during the daylight, and, knowing SPECTRE's thoroughness, Bond assumed they would not halt the patrols when the sun went down.

He took in air and went deep, swimming steadily but not flat out, conserving energy against any panic moment that might come.

On the way in, he surfaced twice, and the second time told him that they had found the speedboat. Their craft had stopped and voices drifted over the water. He had around half a mile to go now, and his main worry was the possibility of meeting sharks—the island would not be named after the creatures if they were not known to haunt the vicinity.

His luck held—at least until he came suddenly against the heavy wire mesh of an antishark barrier around sixty yards from the beach. Clinging to the strong metal, he could see the island's lights clearly—from the bright, large windows in the long, high house, to the floodlights in the grounds. Looking back he saw the spotlight from the patrol boat and heard its engine rise again. They were coming to look for him.

He heaved himself up onto the metal bar that topped the protective fence. One flipper caught, awkwardly, in the mesh and he lost a few precious seconds disentangling himself before finally lowering his body into the water on the far side.

Again, he went down deep, swimming a little more strongly—faster—now he was almost there. He had gone about ten yards when instinct told him there was danger: something close. Then he felt the bump, jarring his ribs, throwing him to one side.

Bond turned his head and saw, swimming beside him, as though keeping station with him, the ugly wicked snout of a bull shark.The protective fence was not there to keep the creatures out, but to make sure that an island guard of sharks remained close inshore—the favorite hunting ground of the dangerous bull shark.

The shark had bumped him, but, so far, had not attempted to turn and attack, which probably meant either that it was well-fed or that it had not yet sized up Bond as an enemy or the chef's special on today's menu. He knew his only salvation was to remain calm, not to antagonize the shark, and certainly not to knowingly transmit fear—though he was probably doing that at the moment.

Still keeping pace with the shark, he allowed his right hand to go down to the knife handle, his fingers closing around it, ready to unsheath and use the weapon at a second's notice. He remembered also that on no account must he drop his legs: If he did that, the shark would know in an instant that he was prey, and the bull shark could move like a racing boat. The most dangerous moment lay ahead, and not very far ahead, when he reached the beach—there he would be at his most vulnerable.

The shark continued to keep station, then, as Bond felt the first touch of sand under his belly, as the water became shallow, he was aware of the shark moving, dropping back. He swam on until his flippers began to churn sand, and, in that moment, he knew the shark was behind, probably even beginning to build up speed for the strike.

Later Bond thought he had seldom moved as quickly in water. He gave a mighty push, sending his body upward, bringing his encumbered feet down, then splashing, racing for the beach, in an odd splay-footed, leg-raising, hopping run dictated by the suit and flippers.

He got to the surf, and then the sand, in one great leap, and as he hit, rolled to the left: just in time, for the bull shark's snout—jaws wide and snapping—broke through the surf, missing him by inches.

Bond continued to roll, trying to propel himself up the beach, for he had heard of bull sharks coming right out of the water to attack. Six feet up, he lay still, the first danger past—panting, feeling his stomach reel with a stab of fear.

Quickly, his subconscious told him to move. He was *on* the

island, and heaven alone knew with what other guardians SPECTRE had surrounded its headquarters and its dying leader. He kicked off the flippers and ran forward, crouched, to the first line of palms and undergrowth. There, he squatted again to take stock.

Before doing anything, he dumped the mask and snorkel with the flippers, pushing them under the bushes. The air was balmy and the sweet smell of night-blooming tropical flowers came to his nostrils like a magic potion. As he crouched and listened he could detect no noises or movement coming from the grounds, which were—now he was close—well-lit and obviously laid out with paths, small water gardens, trees, statues and flowers. There was a low murmur of voices coming from the house—though far away, inside—and the house itself was something that had to be seen to be believed. It was built like a pyramid, lifted high above the ground on great polished steel girders. He could make out three stories, each surrounded by a metal balcony running around the whole of the building.

Behind all of the balconies were large picture windows, some of them partly open, others with curtains drawn, and atop the whole pyramid, a forest of communications aerials stretched up like some avant-garde skeletal sculpture.

Gently, he reached down, opened the waterproof pouch and drew out the ASP, cocking it and taking the safety off. He was breathing normally now, and using the trees, darker patches of the gardens and the statues for cover, Bond inched his way silently toward this vast, slab-sided modern pyramid.

As he got closer, he saw there were several ways into the place— a giant spiral staircase running up through the center, and three zigzagging sets of metal steps, one to each side, which rose from one terraced balcony to the next.

He crossed the final piece of open ground, standing to listen for a moment. The voices had stopped; he thought he could hear the patrol boat, far out to sea. Nothing else.

With great care, James Bond began to climb the open zigzagging stairs to the first level, his feet noiselessly touching the fretted metal, his body to the left to leave his right hand, and the ASP, ready for instant use. At the top, standing on the first terrace, he waited, head cocked. Just ahead of him there was a large sliding picture window, the curtains only partially drawn and one section of the window open.

Moving so that he covered all points of the compass around him, Bond crossed to the window, peering in. He could not believe what he saw, almost speaking his thoughts out loud—"First time lucky."

The room was white and splendidly decorated, with glass tables, white soft armchairs, and what appeared to be excellent original paintings on its walls, a deep pile white carpet covering the floor. But the central feature was a large, comfortable, customized bed— a king-sized sickbed, with controls on a panel at the head, switches and buttons that could, obviously, adjust any part of the bed, from head to foot, to suit the patient who now lay in it, propped up with silk pillows, his eyes closed in sleep and his head turned to one side.

In spite of the now shrunken face, the skin a parchment pallor, Bond recognized the man immediately. On their previous meetings, Tamil Rahani had been smooth, short, dapper and attractive, in a military fashion. Now, he was a shadow of his former self—the heir to the Blofeld fortune, and the organization, SPECTRE, reduced to this human doll, swamped by the seductive luxury of a high-tech bed.

Bond slid the window open and stepped inside, moving like a cat to the end of the bed, gazing down on the man who controlled his greatest enemies.

Now I can have him, he thought. Now, why not? Kill him now and you may not ruin SPECTRE, but at least you'll decapitate it—just as its leader wants you decapitated.

Taking a deep breath, Bond raised the ASP. He was only a few steps from Rahani's head. One squeeze of the trigger and it would be obliterated, and, with luck and cunning, he could be away— hiding up in the grounds—until he found a method of getting off the island.

He began to squeeze the trigger, and as he did so thought he felt a small gust of air on the back of his head.

"I don't think so, James. We've brought you too far to let you do what God's going to do soon enough." The voice came from behind him.

"Just drop the gun, James. Drop it, or you'll be dead before you can even move."

He was stunned by the voice. The ASP fell, with a noisy thump, to the floor and Tamil Rahani stirred and groaned in his sleep.

"Okay, you can turn around now."

Bond turned to look at Nannie Norrich, who stood in the window, an Uzi machine pistol tucked into her lithesome hip.

18

MADAME AWAITS

"**I**'M SORRY IT had to be like this, James. You lived up to your reputation. Every girl should have one." The gray eyes were as cold as the North Sea in December, and the words meant nothing.

"Not as sorry as I am." Bond allowed himself a smile that neither the muzzle of the Uzi nor Nannie Norrich deserved. "You and Sukie, eh? You really did take me in. Is it private enterprise, or do you both work for one of the organizations?"

She replied flatly, any feelings she might have had well under control, "Not Sukie, James. Sukie's for real, and, at the moment, she's out for a few hours, in bed at the Pier House. I slipped her what the old gumshoe movies would call a Mickey Finn—a *very* strong one. We had coffee after we left you. Coffee on room service, and I provided an added service of my own. You'll be well gone by the time she wakes up. If she does wake up."

Bond glanced at the bed. The shrunken figure of Tamil Rahani had not moved. Time. He needed time. Time, luck and possibly some fast talking. None of them were easily obtainable commodities. He tried to be casual. "Originally, a Mickey Finn was a laxative for horses. Did you know that?"

She took no notice. "You look like a black Kermit the Frog

in that gear, James. Doesn't suit you, so—very slowly—I want you to take it off."

Bond shrugged. "If you say so."

"I do, and please don't be fooled. The tiniest move and I'll have no compunction about taking your legs off with this." The muzzle of the Uzi twitched. "Don't worry if you're naked under the wet suit. Remember I've seen it all before."

There were no options. Slowly, and with a certain amount of difficulty, Bond began to divest himself of the wet suit. As he did so, he tried to talk, picking questions with care.

"You *really* did have me fooled, Nannie. After all you saved me several times."

"More than you know." Her voice level and without emotion. "That was my job—or, at least, the job I said that I'd try to do."

"You disintegrated the German—what was his name? Conrad Tempel?—on the road to Strasbourg?"

"Oh, yes—and there were a couple before then who had latched onto you. I dealt with them. On the boat to Ostend."

Bond nodded, acknowledging that he knew about the men on the ferry. "And Cordova—'The Rat,' the 'Poison Dwarf'?"

"Guilty."

"The hoods in the Renault?"

"Took me a little by surprise. You helped a great deal, James. Quinn was a thorn in the flesh, but you helped again. I was simply your guardian angel. That was the job."

He finally pulled off the wet suit, standing there in the slacks and the cotton rollneck. "What about Der Haken? The mad cop."

She gave a glacial smile. "I had some help there. My own private panic button—Der Haken was briefed; he thought I was a go-between for himself and SPECTRE. Colonel Rahani had given me the benefit of the doubt and sent in the heavy mob. They wanted to take you then, but the colonel let me carry on—though there was a penalty clause: My head was on the block if I lost you after that. And I nearly did, because I was responsible for the vampire bat. Lucky for you that Sukie came along to save you when she did. But her arrival gave *me* a hard time with SPECTRE. They've been experimenting with the beasts here. It was meant to give you rabies. You were a sort of guinea pig, and the plan was to get you to Shark Island before the symptoms started to become apparent. The colonel wants your head, but he was quite content to watch you die in agony before they shortened you—as they say." She moved the Uzi again. "Let's have you against the wall, James. The standard position, feet apart, arms stretched. We don't want to find you're carrying any nasty little toys, do we?"

She frisked him expertly, and then began to remove his belt. It was the action of a trained expert, and something Bond had dreaded. "Dangerous things, belts," she said, undoing the buckle, then unthreading it from the loops. "Oh, yes. This one especially. Very cunning." She had obviously detected the Toolkit.

"If SPECTRE has someone like you on the payroll, Nannie, why bother with a charade like this competition—the Head Hunt?"

"I'm not," she said, curtly. "Not on the payroll, I mean. I entered the competition as a freelance. I've done odd bits of work for them before, so we came to an arrangement. They put me on a retainer, and I stand to get only a percentage of the prize money if I win—which I have done. The colonel has great faith in me. He saw it as a way of saving money."

As though he had heard talk of himself, the bundle that was Tamil Rahani, on the bed, stirred. "Who is it? What . . . Who?" The voice, so commanding, confident and firm the last time Bond had heard SPECTRE's chief speak, was now as much of a husk as the body.

"It's me, Colonel Rahani." Nannie's voice stood to attention.

"The Norrich girl?"

"Nannie, yes. I've brought a present for you."

"Help . . . sit up . . ." Rahani croaked.

"I can't at the moment. But I'll press the bell."

Bond, hands splayed against the wall, leaning forward, heard her move, but knew there was no chance of his taking any precipitate action. Nannie was fast and good with weapons at the best of times. Now, with her quarry here in the room, she would be *very* itchy with her trigger finger.

"You can stand up now, James. Slowly," she said a couple of seconds later.

He pushed himself from the wall.

"Turn around—slowly—with your arms stretched out and feet apart, then lean back against the wall."

Bond did as he was told, regaining a complete view of the room just as the door to his right opened.

The hoods who entered first both had guns in their hands.

"Relax," Nannie said softly. "I've brought him."

They were the usual SPECTRE gorillas—one fair-haired, the other balding, but both big, muscular men with wary eyes and cautious, quick movements. The fair one smiled. "Oh, good. Well done, Miss Norrich," his English laced with a slight Scandinavian accent. The bald one merely nodded.

They were followed by a short man, dressed casually in white shirt and trousers, his face distorted by the right corner of his mouth, which seemed permanently twisted toward the right ear.

"Dr. McConnell," Nannie acknowledged him.

"Aye, so it's you, Mistress Norrich. Ye've brought yon man the colonel's always raving about, then?" His face reminded Bond of a bizarre ventriloquial dummy when he spoke, in what was almost a bad stage Scottish accent. A tall, butch-looking nurse plodded in his wake—big, raw-boned, with flaxen hair: the kind of nurse Bond thought would not have been out of place among those who worked in the Nazi concentration camps during World War II.

"So, how's ma patient, then?" McConnell stood by the bed.

"I think he wants to see the present I've brought for him, Doctor." Nannie's eyes never left Bond. Now she had him, she was taking no chances.

The doctor gave a signal to the nurse, who moved toward the white bedside table. The nurse picked up a flat, black control box—attached to an electric cable that snaked under the bed— the size of a man's wallet. She pressed one of the buttons and the bed-head began to angle upward, raising Tamil Rahani into a sitting position. The electronic mechanism made no more than a mild whirring noise.

"There," the smallest hint of glee in Nannie's voice. "I said I'd do it, Colonel Rahani, and I did. Mr. James Bond, at your service."

There was a tired, wheezing cackle from Rahani as his eyes focused. "An eye for an eye, Mr. Bond. Apart from the fact that SPECTRE has wanted you dead for more years than either of us would care to recall, I have a personal score to settle with you."

"Nice to see you in such a bad way," Bond spat out the words.

"Ah!" It was meant to be some kind of laugh. "Yes, Bond. The last time we met, you caused me to jump for my life. I didn't know then that I was jumping to my death. The bad landing I suffered then jarred my spine. In turn this set in motion the incurable disease from which I am now dying. As you've personally caused the downfall of previous leaders of SPECTRE and decimated the Blofeld family, I regard it as a duty, as well as a personal privilege, to see you wiped from the face of the earth—hence the little contest." He was rapidly running out of steam, each spoken word seeming to tire him. "A contest that was a gamble with the odds in SPECTRE's favor, for we took on Miss Norrich, a tried and true operator."

"And you manipulated other contestants," Bond said grimly. "The kidnapping, I mean. I trust . . ."

"Oh, the delightful Scottish lady, and the famous Miss Moneypenny. You trust. . . ?"

"I think that's enough talking, Colonel." Dr. McConnell came closer to the bed.

"No . . . no . . ." Then, weaker still, "I want to see him depart this life before I go."

"Then ye will, Colonel." The doctor bent over the bed. "Ye'll have to rest a while first, though."

Almost in a whisper, Rahani tried to speak with Bond, "You said you trust . . ."

"I trust both ladies are safe, and that, for once, SPECTRE will be honorable and see they are returned in exchange for my head."

"They are both here. Safe. They will be freed the moment your head is severed from your body." Rahani seemed to shrivel even more as his head sank back onto the pillows.

For a second Bond relived the last time he had seen the man— over the Swiss lake, strong, tough, outclassed but leaping from an airship to escape Bond's victory.

The doctor looked around at the hoods, "Is everything prepared? For the—er—the execution?" He did not even glance at Bond.

"We've been ready for a long time." The fair man gave his toothy smile again. "Everything's in order."

The doctor nodded. "The colonel hasn't got long, I fear. A day, maybe two. I have to give him medication now, and he will sleep for about three hours. Can you do it then?"

"Whenever," the balding hood nodded, then gave Bond a hard look. He had stone eyes, the color of granite and twice as indifferent.

The doctor signaled to the nurse and she busied herself preparing an injection. "Give the colonel an hour, he'll no be disturbed by being moved then. In an hour ye can move the bed into the . . . what d'ye call it? The execution chamber?"

"Good a name as any," the fair man said. "You want us to take Bond up?" he added, addressing Nannie.

"You touch him and you're dead," Nannie sounded as though she meant it. "I know the way. Just give me the keys."

"I have a request." Inside, Bond felt the first pangs of fear, but his voice was steady, even commanding.

"Yes," Nannie, diffident.

"I know it'll make little difference, but I'd like to be sure about May and Moneypenny."

Nannie looked at the two hoods. The fair one nodded. "They're in the other two cells. Next to the death cell."

Bond could not help giving a wry smile. "SPECTRE made certain this place contained all modern conveniences when it was designed."

"Oh, they had you in mind," the fair hood grinned. "You, and several other people." Then, to Nannie, "You can manage him by yourself? You're sure?"

"I got him here, didn't I? I lured him . . ."

"But we had to give you a hand with the Austrian cops."

"A temporary matter. Yes, I can manage him, Fin. Don't worry about that. If he gives me any trouble I'll take his legs off. The doc can no doubt patch him up for the headechtomy."

From the bed, where he was administering the injection, McConnell gave a throaty chuckle. "I like it, Mistress Norrich—headechtomy, I like it verra much."

"Which is more than can be said for me," Bond sounded very cool. At the back of his mind he was already doing some calculations. The mathematics of escape.

The doctor chuckled again, "If ye want tae get a head, get a Nannie, eh?"

"Let's go." Nannie came quite near to prodding Bond with the Uzi. "Hands *above* the head, fingers linked, arms straight. Go for the door. Move."

Bond walked forward, passing through the door to find himself in a curving passage, deep pile carpet under his feet, the decor changing from white to a sky blue. The passage, he reckoned, ran around the entire story, and was probably identical to others on the floors above. The great house on Shark Island, though externally constructed as a pyramid, appeared to have a circular core.

At intervals along the passage there were alcoves, Norman in style, each containing some objet d'art. These alone reflected the wealth amassed by SPECTRE over the years, for he recognized at least two Picabias, a Duchamp, a Dali and a Jackson Pollock. Fitting, he thought, that SPECTRE should invest money in surrealist artists.

Finally they came to a set of elevator doors—brushed steel, curved like the wall itself. Nannie commanded him to take up the hands-on-wall position again while she summoned the elevator, which arrived as soundlessly as the doors slid open. Everything appeared to have been constructed in a manner that made silence obligatory.

She ushered him into the circular cage of the elevator. The doors closed and he could hardly tell if they were moving up or down—deciding that up was the only possible way they could go. Seconds later the doors opened again, this time onto a very different kind of passage—bare, with walls that looked like plain brick and a floor that gave the impression of being made of flagstones, though no noise came from treading on them.

As the elevator disappeared, Bond could see that they were in a very small area of the second story, for the curved passage was blocked off at either end.

"The retaining area," Nannie explained. "You want to see the hostages? Okay, move left."

He did so, and she stopped him in front of a door that could have been part of a movie set, yet it was real—black metal, with a heavy lock and a tiny Judas squint. "Be my guest." Nannie waved the Uzi toward the squint.

From what he could see, the interior was comfortable enough— a somewhat spartan bedroom, on the bed of which lay May, asleep, comfortable, her chest rising and falling and her face relaxed.

"I understand they've been kept under sedation—only mild though." He thought he detected a glimmer of compassion in her voice. "They take only a second or two to be wakened for meals."

She ushered him on to a similar door, and through the squint he saw Moneypenny on a similar bed, relaxed and apparently sleeping like May.

Bond drew back and nodded.

"I'll take you to your final resting place, then, James." Any compassion had disappeared, and they went back the way they had come, this time stopping not before a door but in front of an electronic numeral pad set into the wall.

Nannie again made him take up a safe position against the wall as she tapped out a code on the numbered buttons. A section of wall slid back, and Bond was ordered forward. This time his heart and stomach turned over.

They entered a large, bare room. One wall was taken up by a row of deep comfortable chairs, like exclusive theater seats. There was a medical table and a hospital gurney trolley, but the centerpiece, lit from above by large spots, was far from surrealistic: a full-sized, very real guillotine.

Bond's first reaction was that it seemed smaller than he had expected, but that was probably due to all the French Revolution movies, which tended to show the instrument as a blade sliding down very high, grooved posts. This instrument stood barely eight feet in height, making it look like a model of all the Hollywood representations he had seen.

There was no doubt that it would do the job, though, for everything was there, from the stockslike fitment for head and hands at the bottom—with a neat, almost hygienic, plastic oblong box set to catch the dismembered head and hands—to the angled blade, firmly set at the top, between the posts. Even at a distance it was clear that it was razor sharp.

A vegetable—a large cabbage, he thought—had been jammed into the hole for the head, and Nannie, in a fast and precise movement, stepped forward and touched some kind of trigger on one of the upright posts.

He did not even see the blade fall, it came down so fast. The cabbage was sliced neatly in two and there was a heavy thud as the blade settled. The whole thing was macabre and unnerving.

"In a couple of hours or so," Nannie said, brightly.

He nodded, knowing what she meant, realizing that, unless he could pull off some kind of miraculous escape, he would very soon have no head with which to nod.

She allowed him to stand for a minute to take in the scene, then pointed him toward a cell door, similar to the ones in the passage, but at the far side of the chamber, directly in line with the guillotine.

"They've done it quite well, really," Nannie almost sparkled. "The first thing you'll see, when they bring you out, will be Madame La Guillotine." She gave a little laugh. "And the last thing also. They'll do you proud, though, James. I understand that Fin is to do the honors, and he's been instructed to wear full evening dress. It'll be a classy experience."

"How many've received invitations?"

"Well, I suppose there're only about thirty-five people on the whole island—in Shark House, as they call this place. Some, the communications people and guards, will be working. Ten possibly—thirteen if you count me, and should the colonel command that the hostages be present, which is not likely—" She stopped, abruptly, realizing that he could well have asked the question as a means to discover how many men and women SPECTRE had stationed on this remote island off the American mainland—which he had indeed intended.

Quickly, though, she regained her composure. It did not matter if he knew or not, for there was only one possible end to the proceedings—the blade thudding down and decapitating James Bond, separating head from body in the fraction of a second.

"Into the cell," she said quietly. "Enough is enough." Then, as he passed through the door, "I suppose I should ask if you have any last request?"

Bond turned and smiled. "Oh, most certainly, Nannie, but you're in no condition to supply it."

She shook her head. "I'm afraid not, my dear James. You've had that already—and very pleasant it was. You might even be pleased to hear that Sukie was furious. She's absolutely crazy about you, incidentally. I should have brought her along. She would have gladly complied."

"I was going to ask you about Sukie."

"What about her?"

"Why haven't you killed her? You're a pro. You know the

form. *I* would never have left someone like Sukie lying around, even in a drugged stupor. I'd have made sure she was silenced for good and all."

"It's quite possible that I have killed her. The dosage was near lethal." Nannie's voice dropped slightly—sadly. "But you're quite right, James. I should have made certain. There's no room for sentiment in our business. But . . . well, I suppose I held back slightly. We've been very close over the years, and I've always managed to hide my darker side from her. You need someone to like you, when you do this kind of thing: You need to be loved, or don't you find that? You know, when I was at school with Sukie—before I discovered what sex I was, if you follow me—I was in love with her. She's been good to me, but you're right. When we've finished with you, I shall go back and make sure she's not around anymore. She's certainly no danger to me at the moment."

"And how did you manage to engineer that meeting—between Sukie and myself?"

Nannie gave a little puff of laughter. "That really was an accident. I was playing it very much by ear. Knew where you were—we stuck a homer on your Bentley. I had it done on the boat. Sukie really did insist on making that part of the journey alone, and you *really* saved her from a fate worse than death. I was going to set up something, depending where you happened to stay, because I knew you were heading toward Rome, as she was. It's funny, but the pair of you played right into my hands. Now, any further thoughts?"

"Last requests?"

"Yes."

Bond shrugged. "I have simple tastes, Nannie. I also know when I'm beaten. I'll have a plate of scrambled eggs and a bottle of Taittinger, the '73 if that's possible."

"In my experience, anything's possible with SPECTRE. I'll see what I can do," and she was gone, the cell door slamming shut and the heavy thump of the key in the lock. The cell was a simple bare room, but for a small metal bed, covered with one blanket.

Bond waited for a moment before going to the door. The flap over the Judas squint was closed, but he would have to be quick and careful. The silence produced in this place was against him, and someone could be outside the door very quietly without his even knowing.

Slowly, Bond undid the waistband of his slacks. Very rarely did he leave things to chance these days. Certainly, Nannie had removed his belt and found Q Branch's Toolkit—the spare one, which was the special extra piece of equipment he had taken from his briefcase, back at the Pier House, and the *only* secret he had fitted inside the belt.

The black slacks were also made by Q Branch, and contained screened hidden compartments stitched—well-nigh undetectable— into the waistband. It took him just over a minute to remove the Toolkit and other objects from their secure hiding places. At least he knew there was a fair chance of fixing the cell door so that he could get as far as the execution chamber. After that—who knew?

He reckoned half an hour before they would bring the food. So, within thirty minutes, he must at least establish that he could open the cell door. For the second time in a matter of days he went to work with the pick-locks.

Oddly, the cell lock was simple—a straightforward mortise that could be manipulated with ease by two of the picks. He had it open, and closed again, in less than five minutes.

Opening it a second time, he pushed at the cell door and walked out into the execution chamber—eerie, with the guillotine standing, sinister, in the center.

This, he knew, would have to be a reconnaissance, and when he got to the main door, Bond discovered he could find it only because he knew roughly where it was located. The thing was wholly electronic and appeared to be part of the wall itself. If he got the explosives in the correct place he might just do it, but finding the right position to blow the electronic locks would be a matter of luck more than judgment. It was then that he went back to the cell, locking the door behind him, pushing the Toolkit and other items under the blanket on the bed, depressed by the knowledge that blowing the execution chamber door was a gamble with odds of around ninety to one *against*.

In the next twenty minutes, he racked his brains in an attempt to come to some resolution—even thinking of destroying the guillotine itself, yet realizing that this would be a hopeless act of folly, and a waste of good explosives. They would still have him—

and there was more than one way of separating a man from his head.

The food arrived, carried by Nannie, with the balding hood in attendance, his hands almost white-knuckled on the Uzi.

"I said nothing was impossible for SPECTRE." Nannie did not smile as she indicated the Taittinger.

Bond simply nodded, and they left.

As the cell door was closing, however, he picked up one tiny morsel of hope. "The old man's sleeping. We're going to bring him through now," he heard the balding hood say.

Rahani was to be brought up in good time, so that he could wake from his medication already in position. As long as the nurse did not stay with him, Bond might just do it. The idea now formed, whole and desperate, in his mind as he addressed himself to the scrambled eggs—which he rated four out of a possible ten—and the champagne, which was superb, '73 having been an excellent year.

As he was completing this, possibly, final treat of his life, he thought he could hear sounds from the other side of the door. He put his ear hard against the metal, straining to catch the slightest sound, then, almost by intuition, knew there was somebody approaching the door.

Swiftly he stretched himself on the bed, ears still concentrating, so that he was 90 percent sure that he heard the Judas squint move back and then into place again.

He counted off five minutes, then unearthed the Toolkit, leaving the explosives and detonators hidden for the time being.

For the second time, Bond went to work on the lock, and when the door swung open he found the chamber in darkness, but for the glow of a bedside lamp from which he could just see the electronically operated bed of SPECTRE's leader, Tamil Rahani.

He crossed the chamber and, sure enough, Rahani lay there, silent and sleeping. Bond touched the control box that operated the various mechanisms of the bed, found the wire that led below the mattress, and followed it under the bed. What he saw gave him hope, and he crossed back to the cell to bring Toolkit, explosives and the pinlight torch.

He slid quickly, on his back, under the bed, and in the darkness sought out the small electronic sensor box that operated the bed-head, moving it up and down to raise and lower Rahani.

The cable from the control box ran to a main switching box, bolted more or less centrally onto the underside of this luxurious piece of furniture, from which a power lead was carefully laid out to a mains plug in the wall. From the switching box, various wires ran to the sensors that operated the head, foot and differing angles of tilt. He was interested in those that connected the switching box to the bed-head sensor. Stretching forward, Bond quietly turned off the power switch in the wall, and then began to work on the slim wires that joined the main box to the bed-head sensor.

First he cut them and trimmed off about half an inch of their plastic coating. Then he collected every piece of plastic explosive he had managed to bring in. This he molded to the edge of the sensor, finally inserting an electronic detonator, its two wires hanging loose, and short, from the plastique.

All that remained now was to plait the wires, as before, only this time adding a third wire to each pair—the wires from the detonator. In the Toolkit there was a minute roll of insulating tape, no wider than a single book match. It took a little time, but he finally insulated one set of wires from the others, thereby making sure that no bare wire could be touched by somebody moving the bed.

Last, he gathered all the items used from the Toolkit, turned on the mains power again, returned to the cell, locked the door with the picks, and once more hid the Toolkit.

If all went well, the relatively small amount of explosive would be detonated the moment anyone pressed the button to raise the bed-head. When—and he had to admit *if*—the thing worked, he would have to move like lightning. But that would have to be played almost literally on the fly. He could only wait and hope.

It seemed like an eternity, but quite suddenly, there was the clunk of the key in the cell door. The fair hood called Fin stood there, in full evening dress and white gloves. Behind, and to his right, the balding hood—also in tails—carried a heavy silver dish. They were going to do this in style, Bond thought. His head would be presented to the dying Tamil Rahani on a silver charger, just as in all the old legends and myths.

Nannie Norrich appeared from behind the balding man, and for the first time Bond saw her, under the glare of the lights, as she probably was in reality. She wore a long dark dress, her hair loose and face overpainted with makeup so that it looked more like a tartish mask than the face of the charming girl he thought he had known.

Her smile was a reflection of horrible perversity. "Madame La Guillotine awaits you, James Bond," she said. He squared his shoulders and stepped into the chamber, quickly taking in the whole scene, and the positions of everybody there.

The sliding doors were open, and he saw what he had missed before—a small shutter in the wall next to them. The shutter was open to reveal a button combination lock that was a replica of the one in the passage.

Two more big men had joined the party—standing just inside the door, each with the familiar stone face, one carrying a handgun, the other an Uzi.

Another pair—each with a handgun—were placed near Rahani's bed, as was Dr. McConnell and his nurse.

"She awaits you," Nannie prompted, and Bond took a further step into the room. It hasn't worked, he thought, then heard Rahani's voice, weak and thin from the bed. "See . . ." he whined. "Must see. Raise me up." And again, stronger, "Raise me up!"

Bond's eyes flickered around the group again, and the nurse reached for the bed's control box.

He saw, as if in closeup, her finger press down on the button that would raise the bed-head. Then hell and confusion burst about the room.

19

DEATH AND DESTRUCTION

For a few seconds, Bond thought he was blind, deaf and, possibly, dead. He was aware of a burning eruption of flame from the direction of Tamil Rahani's bed. Then the flash and heat seared his eyeballs, and it was as though somebody had clapped cupped hands, hard, over his ears. He could not be certain he had even heard an explosion, though he was aware of the impact of heat and the great blast of scorching air pushing him backward.

Time stood terrifyingly still, so that—once he realized he could see again, and move—everything took on a dreamlike quality, and the actions of all concerned appeared to be telescoped into slow motion. His brain, though, took in the fact that, in reality, events were moving at high speed; also, in the forefront of his mind two things were repeated, over and over—survive, and save May and Moneypenny.

What he saw, in that split second of gathering his thoughts, was the remains of Rahani's bed blazing in the far corner to his right. There was nothing left of Rahani himself and, at first sight, Bond thought most of SPECTRE's leader's remains had been scattered, together with pieces of the bed, over the doctor, the nurse and the pair of hoods who had been standing close to the explosion.

All of them appeared to be oddly decorated. It took Bond a second to realize that what he saw was, in fact, partly the remains of Rahani and partly the remains of those standing near. He was aware of the doctor suddenly keeling over, pitching into the fire that had been the center of the bed; the nurse stood, stock still, her head back, clothes ripped from her body, which was covered in wounds. From her mouth came a ghastly shriek, lasting only for a second before she also fell toward the fire.

The two hoods who had been near their leader were moving, but not of their own volition. One was minus most of his clothes and part of his face, and he seemed to have been lifted up and hurled toward the center of the room, toward the guillotine. The other was also in midair, one arm flapping, half-severed, as he was hurled toward the man with the Uzi, stationed by the door.

This latter guard seemed to be alive, though shocked, for the blast—always unpredictable in any explosion—had knocked him back against the door, his arm jerking forward, hand releasing the Uzi so that it skated across the floor to land just in front of the guillotine, on the side opposite Bond.

The other door guard appeared to be unhurt, but dazed, his hand limp, clutching his pistol.

The hood who had lost part of his face let go of his pistol, which now slid, spinning like a small curling stone on slick ice—heading straight toward Bond.

It was at that moment he realized that, in anticipation of the explosion, he had stepped back into the cell as the nurse reached for the control box. In spite of the ringing in his ears, and the dazzle of his eyes, Bond had been saved any real damage from the blast. Automatically, still not able to see or hear properly, he had stepped out of the cell again.

Fin, the balding man with the silver salver and Nannie were scattered, blown in three different directions and only just—like Bond himself—beginning to react.

He seemed to be looking at the automatic pistol sliding toward him like a man mesmerized. Then he moved, flinging himself at the weapon, a tick of time before Nannie's brain registered the same idea.

He was on his belly, hand grasping the pistol, rolling, firing as he rolled—first at the remaining guard near the door, then at Fin and the balding man. Two rounds apiece, in the approved Service fashion.

He heard the shots as tiny pops in his ears, and knew he had scored with each round—the guard by the door spinning backward; Fin's white evening shirt suddenly patterned with blood; the balding man clutching his stomach, a surprised look on his face as he sat, splay-legged, on the floor.

Bond swiveled, looking for Nannie, and realized that she was doing the only thing possible—making a dive for the Uzi on the far side of the guillotine. She was taking the shortest route, her body flat on the ground, arms reaching above the retaining stocks at the bottom of the instrument of death.

He saw her hands close on the weapon just as he flung himself toward the guillotine, lifting his arm and striking the projecting lever set into the nearest upright post—the lever that Nannie had herself used to demonstrate the diabolical machine.

Even through his deafness, Bond heard the horrific thud and the awful scream as the blade sliced through Nannie's arms, just below the shoulders. He was conscious of the spurting blood, the continued screaming and the fact that the fire, where Rahani's bed had been, was getting worse, pouring out thick, dark smoke.

He paused only to grab at the Uzi and shake off the pair of

detached arms, the hands of which remained clamped around the weapon. It took two hard shakes to free them from the machine pistol. Then he was outside in the passageway, which was also rapidly filling with smoke.

Turning, Bond looked at the numerical electronic locking pad on the wall. At first sight it seemed to be a simple series of numbered buttons, but then he saw the bottom row, which contained red buttons marked *Time Lock.* There was a small strip of printed instructions below it—*Press Time button. Press Close. When doors shut press number of hours required. Then press Time button again. Doors will remain inoperable until period of time set has elapsed.*

His fingers stabbed out—*Time . . . Close.* The doors slid shut. Then, again—*Two . . . Four . . . Time.* Everyone in the execution chamber was either dead or dying anyway. The action of putting the doors on a twenty-four-hour time lock just might hold back the fire. Now, he thought, for the hostages.

As he ran for the cell containing May, alarm bells began to ring, and by now Bond could hear them well enough. Either the fire had set them off, or someone still with strength left had activated them from inside the death chamber.

He reached the door of the first cell, looking around wildly for any sign of a key. There were no keys, so standing well to one side, Bond fired a burst from the Uzi, not at the metal lock but at the topmost hinge and the area into which it was set. Bullets whined and ricocheted around the passage, but they also threw out great splinters of wood, and, with pleasure, Bond saw the door sag as the area around the hinge gave way. He turned the Uzi onto the lower hinge, gave it two fast bursts and leaped to one side as the slab of metal detached itself from the wall, hesitated, then fell heavily to one side.

May cowered back on her bed, eyes wide with fear, looking as though she was attempting to push her body through the wall.

"It's okay, May! It's me!" he yelled, and she gasped out, "Mr. James! Oh, my God, Mr. James!"

"Just hang on there," Bond shouted at her, realizing he was raising his voice too high—a result of the temporary deafness caused by the explosion. "Hang on while I get Moneypenny. Don't come out into the passage until I tell you!"

"Mr. James, how did . . . ?" she began, but he was away, up

the passage to the next cell door, where he repeated the process with the Uzi.

When the door fell, he found Moneypenny in an attitude similar to that in which he had discovered May.

"It's okay, Moneypenny." He was breathless and the passage appeared to be filling with even more smoke. "It's okay. It's the white knight come to take you off on the pommel of his saddle, or something like that."

She looked gray with fear and was shaking badly. "James! Oh, James. I thought . . . they told me . . ." and she rushed to him, threw her arms around his neck, pressed her lips to his and tried to give vent to years of pent-up passion and desire for him. Eventually, Bond had to firmly disentangle himself from his Chief's personal assistant and gently tell her to follow him. "I'll need your help with May, Penny. We've still got to get out of here. There's a fire blazing along the passage, and unless I'm mistaken, quite a number of people who don't really want to see us leave."

He almost dragged her into the passage and pointed her towards May's cell. "Be calm," he said, "and for God's sake, don't show any signs of panic. Just get May out here as quickly as you can, then do as I tell you."

As soon as he saw her respond, he ran through the thickening smoke, toward the elevator doors. *Never use elevators in the event of fire.* How many times had he seen that warning in hotels? Yet, now, there was no alternative. Like it or not, there appeared to be no way out of the passage but by the elevator.

He got to the curved steel doors and jabbed at the button, knowing there was always the possibility that others were making their escape—from the floors above—by the same method; or that the mechanism had already been damaged. His hearing was gradually getting back to normal, making him aware of the roaring of fire from along the passage—from behind the doors of the execution chamber.

Reaching out, Bond touched the curved metal doors and found them distinctly warm. He waited, jabbing again at the button, then checking the Uzi and the automatic pistol, which turned out to be a big Stetchkin, which meant a twenty-round magazine, if full, and he had only loosed off six shots. The Uzi would by now be almost empty, so he switched it under his left arm, holding the Stetchkin in readiness.

Moneypenny came slowly along the passage, supporting May, just as the elevator doors opened to reveal four men, in dark combat jackets. Bond took in the surprised looks and the slight movement as one of them began to reach toward a holster at his hip.

Bond's thumb flicked on the Stetchkin, clicking it from single shot to automatic, and turned his hand sideways—for the Stetchkin has a habit of pulling violently upward on automatic fire. If turned sideways it will neatly stitch bullets from left to right. The burst fired by Bond was a controlled six rounds, and when it was over, the four SPECTRE men were littering the floor of the elevator, leaking blood badly over the carpeting.

He held up a hand to stop Moneypenny bringing May any closer while he quickly hauled the bodies out of the cage with little ceremony, jamming one of them across the doors to keep them from closing.

The whole episode took less than thirty seconds, and when it was done he ushered the two ladies toward the lift, which was rapidly becoming very hot. Pulling the body out, and stepping inside, Bond pressed the *Down* button, keeping his finger on it for five or six seconds.

When the doors next opened, they were facing the first curved passage along which Nannie had taken him from Tamil Rahani's room.

"Slowly," he cautioned May and Moneypenny. "Take care." As though in answer to his warning a burst of machine-gun fire rattled in the distance—from along the passage, toward the room originally occupied by Rahani.

It crossed Bond's mind that something odd was now going on. A fire was obviously blazing above them, yet they would be the only valid targets for any SPECTRE people active on the island. Why, then—he asked himself as he moved, close to the wall, along the passage—was there any shooting going on that was not directed at them?

The door to Rahani's room was open, and as Bond reached it, there was a violent burst of fire from within. Slowly he edged into the doorway. Two men—dressed in dark combat jackets similar to those worn by the men in the elevator—manned a heavy machine gun, set up near the big sliding windows. They were firing down into the gardens, and beyond them Bond could see a mass of activity—helicopters, their lights blinking red and green, hovered around the island, a star shell burst high in the velvet night sky, and three sharp cracks, followed by splintering glass, left him in no doubt that the house was being fired at.

He only hoped that the men out there were on the side of the angels as he stepped into the room and placed four bullets neatly into the necks of the two machine-gunners.

"Stay in the passage! Stay down!" he shouted back to May and Moneypenny.

There was a second's silence, and then he heard the unmistakable sound of boots clanking up the metal steps leading to the terraced balcony outside the window. Holding the pistol low, he now called in the direction of the window, "Hold your fire! Escaping hostages!"

The next thing he saw was the burly form of a United States Navy officer, brandishing what looked like a very large revolver. He was followed by half a dozen naval ratings, armed to the teeth, and behind them the white, frightened face of Sukie Tempesta, who cried out, "It's them. It's Mr. Bond and the people they were holding to ransom!"

"Bond?" snapped the naval officer.

"Bond, yes. James Bond." He nodded.

"Thank heaven for that. Thought you were a goner. Would've been but for this pretty little lady here. Best get out fast. This place'll go up like a fired barn in no time." He was a leathery-faced man, with what used to be called gimlet eyes back in the days when a gimlet was a tool and not just another drink. He reached out, grasped Bond's wrist and propelled him toward the balcony, while three of his sailors hurried forward to help May and Moneypenny.

"Oh, James! James, it's so good to see you." He had been thrown almost straight into the Principessa Sukie Tempesta's arms, and for the second time in a matter of minutes, Bond found himself being kissed with an almost wild, skidding passion. This time he was in no hurry to break away.

"But what happened? How come the Navy—and, I gather, the Coast Guard—got into the act?" Bond asked.

They had been hurried through the gardens, along paths to the small pier and into a Coast Guard cutter. Now, as it drew away, they all looked back at the island. Other launches and cutters were circling, as were more helicopters, rattling their way around and keeping station with one another, some shining spotlights down into the beautifully laid-out gardens.

"It's a long story, James." Sukie looked at him, eyes doing a very sensual foxtrot.

"Jesus!" muttered one of the Coast Guard officers, and Bond turned to look back. The great modernistic pyramid that had been SPECTRE's headquarters was spouting flame like an erupting volcano, the flames growing higher and higher, exiting through the top of the structure.

The helicopters had started to turn away, one making a low pass over the cutter. May and Moneypenny sat in the bow, being tended by a naval doctor. In the weird light from the Shark Island fire they both looked feverish and ill.

Bond took one more look back.

"She'll blow any minute," the Coast Guard officer muttered and, almost as he said it, the building appeared to rise out of the island and hover for a second, surrounded by a sheet of dancing flame. Then it exploded in a flash of such dazzling violence that Bond had to turn his head away.

When he looked again, the air seemed to be filled with burning fragments and a pall of smoke hung across the little hump that had been Shark Island. He wondered if that was really the end of his old, old enemy, SPECTRE, or whether it would rise, like some ungodly phoenix, from the ashes of the death and destruction he, James Bond, had caused.

20

CHEERS AND APPLAUSE

SUKIE TOLD HER story once the cutter was inside the reef, and the noise of waves, wind and engines grew less, so that she did not have to shout.

"At first I couldn't believe my eyes. Then, when Nannie made the telephone call, I knew," she said.

"Just take it a step at a time," Bond was still shouting, as the ringing had not completely gone from his ears.

When Sukie and Nannie had left Bond on the previous night, Nannie had ordered coffee from room service. "It arrived, and I left her to pour it," Sukie told him. She had gone into the bathroom, to touch up her face, but left the door open, and through the mirror saw Nannie doctoring her coffee, from a bottle. "I couldn't believe she was really up to no good, in fact I nearly taxed her about it. Then thought better—thank heaven. One thing, I remember, was that I reckoned she could be trying to do me a good turn and keep me out of danger. I've always trusted her— my closest friend since school days. I never suspected there was anything like . . . well . . . She *was* a very faithful friend, you know, James. Right up to this."

"Never trust a faithful friend," Bond smiled wryly. "It always leads to tears before bedtime."

Sukie had dumped the coffee and feigned sleep. "She stood over me for a long time, lifted my eyelids and all that sort of thing."

But, in the end, Nannie had been satisfied that Sukie was out for the count. "She used the telephone in the room," she continued. "I don't know whom she spoke with, but it was quite clear what she was up to. She said she would go down and keep you under surveillance. She thought you might try to make it to the island without us. 'I've got him, though,' she said. 'Tell the colonel I've got him.' "

Sukie had stayed put for a while, "In case she came back— which she did, and made another call. Very fast. She said you'd gone in the hotel motorboat and that she was following. Told them to keep a watch for you, but that you were her prisoner and she didn't want anyone to take you before she did. She kept saying she'd get you to the colonel in one piece. He could divide you. That make sense?"

"Oh, a great deal of sense." Bond thought of the guillotine blade smashing down and removing Nannie Norrich's arms. "Terrible," he said, almost to himself. "Really terrible. I quite liked her."

"So I heard," Sukie sounded well and truly piqued, and at that moment, the cutter entered the small naval base harbor.

* * *

"And who's paying for all this luxury? That's what I want to know." May was obviously well recovered.

"The government," Bond smiled at her. "And if they don't, then I shall."

"Well, it's a wicked waste of good money, keeping us all here in this verra expensive hotel. Ye ken how much it's costing here, Mr. James?"

"I ken very well, May, and you're not to worry your head about it. We'll all be home soon enough, and this'll seem like a dream. Just enjoy it, and enjoy the sunset. You've never seen a Key West sunset, and it's truly one of God's miracles."

"Och, I've seen sunsets in the Highlands, laddie. That's good enough for me." Then she appeared to soften. "It's guy kind of you, though, Mr. James, for getting me fit and well once more. I'll say that. But, oh, I'm longing for ma kitchen again, and looking after you."

It was two days after what the local newspaper was calling "the incident on Shark Island," and they had all been released as fit from the naval hospital that afternoon. Now, May sat, with Sukie and Bond, on the deck in front of the Havana Docks Bar at the Pier House Hotel. The sun was just starting its nightly show and the place was crowded. As was usual, Sukie and Bond at the huge, succulent shrimp with little bowls of spicy sauce and drank calypso daiquiris. May spurned both, making do with a glass of milk, about which she loudly expressed her hope that it was fresh.

"Lord, this really is the place where time stood still." Sukie leaned over and kissed Bond lightly on the cheek. "I went into a shop on Front Street this afternoon and met a girl who came here for two weeks. That was nine years ago."

"I believe that is the effect it has on some people." Bond gazed out to sea, thinking it was the last place he wanted to stay for nine years. Too many memories were crowded in here—Nannie, the nice girl who had turned out to be a wanton and ruthless killer; Tamil Rahani, whom he had really met for the last time; SPECTRE, that dishonorable society, willing even to cheat others of promised prizes for Bond's head.

"Penny for them?" Sukie asked.

"Just thinking that I wouldn't like to stay here forever, but I wouldn't mind a week or two—perhaps to get to know you better."

She smiled. "I had the same thought. That's why I arranged for your things to be brought up to my suite, dear James." The smile turned into a grin.

"You did what?" Bond's jaw dropped.

"You heard, darling. We've got a lot of time to make up."

Bond gave her a long, warm look and watched the sky turn to blood as the sun dropped behind the islands. Then he glanced toward the doors of the bar to see the ever-faithful Moneypenny striding in their direction and beckoning to him.

He excused himself and went over to her. "Signal from M," she said, shooting a few eye-propelled daggers in Sukie's direction.

"Ah." Bond waited.

"Return soonest. Well done. M," Moneypenny intoned.

"You want to return home soonest?" he asked.

She nodded, a little sadly, and said that she could understand why Bond might not wish to leave just yet.

"You could, perhaps, take May back," he suggested.

"I booked the flight as soon as the signal came in. We leave tomorrow." Efficient as ever.

"All of us?"

"No, James. I realized that I would never be able to thank you as I'd like to—for saving my life, I mean . . ."

"Oh, Penny, you mustn't . . ."

She put a hand up to silence him. "No, James. I've booked a flight for May and myself. I've also sent a signal."

"Yes?"

"Returning immediately, but 007 still requires remedial treatment that will take about three weeks."

"Three weeks should do just nicely."

"I thought so," and she turned, walking slowly back into the hotel.

"You actually had my stuff moved into your suite, you hussy?" Bond asked, once he had returned to Sukie.

"Everything you bought this afternoon—including the suitcase."

"But," Bond smiled. "How can we? I mean, you're a Principessa—a Princess. It wouldn't be right."

"Oh, we could call the book something like *The Princess and the Pauper*." She grinned again—wickedly, with a dash of sensuality.

"I'm not a pauper, though," said Bond, feigning huffiness.

"The prices here could fix that," Sukie laughed, and at that moment the air and sky around them turned crimson as sun took its dive for the day.

From Mallory Square, where crowds always watched the sunset, one could hear the cheers and applause.

NO DEALS, MR. BOND

to my good friend
TONY ADAMUS
with thanks

CONTENTS

1

SEAHAWK

THE NAVIGATION OFFICER, like so many of his Royal Navy counterparts, was known affectionately as Vasco. In the red glow of the submarine's control room he now quietly leaned over and touched the captain's arm.

"Coming up to RV, sir."

Lieutenant Commander Alec Stewart nodded. "Stop all. Planes midships."

"All stopped," came back from the watchkeeper.

"Planes midships," answered the senior of the pair of planesmen, who sat strapped into their seats, like pilots, in front of depth and turn indicators, their hands on the yokes which operated the hydroplanes that controlled the submarine's depth.

"Sonar?" the captain asked quietly.

"Distant activity around Bornholm Island, usual heavy stuff in and out of Rostock, two targets that sound like small patrol boats distant, up the coast at around fifty miles, bearing Zero-Two-Zero. No submarine signatures."

Lieutenant Commander Alec Stewart raised an eyebrow.

He was not a happy man. For one thing, he did not like operating his Trafalgar Class nuclear submarine in forbidden waters. For another he did not like "funnies."

He only knew they were called funnies because he had read it in a novel. In other jargon he would have called them "spooks," or maybe simply spies. Whatever they were, he did not like having them aboard, even though the leader held a Naval rank.

During wargames, Stewart had performed facsimile covert ops, but the real thing, and in peacetime, stuck in his throat.

To begin with, when the funnies had come aboard, he thought the Naval rank was simply part of a cover, but within a few hours he realized that Seahawk, as their leader was cryptonymed, knew a great deal about the sea—as did his two companions.

That fact did not reduce Stewart's annoyance. It was all too cloak-and-dagger for his liking. It was also far from easy work. The orders had been explicit and precise: *You will afford Seahawk and his companions every assistance. You will run silent and submerged, making all possible speed, to the following RV.* This was a latitude and longitude that, after a quick glance at the charts, confirmed Stewart's worst fears—a point some fifty miles along the small strip of East German coast, sandwiched between West Germany and Poland, and around five miles offshore. *At the RV, you will stand by, remaining submerged, under the direct orders of Seahawk. On no account will you disclose your presence to any other shipping, especially DDR or Russian naval units that operate out of nearby ports. On reaching the RV, it is probable that Seahawk will wish to leave the boat, together with the two officers accompanying him. They will use the inflatable they have brought with them, and after their departure you will submerge to periscope depth and await their return. Should they not return after three hours, you will make your way back to base, still running silent and submerged. If Seahawk's mission is successful he will probably return with two extra people. You will afford them every possible comfort, returning to base as instructed above. Note, this operation is covered by the Official Secrets Act. You will impress upon all members of your crew that they will not talk about the operation—either among themselves, or to others. An Admiralty team will debrief you, personally, upon your return.*

Damn Seahawk! Stewart thought. The submarine's destination was not the easiest place to reach undetected: under the North Sea, up the Skagerrak, down the Kattegat, skirting the Danish and Swedish coasts, through the narrow straits—always a tricky navigational exercise—and out into the Baltic for a final fifty-odd miles. Then inland into waters that undeniably belonged to the DDR—East Germany—crawling with Eastern Bloc shipping, not to mention Russian submarines from bases at Rostok and Stralsund.

"Periscope depth." Stewart muttered the order, observing the quiet atmosphere of the silent-running mode of the boat.

The planesmen caressed their aircraftlike yokes, bringing the

submarine up slowly from its 250 feet below the water, then gently
eased off.

"Periscope depth, sir."

"Up periscope."

The solid tubular structure hissed upward, and Stewart slammed
the handles down, flicking on the night-vision switch and doing
one complete circuit of 360 degrees. He could just pick up the
coastline—bleak and flat. Nothing else. No lights or ships. Not
even a fishing boat.

"Down periscope."

He knocked the handles up, took two steps across the control
room to the radio array, and picked up the internal broadcast
microphone, switching it on with his thumb and speaking in
almost a whisper: "Seahawk to the control room, please."

Up in the fore-ends, surrounded by red-marked safety equipment, just behind a bank of torpedo tubes in the only space
available for passengers, Seahawk and his two companions heard
the captain's voice as they lay on makeshift bunks, four feet above
the deck.

Already, having had plenty of warning prior to the approach
to the RV, they were kitted out in black rubber diving suits, each
with waterproof holsters attached to his belt, while the cumbersome
folded inflatable had been unstowed and now lay within reach.

Seahawk swung his feet onto the metal deck and, without undue
haste, made his way abaft to the control room.

Only those inside that magic, confined, inner circle of specialists
that is the global intelligence community would have recognized
Seahawk as Commander James Bond. His companions were members of the elite Naval Special Boat Squadron—officers known for
their discretion and often used by the Service to which Bond owed
his allegiance.

Stewart looked up as Bond stooped to enter the control room.
"We've got you here on time."

His manner showed no particular deference, merely a taut
professionalism.

Bond nodded. "Good. In fact, we're about an hour early, which
gives us a little leeway." He glanced at the stainless-steel Rolex
on his left wrist. "Can you let us go in about twenty minutes?"

"Yes. How long will it take you?"

"I presume you'll surface only partially, so just enough time to get the inflatable blown and paddle out of your downdraught. Ten, fifteen minutes?"

"And we use only the radio signals, as instructed?"

"Three Bravos from you for danger. Two Deltas from us when we need you to resurface and take us aboard again. We'll use the exit hatch for'ard of the sail, as arranged. No problem there, I trust?"

"It'll be slippery on the casing, particularly on return. I'll have a couple of ratings out to assist."

"And a rope. A ladder for preference. As far as I know, our guests haven't had any experience boarding submarines at night."

"Whenever you're ready."

"Right, we'll get shipshape, then." Bond turned and made his way back toward the pair of Special Boat Squadron officers—Captain Dave Andrews, Royal Marines, and Lieutenant Joe Preedy, Royal Marines.

Quickly, they went over the drill again. They lugged the inflatable paddles and the small lightweight engine back toward the metal ladder that would take them to the forward hatch, and from there to the casing and the cold wetness of the Baltic.

Two ratings in oilskins already waited for them, and the entire party stood at the foot of the ladder—one of the ratings ready to scramble up as soon as the order came.

In the control room, Lieutenant Commander Stewart had taken another quick look around through the periscope, and, as it was lowered, gave the order to surface to casing and black light. As the second command was obeyed, the interior of the boat became completely dark but for the glow of instruments in the control room, and the occasional flicker of a heavily shaded red torch. One such was carried by the rating at the foot of the ladder. He began to move quickly up the rungs until the soft voice came from the communications speakers: "Casing surfaced!"

There was a slight clang as the man turned the wheel unlocking the forward hatch; then fresh air poured in, like cold water, from the small open circle above them.

Joe Preedy was first up the ladder, assisted by the dimmed red glow of the torch held by the rating below. Dave Andrews—partway up the ladder—took one end of the inflatable from Bond, hauling it up to Preedy, and together the two men heaved the bulky thick rubber lozenge up onto the casing.

Bond followed them, the rating below him passing up the paddles and the heavily classified lightweight engine. Easy to handle, with small propeller blades, the IPI, as the engine is known, can run effectively, with little noise, on a fuel supply contained in a self-sealing tank that is a standard part of the rear section of the inflatable.

Finally Bond ran the air tube up to Preedy, and, by the time he reached the dark slippery metal of the casing, the inflatable had become its true self—a long, slim, low cutter, complete with bucket seats and hand grabs.

Bond checked that the two-way radio was firmly attached to his wet suit and balanced himself on the casing while the two SBS men launched the inflatable, the rating holding a line from the shallow rounded bow until the paddles and IPI were transferred. Bond then slid from the casing, taking his place in the stern. The rating let go of the line for'ard, and the inflatable was jerked away from the submarine.

They allowed the little craft to drift clear while Bond took a quick compass reading. Then he set the luminous compass—still attached to a lanyard around his neck—onto the plastic well in front of him, and, using his paddle as rudder, he gave the order to make way.

They paddled with long steady strokes, fighting the choppy sea but moving the little boat with speed through the inky blackness. After two minutes, Bond checked their course and, as he did so, heard the hiss of water as the submarine submerged again.

Around them the night merged with the sea, and it took almost half an hour of strong paddling, combined with a constant checking of the compass, before they could distinguish the coastline of the DDR. It was going to be a long pull to the shore, but if all went well they would use the engine for a quick sprint back to the sub's position.

An hour and a quarter later they were within striking distance of the coast, right on course, for Bond could see the inlet, free of rocks with a tiny spit of sand, light against the surrounding darkness. They allowed the craft to drift in, alert and ready, for they were now at their most vulnerable.

Andrews, in the stern, raised his unshaded torch and flashed two fast Morse code Vs toward the small stretch of sand. The answer was returned immediately, four long flashes.

"They're here," Bond muttered.

"I only hope they're on their bloody own," grumbled Preedy, and they allowed the inflatable to drift inland, grinding onto the beach—Andrews leaping into the water and holding the bow rope to steady the craft as two dark shapes came running to the foaming water's edge.

"Meine Ruh'ist hin." Bond felt a shade stupid quoting Goethe—a poet of whom he had little knowledge—in the middle of the night on a deserted, dangerous East German beach: "My peace is gone."

"Mein Herz ist schwer." The answer came back from one of the figures on the beach, completing the couplet—"My heart is heavy."

The three men helped the pair on board and had them quickly seated amidships, while Andrews hauled on the for'ard rope to bring the inflatable around as Bond set the reciprocal course on the compass. Within seconds they were paddling out again. In thirty minutes they would start the engine and give the first signal to the waiting submarine.

Back in the control room of the sub, the sonar operator had been monitoring their progress via a small short-distance signaling device installed in the inflatable. At the same time he swept the surrounding area, while his partner did the same on a wider scale.

"Looks as though they're coming back, sir," the senior sonar operator muttered.

"Let me know when they start their engine." Stewart had no idea what the funny business was about, and he really did not want to know. All he hoped for was the safe return of his passengers—and whomever they brought with them—followed by an even safer, undetected run home to base.

"Aye-aye sir, I think . . . Oh, Christ . . ." The sonar operator stopped short as the signal came loud into his headphones and the blip appeared on his screen. "They've got company." His voice resumed its professional tone. "Bearing Zero-Seven-Four. He's coming from behind the headland on their starboard side. Fast and light, I think it's a Pchela."

Stewart swore aloud, something he rarely did in front of his crew. A Pchela was a Russian-built patrol hydrofoil, and though now elderly, carrying two pairs of 13mm machine guns and the old Pot Drum search radar, these craft were formidable in both inshore water and choppy seas—fast, and using a shallow depth foil.

"It's a Pchela signature, sir, and he's locked on to them, closing rapidly," from the sonar operator.

In the inflatable they heard the heavy thrum of the patrol boat's engines almost as they left the shore, pulling away with the paddles.

"Use the engine? Make a run for it?" Dave Andrews shouted the questions back at Bond.

"Never make it." Bond knew what would have to be done, and didn't like to contemplate the consequences. He was spared making any decision by Andrews, who leaned back and shouted, "Let him come abreast and be ready for the bang. Don't wait up for me. I'll make my way back overland providing the limpet doesn't get me!" He was quickly over the side, disappearing into the sea.

Bond knew that Andrews carried two small limpet charges that, if placed properly, would blow holes directly into the fuel tanks of the hydrofoil. He also knew they would probably blow the SBS man to pieces as well.

At that moment the searchlight hit them, and the patrol craft appeared to bleed off speed, settling on her bows, off the long foils—a skilike structure—that ran under her hull.

The strong pool of light hit the inflatable, dazzling them, and a voice came loud over the closing gap of water, carried by a loudhailer and speaking in German—"Halt! Halt! We are taking you on board so that you can state your business. This is a military order. If you do not stop we will open fire on you. Heave to!"

"Raise your arms above your heads," Bond commanded. "Show yourselves to be unarmed, and do as you're told. There will be an explosion. When it happens drop your heads between your knees . . ."

"And kiss your arse goodbye," Preedy muttered.

". . . and cover your heads with your arms."

The patrol boat was low in the water now, engines at idle as she drifted in toward the inflatable, the searchlight unwavering.

The gap closed to almost fifty yards before Andrews' mines did their work.

The bows of the patrol boat suddenly disappeared in a blinding white flame turning to crimson. The explosion came a second after the flash—a great ripping crump, followed by a deeper roar.

Bond, who had ducked his head at the first flash, now raised it to see that Andrews had set the mines in perfect position. He would, Bond thought. Any good SBS man would have known the exact position for maximum effect on all Russian or Eastern Bloc craft, but this had been exceptionally well done. The boat had already tipped back by the stern. Fire ran its entire length, and the bows with their distinctive foils rose well out of the water as down she went—all in less than a minute.

The inflatable had been affected by the blast, blown sideways to skid over the water and spin like a child's toy. Bond reached down for the lightweight engine, which they had already attached to its fuel line. He lifted it over the stern, pressing the ignition button. The little IPI buzzed into life, the propeller blades whirling. Holding its grab handle, Bond pushed the engine down into the water, then leaned back and manipulated the machine so that it acted as propellant and rudder alike.

The whole area was now illuminated by the flames from the doomed patrol boat. Half a dozen queries went through Bond's mind—had the patrol already alerted other vessels along this closely guarded stretch of coast? Was the inflatable even now locked on to a land-based radar system, or another fast ship? Had Dave Andrews got clear after setting the limpets? Doubtful. Would their submarine have gone deep, preparing to crawl out to avoid detection? That was certainly a possibility, for a nuclear sub was more precious to its captain than Operation Seahawk. He thought on these things as Preedy shouted back corrections, using his own compass to guide them. "Starboard two points. Port a point. No. Port. Keep turning port. Midships. Hold it there . . ."

Bond struggled to control the inflatable's progress by heaving on the engine, which seemed to be trying to pull itself free from his grip. It took all his strength to keep the little craft moving on course, amid constant demands from Preedy to alter to port, then starboard, as they bounced heavily on the water, crashing down, then up again, with the stern low and bows lifting.

He felt spray and wind in his face, and in the final dying light of the patrol boat's last seconds he saw their two passengers, hunched together, huddled in anoraks and tight woolen caps. You could tell by the set of their shoulders that they were terrified. Then, as suddenly as the hydrofoil had ignited and lit the deep black waters, the darkness descended again.

"Half a mile. Cut the engine!" Preedy shouted from the bow.

Now they would know. Any minute they would discover if their mother ship had deserted them or not.

Back in the submarine's control room, Stewart had witnessed the death of the hydrofoil. He wondered if Seahawk and his companions had perished in the explosion, and decided to give them four minutes. If sonar did not pick them up by then, he had to go deep and silent, preparing to edge his way out of the forbidden waters.

Three minutes and twenty seconds later, sonar said he had them. "Heading back, sir. Going fast. Using their engine."

"Prepare to surface low. Receiving party to for'ard hatch."

The order was acknowledged. Then, "Half a mile, sir," from the sonar operator.

Stewart wondered at his own folly. All his instincts told him to get out while they remained undetected. Damn Seahawk, he thought. Seahawk? Bloody silly. Wasn't it the title of an old Errol Flynn movie?

The radio operator heard the two Morse code Ds, clear in his headphones, just as Bond transmitted them from the now almost stationary inflatable. "Two Deltas, sir."

"Two Deltas," replied Stewart with little enthusiasm. "Surface to casing. Black light. Recovery party clear for'ard hatch."

When the Seahawk party had been pulled on board and slithered down the ladder—Preedy last, after ripping the sides of the inflatable and setting the charge that would destroy the craft underwater leaving no trace—Stewart submerged, going deep and changing course. Only then did he move through the boat, toward the fore-ends, to the Seahawk party.

He raised his eyebrows at Bond when he saw they were one short.

"He won't be coming back," Bond said, without waiting for the question.

Then Lieutenant Commander Stewart caught sight of the two new members of the Seahawk team. Women, he thought. Women! Nothing good about having women aboard. Submarine drivers are a superstitious breed.

2

SEAHAWK PLUS FIVE

IT WAS THE best time of the year, spring, and London was at its most seductive—the golden carpets of crocuses in the parks; the girls unwrapped from a particularly hard winter; and the sense of summer just around the corner. James Bond felt at peace with the world as he sat draped in a toweling robe, finishing his breakfast, sipping his second large cup of coffee, savoring the unique flavor of the freshly ground beans from De Bry. The sun glinted into the small dining room of his flat, and he could just hear May humming to herself in the kitchen.

He was on the late shift at Service Headquarters in that tall building overlooking Regent's Park, and therefore had the day to himself. Nevertheless, his first duty of the morning was almost complete, as the multitude of discarded newspapers proved—for, when he was on an office assignment, it was necessary for Bond to go through all the national daily papers, plus one or two of the provincial ones.

He had marked up three small stories that appeared in *The Mail, The Express,* and *The Times* that morning: one concerning the arrest of a British businessman in Madrid; a second consisting of three lines in *The Times* about an incident in the Med; and the third being a whole article in *The Express* by their constant, though often inconsistent, spywatcher, claiming the Secret Intelligence Service was in the midst of a huge row with its sister organization, MI5, over disputed territory.

"Have you no finished yet then, Mr. James?" May, her old and stubborn self, bustled into the room.

Bond smiled. It was as though she took pleasure in harassing him, chivying him from room to room when he had a free morning.

"You can clear, May. I've got half a cup of coffee to finish, the rest can go."

"Ooh, you and your newspapers." She swept a hand over the

papers spread across the table. "There's ne'er a happy bit of news in them these days."

"Oh, I don't know . . ." Bond began.

"It's terrible, though, isn't it?" May pounced on one of the tabloids.

"What in particular?"

"Why, this other poor girl. It's spread all over the front pages, and they had yon head policeman on the breakfast television. Another Jack the Ripper, it sounds like."

"Oh, that! Yes." He had barely read the front pages. They were full of a particularly nasty murder that the police—so the newspapers said—linked to a killing earlier in the week. He glanced down to the headlines—TONGUELESS BODY IN WOODSHED. SECOND MUTILATED GIRL DISCOVERED. CATCH THIS MANIAC BEFORE HE STRIKES AGAIN.

He picked up *The Telegraph,* which had the story as a second lead.

> The body of Miss Bridget Hammond (27) was discovered late yesterday afternoon by a gardener in a disused woodshed near her home in Norwich. Miss Hammond had been missing for twenty-four hours. A colleague from Rightline Computers, where she worked as a programmer, had called at her flat in Thorpe Road on Wednesday night, after she had failed to turn up for work that morning.
>
> The police stated that the case was clearly one of murder. Her throat had been cut and there were "certain similarities" with the murder of 25-year-old Millicent Zampek in Cambridge last week. Miss Zampek's body was discovered mutilated on the Backs, behind King's College. It was revealed at the inquest that her tongue had been cut out. A police spokesman declared, "This is almost certainly the work of one person. It is possible we have a maniac on the loose."

An understatement, Bond thought, tossing the paper to one side. These days, perverted murder was a fact of life. Instant information, through the wonders of modern communications, simply appeared to bring it closer. Then, as the telephone began to ring, he felt a strange sensation—a prickling at the nape of his neck, and an extraordinary sinking in the pit of his stomach, as though he knew something very unpleasant was about to be—as they said in the Service—laid on him.

It was the ever-faithful Miss Moneypenny, using her official voice and speaking in that jargon they had both mastered so well over the years.

"Can you lunch?" was all she asked after he recited his number. "Business?"

"Very much so. At his club. Twelve-forty-five. Important."

"I'll be there." Bond cradled the receiver. Lunch with M at his club, Blades, was a rare invitation that did not bode well.

At precisely 12:40, knowing his Chief's obsession for punctuality, Bond paid off his taxi, taking the usual precaution of walking to Park Street, where that most coveted of gentleman's clubs can be found in almost mysterious splendor behind its recessed, elegant Adam façade.

Blades—as any book on London's clubland will point out—is unique; it was an offshoot of The Savoir Vivre, which was too exclusive to last after its opening in 1774. Its successor, Blades, came into being on the old premises in 1776, and, while noted for its exclusiveness and considerable expense, it has remained one of the few gentleman's clubs to flourish and maintain its standards right up to the present day.

Blades is still an all-male preserve. Its revenue comes almost entirely from the high stakes at its gaming tables, the food is still exceptional, and its half a dozen waitresses have continued to be the most beautiful in the city. They also keep the reputation of being, in the main, not averse to male blandishments, and it is not unknown for one or the other of them to linger on the premises in order to console a lonely soul in one of the twelve bedrooms available to members staying overnight.

Blades' membership includes some of the most powerful and wealthy men in the land, who have been shrewd enough to persuade visiting business associates—Croesus-rich Arabs, well-heeled Japanese, and billionaire Americans—to use the facilities as guests. Literally thousands of pounds still changed hands each evening—on the turn of a card or the roll of backgammon dice.

He pushed through the swing doors and walked up to the porter's lodge. Brevett—the porter—knew Bond as a very occasional guest at the club, and greeted him accordingly. Bond could not help thinking of the man's father, who had been the porter at the time of the great card game in which 007 had, at M's instigation, revealed the evil Sir Hugo Drax as a cheat. The Brevett family had been custodians and porters to Blades for well over a hundred years.

"The Admiral's already waiting in the dining room, sir." Brevett gave a scarcely noticeable hand motion to a young page boy who led Bond up the wide staircase, and across the stairwell into the magnificent white and gold Regency dining room, which has not altered over the years.

M was seated alone in the far left corner, away from windows and doors and with his back to the wall, so that he had a view of anyone entering or leaving the room.

He gave a curt nod as Bond reached the table, glancing at his wristwatch as he did so. "Bang on time, James. Good man. You know the rules, what d'ye fancy?—bearing in mind we haven't got all day."

Bond ordered grilled sole with a large salad, asking for the makings of a dressing, so that he could prepare it himself. M nodded his approval.

The food arrived, and M waited in silence as James Bond carefully ground half a teaspoonful of pepper into the small bowl on the tray of accoutrements. This was followed by a similar amount of salt and sugar, to which Bond added two and a half teaspoonsful of powdered mustard, crushing the mixture well with a fork before stirring in three full tablespoons of oil, followed by one of white wine vinegar, which he dribbled in carefully, adding a few drops of water before the final stir and pouring the mixture over his salad.

"Make someone a damned good husband, Bond." The clear gray eyes showed no apology for mentioning marriage—a topic people who knew Bond steered well clear of, and had done since the untimely death of 007's bride at the hands of SPECTRE.

Bond ignored his Chief's lack of taste, and began to attack his fish with the skill of a surgeon. "Well, sir?" He kept his voice down.

"Time enough, yet not enough time," M said coolly. "Words of our late Poet Laureate, not that you'd recognize Betjeman from Larkin, eh?"

Bond decided to rise to the irascible old spymaster's bait. "I know a few good ribald rhymes though, sir—The Jolly Tinker;

The Old Monk of Great Renown? I can even recite you the odd limerick."

M chewed on his fish—he had ordered the sole also, but with new potatoes—swallowed, and looked at Bond, his eyes cold as a Siberian labor camp. "Then recite me one about Seahawk, Bond. You remember Seahawk?"

Bond nodded. Five years had now passed since that operation. But Dave Andrews had been killed on Seahawk, and Bond would never forget the days and nights spent in the cramped quarters at the fore-ends of the Trafalgar Class nuke, trying to calm and comfort the two girls.

"There once was an Op we called Seahawk . . ." he began, but M held up a hand to stop any further impropriety.

"What if I tell you the truth about Seahawk?"

"If there's need-to-know, sir." All Bond knew in fact about Seahawk was what he had been ordered to do, and what had happened. Take off two agents, he had been told. He remembered Bill Tanner, M's Chief of Staff, saying the two Bond had to rescue were getting out in their socks—which in another language meant leaving in a hurry to save their very lives. Almost to himself, Bond said, "They were so damned young."

"Eh?" snorted M.

"I said, they were very young. The girls we got out."

"They weren't the only ones." M looked away. "We pulled the whole shooting match out over a matter of seven days. Four girls, a young man, and their parents. We did it. *You* brought a couple of the girls home. Now, Bond, two of the girls are dead. You probably read about it this morning. They had new names, new backgrounds, the whole works. Untraceable, the children—you're right, they *were* very young—and their families. But now someone's got to at least two of them. Brutally killed, with the added horror of having their tongues removed. You read about the maniac on the loose?"

Bond nodded. "You mean—?" he began.

"I mean that both the recently murdered young women were rehabilitated after doing sterling service for us, and there are still three out there waiting for the executioner who cuts out their tongues."

"A KGB hit squad, leaving us a message?"

"With each death, yes. They're slicing up *Cream Cake,* James, and I want it stopped—fast."

"Cream Cake?"

"Finish your lunch, then we'll take a stroll in the park. What I've to tell you is too sensitive even for the walls of this exclusive establishment. *Cream Cake* was one of the most audacious things we've done in years. I suppose that's why there's a penalty. Revenge, they say, is a dish best eaten cold. Five years is cold enough, I reckon."

"Cream Cake was a ploy to get our own back." M did not look at Bond as the two of them strolled—two businessmen reluctantly returning to their offices—through Regent's Park. "You know what an 'Emily' is?"

"Of course. The argot's a shade outdated, but I know what it means."

Bond had not in fact heard the word "Emily" for years. It was the name their American sister Service had used to denote special KGB-recruited operatives, mainly in West Germany. Emilies were usually single girls who had thought themselves into a situation common in certain kinds of young women, who imagine they will remain spinsters for the rest of their days. Indeed, some were held back because of an elderly parent, and the lack of romance in their lives was accounted for by the fact that they had little time to spare—work by day, coping with an ailing mother or father by night and early in the morning. But Emilies had something else in common: they usually worked for a government department, mainly in Bonn, and often as secretaries close to the BfV (Bundesamt für Verfassungsschutz), the West German equivalent of MI5, but attached as a department of the Ministry of the Interior; or the BND (Bundesnachrichtendienst), which is the intelligence-gathering organization, working very much in harmony with the British SIS, the American CIA, and the Israeli Mossad.

The KGB had exploited numerous women in the Emily category over the years.

A man would suddenly come into an Emily's life, and quite quickly the drabness of that life would alter dramatically. She would feel wanted; she would find herself receiving gifts, being taken to expensive restaurants, theaters, cinemas, the opera. Then she would be so swept off her feet that the unbelievable would happen—she would sleep with the new friend. She was in love and nothing else mattered—not even when the beloved asked her to do little favors, like smuggling trifling documents out of the office, or copying some trivia from a dossier.

Click, she was trapped, and, before she knew it, an Emily was in so deep that, if things went wrong, she had to flee Eastward with her lover—who, as likely as not, disappeared when she was set up in a new life within the Communist DDR, or even in Russia itself.

"We decided to use the Emily ploy in reverse," M said, cutting through Bond's thoughts. "But our targets were very big guns indeed—senior officers of the HVA, who began the Emily business, after all, and even trained the seducer agents."

Bond nodded. M spoke of the Hauptverwaltung Aufklärung, or Chief Administration, Intelligence—the most efficient organization, next to the KGB, in the Eastern Bloc.

"Senior HVA officers; also, attached KGB officers—including one woman. We had several sleepers who'd been left unused— left so long that they were really past it. Husband-and-wife teams we thought would be of great use. In the end, we found their children would be the best bet. Five families were chosen because of their kids—all attractive, late teens to early twenties, over the age of consent, if you follow me?" M sounded embarrassed, as he always did when discussing sexual traps, or honeypot ops, as the trade knew them. "Sounded 'em out. Satisfied ourselves. Slipped in a bit of on-the-ground training—even brought two of 'em into the West for a while." He paused as they passed a gaggle of nannies wheeling perambulators.

"Took a year to set up *Cream Cake,* and we had great success. Very great success, with a little help from others. Put the bite on the woman, who was pure old-school KGB—or GRU; snaffled a couple of high-grade HVA men. Eating out of the palm of our hands; and there was one very big fish who could still be dangerous. Then it was blown. With little warning. You know the rest. Brought them home. Reconditioned all of them—gave them new lives, golden pat on the back, homes, training, careers. Got a lot out of it, 007. Until last week, when one of the girls was murdered."

"Not one that I—"

"No. But it alerted us. Couldn't be sure, of course. Couldn't tip off the police. Still can't. Now they've got a second one, the

Hammond girl in Norwich." He took a deep breath. "They've signaled loud and clear by this bizarre removal of tongues. Could be KGB, might be HVA—even GRU. But there are still two young girls out there, and one personable young man. They've got to be pulled in, 007. Brought to a safe place, and put under protection until we've rolled up the hit team."

"And I'm the one who's going to pull them?"

"In a manner of speaking, yes."

Bond knew that gruff tone of voice only too well, and M pointedly looked away as he continued, "You see, it's not going to be an easy operation."

"There's no such thing." Bond realized he was trying to raise his own sinking spirits.

"In this case it's worse, 007. We know where two of them are— the girls you brought out, as it happens. But the young man's a different kettle of fish entirely. He was last known to be in the Canary Islands." M gave a frustrated sigh. "One of the girls is in Dublin, by the way."

"I can get the girls quickly, then?"

"It's up to you, James." Again, the use of his Christian name alerted Bond. "I cannot sanctify any saving operation. I cannot give you orders."

"Ah!"

"In the event of anything going wrong we will deny you—even to our own police forces. After the *Cream Cake* debacle, the Foreign Office watchdogs gave strict instructions. The participants were to be Hoovered clean, given a face-lift, and then left alone. We were to make no further contact or aid. If I went to the Powers That Be asking for sanction to protect these people, and possibly use one of them as a tethered goat to deal with the hit team, the answer would come back as callous as the Black Death . . ."

"Let them eat cream cake." Bond spoke somberly.

"Precisely. Let them die one by one, and have done with it. No compromises. No connections."

"So what do you want, sir?"

"What I've told you. You can have names and addresses, I can point you in the right direction, let you delve into the files—even the murder reports, which, naturally, we have, er, acquired. After that, which should take you the rest of the afternoon, I can give you leave of absence for a couple of weeks. Or you merely carry on with your normal duties. Understand?"

"Point me." Bond's voice was gritty. "Point me and give me some leave. I'll pull them in . . ."

"Nothing official. I can't even let you use a safe house . . ."

"I'll see to that, sir. Point me and I'll get them, and the hit team into the bargain. With luck *nobody* will know what's gone on—except the hit team's masters."

The following silence seemed to go on forever. Then M took a deep breath. "I'll give you names, and the file numbers for Registry, as we walk back to the shop. After that, you're relieved of duty for two weeks. Good luck, 007."

3

DARE TO BE CHIC

THE HEADQUARTERS REGISTRY was on the second floor, guarded by girls as statuesque as models, and usually dressed in casual jeans and shirts. Until a few years ago the uniform was twin sets, pearls, and well-cut skirts purchased with Daddy's hard-earned cash at Harrods or Harvey Nichols. M rarely went near the Registry since the rules had been relaxed, but he had been as good as his word regarding the information Bond was to see.

In the park, M had rattled off names and file prefixes, made Bond repeat them, and then told him to take one more turn around the Inner Circle, in which Queen Mary's Gardens are enclosed, before returning to the high, anonymous building where the Service kept its darkest secrets.

Now a tall, unimpressible goddess jotted down the file numbers as Bond gave them to her, taking the slip of paper to the Watch Officer—a striking brunette who sat at a high desk overlooking the other girls, ranged in rows before their work stations. There were no questions, not even a raised eyebrow from the Watch

Officer, whose name was Rowena MacShine-Jones—known to all as Registry Shiner. Ms. MacShine-Jones gave the nod, and the computers and digitizers went through their paces. Within five minutes, the goddess returned with a thick plastic file that was flagged in red, meaning CLASSIFIED A +, followed by the date and the magic words, *These documents must not be taken from the building. Return by 16:30 hrs.* Bond knew that, if he did not obey this command, one of the Registry guardians would seek him out and bring them back for shredding and burning, just as he knew the file's spine contained a "smart card" that would trigger a holocaust of alarms if he even tried to get them out of the file, let alone the building. High tech was the byword these days.

On his office desk he found a similar file, flagged with the same classification, except this one had to be returned to the eighth floor—which meant to M personally.

Within an hour, Bond had been through both sets, making mental notes that were now neatly pigeonholed in his well-ordered mind. He spent another hour rechecking his memory against the documents. After that, it was simply a case of returning the Registry file and taking the second one up to M's office.

"I think he'll see me." Bond smiled at Miss Moneypenny on entering the annex to M's private eyrie.

"More leave, James? He mentioned you might want to take some."

"Only for unexpected family business." Bond looked her straight in the eyes, like any trained dissembler.

Moneypenny sighed. "Oh, that I could be part of that family. I know what sort of business it is when you fabricate this kind of leave." She shaped her lips into a mock pout.

"Penny, if that were true there's nothing *I'd* like better."

The intercom buzzed, and M's voice crackled through the speaker: "If that's 007, Moneypenny, send him in here."

Moneypenny gave Bond a rather soulful look, raising her eyes heavenward. Bond merely smiled at his Chief's crustiness and—seeing the small green light come on over M's door to signify that anyone waiting should enter—gave a small, courteous bow to Moneypenny, and went into the inner sanctum.

"Come to return the grisly papers, sir." He placed M's file on the desk. It contained the police reports on the two murders—complete with photographs. The two girls—Millicent Zampek and

Bridget Hammond—had traveled the road to their respective ends via blunt instruments crushing their skulls from behind. The tongues, of which the press had made so much, had been removed with almost surgical precision after death—the police officer in charge of both cases had queried the *medical knowledge* of the murderer(s). There was little doubt, the reports said, that the same person, or persons, had carried out the executions.

M drew the file toward him with no comment. "Moneypenny said you'd put in an application for two weeks' compassionate leave, 007. True or false?"

"True, sir."

"Good. Then you can leave right away. I trust things'll work out for you."

"Thank you, sir. I think I'll visit Q Branch before I go, but I really do have to get into Mayfair before six."

M nodded, satisfaction flickering for a second in those iceberg-gray eyes. A look of tacit understanding passed between the two men, for they knew that, of the three remaining prospective victims, the nearest—Ms. Heather Dare—owned and managed a beauty salon just around the corner from The Mayfair Hotel. This was a pleasant coincidence, for Bond occasionally dined in that hotel's particularly good Le Château Restaurant, not merely for the excellent food, but for the security offered by its half a dozen special alcoved and very private tables that are well away from the eyes and ears of other clients.

M dismissed Bond with an almost cursory flick of his right hand, and 007 made his way into the bowels of the building where Major Boothroyd—the Armorer, as he was known—kept his iron hand on Q Branch. As it turned out, the Major was away ("In Dorset, looking at some nasty electronic hardware"), and Bond found the Branch operating under the expertise of the Major's assistant, the leggy, bespectacled, but unashamedly delicious Ann Reilly—known to everyone in the Service, somewhat obviously, as Q'ute.

In her early days with Q Branch, Bond and Q'ute had quite a thing going, but with the passage of years and Bond's unreliable timetable they had become mere kissing cousins.

"James, how nice," she greeted him. "To what do we owe the pleasure? Nothing new brewing, is there?"

"On a spot of leave. Couple of weeks. Thought I'd collect bits and pieces." He deliberately played it down. If he had been on normal leave he would have had to sign out with her for a CC500 scrambler telephone anyway. That justified his presence. In reality, he was there to pick her brains and maybe filch some small piece of technology.

"We've got one or two things on test. Maybe you'd like to take away a sample or three." She grinned, looking her most stunning, and Bond wondered if M, in his craftiest mood, had given her guarded instructions.

"Come into my parlor." She made it sound like an open invitation, and they walked briskly down the long room where shirtsleeved young men worked in front of VDUs or peered through huge lighted magnifiers at electronic boards. "Nowadays," said Q'ute, "everyone wants it smaller, with a longer range, and more memory."

"Speak for yourself." It was Bond's turn to smile, though the gesture did not even light up his eyes. His mind was full of the gruesome photographs of two young girls battered to death, even though he knew Q'ute talked of sound stealing, movement theft, concealment, and deadly devices—her stock-in-trade.

He left half an hour later with some small items, plus the obligatory CC500—which, under his current instructions, he would not be allowed to use, for both M and the Foreign Office would deny him entirely until he had everything neatly tucked away and the hit team—KGB, GRU, or HVA—disposed of or sent scuttling back to their homeland.

At the door of her office, Q'ute put a hand gently on Bond's arm. "If you want anything from here—if you *need* anything— just call and I'll bring it to you myself."

He looked into her face and saw that he had been right— instructions of one kind or another had been given to Q'ute by M.

The participants were to be Hoovered clean, given a face-lift, and then left alone, M had said—by which he meant that everybody who had been operationally active during *Cream Cake* was to be debriefed, provided with a foolproof new identity, and then dis- owned. Bond knew what *that* meant. It was like being cut out of some rich relation's will, and, if he fouled up, the same fate would fall on his head like a load of manure.

In the Bentley Mulsanne Turbo, tucked away in the underground car park, he readied himself for what the instructors called street work—checking the ASP 9mm automatic, its spare clips, and the hard steel telescopic operations baton. His getaway case—containing spare clothes for at least a week—was in the boot. So prepared, James Bond started the engine, and the car glided smoothly out of its parking slot and up the ramp into the spring sunshine of London's streets.

Some twenty minutes later, having handed the car over to one of The Mayfair Hotel's blue-liveried doormen—the one with a discreet Parachute Regiment badge in his lapel—Bond walked by Langan's Brasserie in Stratton Street, its garish red neon blazing even in the afternoon. From there, Dare to Be Chic, which lay on the Piccadilly end of Stratton Street, was but a few steps away.

"Dare" he could understand, for the girl's German family name— true or false—had been Wagen, so this was a literal translation. Where the Heather had come from, heaven and the Service resettlement officers alone knew.

The windows of the beauty salon, which had become popular and successful in the last couple of years, were black, the lettering gold with a logo—art nouveau: a bobbed-haired woman sporting a cigarette holder positioned below and to the right of the bold script that dared you to be chic.

Inside the neat single door was a minute foyer, deeply carpeted and with one picture—a Kurosaki woodblock print that, to Bond, resembled a magician's box opened in front of highly regular pyramids. The Kurosaki hung to the right of a gold elevator door, the button of which was neatly labeled with the Dare logo.

He pressed, stepped into the mirrored cage, and was whisked silently upward. Like the foyer, the elevator sported a deep crimson pile carpet. For a finger-snap of time Bond thought it would be a wonderful place to make love to a beautiful woman. Then the cage came to a gentle halt and he was in another foyer. Double doors led to the rooms where women subjected themselves to heat, facials, the expert fingers of hairdressers, and the professional hands of masseurs. The carpet remained red, another Kurosaki hung on the wall to his left, there was a door marked PRIVATE to the right, while in front of him a golden blonde dressed in a severe black suit and blazing white silk shirt sat at a kidney-shaped desk.

The blonde looked as though every pore on her face had been

cleaned out by Dyno-rod, and each strand of hair accurately grown and set for all time by a sculptor. Her lips parted in an encouraging smile while her eyes asked what the hell a man was doing in this woman's preserve. To Bond it was rather like the greeting one had when visiting his sister Service, MI5.

"Can I be of help, sir?" The words came out in that terribly painful, overemphasized drawl that Knightsbridge shop assistants confuse with uppercrust speech, turning "can" to "Ken," and "sir" to "sah."

"Quite possibly." Bond gave her his second most radiant smile— his first was reserved only for the genuine article—"I wish to see Ms. Dare."

The encouraging look became fixed as she said she was most terribly sorry, but Ms. Dare was not in this afternoon. Bond watched her eyes as she said it, noting the tone of voice collapsed slightly, as though she had learned the words by heart. The reply lacked conviction and the eyes flicked a fraction toward the door marked PRIVATE.

He sighed, took out a blank card, leaned over, wrote one sentence on it, and pushed it toward the girl. "Be a darling and take this to her. I'll mind the store. It *is* very important, and I'm sure you wouldn't want me to walk in on her without being invited."

When the girl hesitated, he added that Ms. Dare could look at him on the monitor—inclining his head toward the security camera high up in the corner by the door—and if she did not like what she saw he would move on. The blonde still could not make up her mind, so he added that it was official and flashed his ID— the impressive, fully laminated one with colored lettering, not the real thing, which was plain plastic in a little leather folder.

"If you'll wait one moment I'll see if she's come back. Ms. Dare was *certainly* out earlier this afternoon." She disappeared through the private door and Bond turned to face the camera. On the card he had written, *I come in peace with gifts. Remember the gallant submariners.*

It took five minutes but it worked like a charm. The golden girl showed him through the door marked PRIVATE, along a narrow corridor, up some steps to another very solid-looking door. "She says to go straight in."

Bond went straight in to find himself staring down the wrong end of a piece of gunmetal blue that, by its size and shape, Bond recognized as a Colt Woodsman—the Match Target model: a plinking pistol, as they would say in the US, but a plinking pistol can still kill, and Bond was always respectful in the presence of any such weapon, particularly when it was held as steadily as this, and pointed directly at his most trusted and best friend.

"Irma," he said in a slightly admonishing tone. "Irma, please put away the gun. I'm here to help." As he spoke, Bond assured himself that there was no other exit and that Heather Dare, née Irma Wagen of Operation *Cream Cake,* had placed herself in the correct position—legs slightly apart, back against the left-hand side of the rear wall, eyes open and uncompromisingly steady.

"It *is* you," she said, but did not lower the pistol.

"In the flesh," he obliged with his genuine number-one smile, "though to be honest I wouldn't have recognized you. The last occasion we spent time together you were a bundle of sweaters, jeans, anoraks, and fear."

"And now it's only the fear." She looked very solemn, and, for the first time, Bond realized all manner of things about her.

Heather Dare's accent held no trace of her first language—German—which meant she was the complete professional as far as the secret world was concerned; she was also a very poised, attractive lady—dark of hair and eyes, with a tall, slim frame, most of which, he considered, was taken up by her legs. Her elegance went with the business she had managed to build up over the past five years. All in all, a lady who would turn heads even on the most exclusive beach. Bond also caught an inkling of something else—a grittiness, maybe even a deeply ingrained stubbornness.

"Yes, I understand about the fear," he said. "That's why I'm here."

"I didn't think they'd send anybody."

"They didn't. I was simply tipped off. I'm on my own, but I do have the training and skills. Now, put the gun down, so that I can get you away to somewhere that's safe and under wraps. I'm going to haul in all three of you—the three that are still alive."

Slowly she shook her head. "Oh, no, Mr. . . . ."

"Bond. James Bond."

"Oh, no, Mr. Bond. The bastards have got Franzi and Elli, I'm going to be certain they don't get my other friends." The Hammond girl's true Christian name was Franziska—hence Franzi, Franzi Trauben; while Millicent Zampek had been known, in her life within *Cream Cake,* as Eleonore Zuckermann.

"That's what I said." Bond took a pace forward. "A place of safety, where nobody's going to find you. Then I'll take care of the bastards myself."

"If that's the case, where you go, I go. Until it's over, one way or another."

So, it was a combination of toughness and rock-like stubbornness that motivated Heather Dare. He had experienced enough about women to realize that this mixture could be neither fought nor reasoned with.

He looked at her for a moment, pleased with her slender build and the femininity that lay under the veneer of clothing—the well-cut gray suit, set off at the throat by a pink blouse and thin gold chain with pendant. The suit looked very French: Paris, he thought, probably Givenchy. It would be true to form for Heather to be dressed by the same designer as Frau von Karajan. "You have any ideas how we should handle it then, Heather? I *do* call you Heather, don't I—not Irma?"

"Heather," she breathed very low. A two-beat pause—"I'm sorry, I gave you the other names in their original form. Yes, I've thought of myself as Heather ever since your people sent me out into the real world with a new name. I have difficulties in thinking of the old gang in new guises."

"On *Cream Cake* you were interconscious? I mean, you knew one another? Knew what each target was?"

She gave a brief nod. "By real names, and by street names. Yes, we were interconscious, as you put it—of one another, of the targets, of our control. No cutouts, that's why and how Emilie and I were together when you picked us off that little beach." She hesitated, then frowned, shaking her head. "Sorry, I mean Ebbie—Emilie Nikolas is Ebbie now."

"Yes, Ebbie Heritage, right?"

"Correct. It happens that we're old friends. I spoke with her this morning."

"In Dublin?"

Heather smiled. "You *are* well informed. Yes, in Dublin."

"On an open line? You spoke on an open line?"

"Don't worry, Mr. Bond."

"James."

"Yes. Don't worry, James, I said three words only. You see, I spent some time with Ebbie before this place got going. We made a pact, complete with all the old secret trappings. I told her, 'Elizabeth is sick.' She replied, 'I'll be with you this afternoon.' "

"Meaning?"

"The same as 'How's your mother,' which was the *Cream Cake* warning, slipped into a conversation—'mother' was the trigger: *You're blown. Take the necessary action."*

"The same as it was five years ago."

"Yes, and we're about to take that necessary action again now. You see, James, I've been in Paris. I flew back this morning. On the plane I saw the paper—the murder, *murders.* It was the first I knew of it. Once would have put us on guard, but twice—and with the . . . the tongue . . ." For the first time she sounded unsure, even shaken. She swallowed, visibly pulling herself together. "The tongues made it certain. It's a charming warning, yes?"

"Not subtle."

"Warnings, and orchestrated revenge killings, are seldom subtle, James. You know what the Mafia does to adulterers within a family?"

He gave a sharp nod. "It's not pretty, but it makes its point." For the blink of an eye his mind recalled the last time he had heard of such a murder, with the man's genitalia hacked off.

"The tongue makes a point also."

"Right. Then what does 'Elizabeth is sick' mean?"

"That we've been blown; it is dangerous; meet me where we arranged."

"Which is?"

"Which is where I'm going—on the Aer Lingus flight from Heathrow at eight-thirty tonight."

"Dublin."

Again she nodded. "Dublin. Hire a car and head for where Ebbie will have been waiting since this afternoon."

"And you did the same for Frank—Frank Baisley—or Franz Belzinger? The one now known as Jungle?"

She was still tense, but she gave a little smile. "He was always a joker. A bit of a risk-taker. His street name was Wald, German for Forest. Now his nickname is 'Jungle.' He finds it amusing, and no—no, I could not get a message to him because I don't know where he is."

"I do."

"Where?"

"Quite a long way off. Now *you* tell me—where are you meeting Ebbie?"

She hesitated for a second, probably weighing up the safety of such a breach of their private security.

"Come on," Bond rapped out, "I am here to help. I'm coming with you to Dublin anyway. I have to. Where do you plan to meet?"

"Oh, we decided a long time ago that it would be best to hide in the open—Ashford Castle, County Mayo. A grand hotel—the place where President Reagan stayed."

Bond smiled. It was sound professional thinking—The Ashford Castle Hotel *is* grand, and expensive, and the last place on God's earth a hit team from either Russia or one of the satellites would think of looking, unless they were on your heels and following. "Can we look as though we're having a business meeting?" he said casually. "And can I use your telephone?"

She took a seat behind her long desk, the Woodsman disappearing into some safe place. Then she spread papers around and pushed the telephone toward him. Bond dialed Heathrow and asked for the Aer Lingus reservations desk, was given another number to call—which shows how wonderfully organized they are at Heathrow—dialed the second number, and booked himself onto EI 177, Club Class, in the name of Boldman.

"My car's just around the corner," he said as he put down the receiver. "We'll leave here at about seven. It'll be dusk and, I presume, all your people will have gone."

She glanced at her watch—a neat Cartier—and her eyebrows rose. "They'll be finished very soon now—" and, as though on cue, her telephone rang.

It was the blonde, Bond presumed, because Heather said yes, they should all leave, lock the doors, usual things—she was working late with the gentleman who had called. Yes, she would see them all in the morning.

So they sat, as the glowing spring day took on a chill of evening, and the grumble of traffic from Piccadilly dwindled slightly. And as they sat, they talked, Bond gently probing her about *Cream*

Cake and learning nothing he did not know from the files of that afternoon, except that Heather Dare held herself responsible for the panic call to all five participants: "I'm sorry, Gustav has canceled dinner." She herself had been working their prime target, Colonel Maxim Smolin, who during that period was the second man in the East German madhouse of secrets, the HVA.

She told him, unwittingly, a great deal about herself, and a lot more concerning the inner workings of *Cream Cake,* alerting him to a few deceits left out, or degutted, in the files.

At five minutes to seven he asked if she had a coat, and she nodded, going to the small, built-in wardrobe and slipping into a white trenchcoat that was far too easily identifiable, and very definitely French, for only the French can make raincoats that have flair. He ordered her to lock up the Woodsman. Then, together, they left her office, switching out the lights as they went.

Into the elevator cage, hissing down to street level.

The lights went out of their own accord just as they reached the small ground-floor foyer, and, as the doors opened onto gloom, Heather screamed and the attacker came at her like a human typhoon.

4

DUCKING & DIVING

THE MAN WHO hurled himself into the elevator cage must have been absolutely certain that Heather was alone. Later Bond thought that all the attacker could have seen from his lurking point in the foyer was the white trenchcoat—for Heather had taken a step forward toward the doors as they opened.

Bond was thrown against the glass side of the cage, off balance. He felt his back crack into the glass, saw that the assailant had one hand firmly on the shoulder of Heather's trenchcoat, spinning her around, with his other arm raised high. Dimly Bond could just make out an object that looked like a large hammer held aloft. The whole business had taken a split second—all fury and violence.

Desperately fighting the natural forces of gravity, Bond struck out with his right leg—a hard, straight blow with his heel forced forward and in the direction of the intruder's lower legs. He felt his shoe hit and heard a muffled grunt as the man was deflected from making an accurate downward stroke, missing Heather by inches.

The rear mirror glass of the cage shattered as the wielded hammer struck. It was the attacker's turn to recover his balance. By this time, Bond had made his move, tugging the collapsible baton from its holster on his right hip, flicking down so that the telescoped steel clicked into place—forming a formidable weapon with which he struck out toward the target's neck.

The killer went down without even a cry—just a dull thud as the steel of the baton connected, followed by a scraping noise as the man's head went straight into the already splintered glass, as though following the exact trajectory of the mallet blow.

Suddenly the fury was gone, leaving only the sound of Heather breathing heavy little choking sobs. Bond reached out to see if there was an emergency light switch inside the elevator cage. His hand touched the control panel and, at first, the doors tried to close and then open as the safety buffer came into play, for the sprawled assailant's legs stretched out into the foyer.

The same thing happened three times before Bond's fingers hit some override button and the cage flooded with light.

Heather was shaking, hunched in the far corner away from the inert body, which was clad, from head to foot, in black—jeans, a turtleneck, and gloves. Even the man's hair was dark, but it looked as though some hairdresser had tried to give it a punk style by putting in crimson streaks. The sharded rear mirror reflected the gory patches—the great starlike cracks giving an odd, kaleidoscopic picture of black and red.

With his right foot, Bond heaved the body over, turning it faceup. The man was not dead. His mouth had fallen open and there was a sharp pattern of slashed cuts, from hairline to mouth, where his face had hit the glass. You could hear the quick breathing, and the blood seemed to be flowing normally. Enough, but nothing to worry about. When consciousness returned, he would probably feel more pain from Bond's blow than from the slashes.

"Couple of aspirins and he'll be right as rain," Bond muttered.

"Mischa," Heather said, aloud and with some violence.

"You know him?"

"One of the heavies they kept in Berlin. Moscow-trained. Jack-of-all-trades, as long as the trades have something to do with causing pain, maiming, or killing." As she spoke, Heather seemed to be trying to press her back through the side of the elevator cage, as though attempting to put as much space as possible between her and the man she recognized as Mischa. All the time, the doors kept closing, hitting Mischa's legs, rebounding open again, quiescent for a few seconds, then having another go.

"Persistent things, elevator doors." Bond bent over the unhappy Mischa, probed around, and finally pulled—from under the thug's body—the weapon meant for the back of Heather's skull. "A nice carpenter's mallet." He hefted it in his hand, a large, heavy wooden hammer with a king-size head. "Brand new. Unused," he said after examining it, before wiping the handle off with his hand-kerchief and putting it back on the floor. Bending again, he began to go over the body, searching and feeling wherever another weapon might be concealed.

"Not even loose change, or a pack of cigarettes," he announced, straightening up. "Do we, by any chance, have another way out, Heather? A fire escape or something?"

"Yes. A metal zigzag thing at the back of the salon. It's to do with fire regulations. I had it put in when we refurbished the place." She paused, looked around her, scowled at the thumping elevator doors, and asked, "Why?"

"Because, sweet, lucky Heather—and you've been damned lucky—friend Mischa did not come alone. Not if comrade Colonel Maxim Smolin orchestrated everything for the other two girls and intended you to go by the same unpleasant route."

"But Maxim wouldn't . . ." she began, then changed it to another questioning "Why?"

"Mischa carries nothing else on him. Just the instrument to bludgeon you to death. There's no knife; no little medical gizmo for the swift removal of tongues—and that's the trademark, isn't it?"

She gave a small frightened nod; Bond, kicking the mallet to the back of the cage, grabbed the unconscious Mischa by the scruff of his turtleneck and lifted him without effort, dumping him into the foyer.

Heather had the wit to hold the elevator button, and once the unconscious killer was free of the doors, Bond slammed the heel of his hand onto the UP button.

They made the silent ascent to the beauty salon's entrance, where Heather did things with security alarm switches in a neat metal cupboard set into the wall. Then, with a quick "Through here!" she pushed open the double doors.

"No lights," Bond ordered. "Lead me there," and he felt her hand, remarkably cool for one who had just escaped death, clasp his own palm, as she negotiated her way past the handbasins and dryers of the hairdressing salon, then into a corridor punctuated with doors that stood out clearly in their clinical white.

A final door—EMERGENCY EXIT visible in red overhead—opened with a push-bar safety lock, and the cool of the evening hit them as they emerged onto a metal platform—a black square studded with holes—from which you could almost reach out and touch the other buildings. To the right, narrow and swaying steps zig-zagged down.

"How do we get out? At the bottom, I mean." Bond looked down, seeing nothing but a tiny courtyard—square, surrounded by the backs of buildings.

"Only key holders can use the exit," she panted. "We have four sets, one for each of my head people: hairdressing, beauty consultant, massage—and one for me. There's a door to a passageway that runs alongside the car showroom, and a door at the other end. Same key for both doors."

"Locks?"

"Yales. The far door takes you into Berkeley Street."

"Go, then! Go!"

She turned toward the fire escape, one hand on the guardrail, and at that moment Bond heard heavy running feet thudding toward them from the other side of the door. "Get on with it." He did not raise his voice. "Just get down and leave the doors open for me. There's a British Racing Green Bentley Turbo parked opposite The Mayfair. Go into the foyer and watch for me. If I arrive in a hurry, with both hands in view, run straight to the car. If my right hand's in my pocket, and I'm taking my time,

lose yourself for half an hour, then come back and wait. Same
signals at half-hour intervals. Now, move!"

She seemed to hesitate for a second, then went down the metal
stairs, which seemed to shake precariously as her speed increased,
while Bond swiveled toward the exit, drawing his 9mm ASP,
holding it low against the hip. Friend Mischa, the mallet man,
had not come alone.

The thudding of feet grew louder, and, when he thought the
distance right, Bond pulled back sharply, opening the door.

He did it the textbook way, leaving just enough time to be
certain his targets were not friendly policemen—who were liable
to be unfriendly if they thought he was some criminal intruder.

By no stretch of the imagination were these men police: unless
London's finest had taken to using Colt .45 automatics without
warning.

The men who had been pounding down the passage slithered
to a halt as soon as he showed himself. Oddly, they had put lights
on in the corridor, so they could be seen quite clearly—though
Bond was aware that he was an equally good target, even turned
sideways as they taught on the yearly field small-arms course.

There were two of them—well-muscled trained hoods, one moving fast behind the other, each hogging a different side of the
narrow corridor.

It was the one ahead, to Bond's right, who fired, the big .45
sounding like a bomb in the confines of the corridor. A huge
piece of the doorjamb woodwork, to his left, disintegrated, leaving
a large hole and sending splinters flying. The second shot passed
between Bond and the jamb. He felt the crack of the bullet as it
cut the air near his head, but by this time he had also fired—
low, to miss or do damage to feet and legs with the horrific little
Glaser slugs with which he always loaded the ASP.

The hoods would have been easy meat for that kind of ammunition—hundreds of No. 12 shot in liquid Teflon within the
soft bullet—but Bond had no desire to kill anybody: M had been
clear enough—*In the event of anything going wrong we will deny
you—even to our own police forces.* He had no intention of being
denied by his Service if up for murder at the Old Bailey, so he
squeezed the trigger twice, one shot to each wall, heard a yelp of
pain and a shout, then turned about and hurtled down the fire
escape, glancing below to see there was no sign of Heather.

He thought there was another shout from above him as he reached the first door, which Heather—he thanked heaven—had left open. Bond went through it as though trying to beat all existing records, slammed it after him, and put up the Yale catch before barreling down the passage to the street door. Seconds later he was in the street itself, turning left and left again, both hands in sight.

Within seconds the hotel doorman had come over with the car keys and unlocked the Bentley. Bond tipped him a shade lavishly and smiled casually at Heather as she came across the road from the hotel entrance.

The car was parked facing Berkeley Street, and they slid away, first left, then around Berkeley Square, bearing left again, then right, past that doyen of hotels, The Connaught, and left into Grosvenor Square, Upper Grosvenor Street, and the heavy traffic of Park Lane.

"Keep an eye open," he told Heather, who sat—silent—at his side. "You're trade, like me, so presumably you can spot a tail. I'm going through the park, down Exhibition Road, and then right, toward the M4. I presume you've been trained, so I really don't have to tell you the rules, but in case you've forgotten—"

"I don't forget," she cracked back, like a whip. "We are ducking and diving, yes?"

"That's what the rule book says. Never fly straight and level for more than half a minute; so never walk around without watching your back; always make it difficult for them to follow; always mislead."

"Even when they know you're there," she added tartly.

"Right." Bond smiled, though the streak of cruelty still played around his mouth. "What, incidentally, were you going to do about luggage, Heather?"

"I had a case packed at home. No way, now."

"Have to buy a toothbrush at the airport. Anything else'll have to wait until Ireland. You booked under your own name?"

"Yes."

"Well, you're going to unbook it. Then hope like hell the wait list isn't too long. We'll stop at the service station. We can only presume the other two were also Smolin's men—expecting to find your battered corpse, and do the tongue removal. I got a glimpse of them, and they seemed to be the kind of people who'd enjoy that sort of thing."

"Did you . . . ?"

"Kill them? No, but at least one of them's hurt. Maybe both. Didn't stop to find out. Now, think of a good alias."

"Smith?"

"No. House rules—not Smith, Jones, Green, or Brown. Something with polish."

"Arlington," she said. "Like Arlington Street. Very smart and West End."

"Like the American cemetery," Bond snapped. "Probably a bad omen, but it'll do. We still free of company?"

"There was a Jag XL back there that I didn't like the look of, but it turned off into Marlowes Road. I think we're clear."

"Good. Now listen, Heather. You cancel your Dublin booking, and try to get on in the name of Arlington as soon as we arrive. I'll take care of anything else. Right?"

"Whatever you say." She was reasonably calm, only a razor-thin edge under the cool, collected voice. It was impossible for Bond to deduce how good she really was.

They stopped at the first service station on the M4 Motorway, three miles or so from the Heathrow Exit. Bond shooed her into the one telephone booth that was free while he loitered by the next one, in which a woman was dialing a series of numbers from a little black book. In the end, Bond was able to take Heather's place. She nodded to him, confirming that she had canceled her Aer Lingus flight, and Bond, with a handful of change, delved into his telephone number memory and dialed the British Airways desk, inquiring if there were seats available on the 20:15 shuttle to Newcastle. Assured that there were, he asked them to hold two in the names of Miss Dare and Mr. Bond.

Back in the parking area, using the car for cover, Bond opened the boot and slid the baton and his ASP pistol into the special, lined compartment of his getaway case, where they were 100 percent safe from airport scanners, and 99.5 percent secure from search. If worse came to worst, he would have to use his Service permit, but then every Special Branch officer of the Irish Garda would know he was in the Republic.

Fifteen minutes later he had the Bentley stashed away in the secure long-term park, his getaway case out of the boot, and stood—two paces behind Heather—in the queue for the Terminal Connection Bus. He reflected, not for the first time, on the inappropriateness of the use of the word "terminal" for airports.

During the short drive from the service station to Heathrow, he had explained the diversionary tactics to Heather. "They're remarkably inaccurate about passenger listings on the internal shuttles." He smiled, having pulled the trick before. "You also have to go through the same airside main gate to get to shuttles or the Irish flight." He went on to tell her exactly what to do, including emergency procedures in the event of her not being able to get a seat on Aer Lingus 177.

In the first stages they were to go their separate ways, meeting up only when, as Mr. Boldman, he checked in at the Dublin desk. He also suggested that she try to buy a small carry-on flight bag and the bare essentials. "Not that you'll ever be able to buy anything *really* essential at Heathrow," he added, his mind darting back to those halcyon days when airports and railway stations could provide practically everything around the clock.

They got off the bus at Terminal One. It was just twenty minutes to eight, and both of them moved with some speed—Heather to the Aer Lingus Dublin desk, Bond to the shuttle area, where he picked up the tickets booked in their real names and paid for with his own credit card. Clutching his small bag, he walked briskly back to the Aer Lingus check-in, collected his ticket in the name of Boldman, and loitered until Heather reappeared, carrying a small, very new-looking bag. "Toothpaste, brush, spare undies, and some scent." She grimaced.

"Good." Bond nodded. "Now for the Newcastle shuttle."

As they passed down the ramp and through the gates to the walkway, brandishing tickets at the security guards, Bond checked the departures monitor to satisfy himself that already EI 177 was loading at Gate 14.

There was the usual crush around the shuttle check-in, and he took the boarding cards for both of them. They did not even have to put on an act in order to slip quietly to the back of the queue, and then away through the door and out into the walkway again, this time switching tickets for the Aer Lingus flight, and parting from one another—Bond allowing Heather to go well ahead of him toward Gate 14. If anyone came looking, they would at least show as having bought tickets for the shuttle, and even checked in.

If M had broken the rules further, and had someone watching at a discreet distance, they would not discover the Dublin booking until too late. But he was thinking more of Smolin's people, who could well be searching the airport, and making inquiries already.

That sixth sense, acquired over long years of playing Hare and Hounds with SMERSH, SPECTRE, and a dozen other organizations, was well tuned, and Bond's mental antennae picked up nothing of note. If anyone was on the watch—particularly lurking on behalf of Comrade Smolin—Bond neither felt, nor saw them.

They boarded EI 177 separately, and sat three rows apart, not joining up again until they had gone through the green customs channel at Dublin Airport an hour later.

Outside it was raining and dark, but Bond, undeterred, felt quite ready for the lengthy drive to County Mayo and the famous Ashford Castle.

There were no signs of a reception committee at Dublin, so while Heather went off to see if the main airport shop—which they both knew sold clothes—was open, Bond sauntered over to the car rental desk and organized a car. They had a Saab available—his preference, a Bentley Turbo, was way out of the question—and he filled in the necessary forms, using his Boldman license and credit card. A red-uniformed girl smiled a Colleen-type smile, and had just told him she would take him down to the car, when he turned to see Heather, seven or eight yards away, leaning against a pillar. She looked stunned: her face was chalk-white. As Bond closed in on her, he saw a copy of the Dublin *Evening Press* dangling from her hand. "What is it, Heather old love?" he spoke gently.

"Ebbie," she whispered. "Look," raising the newspaper for him to see the headlines, "it must be Ebbie, the bastards."

Among the chatter and throng of the airport main concourse, Bond felt the hairs on the back of his neck rise. In bold print, four inches high, the headlines shouted their warning—MYSTERY GIRL BATTERED TO DEATH AND MUTILATED IN HOTEL GROUNDS.

He scanned the small print. Yes, it was County Mayo. Yes, it was The Ashford Castle Hotel. Yes, the girl—unidentified—had been battered to death. Yes, one report—unconfirmed—said a part of her body had been mutilated. Yes, Bond thought, it had to be number three—Ebbie Heritage, also known, in another world and time, as Emilie Nikolas, if he remembered the file correctly. Smolin—if, indeed, it *was* the famous Colonel Maxim Smolin behind the murders—must have two teams operating. This, Bond knew as he glanced at the trembling Heather, meant they were not safe anywhere. "Move," he told her, softly. "Move fast. Now! Follow the nice lady in the red uniform."

5

JACKO B

IT WAS NOT what in Ireland is called "soft weather." This was the hard variety, lashing against the windscreen so that you could barely see the taillights of other vehicles. Bond drove with excessive care while Heather sat, hunched, next to him sobbing, her words blurred by grief—"My fault . . . it's my fault. Three of them now. Ebbie now. Oh, Christ, James . . ."

"It's *not* your fault. Get that out of your head." But he knew how she felt, for Heather had told him the whole sorry tale as they waited in the little office high above the intersection of Stratton Street and Piccadilly a few hours, and yet a lifetime, ago. With the news of another violent death spread over the front page of the *Evening Press,* Bond knew it would be folly to head straight for Ashford Castle now. He turned onto the airport exit road, was narrowly missed by a battered yellow Cortina with a wire coat-hanger for an aerial, and then turned off before reaching the main road that runs into Dublin from the North. The sign said INTERNATIONAL AIRPORT HOTEL, and he knew that place of old.

Tucking the car away in one of the vacant slots near the entrance, he turned off the engine and looked at Heather. "Stop crying." It was a quiet command. Not ruthless, or uncaring, but a command nevertheless. "Stop crying, and I'll tell you what we're going to do." At that moment, if pressed, he wouldn't have been able to tell anyone what he expected to do, but he needed the girl's confidence and cooperation.

She sniffed, turning her red eyes toward him, the scarlet accentuated by the hotel park lighting. "What *can* we do, James?"

"Book into this hotel. Now, here, just for the night. I'm not taking advantage of the situation, Heather, but we book *one* room, okay? One room and I lie across the door to guard you—or on a sofa pulled across the door. I also make a couple of telephone calls. We are Mr. and Mrs. Boldman, got it? They'll need only my signature, but you have to know what this is about. I'm taking a double room for your protection and your protection only. Right?"

"Whatever you say."

"Then do something with your face. Tidy up, and we'll go in looking like an ordinary English couple—or maybe an Irish couple, depending on what sort of voice I'm in."

Inside, Bond managed the soft brogue of Southern Ireland and a Dublin accent, booking the room, commenting on the weather, and backchatting the somewhat straitlaced girl at RECEPTION.

The room was functional. A one-night resting place between planes or onward travel: comfortable, but without any frills.

Heather flopped onto the bed. She had ceased crying, but looked weary, tired, and frightened. Meanwhile, Bond had made some quick decisions. M had given him the push toward this job, and underlined that he had no official status; but Bond had his own contacts, even here in the Republic of Ireland, and as long as he did not cross lines with the Embassy, he saw no reason for not taking advantage of them.

"We'll get food shortly." He grinned at Heather, probably a shade too conspiratorially. "In the meantime, why don't you freshen up in the bathroom while I make a couple of calls." Even if it was Smolin, with the entire HVA, GRU, and KGB backing him up, it was unlikely the telephones of the International Airport Hotel had an intercept on them.

Dredging his memory, Bond dialed a local number and was answered, after three rings, by a woman.

"Inspector Murray in?" Bond asked, mentally crossing his fingers.

"Who wants him?"

"One of his lads, tell him. He'll be knowing when he speaks."
Bond still used the Dublin accent.

She made no comment, and a few seconds later the deep
chuckling voice of Inspector Norman Murray, of the Garda's
Special Branch, came on.

"Norman"—Bond smiled to himself as he spoke—"Jacko B
here."

"Oh? Jacko, is it? And where are *you,* Jacko?"

"Not over the water, Norman."

"Lord love you, what the hell're you doing here, then? Not
mischief, I hope—and why didn't I know you were in the country?"

"Because I didn't advertise. No, not mischief, Norman. How's
the charming Mrs. Murray?"

"Bonny. Rushing around all day and playing squash half the
night. She'd be sending her love to you if she knew we'd talked."

"Don't think she should know."

"Then you *are* on mischief. Official mischief?"

"Not so you'd notice, if you follow me."

"I follow you."

"You owe me, Norman."

"That I know, Jacko. Only too well. What can I do for you?"
A slight pause, then, "Unofficially, of course."

"For starters, the Ashford Castle business."

"Oh, Jesus, that's not in our court, is it?"

"Depends, and even then, it could be unofficial. Have they
identified the girl yet?"

"I can find out. Ring you back, shall I?"

"I'll call *you,* Norman. You're there for the next hour or so?"

"You'll get me here. Home after midnight. I drew the late shift
this week, but the wife's out with her squash pals."

"You hope."

"Away with you, Jacko. Call me back. Ten, fifteen minutes,
okay?"

"Thanks." He quickly closed the line, praying that Murray would
not run a check with the Embassy. You could never really tell
with Branch people on either side of the water. He dialed another
number.

This time a jaunty voice answered—chirpy, but oddly guarded.

"Mick?" Bond asked.

"Which Mick would you be wanting?"

"Big Mick. Tell him it's Jacko B."

"Jacko, you rogue," the voice roared at the other end of the line. "Where are you then? I'll bet you'll be after sitting in some smart hotel with the prettiest girl any red-blooded man would fancy right there on your knee."

"Not on my knee, Mick. No. But there is a pretty girl." He glanced up as Heather came out of the bathroom, face scrubbed. "A very pretty girl," he added, for Heather's benefit. She did not smile, but grabbed her handbag and retreated into the bathroom again.

"There, what'd I tell you?" Big Mick's voice gave a great guffaw. "And if there's a woman in the picture, Jacko B, then there's trouble, or I don't know you at all."

"Could be, Mick. Just could be."

"What can I do for you, Jacko?"

"Are you in work, Mick?"

Another guffaw. "Sorta in and out. This and that, if you know what I mean."

Bond knew what he meant. He had known Big Mick Shean for the best part of fifteen years, and while the Irishman walked a very slender tightrope as far as the law was concerned, Bond had a dozen reasons to trust him—or any one of his companions—with his life. In some ways, Bond had trained him in certain nefarious dealings, like backwatching; on-the-ground surveillance; and how to get rid of dubious people who showed more than a passing interest.

"Would you have any wheels, Mick?" he asked, knowing that if Big Mick did not have a car he could soon get one—or three—and have them clean and respectable within twelve hours.

"I might have."

"You'll need, maybe three. With a couple of fellas to each."

There was only a slight pause—half a beat too long. "Six fellas and three sets of wheels. What's in it?"

"Couple of days' work or so. Usual rates."

"Cash?"

"Cash."

"And danger money?"

"If there's danger."

"With fellas like you there's always danger, Jacko. What's the deal?"

"Straight and true as a dog's hind leg. I might be needing you to look after me and the girl—at a distance."

"When?"

"Probably in the morning. As I say, two days, maybe three."

"Give us a ring about midnight, Jacko. If it's you, the cars have to be respectable . . ."

"And reliable."

"I was just going to say that, so."

"A nice little country drive, that's all."

Big Mick appeared to hesitate again; his voice had dropped and become very serious when he next spoke. "It's not to go into the North at all, Jacko, is it?"

"The opposite direction entirely, Mick. No worries on that score."

"Lord love you, Jacko. We don't do politicals, if you follow me."

"I'll call back around midnight."

"You do that."

Bond cradled the telephone just as Heather came out of the bathroom again. She had repaired her face, and the hair now looked fabulous.

He smiled at her, the kind of smile guaranteed to get cooperation. "Pity, you look so good, Heather."

"Why a pity?"

"Because I'd like to take you out to dinner, Dublin boasts some excellent restaurants. Unhappily—"

"We daren't show our faces."

"No. I fear it'll have to be sandwiches and coffee up here. In the room. What's your fancy?"

"Could we make it a bottle of wine instead of coffee?"

"Whatever you say."

In the end he called room service and discovered they made smoked salmon sandwiches, with which he ordered the best bottle of Chablis they seemed to have. He also retrieved the baton and his gun from the getaway case—it was the thought of someone coming to the room with the sandwiches, for the oldest trick in the book was to substitute a man for the waiter. One of the few things they got right in bad movies. But, before the waiter arrived, Bond picked up the telephone and called Inspector Murray as he had promised. Their conversation was short and fairly sharp. In the field never trust anybody, they taught, and he knew exactly how long it would take Murray to get a trace on his number, and therefore pinpoint him at the International Airport Hotel.

"Norman? Jacko. You have anything?"

"It'll be in the morning papers, Jacko. But there's something else I want to talk to you about."

"Just give me what's going in the papers."

"Local girl, Jacko. No form. Part-time chambermaid, name of Betty-Anne Mulligan."

"Ah. They got any ideas down there?"

"None at all. Good girl. Twenty-two years. No current boy-friends. Family's cut up no end."

"And the mutilation?"

"I think you know, Jacko. You've had a couple on your side of the water. Betty-Anne Mulligan was sans tongue. Head bashed in and not a tongue in her mouth. Removed after death. Very surgical—professional—they tell me."

"So. Nothing else?"

"Only the clothes she was wearing. The raincoat and headscarf."

"Well?"

"Not hers, Jacko me boy, not hers. Belonged to a guest at the hotel. Lovely bright day when Betty-Anne went in to work. The rains came midafternoon, and she had a long walk. Two miles and no coat or covering for her head. Guest took pity on her . . ."

"Name?"

"Miss Elizabeth Larke—with an 'e,' Jacko. Would you be knowing anything about that?"

"No," Bond answered honestly, "but I might by tomorrow. If I do I'll give you a call."

"Good man, now—"

"No, Norman. No time. Will the guest's name be in the papers?"

"It will not. Neither will the tongue."

Bond had been looking hard at his watch. He had about thirty seconds to get him clear of a trace. "Good," he snapped. "Your questions'll have to wait. Oh, and Norman, this *is* completely unofficial. I'll be in touch."

He heard Murray cry out, "Jacko—" as he closed the line. For a full minute he sat looking at the telephone, then the room service waiter knocked on the door, breaking the mood.

"Heather, did you often have meetings with Ebbie? I think I asked you before, but I need more details."

They munched at the pile of sandwiches, washing them down with a '78 Chablis that cost a fortune. Certainly it was a good year, but not at that kind of price.

"We met two or three times a year." Heather held out her glass for more.

"And observed precautions? Field rules?"

"Yes. Very careful. Booked hotels under names we concocted . . ."

"Such as?"

"She was always Elizabeth. I was Hetty. Surnames were birds and fish—she was a bird, I a fish."

"Ah. You kept a list?"

"No. Each time we met we arranged the name for the next meeting." She laughed, a jolly laugh, the kind you got from girls who hung around horses, rode, and talked of sales, and roans, and chestnuts. "Ebbie and I were very close. Best friend I ever had. In my time I've been Miss Sole, Miss Salmon, Miss Crabbe—with an extra 'b'-'e'—we always added, if possible, like Miss Pyke spelled with a 'y.' "

"And what are you this time?"

"You've made me Miss Arlington, but I would have gone as Hetty Sharke—with an 'e.' "

"What about the bird?"

Her eyes brimmed and he thought she was about to break down again; he told her to take her time, sounding supportive. She nodded, gulped in air, and tried to speak, then had another go and it worked, but with only a little voice. "Oh, we laughed a lot, she's been Elizabeth Sparrow, Wren, Jay, Hawke—with an 'e.' "

"And this time?"

"Larke."

"With an 'e,' naturally."

She gave a little nod, then giggled as though the wine was getting to her. "We steered clear of Tits, James."

"Yes." The wine was definitely getting to her: a strange mixture of a girl for a former field agent, part completely naïve amateur, and part sharply professional. So, Miss Larke, safely staying at The Ashford Castle Hotel, was Ebbie Heritage. There were other questions, though. Had she just been kind, lending the poor little chambermaid her raincoat and scarf? Had she spotted someone, and if so, would she now get out fast?

"You have a fallback if anything went wrong?"

Heather nodded. "Every time." The professional status was rising again.

"Yes?" He was asking the pertinent question.

"This was an emergency. We made plans for something like this the first time we met after our rehabilitation. If something went wrong, or I didn't show, she was to have gone to Rosslare—the big hotel that looks over the harbor, The Great Southern. In case we had to make a dash for it on the ferry. But, now . . ." she trailed off, the tears close again.

Bond looked at his watch. It was gone eleven. For a second he wanted to put Heather out of her misery—tell her that Ebbie was alive and well and living in—where? But no. Experience told him to play Ebbie's situation very close to his chest.

"Look, Heather, tomorrow's going to be a tough day. I'm going downstairs for a few minutes. You are not to open the door to anyone except me, and I'll give you a Morse V knock—tap-tap-tap-bang, twice. Anyone else, just stay silent. And don't answer the telephone if it rings. Get yourself ready for bed. I'll avert my eyes when you open up—"

"Oh, Lord, James, I'm a big girl. I've been in the field, remember. I'm not shy about you seeing me in my scanties, as they so coyly say." She giggled again, and Bond felt a small signal of worry. This was a trained field agent, who had been entrusted with, possibly, the most important target of *Cream Cake,* yet she appeared to be slightly drunk on less than half a bottle of Chablis. *That* just didn't ring true, like many other things. Very enthusiastic amateur trying hard for professional recognition.

He slipped into his jacket. "Right, Miss Heather Dare. No door, except for my knock. No telephone. I won't be long."

Downstairs, Bond went into the bar and bought a vodka and tonic, offering an English ten-pound note. The change came strictly in Irish money, as though there was no difference in the rate of exchange, so he leaned lightly on the barman for three pounds' worth of ten-pence pieces to feed one of the telephone boxes in the foyer.

There was nobody suspicious either in bar, coffee shop, or

foyer—he took his time checking, walking even into that odd well, spaced out with black imitation leather seats, set back in booths, that occupied most of the foyer like some kind of bunker.

Not a smell. Nothing untoward, as his old friend Inspector Murray would have said. When he was absolutely certain, he went over to the telephone near the door, looked up The Ashford Castle Hotel, County Mayo in the directory, and dialed the number standing with the handful of coins in his other hand.

"I'd like to speak to one of your guests—Miss Larke," he told the distant switchboard operator. "Miss Elizabeth Larke."

"Just one moment." A click on the line, then, "I'm sorry, sir, Miss Larke checked out."

"When? I'm really calling for a friend who was to meet her at your hotel, a Miss Sharke, S-h-a-r-k-e. There wouldn't be a message left for her?"

"I'll have to put you through to Reception." There was a click, and another voice announced that she was "Reception."

Bond repeated his query. Yes, Miss Larke *had* left a message to say she had gone on ahead.

"You don't know where?" Bond queried.

"It's a Dublin address." Reception paused, as though uncertain if she should give it, then relented and rattled off Ebbie's normal Dublin address, near Fitzwilliam Square.

Bond thanked her—wondering what Ebbie had really been up to with an address as good as that—then closed the line and dialed the Garda Special Branch number, right up there in Dublin Castle where all the action was.

"Jacko again, Norman," he said when Murray came on the line.

"You just caught me, I was getting out early. Hang on a minute." The minute stretched a little. Murray was putting a trace on the call.

"Right, man, I wanted a word with you anyway."

"That you'll get, probably tomorrow, Norman. One question: do you think the boys in Mayo will have finished with Miss Larke—the guest who was so kind with her raincoat?"

Pause. One, two, three. He was holding on to give the engineers time. "Well?" Bond chivied.

"I suppose so. If they had her forwarding address. I spoke to the Super in charge of the case. She was no suspect. Gentle as a lamb, he said. Lamb and Larke, eh?" An explosion of laughter.

"Thanks, Norman." Bond quickly put down the phone. Murray knew him as Jacko B on a very official basis. They had worked together a couple of times, and the Special Branch man had no illusions concerning the Service he was dealing with when Jacko B contacted him. They had an edgy, suspicious, though firmly defined relationship. In all probability, Murray would now—after three conversations, and no idea of his whereabouts—be on to the Resident at the Embassy in Merrion Road. Jacko B had been Bond's contact telephone crypto for the Republic of Ireland—his "blower name," as old hands called it—for a long time. In fact, he considered, it must be wearing a shade thin now, but nobody had thought of changing it.

Not yet midnight, Bond thought, but Big Mick was never very far away from a telephone. Piling the loose change on top of the public telephone, he dialed the number. Mick came on straightaway.

"I have the cars and the men," he said, once the bona fide codes were established. "Just give me the details, Jacko."

Bond gave him the number of the self-drive hire car, then, "I should say around ten, maybe ten-thirty, tomorrow. You'll pick us up somewhere around the Green. We'll be parked, and walking up from Grafton Street. What've you got, Mick?"

"A Volvo, maroon; a dark blue Audi; and an old Cortina, dun-colored, with plenty of go under the hood. Where're we going, and how d'you want us?"

"We'll be going to Rosslare—the direct route. I want someone well ahead, let's say the Cortina; with the Volvo and Audi close up to me. Box me in if you can, Mick. Not too tight, nothing out of the ordinary. Flash me if we've got any persistent company. Flash twice if you mark a dark-complexioned man with close-cropped hair, square face, struts rather than walks—"

"He won't be doin' much strutting in a motor," Big Mick sounded caustic.

"Military. German. That's the only description I can give you," Bond said wearily, realizing that a verbal picture of Maxim Smolin was not the easiest thing to paint over the telephone. He had seen the man only once, in Paris about three years ago. Seen him once, and been through his file a dozen times. There were seven covert photographs in the file and even they did not help. "Anyone who looks out of place is a danger," Bond said. "See you tomorrow, and thanks, Mick. Money from the usual place, okay?"

"You're a gentleman, Jacko. Tomorrow, then."

He cradled the telephone, and was about to go up to the room again, when he thought of one more chore—suspicious, perhaps, but necessary, for he felt most uneasy. On the way to the elevator he paused by the internal guest telephone and dialed their room number, scowling as it gave the engaged sound. Heather had disobeyed him, and the thought added more worry to his already overloaded anxiety.

Back at the bedroom, Bond gave the Morse code V knock twice, quickly. The door opened, and a vision of pink and white scampered away, back into the bed. He closed the door, put on the chain, and turned to look at her, lying, with a half smile on her face. The telephone on the bedside table was off the hook. He nodded toward it.

"Oh." She smiled again, moving from under the bedclothes so that they dropped back revealing a bare arm, shoulder, and part of one breast. "I'm terrible with phones, James. Can't stand not answering them, so I took it off the hook." She replaced the instrument and looked at him from the bed, the sheet and blankets falling to reveal both breasts. "If you want to sleep here, James, I wouldn't complain."

She looked so vulnerable that it took a great deal of willpower for Bond to refuse the offer. Heather merely shrugged—a gesture that allowed the covers to fall even lower. Bond recalled some song he had heard, which described breasts, "like virgin moons."

"You're a sweet girl, Heather, and I'm flattered. Bushed, but flattered, and tomorrow's another day. A tough old day as well."

"I just feel so . . . so—alone, and bloody miserable. Oh, you probably think I'm just a tart. What the hell." And, with that, Heather Dare, née Irma Wagen, turned over, pushed her head into the pillow, and pulled the sheets up.

Bond quietly removed one of the spare pillows from the bed, took off jacket and trousers, wrapped himself, first in the short silk robe from his getaway case, then in a blanket he found in the wardrobe. James Bond then literally stretched himself across the doorway, one hand resting lightly on the butt of his automatic pistol.

Sleep eluded him. Heather gave little snorts, as though having a bad dream, but Bond's dreams were reality, there in the darkness, as he thought about the operation that had been called *Cream Cake,* the incongruities of the situation, and the ruthlessness of the man called Maxim Smolin.

He drifted into sleep, waking with a start. It was five o'clock, and someone was gently trying the handle of the door.

6

BASILISK

SILENTLY, JAMES BOND rolled out of his blanket, drawing the pistol as he did so. The door handle continued to turn, then stopped, but by the time it had done so Bond was at Heather's side of the bed, his gun hand shaking her naked shoulder, while the other pressed gently over her mouth.

She made small grunting noises as he bent low and whispered that they had company—she should keep silent, get onto the floor, and lie out of sight. She nodded and he took his hand away, returning to the door, keeping to one side, because more than once he had seen what bullets did to people through doors.

He slipped the chain gingerly and then, standing well back, sharply pulled the door open.

"Jacko? Hello there." Even in the light from the corridor, Bond recognized Inspector Murray's tall frame and the smiling, shrewd face peering into the room.

"What the hell!" Bond moved behind him, shutting the door, snapping the lights on, and pushing the Garda Special Branch man just hard enough to put him off balance, all in one fast movement.

Murray stumbled forward, grabbing for the bed, but Bond had him in a neck choke, the ASP's muzzle just behind the policeman's right ear. "What the blazes are you playing at, Norman? You'll get yourself killed creeping about like that. Or have you got an armed posse surrounding the hotel?"

"Hold it, Jacko! Hold it! I come in peace. Alone, and unofficially."

Heather's frightened face slowly appeared from the other side of the bed, her eyes looking straight into the Inspector's merry face.

"Ah," he said, the mouth splitting into a friendly smile, as Bond slightly relaxed his grip. "Ah, and this would be Miss Arlington, would it, Mr. Boldman?—or may I call you Jacko B?"

Keeping the pistol close to Murray's head, Bond released him from the choke, moving his free hand and finding the Garda-issue Walther PPK in a hip holster. He removed the gun, sliding it across the floor, well out of reach. "For a man of peace, you come well prepared, Norman."

"Oh, come on, Jacko, I *have* to carry the cannon, you know that as well as I—and what's a wee gun, between friends?"

"Death." Bond sounded cynical. "You knew I was here all the time, then?—and Miss Arlington?"

"Ach, man, of course. But I kept it to myself. We just happen to have a red alert on at the moment and your face came up at the airport. Lucky I was on duty at the Castle when it came in on the Fax. I telephoned old Grimshawe—who we all know is the Brits' head spook in Merrion Road—and asked if he had any extra bodies over here, or expected any. Grimshawe tells me the truth. We work better that way. It saves a lot of time. He said no—no spooks, and no extracurricular activities, so I believed him. Then you rang me, and I got interested." His eyes twinkled as he turned back toward Heather. "You wouldn't be Miss Larke's friend, Miss Sharke, would you, dear?"

"What?" Heather's mouth hung open.

"Because, if you are, then it's bloody bad security, and not up to the high standards we've come to know and love. Names like Larke and Sharke attract attention. Stupid—which *we* are not."

Bond stepped back. "Mark him well, dear, stupid he is not," he said, mimicking Murray's accent, which was more lowland Scots than Dublin—as Murray always said, "I was born in the North, educated in the South, holiday in Scotland or Spain, work in the Republic, and don't feel at home anywhere."

"It was a shade idiotic, Norman, to come trying my door handle at this time of night."

"And when else should I try it? Not in broad daylight, when I have to account for every movement I make."

"You could have knocked."

"I was going to knock, Jacko. Another thirty seconds and I'd have knocked. Tap, tap, bloody tap."

The men looked at each other, neither believing the other. "I'm not here for the fun of it." Inspector Murray produced his cheerful smile. "I'm here because I owe you."

"Not because you're as nosy as any other copper?"

"I think your London policemen are wonderful, too. I owe you in a big way, Jacko, and I always repay."

That was true enough. Four years ago, Bond had saved the Garda SB man's life—up on the border, just on the Republic's side, not far from Crossmaglen, but the facts of that would remain buried in secret archives.

Heather still crouched on the floor. Now she pulled the clothes off the bed, wrapping them around her, and trying at the same time to pat her ruffled hair into some reasonable shape. Both men gazed at her in silence.

When she was decent, Murray sat himself on the bed, swiveling his body in a vain attempt to watch both Bond and Heather at the same time. "Look, girl," he addressed Heather, "Jacko'll tell you that you can be trusting me."

"Don't even think about trust, Miss Arlington." Bond's face remained impassive.

Murray sighed. "Right. I'll just be giving you the facts, then I can get home to a cup of cocoa and sleep."

They sat as though staring each other out. Finally Murray spoke again. "Your Miss Larke, now—the one that lent the poor young girl her coat and scarf—"

"What . . . ?" Heather began, but Bond shook his head almost viciously, telling her to say nothing.

"Well, your Miss Larke now appears to have, as they say of foxes, gone to earth."

"You mean she's not—?" Heather began again.

"Shut up!" Bond clipped out with some venom.

"My God, Jacko, can't you be the masterful one when you've a mind?" Murray grinned, took a breath, then started to speak again. "There was a Dublin address." He looked around, first at the girl and then at Bond, his face a picture of innocence. "A nice little address near Fitzwilliam Square."

Silence, as though he was still waiting. No replies, so, with a shrug, he continued, "Well, as they would say in London, somebody's gone and turned over that particular drum."

"You mean this Dublin address given by someone called Larke?" Bond asked.

"Whose name is not Larke, but, I suspect, Heritage. Ebbie Heritage, and what sort of a name is that, I ask you? Sounds like one of these romantic novelists. *Her Heart Lies Bleeding* by Ebbie Heritage."

Heather could not stop herself from letting out a stifled gasp.

"Enough of bleeding hearts." Bond sounded decidedly crusty. "This woman—Larke, or Heritage . . . ?"

"Ach, come on, Jacko, don't play the goat with me. You know bloody well, if you'll pardon me, Miss . . . er—Sharke?"

"Arlington," Heather provided, appearing to have herself under control.

"Yes." He did not believe a syllable of the name. "I've told you, the address provided by Miss Larke really belongs to a Miss Heritage. Both are missing. The apartment—the flat—near Fitzwilliam Square's been done over."

"Burglary? Vandalism?" Bond was exceptionally curt.

"Oh, a bit of both. It's one hell of a mess. Professional, but dressed up to look like enthusiastic amateurs. Interesting thing is that either the owner never had a piece of correspondence, or never kept any—or it was purloined by whoever took the place apart. They even ripped up loose floorboards. Now what d'you think of that?"

"You've come out here, at dawn, just to tell me this?" Bond asked.

"Well, you showed interest in the Ashford Castle business. Thought you should know. Besides, me knowing what kind of work you're engaged in, I thought there was something else I should put your way."

Bond nodded, as if to say, "Go on, then."

"Did you ever hear of a fella called Smolin?" Murray asked, all honey and disinterest. "Maxim Smolin. The Branch in London, ourselves, so I presume the people you work for as well, have him under a stupid code name—*Basilisk.*"

"Mmm," Bond grunted.

"You want this joker's life history, or do you know it already, Jack?"

Bond smiled. "Okay, Norm—"

"And don't you be after calling me Norm, either, or I'll have you in the Bridewell on some trumped-up charge that'll ban you from the Republic for life plus ninety-nine years."

"Okay, *Norman.* Maxim Anton Smolin. Born 1946 in Berlin of a German lady called Christina von Geshmann, by a Soviet General—whose mistress she was at the time—name of Smolin. Alexei Alexeiovich Smolin. Young Smolin took his father's name and, oddly, his mother's nationality. There is some corner of a Russian field that is forever German, if you follow me."

"I'm ahead of you, lad."

"Educated in Berlin, Moscow, and then Berlin again. Mother died when he was only a couple of years old. That your man, Norman?"

"Go on."

"Entered the military via one of those nice Russian schools, I forget which one. Could have been the Thirteenth Army. Anyway, he was commissioned young, then into the Spetsnaz Training Center—the élite, if you like that kind of élite killer. One thing's for sure, young Maxim found his way, by invitation, into the GRU, because that's the only way you get into the GRU—unlike the KGB, who'll take you off the streets if you make them an offer. From thence, by a series of postings, Smolin came back to Berlin—East Berlin. And he returned as a high-ranking field officer of the HVA—the East German Intelligence Service."

"Our Jacko's got one of those photogenic memories, as my old mother would say," Murray muttered.

Bond took no notice, hardly pausing for breath. "He's everything, our Maxim. A mole within a warren of moles: working with the HVA, which has to work with the KGB, yet all the time he's doing little jobs on the side because he's really a member of the GRU—that most secret arm of Military Intelligence."

"You have the man to a T." Murray beamed at them. "You know what they say about the GRU, which in many ways is to be feared more than the jolly KGB? They say it costs a ruble to

join, and two rubles to get out of. Almost an Irish saying, that.
Very difficult to become a GRU officer. Bloody difficult to jump
over the wall once you're in, because there really is only one way
out—in a long box. They're also very fond of training foreigners,
and Smolin is only half Russian. They tell me he holds great
power in East Germany. That even the KGB men there are in
awe of him."

Bond half nodded. "That's really a matter for speculation, but
who better to be well placed in the East German Secret Service?
Him being a member of the Russian Military Intelligence with a
lot of experience?" He stopped for four beats. "But what of this
little man, Norman? Have you something to tell us about him?"

"You know, Jacko, the whole world imagines that we have but
one problem on this divided island—the North and the South;
the lads and the forces of law and order. They're wrong, and I'm
sure you're aware of it, so. Your man—Basilisk—arrived in the
Republic two days ago. Now, Jacko, when I heard of that terrible
thing at Ashford Castle, I recalled there'd already been two just
like it over the water, and a little quotation came to mind."

"Yes?"

"There's something most pertinent been said, and written, about
your Soviet General Staff Chief Intelligence Directorate—your
GRU. The fella was writing about people who can't keep quiet;
who leak secrets. He wrote, *The GRU knows how to rip such
tongues out!* Name of Suverov, that fella. GRU defector. Interesting, Jacko?"

Bond nodded, looking solemn. The amateur and professional
historians of the secret world always tended to dismiss the GRU
as having been swallowed by the KGB. *The GRU (Soviet Military
Intelligence) is completely dominated by the KGB,* one such writer
had maintained. *It is an academic exercise to consider the GRU
as a separate entity,* another had written. Wrong, on all counts.
The GRU fought hard, and constantly, to keep a separate identity.

"Penny for them, Jacko?" Murray was making himself comfortable on the bed.

"I was merely thinking that the cream of the GRU are richer—
and more deadly—than their KGB counterparts. Men like Smolin
are better trained, and have no scruples at all."

"And Smolin's here, Jacko, and"—he paused, the smile wiped
from his face to be replaced by the look of a hard man—"and

we've lost the bugger, if you'll pardon the language again, Miss Dare."

"Arlington," Heather mumbled without conviction. Bond saw that she looked both nervous and a little sad.

Norman Murray lifted his hand and tilted it. "Dare, Wagen, Sharke, so who's counting?" He yawned and stretched. "It's been a long night. I must away to my bed."

"Lost him?" Bond asked.

"He did the vanishing trick, Jacko. But Smolin's always been good at vanishing—he's a proper little Houdini; and talking of Houdini, Smolin's probably not the only one of his breed that's on the loose in the Republic."

"Don't tell me you've lost the Chairman of the Central Committee as well?"

"It's no time to be caustic with me, Jacko. But we've had a small tip-off. Nothing elaborate, mind you, but a strong straw in the wind."

"A straw to clutch at?"

"If it's the truth, you wouldn't be after clutching at this one, Jacko B. This one's a walking mortal sin that doesn't go by any fancy cryptonym. Just a word, that's all."

"Well?" Bond waited.

"The word is that someone much higher up the ladder than Smolin is, at present, in the Republic. I've no collateral; nothing firm. But the word's strong enough. Someone from the top; now, that's all I can give you." He rose, walked to the corner, and retrieved his Walther. "I'll be saying goodnight to you both, then. And sweet dreams."

"Thanks, Norman. Thanks a whole bunch." Bond walked him to the door. "May I ask you something?"

"Ask away. There's no charge."

"You've lost sight of Comrade Colonel Smolin . . ."

"This is true. And we haven't even had a sniff at the other one—if he's here at all."

"Are you still looking for him—them?"

"We are that—in a desultory way, of course. Manpower, Jacko B, manpower's your problem."

"What would you do with them if you cornered either one?"

"Put them on an airplane to Berlin. But those fellas'd complain and dodge into that den of iniquity in Orwell Road—you know, the one that's got about six hundred bits of aerial and electronic dishes on the roof. Bit of irony, isn't it? The Soviets having their embassy in Orwell Road, and building a forest of communications hardware on top of it. That's where your man'd hide."

"And he's not there at the moment?"

"How would I know, so? I am not my brother's keeper."

"But you *are,* Norman. That's exactly what you are."

They came into St. Stephen's Green from Grafton Street, with Heather clutching shopping, the carriers announcing to the world that she had bought all a girl needs at Switzers and Brown, Thomas & Co.

Bond walked two paces behind her and a shade to the left. He carried one small parcel and his gun hand hovered across the front of his unbuttoned jacket. Ever since Norman Murray had left the hotel Bond had worried—anxious about a dozen matters that just did not add up.

At first, Heather had nagged him, furious that he had not told her Ebbie was alive and not victim of the mallet and scalpel— maybe some special curved surgical instrument, he thought.

"But you didn't tell me, you bastard. You knew how I felt. You knew she was alive—"

"I knew she was *probably* alive."

"But why couldn't you have the decency to tell me?"

"Because I wasn't one hundred percent certain; and because your precious operation *Cream Cake* strikes me as having been a lash-up from start to finish—and it's still a lash-up!" He stopped himself from saying more, for his temper was rapidly fraying at the edges.

After a few more exchanges, Bond finally told her to shut up and get at least an hour's more sleep. "You're going to need it."

She dozed off, but Bond remained awake, turning the problems over and over in his mind.

In theory, *Cream Cake* was a good operation, but if Heather was typical of the five young people chosen to carry out the seductions, the Operations Planners were criminally at fault.

The germ of the idea had been fair enough: after all, the HVA and KGB had been seducing little Emilies working for West German Government agencies for years—had not they even seduced old Willy Brandt's confidential aide? Though you could hardly call him an Emily.

The trouble with *Cream Cake* lay in its team—four young girls and a youth: there would never have been time to train them properly. Their parents were in place, as the Planners liked to say, so that was considered to be enough.

Their names spun in Bond's head like a gramophone record revolving with the needle stuck in a groove—Franzi Trauben and Elli Zuckermann, both dead, skulls crushed and tongues neatly removed; Franz Belzinger—who liked to be called Wald—and, of course, Irma Wagen herself, and Emilie Nikolas, a real Emily who should be in Rosslare.

He told himself that he must start thinking of them all by their refurbished English names—much good those had done them. Then he asked himself why Franz—Frank, he corrected himself—liked being nicknamed Wald? No, he had to think in English—the dead Bridget and Millicent. The living Heather and Ebbie. The presumably living Jungle Baisley.

Four young girls and a youth—tethered honeypots—plunged headlong into an Emily ploy that came unstuck. He would go over it again with Heather. He must go over it again.

And, in those early hours of sleeplessness, while the five characters in this drama called *Cream Cake* came and went in his head, Bond was conscious of the other dark figures, appearing out of all proportion, as is often the case within an active mind half awake just before dawn. The sixth actor—Maxim Smolin, whom he had seen so many times in grainy surveillance photographs, or jumpy films, distorted through fiber-optic lenses, and once—once only—in the flesh as he came out of Fouquets on the Champs-Elysées.

Bond had been sitting almost opposite—at a pavement café with another officer—and, even at the distance provided by that wide street with the distractions of its traffic, the short, tough, military figure of Smolin had a profound effect on him. It was possibly the way he carried himself—like a professional soldier, but more so; or, maybe it was his look, the eyes never still, the hands held just so, one fist clenched, the other flat as though making a tough cutting edge. In those few brief moments when Bond saw him, Smolin appeared to radiate energy and a malevolent power.

Then there was the seventh protagonist, the someone higher up the ladder than Smolin, unnamed by Norman Murray. The possibility that an even more senior officer—GRU or KGB—was here threw a considerably darker shadow over the entire business.

But those were predawn thoughts, when the enemy assumed near-nightmare proportions. Now it was day, and their car was parked on the far side of St. Stephen's Green; Heather had bought everything, from the flesh out and then some, and, before that, Bond—to Heather's amazement—had gone through his ritual exercises and eaten his predictable breakfast, commanded, rather than ordered, from room service, and sent back twice until they got it right.

The rain had gone, yet there was a chill in the air and drifting gunfire-smoke clouds raced each other over the rooftops.

En route to the parked car, they paused for the traffic lights, and Bond caught a glimpse of the piratelike, black-bearded, tousled-haired Big Mick Shean at the wheel of a maroon Volvo. The Irishman showed no sign of recognition, but he was sure to have already identified the parked car, and Bond with the girl as they waited for the lights to change.

They crossed the road on the green light and began to walk slowly—"Don't rush it," he had told Heather. "It should be the same routine you use when lighting a fuse on an explosive charge: walk away, never run, lest you trip." She nodded, and obviously knew something about explosives, so there had been *some* training out of the field, Bond judged. During the ride to Rosslare he would go through it piece by piece.

They did not cut across the Green, but sauntered along the North side, heading East—for the car was parked on the Eastern side of the square that forms that Dublin landmark.

As they drew level with The Shelbourne Hotel, Bond almost froze. He glanced across at the renowned hostel—once Noël Coward's favorite, and often likened to New York's Algonquin because of its attraction for the arty and international set—and saw, for only the second time in the flesh, the precise, compact figure of Colonel Maxim Smolin, accompanied by two men who could only be described as thickset, and even that was an underestimation. "Don't look toward the hotel," he muttered under his breath. The three men were now descending the steps, looking left and right as though for expected transport. "No, Heather, don't look," as she reacted by starting to disobey his order. "Just keep walking," quickening his pace, "your ex-lover just came out of his cave."

To himself, he thought, Basilisk is here, now, and deadly.

7

ACCIDENT

THERE WAS NO point in trying to hide or run. Smolin knew Heather by sight. He could have recognized her, clothed or unclothed, at half a mile in a Scottish mist; and Bond reckoned that the HVA man would know *him* on sight as well. After all, his photograph was in the files of practically every intelligence agency in the world. All he could pray for was that, in the traffic, and with Smolin's obvious concern over his own transport, he would not have spotted them. But with a man like Smolin he knew the chances were slim. Smolin was not just a professional, but a hyperprofessional, trained to single out the most unlikely faces among a crowd of thousands.

Gently taking Heather's arm, Bond guided her around the corner, turning right—their backs to The Shelbourne now—not hurrying her unduly, but almost imperceptibly increasing their walking pace toward the car, which was parked, nose inward to the pavement, on one of the many meters that stood like detection devices along the East side of the Green.

He felt the familiar, unpleasant tingling around the back of his neck—like a dozen small, deadly spiders unleashed in the nape hair. It was not 100 percent accurate, but Bond was realistic enough to know the odds were very high on Colonel Maxim Smolin's eyes watching their retreating backs. He was also probably smiling at the coincidence of catching sight of his former lover in the middle of Dublin. Or, Bond wondered, was it simple coincidence? In this business coincidence was usually a dirty word. M always maintained there was no such thing, just as Freud had once said that, in conditions of stress and confusion, there was no such thing as an accident.

They reached the car and, once in, Bond scanned the mirror while twisting the key in the ignition and clipping his seat belt on. The traffic was heavy, but he just caught the flash of a dun-colored Cortina passing behind them, with a dark blue Audi close on its bumper. Already he had seen Big Mick at the wheel of the maroon Volvo, so all the cars were circling the Green. The trick would be to get out and onto the road to the outskirts of Dun Laoghaire, then on along the coast. The route would take them through Bray and Arklow, Gorey and Wexford, then down to Rosslare—that untidy crop of buildings that stood above the harbor. A trick it certainly would be, for they might well have to circle the Green more than once to get into position: and that meant passing The Shelbourne again.

Gently, Bond started to back out into the traffic, waiting with not a little impatience for a gap to appear. When one finally did he reversed the car unforgivably fast, slamming the gears into first again and taking off at some speed. Seconds later he was tucked neatly in behind the Audi.

They circled the Green once and there was no sign of Smolin and his two large associates outside The Shelbourne. The Cortina left at that junction, going straight on, heading for Merrion Row and Baggot Street.

By the time they reached the same point a second time, Big Mick was behind them, so that they were tightly boxed in—with the Cortina well ahead and out of sight as the forward scout. Bond, glancing in the mirror, saw Big Mick's craggy face split into a grin at the successful fast linkup of the team. Behind them, in the back seat, Heather's purchases rolled around, slipping and sliding as Bond threw the car from one lane to another. He wanted to get out of Dublin's main environs as soon as possible.

"Why did he like to be called Wald?" Bond asked suddenly. They were now well away, mixed up in a steady stream of traffic, but approaching Bray with its great, ugly church dominating the small town, looking almost French and certainly too large for the community.

Heather started in her seat. She had been silent, allowing Bond to concentrate.

"Wald? You mean Franz? Jungle?"

"I'm not talking about the Black Forest, old love." Bond drove like a fighter pilot, eyes scanning the road ahead, the mirrors and instruments, making regular checks at least every thirty seconds. Yet his mind was balanced between driving, watching, and the short interrogation he wanted to conduct.

She paused, as though she needed to think of the answer. "It was odd. You've seen his photograph? Yes, well, he was so good-looking—blond hair, clear skin, fit, tall and slim, strong, and with a fine face. He looked like those old photographs you see of Hitler's ideal Germans—a true Aryan."

"So why did he like to be called Wald?" There was impatience in Bond's voice, and it showed. Her description was colored by her new business interest—the beauty salon—not her old profession as tethered honeypot. "Why Wald?" he repeated.

"He was vain." She made it sound that simple.

"And what's that got to do with it?" They had stopped for some traffic lights, Bond's car close on the Audi's rear, with Big Mick's Volvo separated from them by two trucks.

"About the work, he was vain. He said he could always hide from anybody. He had this idea that no one could ever find him if he didn't want to be found—like searching a dense forest. I think it was Elli who said we should call him Wald, and that pleased him. He is a little full of himself—is that the right phrase?"

Bond nodded. "Hence Jungle Baisley now. Looking for him would be like looking for a particular tree?"

"That's about it. Or like a needle in a haystack."

Now Bond was even more concerned. "You say Elli gave him the nickname. The five of you met together regularly?" That would have been almost suicidally bad security, he thought. But there were many things about *Cream Cake* that pointed toward bad security.

"Not a lot of times, no. But there were meetings."

"Called by your case officer—your controller?"

"No. Swift saw us one at a time. We had regular meetings. Safe houses. Rendezvous in shops or parks. But you must understand that we all knew each other—since children."

Bond thought they were almost children when this monstrous plan was conceived. Two were dead for sure, the others had prices on their heads and their tongues. Smolin would not rest until they were all safely in their coffins. And what of Swift, their case officer, their control? There had been a great deal about Swift in the files M had put his way. Swift was a street name, and the real identity was carefully hidden, even in the official documents. But Bond knew the man behind the masked name—a legend among case officers; one of the most experienced and careful people in the business. So much so that he was cryptoed Swift because of the speed at which he worked on his clients: swift and surefooted. Not the kind of man to make errors. Yet, if Heather had told him the truth about how *Cream Cake* had come to its chaotic end, Swift's judgment had let him down at last.

They passed through lush green countryside, littered with trees and the occasional cottage sending up calm and drifting smoke signals from its turf-burning fire. It was a land that appeared tranquil, if untidy—just as untidy as *Cream Cake*. Quickly, Bond went through it again in his mind, thinking of the network by their English names.

All five had parents who had been, if not sleepers, then dozing agents—men and women who handed over the odd piece of useful intelligence; yet all of them very well placed. Bridget's father was a lawyer, with some bigwig officials among his clientele; Millicent's parents were both doctors, with a number of intelligence community people on *their* books; the other three came from military or paramilitary families—Ebbie's father was an officer with the Vopos; Jungle's and Heather's were in the thicket of secrets— German officers working out of Karlshorst, that area of East Berlin that housed both military barracks and intelligence buildings as well as the Soviet HQ in Eastern Germany.

It was easy to see how—a few years ago—those five young people had glistened like gold when the Planners thought up the idea of compromising people in East Germany: just as the Soviet and East German agencies had done to intelligence departments in the West.

Bridget was to set her cap at a member of the East German Politburo; Millicent was to "make herself available" to one of the seven KGB officers serving under a paper-thin "advisory" cover at Karlshorst; Ebbie had a Major of the East German Army in *her* sights; while Jungle and Heather were in charge of the greatest prizes—Fräulein Captain Dietrich, the woman officer in charge of the civilian executive staff of the HVA, well known for her taste in younger men; and Colonel Maxim Smolin, to whom some referred, with a dark gallows humor, as The Plague Master of the HVA—for Smolin was responsible for rooting out and destroying clandestine agents of the Western organizations. Next to the Director of the HVA—and the leading politicians—he was probably one of the most powerful men in East Germany, with a hire-and-fire brief that made his law absolute in the seamier, and more deadly, side of the secret labyrinth—except, perhaps, for this more senior officer hinted at by Murray.

But back to Maxim Smolin, who had fallen for Heather—hook, line, and proverbial sinker. Or so the record said. Bond recalled every detail of *that* file—*Basilisk set the girl up in a small apartment, five minutes' drive from the Karlshorst Headquarters, where he spent most of his off-duty hours with her. After any "business" trip abroad he brought back luxuries*—there had followed a list that ranged from expensive hi-fi equipment to what the French term "fantasy" gifts from Paris. The list, attributed to Swift, was amazing in its detail: dates and items given in one column, time that Basilisk spent away in another, with a full list of his movements. It was the only one so itemized.

Fräulein Captain Dietrich also gave presents to Jungle, but Swift did not appear to have such good and knowledgeable intelligence about those. There was, also, far less information concerning the relationships between the other three *Cream Cake* operatives and their targets. From the beginning, Bond had wondered if this was really a team business, or were they only after two people—Dietrich and Smolin—with the rest merely makeweights, or even distractions?

Bearing in mind the way Swift had misjudged the operation, Bond had to go over the whole thing, again and again.

"Tell me about it one more time, Heather." They were passing through a village that looked as though it had a cathedral, twelve garages, twenty bars, and around five hundred inhabitants.

"I've told you. All of it." She spoke in a small voice, weary, as though she did not want to speak of *Cream Cake* ever again.

"Just once more. How did you feel when they told you?"

"I was only just nineteen. Precocious, I suppose. I saw it all as a joke. It wasn't until later that I realized how deadly the whole business really was."

"You were a virgin?"

She gave a little snort. "Of course not."

Bond did not pursue that line. "But you felt excited?"

"It was an adventure, for God's sake. If you were just nineteen and they told you to seduce a not unattractive woman older than yourself, wouldn't you have been excited?"

"Depends which way my political feelings ran—uphill or down."

"What's that supposed to mean?" She was showing shredded nerves now.

"Were you a politically aware young woman when they approached you for this exciting adventure?"

She gave a long sigh. "If you really want to know, I was disenchanted with the whole political scene. To me, everyone talked pigswill—East, West, North, South, whatever—the Communist Party, the Americans, the British. Maxim used to say, 'When it comes to politics and religion, it's a fairground.' "

"Really?" He was surprised at this sudden revelation about Smolin's views. "And what did he mean by that, I wonder?"

"He meant you paid your money and took your choice. But he used to say that once you'd taken that choice it bound you hand and foot. He said that Communism was the nearest thing in politics to the Roman Catholic Church. Both of them had rules from which you could not deviate."

"But you were trying to deviate him. You were doing your best to make him a convert."

Another sigh. "In a way, yes."

Bond grunted. "You had met him before—Smolin?"

She sighed. "I've told you. He was a regular visitor—social functions at the house, of course."

"And he'd shown an interest?"

"Not particularly." She stopped, then launched into a long speech—yes, Colonel Smolin may not have been the greatest-looking man around, but he *was* attractive. Not really a physical thing at first sight, but he had *something*. She used the word "indefinable." Then Smolin had appeared even more attractive when the matter was fully explained to her, first by her father, who had said he was fighting against the powers that had split her rightful country in two; then by the man she had come to know as Swift, her controller. He had been more blunt with her.

"He's a bastard," Swift had said at her first briefing. "A grade A, platinum bastard who wouldn't think twice about hanging his own mother with piano wire. He's a professional spycatcher, spyhunter, and spykiller who doesn't mind if he's wrong from time to time. We're asking you to get yourself into his bed, make him rely on you, share his thoughts with you, share his fears, and, at the last, his secrets."

"Maxim wasn't really as bad as Swift painted him." She still clung to some hidden, probably sentimental, sadness about the affair with Smolin. Bond had sensed it before.

"I expect the executioners' mistresses at Auschwitz and Belsen said similar things while they ate their *Kirschtorte* as their loved ones were operating the gas chambers," Bond said brusquely. He had no time for sentiment as far as men like Smolin were concerned.

"No!" Heather almost shouted. "Read my report. It's all there. Maxim was an odd mixture of a man, but a lot of the stories about him are just not true."

"So that's why he's got a team out now—hunting down your friends, and yourself? That's why he's tearing tongues out?"

She remained silent, staring ahead. Bond gave her a quick glance. He could have sworn that there were tears glistening in her eyes.

"What were they really after?" Bond asked after a while, though the question was as much to himself as to Heather. Already he had a theory about *Cream Cake*. It was not just a series of dangling honeypots to turn a handful of East German bigwigs into doubles, or to compromise them in such a way as to make them run so hard that they would never be any trouble again. There was some more devious motive. Again, aloud—knowing that Heather had not the remotest idea about what they were after, for the whole thing had ended in chaos—"And you just went out and caught him, netted him, bedded him, and reported the pillow talk back to Swift?"

"I've told you!" she almost shouted at him. "How many more times, James? Yes, yes, yes. I hooked him. I even became fond of him. He was good to be with: kind, thoughtful, gentle, and very loving. Too loving."

"Because you misjudged the moment of truth?"

"Yes!" Angry now. "Yes, must I go through it again and again? I told Swift that I thought he was ready. God . . ." She *was* near to tears, and they were on the Arklow road now. "Swift told me to bring him home. Lay the news on him. His actual words were, 'Spear him and drag his soul to me.' "

Bond concentrated on the road. He had first read the bones of the story in the files, and heard the inside guts of the events from Heather in the offices of the beauty salon, Dare to Be Chic, high above Piccadilly, a lifetime ago—yesterday. Now he needed to hear it again. "Spear him and drag his soul to me." "And what happened when you laid the news on Maxim Smolin? When you tried to spear him and drag his soul to Swift?"

She took a deep breath, opened her mouth, and, as she did so, they started to go into a bend leading onto a long stretch of open road flanked by scrubby hedges. Big Mick, a couple of hundred yards behind, suddenly flashed his lights, and in the driving mirror Bond saw two cars at speed, squeezing in on the Volvo so that the whole road was filled with the three vehicles. Though he had not driven this route for years, Bond had an odd sense of déjà vu. In his mind there was a picture of an accident, flashing blue lights, police flagging them down. Before even seeing what lay ahead, he knew and felt the fear tighten in his stomach. Behind, the two flanking cars appeared bent on squashing the Volvo.

Then they were round the bend and onto the mile or so of straight road that was—just as he expected—not empty, but littered with debris, warning signs, and the flashing lights of catastrophe. He shouted to Heather, yelling at her to brace herself. Ahead, there was a Garda car, an ambulance, the remains of a dun-colored saloon that could have been a Cortina, and an Audi on its side crushing the hedge. There was also a heavy truck across the road. Bond was in no mood for trucks. He braked, left-footed, and tried to spin the car, even though he knew that by now the road behind him would be blocked by a crushed Volvo—unless Big Mick had supernatural powers.

Heather screamed, the car slewed sideways on, and then just kept going, gathering speed in spite of Bond's attempts to control it. Too late, he realized that the road surface had been neatly treated with a thick slick of oil.

The group of mangled vehicles—plus the ambulance and Garda patrol car—seemed to be coming up with amazing speed. Bond fought the wheel, feeling the rear coming round much too fast, and knowing there was no way to avoid collision. When it came, there was almost a sense of anticlimax—a grinding crunch and a sudden stop, taking them from around fifty mph to zero in a split second.

He automatically reached for his gun, but even that was too late, for the doors were wrenched open and, with professional ease, two men in Garda uniform had both Heather and Bond out of the car, each using a neat armlock that caused considerable pain. Dazed, Bond wondered where his gun had gone—disappeared like some magician's prop. He tried to shake off the pain and resist, but, almost unaware of the movement, he found he and Heather were both being hustled into the ambulance, where four other figures waited to take over.

For members of an ambulance team, they did not appear to be at all concerned about injuries. In fact, one of them seemed more intent upon causing pain than preventing it, for by this time Heather was screaming fit to wake the dead. Then she stopped, suddenly and completely as one man chopped her expertly on the side of the neck with the cutting edge of his extended hand.

She went down just as the doors closed and the ambulance began to move, but the man who had hit her also caught the falling body and hoisted it onto one of the two stretcher beds on either side of the interior.

From the gloom up front a fifth man appeared, yet they seemed in no way crowded. Later Bond realized that it was a very large ambulance—probably a resprayed, refurbished military vehicle.

The ambulance picked up speed, its siren hee-hawing. Above the wail, the fifth man spoke.

"Mr. Bond, I believe. I'm afraid there's been a small accident, and it's necessary to get you away from the site as fast as possible. I'm truly sorry to inconvenience you, but I fear this is essential to all of us. I'm sure you understand. So, if you would just sit down and remain quiet, we'll get along nicely, I'm certain."

There was no doubt about it—Colonel Maxim Smolin had a great deal of charm, even when it was laced with threats.

8

COCKEREL OR WEASEL

THE AMBULANCE SWAYED and bounced, slowed, swayed again, then accelerated. Bond reckoned they had very quickly left the main road and were probably doubling back—possibly edging up into the hills, maybe even climbing through the wild and craggy Wicklow Gap.

Bond glanced at Heather, who lay unmoving on the stretcher bed, and hoped that the force of the blow had not done any serious damage.

"She'll be fine, Mr. Bond. My men had orders not to kill, merely to render unconscious." Close up, Smolin seemed an even more commanding figure, and his quick response to Bond's anxious look showed an intelligent and observant awareness.

"And your people're well trained in how to kill and not *quite* kill, I'm sure." He almost added Smolin's name, but held back.

"Trained to perfection, my dear fellow." For a man of his background, Smolin spoke near-faultless English, though the trained ear would undoubtedly pick up the fact that it was just a shade too perfect. There was a charm in his manner that took Bond by surprise; yet, behind the charm, one sensed a diamond-hard interior: not so much a ruthlessness as a feeling of absolute power and confidence—a man who expected to be obeyed; one who knew, without second thoughts, that he could maintain his balance at the sharp end of life.

He was a shade taller than Bond had realized from his previous two sightings, and his body was strong, fit, and well-muscled under the casual—if expensive—anorak, cavalry twill trousers, and turtleneck.

Smolin now looked hard at Bond, and there was the trace of a bright twinkle in his dark, slightly oval eyes, while the smile around his mouth appeared not mocking but amused.

"Might I ask what all this is about?" Bond had to speak loudly above the engine noise and rattling as the ambulance continued to sway, accelerating, then slowing. The driver was either unused to handling such a vehicle, or they were, indeed, on a difficult mountain road.

The smile turned into a chuckle—short and almost pleasant. "Oh, come on now, James Bond, you know well enough what it's about."

"I know that I was giving a lift to a lady friend of mine, and suddenly I find we're kidnapped." He paused, then added with mock puzzlement, "And you know my name! How the hell do you know my name, anyway?"

This time there was a full-blooded belly laugh. "Bond, my dear good fellow, don't make me into a fool." He nodded his head toward the still-unconscious Heather. "You know who your lady friend is, and what she's done? I suspect you know *exactly* what she's done, and *exactly* who I am—after all, my file is with many foreign agencies. Surely the British Secret Intelligence Service has a dossier on me just as my own Service has one on you. Try telling your grandmother to suck eggs, James Bond. You know everything about the operation called *Cream Cake,* and I would be most surprised if you did not have all the details of the punishment at present being dealt out to its protagonists."

"Cream Cake?" Even Bond was pleased with the way the words came out in a cross between question, puzzlement, and surprise.

"Operation *Cream Cake.*" Smolin paused for breath, then laughed again as though he found the whole thing as funny as a Marx Brothers' movie.

"I know nothing about cream cakes, or chocolate éclairs!" Bond was pacing himself now, allowing time to build up a good, healthy anger. "I do know that Heather here asked me to give her a lift—"

Smolin gave a rueful smile, his laughter diminishing. "Would this be after the little problem in her beauty salon last night?"

"What problem?"

"You're trying to tell me that you were not the man who was with her when some ill-advised idiots tried to kill her in London? That you're not the man who drove her to the airport . . . ?" The smile had faded into just a hint of uncertainty.

"Bumped into her in the departure lounge." Bond locked eyes with him. "I mean, I've only met her once before. Look, what's this really all about? And how did you set up that police roadblock? You a terrorist or something? To do with the North?" He was sizing up the opposition while playing a somewhat ridiculous game for time. Heather still lay unconscious, Smolin sat quite close to him, and the other four hoods were ranged around the ambulance—two up front, the other pair by the doors: all clinging on because the ride was more like being on a rollercoaster than in a large vehicle. They had disarmed him, and he could not drag the charade on for much longer, or even contemplate escape as yet.

"If I didn't *know* who you are, and had not watched you set up your own security precautions, I might just wonder if I'd got the wrong man." Smolin was smiling again. "But the setup, together with the weapons you were carrying. Well . . ." He allowed matters to hang in the air.

"And what of *your* setup?" Bond asked, seemingly without guile.

"I suspect they were exactly what you would have arranged in similar circumstances. We had a backup watching you, in radio contact while we went on ahead. Then we simply closed off the far end of the road, a mile or so on; and shut off the road behind you when you passed into our zone of operations—the old funnel principle, with plenty of debris, an oil slick, and some fancy-dress Garda uniforms."

Bond could dissemble no longer. "They teach you those kinds of skills in that center of yours on the old Khodinka airfield, do they, Colonel Smolin? The place where most of you end up, one way or another—in the crematorium, either neat in a box, or alive and screaming because you've betrayed your service—the organization you jokingly call The Aquarium?" He said calmly, "Or do you learn them at your offices on Knamensky Street?"

"So, Bond, you *do* know about my service—you know about GRU. And you know about *me* also. I'm flattered—but happy that I was right about you."

"Of course I know, together with anyone who takes the trouble to read the right books. We have a saying in *my* Service, that the tricks of our trade are far from secret; you only have to find the right bookshops in Charing Cross Road, or Piccadilly, and you can learn it all—tradecraft, addresses, organization. It takes only a little reading."

"A little more than that, I suspect."

"Possibly. The GRU likes to let the KGB have the glory, pretending to be backseat boys who bow to the gray men of Dzerzhinsky Square. Yes, we do know you're more fanatical, more secretive, and therefore more dangerous."

Smolin's smile was overtly happy. "Much more dangerous. Good, I'm glad we know where we stand. It has been a long ambition of mine to meet you face-to-face, Mr. Bond. Was it you, perhaps, who concocted the idiotic *Cream Cake* business?"

"There you have me, Colonel Smolin. I know nothing of such an operation."

One of the hoods shouted something from the front of the ambulance, and Smolin said, almost apologetically, that they would soon have to take measures to ensure silence and blindness. "We're coming up to the point where we change cars." The smile seldom left his lips, as though it had been neatly cut to shape by a plastic surgeon.

The ambulance slowed down, lurched, leaned heavily to the left, so that everyone had to grab on to whatever was at hand in order to remain either upright or seated. Gradually they rumbled to a halt on what Bond presumed was rough ground.

From the front came the sound of the cab door being slammed shut. Then the rear doors opened and a short, red-faced man dressed in the dark uniform of an ambulance driver peered in.

"They are not here yet, Herr Colonel." He addressed Smolin in German.

The Colonel merely nodded in an offhand way, and told them to watch and wait. Bond craned his neck in an attempt to see out of the back, but only glimpsed trees, backed by rocky slopes that bore out his original feeling that they had taken a route into the bleak Wicklow hills.

"Get the girl ready." Smolin half-turned his head, giving the order to one of the men up front. The man fumbled with a briefcase, and Bond saw a hypodermic being made ready. He made a slight threatening move toward the syringe-bearer, whose partner immediately performed a small magic act with an automatic pistol. One moment his hand was empty, the next it was full of gun, the one-eyed muzzle of which pointed steadily at Bond.

Smolin raised an arm, as though both protecting and restraining Bond. "It's all right. The girl will not be harmed. I merely think she should be put under a mild sedation for a while. We have a long drive ahead, and I really don't want her to be conscious. You, friend Bond, will lie on the floor in the back of the car that will arrive at any minute. You will have your face covered, and as long as you behave no harm will come to you." He paused, smiled, then added, "Yet!"

There was a long silence, during which Heather moved slightly and groaned, as though regaining consciousness, and the hood with the syringe quietly prepared her for the injection, which he gave with some skill, the needle sliding through the skin of her bared forearm at a neatly calculated angle.

"So, James Bond, you say that you know nothing of any operation coded *Cream Cake?*"

Bond replied by shaking his head.

"And I suppose," Smolin continued, "you've never heard of Irma Wagen?"

"Not a name known to me."

"But you do know Heather Dare?"

"I met her once, before the airport departure lounge, yes."

"And where did you meet her, *once before the airport departure lounge?*"

"At a party. Through friends."

"Friends, as in professional friends?—I believe, in the jargon of your Service, friends are other members of that Service. Or, at least, your Foreign Office refers to them as The Friends."

"Ordinary friends. A couple called Hazlett—Tom and Maria Hazlett." He added an address in Hampstead, knowing it could be checked out with impunity, for both Tom and Maria were an active alibi couple. If asked—even in a roundabout way—whether they knew either Bond or Heather they would answer, "Yes, and isn't Heather wonderful?" or, "Of course, James is an old friend." They would also have a surveillance team on to the questioners in double-quick time, for both had that particular knack of second-guessing friend or foe, and covering for people in the correct manner. After all, that was what the Service had trained them to do.

"So, in that case you would claim you did not know Irma Wagen and Heather Dare—of the Dare to Be Chic beauty salon— are the same person?"

"I've never heard of any Irma Wagen."

"No. No, of course you haven't, James—you must call me Maxim, by the way. I do not respond to the diminutive, Max. No, you haven't heard of Irma, nor the doomed *Cream Cake* operation." His smile did not alter, but the disbelief shone through his words. Then he came out and said it aloud, "I just do not believe you, James Bond. I do not, cannot, believe you."

"Please yourself." Bond gave the impression of complete disinterest.

"Then where were you driving the fair Fräulein Wagen, whom you know as Heather Dare?"

"Enniscorthy."

"So, why should she want to go to Enniscorthy?" He shook his head, as though to underline his disbelief. "And where were you going that enabled you to give such a service to this—this damsel in distress?"

"She was in no distress," Bond said levelly. "We merely recognized each other at the airport, and sat next to one another on the plane. I told her I was going to Waterford and she asked if she could cadge a lift. What she actually said was, 'Can I bum a ride?' "

Smolin wrinkled his nose.

"Yes, I agree. Nasty phrase." Bond smiled back pleasantly.

"And what were you going to do in Waterford?" Smolin remained comfortable on the other stretcher bed, beside Bond.

"Buy glass, what else? I'm very fond of Waterford crystal."

"Of course you are. And it's so difficult to buy in London, isn't it?" With heavy sarcasm like that, Smolin betrayed his Russian side.

"I am on leave, Herr Colonel Smolin. I repeat, I know of no Irma Wagen, and have never heard of an operation called *Cream Cake.*"

"We shall see," Smolin replied smoothly. "But, just to clear the air, I will tell you what we know of this ludicrously named operation. It was what used to be called a honeytrap. Your people baited it with four very young and attractive girls." He held up four fingers, grasping one for each name, as though ticking them off. "There were Franzi Trauben, Elli Zuckermann, Irma Wagen, and Emilie Nikolas." He laughed his pleasant chuckle again. "Emilie—a good name, when you consider that we always spoke of *our* honeytrap *targets* as Emilies—but you know all that." He ran a hand through his dark hair. "Each of these girls had a well-placed target, and they might just have got away with it, but for the fact that I was included among the targets." Quite suddenly his whole demeanor altered. "They used *me* as a target for their games. *Me,* Maxim Smolin, as though I could be caught and netted by a slip of a girl with about as much idea of how to set up an entrapment as a raw recruit." His voice rose. "That's what I can never forgive your people for doing! Putting an amateur onto me! So amateur that she gave the game away within minutes of her first pass at me, and eventually brought down the whole nasty little network. *Your* Service, Bond, took me for some kind of a fool! A professional would have been different, but an amateur, like her"—his finger rose, pointing toward the prone body of Heather—"an amateur I can never forgive!"

So, Bond thought, this was the real Smolin—proud, arrogant, and unforgiving.

"Surely, the Glavnoye Razvedyvatelnoye Upravleniye also uses casual labor from time to time, Maxim?" He asked the question with the ghost of a smile.

"Casual labor?" A fine spray of spittle clouded the air in front of Smolin's lips as he spat the words out with utter contempt. "We would *train* casual labor. But *never* would we use casual labor against a target of my importance."

There he had it. *My importance.* Colonel Maxim Smolin regarded himself as inviolable; essential to the smooth running of the second most dangerous of the secret organizations within the structure of the Soviet Union—the first being Bond's older enemies, the one-time SMERSH, now totally reorganized as Department 8 of Directorate S following their total loss of credibility as Department V, as in Victor.

Smolin was breathing heavily, and Bond felt that old and ice-cold hand trace an invisible finger down his spine, an indication of fear. The chiseled stone face of a killer, the hard muscular body, that brightness in the dark eyes.

From far away came the sound of a car's horn. Three short blasts followed by a longer one.

"They're here." Smolin returned to his native German.

The ambulance doors opened, fully revealing the view of green slopes, strewn with the gray of rock outcrops, and the half circle of trees in which they were parked, well off the road down which two cars—a BMW and a Mercedes—were making slow progress toward them.

Bond looked at Smolin and cocked his head toward Heather. "I truly have no knowledge of this *Cream Cake* business." He spoke quietly, hoping that in his moment of rage Smolin might even believe him. "Sounds more like a BND job rather than our people . . ."

Smolin turned. "It *was* your Service, James Bond. I have proof. Believe me, just as you must believe we'll sweat you until your very bones turn to water. There are still a couple of mysteries that need solving, and I'm here to solve them."

"Mysteries?" The cars were near now, and two of the hoods had descended from the ambulance, readying themselves for the transfer of their prisoners.

"We have dealt with two of that nest of bottled spiders—the Trauben girl, and the Zuckermann bitch. You might recognize them better as Bridget Hammond and Millicent Zampek. Small fry, but squashed. This girl—*my* girl—might hold some of the answers in her pin brain; and there's another yet to come. The Nikolas cow—Ebbie Heritage. Those two, with yourself, should fill in the gaps, and put the final pieces into the jigsaw before the three of you go to hell and damnation." Smolin started to chuckle, and the chuckle turned into the old belly laugh.

If he wanted Heather and Ebbie alive, why the thug with the mallet, and the chase down the fire escape—the shooting and dicing with death in London? Smolin had spoken of the incident earlier as "some ill-advised idiots trying to kill her."

The most devious of ideas began to permeate Bond's brain as he watched while two of the hoods carried Heather to the Mercedes. He was also surprised to see the ambulance driver loading the pile of packages they had bought in Dublin into the boot. They had moved with great speed, Bond thought, to get everything out of his rented car in what seemed to be so short a time. But, then, the GRU were organized on military principles, and all true members were trained soldiers—but for recruited talent operating in foreign countries.

In Moscow, they worked out of that decorative mansion at 19 Knamensky Street—once the property of a Tsarist millionaire—and were at constant loggerheads with the KGB, who always claimed to have the upper hand, even though the GRU, by virtue of its military roots, was effectively set apart from the larger and better-known intelligence and security service.

He felt Smolin's arm on his shoulder, hearing him hiss, "Your turn, Mr. Bond."

They frog-marched him to the car, drew a thick sack over his head, handcuffed his wrists securely behind his back, and forced him onto the floor of the BMW. The sack smelled of grain, drying his throat in a matter of minutes.

He heard the sound of the ambulance starting up, and then Smolin's feet pressing down on his back as the Colonel took his seat. A moment later, the car started, and they began to move away.

Why? Bond asked himself. Smolin had said that the "honeytrap" was "baited . . . with four very young and attractive girls." Only four had been mentioned. Only the four girls. He had not even bothered with Jungle Baisley, né Franz Wald Belzinger, and his target—Fräulein Captain Dietrich—whom Heather had described as one of the two prime targets. Why? The germ of a terrifying and sinister scenario became more clear in Bond's mind as he concentrated on trying to deduce their speed, mileage, and direction. Was Jungle an undiscovered and successful member of the network? Had M performed a neat piece of misdirection when briefing him, or was something more dangerous at work here in the peaceful lush greenery of the Republic of Ireland? Did it all have something to do with Norman Murray's rumor that an officer, more senior to Smolin, was in the field? Was Smolin under pressure?

He also remembered Murray's smiling face—"Maxim Smolin . . . a stupid code name—*Basilisk*." Now, Bond delved into what little he knew of mythology. The Basilisk, he remembered, was a particularly revolting monster—hatched from a cockerel's egg by a serpent. Even the purest human perished at a glimpse from the Basilisk's eyes. The creature would lay the whole world to waste but for its two enemies, the cockerel and the weasel. The weasel was immune, and the Basilisk died at the sound of the cock's crow.

Bond wondered what he was—a cock, a weasel, or neither.

9

SCHLOSS GRUESOME

By BOND'S RECKONING, they drove for roughly three hours. After eighty minutes or so he lost all sense of direction, except that his instincts told him they were crossing their own path time and again. In the dark choking stuffiness of the sack, with his body unnaturally curled, cramped, and uncomfortable on the floor of the car, he tried to clear his mind, concentrate, and work out exactly what headings they were on. When he was forced to abandon this, he began to examine the various theories that had first come to mind back in the ambulance.

He did not doubt that Smolin's threat, to get a full rundown on *Cream Cake* from Bond and Heather, was in any way idle. The man's reputation was enough.

It was quite possible—if Norman Murray's vague and obscure information was accurate—that Smolin was not entirely his own man. If the huge arrogance he had shown in the ambulance had been dented, it could be that the GRU officer might well act irrationally, and that could be Bond's lever. Somehow, he knew that it was now up to him to make things happen.

Bond could not know that, the longer they were on the road, the more difficult and complex the situation was to become.

They stopped once, and Smolin—who did not leave the car—spoke calmly to Bond. "Your lady friend appears to have woken up, so they're taking her for a short walk. She is quite safe." He gave an amused snort. "She should remain docile for a while yet."

Bond moved, trying to shift his position, but Smolin's heel came down hard on one shoulder, almost causing him to yelp with pain.

When it came, the interrogation would probably not rely on the more sophisticated methods of that dark art. Rather, it would be conducted in the atmosphere of brutality.

Eventually, they seemed to leave the smoothness of a well-made road—Bond had sensed they had been climbing for some eight or ten minutes—and moved onto a rougher track, going at around thirty miles an hour and bouncing a good deal.

Then they were back on a good surface, turning slightly and coming to a halt. There were the sounds of engines dying and doors opening. He felt fresh air on his body, Smolin moving, and hands pulling away the sack and unlocking his handcuffed wrists.

"You can get out of the car now, Mr. Bond." Smolin was obviously already out, and Bond blinked, adjusting to the bright lights as he tried to massage life back into his arms.

Stiffly, he pulled himself onto the seat and then through the door. His legs felt as though they did not belong to him, while his back and arms ached so that he could hardly move, and had to clutch at the car to steady himself.

It took several minutes for him to even stand properly, and he used the time—making more of it than necessary—to examine the surroundings. They appeared to be on a large turning circle in front of a great gray solid building, oblong but decorated with a square tower at either end. Above the roofline the top of the walls—like those of the towers—were castellated: great rows of thick toothlike battlements.

The main front door was of heavy oak, set in a Norman arch, while what windows could be seen were also built within ornate arches. The whole, Bond thought, added up to one of those strange buildings erected in Ireland during the late Georgian or early Victorian period by landed gentry who felt it necessary to refer to their homes as castles.

This one, he noted quickly, had a number of twentieth-century refinements, like a large number of antennae sprouting from one tower, and a big satellite dish aerial on the other.

The whole pile was set in a green bowl at least three miles wide, with the ground curving upward in sloping hillocks on all sides. All traces of trees, or other cover, had been neatly removed.

"Welcome." Smolin was in peaceful mood now, seemingly at his most charming.

As he spoke, Bond saw Heather being helped from the Mercedes parked in front of them. He was also aware of the undisciplined barking of dogs coming from behind the front door, together with the sound of bolts being drawn back.

Seconds later the doors swung open, and three dogs crashed onto the graveled turning circle—German shepherds to whom Smolin called, "Hey, Wotan, Siegi, Fafie. Hey-hey!"

The dogs—big, sleek-coated creatures—bounded toward Smolin with obvious pleasure. Then, as they sensed Bond, one of them turned and bared its fangs, growling with some menace.

"Good, Fafie, good! Stay! Watch!" All this in German, then to Bond, "I should not make any sudden moves, if I were you. Fafie can be particularly vicious once I've told him to watch someone. They're well trained, these animals—all with good killer instinct—so take care." He stopped petting the other two shepherds, quietly motioning toward Bond. "Siegi, Wotan. Watch! Yes, *him.* Watch!"

Two men had come through the door, then there was a female

voice and a young girl, pert with fluffy blond hair, appeared. She was dressed in a claret-colored tight silk shirt, and a pleated skirt that lifted and flared around her legs as she started to run toward Heather, calling out in German, with eyes twinkling and her face a picture of happiness. She looked a wholly delightful child of nature, Bond thought as he watched her: the breeze blowing at her skirt, showing the tantalizing molding of her thighs. She turned, moved, and stood with an almost innocent sexuality, as though unaware of her body and its beautiful proportions.

Then Bond's heart sank as he heard her words—"Heather—Irma—they have you safe as well. I thought we were going to be left out in the cold. But they haven't let us down. I always said the British wouldn't let us down." She was close to Heather now, embracing her.

"A small deception, I'm afraid." Smolin looked at Bond, as Heather gasped, "Ebbie? What—?"

"Inside!" Smolin's voice cut loudly across the mix of conversations that had started up between his men, and also the bewildered girls. "Everybody inside! Now!"

The hoods closed in, the dogs circling as though on guard. They seemed to be particularly concerned with Bond and the two girls, moving them like sheep through the door, into a vast, high hallway, flagstoned and surrounded on three sides by a gallery fashioned in stripped pine, as was the wide staircase that reached up to it, curving down to the far right of the hall.

Heather appeared to be quite calm—the effect of the drugs, Bond supposed—but Ebbie trembled visibly, horror in her wide blue eyes as she looked toward Bond. Recognition slowly dawned as she recalled that night, five years before, when Bond and the Special Boat Squadron men had plucked Heather and herself from the German coast.

"Is he—?" Ebbie spoke loudly, turning toward Heather, half raising a hand to point accusingly at Bond. Heather shook her head and said something quietly, glancing quickly, first at Smolin and then at Bond, whose eyes flicked around the hallway, taking in everything: the dark blue velvet of the drapes, the three doors and one passage that led off to other parts of the castle; the large paintings—eighteenth-century men and women staring sightless from their oil-created eyes, trapped on canvas and set within ornate gilt frames.

Smolin snapped orders at the two men who had come out with Ebbie, while the other group—the four men from the ambulance, plus the pair of thugs who had driven the Mercedes and BMW—stood near the door.

All were armed, you could see it in their manner and in the clothes they wore—the distinct bulges beneath either uniforms or jeans and short denim jackets.

Armed to the teeth, Bond thought, and, as though the very idea produced proof, he saw a folded machine pistol appear from behind one of their former drivers' backs. There would be more of those, and probably other men as well—watchers on the rim of the grassy bowl in which the castle stood. Men, guns, and dogs; locks, bars, and bolts; plus a long haul across open ground even if they were to get past this lot. All his senses were directed toward the possibility of escape, while at the back of his mind, buried in that constantly working computer of the brain, he still examined the various theories that had first come to him in the ambulance.

"Irma, my dear, bring Emilie over here, though I think she knows Mr. Bond." Smolin called across to the girls, and Bond was pleased to note that Ebbie had regained wit enough to cloud her face with a puzzled expression—"I don't think . . . ?" she began.

Smolin spoke coldly. "Remiss of me. Mr. Bond, you do not know Fräulein Nikolas—or Miss Ebbie Heritage, as she now prefers to be called?"

"Haven't had the pleasure." Bond walked over with his right hand outstretched to give Ebbie a comforting, reassuring squeeze. "And it *really* is a pleasure." He meant this last remark, for, now that he was close to Ebbie Heritage, Bond sensed a desire he rarely felt at first meeting a girl. Through his eyes he tried to convey that all would be well, a difficult task as the three German shepherds moved with him, not growling or showing signs of attack, but letting him know they were there and ready.

"Strange," Smolin rasped, "I could have sworn that she recognized you out there, Bond."

"He . . ." Ebbie began. Then, as a tincture of confidence returned, "He reminded me of someone I used to know. Just for a second. Now I see he's English, and I've not met him before. But, yes, for me also it is a pleasure." A flash of static seemed to pass between them.

Good girl, Bond thought to himself, glancing toward Heather and trying to pass on a reassuring look to her. Heather's eyes did not appear to be properly focused, but she managed a firm and very confident smile. For a moment, Bond could have sworn that *she* was trying to give *him* a message not merely of hope, but also something deeper. It was as if they had already reached a mutual understanding.

"So." Smolin was standing beside them. "I suggest we all eat a hearty meal. A full stomach before work, eh?"

"What work, Colonel Smolin?" Bond saw the glint of evil deep in the man's eyes.

"Oh, Maxim. Please call me Maxim."

"What kind of work?" he repeated firmly.

"There is much talking to be done. But first you must see your quarters. The guest accommodation is good here in . . ." He paused, as though stopping himself from giving away their actual location. Then, "Here, in Schloss Varvick," a contented smile. "You recall Schloss Varvick, James?"

"Familiar." He nodded.

"As a boy you probably read of it—Dornford Yates, I forget the book, but one of his many improbable tales of derring-do included such a castle."

"So, for the want of a better name, Maxim?"

Smolin nodded. "For want of a better name."

"Your base in the Republic of Ireland? Schloss GRU?" Bond did not smile. "Or, perhaps, Schloss Gruesome."

Smolin exploded in a burst of laughter at Bond's rather heavy-handed humor. "Good. Very good. Now, where is our house-keeper? Ingrid!" He shouted, and again, "Ingrid—where is the girl? Somebody get Ingrid."

One of the retainers disappeared through a door that obviously led into the bowels of the castle, if you could dignify the bizarre place with such a name. In a few seconds, he returned with a tall, angular woman, dark-complexioned, jet-black hair worn long and tidy; but with a face so sharp that there could be no other description for it but hatchet.

Smolin ordered her to show his guests to their quarters, adding that Miss Heritage was already nicely settled in. "You'll not be cramped." He stood, hands on hips and head thrown back. "There is a communal sitting room, but you each have a separate bedroom, so all will be kept decent."

Two of the hoods closed in on them as Smolin ordered Fafie to follow, and the thin figure of Ingrid moved up the stairs silently, as though she was on a cushion of air. Yet there was no grace about her, rather something sinister, all sharp angles under her long black dress, a veritable Mrs. Danvers from Daphne Du Maurier's *Rebecca.*

"It *is* very comfortable." Ebbie's voice was strong and pleasant, with no hardness in her accent. "I quite enjoyed it last night— but, then, I thought it to be sanctuary." Her English was not quite as flawless as Heather's, but she did seem, on the face of it, to have a more outgoing personality. For all her svelte, dark, model-girl appearance, Heather—he felt—had disappeared into the shell of her long legs, slim body, and attractive mask of a face. Ebbie, on the other hand, was full of fun, laughter, and with a sense of her own sexuality. She held her shoulders well back, as though to show off her fine, obviously unrestrained breasts, which pushed out hard against the silk of her shirt.

The little group, followed by Fafie, climbed to the gallery and turned right, treading on polished pine boards until they came to an open corridor that ended, some ten paces from its entrance, at a heavy door, also in pine.

This, in turn, led into a large sitting room, heavily decorated— flock wallpaper, a large, buttoned settee with matching chairs, and solid-looking side tables. What space remained against the walls was taken up by other pieces of furniture—a card table with ball-and-claw feet; a Gothic breakfront bookcase reaching almost to the ceiling, containing nothing but magazines crushed and piled into the shelves; and a very big, equally Gothic bureau, the top of which came to just under Bond's chin.

It was all very Germanic, as were the three pictures that hung lowering on the walls—dark prints of mountain scenes, clouds gathering between valleys—Victorian German in great, ugly wooden frames. The floor was of the same polished pine, but sported a number of thick rugs, placed haphazardly around a larger center oblong rug. Bond was always deeply suspicious of rugs. It also concerned him that the room had no windows.

Not counting the entrance, there were three doors—one to each of the walls—which Bond took to be the bedrooms.

"I have the one over here." Ebbie went to the door set almost opposite the entrance. "I hope nobody minds this?" She looked straight at Bond, hard in the eyes, then through slightly lowered lashes, as though inviting him to use the room with her. She stood with one leg forward, bent at the knee, once more showing the curve of thigh under the thin material of her skirt.

"First come, first served, as my old Nanny used to say." He nodded at her and then, turning to Heather, he told her to take her pick. She shrugged and went to the door on the left. Sinister, Bond thought, recalling the old theatrical tradition of the pantomime devil making his entrance stage left—*a sinister,* the side of the evil omen.

The whole caldron of theories, left bubbling on the back burner of his mind, came into the open again together with the possible answers to many questions—where did Jungle Baisley fit in? Had M misled him? Had *Cream Cake's* former controller—Swift— really made a terrible error of judgment in telling Heather to activate Smolin? How was the said Smolin so well briefed concerning his movements? and why had he felt it necessary to distance himself from the so-called London incident, when Heather had almost died like the two other girls from the network? Had the fluffy and edible Ebbie lent her raincoat and scarf to one of The Ashford Castle Hotel chambermaids on purpose?

He entered the bedroom, which had a bathroom *en suite*—as they said in the best middle-class estate agents' advertisements— and found the furniture as oppressive as anything in the castle. A huge bed, the head in solid oak, carved with intricate whirls and circles; a freestanding wardrobe, solid and ornate; and an old-fashioned washstand, complete with a solid marble top that had once carried a bowl and jug, doubling as a dressing table.

The bathroom was modern—two-star hotel, in unlikely avocado green, with pine laminates around the tiny cupboard, a tub built for a midget, and even a bidet squeezed between bathside and sink.

Bond went back into the bedroom to find one of the hoods standing in the doorway, holding his getaway case.

"The lock is, I fear, broken." The man's English was far from good. "The Herr Colonel ordered the contents inspected."

The Herr Colonel can stick it, thought Bond. Aloud, he thanked the man. It was highly unlikely that they had found anything to interest them. After all, his two overt weapons—the ASP and the baton—had been removed, but they had left him cigarette lighter, wallet, and pen, all three of which he had from Q Branch with Q'ute's blessing.

Another thought struck him. It was odd that, so far, Smolin had not subjected him to a body search, which could easily have revealed items secreted in his clothing. Smolin was a dedicated and careful operative, and this oversight was well out of tune with his reputation.

They had wrecked the locks on his case, and he was about to open it when he heard the two girls talking loudly in the sitting room.

Quickly he went out, motioning them to stop, pointing at the telephone, two standard lamps, and the overhead lighting in order to remind them that the suite of rooms was almost certainly bugged—though not, he felt, in those obvious and traditional places.

There had to be some way of talking unheard with the girls, for he needed a lot of information—the three key questions Heather had been instructed to ask Smolin, as well as some pertinent details concerning their case officer, Swift.

Traditionally, they should have crowded into one of the bathrooms, turned on all the taps, and talked—but that old dodge had long gone out of the window with modern filtering systems that cut out extraneous sound. Even talking in whispers with a radio on at full volume was no longer safe.

Quickly he strode to the bureau and tried the flap. It was not locked, and sure enough writing paper and envelopes had been left in the pigeonholes. Taking some of the paper, he gestured at the girls to sit down near one of the heavy side tables and carry on talking while he went to the door and peered out. They must have been very sure of themselves, he thought, for the door was unlocked and there appeared to be no guards in the corridor.

Back at the table—seated between the girls—he bent over the paper, taking out his pen and writing quickly, trying to make some logic of his own confused suspicions, and set questions in a definite order of importance.

The girls were flagging, their conversation becoming stilted, so he asked Ebbie how she had been picked up.

"The telephone. After the terrible thing that happened. Heather says you know about it, the girl's murder." Ebbie moved a fraction closer to him, a hand brushing his arm.

Bond started to write his questions, two to each sheet of paper, and double sets—one for Ebbie, another for Heather."

"They telephoned you?"

"*Ja*—yes. They said I was to leave as soon as the police had no use for me. I was to drive to Galway—to The Corrib Great Southern Hotel—they would contact me there." She allowed her shoulder to press hard against his arm, leaving in its wake a tingling sensation that he found decidedly pleasant.

Bond passed two sheets of questions to Heather, and a couple more to Ebbie, miming for them to write replies. Heather had a pen, but Ebbie looked lost, so Bond gave her his, carrying on the conversation, as though desperate to know the answers. "And they said they were from Britain?"

Hesitation, for Ebbie was trying to write. Then, "Yes, they said from the people we used to work for." She smiled at him, revealing small, perfect teeth and the pink tip of her tongue.

"You had no doubts?"

"None. They seemed *very* English gentlemen. They promised one night at a safe place, then an airplane would come. I would go to some other place." She frowned and continued to write, still allowing her arm to press against Bond's shoulder.

"They say anything about your friend here—Heather?"

An agonizing silence while she wrote some more. "Safe. They say she is safe and will be coming soon. I never . . ."

He turned to Heather, who had been writing quietly, and seemingly efficiently. "You were unconscious in the ambulance." He gave her a broad wink, so she would not be disturbed by what he was going to say. "Smolin talked to me about something called *Cream Cake,* you know about that?"

Her jaw dropped, the mouth starting to form the word "but"—as in, "but you know all about *Cream Cake,* James," then she realized it was for the listeners, and said she was not to speak of it. The whole business had been a despicable trick; that neither she nor Ebbie was responsible for this thing. "A mistake," she repeated, "a most horrible mistake."

Bond leaned over and began to read what they had already written, his eyes moving quickly, first down one page, and then the other.

As he read, so the worm of suspicion and deception, which had sprung to life earlier, started to move in his brain, and at that moment the door burst open to reveal Smolin, flanked by two of his men. There was no point in trying to hide the papers, but Bond drew them off the table, trying to misdirect Smolin's gaze by rising to his feet.

"James, I'm surprised at you." Smolin's voice was soft, almost soothing, and therefore more threatening. "You think we only steal sound from what we call our guest suite? *Son et lumière,* my friend. Sound and pictures." He gave one of his regular laughs. "You will never guess the times we've compromised important people in one or another of these rooms. Now, be a good fellow and hand over the papers." One of the men stepped toward them, but Heather snatched the sheets from Bond and headed for her bedroom door, light and very fast on her feet.

The hood sprang at her in a rugger tackle, missed, and ended against the wall as her door slammed, followed by the noise of the key turning in the lock.

Both Smolin and the still-upright hood had automatics in their hands, and the man who had fallen was back on his feet, pounding on the door, shouting in German for her to come out. But there was no sound until, eventually, the lock clicked and Heather—haughty as ever—stalked into the room. From behind her door, smoke curled out of a metal waste bin. "They're gone," she said in a matter-of-fact tone. "Burned. Not that they could have meant much to you, Maxim."

Smolin took one pace forward and lifted his arm, hitting her hard in the face, first with the back of his hand, then the palm, smashing into her cheeks. She rolled with the blows, staggered, and then straightened up, her face scarlet.

"That's it. Enough!" Smolin drew in a breath through his clenched teeth. "We won't wait for food. I think the time has come to talk—and talk you will. *All* of you." He turned back to the door, shouting for more of his men, who came noisily up the stairs, weapons drawn.

"You first, I think, James." Smolin's finger was aimed like a dagger.

There was little point in struggling as two of the men locked Bond's arms and hustled him out along the corridor and down the main staircase.

The angular Ingrid stood near the front door, as though overseeing the whole thing, like a thin black insect, while the dogs growled, ranged around her. Then they pushed Bond through one of the other doors and down another pine staircase. Along a passage and into a small room, bare but for a chair bolted to the floor.

They sat him down, snapping cuffs on wrists and ankles, shackling him to the arms and legs of the chair, which, he quickly discovered, was made of metal.

He was conscious of the two men standing behind him, preparing Lord knew what, and of Smolin, face set in a burning cold anger, directly in front of him.

Bond braced himself for physical pain, or even that worse possibility—the thing the Soviets always spoke of as a chemical interrogation. He emptied his mind, did all the things they had taught him, putting in layers of rubbish, forcing truth deep into his subconscious.

Then, when it came, Bond was shocked into mind-bending fear, for Colonel Maxim Smolin of the GRU, the main target of *Cream Cake,* spoke very quietly. "James," he began. "When M took you to lunch, and then for that walk in the park, explained *Cream Cake* to you, and bluntly said they would deny you if anything went wrong—now, James, what was your first thought?"

Smolin had begun at the point that Bond had neatly hidden away, and would have given to his interrogator only under the heaviest of pressures—physical or drug-induced.

10

INTERROGATION

FOR WHAT SEEMED an eternity, Bond felt as though his mind had been struck by a whirlwind—the enormity of the situation exploded in his brain as he tried to put some logic into Smolin's question. Listening devices planted in M's club, Blades? directional microphones? sound stealing in the park? a penetration of M's office? Impossible. M himself? Equally impossible.

Yet Smolin *knew.* There was no getting away from that central point. In the beginning was M's private briefing in the park. The beginning was the last thing Bond would have revealed. But Smolin had it, and if he was party to that knowledge, what else did he know, and how?

Bluff would not last long—"What briefing? What park?" Spin it out, he thought. All ideas of taking any initiative dissolved rapidly.

"Come, James, we both know better than that. I'm a GRU officer with considerable experience. Case-hardened, you might say. We're both aware of the way our organizations can be—have been—penetrated. Let us just say that *Cream Cake* was detected long before we allowed the four girls to discover they were blown."

"As I know nothing of this *Cream Cake,* I can't be any help to you." *Four girls,* he thought—still only four, and no mention of the one man.

Smolin shrugged. "Do you want me to do it the hard way, James? We all make mistakes from time to time. Your people made a mistake with *Cream Cake.* We made a blunder in letting the network get away in their socks, as your people say." He gave his most unpleasant laugh. "In the case of *Cream Cake,* I suppose we should say they got away in their stockings, eh?" His eyes locked with Bond's, and it was as though *he* was now trying to pass some secret message. "*All* of them being young women, eh?"

What about Jungle? Bond's mind still spun in disbelief. "I don't know what you're talking about," he said quietly. "I haven't the faintest idea what this *Cream Cake* business is, or was. I gave a lift to a girl I met at a party, and ended up with the GRU around my neck. I haven't denied what you obviously *do* know—that I'm a member of one of Britain's supposedly secret departments. But we're not all privy to every harebrained scheme that goes on. We work on a need-to-know basis . . ."

"And your most secret Head of Service—M—decided that you had need-to-know, James. Yesterday, in Regent's Park after lunching at his club, he told you the whole story, with many of its twists and turns—not quite all of them, though. Then he said he'd be obliged if you'd tidy things up—bring in the members of the *Cream Cake* team, and make them safe. Defuse the time bomb. He offered you the information, but said he could give you no sanctification. If you got into a mess neither he, nor the

Foreign Office, could bail you out. On the contrary, they would deny you and, unlike Saint Peter with Christ, not just thrice, but for all time." He twisted the left side of his mouth in a smirk. "It was up to you, and like the headstrong field man that you are, you took him up on it. Now, my question was, what did you feel when he laid that little lot on you?"

"I felt nothing, because it didn't happen." This was surely a nightmare. Any minute he would wake in his comfortable flat, with May preparing breakfast.

There was a long pause as Smolin sucked in air through his teeth. "Have it your own way. I'm not going to play any games. No strong-arm stuff. We'll do it with a small injection. I haven't got time to waste. My report has to be ready by later tonight when a *really* important visitor is expected." He turned, speaking to the pair of guards in a mixture of German and Russian. From what Bond could understand he was telling them to bring in the medical tray, then leave him alone to do the work.

The taller of the two men asked if he did not need assistance. "I shall do my own recording. The prisoner is secure. Now get on with it." Smolin's commanding manner made them jump to obey, and one was back in a few seconds wheeling a small medical trolley, like a butler serving tea.

Smolin dismissed the man, and once the guard had left, the GRU officer moved into Bond's line of sight, toward one of the walls. For the first time, Bond saw a row of small switches, which Smolin carefully threw down, turning back to the medical trolley and starting to do things with a hypo. As he worked, so he spoke, very softly, not even looking in Bond's direction.

"I've turned the sound off, so that we cannot be overheard. One of those guys is KGB—very bad news; and there are others planted in the team I've been given—only two of them can be trusted as GRU men, and even they might find themselves in a situation where they cannot obey my orders. While I'm getting things ready, you should know that the injection is to be nothing more worrying than distilled water. It was the only way I could engineer matters so that we could be alone." The eyes lifted slightly in a conspiratorial glance.

"What the hell're you talking about?" Bond found his own voice dropping to a whisper, realizing that in the one short sentence, Smolin had revealed yet another persona.

Careful, he cautioned himself. When you sup with the devil use a long spoon.

"I'm speaking to you about truth, James Bond." He lifted the hypo and a small vial, slid the needle through the skin of the vial, filled it, and squirted a small spray from the hypo to clear any air. "I'm talking about how I escape—with Irma. I'm sorry, I mean Heather. I've been able to hide the fact that Wald Belzinger—your Jungle Baisley—was ever part of the *Cream Cake* network. I did that to shield both myself and Susanne."

"Susanne?" Bond queried as Smolin readied his arm to take the injection.

"My colleague, Susanne Dietrich. I hid her little affair, and the conspiracy. I also warned the four girls, so they could get out before KGB caught up with them. That was none of Heather's doing—though, of course, she imagines it was her fault: that she made the final play for me too soon." He slid the needle home and Bond did not even feel it go in. "If anyone else should arrive in this room, act as though you're doped to the eyeballs. In fact, it would be a good idea if you just let your head go back and closed your eyes, anyway."

"As I understand it," Bond still talked in almost a whisper, "it was you, the so-called Plague Master of the HVA, and resident GRU mole within that organization, who blew the whistle on the girls." Christ, into the trap, he thought. I've admitted it.

Smolin bent low, near his ear, pretending to make the supposedly drugged Bond comfortable. "Yes, I *had* to blow the whistle, as you put it. Believe me, James, I only blew it a matter of seconds before KGB sounded their own alarm. And now? Well, I can't keep the heat off much longer. First, it *is* a KGB team—two teams, to be exact—who are quietly killing off the former members of *Cream Cake*. Also, I should imagine that, when our honored guest arrives tonight, he will bring with him tidings that the fifth, hidden and male, member of the network has—as I understand the London criminal fraternity would say—had it away on his toes with my good colleague and close friend Fräulein Captain Susanne Dietrich."

"Really?" Bond wanted to listen, not comment. Already he had gone too far.

"She went on leave two weeks ago, and has not returned. The KGB officer in charge of sweeping up the case will have put two and two together by now, and there will be, like in American gangster movies, an APB out on friend Belzinger, or Baisley, or Wald, or Jungle. It also puts me right in focus, which means I too must jump, as I have promised, if the going gets rough."

"Promised whom?"

"My dearest Heather, for one. Her case officer—Swift—for another. And your own beloved Chief, M, for good measure."

"You're trying to tell me, Maxim, that you have been a defector in place for the last five years?"

"Quite."

"And you expect me to believe you? *You*, the half-Russian, half-German scourge of the DDR's intelligence service? *You*, hated by more people than either of us would care to count? The dedicated officer with allegiance only to Moscow? I can't buy that, Maxim. There is no way I can buy it. Just doesn't add up."

"That is exactly *why* you should buy it, James. It is the only thing you can buy, because if you don't you're dead—so am I, come to that. You, Heather, Ebbie, myself, and, eventually, Susanne Dietrich and her lover Jungle Baisley. We're all booked for oblivion if you don't buy it and act on it."

"Prove it to me, then, Maxim. Give me proof."

"Haven't I done that, James? Haven't I done it by asking you the question about your reaction to M's very private briefing? There was no way for me to get that except from the horse's mouth. I can give you chapter and verse if you want."

Bond waited, the voice within still telling him to take care. He felt no ill effects from the injection, but that didn't mean a thing. Now he dug deep into his mind, focusing attention on Smolin at the same time as he examined his own mental and emotional state. No, he was not drugged. This was all very real, and the likelihood of Smolin's story became more probable as each second passed.

"James, the job we're in—it's like living within a set of Chinese boxes and never knowing exactly who or what is in which box. I know about the telephone call you received yesterday morning; your lunch at Blades; your walk in the park; your afternoon spent going through the files; and the incident at Heather's beauty salon." He paused, looking very serious now. "I tried very hard to head off that bloody KGB team of assassins, but it was too late. I know about the escape; your double switch at Heathrow; your telephone conversations with friends here—including Inspector Murray of the Garda Special Branch." He leaned both his hands on the chair arms, putting his face close to Bond. "You see, I have committed the cardinal sin within any intelligence organization. I *knew* what Heather was when she made her first pass at me; I checked out the others. At any moment I could have hauled them all in, but I did not."

"Why?"

"Because, when I was approached I *wanted* to be approached. I wanted to get out; knew it; had to live with it. Heather offered me a way of escape and, like a fool, I took it. And what happened? They asked me to stay in place; to become even more of a monster than ever before. What better cover, James?"

"Who asked you?"

"Heather, whom I love dearly. Then Swift, and, last of all, your own boss—M."

"Where?"

"In a safe place on the West side of the Wall. A day trip. He agreed to keep Heather under wraps. I agreed to work for him. In Berlin we set up codes, contacts, cutouts, and so it was, until the KGB began to sniff around what had really been going on five years ago within their sister service in the DDR. It is only a matter of time before they find my name computes with *Cream Cake*. After that, unless I can jump, it's Moscow, a quick bullet if I'm lucky; one of the cancer wards or the Gulag if I'm not." He wagged a finger in front of Bond's nose. "The same goes for you, James. For all of us."

In spite of his feelings, Bond had yet to be convinced that this was the whole and complete story. "If this is true, why wasn't I told?" For a stomach-churning second, he again realized that even in discussing events with Smolin he was answering questions, providing a skilled interrogator with all he required.

"Need-to-know. Your cunning old M is too wily a bird. You were the man for the job, but you did not *have* to know about me. It was a chance in a million that we would meet. M's instructions to me were to watch from afar and let you get the girls out—then pick up Jungle." His eyes narrowed below a wrinkled forehead, replete with anxiety. "I don't think he realized that I was so surrounded by KGB; and I couldn't call off their hit team. Also, up to late yesterday, he had no idea of the latest developments. We spoke during the early hours this morning—first through Murray, who had contacted him, and later on a secure line. M thought I might still have a chance of staying in place. That is what *he* reasoned. But he is wrong; I've been blown, James—or, at best, almost blown—and I must get out, and to get out I need your help, because we have not just been penetrated by KGB, but impregnated by them. I've told you—at least one is in my team: most probably more than one. The real threat, here in the castle, is that bitch of a housekeeper, Ingrid. She's very definitely KGB. Black Ingrid, as they call her in certain circles, is deputy, and, I suspect, mistress of the man who is running the rout of your *Cream Cake* team. Beware of her, my friend. It might look as though those damned dogs regard me as their master, but I assure you the dogs are also doubles, and Ingrid's their real case officer. She can countermand my orders to them in a second, and they will obey." He gave a humorless smile. "And before you ask it, yes, the dogs *were* trained in that almost windowless complex you have described—the one outside Moscow, behind the walls and wire on the old Khodinka airfield."

What had he to lose—Bond thought—or for that matter, what to gain? "If I believe you, Maxim, what do you need from me? You have a plan, have you? Like getting me to take you, and the girls, to Jungle Baisley's hideout so you can put the lot of us in the bag?"

"Don't be stupid, James. You think KGB won't know where he's hiding out by now? You think they won't have double-checked Susanne's movements? I should imagine that, by this time, those two're probably as near to being in the bag as we are."

"And who's this honored guest you've been talking about? The one due in tonight?"

"I thought you'd never ask, James." He stopped, his eyes clear and calm, but Bond had the impression that this was the kind of terrible calm you get before a hurricane strikes.

"Well?"

"You know *me* as Basilisk, yes? Cryptonym, Basilisk, yes?"

"Yes."

"Do you, then, James, happen to know the cryptonym Black-friar?"

Bond felt his heart thump and stomach turn over wildly. "Christ!"

"Quite. Our guest is Blackfriar."

It took a few seconds for Bond to assimilate the information. "Konstantin Nikolaevich Chernov. *General* Chernov." Smolin supplied the real name.

"Christ," Bond repeated. "Kolya Chernov?"

"As you say, James, Kolya Chernov—to his few friends. The Chief Investigating Officer of Department Eight, Directorate S, which was once Department V, and before that—"

"SMERSH!"

"With whom you have had dealings on several occasions." Smolin spoke slowly, as though each word had a hidden meaning. "And Konstantin Nikolaevich has a reputation that makes my own appear as blameless as Little Red Hooding Ride."

"Riding Hood," Bond corrected. He had noticed that Maxim Smolin's faultless English had developed flaws under the stress of their conversation. Bond's brow crinkled, for he was not only aware of General Chernov's reputation, but knew his file intimately. Kolya Chernov was responsible for dozens of black operations, causing death and mayhem within both the British and American intelligence communities. He was also a man of crude and cruel cunning—hated, Bond guessed, by many within the Russian services as well as abroad. Blackfriar was a living nightmare to Bond's Service.

In his mind he saw the set of photographs that took up several pages of the file they held at the Regent's Park Headquarters. A slim man, tall, with his body well-honed by much exercise, Blackfriar was a known health fanatic who neither smoked nor drank alcohol. His IQ went off the scale, and he was well established as a dirty-trick planner of immense ingenuity. He was also a tenaciously shrewd investigator, and his file showed that he had sent at least thirty members of both the KGB and GRU to either their deaths or the Gulag for both major and minor infringements of discipline. "Being what he is, Blackfriar has the knack of scenting even the most tiny deviation at ten paces, and he follows it up like a hellhound," one defector was on record as saying.

Bond closed his eyes and let his head droop. Suddenly he felt both exhausted and fearful: not for himself, but for the two girls. "It *must* be important if he's actually coming into the field," he murmured.

"It is the first time in my own memory." Either Smolin was a very good actor, or he was filled with dread by even discussing the General. "Let me tell you, James, when I first blew *Cream Cake*—admittedly not for simply altruistic reasons—it was a matter for the Germans, for HVA and, naturally, GRU, me being who and what I am." Another humorless smile. "Or what I was. It has taken time for KGB to sniff out the more devious moves, the hidden secrets of *Cream Cake*—the existence of Jungle; the turning of Susanne Dietrich; and, of course, the turning of Maxim Smolin." He banged his own chest with a balled fist.

"It's taken them five years." Bond's voice was flat, as though his mind worked elsewhere.

"Four, to be exact. It was last year that KGB reopened the files and decided to investigate the case, going over our heads. They do not like GRU to feel they are an élite body; they dislike our methods, our secrecy, our way of recruitment from within the Army. I have heard Chernov himself say that we smack of the hated SS from the Great Patriotic War."

At first, Smolin said, the reinvestigation had been fairly low-grade—"A few simple dates, some cross-checking here and there." Then, out of the blue, General Chernov—Blackfriar himself—arrived in Berlin, "like an insidious disease. I flashed warnings to your people, but I dared not make a move. After only a week there were a number of field changes, and it didn't take great intellect to deduce that KGB were boxing me in. James, I have been watched and monitored for the past six months. It is Chernov's own revenge team who are on the loose, and Chernov's orders are that the girls are to be rooted out, killed in a particular way, and left with their tongues cut from their mouths—as the French say, *pour encourager les autres.*"

"So you do all in your power to assist Blackfriar, eh, Basilisk? You pick up Ebbie, and go to great lengths to trap Heather and myself on the road."

"On Chernov's orders, and only on *his* orders. I've told you, they're all around us, KGB. I thought of botching the job, but how could that help? James, I want your help. I need to get out *now.* Take you and the girls with me. Naturally, in front of the others I have to keep up a pretense—I must be seen to obey Chernov's orders. But not for long now."

"So, if you're giving me proof of your intentions, Maxim, tell me where we are. The location of this castle?"

"Not all that far from where we picked you up. The track to

the road is about two miles. At the entrance we turn left, and it's straight downhill until we reach the Dublin–Wicklow road. An hour, two hours at the most, we can be at the airport and away."

"If I accept your version"—Bond still lay back, with his eyes closed—"I also need help."

"You have it. Don't move suddenly, but I'm unlocking the cuffs now. I have your gun with me—a nice piece of work the ASP 9mm. There . . ." Bond felt the heavy metal drop into his lap.

"So we just shoot our way out?"

"I fear we would be a little outnumbered. It is possible we could bluff most of my own men, but certainly not Black Ingrid, and those whom Chernov has infiltrated."

"Again, assuming I accept your word, how long have we got?" Bond's hands were free now. He could feel the cuffs drop away.

"An hour. Hour and a half with luck. He has to land here while there is still light."

"And the girls, where are they being housed?"

"They've been locked in the guest suite, I should imagine. Those were my orders. The problem is getting to them. After such an interrogation as I am supposed to be making, you would be semi-conscious. They'll be waiting with a gurney trolley to take you along the passage. Then they'll carry you up the stairs. There." Bond felt the shackles on his legs being freed.

"Any suggestions?" Bond slid his hand onto the ASP, weighing it carefully to be certain there was a real magazine in place. It was something he had practiced many times—even in the dark—with empty magazines, or ones loaded with blanks, and the real thing. It *was* fully loaded.

"There is one way . . ." Smolin began, then stopped, his head and body turning as the door smashed open to reveal Ingrid, still in her Mrs. Danvers drab garb, but with the three dogs straining at their leashes.

"Ingrid!" Smolin used his most commanding tone.

"It's all been very interesting." Ingrid's voice was distinctly unfeminine—like her face, it was thin and sharp. "I have made certain changes to the interrogation room since you were last here, Colonel—on General Chernov's orders, naturally. For one thing, the switches, in here for the recording facility, have been reversed. He's going to be fascinated by the tapes. But we have listened long enough. The General will be here soon, and I want you *all* tightly locked away before he arrives."

As though reading each other's thoughts, Smolin leaped to the left, while Bond rolled out of the chair, moving right, as Ingrid shrieked, in German, at the dogs—*"Wotan, Rechts! Anfassen! Fafie, Links! Anfassen!"* The dogs sprang, snarling and, as Fafie's teeth fastened on his gun arm, Bond had a fleeting view of men standing behind Ingrid, and the third dog—Siegi—straining at the leash to go in for the kill.

11

DOG EAT DOG

He felt a tearing rip of pain as Fafie's jaws fastened on the lower part of his arm, making the fingers of his right hand open involuntarily, so that the gun dropped heavily onto the floor.

Beyond the pain, Bond was aware of several things—Ingrid's raw voice shouting above the snarling of the dogs; Smolin cursing in both Russian and German; the stale, stinking smell of Fafie's breath on his face, and the dog's weight as he held on—still growling—head moving from side to side as though trying to wrench Bond's arm from its socket.

He reflexed, like any trained man, smashing his free hand with full force into the dog's genitals. That's what you were taught, but training was different—for one thing, your arms were well protected, and you did not follow through on the blows. The trainer was always around and, once you had gone through the moves, he called the animal off. But this was for real, and he felt Fafie react to what must have been an exquisitely painful contact. The growl changed into a yelp of unexpected pain, and for a second the jaws relaxed.

Bond used that brief moment to roll and bring his right hand up to the animal's throat—thumb and fingers finding the windpipe and pressing as though he wished to tear out the dog's larynx. His left arm whipped around, catching the beast by the scruff of the neck but, by this time, the shock of pain and the full instinct of real danger had given Fafie renewed strength.

The yelp changed back into a series of chilling snarls and it took all of Bond's depleted reserves just to hang on. He could feel the deepening pain where Fafie had lacerated his arm, and the weakness that came from it. But, like the dog, he knew he was fighting for his life, and he increased the pressure with thumb and fingers—"You never throttle anyone, or anything, like they do in the movies, with both hands. Always use the one-handed choke for good results." He could hear the little leathery instructor from the training school as clearly as he had heard him long ago, during the first of many kill-or-be-killed courses.

Screw in with the hand on the windpipe and use all your strength at the back of the neck with the other hand—he put action to the thought, as Fafie was thrashing around in an attempt to pull clear. It was like wrestling with a tiger, and for one brief, darkened moment, Bond allowed his natural love for animals to creep into his consciousness, but for no more than a second. This *was* life and death.

As he wrestled, aware of the pain, noise, and confusion around him, Bond's mind clung to the one thing that would keep him going—Fafie wanted blood. His blood and his death.

"Fafie! Anfassen! Anfassen!" Ingrid shrieked over everything— "Fafie! Hold him! Hold him!"

But Bond had summoned a last great surge of strength, his fingers cutting in through the thick fur of Fafie's coat, the left arm pressing with increased power.

He could feel the animal begin to lose consciousness. Then, almost with lightning suddenness, Fafie's jaws relaxed, and the body became a dead weight.

Though he knew he had won this round, Bond continued to act as though he was wrestling with the dog, glancing sideways to lock on to where the ASP had fallen.

He rolled, grunted, and moved, trying to give the impression that Fafie was still fighting him. He felt strangely cool and calculating now, conscious of pain, but determined to get his hands on the automatic that lay to his right, just within his grasp.

He relaxed, looking toward Smolin to see, with some horror,

that the GRU man was lying back, with Wotan covering him, fangs bared ready to be buried into his victim's throat if Smolin showed further resistance. That one look told Bond that the Colonel was not going to risk even the twitch of an eyebrow, for there was also Siegi being held on a choke chain, in reserve. After Siegi, there would be the men he had seen crowding in behind Ingrid. The moves would have to be carefully calculated and coordinated—all this was seen, digested, and comprehended in the wink of an eye.

There was no question of choosing the right moment, for the right moment was any moment.

Using the now dead Fafie as his only available shield, Bond broke through the barrier of pain that leaped from his damaged arm. He rolled to the right, reached for the weapon, rolled again, and fired—two shots for the straining Siegi; another single round as Wotan turned from his captive, catching the full force of a Glazer slug—knocking the vicious, trained killer animal back against the wall—then a fourth shot, low and toward the door, where it struck the jamb, carving a great hole through wood and plaster.

The sudden, unexpected deaths of all three animals had frozen Ingrid in the doorway, shock rooting her to the floor; but the men behind her had scattered.

"No more!" Smolin shrieked, on his feet now, lunging toward Ingrid, catching one wrist and jerking her arm down hard, then toward him and away, so the luckless housekeeper hurtled across the room, thudding into the far wall with a bone-cracking sound.

As she hit, Ingrid made an odd noise, part scream, a commixture of rage, frustration, and agony. Then she silently slid down the wall to sprawl, a black heap, on the floor.

Smolin had an automatic in his hand and was shouting toward the shattered doorway: "Alex! Yuri! I know you're good and sworn GRU men. I am your senior officer. KGB have mounted a despicable plot against us. You are with KGB men now. Turn. Turn on them. They are traitors and can only bring discredit, and death, upon your heads. Turn now!"

For a couple of seconds, silence hung in the passageway, like some deadly gas, then there was a cry, followed by a shot and the sound of blows.

Smolin nodded at Bond, signaling for him to take up a position on the right of the door, while the GRU man pressed himself against the wall on the opposite side.

Another shot. A shout, and the noise of a struggle, the unmistakable sound of a fist pounding against flesh and bone, and a voice calling in Russian, "Comrade Colonel, we have them. Quickly, we have them!"

Smolin nodded toward Bond, and together they threw themselves into the passage. As they jumped, so Smolin yelled in English, "Get them *all*, James! All!"

He needed no second bidding. On his side, to the right of the passage, one man lay unconscious while two struggled with a fourth, attempting to overpower him.

It required three quick shots from the ASP to dispatch the group. The terrible, efficient Glazer slugs did their work—the first exploded in the right side of one of the struggling men, spreading half its load into the stomach of the one grappling with him; the second took out the man on the floor; while the third dispatched the fourth man, who did not even have time to know what hit him.

The noise of the shots was deafening within the narrow passage walls. Doubly so, as Smolin loosed off two rounds from his automatic. Bond turned, to see he had also scored, the couple of fresh corpses—one spread-eagled, the other an untidy pile of remains—bore witness to the GRU officer's accuracy.

"Pity," Smolin muttered. "They were good men, Alex and Yuri."

"There are times when you have no option." Bond looked grimly at the carnage, realizing that he felt more for the dogs he had been forced to kill than for the thugs. "How many upstairs, Maxim?—You've proved yourself now."

"Two; I should think they're with the girls."

"They'll be down any minute, then."

"I doubt it. Up there, you don't hear much that goes on down in this basement." He was breathing hard. "We've used it many times, James. Strong men have screamed down here while people in the rooms above have made love and heard nothing."

Bond could hear Smolin, but the world around him began to swim and go out of focus. He was aware of the hot stickiness of his arm and a blinding pain that started at the source of the heat and spread throughout his body. He retched twice, heard Smolin calling his name from a long way off. Then the darkness covered him.

He dreamed of snakes and spiders. They slithered and crawled around him as he tried to get out of a dark and twisting maze, ankle-deep in the revolting creatures. He had to make it, and there was light, dim at the end of the tunnel. Then the end would disappear, and he was back where he had started, far below the earth, surrounded by a red glow. There. There it was again, the light at the end, but a large snake was dragging at his legs. He had no sense of fear, just the knowledge that it was essential for him to get out. But another snake had joined the first, while smaller reptiles wrapped themselves around his legs, pulling him down, hissing as he lost his balance.

Now, one of the reptiles had him by the arm, squeezing, sinking fangs into it, causing a pain that broke through the blackness. He looked, and a nest of spiders crawled into the wound made by the snake. Other spiders—large, fat, and furry—were on his face, stuffing themselves into his nostrils and prizing their way into his mouth so that he had to cough, splutter, and spit them out.

He was gagging on the spiders, but somehow he must have managed to get nearer to the tunnel's end, for light was hurting his eyes and a voice called his name—"James! James Bond! James!"

The snakes and spiders were gone, leaving only a wrenching pain where they had ravaged his arm, and something else was swimming into his vision—a face. The face of a girl. An angel? Was he dead? The lips moved. "James? Come on. It's okay." The face went out of focus and said, "Heather, he's coming round."

"Thank heaven for that."

Bond's eyes fluttered, opened and closed, then opened fully to see the pert pretty face of Ebbie Heritage filling the entire screen of his vision.

"What?" he said.

"You're okay, James. It's okay now."

He moved and was aware of the throbbing in his right arm and a feeling that something was constricting it.

"There's not much time." It was Maxim Smolin, easing Ebbie to one side. "You'll be fine, James, but . . ." He looked at his wristwatch.

Everything came flooding back in sharp detail, as though some-one had opened a set of gates in his memory.

Smolin straightened up. He stood looking down at Bond, one arm around Heather Dare's shoulders.

Bond took a deep breath. "Sorry, did I pass out on you?"

"Not surprisingly." Smolin smiled. "That damned dog's teeth went deep. How does it feel?"

He moved his arm. "Numb. Uncomfortable, but I can use it."

"Ebbie played Florence Nightingale." It was Heather speaking now. "We all have a lot to thank you for, James. Maxim's told us what happened down there."

"I only cleaned the wound." The Sirens, with their sweet, alluring, and seductive voices, must have sounded like Ebbie, Bond thought, stupidly dazed, as she continued, "The dogs were in good condition. I don't think there's any danger of poison. We used the strongest antiseptic known to man."

"And the most expensive." Smolin gave a wry smile. "The last of the Hine 1914 vintage. Smooth. Very smooth."

Bond groaned, "Smooth, magnificent, and far from intoxicating. I'm sorry."

"It went for a good cause," Smolin said with a nod. "Can you sit up? Stand?"

Unsteadily, Bond eased himself up. They had laid him on the settee in the guest suite. He tried to stand, but his legs felt as though they had been filleted. At first he had to cling to one of the settee arms to steady himself. Ebbie rushed to his side, her hands strong and experienced.

"Thank you, Ebbie. Thank you for everything." He moved with care, trying the muscles and thinking he must look like a small child learning to walk. Slowly the power returned. "Thank you, Ebbie," he repeated.

"We're in *your* debt. This was nothing."

"The others?" Bond turned to Smolin again. "Your men up here?"

"Taken care of." The GRU man's face went blank, reminding Bond of his own mind and emotions when a nasty piece of work had been done. It was always best to erase that kind of thing from memory. People who recalled too much either started to enjoy it and were engulfed by madness, or cracked under the guilt.

"Ingrid?" he asked, just for the record.

"Alive. Resting. Conscious, but she won't be going far. Several bones're broken." He became urgent. "James, we have to get out. You remember? Blackfriar? He could arrive anytime. We really should try to be away before he lands."

"Who's Blackfriar?" From a startled Ebbie.

"Satan himself." Smolin's mouth was set grimly. "General Chernov. From KGB's darkest side of the moon."

Bond nodded. "I'll be okay. Blackfriar is as Maxim says. Evil, clever, and very good at his work—which he appears to enjoy." He took several deep breaths and glanced, smiling, at Ebbie. She looked less sophisticated than Heather, but Heather appeared to have abandoned her haughty side as she now gazed at Smolin with wide, dark, and adoring eyes.

"Yes, I'm sure you'll be okay, James." Smolin had developed some acid in his manner. "You're the one who's had an injury, but you'll survive. I'm thinking of the rest of us."

"The cars are . . .?"

"Here, yes." The Colonel gave a petulant shake of his head. "We have cars, James. What you don't seem to realize is that we're sitting in a natural bowl of earth. It's overlooked on all sides and there are, to my knowledge, at least ten men out there with sniperscopes, automatic weapons, the full works. They're also KGB, not GRU. Four of them at the main entrance alone. We start to drive away, they'll want to know why, and I really don't think they'll stop to question us. KGB have special men for that. The guys up on the rim of those hills—and at the entrance—are not questioners, either; they're shooters, killers."

"Dog eat dog, eh?"

"Shoot first. Worry about the questions later."

"Would they shoot at a really prime target?"

"Yes. You, me, or the girls. No doubts at all. Blackfriar has been in constant touch with this place—its real name is Three Sisters Castle, incidentally, and it's been used by KGB and GRU for the past ten years. But he's been on the radio link. I've had a look at the scratch pads in the Communications Room. Your name's been passed along the line. So has mine, and his last order was that nobody leave until he gets in. Anyone who tries *must* be stopped."

"I said *prime* target," Bond repeated. He was gradually starting to feel better, his mental processes becoming sharper. "Really prime—like General Konstantin Nikolaevich Chernov. Would they endanger his life? Put him in the line of fire?"

"You mean take him with us? Wait, and grab him?"

"Why not?"

"Because he will not be alone."

"Well, why not simply use him as cover? How's he coming in?"

"Helicopter. He's got plenty of unofficial transport over here—all *very* legal of course; the Republic's not the kind of place to play games using illegal transport. But he won't risk coming in when it gets dark—there are no facilities here for light aircraft or choppers once the sun's gone."

"He'll land near the castle?"

"We usually come in directly in line with the main entrance and fly up it. Then land out in front—close to where the cars are now."

"Who'll be with him?"

"At least two bodyguards—possibly more—his adjutant, and a skilled interrogator. They'll be armed. And they're all highly efficient."

Bond thought for a moment, and his arm gave a sudden stab of pain, making him wince.

"James, you all right?" Ebbie was at his side, one hand resting on the injured arm, her face troubled.

She had the kind of deep blue eyes in which a man would not reject the chance of drowning, and lips that cried out to kiss and be kissed. Bond nodded, saying it was just a twinge, nothing serious.

"We've *got* to get out." He reluctantly dragged his eyes from Ebbie, back to Smolin. "So we have to run the gauntlet, whatever the risks. Strikes me that the risk is lessened if we go just as the General arrives. Which of the cars, Maxim?"

"The BMW. It's good to start with, but this one's been souped up a little, as I believe they say."

Bond began to pat his clothes. "My gun?" he asked, and Smolin produced the ASP from the table, together with the spare magazines and the baton. As he dismantled and reassembled the weapon, Bond surreptitiously checked the more secret parts of his clothing, to make sure that certain other items had been left in their hiding places. "We agreed, then? We make a run for it as soon as the chopper appears?"

The others nodded, but Smolin did not look altogether happy. "Maxim?"

"Yes, it's the only way—or go now and risk their full firepower. I'd be happier if we'd had the time to take them out."

"You going to arm the girls?"

"He already has." Heather had certainly become more confident. Bond made a mental note to ask her why she had offered herself to him, so blatantly, at the Airport Hotel—but that was a question he would not put to her in front of Smolin, to whom he now turned. "And you have the BMW's keys?"

Smolin nodded.

"Then what're we waiting for? We should get down to the main doors. Maxim, when we go down, why don't you walk out to the car? That would be natural enough. Play around with it, and give us a yell as soon as the chopper appears."

They went down the stairs, and the castle suddenly seemed very cold and cheerless. Outside there was still plenty of light, though the sky was just starting to redden in the West; but the flagstoned hall retained an almost ghostly chill.

"Going to be a lovely sunset." Bond smiled cheerfully, mainly to keep the girls in good spirits. He knew from Smolin's face that escape from this place was not going to be easy.

At the door Maxim asked how they should sit when they reached the BMW. "Okay if Irma—sorry, Heather—comes in front with me? You, James, in the back with Ebbie. I suspect we should all keep as low as possible once it's started."

"That's fine by me." Ebbie grinned happily at Bond, who suggested that all the windows should be opened—"In case we have to return fire."

"Right." Smolin gave a curt nod. "I think that would be most wise. None of this is going to be easy."

"You've made the point, Maxim. But I really don't fancy swimming into Kolya Chernov's shark-infested waters at the moment. Now, a private word with you." He took Smolin's arm and pulled him to one side, away from the girls. "If we *do* get clear, where do you think we should head for?"

"Out of this country, for a start. But there's no hiding place from Chernov—not in the long run."

"You got any ideas about Jungle and your colleague—Susanne, is it? Where they might be?"

"You know where they were last sighted?"

"Yes, and you?"

"The Canary Islands."

"That's what I had, but I should imagine it's old news by now."

"It was a week old when M gave it to you. I think they'll have moved on, but once we're clear—and that's no foregone conclusion—I'll have burned my boats. We'll have to try to follow their spoor, and that will mean doing it alone. No help from my people—"

"And very little from mine, if we're sticking to M's rules."

"Chernov'll expect us to head for Dublin, Shannon, or one of the ports—Rosslare or Dun Laoghaire."

"Which we'll have to do eventually, if we're going to get out."

Smolin gave him a fast sideways glance. "Not necessarily. I still have some contacts we can use. Come to that, so do you. But I could get us out quietly."

It was Bond's turn to look anxious. "I can't go into the North, you do know that? Even if M's sticking to the brief he laid down about denying me, I still daren't go into the North. Off-limits to my department. Strictly MI5 territory. We've had too many internal battles about that one already. I would *really* be persona non grata if I turned up there. 'Five' are very touchy about it."

Smolin made pushing movements with the flat of his palms. "I'm not thinking about the North. Again, *if* we do get out, we'll have to pull some kind of deception. Make them think we're heading for Dublin, then double back. I want to get us into West Cork. From there I know how we can be moved out with the minimum fuss. Okay?"

Bond nodded. "You'll be at the wheel, so you lead."

Smolin gave his first cheerful smile for some time. "At least I know where we can switch cars," he said with some glee, as though he had only just thought of it. "I also know a nice quiet hotel where they're unlikely to come looking for us."

"Well," Bond began, then changed his mind. "How many telephones have they got in this place?" he asked, as though suddenly struck with another idea.

"One here, in the hall." Smolin pointed to a small table set under the stairs. "There's one in the control room—the door to the left, on the gallery at the top of the stairs—and one in the main bedroom, that's the next door along."

"They're all linked to the same number?"

"Yes." He recited the number, which Bond instantly committed to memory. "The line in is the one in the control room, where they keep the communications equipment. The others—in the hall and main bedroom—are extensions. Why?"

"Just a little idea. Keep the girls happy. Get them outside with you. It'll only take ten minutes."

Smolin raised his eyebrows. "If we've got ten minutes. This is necessary?"

"I believe so, yes." Bond gave a cheerful smile and turned away, taking the stairs as quickly as he could. The arm did not hurt so much, but he still felt weak.

The control room was small, with most of the space taken up by great banks of radio equipment, tape machines, and a large computer, all of which were ranged against the longest wall, on professional wood and metal desks, each with a high-backed office chair. On the desks were scratch pads, blotters, calculators, and the like. The telephone stood on the center desk, in front of the main radio gear.

Almost before he was in the room, Bond had unclasped his belt to seek out and remove the ingeniously hidden miniature tool kit, put together by Q'ute some time ago. It contained an assortment of compact tools, detonators, picklocks, wire, and fuses, and folded into an almost flat leather container.

From what was at his disposal, Bond took a small plastic cylinder, removing the top to display several different screwdriver heads. He selected one that would easily fit the screws on the underside of a standard telephone, and slid the driver into the other end of the tiny cylinder, which became a handle. Thus equipped, he removed the four screws at the base of the instrument.

Once he had opened up the phone, he took out his wallet and extracted a small packet—given to him by Q'ute just before he had left the headquarters building and was starting off for Heather's beauty salon, Dare to Be Chic.

The packet contained what appeared to be six black grains of wheat, each with two tiny wires trailing from it. Again he changed the screwdriver head, this time using the size normally associated with jewelers.

Each of the wheatgrain-like objects was, in fact, the latest advance in what at one time was known as a harmonica bug—small now being beautiful in the eyes of all concerned with surveillance and sound-stealing devices.

It took Bond less than two minutes to attach one of the bugs to the requisite terminals within the telephone, and another two to close the whole thing up. He breathed a silent thank-you for these skills, which he had learned many years ago at the hands of Q Branch's special telephone instructor—a perky cockney called Philip, known to all at the Regent's Park HQ as Phil the Phone.

He then went to the main bedroom, quickly located the telephone, and inserted another of the tiny—well-nigh undetectable—devices.

Downstairs again, he went through the same routine with the third telephone. Smolin and the girls were outside, watching for Chernov's arrival, which could now be any minute, for the sun was quickly sinking and the light had started to go.

He had hardly completed the work on the last telephone when Smolin reopened the door, calling out, "I'm going to the car, James. He should be here by now. Right?" He squared his shoulders, pushed at the heavy front doors, and walked slowly toward the BMW, playing around with the boot for a while before going to the interior of the car, activating the windows to open, and climbing behind the wheel.

They heard the first sound of the helicopter's engine in the distance. Smolin started the BMW, leaning over and opening the passenger door, shouting for them to come on.

Hardly had they reached the car—with the helicopter clearly visible, an insect against the blood glow of the sky—when the first shots came down, from the rim of overlooking hills. They were warnings, smacking against the hard tar of the turning circle, well away from the car.

Inside there was heavy breathing, Maxim Smolin crouched over the wheel and the others as near to the floor as they could get; Ebbie, close to Bond, tensing as a second strike of bullets hit the ground nearby.

Smolin took off like a racing driver, weaving as he went, building up speed to take the bumps along the rough track that led, some two miles on, to the main entrance.

The helicopter had turned away from its run in, as though alerted by the gunfire, circled low, and, as Bond had hoped, came between them and at least some of the marksmen. He could now see that it was a version of the big twin-finned, double-rotored KA-25, and that it carried civil markings—the Hormone, as NATO dubbed it.

"If we do get out," Heather shouted, "where're we heading for?"

"*If* we make it!" Smolin yelled, and at that moment they heard the roar of the helicopter just over the roof, and the sudden rattle of automatic fire, kicking up the dust and stones to their right. Bond raised his head and watched as the squat, cumbersome-looking machine turned on its own axis and started to run in again, toward them—its two huge rotors whirling fore and aft.

Bond had the ASP clasped in his right hand, and felt the downdraft of the Hormone battering at the car like a gale. It was low, and chopping in alongside them, one man half out of the rear sliding door, manning a machine pistol. The ASP kicked and banged twice, and the marksman was cut straight out of the door, while a small amount of the helicopter's fuselage went with him. Bond steadied his hands, lifted the weapon slightly, and loosed off another two rounds, aimed at the lower rotor blades.

The Hormone faltered and began to fall away—the forward rotors whining as a hunk of one blade was torn off by a Glazer impact.

Smolin let out a gust of laughter. "You got the bastards," he shouted, "the stinking, rotten bastards! There they go . . ."

Bond glanced back through the rear window to see the helicopter put down heavily, with a jolt that almost crushed one of the wheels of its undercarriage, sending it into the fuselage. "They won't get that fixed in a hurry at the handy local garage," he muttered. Then the bullets started to come down around them again and he had to fold himself flat on the floor, so close to Ebbie that he could smell the scent of her hair. It reminded him of summer in the fields of Kent.

"Let's get the hell out of here," Smolin called. "Hang on! Hang on, tight! I'm going to take a shortcut."

STRANGE MEETING

THE CAR LURCHED—first right, then left as Smolin dragged it around rough grass. At one point there was a thump and bang, which knocked the vehicle precariously to one side, so that the girls screamed, and for a second even Bond thought they were going to turn over—he knew it was the impact of a heavy-caliber bullet, and what *that* was capable of doing.

Dusk was rapidly turning to night, but the grounded helicopter had its forward lights on, a glaring immobile cone that lit the main track toward the entrance, barring exit there, unless Smolin decided on a suicide dash along the beam.

But he heaved the BMW away from the track, swinging it over the uneven rutted meadow, moving closer to the rising ground as he did so. The castle was to their left now, and the helicopter a long way behind—to the far left of the building.

Another three shots came down around them, one hitting the front passenger side door, passing through but appearing to do no damage. The long-range snipers were almost certainly using night scopes.

"Should we try it on foot?" Bond shouted to Smolin above the noise.

"On foot they'd get us. There used to be a gap along this side—overgrown, but not properly sealed off." He sounded perfectly calm as another shot, from somewhere above them, ricocheted past. "It's about our only chance."

He drove without lights, craning forward to peer into the darkness, the engine whining under stress and the whole car bumping and grinding, slewing like a small boat in very choppy water.

"There!" Smolin's voice was full of glee. "Now we pray." The car slowed as he began to change down, pumping at the brakes. They were moving right, wheels protesting and the back swinging violently.

"Ever done any rallying?" Bond called casually, as though to take the girls' minds off the alarming experience.

"No!" Smolin laughed. "But I've done the GRU course—*Scheiss!*" It looked as though they were now hurtling toward an impenetrable wall of trees.

"Down! Hang on!" Bond shouted.

The car struck and there was a grinding noise as the underside hit the hard roots of bushes and undergrowth, followed by the whisper of branches and foliage parting against the vehicle.

There were no solid trees, however, and, while the dense growth had slowed them, the car did not stop. It crunched, bounced, and made some impressively terrifying noises, but kept going to the point where Smolin had to change right down to first, with his foot hard on the accelerator. Then, as suddenly as they had struck the barrier, they were through, but with a heavy pole and barbed-wire fence facing them, towering a good seven feet above the ground.

"Keep praying." Smolin's voice dropped a shade as he changed up, accelerated, and rammed the fence head-on. This time the impact was more dramatic—Smolin and Heather were thrown against their seat belts, while Bond catapulted hard against Smolin's seat back.

Ebbie came off best, having stayed on the floor, though she reacted with touching concern as Bond gave a small cry of pain as his injured arm banged against the driver's seat—"James? Are you—*ouch*"—as she was rolled back by the jolt.

The car kept going, then, tangled in wire, spluttered and stopped, halfway onto the road ahead of them.

Smolin forced his door open, pushing it against the broken wire to get it free. "Get out—if you can!" he yelled, and Bond tried the door on his side. It opened halfway, then became trapped in the wire, so, following Smolin, he shoved hard until both of the men were out, scrambling around the car, grappling at the wire with bare hands, which in moments were cut and bleeding from the vicious barbs.

Each cursed in his respective language, under panting breath, as the car was slowly cleared of the tentacles that seemed almost alive, springing up and waving about as each new strand was loosened.

"Where now?" Bond breathed heavily.

"Dump this car, and get another one." Smolin ducked to avoid a snake of wire that shot up, missing his face by inches as he freed it from the back wheels.

"Where?"

"I have a good British-made Rover Vitesse stashed away—that is correct, yes? Stashed?"

"Yes." Bond tugged the last piece of wire from around the rear bumper. "You've certainly got this country sewn up, Maxim—cars stashed away, covert routes in and out."

Smolin was heading back for the driving seat. "Not just me. I'm sure Chernov has more transport near at hand. We'll be running another gauntlet."

They were both back in the BMW with Smolin twisting the ignition key in a vain attempt to start again. The engine coughed and died several times, then—to everyone's relief—fired. As though nothing had happened, Smolin slammed the gears and edged the car onto the road, driving with no lights, turning left—which, Bond recalled, would take them to the Dublin–Wicklow road.

"They'll send the Mercedes after us first, and probably organize another couple of teams," Smolin continued. "But our switch in cars should help. This one I kept up my sleeve. It's private, *nobody* knows I have it. Did the whole thing alone."

"Far?" Bond asked, thinking of other things. Personally he badly wanted a telephone.

"Fifteen minutes as the crow flies—but have you noticed how many crows there are in this country? And they don't seem to fly. They litter the roads and walk out of our way." At long last, he switched on the headlights, while still treating the car, road, and his passengers in an unnervingly cavalier fashion.

They were moving swiftly through lanes that appeared to have been constructed from several sets of leftover S-bends, overhung by bushes and hedges. Nobody spoke, though Ebbie's hand stole softly into Bond's palm, then was snatched back again as she peered in the half-light at the blood flowing from what seemed to be hundreds of cuts and gashes.

Without a word she reached down, lifted her skirt, exposing a generous segment of thigh—unmistakably white against the semi-darkness—and started to tear at her slip. When she had a sizable piece of light-colored silk, she put it to her mouth, biting to rip it into two pieces, which she then tenderly bound around both of Bond's damaged hands. "Poor you," she whispered. "I'll kiss them better." So saying, she bent her head and ran her lips over the exposed part of his fingers. First one hand, then the other, her tongue licking the flesh and her lips closing over the middle finger of one hand.

"I don't think anyone's ever made love to my hands before," Bond whispered. "Thank you, Ebbie."

Breaking the spell, she looked up at him, her eyes wide with innocence. "Hope your tetanus shots are up-to-date," she murmured—and even that sounded stimulating.

After a couple of miles they turned off, abruptly and with no warning, onto another narrow road that led into a forest of some size. The night had closed in fully now, and the trees on either side lost their color in the headlights. Every few hundred yards, timber was stacked neatly on wooden bunkers by the roadside, and half a mile on they turned again, straight onto a track leading into the trees, ignoring a notice that plainly said, NO MOTOR VEHICLES. PEDESTRIANS ONLY.

"You see that, Maxim?" Bond asked with no trace of criticism.

"We're in Ireland, James. Notices like that don't mean what they say. Anyway, I figured out it would be best to hide a car where no cars drive."

"And no birds sing," Bond muttered reflectively. "The GRU teach you that as well?"

"I suppose so. But I'm pretty certain that, for all their clever ways, Chernov's lads'll be out looking single-mindedly for this BMW, not for the pretty lady over here." He flung the car sideways on, almost brushing against the thick trunks of two fir trees, then another, and a third pair before the headlights revealed a small clearing containing what seemed to be a mound of branches.

"Okay, everybody out. Uncover that car, then use the stuff to hide this one. I must look to my maps."

It took less than ten minutes, and when it was done, a dusty but patently new black Rover Vitesse stood in the clearing, while the pile of branches covered the BMW.

Smolin, ever cautious, paced out a number of steps from the nearside front wheel of the Rover, dug in the moss and bracken, and retrieved a small package containing two sets of keys. Bond, standing over him, spoke in a low voice. "Get the girls into the car, Maxim. We need to talk."

Smolin nodded, carefully ushering Heather into the front and

Ebbie to the back. Then he walked over to Bond, a short distance from the Rover, where the girls could not hear them.

"First"—Bond moved very close to him—"when you were in Berlin, did you have a sidekick called Mischa? Because if you didn't, Maxim, you should look to your lady."

Smolin nodded. "Yes, Mischa was around, but he was KGB plant on me. You should know, James, that nothing can ever be straightforward between KGB and GRU. We are up to our ears in suspicion concerning one another. You ask about Mischa because he's one of Chernov's killing party. He was in London, yes?"

Bond nodded. "Okay. Now, further plans. I just about trust you, Maxim, but I need to know what we're up to. You mentioned throwing them off the scent and getting to West Cork."

Smolin smiled in the gloom. "You have special contacts, James. I also. I run two people in Skibbereen. They have a light aircraft. By night we can fly very low—escape all detection and land quietly, and without anyone knowing, in a field—glorious Devon. I have done it several times."

It was feasible, Bond knew it. Hadn't Special Branch and "Five" suspected illegal entry by light aircraft for some years now? Nobody could ever pinpoint places, yet they knew it was done by the lads from the North and, they thought, other interlopers.

"Right." Bond knew what he needed from this situation. "Chernov wants us, the girls, and, presumably, Jungle together with his lady friend, Dietrich. If we drive to Skibbereen now we won't make it until the very small hours. That'll mean holing up close to our departure point, not the best thing. I agree that—given the KGB's form—they'll be looking for four people in a BMW. So, using the Rover we've partially thrown them."

"Completely thrown them." Smolin was firm.

"You, of all people, Maxim, should know better than that. The girls—and, I suspect, ourselves—need some rest. There are also things I have to do. The telephones at the castle, you follow?"

He saw Smolin's head move.

"Why don't we drive partway tonight"—he peered at his watch—"it's eight-thirty now. We could be in Kilkenny by ten o'clock. Stay overnight, then continue the journey tomorrow—late afternoon. You can get hold of your people by telephone, and they're contained, I presume?"

"How contained?"

"From KGB doubling."

"KGB cannot know of them. They're personal. Mine alone. This will be the first time I've taken anyone in with me, okay?"

"Okay. They won't be looking for a black Rover, but they will be on the trail of four people. Once we're on the road we could telephone ahead—"

"If we find an unvandalized telephone, yes."

"Book in at two different hotels. You can drop Ebbie and myself off near one, and take the car to whichever watering hole you choose. We can make contact and arrange a meeting for the morning."

He saw Smolin nod like a wise owl. "That seems good. Also, I have two cases in the boot—sorry we did not have time to pick up yours, James. There's nothing that will fit you, but it will make the right impression, yes? The girls can shop in Kilkenny tomorrow, as long as they're careful. Ebbie has some stuff in that big shoulder bag, so she may be okay for a day or two."

"What kind of papers you carrying, Maxim?"

"British passport. International driver's license. Credit cards."

"Are they good?"

"The best forgeries ever to come out of Knamensky Street. My name is Palmerston. Henry J. Temple Palmerston. You like it?"

"Oh yes." Bond's voice was heavy with sarcasm. "You just pray that no passport control officer is a student of nineteenth-century British politics."

"Correct." He could feel Smolin's broad smile in the dark. "They are mainly people whose interests lie elsewhere—airplane modeling, railway trains, the novels of Dick Francis and Wilbur Smith. Very few of them graduate to Margaret Drabble or Kingsley Amis. We ran a thorough check—through the mail. Simple questions, but effective. Eighty-five percent filled in our little forms. We said it was for market research and offered a prize of five thousand pounds sterling. A man working at Heathrow won the lucky draw, and all others got small consolation prizes—Walkmans, pens, diaries. You know the kind of thing."

Bond sighed. At least the Soviets were sometimes thorough. "Well, Mr. Palmerston, don't you think we should get going?"

"If you say so—Mr. Boldman."

* * *

They arranged that Smolin and Heather should not stay in Kilkenny, but at The Clonmel Arms Hotel—thirty minutes away. "It will be best to be completely separated," was Smolin's judgment. They had, to everyone's surprise, come across an unvandalized white and green booth marked TELEFON only fifteen minutes after leaving the dense wood.

Bond and Ebbie were booked into The Newpark, near to the famous castle, in Kilkenny. "You can have the bed," he told her. "I'll sit up and keep watch."

"Let's wait and see." Ebbie's hand slid into his again. "I do know you're a gentleman, James. But perhaps I don't want a gentleman."

"And I have certain professional duties," he replied calmly.

Ebbie grinned. "Duties, I might like. I'm sure you do everything like a professional."

Arrangements were made between the two men concerning contact by telephone, simple code phrases and the like. They arrived in Kilkenny just before ten and Smolin passed The Newpark, stopping a hundred yards or so further on. He got out, unlocked the boot, and hauled out a black travel bag. "A few clothes of mine, and there is a razor and toothbrush." He smiled. Ebbie had a large shoulder bag that she had carted with her from The Ashford Castle Hotel to what she imagined was to be sanctuary at The Three Sisters Castle. "It's got warpaint, another shirt, and some jeans in it," she explained, somewhat archly, opening her eyes widely and adding that it also contained *Unterkleidung,* as though this was a very daring admission. "Very small." She giggled, holding her hands close together with forefingers extended, about two inches apart.

As Mr. and Mrs. Boldman, they were greeted with great friendliness at the hotel, told that the restaurant was closed, but the chef could "knock you up anything you might fancy, so."

Bond suddenly realized he was ravenous, while Ebbie also reacted to the idea of food rather in the manner of someone who is starving but wishes to be polite—"Well, a little something," she said. "Steak, perhaps, with potatoes and a green salad. Possibly some mousse, or profiteroles to follow—oh, and coffee, bread, maybe some wine."

"Anything at all, madam." The receptionist smiled. "Anything, so long as it's Escalope Holstein, French fries, green salad, and fruit salad."

"That'll do nicely," Ebbie said quickly. Bond nodded agreement, also choosing a white Burgundy of vague vintage and dubious nomenclature.

Ebbie also asked for, and got, some bandages and disinfectant—"We had a small trouble with the car, and my husband burned his hands." All in all, Bond decided, Ms. Ebbie Heritage was a treasure.

Treasure or not, he could not wait to get to the telephone once they were shown to their room: pleasant, if somewhat lacking in originality—no surprise, for the hotel's foyer was decorated adobe style, with a distinct Spanish influence.

"I must do those hands," Ebbie pleaded, "and, James, they'll be here with the food any minute."

Bond quietened her, reached up to the top button of his Oscar Jacobson jacket, and, using a thumbnail, prised off a thin strip of gray plastic—around an inch in length and a quarter of an inch thick.

He dialed for an outside line, and then the number of Three Sisters Castle, committed to memory when Smolin had given it to him.

As he heard the automatic exchange click through, a second before the ringing tone, Bond put the piece of plastic to the mouthpiece and pressed hard. For two seconds it emitted a tiny, piercing beep not unlike the sound of a muted harmonica. The earpiece of the phone gave a small beep back, meaning that the black grains of plastic wheat he had planted in the castle telephones reacted to the tone and grew ears. With the tiny harmonica bugs coming to life it was now possible for him to listen in, not just to telephone conversations, but to any speech or noise within thirty feet of each bug. He could have been far away—in Australia or South Africa—and the same thing would happen. These powerful tiny transmitters, if not detected, can be activated from thousands of miles away, making the telephone in which one has been implanted into a live, ever-ready microphone. Theoretically, you could obtain infinite intelligence. But now, even though the tone had reassured him that the transmitters were active, Bond could hear nothing at the other end but odd noises, far away, probably from one of the many other rooms that contained no phone.

Softly, Bond put down the receiver, glancing at his watch, knowing he must go on activating the bugs again and again until he got a result.

Ebbie had been hovering, looking perplexed, her hands clasping bandages and the disinfectant. "James, will you let me do your hands? Please."

Bond nodded, his face grave as he debated whether he should telephone Smolin now. Somebody would certainly be in the castle, if only to tend the injured Ingrid. But the fact that he could pick up nothing else meant one thing only—Chernov had every available man, including himself, scouring the countryside for them.

"Yes, okay, Ebbie. Do your worst." He sighed.

She in fact did her best. Soothing, soft, gentle, and very disconcerting. In the middle of her ministrations the food arrived, and they set to eating once she had finished.

"I shall bathe after this." She spoke with her mouth half full. "I'm sorry, but I was so hungry."

"That's all right, Ebbie. You've been very kind."

She looked across the little table that had been brought in for them. Her head was bowed, but she lifted her eyes, half-hooded, then opening wide. "I want to show you every kindness, James. You were wonderful back at that awful castle."

"I don't need payment, my dear."

"Oh, I liked you all those years ago—on the submarine. You've bugged the phones at the castle, yes?"

"You're very astute, Ebbie."

"Astute? What's astute? Is it sexy? I find you very . . ."

"It means you're very shrewd—clever at spotting things."

"But it was obvious, what you were doing just now—we were taught about it when we prepared for . . . for *Cream Cake*—that is such a stupid name. But you have listening devices in the castle, yes?"

"Of course I have."

"Then you're a very clever little bugger, James, to be able to listen to things in the castle from this telephone."

"I think you have the wrong word, Ebbie, but no matter." He smiled, and her face lit up.

"James, dear man, I hope you don't have to listen to them all night?"

"It depends. At the moment there's nobody there."

"I hope you don't. Oh, I do hope you don't."

"We shall see. I must keep trying."

They finished eating and Ebbie disappeared into the bathroom, while Bond wheeled the debris-cluttered room service table into the corridor. He was about to dial the castle again when Ebbie came out of the bathroom, dressed only in what she would have called her *Unterkleidung,* and very fetching she looked as she grinned unselfconsciously, gathered up her bag, and disappeared again.

He tried the castle once more, and this time caught a short conversation—a man talking in Russian to the obviously weak Ingrid. It amounted to nothing, and he waited for fifteen minutes, but there was no other sound.

At last, he put down the telephone and lay back on the bed, feeling tired and now very aware of the pain in both arm and hands.

Closing his eyes, he wondered what the next move would be. Like it or not, he would have to reactivate the bugs at regular intervals, and his experience told him that within a few hours they should all be on the move if there was no further news from the sound-stealing devices. If they got back to England in one piece he could park the girls in one of his *own* safe houses—which he kept well hidden from the Service—and report to M with Smolin. At least two-thirds of the mission would have been accomplished.

At the moment he started composing his apologia to M, Ebbie returned to the bedroom, hair glistening and her body only partially covered by an oyster satin negligé.

"The bathroom's free now, James." She allowed the negligé to slip from her shoulders. "Unless you have something better to do."

Bond looked at the young fresh body, which held for him that same urgent attraction of innocence he had felt earlier. Slowly, he moved from the bed and into her arms. Their first kiss lasted about a minute, though it seemed like a lifetime, or a departure from one kind of life to another. His hands slid down to the neat silky little buttocks, and he felt his mind shrinking to one great need as Ebbie returned his kiss, her tongue darting and reaching hard into his mouth.

He pulled away, looked into the wide-open blue eyes. "With these bandages on, it might be difficult for me to take a bath," he said, his throat dry. "I wonder if you could . . ."

"Why don't we have a bath together?" Ebbie's firm hand closed around his wrist and she led him, unprotesting, into the bathroom.

She drew the bath and Bond allowed her to undress him. When he was lying in the warm water she stood over him, naked, to soap his body—her hands and fingers exploring him as she did so. When he was washed clean she stepped into the narrow tub, sliding onto her side and lifting one leg over his so that he took her beneath the warm water.

When it was over, Ebbie dried him with a rough towel, and redressed his hands. This time, he led her back to the bedroom. With all her innocent looks, she was like a woman who had just discovered the secret joys of life for the first time. It was soon obvious, however, that she was far from innocent, for she showed not only great stamina, but also imagination and invention. Through that night they made love three more times, once with a stormy wildness, then with passion—Ebbie above him, reciting a sensuous poem to the rhythm of her own body.

Between the lovemaking, when she left him to visit the bathroom, or lay back happy and panting on the bed—Bond tried the castle several times. Still with no result. In the end he gave up, drifting to sleep with Ebbie twined around him.

He woke with a start, realizing that, while it was still dark, dawn was not far away. Gently, Bond disentangled himself from the smoothness of Ebbie's body and looked at his watch. Five-thirty in the morning.

Sliding from the bed, he quietly padded to the bathroom. His hands felt better, though the arm mangled by Fafie still throbbed. Washing was easier than he expected, and by six o'clock, with dim light starting to show outside, Bond was dressed and equipped with the ASP, baton, and other hidden items.

Ebbie still lay supine in a deep sleep, her fair hair ragged on the pillow, her face tranquil with content. She might need all the rest she could get that day, so Bond pocketed the room key and went silently into the corridor.

The room service table had gone, and the whole hotel seemed wrapped in silence. As he made his way down to the main lobby the calm was broken by occasional sounds of movement from below, as the kitchen staff prepared breakfast.

Nobody appeared to be on duty at Reception, so he quickly made his way to the coin-operated telephone, dragging a pile of Irish change from his pocket.

A decidedly sleepy and disgruntled voice answered from The Clonmel Arms Hotel, and he had to repeat his request to be put through to "Mr. and Mrs. Palmerston."

There was an unduly long wait for any response and, finally, the operator came back on the line. "I'm sorry, sir, but they've checked out."

"When?" Alarm bells sounded in his head.

"I've just come on duty myself, sir. But some friends of theirs arrived unexpectedly, so I'm told. Mr. and Mrs. Palmerston left around a half hour ago."

Bond's nerve ends shrieked as he quickly thanked the operator and hung up. What friends? His Service, alerted from afar, or Blackfriar? The queries in Bond's mind were rhetorical, for he already knew the answer—Blackfriar. General Chernov had caught up with Smolin, and, if that had occurred, it would not be long before they reached Ebbie and himself. He might have half an hour or ten minutes, yet in that time it was essential he take some action to put himself back in control of the situation.

Within seconds he was dialing a Dublin number that rang and rang before the voice answered sharply, "Murray."

"Jacko B. There're problems. I have to make this official."

"Where are you?" Norman Murray sounded on edge.

"Kilkenny. Newpark Hotel. I think your friend—and mine—Basilisk's been lifted, with the girl you saw at the airport. The rumor about the other one, who I'd bet you already know as Blackfriar, is true. There's a place called Three Sisters Castle . . ."

"We know all about Three Sisters. No jurisdiction. It's Embassy property. Bit of a fracas there, Jacko, was that you, now?"

"Some, but I'm here with the girl from The Ashford Castle Hotel, got me?"

"Right. The girl with the romantic name."

"We're also due to be lifted. If you can—"

But Murray was way ahead of him—"I know all about Basilisk,

and it's a lash-up. I'll do what I can, Jacko. Watch your back. Official now, you say?"

"Very official, and *very* dangerous."

"I doubt it, but get out and head for Dublin. We don't have orders to lift *you.*"

"What d'you mean?"

"We were lifting Basilisk, and it's gone sour. Now, will you get going."

"No transport."

"Well, you'll have to steal something, Jacko. I hear you're good at that kind of thing." Murray gave a quick laugh and closed the line, leaving Bond looking at the dead telephone in his hand.

Ebbie, he thought. Get her out, even if we have to hide in the hedgerows. Yet, as he turned, another thought struck him. One more try for the harmonicas in the castle. He peeled the activator from its button, dialed the number, and bleeped the tiny plastic gizmo into the telephone. Suddenly the earpiece was filled with a confusion of noise—several people talking in different parts of the castle. What he could hear made him tighten his grip on the phone.

"They've lost the traitor Smolin, and his girl—shit . . . ." Spoken in Russian.

A laugh, undoubtedly the sinister Ingrid. "The General's going to be very happy."

Then, clear, probably from the control room.

"Yes, message received and understood," this in German. "Hans," the voice shouted loudly, and an answer came from far away, and then close. "Hans, the team in Rome have tracked them down at last—Dietrich and the man Belzinger. Took a flight out last night. Can you get the Chief?"

"He's trying to locate the other pair—radio silence."

"Break it. Dietrich and Belzinger are headed for Hong Kong."

"Christ, I don't believe it."

"Neither will the General, but get him. Get him quickly."

Hong Kong, Bond thought. Jungle and his lady Captain were really distancing themselves from Europe. The sooner he got Ebbie out, the better it would be for all of them. He turned and took the stairs at a run, reaching their room, unlocking the door, and heading straight for the bed.

"Ebbie! Ebbie, wake up . . . !" His voice trailed off, for the bedclothes were pulled back and Ebbie was gone.

The alarm bells sounded again, but before he could react to the prickle of danger a voice whispered close to his ear. "Don't even think about going for the gun, Mr. Bond. You are of little use to me and I'd blow you away, now, in this room, if I had to. Hands on your head and turn around slowly."

He had heard the voice once before, on tape, so knew as he turned that he would be gazing into a face seldom seen in the West—the clean-cut, almost French-looking features of General Konstantin Nikolaevich Chernov, Chief Investigating Officer of Department 8 of Directorate S, KGB: Blackfriar himself.

"A strange meeting, Mr. Bond, eh? After following each other in office paper chases all this time." Chernov had a smile on his face and a large automatic pistol in his hand, while behind him three big men crowded in, like hounds gathered for the kill.

13

BLACKFRIAR

"WELL"—BOND LOOKED straight into Chernov's green-flecked eyes—"you're out of your usual territory, Comrade General. It must be odd to be away from your comfortable office in the Square, or have they moved Department Eight out to that modern monstrosity off the ring road—the so-called Scientific Research Center?"

A wisp of a smile appeared on Chernov's lips. Anyone, Bond thought, could have taken him for an influential, wealthy businessman: the powerful body under a beautifully cut gray suit; the tanned, slim, and undeniably good-looking features; the personal magnetism of the man combined with his height—he was well over six feet tall—to make him a particularly commanding personality. It was easy to see how this man had become the Chief Investigating Officer of what had at one time been SMERSH.

"You read the right books, Comrade Bond. If I may say so, the right kind of fiction." He lowered the pistol, a heavy Stetchkin, turning his head in a slightly diffident manner to give a crisp instruction to one of the men behind him. "I'm sorry." He smiled again, as though he genuinely liked Bond. "I'm sorry, but your reputation goes ahead of you. I've asked my people to remove any obvious toys you might be carrying." His free hand went up to brush one of the graying, thick wings of hair that Headquarters always pointed to as one of his principal identification marks— *the hair is thick, graying at the temples, unusually long for members of the Russian Service, but always well groomed, and distinguished by the wings that almost cover his ears. It is swept straight back, with no parting.* Bond knew most of the senior KGB and GRU officers' profiles by heart.

One of Chernov's men, obeying the order, caught hold of Bond's shoulders, turning him around roughly and ordering him—in cumbersome English—to place his palms on the bedroom wall.

Chernov snapped another command, then, "I'm sorry, Mr. Bond, he was instructed to handle you more gently." His accent could easily have been acquired at one of the older British universities, the whole manner near to being deferential—the voice, usually quiet and calm: a trait that made him even more sinister.

The man conducting the body search was all too thorough— first the ASP and Concealable Security Baton; then the more devious tricks of the trade: pen, wallet, and the precious belt that contained so many secrets. He felt the lining of Bond's clothes and then his shoes, one at a time, each removed, examined, and returned. Within a matter of minutes Bond was left only with the tiny harmonica beeper still attached to the top button of his jacket. Everything else of any value to him had been taken.

"It's interesting, isn't it?" Chernov said in his near-languorous tones. "Interesting how our masters are always dreaming up new little pieces of technology for us?"

"With respect, you're one of the masters." Bond willed himself to show equal calmness, for Chernov would be like an animal who could scent fear at fifty paces.

"So I am." He laughed, low-pitched.

"One to be admired, so we are told."

"Really." He did not sound flattered.

"Isn't it true that you are practically the only senior officer to survive the 1971 purge, after Lyalin's defection?"

Chernov shrugged. "Who knows about Lyalin? Some say that was a put-up job to get rid of us altogether."

"But you *did* survive, and helped to build the Phoenix out of the ashes of your department. You're to be admired." This was not mere flattery on Bond's part, for a man with Chernov's track record would never fall for flattery.

"Thank you, Mr. Bond. The feeling is mutual. You have also been resurrected against much criticism, I gather." He sighed. "What a difficult thing our job is. You realize what must be done?"

"The price on my head?"

"There's no price—not this time." He chuckled. "However, you *are* on a list. Therefore, I would be failing in my duty if I did not see that your execution was carried out. Preferably at the Lubyanka, following some question-and-answer sessions." He shrugged again. "But I suppose that could prove difficult. To dispose of you will not be a problem; yet my career demands that justice must be seen to be done. Your death has to be public rather than in the privacy of the Lubyanka cellars."

Bond nodded, knowing the longer he kept the man talking, here in the hotel, the more chance Murray would have to be the US Fifth Cavalry and ride in, at the eleventh hour, to his rescue. Official or not, Murray would certainly do all that was possible—did he not owe Bond his own life?

"I'm glad you are philosophical about it, Mr. Bond. You say you admire me, and it would be unjust if I did not admit to holding you, your ingenuity, speed, and resourcefulness, in some awe. As the American criminal fraternity would say, you must understand that there will be nothing personal about your death. It's just business."

"Of course." Bond hesitated for a moment. "Might I ask what has happened to the lady?"

"Don't worry about the lady." He smiled, inclining his head to one side in a condescending gesture. "Eventually she must also pay a penalty—together with the turncoat Smolin and his whore—not to mention our other traitor Fräulein Captain Dietrich, and *her* gigolo, Belzinger—or Baisley, as he now likes to be called. My duty is to see justice done to them. You are a most delightful bonus." He looked around him, at his lieutenants. "We should be on our way. There is much to be done."

"I'm ready when you are." Bond realized that he must have sounded a shade too confident, and saw his error in the worm that stirred deep in Kolya Chernov's eyes.

For a second the General looked at him suspiciously, then turned on his heel, flicking his hand in a gesture that was itself an order for his people to follow with Bond.

They took him along the corridor, away from the main exit, and down two flights of stairs that were meant for emergencies only. Behind the hotel stood two cars—a Renault of some kind, and a sleek black, official-looking Jaguar with customized darkened windows.

Chernov walked straight toward the latter vehicle, and Bond's captors pushed him in the same direction. The Renault was obviously either the trail or scout car. Bond was to travel in the comparative luxury of Chernov's Jaguar. A man detached himself from the driving seat and strolled over to open the rear door. He wore a black turtleneck and his head was bandaged. Even from a distance, Bond recognized Mischa, the killer who had made the abortive attempt on Heather's life in London. The bandages made him look more piratical than ever, and he stared at Bond as a jackal might view his cornered victim.

General Chernov ducked his head and climbed into the rear of the Jaguar, while the others pushed Bond around to the far side. There was no sign of Ebbie.

Another man climbed from the offside door, standing to one side as Bond was bundled in next to Chernov.

Chernov sighed. "The ride will not be that comfortable; it's a shade cramped with three people in the back."

The guard climbed in after Bond so that he was sandwiched between him and Blackfriar. Mischa returned to the driving seat, while one of the other men took the front passenger seat: riding shotgun.

Being a realist, Bond did not think about what might happen if Murray missed his cue.

Mischa started the engine, and the Renault pulled away in front of them—a forward scout, Bond thought. It was exactly how he would have played it.

Within minutes it became obvious that they were taking the

road to Dublin. In a matter of hours they would be back at Three Sisters Castle.

Mischa drove with almost exaggerated care, keeping around a steady thirty yards behind the Renault. He did not look back at Bond, though you could feel the malevolence coming from him like static. The hood next to Bond kept one hand inside his jacket and occasionally Bond could glimpse the butt of a pistol grasped firmly in his paw. The General dozed, but the fellow riding shotgun remained alert, occasionally turning round, or watching the rear from the vanity mirror set in the sun visor, which he had pulled down.

Time dragged, and Bond tired of the views of lush greenery, and the untidy towns and villages through which they passed. His mind ranged through every possibility. There was no way he could escape from the car in one piece—that was sure: certain death, even on the main roads of the Republic of Ireland. Murray, he kept thinking, if only Murray would turn up there might be a way. For the present the ball was out of his court, and he had lost control over the situation.

But they covered the miles without incident, finally passing through the narrow streets of Arklow.

About three miles on, the Renault turned off to the left, up a very narrow road bordered by high trees and hedges, and with barely space for two cars to pass comfortably. Bond had a sense of déjà vu, knowing that this was the road leading to the main castle entrance.

Chernov—Blackfriar—stretched and woke, telling Mischa he had done well, sharing a joke with him in Russian. Ahead, the Renault turned a sharp bend, and as the Jaguar followed, Mischa let out an obscenity. On the other side of the bend, the Renault had been forced to pull up sharply. There were two Garda cars angled across the road, and as Mischa applied the brakes, Bond glanced behind to see an unmarked saloon slewing to their rear.

"Stay calm. No weapons!" Chernov ordered, his voice cracking like a whip. "No shooting. Understand!"

Half a dozen uniformed Gardi were surrounding the Renault, and another four now approached the Jaguar.

With a slow insolence, Mischa activated the window, and a uniformed officer bent to speak with him.

"Gentlemen, I'm afraid this road is closed to all but the diplomatic traffic. You'll have to get the car turned around."

"What appears to be the trouble, officer?" Chernov leaned forward, and Bond noticed that both he and his guard, in the rear, had placed themselves in a vain attempt to hide their passenger's face.

"It's diplomatic trouble, sir. Nothing serious. There were some complaints last night, so we're having to keep the road well shut down for a while."

"What kind of diplomatic trouble? I carry a diplomatic passport, as do my fellow passengers. We're heading for the Russian Embassy property at Three Sisters Castle."

"Ah, well, that makes a difference, then." The man took a step back. Already, Bond could see the cars ahead of them had been moved slightly, to let the Renault through. He was also aware of men in civilian clothes close to the car. One of them now leaned forward to the rear window that Mischa had been forced to open. Bond did not recognize him, but he had the roving, relaxed eyes of an SB man.

"There were reports of shooting around here last night. You'll understand that people get a bit nervous of that kind of thing. So I'll have to see your credentials, sir, if you'd care to—"

"Certainly." Chernov fumbled in his coat and pulled out a wedge of documents, including his passport. The Irish SB man took them, examining the passport carefully.

"Ah!" He looked hard at Chernov. "We knew you had arrived, Mr. Talanov. It's your Foreign Ministry you're from, is it not?"

"I am Inspector of Embassies, yes. Here on the usual annual visit."

"Now, it wasn't you who came last time, though, was it, Mr. Talanov? If I recall correctly, it was a short man, now didn't he have a beard or something? Yes, a beard and glasses. Name of . . . God love me, I'll forget my own name next, so I will."

"Zuyenko," Chernov supplied. "Yuri Fedeevich Zuyenko."

"That's the fella, now. Zuyenko. He's not coming this year then, Mr. Talanov?"

"He is not coming anywhere." Bond detected a slight edge. Chernov, with his experience, would know by now that the garrulous Special Branch man was playing for time. He obviously was already irritated by it. "Yuri Fedeevich died. Suddenly. Last summer."

"Lord rest his soul, poor man. Suddenly, last summer, eh? Did you ever see that filum, sir? It had the lovely Katharine Hepburn in it, and Miss Taylor—you know she has a cottage hereabouts, did you know that?"

"I really think we should be moving. Especially if there has been trouble up the road—at Three Sisters?"

"Bit of something and nothing, I should think, Mr. Talanov. But, before you go . . ."

"Yes?" Stern, his eyes glittering with more than a hint of anger.

"Well, sir. We do have to check *all* diplomatic credentials."

"Nonsense. I vouch for all in the car. All are under my care."

As Chernov spoke, Bond felt the hard metal of the guard's pistol in his side. He could not yell or make a fuss—though, heaven knew, Chernov would not want a killing incident on his hands out in the open.

Another face replaced the one who had been speaking to Chernov. "I'm very sorry, Mr. Talanov, as you call yourself, but we'll be taking that gentleman there." Norman Murray pointed at Bond. "You're keeping bad company, sir. This man's wanted for questioning, and I think you'll agree he's not a Russian citizen, and certainly no diplomat. Am I right, so?"

"Well . . ." Chernov started.

"I think you'd better let him come quietly. Out of the car, you!" Murray reached in across the guard and took hold of Bond's jacket. "You'll come quietly, won't you, me boyo? Then the other gentlemen can get on their way."

"Quits now, Norman?" Bond did not smile at the Special Branch man. He could see that something had gone seriously wrong—had seen it as soon as Norman Murray led the way to his private car, and nodded for Bond to get in, before taking the wheel, leaving the other Gardi and SB officers to see Chernov's car through to the castle.

"More than quits, Jacko. I'll be for the high jump tomorrow, no doubt about that. There's little I can do for you. I doubt if I could walk the length of my shadow for you, and that's a fact. Though there's some very funny business going on, I'll tell you."

"What's happened?" Bond knew Murray well enough to see the man was engulfed in a strange mixture of anger, frustration and concern.

"It's what didn't happen. First, I was wakened before dawn with a message about your man Basilisk. Your friends across the water wanted him pulled in and delivered to them on the quiet, right, and seeing as how we do favors for one another, a couple of cars were dispatched to The Clonmel Arms where, we were reliably informed, Basilisk was staying with your young woman—the one I met at the hotel in Dublin."

"You didn't say anything when I telephoned you."

"Because you said they had been lifted. I thought it'd be a nice surprise for you to know *we* had lifted him."

"You took the girl as well?"

"Didn't get either of them. They weren't there. I had a call five minutes after you got in touch. The people at the hotel were like the proverbial clams—said friends had picked them up. But later they changed their tune. It appears that Basilisk made a large number of telephone calls during the night. Then he and Heather came down around three-thirty in the morning, paid the bill, and left."

"What about the girl I was with?"

"Neither hide nor hair. There really were complaints about shooting and explosions at Three Sisters, and one of our people spotted you being brought out of the hotel. But it's a great chance I've been taking meddling with the fella you were with."

"None of this is good." Bond felt foolish at his understatement.

Murray laughed. "You've yet to hear the really bad news, Jacko. Your Service refused to make you official."

"Damn!"

"You're on leave. No sanction for you to be in the Republic, operational. That's what I got. On no account are you to give this officer assistance. On *no* account, Jacko. That's what they said."

In the event of anything going wrong we will deny you—even to our own police forces. He heard M's voice, gruff as it was when he first said the words as they walked through the park. "Our own police forces" implied everyone else's forces as well. But why? M had held out on the turning of Basilisk—Smolin—though that had, in some measure, been explained. There had been contact between M and Smolin, using the offices of the Irish Special Branch, probably through Murray, who was the most pliable Irish SB man the Service had on tap. Already Bond had run Smolin and two of the girls to earth. Why in heaven's name would the old man go on denying him?

"Norman, you realize who that was in the car?"

"I know exactly who it was, Jacko."

"Then why didn't you—?"

"Hands off. Those were the instructions from *my* people, and I gather they liaised with your own folk across the water. Take in Basilisk and deliver him to us, but don't touch Blackfriar. That's what was asked of us. Well, Basilisk's disappeared, and—"

"And the girls as well. The girls were my real collateral, Norman."

"I don't want to know."

"You're not going to know. Except that I have to find those girls, and someone else."

"Well, you won't be finding them here, not in the Republic. I'm to get you to a secure place we have at the airport and move you on—with a giant boot up the backside."

"What?"

"You heard, Jacko. We don't want you here. So off you go. Even your Embassy doesn't want you here."

Bond's mind reeled with the queries that gnawed at him. "If we come to a phone, will you stop for a minute, Norman?"

"Why should I?"

"Old times' sake."

"We're square."

"Please," he said with gravity. Smolin and Heather had disappeared off the face of the earth. Ebbie had vanished in minutes from their room and her place taken by Chernov. Nasty question marks, and even nastier answers, were starting to form in his head.

Slowly Murray nodded, and a couple of hundred yards along the road they came to a telephone booth and he pulled over. "Quickly as you can, Jacko. And no stupidity, we've enough trouble and duplicity without you going walkabout."

Bond already had the plastic harmonica bleeper unpeeled from the button before he even got to the box, which—praise heaven—was unvandalized. By now, Blackfriar should be back in the castle, and Bond reckoned the General would immediately have the phones checked. In many ways he was surprised it had not already been done, for Chernov was obviously scrupulously careful in the field.

But, no. The bugs grew their ears again, bringing the usual chaotic commixture of voices into the earpiece. He could make out very little, and was about to replace the instrument when he suddenly heard Chernov's voice, very clear, as though he stood over one of the activated phones—"I want every man we have on the streets of Dublin." His tone was calm, but laced with authority and threat. "The man Bond—and Colonel Smolin—*must* be found, and soon. I want them both. Understand? They took him from under my nose. We've also got the added trouble of those two German whores, the damned *Cream Cake* business. What have I done to deserve such idiots?"

"Comrade General, you had no option. It just couldn't be helped." The conversation was in Russian. "Your orders have been obeyed to the letter. Everyone knows who, when, and why. Once we run everyone to earth it will be simple. But the firefight, last night, has caused almost a diplomatic incident."

"Diplomatic nincompoop!" Chernov all but snarled.

Now there was another voice, close to Chernov. "We've just had a message from one of our Hong Kong people, Comrade General."

"Yes?"

"They've tracked Belzinger and the traitor, Dietrich. She's opened up the house on Cheung Chau Island. The GRU house."

"Has she, by Lenin. I always thought Dietrich was an over-confident bitch. We shall have to move fast. Get a message to Hong Kong. Tell them to watch at a distance. I don't want anyone going in there until I arrive."

The line began to break up, and another thought stole into Bond's mind. Now, above all else, it was essential for him to take the initiative. Delving into his pocket, he pulled out the few Irish coins that Chernov's man had left him. Closing the line he reopened it again, dialing the castle number, letting it ring without activating the harmonicas.

When it was picked up, he spoke quickly in Russian, asking for General Chernov by name, saying it was urgent—"Most urgent! A life-and-death matter."

Chernov was on in a few seconds, quietly cursing and talking about secure lines. "We don't need a secure line, Comrade General,"

Bond said in English. "You recognize the voice?"

There was a short pause. Then, cold as Siberia, "I recognize."

"Just wanted to say that I look forward to meeting you again, Blackfriar. Catch me if you can. North, South, West, or *East*." He put the accent on East, goading Chernov. After replacing the instrument, Bond left the box, walking rapidly to the car. Chernov would know Bond was calling him—like a man playing poker. He would also be aware that Bond had an edge, and some knowledge of Chernov's likely movements. M would probably have said the call was an insane move, but M was also playing a devious game.

"For a minute there I thought you were after playing games with me, Jacko. They've been on to me from Dublin. What country do you want?"

"What d'you mean, what country?"

"You're being deported, Jacko. Your own folk in London have said we can send you to the moon as far as they care. Even your old boss—who, as you know, I have dealings with—says you're to take the rest of your leave elsewhere."

"He used those words?"

"Those exact words. 'Tell the renegade to take the rest of his leave elsewhere. Tell him to be missing.' That's what the auld divil said. So where's it to be, Jacko? Spain? Portugal? A couple of weeks on the Canary Islands?"

Bond glanced at him, but Murray showed no sign of any particular knowledge concerning the Canaries—where they had thought Jungle to be before he had stolen the latest news, fresh from the presses at Three Sisters Castle, via the tiny transmitters.

"Let me think for a minute or two, Norman. Wherever I choose, you can get me out really quietly?"

"As the grave. You'll go so still that not even the Dublin airport controllers'll know."

"Give me a minute, then." Already he knew exactly where he wanted to go, but first Bond needed to turn his mind to the whys and wherefores of M's attitude. All controls worked on the basis of need-to-know, so why had M decided—from the outset—that Bond should be told he was on his own? And why, when M must know two of the girls had been found, and then disappeared, was he still denying Bond had any rights in the field? Bond was never supposed to meet Smolin, so he did not need to know about him.

Was this a case of Bond *not* needing to know something else?

He tried to be logical, going through the events and then turning back to elementary trade and fieldcraft. When did a control deliberately withhold some piece of vital information from his agent—even when it might put his man at a grave disadvantage? There was only one set of circumstances that allowed this kind of risk, and already there had been a hint of it in the conversation overheard through the harmonicas. You withhold one kind of information only—that a trusted person might well be a double. You withhold that when you do not know which person could be guilty. Bring them all back, M had told him. *All.* Which meant Ebbie, Heather, or Jungle could be doubles. It had to be the only answer—one of the *Cream Cake* team had been turned, and, knowing the ingenious way M's mind worked, Bond had to include Smolin and Dietrich among the suspects.

They reached the outskirts of Dublin, sashaying their way through the heavy traffic. Why deny him? Simple. Deny a field agent only when the Foreign Office and their political masters would be gravely embarrassed; or deny him when his targets *know* he is getting no assistance. Damn M, Bond thought, he's playing it very long indeed—long and dangerous. Any other officer would have called it a day, gone back into London with his spoils, and laid them, like a gun dog, at M's feet. But not Bond. M was putting all his money on Bond seeing it through until the end; risking his man like a gambler, knowing the stakes had risen dramatically once Blackfriar had shown himself.

"Is there a secure telephone at this place you have at the airport, Norm?"

"I told you not to be calling me Norm." Murray sounded annoyed.

"Well, is there?"

"Safe as you can get." He glanced toward Bond, giving a large smile. "We might even let you use it, if you've decided where you want to go."

"Can you get me into France—as near to Paris as possible?"

Murray laughed, loudly. "You're asking for miracles, so. You know what the DST is like, non-bloody-cooperative."

"You live in a country of miracles, Norman. Me, I'd rather be going back across the water to the good life—you know, click of the willow against a villain's head; the roar of the riot, the smell of tear gas; the scent of new-mown grass snakes."

"Lord love you, but you're turning poetical, Jacko. Thank heaven the blessed St. Patrick rid us of snakes."

"Did he?" Bond returned the grin, knowing he was about to have all his requests fulfilled.

The secure quarters were inside the airport itself, in an area well away from any possible prying eyes. A small walled compound hid any cars or their passengers from possible surveillance teams, and, when they reached the approach road, Bond realized there were more than the usual number of Garda patrols around.

On the face of it, Dublin has one of the most open airports in Europe. In fact, it boasts discreet and powerful security, the bulk of which is hidden from public view.

Inside there was a comfortable waiting room—with armchairs and magazines. Bond thought of dentists. There were also a couple of plainclothes men who showed a certain amount of deference to Norman Murray.

"There's a soundproof booth over there. One of the most secure telephones in Ireland." The Special Branch man pointed. "Use it now while I set everything else up."

"Not until I'm certain you can get me into France, and that I can be in Paris by tonight." Bond looked at him as though calling a bluff.

"It's as good as done, Jacko. You do your telephoning. You'll be on your way with nobody the wiser within the hour."

Bond nodded. Norman Murray was a very convincing officer.

Inside the booth, Bond dialed a London number. The female who answered asked straightaway if they were scrambled, and he said probably, but it was totally secure.

Q'ute had made the offer of help when he last saw her. Bond had known then that it was no idle remark. Q'ute was primed when, just before he left on this unofficial mission, she said, *If you want anything from here—if you* need *anything—just call and I'll bring it to you myself.*

He was calling now, with a longish shopping list and an almost impossible delivery time and place, but Q'ute took it in her stride. When he finished talking she merely said, "It'll be there. Good luck," and closed the line.

Murray was waiting for him, a set of white overalls in his hand.

"You put these on"—it was a command—"and you listen carefully."

Bond did not argue, and Murray continued. "The passage through that door leads to the flying club. You're going on a spot of cross-country with an instructor. The flight plan is filed. Permission has been given for you to overfly Northern France—they do it all the time, here. This time, you'll have a small problem. Engine trouble near Rennes, which is your turning point. You won't be able to make an airfield, so your instructor'll put out a Mayday and you'll glide into a field—not any old field, but a particular one. There'll be a car and someone to take your place in the aircraft for when the gendarmes and customs arrive. It's got to go like clockwork. Do as you're told and it should be okay. But, if you're asked, I had no hand in this—you follow?"

Climbing into his white flying suit, Bond nodded. "Thanks, Norm."

"And don't you be calling me Norm. The aircraft's directly in front of the building, with engine running and cleared to taxi. A nice little Cessna 182. Take four at a pinch. Good luck, Jacko."

Bond took the firm hand and shook it, thanking his old Irish colleague and knowing that, somehow, M was still with him, for a reason best known to the old man himself.

The aircraft was drawn up very close to the buildings, and Bond kept his head well down as he walked quickly toward it, ducking under the wing and climbing up beside the instructor—a young, happy-looking Irishman who grinned at him, shouting that it was about time.

He had hardly strapped himself into the pupil's position to the instructor's left before the Cessna was taxiing away, quite quickly, toward the short runway on the far side of the field.

They waited for a few minutes as an Aer Lingus 737 came in from London, then the instructor opened up the engine and the light plane took to the air almost of her own accord.

They turned out to sea, and began to climb. At two thousand feet the instructor leveled out. "There we are," he shouted, "all set for the fun and games. I'll be turning onto course in five minutes." He moved his head. "You okay back there?"

"Fine."

Bond turned to see Ebbie's face peering over the back of his seat, where she had been hiding. "Hello, James. Pleased to see me?" She planted a kiss on his cheek.

14

DINNER IN PARIS

EVERY FIELD AGENT worth his salt has his own special left-behind sources—a bank account in Berlin; weapons cached in Rome; passport blanks in a strongbox in Madrid. With James Bond it was a safe house in Paris—not really a house, but a small apartment owned by good friends who were willing to leave their home at a moment's notice and with no questions asked.

The apartment was on the fourth floor of one of those old buildings off the Boulevard Saint-Michel—the Boul' Mich—on the Rive Gauche.

They arrived just after six in the evening, following a series of events that had gone almost too smoothly for Bond's peace of mind.

The instructor had piloted the Cessna all the way, and Bond noticed that, once over the French coast, he allowed their flying height to become erratic, to a point where the Paris ATC people were constantly calling him up to remind him of the altitude he was allowed to maintain.

The RV itself had been well picked, a lonely spot west of Rennes over which they circled for fifteen minutes, gradually losing height until their pilot was certain his contact was in place.

He's done this before, Bond thought, wondering when and in what circumstances. Maybe Murray had something on the man—smuggling, or even a tricksy business concerning the lads, as the Provos are always referred to in the Republic.

Whatever the circumstances, it went like clockwork. ATC called up again, anxious about loss of height. The pilot waited for around four minutes as he turned, bleeping his engine, positioning himself for a landing, then began his Mayday call, giving a heading and fix that was around ten miles out, so that the authorities would take longer to reach them.

"When we're down, you've got around five minutes to get going," he shouted at Bond, cutting the engine, then giving it another burst. "A bit of realism for the paying customers," he said, grinning. "Only I hope there aren't any paying customers."

They drifted over some flat farmland with no sign of life for five or six miles, and touched down to taxi toward a clump of trees and a ribbon-straight road lined with poplars.

A battered elderly Volkswagen was parked near the trees, almost out of sight from the road, and a figure, wearing a white coverall identical to the one Bond had been given, detached itself from the trees, arriving at the Cessna just as the engine stopped.

"Go! God be with you." The pilot had already begun to climb out.

Bond helped Ebbie down into the field, stripped off the overalls, and looked at the man who had joined them.

The replacement merely nodded, inclined his head toward the VW, handed over the keys, and said there were maps in the car.

Taking Ebbie by the hand, Bond set off at a trot. The last they saw of the two intrepid flyers was from the car. They had part of the cowling off and were fiddling with the engine. But by this time, the VW was already on the road, heading for Paris.

"Right, young lady." Bond allowed himself time to get used to the car before he spoke. "How, and why, did you turn up again?" It had been impossible to carry on any detailed conversation on the aircraft, and he was now vastly suspicious of Ebbie's dramatic reappearance—even if it did have Norman Murray's blessing.

"That nice policeman thought it would be a good surprise for you, darling James."

"Yes, but what happened to you at The Newpark—in Kilkenny?"

"He didn't tell you?"

"Who?"

"The inspector. Murray."

"Not a word. What happened?"

"At the hotel?"

"Well, I'm not talking about your daring escape from Germany, Ebbie," he replied with a certain crustiness.

"I woke up." As though that explained it all.

"Yes?" he coaxed.

"It was early, very early, and you weren't there, James."

"Go on."

"I was frightened. Got out of bed and went into the passage.

Nobody was there, so I went along to the stairs. You were using the telephone. Down in the lobby. I heard your voice, then other things—people coming in at the other end of the passage. I was very embarrassed."

"Embarrassed!"

"I only had—only little . . ." She indicated what she had been wearing. "And nothing up here at all. So, there was a cupboard— is that right? A closet, where they keep cleaning things."

Bond nodded, and she continued. "I hid. It was dark and not nice. But I hid for a long time. I heard other voices and people walking along the passage. When it was silent I came out again. You had disappeared."

He nodded again. It could just be true, and she was convincing enough.

"I dressed." She gave him a small, uncomfortable look. "Then the policemen came and I told them. They used the radio in their car and told me there were orders. Then they brought me to the airport—James, I have no clothes. Only what I stand up in, and my shoulder bag."

"Did Murray—the inspector—tell you what would be happening?"

"It was a risk for me to stay, he said. For me to remain in Ireland. He said I should go with you, but to give you a surprise. He has a sense of humor. Very funny man, the inspector."

"Yes, exceptionally droll. Hilarious."

Now, as they arrived at his safe apartment, which he had telephoned from a service area on the A-11 Autoroute, Bond still had no way of knowing whether to believe her or not. In these circumstances there was only one course of action he could take— stick with her, keeping her in the dark as much as possible, and behave normally.

There was food in the large fridge, two bottles of a good-vintage Krug, and clean linen on the double bed. No notes or messages. That was always the way—the quick telephone call, giving time and possible duration of the stay, and his friends would be gone by the time Bond arrived. He did not ask where they went, nor did they ever question him: the husband was an old Service hand anyway, but the trade had never been mentioned by either side. In eight years the routine rarely changed. Everything was invariably ready, and this time—in spite of the very short notice—was no exception.

"James, what a beautiful little apartment!" Ebbie appeared genuinely enthusiastic. "This is all yours?"

"When I'm in Paris, and when my friend is away." He had not allowed her to be privy to the telephone call. In the main room he went to the desk, opened the top drawer, and removed the false interior, under which he always kept a float of around a thousand francs.

"Look, there is steak." She was exploring the kitchen. "I cook us a meal, yes?"

"Later." He looked at the stainless-steel Rolex. It would take him the best part of half an hour—given a favorable wind—to get to the RV arranged with Ms. Ann Reilly, better known by her nickname, Q'ute. "Thank heaven there are shops that stay open late in Paris. Ebbie, I want you to make a list of the absolutely necessary clothing you need, and your sizes."

"We are going shopping?" She gave a little jump, like a small child looking forward to a sudden treat.

"*I* am going shopping," he said with great firmness.

"Oh. But, James, there are some things you cannot get. Personal items . . ."

"Just make the list, Ebbie. A lady will get the personal things."

"What lady?" She bridled. Ms. Ebbie Heritage was either one hell of a good actress, or a really jealous woman. Bond would have sworn the latter, for her cheeks had gone scarlet and her eyes were brimming. "You are seeing another woman?" A small stamp of the foot.

"We haven't known each other for long, Ebbie."

"That's got nothing to do with it. You have been with me. We are lovers. Yet, as soon as we come to France . . ."

"Whoa. Hold on. Yes, I am going to see another lady. But I'm seeing her for strictly business reasons."

"*Ja*—Yes, I know. The funny-business reasons."

"Nothing like that. Now, calm down, Ebbie. I want you to listen to me." He realized he was talking to her as he would speak to a child. "This is very important. I must go out. I shall take your list with me. You must *on no account* answer the door or the telephone. You keep the door locked until I return. I shall give a special knock, like so." He demonstrated: three quick raps, pause, another three, pause, then two harder raps. "Got it?"

"Yes." Almost sullen.

"Then show me."

She gave a small shrug and repeated the pattern of knocks.

"Right. Now the telephone. Do not touch it unless it rings three times, goes silent, and then starts ringing again." The codes were as simple as lovers' signals, but they were equally easy to remember.

Bond went through it again, then sat her down at the table with pen and paper while he went round the apartment closing shutters and drawing curtains. By the time he had finished, she held up the completed list.

"How long will you be gone?" she asked in a very small voice.

"With luck, about two hours. Not much longer."

She pulled herself up very straight. "Two hours, and I shall smell this other woman's scent on you if you are making love with her. You be on time, James. Dinner will be here—on this table in two hours exactly. Understand?"

"Yes, ma'am"—he gave her a winning smile—"and don't forget what I told you—the door and the telephone. *You* understand?"

She lifted her face, hands behind her back, raising herself on tiptoe, and turning her cheek toward him.

"Don't I rate a proper kiss?"

"When you come back in time for dinner we'll see."

He nodded, kissed her cheek, and let himself out, walking down the four flights of stone stairs to street level. He always avoided elevators in Paris; in these old apartment blocks, nine times out of ten the lifts were on the blink.

He took a taxi to Les Invalides, then went on foot back to the Quai d'Orsay, crossing the Seine and walking toward the Tuileries Gardens. Only when he was certain he had not picked up a tail did Bond flag down another cab, which he ordered back to the Boul' Mich.

Ann Reilly was sitting in the corner of the small, crowded bistro he had named, only a ten-minute walk from the apartment where Ebbie was, he presumed, cooking dinner.

Bond went straight to the bar, ordered a *fine,* and crossed to Q'ute's table. It did not look as though they were being watched, but he spoke low. "Okay?"

"Everything you ordered. In the briefcase. It's just by your right foot, and it's safe. Nothing will show on the X-ray machines, but

I'd unpack and put the whole lot in your suitcase."

Bond nodded. "How are things back at the buildings?"

"Hectic. There's some kind of flap on. M's been closeted in his office for three days now. He's like a general under siege. The powdervine says he's sleeping there and they're taking crates full of microfilm to him. The main computer's been barred to everyone else and the Chief of Staff's been with him all the time. Moneypenny hasn't been out, either. I think she's lying across his door with a shotgun."

"That figures," he muttered. "Look, love, I've a favor to ask." He passed over Ebbie's list. "There's a supermarket one block down, on the corner. Just do your best, eh?"

"I use my own money?"

"Put it on expenses. When I get back I'll fix."

Q'ute looked at the list and smirked. "What's her taste in—?" she began.

"Sophisticated," Bond cut in quickly.

"I'll do my best, being a plain and simple girl myself."

"That'll be the day. I'll set up a drink for you—oh, and get a cheap case, will you."

"Sophisticated *and* cheap?" Ann Reilly left the bistro, hips moving almost suggestively. Bond made a mental note to buy her dinner once this was over and he was back in London.

She took just under half an hour, coming in with a flurry. "I've got a cab waiting outside. I can catch the last Air France back to LHR if I get a shift on. The case is in the cab. Give you a lift?"

Bond was on his feet, following her to the door and telling her to drop him off a couple of blocks away. She kissed him full on the mouth, whispering good luck when he left, carrying the suitcase and briefcase.

He took forty minutes of back-doubling, riding the Métro, walking, and using another cab, before he got back to the apartment, within ten minutes of Ebbie's childish little deadline, and a lot of Q'ute's lipstick on his handkerchief.

Ebbie sniffed him suspiciously, but could only smell the brandy and so softened slightly—particularly when he gave her the suitcase and told her to open it. Once more there was a chirping of ooh's and ah's as she examined Q'ute's purchases, giving Bond time to check his own clothes—always kept in a particular part of the bedroom wardrobe. A case was no problem, there was always a spare in the flat. He could pack, and repack the items from the briefcase later, at leisure.

"The dinner will be ready in five minutes," Ebbie sang from the kitchen.

"One phone call and I'll be with you." He used the extension in the bedroom, dialing the Cathay Pacific desk at Orly. Yes, they had two first-class seats on their flight to Hong Kong tomorrow. Certainly they would reserve them in the name of Boldman—he gave them his Amex number. "Thank you, Mr. Boldman, that'll be fine. Just pick the tickets up at the desk by ten-fifteen. Have a nice flight."

He peeped inside the briefcase, checking that Q'ute had not forgotten the small rubber stamp with which he could doctor their passports. A sudden horror struck him. "Ebbie!" he called. "Ebbie, you have got a passport with you, yes?"

"Of course. I never travel without it."

He went into the main living room. The table was set for an intimate dinner for two—candles, the lot. "You've been a busy girl, Ebbie."

"Yes, are we going somewhere?"

"Not until the morning. Tonight it's a romantic dinner in Paris."

"Good, but in the morning where are we going?"

"Tomorrow," he said quietly, "we're off to the mystic East."

15

THE MYSTIC EAST

THE CATHAY PACIFIC 747—Flight CX 290, ex Paris/Orly—located the primary ILS, bringing it onto a heading descending over Lantao Island toward the mainland of the New Territories. There the great jet began its almost one-hundred-degree turn to the final-approach ILS taking it right across Kowloon and so down onto

Kai Tak, Hong Kong's International Airport, with its long finger of runway thrusting out into the sea.

As the engines whined, giving the machine the last ounce of extra thrust to carry it over the rooftops, James Bond peered out of the window, craning to see the Island of Hong Kong below, with the Peak shrouded in cloud.

They would be low over Kowloon Tong now, and he thought of its translation—Pool of Nine Dragons—and the story that the late Bruce Lee had consulted a fortune teller before buying an apartment in this exclusive district. The young Kung Fu film star had been told that, should he buy the flat, he would have only bad joss, because his name meant little dragon, and nothing good could come of a little dragon going to live in a pool with nine dragons. Nevertheless, Bruce Lee bought the apartment, and within the year he was dead. Bad joss.

The Boeing touched down, the reverse thrust coming on with a huge roar, flaps fully extended as the speed bled off, and it slowly rolled to a halt at the far end of the runway—buildings towering to the left, and boat-littered water stretching out to the right between the mainland and Hong Kong Island—Fragrant Harbor.

They had arrived in the mystic East, though there was little mystic about it these days.

Within twenty minutes of landing, Bond found himself standing, with Ebbie clutching at his hand, in the somewhat garagelike surroundings of Passport Control, where serious, and scrupulous, Chinese officers scrutinized documents.

From the moment they had left the aircraft, he had done his best to try to spot likely watchers in the airport buildings, but in the sea of faces—European, Chinese, and Eurasian—*everybody* was a potential lookout.

A large Chinese in slacks and a white shirt held a board that announced that he waited for MR. BOLDMAN. Taking Ebbie's arm, Bond steered her forward.

"I'm Mr. Boldman."

"Ah, good. I take you Mandarin Hotel." The Chinese grinned widely, showing what appeared to be several sets of independently working teeth, most of them filled with gold. "Car here. Inside please, never mind." The driver ushered them toward a limousine, opening the door. "My name is David," he supplied.

"Thank you, David," Ebbie said prettily, and they climbed in.

Bond glanced out of the rear as they moved away, to see if he could spot any other car positioning itself behind them. The search was fruitless, for cars left the airport arrivals rank all the time, and most seemed to have just picked up passengers. What he was looking for was some nondescript vehicle with two people up front . . . He caught himself in time—that was what he would have looked for in Europe; in Asia things were different. He recalled an old China hand once saying, "As for watchers, they're most likely to be the people you least expect. East of Suez they watch in plain sight, and they're a bugger to spot."

There were no positive signs as they entered the cross-harbor tunnel, which was jammed with the usual traffic—a whole dictionary, in fact, of transport: cars, trucks, both ancient and modern, and those open 15 cwt. trucks that seem beloved of the Hongkongese, some with tattered awnings, flapping and displaying Chinese characters.

Nowadays you only have to return to Hong Kong after an absence of a few weeks to notice changes. It was a couple of years since Bond had been in the Territory—few refer to it as the Crown Colony since the agreement with China for its return in 1997— so he saw huge differences as they came into Connaught Road, in that part of the island known as Central. Whatever the changes, flying into Asia always causes a subtle culture shock, which often does not make itself felt quickly, but comes as a gradual revelation.

Ahead, to their right, the massive Connaught Centre rose with its hundreds of porthole-like windows, making it look as though it had been designed by an optician; and behind that the almost completed glass triple towers of Exchange Square. The traffic was still as heavy as the heat outside, while the sidewalks and futuristic linking bridges over the main roads were crammed with scurrying people. On the left he caught a glimpse—through Chater Square, with its very English War Memorial—of the new huge and unusual Hongkong and Shanghai Bank Building, erected like a large Lego kit on four great, tall cylinders.

Then they were pulling up in front of the main doors of The Mandarin, which, next to the highrise opulence, appeared quite insignificant. But this feeling vanished, as it always did, when they stepped through the glass doors into the main lobby and a world of crystal chandeliers—one seeming to literally drip from the high ceiling—Italian marble, onyx, and the luster of the past reflected in one wall encrusted with highly detailed golden wood carvings.

Ebbie's eyes, which had been alive and full of wonder all the way from the airport, widened like a child's. "This is really fantastic, James," she began, then took in a sharp breath.

Bond, who had been steering her toward the black-suited Chinese gentlemen at Reception, saw her eyes narrow as she peered across the marbled floor at the concierge's desk.

"What is it?" he asked quietly.

"Swift," she breathed. "Swift's here. I just saw him."

"Where?" They had almost reached the main reception desk.

"Over there." She nodded toward the far end of the lobby. "He was there. Typical of him. He was always a—how do you say it? will-o'-the-wisp?"

Bond nodded—a good name for Swift, he thought, starting to complete the hotel's check-in form. Swift had always been a will-o'-the-wisp; a tortured soul trapped between heaven and hell who led people to destruction with his little lights of burning coal. Swift's expertise in the handling of agents in the field had led many members of opposition intelligence services to destruction.

In a fraction of time all the contradictions and hidden secrets of *Cream Cake* rushed through Bond's mind yet again. M had asked him to take on a job that, because of its delicacy, could not be an official operation. Yet there were things official about it. Already, the conclusion that he was there because someone within the *Cream Cake* setup had been turned had hardened in his mind. But for the two luckless girls who were now dead it could be anyone, and M, like Bond, had no idea of the traitor— Heather? the already doubled Maxim Smolin? Jungle Baisley, whom Bond had yet to meet? Baisley's target, Susanne Dietrich? Even Ebbie. Damn, he now thought, signing the check-in card, why had he been foolish enough to allow Ebbie to come with him to Hong Kong? By all the rules she should have been popped into some form of safety, yet he—James Bond—had not thought twice about her coming with him. Intuition, or merely his growing affection for Ebbie? How stupid could a man be, when led by emotions? But then, he had not been led by anything. Ebbie had, in a manner of speaking, been foisted on him. And now there was Swift. Could Swift be the key? Hardly.

"If you will follow me, Mr. Boldman, Mrs. Boldman."

Bond realized that the under manager at Reception was repeating his courteous words.

"Sorry. Of course." He snapped out of the confusion of thoughts, and, taking Ebbie's arm, followed the man, who was armed with papers and a key.

They went toward the far end of the lobby past the concierge's desk, turning left to the banks of elevators. "Tell me if you spot him again," Bond whispered, and Ebbie nodded.

Around them the hotel was functioning with a disciplined ease and efficiency—gold-jacketed page boys moved swiftly, with fixed smiles; one of them, wearing a form of skullcap that set him apart from the rest, marched through the lobby bearing a bell-hung tinkling board displaying the fact that he was looking for a Mrs. David Davies. An American couple argued softly near the elevators—"Whaddya want, then? We're in a hotel—you want we should move to a different hotel?"

The elevator lifted Bond and Ebbie imperceptibly to the twenty-first floor, to a light and airy room, the balcony of which looked out upon the thousand eyes of the Connaught Centre building and a very large slice of the harbor over which ferries, motorized junks, and sampans plied their way.

The under manager hovered, making certain the room was to their liking, until the room boy arrived with the luggage, asking if he could unpack for them—an offer they both declined.

"You're sure it was Swift?" Bond stood close to Ebbie once they were alone.

"Certain. God, I'm tired, but it *was* Swift." She opened the balcony windows, letting in the sound of Hong Kong's traffic, deafeningly loud even from the twenty-first floor.

Bond joined her on the balcony, feeling the blast of heat as he passed through the doorway. Below, the traffic streamed unendingly; the water of the harbor twinkled in the morning haze; the white wakes of churning propellers, now joined by the long, creamy trail of a hydrofoil sweeping west, and the muddy bow waves of three towed barges, low in the water, weighed down by piles of containers—chugging toward one of the world's largest container ports.

To the left, across the road, everything was dwarfed by the high-rise Connaught Centre and the even larger Exchange Square building—the complex connected to The Mandarin side of the street by an elegant tubular pedestrian overpass. In the foreground, and to the right, the most fabled view in the world—Kowloon, Hong Kong, and the water between—the Fragrant Harbor—dazzled the eye. A pair of helicopters swept down, low, inland—one hovering while the other chopped in to land at Fenwick Pier, below Bond and Ebbie and to their right. The entire scene—buildings, ships, vehicles, helicopters—had a futuristic look about it, almost like a huge set for a twenty-first-century movie. As he gazed, Bond suddenly realized that the elusive familiarity he always felt in Hong Kong came from images of the distant past, when he saw Fritz Lang's *Metropolis*—that classic film made, incredibly, in the 1920s.

"Come on"—he touched Ebbie's arm—"we've got work to do." The air smelled moist, with traces of salt, spices, dust, fish, pork, and money.

"We have to go out?"—excited at the prospect.

"Just wear something casual." Bond smiled, but she did not understand he was joking, and rushed to her suitcase. "Jeans and a T-shirt'll be great," he quickly added, standing by the bedside telephone, delving into that memory bank of telephone numbers that he carried constantly in his head. Even in Asia he had contacts outside the normal Service channels, and this one was important.

Picking up the handset, he quickly punched in the numbers. The call was picked up on the fourth ring.

"Weyyy?"

"Mr. Chang?" he asked.

"Who wants him, *heya?*" The voice was deep, almost gruff.

"An old friend. A friend called Predator."

"Ayeeya! Welcome back, old friend. What can I do for you, *heya?*"

"I wish to see you."

"Come, then. I am in my usual place. You come now, *heya?*"

"Fifteen minutes, never mind." Bond smiled. "I shall have very pretty lady with me."

"So, times never change. My people have saying, *When man visits a friend once with woman, he seldom returns alone.*"

"Very profound." Bond smiled again. "Is that an old saying?"

"About thirty second. I just make it up. Come quickly, *heya?*"

* * *

In another part of Hong Kong's Central District, Big Thumb Chang put down the telephone and looked up at the man standing beside him.

"He comes now, just as you predict; he also brings a beautiful woman, though if she is European I fail to see how she can be beautiful. You want I should do something special with him?"

"Just do as he asks," the other said. He had a slow, calculating voice. "I shall be near. It is essential that I speak with him in private."

Big Thumb Chang grinned, nodding like a toy with a spring in its neck.

16

SWIFT

BIG THUMB CHANG was so called because of a deformity to his right hand. The thumb was almost as long, and twice as thick, as his index finger. Enemies said it had grown like this from counting the large sums of paper money that came his way from many, and varied, business deals.

He could usually be found—when there was money involved—at a small ground-floor hovel, consisting of two rooms off one of the many dauntingly steep streets that step upward at a thigh-aching angle from Queen's Road.

Bond took Ebbie by the scenic route. They rode the elevator down to the mezzanine floor, walking through the sumptuous hotel's shopping arcade, over the pedestrian bridge, from which they viewed the gaudily decorated trams cramming Des Voeux Road, and on into the opulent Prince's Building and through another walkway into Gloucester House and The Landmark—one of Central's most splendid shopping malls.

Ebbie—who had already been gasping with amazement at the glittering shops and the near Swiss-like cleanliness of the buildings—gave a hoot of joy as they entered The Landmark on its fourth tier. Indeed, the hundreds of shops and restaurants around the square, the escalator-linked terraces, combined with fountains, decorative plants, and airy space made London's Bond Street look downmarket, and the famed Los Angeles malls seem ordinary by comparison.

Below them, by the big circular fountain, a jazz combo was playing "Do You Know What It Means to Miss New Orleans?"

They went down to the ground floor, pausing only for Bond to make a quick purchase—a holdall with a long shoulder strap—before taking the exit to Pedder Street, and so into the noisy, crowded sidewalks of Queen's Road.

It took all of fifteen minutes to reach Big Thumb Chang's door, which was open; Chang himself was seated behind a table within the small dark room, which smelled of sweat and old cooking odors, relieved only marginally by the joss sticks burning before a small shrine to a household god in the far corner.

"Ah, old friend." The fat little Chinese gave a grin that displayed discolored teeth. "Many years since your shadow crossed my miserable door. Please enter my slum of a home."

Bond saw Ebbie wrinkle her nose with disgust.

"You forget, most honorable Chang, that I know your real home is as rich as any Emperor's palace." Bond's eyebrows lifted. "So it is I who am humbled by coming to your office."

Chang waved a hand toward two hard and not very clean chairs. "Welcome, beautiful lady"—he grinned at Ebbie—"welcome to both of you. Sit. Can I offer you tea?"

"You are most kind. We do not deserve such lordly treatment." Bond observed the complex rules of negotiation as Chang clapped his hands and a thin, young girl in black pajamas materialized from the street behind them. Chang jabbered instructions to her, and she bowed and left.

"My second daughter by third wife," Chang explained. "She is a lazy, good-for-nothing girl, but out of my duty and good nature I allow her to do small jobs for me. Life is difficult. Never mind."

"We have come to do business," Bond began.

"Everyone wishes to do business." Chang gave him a weary look. "But seldom is this profitable, with so many to support, and gossiping wives and children always wanting more than I can give."

"Well, we need your help." Bond looked equally grave. "It must indeed be hard to live as you do, honorable Chang."

Big Thumb Chang gave a protracted sigh, and the girl reappeared with a tray bearing bowls and a teapot, placing it in front of Chang, receiving his directions to pour the tea, which she did, making heavy weather of it, as though she also was bowed down with care and fatigue.

"Your kindness surpasses our miserable needs." Bond smiled— tapping twice on the table with his fingers to signify thanks to the girl—before sipping the bitter tea: hoping that Ebbie would drink it without comment or any facial expression of dislike.

"It is good to see you again, Mr. Bond. How can I be of service to you and this wondrous lady?"

Bond was surprised that Chang had come to the point so quickly. It was not unusual to spend an hour or more in pleasantries before getting down to business. The fast response put him on his guard.

"It is probably impossible," he said slowly. "But you have done such favors for me in the past."

"So?"

"I am in need of two revolvers and ammunition."

"*Ayeeyah!* You wish to see me imprisoned? Taken away in chains and kept for the bureaucrats of Beijing who will come in 1997 anyway, never mind?" Already, in Hong Kong they were using the true Chinese name for Peking—Beijing—as the year approached for power to be transferred back to the People's Republic. It was ironic that the street hawkers were now selling green caps, emblazoned with the red star, among their usual tourist junk.

"Respectfully," Bond lowered his voice, still playing the game expected of him, "this has never bothered you in the past. Big Thumb Chang's name is well known in my profession. It is held in great reverence, for it is a password to obtaining certain items forbidden in the Territory."

"Certainly it is forbidden to import arms, and in recent years the penalties for such things have been great."

"But you can still put your hands on them?"

"*Ayeeyah!* With the greatest of difficulty. One revolver and a few miserable rounds of ammunition I might *just* be able to find—

and that at great cost—but two! Ah, that would be miraculous, and the cost truly exorbitant."

"Let's pretend you *could* lay your hands on two good revolvers— say a pair of very old Enfield .38s—with ammunition, of course . . ."

"This is impossible."

"Yes, but if you could get them . . ." He paused, watching the Chinese shake his head in what appeared to be not only a negative reaction, but also the sign of one who wonders about the sanity of the person with whom he is dealing. "If you *could* get them, how much would it cost?"

"A veritable fortune. An Emperor's ransom."

"How much?" Bond pressed. "How much in cash?"

"One thousand Hongkong for each weapon—the size not count-ing—and another two thousand Hongkong for fifty ammunition, making four thousand Hongkong dolla."

"Two thousand, for the lot." Bond smiled.

"*Ayeeyah!* You wish my wives and children to go naked in the streets? You wish my rice bowl empty for all time?"

"Two thousand," Bond repeated. "Two thousand and the weap-ons returned to you before I leave, with an extra thousand HK on top."

"How long you here, never mind?"

"A few days only. Two, three at the most."

"You will see me beggared. I shall have to send my best daughters onto the streets as common whores."

"Two of them were already making good money on the streets the last time I was here."

"Two thousand dolla, with two thousand when guns are re-turned."

"Two thousand, and one more on return," Bond said firmly. There were two reasons he asked for revolvers. First, parted from his ASP 9mm, he would not trust an automatic pistol begged, borrowed, hired, or stolen, even from Big Thumb Chang. Second, he knew that Chang could supply only basic weapons.

"Two, with *two* thousand when you return."

"Two and one. That's my last and only offer."

Big Thumb Chang threw up his hands. "You will see me begging in Wan Chai, like No Nose Wu or Footless Lee." He paused, eyes pleading for a higher bid. None was forthcoming. "Two thousand, then. And one when you return the weapons, but you will have to leave five hundred HK as deposit in case you do not come back."

"I've always come back."

"There is the first time. Man always comes back until the first time. What else will you steal from me, Mr. Bond? You wish to sleep with my most beautiful daughter?"

"Take heed." Bond gave him a withering look. "I have a lady with me."

"A thousand pardons." Chang realized that he had gone too far. "When you wish to collect the items?"

"How about now? You used to keep an arsenal under the floor in your back room."

"And many dolla it cost me to keep away the police."

"I don't think so, Chang. You forget that I know exactly how you work."

Big Thumb Chang gave a sigh. "One moment. Excuse, please." He rose and waddled through the bead curtain that separated the rooms.

Ebbie started to speak, but Bond shook his head, mouthing, "Later." It was dangerous enough to have her there at all, now he had made up his mind that *anyone* from the old *Cream Cake* team was suspect.

They heard the Chinese rooting about in the other room, then, quite unexpectedly, the bead curtain parted and, instead of Chang, another man appeared—a European, dressed in slacks and a white shirt; a tall, slim man in his late fifties, but with iron-gray hair and eyes to match. The eyes twinkled brightly as Ebbie breathed, "Swift!"

"Good day to you both." The voice was English, flat and unaccented.

Bond moved quickly, standing and placing himself between Ebbie and the newcomer, who held up his hand. "I come in peace, bearing messages," Swift said softly. "Our mutual Chief told me I would probably make contact with you here. If that happened, I was to say, *Nine people were killed in Cambridge and an oil fire started at Canvey Island.* That mean anything to you?" He paused, the gray eyes holding Bond's face, unblinking.

Unless they had old M tied up in some safe house, and pumped to the eyebrows with sodium pentothal, Swift was truly Swift—a noted member of Service, who had indeed received orders directly from M. By mutual arrangement, Bond always carried in his head some meaningless identification code from his Chief. Anyone repeating the code to him would be genuine, as it was always concocted in ultrasafe conditions. The one running at the moment—unchanged for six months—had been given to Bond in M's office, without a word passing between the two of them.

"Then I am to reply that the sentence comes from Volume VI of Gilbert's excellent biography of Winston Churchill." Bond put out his hand. "Page 573. Okay?"

Swift nodded. He had a firm grip. "We must speak alone." He clicked his fingers, and the girl—Chang's second daughter by his third wife—appeared behind him.

"Ebbie." Bond smiled at her convincingly. "Ebbie, I wonder if you would go with this girl. Just for a few minutes, while we have some man's talk."

"Why should I?" she bridled.

"Why should you not, Ebbie?" Swift's eyes commanded her. She held out for around fifteen seconds, and then meekly followed the girl. Swift glanced back through the curtain. "Good, they have all gone out. We have ten minutes or so. I am here as M's personal messenger boy."

"Demoted?" Bond asked lightly.

"No, only because I know all the participants. First, M apologizes for having put you in such an intolerable position."

"Good of him. I *am* getting a little tired of playing the odd man out. I didn't even know about Smolin."

"Yes, so he told me. M has asked me to find out how much you *do* know first, and then how much you have put together."

"First, I trust nobody—not even you, Swift—but I'll talk because it's unlikely you could get that personal code phrase from anyone but M. What I now know, or at least suspect, is that there was something terribly wrong about *Cream Cake.* So wrong that it had to be taken care of when two of its former agents were murdered. I can only presume that the truth lies in one or more of those left living. One, or more, have been turned."

Swift nodded again. "Almost correct. One or more was always a double. That became all too apparent after Smolin was left in place; and, yes, the Head of Service has no idea which one. But there's a good deal more to it than that."

"Go on."

"M is being leaned on very heavily. So heavily, in fact, that certain people in the Foreign Office are calling for his resignation. A lot of things have gone wrong for him, and when the *Cream Cake* business resurfaced he saw yet another debacle heading toward him like an avalanche. He put a plan up to the Foreign Service mandarins and they turned it down flat—too dangerous, and nonproductive. So he had to go it alone. He chose you, underbriefed you, even withheld a large wedge of intelligence from you, because he believed that you—his most experienced operator—would eventually put two and two together."

That sounded like M at bay. No wonder the old boy was so firm about the operation not having his blessing. He remembered Q'ute's description of the situation, in Paris—*M's been closeted in his office for three days now. He's like a general under siege.*

As though reading his mind, Swift continued, "M is still under siege. In fact, I'm surprised that he even talked to me—which he did under tremendous security precautions. But he won't last another scandal. He stands no chance of weathering the storm if another double is found within his house, or even near to it. You follow?"

"Does, say, Chernov—Blackfriar—know this?"

"Quite possibly. What you haven't figured out yet, I am supposed to tell you. He's pleased with what you've done so far—M, I mean. But now you have a need to know two things." He paused, as though on the brink of disclosing the most secret thing ever known to him. "First, the double within *Cream Cake* has to be eliminated—with no comebacks. Understand?"

Bond nodded. This was not an order M could have given to him directly. Under the relatively new Foreign Office and Government instructions, assassination was never to be used. It had been the end of the old Double-Oh Section, though M maintained that he always thought of Bond as 007. Now he was being told to kill for the Service—and, in particular, to save M's neck. "That means I've first got to finger the double." He felt quite calm about it, for Swift's disclosure had given him a new impetus. M was a shrewd and tough old devil. He was also quite ruthless. His head was on the block, and Bond had been chosen as the one to save his neck. M knew that, of all his people, James Bond would fight shoulder to shoulder with him right up to the end.

"Right"—Swift gave a fast nod—"and I can't help you there, as I haven't a clue, either."

It could be any one of them, or all of them, Bond thought once more—Smolin, Heather, Ebbie, Baisley or Dietrich, both of whom he had yet to meet. "Good Lord!" he said aloud.

"What?" Swift took a step toward him.

"Nothing." Bond closed up like a clam, for he suddenly realized there was yet another contestant. It could be one of them, or all of them, or . . . He did not even allow himself to think of the ramifications of the idea that had just sprung into his head.

"You sure it was nothing?" Swift pressed.

"Certain."

"Good, because there's something else—someone else. To add weight to his position as Head of SIS, M requires a coup. The *Cream Cake* investigation provided the man and the means. He wants Blackfriar, and he wants him alive."

"We could've taken him in Ireland."

"And risked one devil of an incident on foreign soil? True, the Irish Special Branch, in the Republic, are most cooperative, but I don't think even they would have been *that* cooperative. No, we have to take him here, on what is still British territory. Here we have rights. That's another reason M sent *you* into the field, James. As soon as he discovered Blackfriar had been tempted to leave Soviet territory to follow up on *Cream Cake,* he baited the trap with you."

"Because I'm on his department's hit list?"

"Exactly."

That also made sense. M was never squeamish in putting men like Bond into dangerous situations.

"And to help things on their way, I was told to instruct Jungle to head East. Chernov's a determined devil, and he's fallen for it."

"You mean *I* fell for it." Bond looked at him coldly.

"I suppose that also. If you hadn't got out, James, I would probably be dealing with this alone, because General Chernov's already here."

"On Cheung Chau Island?"

Swift gave him a quick, surprised look. "You're very well briefed. I thought that would be my little surprise."

"When did he get in?"

"Last night. But there have been a number of arrivals in the past twenty-four hours. Some came in via China—in all, Black-friar's got quite an army here. He has also taken prisoners. Even brought some—Smolin and Heather. By now I should imagine he has Jungle and his German girl under lock and key out on the island. It's up to us, James. We're very much on our own, so I suggest we meet at around ten-thirty tonight—in the lobby of The Mandarin? Okay?"

"If you say so."

"I'll organize a way to get us out to Cheung Chau—they call it Long Island, or Dumbbell Island, here—it's roughly shaped like a dumbbell. The house is on the eastern side of the island, perched on a promontory at the northern end of Tung Wan Bay. It's very well situated and custom-built for the GRU, so Chernov's probably laughing his head off now he's there—at least, I presume he's there."

"Ten-thirty, then." Bond glanced at his watch. "I have one or two surprises for Blackfriar."

"You're also willing to give your life for M, aren't you?" Swift was not smiling.

"Yes, and damn him, he knows it."

"Thought so." Swift gave a bleak smile, turned his head, and called loudly through the bead curtain. At the back of the building, a door opened.

Ebbie was the first to return. "And how's life been treating you, Emilie—I'm sorry, I should say Ebbie?" Swift greeted her.

"Like always. Danger. I feel that the Soviets have a revenge with me. Is that right, a revenge?"

"A vengeance," said Bond, and at that moment Big Thumb Chang came back into the room carrying several items wrapped in oilskin, which Bond immediately began to transfer to the holdall.

"You not examine the weapons, never mind?" Chang looked momentarily shocked.

Bond tossed several packets of notes onto the table—money had been only a small part of his shopping list to Q'ute. He gave the Chinese a twisted, cruel smile. "Between trusted friends it is not necessary to count the money—*very* old Chinese proverb, as you well know, Big Thumb Chang. Now, please leave us in peace."

The Chinese cackled, scooping up the notes and backing into the inner room.

"When we leave, I suggest you and Ebbie go first." Swift's voice had been very soft throughout his conversation with Bond. Now it became almost soporifically calm. The voice was recognizable from his file (*Always calm and usually speaks quietly,* it read), for Bond had seen this agent's profile and followed his fingerprints over many an East German operation.

Bond moved to the beaded curtain, glancing into the inner room to make sure that Chang had retreated through the rear exit. Satisfied, he spoke rapidly. "Ten-thirty, then?"

"Count on it." With an almost imperious nod of the head, Swift sent them on their way, back down the steep steps flanked by the stalls of street traders and dim-sum sellers.

"Swift," said Ebbie, pronouncing it Svift and almost running to keep up with Bond.

"Yes?"

"That is where Heather and I got the idea for names, for using fishes and birds."

"From Swift?" Bond turned his head away from a dim-sum stall. The food was probably wonderful, but to his sensitive nostrils it smelled too pungent.

"*Ja.* Yes, Swift is a bird and Heather said we should use code names like animals and birds. In the end, birds and fishes."

Bond grunted, quickening his pace so that Ebbie clung to his arm, struggling to keep up with his fast, long, and purposeful strides. They took no shortcuts, going straight back along Pedder Street, dodging the traffic into Icehouse Street, and so to The Mandarin. During the whole walk, Bond's eyes roved the crush of Chinese in the streets, feeling a million watchers around them, a thousand imperceptible signals passing between them.

Back in the hotel, Bond went straight to the elevators, almost dragging Ebbie with him.

"Wait by the door," he ordered when they reached their room. It took less than four minutes for him to transfer the main items provided by Q'ute from his suitcase to the canvas holdall. Then they were off back to the elevators and the hotel foyer. He strode to the main desk, Ebbie panting in his wake. A pretty Chinese girl who looked all of fifteen years old glanced up from a computer keyboard and asked if she could help him.

"I hope so, is there a ferry to Cheung Chau?" Bond asked of the girl.

"Each hour, sir. Yaumati Ferry Company. From Outlying Districts Services Pier." She gestured with her hands.

Bond nodded and thanked her. "We must go. Go now." Turning to Ebbie.

"Why? We are to meet Swift. You arranged . . .?"

"I'm sorry, yes, I did arrange. Just come. You should know that I've ceased to trust anybody, Ebbie. Even Swift—and even you." He became vaguely aware of police sirens close at hand, and, as they reached the main doors of the hotel, a knot of people was already gathering across the road in the decorative square that surrounded the Connaught Centre.

Dodging traffic at great risk, they dashed toward the crowd just as two police cars and an ambulance drew up.

Pushing through the throng, Bond managed to get sight of the trouble. A man lay spread-eagled on his back, blood seeping onto the paving stones. There was a terrible stillness about him and the gray eyes looked steady and sightless into the sky above.

The cause of Swift's death was not immediately apparent, but the killers could not be far away.

Backing from the crowd, Bond caught Ebbie by the forearm, propelling her away and to the left, in the direction of the Outlying Districts Pier.

17

LETTER FROM THE DEAD

THE SAMPAN SMELLED strongly of dried fish and human sweat. Lying close together for'ard, looking back toward the toothless old lady who sprawled across the tiller, and the twinkling stars that were the lights of Hong Kong behind her, Bond and Ebbie could feel the fatigue and tension emanating from each other.

The afternoon, with its sudden violent changes, seemed far away, as did the sight of Swift's body in front of the Connaught Centre building.

After the shock of seeing the man lying dead, Bond's thoughts had been unusually imprecise and jumbled. He was certain of only one thing—that unless Chernov had shown monstrous cunning, Swift had been straight. There were moments during the conversation at Big Thumb Chang's when he had doubted. But there were other people he also doubted. All things were possible. Now he was on his own, and the one chance of fingering the *Cream Cake* double, and getting Chernov alive, lay in putting himself on offer—a living lure.

His first instinct was to give chase, to head for the island by the quickest possible means. He was in fact halfway toward the Ferry Terminal when he realized that this was just what Chernov might want.

He slowed his walk, keeping the holdall close to his left side, and Ebbie fast by the arm to his right. She had not seen the body and thus kept asking what was wrong, and where were they going. Angrily, Bond continued to drag her along until the moment when his fragmented thoughts came together, and a certain peace reigned within his mind.

"Swift," he said, surprised at the calmness of his own voice. "It was Swift. He looked very dead."

Ebbie gave a little gasp and asked, in a small voice, if he was sure. He told her what he had seen, not being kind, in a way wanting the picture he drew to be shocking.

Her reaction had been unexpectedly good. After a lengthy silence, as they almost strolled along the waterfront—picturesque, with little arbors and a pyramid fountain below them—she merely muttered, "Poor Swift. He was so good to us—all of us." Then, as though the full implication had struck her, "And poor James. You needed his help, didn't you?"

"We all needed his help."

"Will they come for us also?"

"They'll come for me, Ebbie, but I don't know about you. Depends which side you're working for."

"You know which side I'm on. Were they not trying to kill me at the hotel, The Ashford Castle Hotel, when I was lending my coat and scarf to the other girl?"

She had a point. Even Chernov would not be so stupid as to

kill an innocent bystander in the Irish Republic. Bond had to put trust in at least one other human being. Ebbie was apparently straight—had been from the outset. So, with some reluctance, he would have to accept her.

"All right. I believe you, Ebbie." He swallowed, and then went on to tell her the briefest details—of how Chernov was certainly on the island, with others; that he was holding Heather and Maxim Smolin prisoner, and almost surely Jungle and the Dietrich woman as well. "We're probably under some form of surveillance now. They might even expect us to go charging over to Cheung Chau straightaway. I'll say this for the KGB, they've got quite classy lately when it comes to psychological pressure." He went on to explain that *they* were being put under stress at their weakest physical and mental moment. "We're both tired, disoriented, jet-lagged. They'll expect us to make moves automatically. We need time—time to rest, organize, and work out some more logical way."

But where to go? What to do? In this place, even though the crowds were constant, you could not get lost, for you could never be quite certain who was watching. He had no safe house at his disposal. Only his own experience, the weapons, and other items in the holdall; and Ebbie Heritage, whose form in the field he did not know.

The only possible chance would be to go through the complex business of throwing a tail—even though he could not spot one. After that, well, it would be a matter of luck—another hotel, possibly. At least they could try it.

He pulled Ebbie closer to him, leaning on the wall and looking out over the harbor. Three low barges were being towed across the center of the bay; the usual junks and sampans plowed and turned; one of the high double-decked car ferries was nosing out to their left, while two of the Star Ferry boats, which ran every ten minutes between Hong Kong and Kowloon, hooted as they passed one another in the center of the harbor.

Asking Ebbie to stand still for a moment and keep quiet, Bond went through the various means of running the back-doubles in Hong Kong. The Mandarin was out as a resting place, for they were certain to have watchers back there. Kowloonside seemed the best idea.

Very carefully, he explained to Ebbie what they must do. Then he went over it a second time, for luck. Smiling down at her, he asked if she was up to it.

She nodded. "Oh yes, we'll show the devils. I have scores to settle with them, James. At least two—three, if you count the poor Irish girl to whom I loaned my scarf and coat." She gave a little smile back. "We will win, won't we?"

"No contest." He tried to make it sound casual, though his mind told him that to win, here in Asia, against the kind of people Kolya Chernov had at his disposal—and with at least one of the *Cream Cake* team as his ally—would take very good joss indeed.

Together they started to walk back along the harbor front, dodging up the open stairs near the central post office to get onto the covered overpass that brought them out on The Mandarin Hotel's side of Connaught Road. The offices were closing, and the crowds had thickened, yet—even among so many people—there was a strange orderliness.

"Keep your eyes open. Watch shoes more than faces," Bond advised her, though now that they were actually doing it he realized how many people wore trainers. A Chinese team would almost certainly be wearing them.

At the hotel they turned right, into Icehouse Street again, but this time they were heading for the smart, red-brick, ivy-covered entrance to the Mass Transit Railway station, less than a hundred yards behind the hotel—to the right, in Chater Road, behind Swire House. It was the Hongkongside, end-of-the-line station, known as Central.

The MTR is, rightly, Hong Kong's pride and joy, and the envy of many cities, for in efficiency and cleanliness there are few underground railways in the world that compare with it. Certainly Moscow has its huge baroque stations; Paris its fabled Louvre station with the objets d'art on view; London has its somewhat dingy charm; and New York its blatant air of danger. But Hong Kong has bright, shiny trains, air-conditioned, with a sense of order and cleanliness—ranging from the electronic turnstiles to the passengers themselves.

They dodged down the steps from the street into the high-ceilinged modern complex. Bond went straight to the booking booth, flashed his Boldman passport, and purchased two special Tourist Tickets, slapping down the HK$30 and receiving a pair of colored-plastic smart cards in return. All tickets are the size of credit cards, but they contain electronic strips recognized by the turnstiles when each journey has been completed, and swallowed up so that they can be reissued, creating a saving of thousands of dollars a year. The Tourist Tickets, however—each with a printed view of the harbor—allow unlimited travel for a certain period, and so save much time. There are high penalties for damaging the plastic smart cards—as there are for smoking, or bringing food and drink into the hallowed, cool atmosphere of the MTR system, hence the scrupulous cleanliness.

Still keeping both the holdall and Ebbie close to him, Bond headed toward the trains—down more stairs, and onto a platform. A train heading for Kowloonside hissed in.

They just made it, settling themselves on the somewhat spartan seats and studying the simple map that Bond had picked up when purchasing the tickets. Now he pointed a finger to the station at which they would get out, and set about casually looking around. Few people took any notice of them as the train pulled into Admiralty station, and then out again to start the crossing, directly under the harbor to Tsim Sha Tsui, a short way up the famous wide Nathan Road. This was where they planned the first jump-off and, when it came to it, the point where Bond spotted at least one pair of watchers.

The trains traveling over to Kowloon followed the same route until the split in the line at Mong Kok or Prince Edward—at the southern side of Kowloon, where the railway branched to the Tsuen Wan line, to the West up the coast, or to the Kwun Tong line, which followed a great curve to the Northeast. The one on which they traveled was bound for this third line, which would take them too far from the center of things. Bond reasoned that, if he could contain matters within a relatively small area, life would be easier.

As they alighted, he noticed, bunched among the crowd of passengers, two well-dressed young Chinese, their eyes undisguisedly averted from Bond and Ebbie, yet somehow appearing to follow their progress. He turned left, as though to make for the exit, the Chinese duo getting closer.

"Back on again, at the last minute," he whispered as they came abreast of a set of carriage doors. It was an old trick, but it could still work. As the doors began to close, he pushed the girl in, following her quickly and seeing, to his frustration, the two Chinese do the same thing, one carriage down.

He told Ebbie to get off at Jordan, the next station, but to leave it until the last moment. When they did so, it took but a few moments in the scurrying crowd to realize that the two men were still there, keeping pace with them, and too close for comfort.

Both watchers wore light gray suits, neat collars, and ties, even in the afternoon heat. They could easily have been taken for two businessmen returning to the office. But to Bond's practiced eyes, they worked with a precision that gave him not only cause for alarm, but also the feeling that another team was at work—possibly in front of them.

They came out of Jordan station and went right, into the noisy, bustling Nathan Road, Bond edging Ebbie to take the harbor direction. Smiling, he quietly told her that they were being followed and that there could be a team somewhere ahead of them. "Stay casual," he said. "Stop and look in the shop windows, move slowly. At the bottom end of the road we come to The Peninsula Hotel. We'll try to lose them there."

The sidewalks were tight with people, more Chinese and Indians than European, for Nathan Road seemed to be a strange cultural meeting place. Garish banners overhung the street; on ground level modern shopfronts squeezed together, yet above them there could still be seen the old ramshackle buildings dating back to the 1930s or even '20s. Neon and paper signs hung drunkenly at angles, sprouting out to catch the eye, while the omnipresent food stalls added an amalgam of smells. There were more camera and electronics shops here on Kowloonside, so Bond and Ebbie were able to stop regularly, as though comparing prices, while they watched for the watchers.

Ying and Yang, as Bond had mentally christened the two surveillance men, kept pace with a cunning that bespoke good and thorough training. But, within five minutes, Bond thought he had latched on to the team in front—a girl and boy, around eighteen or nineteen, seemingly wrapped in each other's company but always stopping when Ebbie and Bond stopped. The boy wore a long, loose shirt outside his jeans, enough cover for a weapon. Ying and Yang, in their tailored gray suits, had plenty of hiding places for handguns. The thought crossed Bond's mind that they could just as well be an execution squad—had it not already been done to Swift? No, he reasoned. Chernov would wish to be present at the end. There should be witnesses from within Moscow Center.

At last they reached The Peninsula, entering by one of the side doors that led into a bright shopping arcade.

As they turned to climb the stairs to the main lobby, so Ying and Yang followed them in. Doubtless the younger pair had made for the front of the hotel to complete the box. "Go ahead," Bond muttered to Ebbie. "Take the armory with you," he added, handing her the holdall. "Make for the loo. I'll be in the lobby as soon as I've dealt with this." At least this would be a thorough test for Ebbie's loyalty, and he nodded to her, smiling and relaxed as he reached for his cigarettes, placed one between his lips, and began to pat his pockets for matches or lighter.

Ying and Yang looked slightly startled as they saw him stop, but, being committed, came on, paying no attention until Bond stepped in front of them and, in English, asked if they had a light.

Close to, they looked like twins—jet short hair, round faces, but with darting, cruel eyes. For a second they paused, and Ying muttered something as his hand went up to reach inside the unbuttoned jacket. When the arm was almost level with his lapel, Bond grabbed the wrist, twisted hard, then pulled down, his right knee coming up with all his strength behind it.

He could almost feel the man's pain as the knee smashed into his groin; he certainly heard the gasp of agony, but, almost before that came, Bond had spun the man around and jerked him forward toward Yang, propelling him downward so that the top of his skull caught Yang's face—head-on. Bond heard the crunch and felt Ying's body go limp in his grip.

By the time anyone came out of the shops along the arcade, both Ying and Yang lay only partially conscious—Ying doubled in pain from both groin and head; Yang's face looking as though he had met a heavy lump of concrete: there was blood pouring from a broken nose, and possibly a cheekbone had been cracked.

Loudly Bond shouted for someone to get the police. "These men tried to rob me!" he shouted, and there was a jabber of Chinese and English.

He bent down, reaching inside each man's jacket. Sure enough, they were armed, with neat, stubby-looking .38 revolvers, easy to conceal and twice as lethal as larger guns. "Look!" he said loudly.

"Somebody get security, these men are bandits."

The outraged noises from the small crowd gathered around them told Bond that they were most certainly on his side. He edged back into this growing circle, dropped one of the weapons, slid the other into his belt, inside the short Oscar Jacobson jacket he wore over shirt and slacks, and slipped away up the stairs. "Down there," he said to the two security men who were descending, almost bumping into him. "Couple of brigands just tried to rob my friend."

Ebbie waited inside the doors, in the corner of the vast, gilded hotel foyer where waiters scurried around tables, serving late tea, watched over by a silver-haired maître d' while a four-piece orchestra—seated high up in what looked like a royal box—played selections from musicals, old and new. Mainly old.

He took the holdall, muttered that they should move fast, and headed toward the main doors, his eyes swiveling around to spot the young couple whom he had fingered as the backup team. But there was no sign of them, either in the lobby or outside in the forecourt.

They crossed the road when the heavy traffic allowed, heading toward the harbor front, among the many building sites giving Kowloon a constant face-lift, Bond's eyes still restlessly moving to try to spot the other team.

"I think maybe we've thrown them." He squeezed Ebbie's arm. "Come on, keep going left. The least we can do is treat ourselves to a decent hotel for a few hours, and The Regent's just along here—great brick blockhouse of a place, but I'm told it's a strong rival to The Mandarin."

The view to The Regent was blotted out by vast hoardings enclosing building works, but as they reached the end of these they saw the hotel, with its driveway sweeping upward, and the forecourt awash with Rolls-Royces and Cadillacs. It was not the only thing that came into view. As they turned the corner, the young man and his girlfriend stepped out directly in front of them.

Bond grasped the revolver butt and was about to draw the weapon when the young man spoke—his hands clearly empty and the girl obviously watching his back.

"Mr. Bond?" he asked.

Bond took one step back, ready for the next move. "Yes." He nodded.

"Do not be alarmed, sir. Mr. Swift said that, should any ill befall him, I was to give you this, never mind." Slowly his hand went to his pocket, from which he drew an envelope. "You might already know that Mr. Swift had serious accident this afternoon. My name is Han. Richard Han. I worked for Mr. Swift. All arrangements are made. I presume you dealt with the two no-good coolie hoodlums who were following you—we heard large commotion . . ."

"Yes," said Bond, still a shade wary.

"Good. There will be a walla walla down by Ocean Terminal at ten-forty-five. I will be there to see you both aboard. Ten-forty-five, near the Ocean Terminal. Okay, *heya?*"

Bond nodded, and the young couple smiled, linked arms, and turned away.

"What's a walla walla?" Ebbie asked later as they lay resting naked in a room high up in The Regent.

"Motorized sampan." Bond chuckled. "Some people'll tell you they're called walla wallas because of the noise of the engines. Others say it's because the very first one was owned by a guy from Washington, D.C."

"You are clever." Ebbie snuggled up to him. "How do you learn all these things, James?"

"From the official Hong Kong Guide. I read it while you spent all that time in the bathroom."

They had encountered no difficulty in getting a room at The Regent—especially when Bond flashed his Amex Platinum Card in the name of Boldman, and said that price was no object.

Nobody even queried the lack of luggage, though Bond supplied a story about it coming on from the airport later, casually showing the holdall—which he refused to let anyone else carry for him.

After ringing room service—ordering a relatively simple three-course European dinner for two—he opened the envelope. Inside was a single sheet of paper that contained a short message and a map of Cheung Chau Island.

> *In case anything happens, I have given this to a*
> *young colleague. Richard Han will assist in any way*
> *he can. I have arranged transport to Cheung Chau.*

The woman will drop you at the harbor, which is to the west of the island. You want a white villa that stands almost opposite The Warwick Hotel on the eastern side—ten minutes' walk over the narrow isthmus. Take the lane through the houses just right of the ferry landing stage. The villa is well placed, high up on the northern side of the bay of Tung Wan, looking out across a rather beautiful stretch of sea and sand—needless to say, The Warwick is on the southern side. To my knowledge there are no warning devices, but the place is always well guarded when anyone's in residence. It has at least one telephone, and the local number is 720302. Remember the nine killed in Cambridge, and the fires started at Canvey Island. If you get this, I will not be there to wish you luck, but you have it anyway.

Swift.

Bond had no alternative but to accept the note, the map, and the person of Richard Han as being genuine. At least this was a way of getting to Cheung Chau and finding the house. After that, who knew?

Before the food arrived, he went into the bathroom, checked the weapons and equipment in the holdall, and decided to arm Ebbie with one of the .38s. He would keep the similar weapon taken from Ying and Yang. The rest could be carried in the holdall. Once the villa was located, he knew what should be done. You could not take further chances with a man like Chernov. He went back to the bedroom, ate a hearty meal, waited for Ebbie to use the bathroom, then stripped and took a shower. They had no change of clothes, but at least they were both refreshed and clean. Bond stretched out on the bed, where, in spite of their tiredness, Ms. Heritage displayed a great deal of inventiveness in the practice of body language.

Now, after a short doze, Bond went over the essentials for the rest of the night. "You understand?" he asked at the end of this little briefing. "You will stay where I tell you until my return. After that, we play it by ear." He gave her a light kiss on each ear, as though to underline the point.

They dressed, armed themselves (he was pleased to note that

she handled the revolver and spare ammunition professionally), and left the hotel just after ten o'clock.

On the dot of ten forty-five, Richard Han met them by the large and sprawling shopping mall, hard by the Star Ferry, known as Ocean Terminal. He led them away from the normal piers, down a path to the harbor, where the toothless old woman in black pajamas waited with her sampan.

"She knows where to take us?" Bond asked.

Han nodded. "And you must give her no money," he said. "She has already been paid enough. The trip will take the best part of three hours. I'm sorry, it's only one hour on the ferry, but this is the best way."

In the event, it took nearly four hours, the woman not speaking a word to them but leaning back, relaxed, at the tiller.

So it was that around three in the chill morning that James Bond and Ebbie Heritage were landed on Cheung Chau Island, around seven and a half miles west of Hong Kong. The sampan had bucked and rolled in the sea, but, once it neared the harbor, the old woman cut the engine, working an oar to bring them noiselessly in through a throng of junks and sampans, some lashed together, others riding at anchor. At last they reached the harbor wall, and the woman whispered something the meaning of which was obvious. Together, they scrambled up onto the wide stretch of concrete that fronted the harbor, Bond lifting an arm in farewell to the woman.

18

TUNG WAN BAY

THE ISLAND, AS Bond had already seen from the map, was shaped roughly like a dumbbell—the south side much wider than the north, with a short spit of land, less than a mile wide, that ran between the two main areas.

Their eyes had adjusted to the dark long before landing, so Bond could make out the buildings ahead. He took Ebbie's hand, made certain that she had her revolver ready, and guided her toward the first dark gap, leading to a narrow lane. As they drew near, he could make out the shape of a clear-glass telephone booth, which he considered using once he had carried out the reconnaissance on the villa.

"You stay here. Don't move, and make sure nobody sees you," he whispered. "I'll be back within the hour." Through the darkness he saw her nod. Ebbie was certainly proving to be less nervous than he had any right to expect. Squeezing her hand, Bond set off up the lane, feeling very closed in by the buildings—shops by day—that made up the sides of this gulch. After a couple of hundred yards, the lane narrowed even more.

There was a large tree to the right, and Bond became conscious of someone near at hand. He stopped, moving only when he realized that it was an old Chinese, flat on his back, snoring under the tree.

In all, it took around twelve minutes before the buildings gave way to a wide strand of pale sand, with the sea, soft and shimmering, directly in front of him. Tung Wan Bay.

Keeping to the cover of the buildings, he edged forward. To his right a glitter of lights indicated The Warwick Hotel. He waited, peering around the bay and up to the promontory on his left. High up, he could see a small splash of gray with two lights burning—certainly the villa Swift had marked with an X.

Staying in dark cover and praying that nobody was using infrared night glasses from the villa, Bond slowly made his way along the buildings to his left until he reached open ground. The sand stretched out, white in the blackness, toward the promontory, the villa still in view.

He guessed that roughly seventy yards of open sand separated him from the shadows to the foot of the bluff—fifty yards of which could be viewed from the villa. Taking a deep breath, Bond sprinted forward, slowing down to a walk once he was in dead ground. The sand petered out, turning to a steep climb on short, spiky grass. Settling the holdall's strap more comfortably on his shoulder, he began the climb. The grass had no sweet smell to it, the roughness scratched at his hands, and occasionally he felt a softness beneath it, as though the whole promontory was nothing but an overgrown sandbank. It took a good ten minutes of hard work before the angle of the climb gave way. He was now on flat, rising ground—still dead to the villa, which did not come into sight for a good thirty yards, and as soon as the first outlines of the building appeared against the lighter sky, Bond dropped onto his belly, adopting a crawl for the next ten yards or so.

He was now quite close—the building being only a few strides away. He lay for five minutes examining the target. It seemed to be a low white bungalow, with a terracotta roof and a series of arches running along the side, making it look more Spanish than Chinese. It also appeared to be set in a circular garden, surrounded by a small wall—some four or five bricks in height.

As he continued to watch, it became apparent that the arches were a kind of cloister that seemed to run round all four sides of the villa. The lights he had seen from below came from a large pair of what looked like sliding glass doors on the side overlooking the bay. There was movement behind the glass, and he thought he could make out Chernov himself, walking to and fro, speaking with somebody hidden from view.

Bond lay there for some time, judging distances and impressing the whole setting on his mind. To the left the ground ran upward— that had been clear when viewing the skyline from the beach below. Recalling the map, he knew that, should he choose to go in that direction, he would eventually find himself on a path that led back, round to the harbor, passing the temple for which the island was well known.

He worked out that if a man moved from the villa toward where he lay at this moment, it would take around fifteen long strides before he could disappear below the skyline—fifteen or sixteen yards, then he would have to slow and stop, as a headlong dash would bring him to the steeply angled ground, and probably a long, unpleasant fall down the slope to the beach below.

If Bond was to outwit Chernov, he needed to take precautions now, in the hope of being able to make use of them later. Carefully he crawled back until he was well hidden from the villa, and in the darkness his hands moved around, seeking soft earth. Eventually the palm of his left hand touched a stone. He shifted until he was lying directly behind it—a rough, circular stone about two feet across and a foot high, with an irregular surface.

Unslinging the holdall, he quietly opened it, removing a small oilskin package—a carefully prepared parcel of goodies made up by Q'ute and delivered to him in Paris. Most of what it contained was backup material—sophisticated lethal extras, all mirroring equipment already hidden in a duplicate belt around his waist, or posing as everyday items spread through his clothing. Digging into the sandy earth behind the rock, he deposited the oilskin package, secured with wraparound tapes. Covering this emergency pack with loose earth, Bond now eased himself forward again, taking mental bearings, hammering them into his head so that, should he have need of it, he could locate the package quickly in relation to the house. Only when he was certain of angles and distances did he retreat again, making the slow descent to the beach.

Some twenty minutes later he was back with Ebbie, whom he found well hidden in the shadows of the buildings fronting the harbor.

"All set," he whispered, adding no explanation. The less she knew, the better it would be.

"Are they there?" she asked, her voice just audible.

"Well, Chernov's there, and where he is I suspect we'll find the others." He had one of the revolvers in his belt, the barrel slanting to one side. Softly, indicating that Ebbie should stay where she was, he padded over to the harbor wall and dumped the holdall into the sea. They were now both armed, with ammunition to spare.

"We're going to show ourselves," he told Ebbie. "Just let ourselves be seen, and avoid actual contact for the time being—Swift's way: like a will-o'-the-wisp. Our job is to draw Chernov out. The house is quite small, but difficult to assault. If he's got a few good men there it would be madness for us to attempt any kind of attack. The ground around it is too exposed, so it would be suicidal."

"Should we not send for the police? This is British territory. Couldn't you have that terrible man arrested?"

"Not quite yet." He did not want her to know that before Chernov was nailed for them someone had to die—whoever was the traitor within *Cream Cake* needed to be disposed of, even if it looked like an accident. That had been implicit in Swift's briefing. The double could not be publicly exposed if M was to be brought into safe waters again. What was it Swift had said? *M is still*

under siege. . . . He won't last another scandal. He stands no
chance of weathering the storm if another double is found within
his house, or even near to it. And now Bond's only way of proving
the *Cream Cake* traitor's identity was to offer himself—and Ebbie—on a plate.

"We'll go in a minute." He put his finger to his lips and headed
for the glass telephone booth noted on their arrival. Digging in
his pocket for the silver cash he required, Bond carefully dialed
the number given in Swift's note—720302. The ringing started,
and the distant instrument was picked up. Nobody spoke. He
slowly counted to six and then, in Russian, he asked for General
Chernov. It was Blackfriar himself who had answered.

Very softly, Bond hissed into the phone, "I'm close. Catch me
if you can," and immediately cradled the instrument.

Returning to Ebbie he led her back along the lane that would
take them onto the beach of Tung Wan Bay. This time, he did
not bother to take any precautions. Instead of keeping well in
shadow, Bond steered Ebbie onto the beach itself, and then to
the left, slowly walking toward the promontory, and finally starting
the upward climb—but this time much further to the right than
before. Unless they had accidentally spotted him on the first
reconnaissance, he wanted to keep Chernov's people well away
from the area he had already covered. But it would be necessary
to take risks in order to draw them from the villa, and so deal
with them well in the open.

Eventually, they reached the flatter ground, crawling together
toward the house and stopping only a few yards from the low
wall, just hidden from view.

All the lights were on now, and the sky in the east had already
started to lighten. In a matter of minutes, daylight would make
them completely visible.

Turning on his side, Bond said he thought they should work
their way around to the back.

"We should do this soon, I believe." Ebbie's eyes were clouded
with concern. "The ground is very open here. I think they could
see us easily from the house if they are awake and looking."

The voice came from behind them—"We seldom sleep for long,
here on Tung Wan Bay. How nice of you to join us. Now I have
the full set."

Bond rolled, the revolver up and ready to fire.

There were three of them: Mischa and one of the thugs who had been with Blackfriar when they picked Bond up at The Newpark. The third, dressed neatly in well-fitting cavalry twill trousers, shirt, and a dark jacket, was of course General Kolya Chernov himself, smiling at his triumph—and pointing an automatic pistol straight at Bond's head. "You invited me to catch you, Mr. Bond; and I have cordially accepted your invitation."

19

MEET THE ROBINSONS

LIKE MANY A safe house in Europe, this villa—set on its promontory and presumably worth hundreds of thousands for the view alone—was spartan once you passed inside. Certainly there were the usual signs of soundproofing—heavy unnatural-looking wallpaper decorating the main living room, which they entered through the large sliding doors that Bond had first observed during his reconnaissance. The rest was functional—chairs made of bamboo, one table of some very solid wood. No pictures adorned the walls. No birds sang.

Bond had dropped the revolver as soon as he knew the odds. He had also turned to Ebbie, signaling with his eyes that on no account should she open up and say anything that mattered. When he spoke at last, it was to Ebbie—"Ms. Heritage, the gentleman pointing the gun at us has what we call star quality. May I introduce you to General Konstantin Nikolaevich Chernov, Hero of the Soviet Union, Order of Lenin—the list of decorations is very long, but he is at present Chief Investigating Officer of Department Eight, Directorate S of the KGB. The Department that was, at one time, known as SMERSH. I suspect the General would prefer it to be still called by that emotive name."

Chernov gave him a pleasant smile, nodding to Ebbie even as in two words he instructed the men to take them into the villa.

Now, inside, he spoke to Bond. "I cannot tell you how glad I am to see you again." Then, switching his attention to Ebbie, "I've also been looking forward to meeting you. By some stupid oversight we missed you in Ireland, Miss Heritage—or should I rightly call you Fräulein Nikolas?"

"Heritage," she answered calmly.

Chernov shrugged. "As you like. However, I am also *very* pleased to see you—the last piece of the ludicrous *Cream Cake* business. All the chickens have come home to roost—and make their final payments, eh?"

Bond had already decided on his strategy. He cleared his throat, coughed, and said, "General, I am empowered to negotiate."

"Really?" The shrewd eyes met Bond with an amused glitter. "You have bargaining powers?"

"Within certain parameters, yes," he lied. "Certain exchanges can be offered for those you hold here—for Ms. Dare, Ms. Heritage, Maxim Smolin, Mr. Baisley, and Fräulein Dietrich. I'm sure you would like some of your own people back, we have quite a number in stock."

Mischa laughed, a quiet, evil sound, while Chernov gave a throaty chuckle. "Everyone connected with *Cream Cake,* eh? All of those under sentence of death."

"Yes."

Mischa laughed again, then spoke—"So, what do we do first, Comrade General? Deal with the traitors and spies, or put your tame puppets to the test?"

"Well, there's plenty of time, Mischa. Relax, this is a pleasant place. Today will be hot. When the sun goes down we'll put the puppets to work. When that is finished, there'll be time to perform the little ritual you seem to long for. With all of them confined here we can be lazy about it. They deserve to go slowly. Really, they wanted us to take Smolin and Dietrich back to Moscow; however, we could be a little pressed for that." He sighed, then looked slyly at Ebbie. "Now, the Nikolas girl here could well provide me with a morsel of pleasure before we extract her tongue and dispatch her with a shade more speed." He turned to Bond. "Don't you agree?"

"I wouldn't know what I'm agreeing to."

"Really? Let's have some coffee and rolls. I can explain while we're eating." He asked Mischa if the Chinese amah had yet arrived with the day's provisions. He nodded, yes—"But I've sent her away again," he added. "Today I felt we had no need for outsiders."

"Quite right, Mischa. Some coffee, then? rolls? preserves?"

"You should have brought your servant, General."

"Perhaps. One of these idiots will help you." He nodded to the man who stood impassive by the door. And at another who seemed to have materialized near the window. Both held machine pistols at the ready. Mischa tapped the arm of the one by the door, and spoke to him in Russian. The man shouldered his pistol by its strap, and was about to follow Mischa out when Chernov intervened. "He can help, but first I think the young lady should join her companions. They probably have a lot to talk about. You should make the most of it." He smiled at Ebbie—this time there was a horrible chill around the eyes—as Mischa called her over and the guard prodded at her with his pistol.

Ebbie nodded, uncurled herself from the chair in which she had been sitting, looked first at Bond, then at Chernov, paused, and went up close to the General, spitting full into his face. He reeled back in disgust, then moved so quickly that even Bond did not see his hand come up to slap Ebbie's left cheek and backhand her right.

The little blonde hardly made a sound, riding with the blows, not even putting her hand to her face. Both the hoods sprang forward, but she merely turned and meekly followed the frowning Mischa from the room, one man behind her, the other returning to his place by the sliding doors. Chernov was wiping the spittle from his face.

"Foolish girl," he muttered. "I could have made the inevitable a little easier for her."

"For all your veneer of sophistication, you're really a cold-blooded bastard, Chernov, aren't you?" The man's dossier and profile at the Regent's Park Headquarters adequately described his devious ruthlessness, but the words did little to reflect the degenerate nature of the man who, for all his cunning intellect, could well have been equated with the most callous and perverted KGB head of all time—the infamous Lavrenti Pavlovich Beria.

"Me?" Chernov's eyebrows shot up. "Me, cold-blooded? Don't be stupid, Bond. These little girls were used by your own cold-blooded Operations Planners, so presumably it was explained to them what risks they were taking." He gave a snort. "You and I know what *Cream Cake* was about—it was about securing the defection of two highly trained and experienced officers, Smolin and Dietrich. To muddy the waters, your people added an extra pair of targets for makeweight, to confuse the issue if need be. Well, it worked! But now, the operation is about to be canceled out. We—KGB *and* GRU—just cannot leave the matter there. Surely you understand that justice must be seen to be done. Two of the girls have been disposed of. It would be greatly unfair to let the rest off with a caution. The intelligence communities of all countries must see that we will not stand by and allow people to get away with this kind of thing." He gave another of his shrugs. "In any case, I have direct orders from my Chairman to carry out summary executions—the bodies left as a warning, with special marks: a kind of ritual. You understand?"

Chernov spoke in a calm, rational tone, as though the murders of Heather, Ebbie, Jungle, Dietrich, and Maxim Smolin—together with the horrors that would take place, such as the ripping out of their tongues, probably while they were still alive—were of as much consequence as imposing a fine on a luckless driver for exceeding the speed limit.

"We cannot negotiate, then?"

"You cannot negotiate with dead people."

"What of me, General?"

"Ah!" He turned, the finger of his right hand raised pointing at Bond, but before he could say more there came a tap on the door, which opened to the hood carrying a large tray, heavy with a coffee pot, cups, a basket of bread rolls, and some large jars of jams and preserves. He was followed by Mischa, who held the man's machine pistol, demonstrating that he was not going to act as butler for anybody, not even General Chernov.

The finger came down. "Ah!" Chernov repeated. "Breakfast."

Mischa left with the other man, and Bond saw that the big fellow who stood guard at the window eyed the food with some envy. "You were saying, General?"

"Oh, after we've eaten, my dear Bond. Enjoy my hospitality while you can." And with that, he refused to enter into any further conversation. In fact, it was the last he was to say about Bond's future for many hours, for as soon as they had eaten, Chernov rapped out several commands. The other hood came back into the room and, with no warning, both men took Bond by the arms and hauled him into the passage outside, and from there down two flights of stone steps. Finally they opened a stout, heavy door, and threw him into a small cell that was completely bare but for a light recessed in the ceiling and covered by a thick metal grille— no windows, no furniture: just an empty room with unpainted block walls and ceiling, and about enough space for a man to stand and spread out his arms.

Mischa appeared in the doorway. "Mr. Bond." For the first time, Mischa displayed an effeminate lisp. He clutched at a bundle of clothes, which he then threw onto the cell floor—a pair of dark blue overalls, nylon socks, underwear, and a pair of cheap moccasins. "They're your size, Mr. Bond. We checked with Moscow. The General would like you to strip and put these on." He gave a toothy smile. "You have a reputation as a bit of a magician— things up your sleeves and that kind of thing. So the General felt it would be safer this way. Just change now, please."

There was no option. As slowly as possible, Bond discarded his own clothes—together with the precious equipment concealed in them—and climbed into the overalls, which made him feel foolish. Mischa and the guards took his clothes and slammed the door. He heard a heavy deadlock clunk into place.

For a while, he took stock. There was a tiny hole, no larger than a pencil, set over the door, so he knew from experience that he was almost certainly being observed by a monitoring system, using minute fiber-optic lenses. The cell was obviously located deep in the ground, under the villa. There was no chance of escape from this place. Now his only hope was that, by some means, he could get to the backup equipment hidden in the earth outside the house. He had hoped this would not be necessary, but at least it was there, and he thanked whatever fate looked after people of his profession for giving him the foresight to have Q'ute bring in the stuff to Paris. Then, once he had accepted that even the equipment hidden outside might be of no use to him, Bond crossed his legs and sat, impassively, emptying his mind of all thoughts and anxieties of what might come; and mentally preparing himself by centering his whole being on nothingness.

He did not know how much time had passed before they came again—the two guards, with more food, which he refused. The men accepted this with ill grace but withdrew.

Time passed, and Bond controlled both body and mind, knowing that, whatever trial the General had in store for him, he would need all his experience and all his mental and physical attributes to combat it—even turn it to his advantage, if he was to save the *Cream Cake* team, and himself, from the certain death that awaited them. All, of course, except the unknown traitor.

In his bones he felt the waning of the day, and at last the door was unlocked and the same men dragged him out and up the stairs to the main room where he had last sat with Chernov.

This time the place appeared smaller, and it was full of people. Outside he glimpsed the long slash of white sand being turned red by the blood from the day's dying sun.

Looking around him, Bond saw Chernov sitting on a bamboo chair in the center of the room. The others—guards apart—were chained together, and he realized there were two new faces. It took Bond almost a full thirty seconds to recognize the man as Franz Wald Belzinger—otherwise Jungle Baisley. The face was certainly the one he had studied on photographs during that first fatal afternoon, following the lunch with M at Blades. The surprise came when he saw that Baisley was a huge man—Bond reckoned over six feet tall, and broad in the shoulders. He looked even younger than his twenty-seven years, possibly because of a shock of red hair that, even though well combed, seemed to be impossible for him to rule. He grinned broadly at Bond, as though welcoming him.

"I think you know everybody, except Fräulein Dietrich and Mr. Baisley, as he likes to be called."

Susanne Dietrich was a slim woman, older than he expected and with light-colored, untidy hair. She gave Bond a frightened look, while Jungle tried to rise and grinned an American coed's grin. "Hi, Mr. Bond. I have been hearing much about you." The voice had German undertones, but more to do with syntax than accent, and he certainly was not going to let anyone know he had an ounce of fear in him.

Bond nodded and smiled, trying to be reassuring. He looked along the line, at Maxim Smolin, Heather, and Ebbie. Heather smiled back; Smolin winked; and Ebbie blew him a kiss. It was good for him to know the trio were obviously going to face their fate with a great deal of dignity. He asked if they were okay. They said nothing, but each nodded resignedly.

"So, I call this meeting to order." Chernov laughed, as though this was the joke of the decade. "Or should I call it a court, rather than a meeting?" he added.

Nobody spoke, so, with a wry smile Chernov continued. "The five prisoners here already know what is to happen to them. They have been informed of their guilt and the reason they are to die. They also know the method of their deaths, which will take place at dawn tomorrow." He paused, savoring the thought. Then— "As for this officer, for we must dignify him with that title, Commander James Bond, Royal Navy, Secret Intelligence Service, as for him—well, the department I represent has had an execution order out on him for many years now. Do you understand that, Commander Bond?"

Bond nodded, thinking of the many times he had outwitted and damaged that part of the Soviet Service sometimes referred to as the black heart of the KGB, and once known as SMERSH.

"Let us not be hypocritical about Commander Bond." Chernov's face was revealed in its serious mode. "He has proved himself a valiant enemy. Resourceful, highly efficient, and brave. It would, therefore, not be in keeping with the principles of the department I represent if we simply dispatched him with bullet, knife, a cyanide spray, or an injection of Racin, the drug our Bulgarian cousins favor. As in a bullfight, Commander Bond should, I believe, be given a fighting—if outclassed—chance." He turned his eyes, and the sinister smile, onto Bond's face. "Commander Bond, do you know what a 'puppet' is—in an operational sense, I mean?"

"One who is easy to control?" Bond tried.

Chernov laughed aloud. "I am not being fair to you, James Bond. It is the Red Army's Special Forces, the Spetsnaz—which we believe to be the equivalent to your SAS, or the Americans' Delta Force—who use the word 'puppet.' Puppets are of great assistance during their training. The puppets, or their equivalent, have been used in the USSR to great effect for more than fifty years now. In the beginning, our noble ancestors, the Cheka, called them gladiators; then the NKVD spoke of them as volunteers— though they are hardly that. SMERSH, under all its different guises, has always called them by an English name, which is strange, eh? We call them Robinsons, Commander Bond. You might be more familiar with them under that appellation. So, I ask you again, do you know what Robinsons are?"

"I've heard rumors." He felt a tightening of his stomach at the thought.

"And you believed the rumors?"

"I think so, yes."

"You would be right to believe them. Let me explain. When somebody is sentenced to death in the Soviet Union, it depends upon his usefulness to the community whether he dies quickly, or if his death can serve the state." Again, the grim and chilling smile lit Chernov's eyes with black ice. "Unlike the decadent and sloppy British, who are so neatly delivering themselves into our hands by their self-indulgence, their laxity, their failure to see how we will finally take complete control of their politics"—his voice rose to a slightly higher pitch—"unlike the British, who are too squeamish to use the death penalty anymore, we use it to advantage. True, old men and women are executed almost immediately. Others go to medical centers; some to assist in the building and running of our nuclear reactors—to do the dangerous jobs. The stronger, fitter, and younger men become puppets, or come to us as Robinsons. It provides good training for our men. Until a soldier has proved he can kill another human being, one cannot be certain of him."

"That's what I'd heard." Bond's face felt frozen, as though injected by a dentist. "We are told that they provide living targets on exercises . . ."

"Not simply targets, Commander Bond. They can fight back—naturally, we keep them under great control. They know that, should they try to escape, or turn their weapons on the wrong people, they will be cut down like wheat. They are, for the time of one exercise, real, live opponents. They kill and get killed. If they are really good, they can survive for some time."

"Three exercises and they are reprieved?"

Chernov smiled. "An old wives' tale, I fear. Robinsons never survive forever. They know they are under sentence, so they fight harder if they *think* a reprieve will come after being put up against our people for only three times." He looked closely at his fingernails, as though inspecting them for some deformities.

The room seemed charged with tension. Chernov turned, nodding to the pair of hoods who went out, carefully closing the door behind them.

"When we heard that you—a man on our death list—had been

attached to the clearing up of *Cream Cake,* I made a request to Moscow Center. I asked for some Robinsons. Some very good men. Ones who had lasted for two exercises and imagined they had only one more to win before reprieve. I asked for young men. Mr. Bond, you should feel honored, this is the first time our people have allowed Robinsons to operate outside the Soviet Union. Tonight, from midnight until dawn, you will be out on this little island, with our four best Robinsons intent on killing you. They will be armed, and we are allowing you a small weapon also. But for six hours, in the dark and on ground that you do not know—and, incidentally, they do—you will be hunted. James Bond, I would like you to meet your Robinsons." He shouted a command and the door was opened by one of the men outside.

20

ZERO HOUR

AT FIRST SIGHT, the four Robinsons looked docile enough. They were not shackled or under any form of restraint—apart from the two guards with their machine pistols.

"Come in," Chernov beckoned, speaking Russian.

If he had expected shuffling cowed prisoners, Bond would have been disappointed. The quartet marched into the room, their bearing military, eyes fixed ahead.

All four were dressed in loose black garments—lightweight trousers and shirts. They even wore black trainers, and Bond reckoned that their faces would also be blackened before the night was over. There had been no moon last night, and there would be none tonight. The Robinsons would become invisible out in the darkness of the island.

"You see, Commander Bond, they are a good little team. They have worked together before, and to good effect—once against a Spetsnaz group of six trained soldiers: five are dead, and the sixth will not walk again. Their second mission was with KGB trainees. Man to man, four to four." He gave his now constant shrug. "KGB are four trainees less. Need I say more?"

Bond stared at the men, sizing them up. All were well built, alert, and clear-eyed, but one stood out from the rest, mainly because of his height—around six-five, towering over the others who were closer to six feet. "What were their crimes?" He tried to make the question sound casual, as though he was a racehorse dealer checking on pedigree.

Chernov smiled. Until this moment, Bond had simply recognized that smile as being somehow humorless and sinister. Now, he realized why. The smile reminded him of the famous *Mona Lisa*. Art experts raved about the look of that painting's lips and eyes— describing them as enigmatic, beautiful, and secretive. Certainly he agreed with the last of these descriptions, but to Bond it had always been something else, as though the lady was smiling at a secret so hideous and appalling that it could never be translated into words. He hated that painting, and knew, instinctively, that it was probably some deep reaction to his own kind of work that caused this particular loathing.

"I have to think," Chernov said, his eyes running along the line of men who stood, statue-still, in front of them. "The big fellow, Yakov, was condemned for six offenses of rape: all very young women, girls almost. He also strangled his victims after using them. Then we have Bogdan—also a killer, though not a rapist. Young men were his specialty. Bogdan broke their necks and tried to dispose of them by cutting up the bodies and spreading the pieces in woodland near his home. He's a peasant, but strong and with no moral sense where death is concerned."

Bond stopped himself from blurting out the obvious—"Like you, Kolya. Just like you."

Chernov continued down the line. "Pavl and Semen are less complex. Pavl, the one with the bulbous nose, was an army officer who took to converting military funds for his own use. Five of his comrades discovered the truth, over a period of two years. Four have never been found. The fifth managed to pass on the information. As for Semen, he is a straightforward murderer— three counts: his lady friend, her lover, and her mother. Very good with a meat cleaver, that's Semen."

"All part of life's rich pattern." Bond knew the only way to fight Chernov was to make light of these four monsters who, in a matter of hours, would be out to kill him. "You say they will be armed?"

"Of course. Two will carry handguns—Lugers, if you want the details. One will be equipped with a knife—a killing knife, similar to the Sykes-Fairbairn Commando dagger, which we know is familiar to you. And one will be given a weapon that he likes, a type of short mace, similar to the old Chinese fighting irons, a spiked steel ball hanging from a rather sharp blade, attached to the end of a two-foot handle. Unpleasant."

"And what about me?"

"You, my dear Bond? Well, we wish to be fair. You'll have a Luger pistol. A Parabellum. In good condition, I assure you."

Eight rounds, Bond thought. Eight chances to kill, if he could put himself in the right position.

Chernov was still speaking. "We have provided you with one magazine—half full. Four 9mm bullets. One for each of the Robinsons, should you be lucky enough to get within range before one of them comes screaming out of the night at you. As I have already implied, this team has been given a walk over the ground. As far as I know, you have not."

"What if they decide to make a run for it? Grab themselves a boat—a sampan—and clear off?"

Again the tantalizing smile. "You still do not understand, do you, Commander Bond? These men are trained and have nothing to lose but their lives—which they keep once you are dead."

"They *think* they'll keep their lives."

"Oh, Bond, don't try to spread dissension. It will *not* work, my friend. They cannot be turned; they will not run; nor will they believe any stories you might try to tell them—in any case, they won't give you the time."

And you know I won't run, either, Bond thought. You think you know me inside out, Comrade General. You know I won't run because, if I can possibly outwit your deadly foursome, I shall return here and try to save the others. Mentally he sighed, thinking that Chernov *did* know him, for that was exactly what he would do. He wondered if Chernov also knew he would try to return in order to unmask the traitor among the other prisoners?

Chernov gave a signal, and the Robinsons were marched out, each one meeting Bond's gaze upon turning toward the door. Was it imagination, or did he detect a bleak hatred in those four pairs of eyes?

"You have a couple of hours to rest before the ordeal." Chernov rose. "I suggest you make your peace with the world." One of the hoods came back into the room, ready to lead Bond away, but Chernov took a step forward. "Let me say something else, just to make certain you are familiar with the rules of this drama. Do not try to be clever. It is possible that you have thought of the obvious scheme. To leave and drop below that little wall that encircles the house, then pick off the Robinsons as they come out—we know you are an excellent marksman. Please, do not even think of trying that. When you are given the order to run, then you run. Any other little tricks and my two guards will cut you to ribbons. Should you, by luck or skill, manage to avoid, or kill, my Robinsons, I would advise you to go on running, James Bond. To run as far as you can. We will kill you tonight, I am certain of that, but if I am wrong, the time will come again and I, personally, will kill you. My department will never rest. Understand?"

Bond nodded, curtly, and left with dignity.

Back in the cell, he began to go over his assets. For a while, up there with the deadly Robinsons, he had almost allowed despair to reach him. Now, alone again, he began to plan.

They were giving him a Luger Parabellum with four rounds of ammunition. Well, that was a start. But there was more, if he could get to the already hidden backup package.

The package, worked on by Q'ute and other members of the Service, was for use only in the event of absolute necessity, in the field and almost certainly only in wartime, for it consisted mainly of killing devices.

Constructed on the principle of the old-fashioned Royal Navy "housewife"—always pronounced "hussif"—the COAP, Covert Operations Accessory Pack, was basically a thick oilskin oblong, measuring one foot three inches by eight inches, with two long tapes running out from the left-hand side.

When laid out flat, the COAP contained five pockets, each made to an exact size to fit the object it contained. On the far left were two objects that, unless examined under laboratory conditions, looked like a pair of squat, stubby HP11 batteries. One of these was in fact a powerful flare to be held firmly in the hand, at arm's length, and activated by pressing the little button that looked like the battery's positive nipple. It would shoot a pure white-light flare to around twenty feet. Anything within a quarter of a mile radius was illuminated like daylight. Fired at the right trajectory, the flare could also have a blinding effect.

The second battery was operated like the first, though you did not hang on to it, for within seven seconds the thing exploded with almost twice the power of the old Mills hand grenade.

Both batteries contained the plastique substances that so concerned antiterrorist organizations in these troubled times, for the plastique could not be detected in any conventional way—by X ray or sniffers, either electronic or canine.

Moving on to the third pocket, one came to a six-inch knife blade—again, undetectable by airport security because it was fashioned from toughened polycarbon. The blade was protected by a scabbard that, when removed, could be screwed to the blade, thereby producing a killing knife.

The fourth pocket was almost flat, containing a saw-toothed garroting wire; the last pocket held probably the most deadly weapon of all—a pen. Not an ordinary pen, but one made in Italy that also had security men worried. With one quick twist, the pen became a small projectile-firing gun. It was operated by compressed air, and could be used only three times to fire toughened steel needles—each the size of a ballpoint, every one a killer if it entered the brain, throat, lung, or heart from around ten paces.

When rolled up, the COAP was tied with the tapes, using a quick-release knot, and now—in his mind—Bond rehearsed where each of these items could be found in the open sheet, remembering the many times he had trained in the dark, handling and using all the items by feel alone, and comforted by the fact that he knew he could have everything stowed away on his person, or in use, within less than a minute. There was nothing like the threat of death, he considered—as many had done before him—to concentrate the mind.

Having gone through the positions in the COAP several times, he could now do no more but prepare himself mentally for the test. So he sat as before—legs crossed, eyes closed—but, this time, going over his memories of the map Richard Han had passed on from Swift. He knew where the house lay in relation to the remaining terrain, and, within the hour, he knew what he would do. If luck and his expertise were with him, there was a chance—a slim chance—that, before the night was over, he would have won.

They told him that it was eleven-thirty when they came for him. The hoods spoke no English, but while one covered him with the machine pistol, the other raised his arm, grinning proudly at his brand-new eight-function digital watch.

Chernov was waiting alone in the main room. The doors had been opened, and a few lights twinkled from the cluster of houses around the center and above the beach of Tung Wan Bay. Across the water, on the southern promontory, The Warwick Hotel had a lot of lights gleaming.

"Come and listen." Chernov beckoned him toward the doors, and the two men stepped outside into the warm night air. Bond thought, Why not kill him now with your bare hands, and be done with it? But that would serve no purpose. He would follow Chernov quickly to the grave, cut down by the man who had stayed in the room behind them.

"Listen," Chernov repeated. "Hardly a sound. You realize that around forty thousand people still live on this little island—most of them on the junks and sampans in the harbor—yet after midnight few people stir. There is little nightlife on Cheung Chau."

As Chernov spoke, Bond took his bearings—reciprocal bearings. Directly in front of them the ground slid away flatly to the place where he had hidden the COAP during his first reconnaissance. He could, thank heaven, pinpoint exactly where he should cross the low wall. Below, the strand circled the bay, while to the right the ground sloped sharply upward. He knew that, once over that rise, it was only a few hundred yards to a rough road that weaved downward toward the central isthmus where the main village was built—its harbor and most of its buildings being on the western side. To reach it, the road swept down, passing the famous Pak Tai Temple onto the Praya, or waterfront, with its fish-processing factory and hundreds of fishing junks.

Chernov slapped him on the shoulder. "But we'll *give* them a little nightlife, eh, James Bond?" He glanced at his watch. "It is almost time." He turned, shepherding Bond inside again.

"Do I get a last request?"

Chernov looked at him, a worm of suspicion in his eyes. "That depends."

"I would like to say goodbye to my friends."

"I think not. It would be emotional for them. They are well controlled—particularly the women. I would not like to risk unbalancing that. You realize it is not a pleasant job I have to do in this place tomorrow. It will be best if those under sentence bear pain—and the inevitability of death—with fortitude. It will make the whole business easier for me. You understand?"

Yes, thought Bond, the last thing you want is for me to see them now, because, like as not, they are one short. The traitor will have been pulled out. Aloud, he said, "You're a butcher, Chernov. Let's get on with it."

Chernov nodded, looking solemn. "You have my word that a full five minutes will pass before the Robinsons are unleashed on you. Come, the weapons are here."

As though by magic, the table was now littered with the means of death—three Luger pistols, the long gunmetal dagger—perhaps an inch longer than the old Sykes-Fairbairn Commando knife—and the unpleasant fighting iron: a wooden haft, some two feet in length, with a reinforced handgrip at one end, and a sharp movable steel blade at the other. The blade was flat at its far end, to which a short length of chain was attached. From the chain dangled a mace, twice the size of a man's fist and covered with sharp spikes. Chernov touched the mace and laughed. "You know what they used to call these?"

"Morning stars, as I recall."

"Yes, morning stars, and"—he chuckled mirthlessly—"and holy-water sprinklers. I prefer holy-water sprinklers." His hand hovered over the weapons, coming to rest on one of the Lugers. "Yours, I believe." He slipped the magazine out before handing it to Bond. "Please make certain the action is in working order, and that the firing pin has not been removed."

Bond checked the weapon. It was well oiled and in good condition. Chernov held out the magazine. "Count the four rounds. Reload the magazine yourself. I insist on fair play."

Bond did as he was bidden, aware that the thug with the machine pistol had stiffened in readiness, and that the Robinsons were being brought into the room behind him. He also knew that the whole setup was designed to add tension to the drama. Chernov was a good stage director, and all this by-play had a point.

"You may load the weapon and put the safety on."

Bond did so, holding the automatic loosely in his right hand as Chernov completed his speech. "When we are ready, I shall stand you by the doors and count down, from ten to zero. At zero the lights will be switched off, and you will begin your run. Do not forget what I've already told you about tricks, James Bond. They will do you no good. I do promise you again, though, on my word as an officer, that the Robinsons will not be unleashed for a full five minutes. I should make the most of your time. You are ready?"

Bond nodded, and, to his surprise, Chernov extended a hand for him to shake. Bond just looked at it, then turned to face the door. Chernov paused for a moment, as though hurt by his refusal, before he began to count. "Ten . . . nine . . . eight . . ." and so on to the final "zero!" The lights went out. Bond hurled himself forward into the sudden darkness.

21

EMPEROR OF THE DARK HEAVEN

BOND JUDGED THE leap over the wall with both skill and luck. Having done his calculations while standing outside with Chernov, he was able to count off the paces as he ran in what he knew to be the right direction.

In the event, he took it in his stride and went pelting straight across the flat scrub until he came to the slope. He went down, rolled rapidly about four times until he was sure his silhouette was well off the skyline. He was certain he had landed within a few feet of his goal, and so felt the ground around him with the palms of his hands. There were a couple of seconds of near panic, then his left hand touched the rock. He rolled toward it, scrabbling in the earth and dragging out the oilskin package.

On his feet again he turned left and began to pelt over the slope, aiming to get above the villa in record time, putting as much distance between himself and the safe house as possible.

Throughout the run he counted, using the old childhood recipe of "One Elephant . . . two Elephant . . ." to gauge the seconds. He had given himself two and a half minutes. Wherever he was at that point, he would stop.

He judged that the point reached in that time was around thirty yards above the villa, and it was there that he fell to the ground, placed the pistol where he knew he could grab it, threw the COAP onto the ground, slipped the tapes, and unrolled the oilskin . . .

By feel alone, in the darkness, he located each item, pulling them in turn from their holders, and distributing them around the pockets of his overalls—leaving the batterylike flare in his hand. Breathing heavily, Bond held out his arm, angled the little object toward the house, and pressed the firing button, and then reached for the Luger.

He judged the flare would explode at five minutes twenty seconds since he had left the house.

There was an open pocket on the right thigh of the overalls, and he jammed the Luger into it. Then, grabbing at the second battery—the small grenade—he waited.

The flare gave a thumping kick against his hand, then went up in a dazzling white flash of light. Bond closed his eyes as the projectile left his hand, then opened them immediately the moment the vivid first flash was over. It was as though someone had bathed the villa and its immediate surrounding area in a floodlight, just as he had intended. There, for anyone to see, were the Robinsons—one pair heading up the rise, toward him, the other two going down in the direction of the beach.

One of the men coming in Bond's direction threw up an arm to shield his eyes, but both kept going, like automatons. Bond could see clearly that the second pair were in no way deflected from their progress down toward the beach and isthmus.

Bond lay still and silent, clutching the tiny bomb. Already he could hear the men's heavy breathing as they came on toward him, their shapes visible in the dying moments of the flare's light.

This had to be judged to the second. It would be obvious tactics for one of each pair to be carrying a pistol, and, if the grenade did not explode at the right moment, taking out both men, he might be forced to use his own Luger—at least one precious shot that he could ill-afford to lose.

The panting and heavy footfalls grew nearer, and now he had only his own judgment to go by, for the flare had long gone. Bond prayed to heaven that he had their measure, pressed on the arming nipple, and aimed his throw in the precise path of the oncoming men.

He caught a quick glimpse of the pair—too close together for their own good—as the tiny cylinder packed with plastique exploded in the air directly in front of them. He ducked his head, feeling the burn and shock across his own scalp and the terrible ringing in his deafened ears. He thought a scream reached him through the explosion, but could not be certain. Stumbling to his feet, he half-walked, half-staggered forward until his foot hit something. He bent to feel a soft wetness he identified as body and blood.

On hands and knees, Bond carefully felt around in the scrubby grass, straining through his buzzing ears for any sound, and trying to condition that other sense of danger so necessary for men in his profession.

It was at least two minutes before he found the knife, and another two or three before locating the gun.

The charge had, as he hoped, exploded directly between the men, and very close to them. Before his hand closed on the Luger, it encountered unpleasant debris from the small bomb—Bond would never get used to the effects of explosions, particularly nowadays, when only a very small amount of modern plastique could do so much damage to human beings.

His head started to clear, and with his original pistol still tucked into the overall pocket—the other weapon clasped in his right hand—Bond began to race westward, heading for the road that would take him down to the Praya.

Chernov had made a point of telling him about the deadly experience of these four men—now there were only two, and it was reasonable to consider that, under discipline, the killers would stick to their route and then probably separate at the village, hoping to catch their prey in the open, or among the buildings running the length of the Praya.

Bond had his own plan of campaign. If he could make the Pak Tai Temple, which was a good vantage point, he would wait there. Let them come to him. It was far and away the best thing to do.

His ears still sang from the explosion, and he was aware that his clothes were stained with the blood of the two Robinsons who had died, but he reached the road without mishap, moving from the rough and stony surface—for it was not a road in the traditional sense—onto the softer grass at the side.

Bond stopped running now, trying to march at speed, taking great gulps of air in an attempt to regulate his breathing, as it had been a hard dash across undulating ground.

After ten minutes or so he thought he could make out the shapes of buildings ahead. Five minutes later he reached the edge of the village, cutting between dark bushes and feeling gently along a stone wall he knew must be the temple.

Working his way to the front of the building, Bond reflected on the fact that at least he had some gods he could pray to now, for Pak Tai is the Supreme Emperor of the Dark Heaven, and the temple in his honor also houses his martial gods—Thousand Mile Eye and Favorable Wind Ear. He could do with the help of all three tonight, for it was black as pitch, and he required the Emperor on his side with his colleagues to radar in on the last pair of Robinsons.

The temple fronted onto an open piece of land, and for the first time since the flare and explosion Bond felt his eyes adjusting to the dark. Within a few minutes he could make out the flat square and the shape of steps below him—the temple steps, guarded by traditional dragons.

Gently, he felt his way toward the top step, and, on reaching it, he retreated once more into the cloaked darkness of the temple doorway, moving to his right, sheltering at a vantage point behind one of the two great stone pillars. There he waited.

Minutes filtered slowly by, and he could but presume that the two other Robinsons were also taking their time, adjusting and moving slowly, silently through the night streets.

At least one hour passed. Then the best part of another. Self-discipline held him from even glancing at the luminous dial of his watch as he conducted a careful, regular search—from right to left, then left to right, moving his head and eyes very slowly, his body becoming cramped by standing so still for so long.

Finally, he broke the habit and looked at the Rolex. Ten to five in the morning. Just over an hour before the game was up and Chernov would be doing his butchery.

Bond's stomach turned over at the thought, and, as the horrific picture of Chernov at his work slid through his mind, so he caught movement, out of the corner of his eye. It came from the far right of the square, close to the houses—a fleeting figure, there for a second, a shadow against the lighter band that was the sea.

Slowly Bond moved, lifting the Luger, eyes riveted to the area where he had seen the shadow. For a moment or two he thought that he had imagined it. Then, there it was again, hard against the wall, moving at a snail's pace, using the full darkness.

He shifted position again, bringing the Luger up as the shadow detached itself from the wall and began to move nearer to the temple steps. It was then that, for all his training and experience, Bond made his first error of the night. Take him out now, part of his mind commanded. No, wait, where's the other bastard? It was this one second of mental confusion that brought about the next terrifying minutes.

Take him out now—his training overrode all else. He centered the Luger's sights on the advancing shadow. His finger took up the first pressure, then his sixth sense warned of closer danger.

He was standing in the classic side-on position, both arms raised in the two-handed grip, and the pain seared through his left arm as though someone had run a burning brand across it.

He heard his own scream of pain, feeling the gun drop from his right hand as he reached across to the injured arm. And, as he swiveled, he saw the Robinson with the fighting mace poised for a second blow.

The reaction was automatic, but everything seemed to go into slow motion through the blur of pain that was his shattered left arm. He could not recall the man's name, though for some obscure reason his mind wrestled with the problem. He thought it was Bogdan, the one who had broken young men's necks and then tried to dispose of them by cutting them up and spreading the pieces around the forest. He could hear Chernov's voice quite distinctly—*He's a peasant, but strong and with no moral sense where death is concerned.* And all the time Bond was looking into the man's eyes the mace was rising, very slowly, above his head. Then it started to come down, the big steel-spiked ball—the holy-water sprinkler—hard down toward Bond's skull. His right arm seemed to move very slowly, with the right leg going back, hand grabbing the butt of the Luger in the overall pocket, finger feeling for the safety catch. The spikes hissing through the air, nearer. The Luger sticking, then coming free, and his hand twisting, finger curling, and two sharp explosions—two shots, just as they were all trained—the scent of cordite and the sharp ting as spent cartridge cases clanged against the steps.

Then the slow motion ended, and things moved very fast indeed.

The two bullets lifted Bogdan off his feet, popping his arms into the air as though he was some obscene jack-in-the-box. The fighting iron was thrown back and Bogdan's body—the chest throwing blood toward Bond—bumped against the door of the temple.

At the same moment, the pain shrieked back into Bond's left arm, and with it another sound, a quick double crack and thump. Pieces of stone flew off the pillar near to where he had taken up his firing position. The other Robinson was firing from the square.

Bond doubled up with the pain, retching, vision blurring. As he almost keeled over, he saw the shape of the second Luger on the steps. He forced himself to turn—his gun, with two rounds still in the magazine, clutched in the right hand. As he went, so he found himself losing his balance, reeling like a drunk with shock and agony. A voice seemed to whisper, near to his ear, Get him. Take him out, now. Automatically, he squeezed the trigger, aware that the weapon was up, and his right arm straight. Two shots at a ghost, he thought. Drop the gun. Everything was in reflex and done by numbers. Drop the gun and pick up the other one. He went through the routine, and just as he ducked down another bullet whined over his head. His hand caught the Luger's butt, and he couldn't straighten up, dropping onto one knee.

Bond raised his head and saw the other man standing over him taking careful aim, saying something in Russian, the Luger huge in Bond's vision.

Then the explosion and what Bond imagined was his own last cry echoed around the pillared entrance to the Temple of the Supreme Emperor of the Dark Heaven.

22

DEATH OF A DOUBLE

IF YOU ARE dead, Bond reasoned, you should not feel pain. His last memory was of the Robinson standing a couple of feet away from him, with the Luger pointing at his head, ready for the coup de grace, then the dull explosion. I saw, I heard, therefore I am dead. But he could sense the waves of nausea and the stunning pain in his left arm. He also knew that he could move, his eyelids were moving. He heard. A voice calling to him—"Mr. Bond? Mr. Bond? You okay, Mr. Bond?"

He allowed his eyes to open fully. The sheer blackness was giving way to the first light of day. He lay on his side and two things swam into vision—the soles of a pair of black trainers and a gray-black hump behind them, which he knew was a body; and the toes of another pair of trainers. He turned his head, eyes traveling upward from the shoes.

"You okay, Mr. Bond?"

From this angle he could not see the face properly; the figure went down on one knee. "Think we should get out of here pretty damn chop-chop." The dark-haired Chinese boy grinned. "You remember me, Mr. Bond? Richard Han. Swift's man. Good thing I followed you. Mr. Swift say that, if anything happen, you might need much help, never mind. He said you would be here, Cheung Chau Island. Also I should watch your back."

"You killed the Robinson?" Apart from the excruciating pain in his left arm, Bond felt distinctly better.

"That his name? Robinson? Okay, yes, I kill him. You killed man with fighting iron. I shot this one." Han held a very large Colt .45 in his right hand. "It was correct that I kill him?"

"Too damn right it was correct. Hell!" Bond squirmed, shifting his head to squint down at his left wrist. The Rolex said five-fifteen. Forty-five minutes, or near enough, before Chernov would have the others in his killing jar.

Shakily, Bond pulled himself upward, testing his weight gingerly.

All seemed well, except for the arm. "Give me that gun—the one on the ground."

Han reached out for the Luger.

"There should be another one." Bond peered into the gray light. His would-be killer's weapon lay to one side of the body. Han picked it up.

"Quickly," Bond urged him. "Take out the magazines and put all cartridges into one. Okay?"

"It's okay. Mr. Swift taught me much about guns. Said I was good shot."

"I agree with him. Look, Han, you know the house to the north of Tung Wan Bay? The house where they kept me?"

"No," the boy said blankly. "Swift say you will be here. I watch your back. So, I come here and nobody seen you. I stick around, then late I see these men behaving like they were looking for butterflies in the dark. Very strange. I think, Richard follow these, they are up to no good."

He would have gone on, but Bond stopped him. "Listen, Han, there is this house . . ." He explained exactly where it was. "Get the police. Tell them it is a security matter . . ."

"Swift gave me a police number Hong Kong. He said it was special police."

"Special Branch?"

"Yes. I am stupid. I think first it is some kind of magic root. Then he explain."

"Okay. You can find a telephone on this island?"

"My father's fourth sister lives here. Has small shop with telephone. I shall wake her."

"Ring your number, but tell him to get local police to that house pretty damned fast—chop-chop. Okay."

"They be there very fast. You going?"

Bond took a deep breath. "While I've got the strength I'm going, yes. You get police there. Tell them to hold everyone." Han was already on his way, so Bond had to shout after him, "Tell them the people at the house are armed. They're very dangerous."

"Okay, I tell them, *heya?*" Han turned, one arm raised, and then, in the first light of dawn, the picture in front of Bond turned to one of carnage. Two heavy thumps, and Richard Han's head appeared to burst open, leaving a mist of blood above the body, which continued to run—three . . . four steps—before it hit the ground.

There was the sudden rattle of a machine pistol. Bullets were chipping and smashing into the temple wall around Bond. His reflexes and training came into automatic action. The muzzle flash was from quite near, to his right. Expecting yet another burst of fire any second, Bond wheeled, loosing off two rounds in the direction of the flash. There was a hideous scream, followed by the noise of someone going down: the crash of metal on stone, then a thud and a series of moans.

He dropped onto one knee, waiting, silent and still, head cocked to pick up any other noises, but only the moans continued. Slowly he raised his right hand, more conscious now of the acute pain in his other arm. Gritting his teeth. Listening.

The moaning had stopped, so, once more, Bond rose, taking a pace forward before he was stopped dead in his tracks by another, recognizable voice—"Move one more muscle and I'll blow your head off, Bond. Now drop the gun."

She was very close indeed. To his right.

"I said drop the gun!" Sharp. Commanding.

Bond opened his fingers, and heard the Luger hit the steps just as Heather Dare—originally Irma Wagen—stepped from the shadows.

"So?" Bond breathed, feeling the horror of her deception wash over him.

"Yes. So. I'm sorry, James, but you didn't really think the General was going to take any more chances. You did very well. *I* didn't think you'd be able to get the better of those men. But Chernov was worried. He seemed to sense the possibility."

"Bully for Kolya Chernov." He cursed himself for not having seen through it before. The white raincoat in London—*that* had worried him at the time, for nobody on the run, and with elementary training, would have worn such a garment. Then there was the offer to share her bed—that too had nagged, particularly when he saw her with Smolin, the two lovebirds. "No wonder the General was so well advised of our movements," he said aloud, hoping to bring her closer.

"I led him like a dancer—led you as well, James. Just as I managed to hook Smolin into revealing *his* treachery. We'd better get on with it, I think. My orders are to kill you here, though I hoped the precious Robinsons would have done the job for me."

"How long . . . ?" Bond began.

"Have I been KGB? A long time, James. Early teens. *Cream Cake* was blown from the start. When we all had to get out, the orders were to leave Maxim and Dietrich in place. They could have been taken out at any point, but Center thought London might use me once I was in England. They didn't, as you know, so it was decided to deal with all the others. *You* were a bonus. Chernov came out of safety just for you, James. You find that flattering?"

"Very."

"On your knees, then. We'll do it the Lubyanka way. A bullet in the back of the head."

He took a step forward, as though preparing himself. "And the attempt on your life in London was . . ."

"A small charade to help you trust me. Mischa underestimated you, though. He's very angry. Now he'll be pleased." She took another step closer to him, and Bond shrugged, the pain again angry, tearing at his arm.

"I'll lose my balance if I try to get down. That bastard's smashed my arm badly."

"Then just turn around, slowly." She was calmer than he expected, but she was coming even closer, as though drawn toward his voice.

He started to turn, mind reeling with the odds on him being able to take her with only one arm. Then, as she stepped in, right hand raised holding the pistol high, he moved.

Turn in. Always turn in toward the body but away from the weapon. It was what the experts taught, and if anyone was foolish enough to get that close with a pistol they deserved all they got. He wheeled right, knowing the position was good as he turned, like a ballroom dancer executing a complicated step.

It had to be very fast, and he knew his reactions were slightly impaired by the left arm, but he got it right. Her gun arm remained rigid for just the needed amount of time so that, when he came close to her the arm, and weapon, were to the right of his neck.

He brought his knee up hard. It was never as effective with a woman, but it still caused a lot of pain. He felt the breath go out of her, and could smell her, feel her body close against his.

As Heather doubled from his knee's impact, his right hand came up to grasp at her wrist. Even with one arm, he could execute a lot of force with the downward pull. She gave a little cry as he broke her arm against his knee—the pistol dropping to the ground, bouncing away down the steps.

Bond flicked his knee up again. She was off balance, in pain, and moving downward, so that her spine presented an ideal target. His knee caught her in the small of the back, so hard that he actually heard the spine go. Then she fell away, breath coming in little panting jerks. Though unconscious, she whimpered loudly.

He should have known that Heather was the obvious choice. The one who had taken the most prized target—Maxim Smolin. He should have seen it from the start.

Reaching out for the Luger, Bond did not hesitate. One bullet only. Straight to the lovely head. He felt no qualms about it. Death was sudden, and in a moment it was all over. What little nausea he felt came from the roaring pain in his left arm.

He slowly walked over to where he had hit the other man— the second half of Chernov's backup team. It was one of the two guards. He had hoped it would be Mischa. The man was dead, both bullets having caught him in the chest.

He looked at his watch again, and at the fast-lightening sky. Time was really running out now. He would be lucky to make it.

Taking another deep breath, Bond clenched his teeth. It was going to be one hell of a run, and Lord knew what he could do when he got to the villa. Yet part of the job was done—the traitor found and dealt with. The odds on him saving the others were small, but he *had* to try.

23

CHINESE TAKEAWAY

He THOUGHT HIS lungs were going to burst with the effort, for he ran faster than he had since leaving the house with the Robinsons at his heels. The pain in his lungs, combined with the increasing discomfort in his thighs and legs, helped, in a strange way, to take his mind off the agony of his torn and broken arm. Somehow he had managed to take hold of his left hand and secure the arm inside the overall. The good right hand held the Luger and he forced himself on, scuffing the stones and sending up dust from the road that would take him almost to the promontory and the villa.

He did not even try to calculate how much time had passed, but Bond knew he would be cutting it very close. Then, after what seemed an eternity, he crested the rise above the villa, sinking to his knees and sliding back from the skyline. Using his right shoulder as a prop, he pulled himself up to peer at the terracotta roof and that section of the front that was visible.

Only a few yards below were the remains of bodies, broken and strewn as though some willful child had dismembered a couple of dolls—the two Robinsons he had killed in the night.

He caught a movement from the front of the villa. The one guard Heather had left behind—machine pistol at the ready—was crouching near the front wall, circling, watching, and obviously very alert. Chernov must be edgy, Bond thought. They would know of the two Robinsons taken out close to the villa, and the other pair had not returned to report success. There would be itchy fingers down there, though he suspected they would be watching for Heather's return. The odds had been so heavily stacked against Bond that nobody in his right mind would have expected him to live.

Chernov would have Mischa inside with him, to help with the ritual killing.

Slowly and painfully, Bond started to work his way around to the rear of the house—aware of the time bomb that was ticking away inside the place. It must be very near to the moment of execution now.

He edged downward and pulled himself to his feet once more. The back of the house was some fifty yards away, and he covered the ground quickly, loping somewhat lopsidedly as he had done all the way back from the Pak Tai Temple. Odd, he thought, how your sense of balance went with one arm out of action.

By the time he reached the low wall nobody had spotted him.

He moved silently, as though walking on eggs, toward the house. When it happened it came suddenly, with no warning.

The sound echoed from the other side of the house, the noise he had dreaded from the beginning of his journey back—a terrible, piercing scream—female, but like an animal in dreadful pain. His mind was lanced by a vivid picture of Ebbie having her mouth forced open, with Chernov wielding a scalpel for the obscene punishment. The scream seemed to go on and on, and as it rose in a high, pleading pitch, the guard came round the corner of the house to check the rear.

The man stopped, his jaw dropping open as though he was staring at a ghost. The machine pistol came up but, before the guard could fire, the Luger jumped twice—two bullets crashing into the man's chest, knocking him down like a skittle. As Bond stepped forward, he thought there was movement to his right, for a second and at the edge of his vision, but when he turned, Luger ready, there was nobody there. A trick of the early morning light.

There was a shout from the front of the garden and the sound of running feet, but before anyone could even get to the angle of the wall, Bond was on top of the man he had just killed, wrenching at the machine pistol, identifying it almost by feel alone as an Uzi—the mini, scaled-down version with the stock folded back—and wondering why the KGB were using Israeli weapons.

All this in less than two seconds. Mischa came pounding around the corner as Bond lifted the Uzi, one-handed, giving Chernov's right-hand man a squirt that almost cut him in two.

He fired on the run, and was at the front of the house almost before he knew it, yelling at Chernov, who stood undecided outside the window, unarmed except for a scalpel, his face pale and shocked.

"Drop the cutter and freeze," Bond yelled.

Chernov made one pitiful shrug, then threw the scalpel into the garden, raising his hands, shoulders drooping.

Maxim Smolin, Susanne Dietrich, and Jungle Baisley were still chained together, dumped and wide-eyed in the corner, while Ebbie lay strapped to a wide plank set astride three sawhorses.

"My God, you *really* meant it!" Chernov backed away, for Bond's voice had risen to an uncontrolled, murderous yell. "You bastard, Chernov, you must be crazy."

"Vengeance is not just the prerogative of the gods." Chernov's voice was shaky—but his eyes blazed with a commingling of fury and frustration. "One day, James Bond. One day all the ghosts of the old SMERSH will rise and crush you. That will be vengeance."

Bond rarely felt the true desire to inflict pain, but in that moment he pictured Chernov being hit by the three horrific steel darts from the pen gun in the front pocket of the overalls—one into each eye and one in the throat.

But Chernov had to be taken alive.

"We'll see about vengeance!" Bond started back. Then, nodding: "The keys, General. I want those chains undone."

Chernov hesitated for a second, then his hand moved toward the table, and Bond saw the keys lying there. "Pick them up gently"—under control now—"and unlock them."

Again, Chernov hesitated, his eyes flickering to a point behind Bond's shoulders. No, Bond thought, you don't fall for an old trick like that. "Just do as I say, Kolya . . ." he began, then the hairs on the nape of his neck prickled and he turned.

"If I were you, Jacko, I'd simply be putting your gun down on the table very carefully." Norman Murray faced him, having come quietly in through the door, his police-issue Walther PPK steady in his right hand.

"What—?" Bond could hardly credit it.

"Kolya," Murray said calmly. "I'd leave the keys where they are. Whatever vengeance you're wanting'll have to wait, because I've a feeling we're going to get some visitors up here soon enough. I'm sorry that I'm so late, but it was a bit of a teaser, avoiding my own people and the Brits. Not an easy job."

Chernov made a tchah-ing sound.

"Well, when it comes to us getting out safely, we'll have to use your man, Bond, as collateral, will we not?"

Bond backed away. "Norman? What in God's name—?"

"Ah, Jacko, the evils of this wicked world. You recall that lovely book of Robert Louis Stevenson—*Treasure Island?* Grand book, that. You remember the bit where young Jim Hawkins meets the castaway, Benn Gunn was his name? Well, auld Benn Gunn tries to explain to Jim how he got started on his iniquitous life of piracy. He says, 'It begun with chuck-farthen on the blessed gravestones'—playing what we'd be after calling shove-ha'penny on the gravestones. Well, I suppose it was like that for me—now will you put that cannon on the table, Jacko Bond."

Bond turned his back carefully, placing the Luger near to the keys.

"Now, hands *on* your head, Jacko."

"I've got a broken arm."

"Well, *hand* on your head then. You're a pedantic divil, Jacko."

By the time Bond turned again, slowly raising his right hand, he had slipped the pen from the breast pocket of the overalls, covering it with his right palm. Two traitors, he thought, not just one but two—and the second one an officer of the Republic of Ireland's Special Branch. A man who had a special, secret relationship with the British Service over matters of intelligence, even cooperated with M himself.

"Good," Murray continued. "As I was saying, Jacko. It started by playing shove-ha'penny on the gravestones for me, after a fashion; only, my game was the horses. The auld, auld joke— slow horses and fast women. The debts and the lady who, one night in Dublin, had me compromised and trussed neat as a turkey at Christmas. I just want you to know it wasn't a political thing with me—more a matter of money."

"Money?" Bond sounded disgusted at the thought. "Money? Then why bother to rescue me from Chernov?"

"Now, that was a bit of cover. None of us ever think we'll blow our cover, do we, Jacko? And I was playing it three ways—my own people, you Brits, and these fellas. I'm a treble, really, Jacko, and I didn't know the cover had gone until I got you to Dublin airport. So, that's water under the bridge now."

"It doesn't matter, Norm—and don't tell me not to call you Norm again, because you're Comrade Norm now."

"I suppose you're right. I don't know how I'm goin' to like it in yon country, it's goin' to be awful cold there, so it is. But, you see, Jacko, they're most of them on to me now. Your man M's on to me for sure, so I'm getting a lift out with Kolya here." He turned toward Chernov—"And don't you think we should be getting a move on, Kolya? The porpoises must be close behind me now. Treading on my tail, so they were when I left Dublin."

Chernov nodded gravely. "We go as soon as the business is completed here."

During the momentary distraction, Bond used the first finger and thumb of his right hand to twist the two sections of the pen counterclockwise, then turn it so the weapon faced forward, his thumb moving to the back, where the push trigger was located. "Norman!" he called, swiveling his body so that he was aligned with Murray's head. He pressed the trigger twice, in quick succession. "Sorry, Norman," as the two steel darts left tiny red pinpoint holes in the Special Branch man's head, just above the eyes.

"Jacko!"

The word came as a reflex, for Murray must have been dead as he spoke, pitching forward, the gun dropping from his hand at the same moment as Bond reached out and retrieved the Luger from the table. Now it was done. Those who might cause scandal were dead. Chernov would be a coup. All that needed to be done was the tidying up, and some plausible explanations to the press.

"Now, Kolya Chernov." James Bond's voice was not as steady as it might have been, for he had liked Murray, yet his part in the business also explained many things—both past and present. "The keys. Just unlock these good people." He looked at Ebbie. "When you're free, go to the phone, darling, and dial the number I tell you. It's my own department's Resident here in Hong Kong. You'll have to cover the General here, while I do some very fast talking. We have to go official on this."

Chernov began to unlock the shackles, and Ebbie went to the telephone. The conversation took three minutes, during which the others were freed—Jungle and Smolin using their initiative and securing Chernov with the chains. He seemed cowed now, as though all the fight had gone out of him.

Bond put down the telephone, resting his good hand on the table. There was a light touch on his shoulder, the hand sliding down to lie on top of his own.

"Thank you," Ebbie said, her voice breaking. "James, I have to thank you so much."

"It was nothing," he replied.

The pain returned, the dizziness took over, and his legs buckled under him. In a far corner of his mind he welcomed the oblivion.

James Bond became conscious in a private hospital room. The Service Resident was by his bedside, and it did not take Bond long to realize that his left arm was encased in plaster.

"It's broken in two places, and there are some torn muscles." The Resident was well known to Bond. They had worked together, once in Switzerland, and again in Berlin.

"Apart from that"—Bond smiled—"how did you enjoy the play, Mrs. Lincoln?" It was a very old joke they had shared in the past.

"M sends congratulations, together with some harsh words about you allowing that girl to travel here with you."

Bond closed his eyes, feeling very tired. "Girls like Ebbie are not easy to stop. Don't worry, it wasn't my only mistake."

"He wants you back in London. The doctors say you can leave the hospital tomorrow, but they also say you're to stay here for a couple of weeks. Reluctantly our Chief has said okay. The quacks just wish to keep an eye on the arm, if you follow me."

"The others?" Bond asked.

"Everything's tidied up. No mess. No questions. Chernov was flown to London this afternoon. You've been out for the best part of a day, incidentally."

"Open him up." Bond's mouth turned down, betraying his innate cruel streak.

"We're denying all knowledge at the moment. Our people'll put him through the mill before we go public—if we ever do. Ms. Dietrich, young Baisley, and Maxim have gone as well. Smolin's no use in the field anymore, but they'll find plenty for him to do on the Eastern Bloc desk at Headquarters. You just rest now, James. You've wrapped up the last crumbs of *Cream Cake*, and all's well with the world."

"Ebbie?"

"I have a surprise for you."

The Resident winked and left the room. A minute later, Ebbie Heritage came in. She stood looking at him, then approached the bed.

"I put my feet down." Her face broke into a smile. "I put my feet down and said I would take care of you. My surprise was great. They told me yes, okay. We are very grand, James. We even have bodyguards until you're well enough to travel."

"I guess I might need one." He smiled and she laid the palm of her hand on his brow.

"That feels very nice." Bond's arm might be damaged, but he knew other parts of his body were in working order. "Your hand's so cool."

"There is old Chinese saying." She looked at him. Butter would not have even softened on her lips. "Woman with cool palm has fire under skirt."

"Never heard that." Bond's eyes twinkled.

"Really?"

"Never."

"It's a true saying. I know, because an elderly Japanese gentleman once told me."

In spite of the plaster cast, they spent a very active couple of weeks together, staying at The Mandarin, and eventually leaving by Cathay Pacific.

As the carpet of lights that was Hong Kong disappeared from sight, the jolly female Cathay purser came over to introduce herself. "Mr. Bond? Ms. Heritage? Welcome aboard." She had a broad grin and infectious laugh. "You have had a good time in Hong Kong?"

"Wonderful," said Ebbie.

"Full of surprises," Bond added.

"Holiday?" the purser asked.

"A sort of working holiday."

"So now you return to London." The purser gave what was almost a guffaw of laughter. "This route has a special name in Cathay Pacific, you know."

"Really?" Ebbie sipped her champagne.

"Yes. We call this route from Hong Kong, Chinese Takeaway, ha!"

Ebbie giggled, and Bond gave a wry smile. "No doubt we'll be back," he said. "One day we'll be back."